The Late Hector Kipling

'A hugely inventive and entertaining tale with a rich tapestry of well-drawn characters. It is also often laugh-out-loud funny. An exceptionally fine debut.'   *Morning Star*

'An intelligent, yet never verbose or pretentious novel which has perfectly formed characters, good twists and is littered with wonderfully odd scenarios.'   *London Lite*

'Thewlis has taken the turn-of-the-millennium London art scene and eviscerated it and the resulting gore makes for wonderful entertainment . . . This is a funny and successful satire of the contemporary art world, but at its core, it is a novel about the over-indulged and fragile artist's ego, about insecurity, about the darker layers of human relationships. Lenny Snook, despite his many pretensions, is a decent and considerate friend, but is none the less the undeserved subject of the unpleasant Hector's rabid, frothing rage. Thewlis has written with a black and cynical honesty about the triumph of bitter competitive destruction over our own will to succeed, as most around us aspire not simply to do well, but to do better as we stumble.'   *Observer* **Review**

'An accomplished debut . . . Thewlis . . . has successfully transferred his talents to the page, displaying a sharp ear for dialogue and a scabrously satiric prose style reminiscent of Howard Jacobson.'   *Daily Mail*

'[Thewlis'] great debut novel is a wry account of a spoilt middle-aged man's collapse.'   *InStyle*

David Thewlis studied at the Guildhall of Music and Drama and has appeared in films as diverse as Mike Leigh's *Naked* and *Life is Sweet*, Ridley Scott's *Kingdom of Heaven*, the Coen Brothers' *The Big Lebowski* and Bertolucci's *Beseiged*. He has also starred in *Seven Years in Tibet* and several of the Harry Potter films. In 1995 he wrote and directed a short film called *Hello, Hello, Hello* (which was nominated for a BAFTA) and, in 2003, *Cheeky*.

DAVID THEWLIS

The Late Hector Kipling

PICADOR

First published 2007 by Picador

First published in paperback 2008 by Picador
an imprint of Pan Macmillan Ltd
Pan Macmillan, 20 New Wharf Road, London N1 9RR
Basingstoke and Oxford
Associated companies throughout the world
www.panmacmillan.com

ISBN 978-0-330-37338-8

A CIP catalogue record for this book is available from
the British Library.

Typeset by Intype Libra Ltd
Printed in the UK by CPI Mackays, Chatham, ME5 8TD

Visit www.picador.com to read more about all our books
and to buy them. You will also find features, author interviews and
news of any author events, and you can sign up for e-newsletters
so that you're always first to hear about our new releases.

FOR ANNA AND GRACIE

Illness, insanity and death
were the black angels that
kept watch over my cradle,
accompanied me all my life.

Edvard Munch

TATE MODERN, LONDON

'So New York was a success?' I say.

'New York?'

'You said the other night that it was a big success and everyone loved you.'

'Oh, it was a bit special,' says Lenny, and pulls his coat around him. He's come out in a long red leather coat – jacket – maybe it's a jacket. Whatever it is, it's got a belt, and he looks a fool. 'New York's always amazing, though, isn't it?'

'I've always thought so,' I say, and think about administering a brutal volley of spiteful little kicks to his pompous, self-satisfied shins.

'It gets better every year.'

'Doesn't it?'

'I mean, people say that it's not what it used to be, but you know what, Hec?'

'What, Lenny?'

'I regard that as a tautology.'

'Well, not really. A tautology is—'

'I mean, what is?'

'What is what?' and I'm limbering up for that first important kick.

'What is *not* what it used to be, if you're gonna look at it like that? I mean, really, if you think about it?'

'Hmmm.'

'I mean you could say that about the potato, or the Pantheon, and I'm sure there're lots of people who do; but you could say it about the moon – "It's not what it used to be" – well, yeah, I suppose, by definition, but you know what? Fuck off! The moon's not what it used to be? Fuck that right off.'

'Tautology, though, is when—'

'So when people say that about New York, it's just—'

'Fuck off.'

'Exactly.'

'So it was good, then?'

'Better than ever.'

'Good, I'm glad.'

'I mean, there was this show, in Chelsea, couple of galleries down from the Gagosian; new lad, early twenties, first exhibition – fucking phenomenal.'

'What was it?'

'Minimalist. Genius, Hec.'

'Genius?'

'Total genius.'

'Like what, then? What'd he done?'

'He'd flooded the entire space with broken eggs. The walls, the ceiling. Twelve thousand broken eggs. They gave you a pair of galoshes to walk round it. The floor was a-fucking-wash with smashed-up fucking egg.'

'And that's minimalist?'

'Well, isn't it?'

'Sounds excessive.'

'It's definitely minimalist, Hec. Twelve thousand broken egg whites and yolks, all squished up all over the fucking place. He called it *Miscarriage* er . . .'

'*Miscarriage*?'

'*Miscarriage Of Just This*.'

'Fuck!'

'Exactly! And the smell!'

'The Gagosian?'

'Couple of doors down.'

'Eggs?'

'Eggs, Hec, eggs.'

'You're right, Lenny . . .'

'*Miscarriage Of Just This.*'

'Fucking genius.'

Suddenly Lenny stops in his tracks, arrested by the sight of Lichtenstein's *Whaam!*. He takes a step or two back and begins to nod his head, like a novelty dog. 'Lichtenstein was forty when he painted this.'

'So what,' I say, 'it's dung.'

Lenny doesn't comment upon whether he thinks it's dung, he just stands there squinting at it, through his tinted specs, as though some other thing is hidden beneath, or above, or just to the side of the only thing that it is – which is tired.

I'll tell you what: Lenny's father died when Lenny was twelve. He was torn to slivers at an air show in Lossiemouth. A faulty red helicopter burst into flames, split in half, dropped from the sky and landed on his umbrella; and I'll tell you what: I hope Lenny isn't trying to tell me that this reminds him of it.

'*Whaam!*' he says, and nods. He takes off his silly little blue-tinted specs and swings them around on his finger. Girls look at him. Women look at him. Middle-aged women, old women, a few men. I look at him, and to say that he's getting on my nerves doesn't do it justice; he's finding footholds on every fucking synapse. Standing there like a rock star in his long red leather coat. The bald get.

We pass through a room of Modiglianis. I'm looking at the skirting board, Lenny's looking at the lights. Modigliani can bog off. And Giacometti, he's in there too with his horrible little thin things. Next thing you know, we're in a dingy little side gallery riddled with huge and gloomy maroon abstracts. I begin to huff and tut, and eventually, and not before time, Lenny asks me what the problem is.

3

'Why does Rothko always get his own room?' I say.

'I don't know, Hector,' say Lenny, 'you tell me, why does Rothko always get his own room?'

'It's not a joke, Lenny, I mean it. Why does Mark Rothko always get his own room?'

'Yeah, Hec, I know.'

Silence. He puts a fist up to his lovely lips and affects a cough. He must think that I've finished with him.

'Lenny, it's not a joke and it's not rhetorical. I'm just asking you, plain and simple, man to man, as one artist to another, why does Mark fucking Rothko always get his own fucking room?'

'Oh, I see.'

'Well?'

'Er, well . . .' and he sets about stroking his cheek as though the answer might be written in Braille on his pale and gorgeous chops. 'Because he killed himself?'

'No! No, no, no. Van Gogh fucking killed himself, he doesn't get his own room.'

'Sometimes he does.'

'Only in fucking Amsterdam, or if there's a retrospective.'

'Everyone gets their own room if they've got a retrospective.'

'That's my point.'

'Well, I don't know, what the fuck, Hec? Because he's spiritual?'

I do a little dance. 'Spiritual? Because he's spiritual?' I say. 'I'm fucking spiritual, but I don't get my own fucking room.'

'Maybe if you killed yourself.'

'Maybe if I killed myself?'

'Yeah, Hec,' and he smirks and straightens up his back, like he might have a point, 'maybe if you killed yourself.'

'Yeah,' I say and stick out my gut, 'or maybe if I killed you.' And I leave it right there.

Before we'd tipped up at the Tate we'd stopped off at Trafalgar Square so that Lenny could suitably probe and thoroughly fetishize the Fourth – capital letters – Plinth. It's not like he's been commissioned or anything; he was doing a just-in-case kind of recce, I suppose. The sky was fat and black, and Nelson, if you could have got a good look at him all the way up there, looked about as unimpressed as I was. Lenny, bless him, paced, frowned, gurned, fingered his chin, fiddled with his specs, and then, just in case I was missing the point, unfolded his fancy two-grand German camera and took a lot of tedious photographs of the space between nothing much and nowhere at all. After two minutes of this posturing fucking nonsense he pulled out a big industrial tape measure and something that looked worryingly like a sextant. I was having fuck all to do with it and wandered off through the filthy rain to scream a little scream against my tongue and gums and stare down the lions.

We move on from the Rothko room, turn a corner, snort at a Leger, howl at a Degas, and that's when I see it.

I don't know what it was that made me cry. I don't think I've ever cried in public before, and I know that I've never cried at a painting. Apart from my own. But that was in private. And they were tears of despair. Worst of all, the whole fiasco was played out in front of Lenny. I wept in front of Lenny Snook and he shuffled away, well away, to gape at a Matisse, ashamed to be seen with me. I swear to God, I don't know how all this has come about. Why did I cry? Why did I suddenly buckle like that?

It was quite a spectacle, quite a performance. Some woman (who may or may not have been Eleanor Bron) scuttled across the room to hand me a tissue. I used it up before it had left her hand and she went into her bag for another. At one point I had to lean against the wall. I'm leaning against the wall (Lenny's already in the doorway) and I realize I've woken up the guard, who asks me to step away from the paintings and make my way to the lobby. In the lobby I'm drawing a small crowd and I'm advised either to leave the building or take myself off to the toilets. I'm in the toilets now, trying to make some sense of it all. I'm having no luck.

Lenny hasn't come down, I notice. He saw me sobbing in the lobby, I know he did. He was watching me from behind a pillar. My hands were over my face and I saw him through the slits of my fingers. Then, as I made my way to the stairs, I glimpsed him nipping out front for a fag. I assume it was for a fag; I saw one behind his ear. Either that or he's just gone and fucked off. It wouldn't be the first time. He fucked off last Thursday, the night he came back from New York. There were the three of us: me, Lenny and our friend Kirk in a back room at Blacks club in Soho. Lenny was telling us about how he'd spent an evening with Jeff Koons, getting pissed on Manhattans, puffing Havanas, exchanging ideas. He put on Koons's voice and at one point he pulled out a Polaroid of him and Jeff snuggled up in some dark booth. Kirk snored and lolled his head. I questioned the word 'exchanging'.

'You know, exchanging,' said Lenny, 'like sharing. I told him some of my ideas and he told me some of his.'

'Ideas about what?' said Kirk.

'You know . . .' said Lenny, and me and Kirk couldn't believe he was going to say it, but he looked like he might, he looked like he might, and then suddenly he did, '. . . art.' He picked up his bottle and took a big swig.

'Wanker,' said Kirk, and laughed. I should mention that he laughed. And I should mention that I laughed when I said: 'So does that mean that now you'll be nicking work off Koons as well?'

And that's when he fucked off. Just stood up and walked out of the club, into the night, like a mental head, like a moody fucking get. Like a ponce. It was that 'as well' coming after Koons that got him. Good that it got him. I'll always get him with that one. Always. He'd better get used to it.

So where is he now? Where's he gone? He can't walk out on me just cos I've gone and got a bit of a monk on over some soft painting in the Tate, can he? It's a big fag he's having out there. Why doesn't he come down? What's he doing? What's happened? What's happening? Why am I crying in a public toilet? And such an ugly public toilet. You'd think they might make an effort, given it's the Tate. Considering the ubiquity of the lavatory in art, they're missing a few tricks, aren't they?

The mirrors are enormous and vicious. I look at my feet, worried that they're too small. I look at my hands, worried that they're too fat, too blue. I look at my ears. I look at my chin. Monkey-black hair. Hopeless shoulders. I've bought this horrible old Crombie, and I'm wearing it now, and it is – it's horrible. I've been putting it off, but suddenly my eyes catch a glimpse of themselves. All pink and liquid. Squandered. Blunt. And then the face. The face, and then the whole. The whole rotten thing. The whole peculiar thing that I, and others, sometimes refer to as 'me'. What do I look like? I look like I live on a diet of sand.

There's the flush of a toilet and a tall, lopsided, foppish-looking fella steps out of a cubicle. I activate the hand dryer and dry my dry hands till they scald. He smiles at me and asks me if I have the time and I tell him that I don't wear a watch. 'Oh,' he says. For some reason I add that I never wear a watch. He asks me why. I tell him that I don't like to. He asks me why I don't like to, and I tell him that I just don't. He asks me if I'm feeling all right. I tell him that I'm feeling just fine. 'Aren't you Hector Kipling?' he says, and I tell him that I am. 'Thought so,' he says, 'I've seen your stuff.'

'My stuff?' I say.

'Yeah, your stuff,' he says and turns on the tap. He begins to splash his face with water and takes no further interest in me, nor I in him. I walk to the door and make my way up the stairs.

Stuff!

After a long search, during which I nod apologies to anyone who'd caught the earlier sob-show, I find Lenny lingering before a Pollock, specs off, toecaps in the air, hands behind his back, like the Duke of fucking Edinburgh. What the hell is he doing? Looking at it? Looking at what? What the fuck does Lenny Snook know about painting? He couldn't paint his fucking toenails. What's he looking for? Detail? Technique? I'll tell you what he's looking for: most of the time the only thing he's looking for is his reflection in the glass. I swear there was one time I caught him gazing into a painted mirror on the back wall of a Vermeer, baffled, totally fucking perplexed because he couldn't see himself in it. That's how much Lenny fucking Snook knows about painting. True story. But that never held him back. That never deterred the critics and the judges. Oh no. That never stopped him from making an 'outstanding contribution to art in Britain in the previous twelve months', did it? No it fucking did not!

'Sorry about that, Len,' I say, appearing by his side. He moves on, and I follow him towards a Hockney. 'Weird,' I say, 'very strange.'

'Hockney?' he says.

'No, I mean what just happened.'

He glances at me out of the corner of his eye. Not at my face, at my chest. He gives a quick glance to my chest and then back to the Hockney, as though he's got no idea what I'm talking about. He moves on to a Bacon, hesitates for about three seconds and then looks around for somewhere to sit.

'Don't know what all that was about,' I say.

He slumps down onto one of the leather couches. 'Stendhal,' he says and begins to fiddle with his laces. He's wearing a pair of wizened old Docs that he bought in Los Angeles. I know that they're from Los Angeles cos he told me, one night in Quo Vadis. It seemed important to him that I should know that.

'Stendhal?' I say.

'Stendhal syndrome,' he says.

'You've lost me,' I say.

'Prominent in Florence,' he says, straightening up and waving his specs in the air. 'People pass out in the presence of beauty.'

'They pass out?'

'People collapse,' he says, 'tourists are carried out of the museums on stretchers. The Stendhal syndrome,' he says, 'it's called that.'

'But I didn't collapse,' I say.

'No, but you cried. Sometimes people just cry. Or it starts with crying, and later they pass out.'

I sit down beside him. 'How much later?'

'Sometimes hours later,' says Lenny.

'But it wasn't beauty.'

'It's a psychiatric disorder. It's a kind of—'

'But I wasn't crying about beauty.'

'Who's to say?'

'It was a fucking Munch, for fuck's sake.'

'Who's to say?'

'I don't give a shit about Munch. I couldn't care less about him.'

'Like I say,' says Lenny, 'who's to say?'

I feel like pushing him off the couch, but I don't, because that would be ridiculous.

'Beauty's not the point,' I say. 'If I thought that beauty was the point do you think I'd paint the way I paint?'

There's a silence. Lenny looks at the floor. I close my eyes. Sick of it all. Sick of all this looking.

The silence digs its heels in. I know what he's thinking. He's thinking what I'm thinking.

'Perhaps,' he says, 'perhaps you paint the way you paint because you know that beauty *is* the point.'

Well, maybe he isn't thinking what I'm thinking after all, because he's breaking it; he's breaking the Agreement. He's breaking the Douglas–Quinn Agreement. Ever since our early twenties we've always abided by the Douglas–Quinn Agreement. Kirk Douglas, Anthony

Quinn. Whenever we found ourselves talking seriously about what art should or should not be, one of us would be entitled to dance in Greek, like Zorba, though I don't know why, cos that's a different film and somewhere along the way we got confused between Anthony Quinn as Zorba and Anthony Quinn as Gauguin. But anyway, all that stopped when I fell in love with Eleni, who's from Crete, and the whole thing became a bit distasteful. The point is that there was always the Agreement and right now all I can hear is the pulse of a santuri and the stamping of boots around a bonfire.

'You paint against beauty,' continues Lenny, oblivious, 'because you know that beauty *is* the point. If you really thought that beauty wasn't the point then you'd paint in favour of beauty, not in opposition to it.'

'Fuck off, Lenny,' I say.

He shrugs his shiny red shoulders and runs his hand across his scalp in a manner so reminiscent of Brando's Mr Kurtz that it's difficult not to take it as a reference. 'Well . . .' he says.

I've known Lenny since I was seventeen, and he was going bald even then. But Lenny being Lenny it's never been a problem cos he's got the head for it and it suits him cos he's a handsome fucker. He was handsome back then and he's handsome now. More handsome now than then. And he'll carry on being handsome. The older he gets the more handsome he becomes. He'll be handsome in middle age and he'll be a handsome pensioner. An 'exquisite corpse'. Bald and handsome. All the more handsome for being bald. All the more bald for being handsome. Whatever that means. It's a pain in the arse.

'Sorry.'

'What?' says Lenny.

'Sorry,' I say, 'sorry for saying fuck off.'

He looks at me. And then he looks off to the side of me. 'It's OK.'

I've been in therapy for the past three months and so far she's taught me to apologize.

'And sorry for crying.'

'You've always been very emotional,' says Lenny and stands.

I stand too. 'You say that like it's a criticism.'

'No,' he says, 'no I don't,' and wanders out through the door. We're back in the lobby. He reaches into his pocket and drops a coin into the donations box. A gaggle of Japanese schoolgirls waddle over and beg him to sign their gallery maps. He pulls out a gold fountain pen and gets down to it. Twelve in all. I try to catch his eye so that we can smirk at each other, but he's having none of it. Smirking, it seems, is a thing of the past. He's got his head down and he's asking them their names.

Outside the sky has darkened into a blurred and sooty purple. The river is salted with seagulls. I love seagulls. They remind me of home.

'I love seagulls,' I say, 'they remind me of Blackpool.'

'Being told not to pick up dirty feathers off the tram tracks, that's what they remind me of,' he says and lights a fag.

We're almost at the bottom of the steps when this young French couple ask if they can have their photograph taken with Lenny. They 'appreciated' his show in Marseilles and would love to have their photograph taken with him. Lenny goes all bashful in his red leather coat-jacket, china-blue buttons, puts his arms around their shoulders and indicates that they should hand the camera to me.

I take it. That's what I do.

It's been raining all day and the river sits nicely with the puddled embankment. The couple embrace. Terrible teeth the two of them. And there's Lenny peeping over the top. The girl's gone mad and grabbed his hand.

I frame them out. That's what I do. I crop the river and the top half of their bodies. I take them from the waist down, their silly French shoes on tiptoe and Lenny in his Californian Docs, and some scabby pigeon pecking at a bus ticket. That's what they'll get when they pick up their prints.

I pass them back their camera and smile. They return the smile and almost bow.

On we go. Lenny removes his specs and dries them on a scrap of pink velvet. He replaces them with august ceremony and stares out across the river.

'St Paul's,' he whispers, 'sublime.'

How come he needs these specs to look at paintings *and* to walk around the streets in? OK, so sometimes he takes them off to look at a painting, but most of the time he leaves them on, and he wears them to read, but then he drives in them and watches films in them. So what's going on with these specs? What kind of specs are they?

He found them, he says, under some floorboards in the Chelsea Hotel. What he was doing lifting up floorboards in the Chelsea Hotel, fuck knows, but he found them there and took them into some optometrists (his word, not mine) and asked them to fit his prescription. They obliged, for a price, and he's come home in them. Ludicrous things they are; little Crippen specs, bendy silver wire, creepy, like he's got an insect strapped to his face. 'They've really changed the way I see things,' he said the night he came back from New York. 'They must have belonged to someone who stayed there. They could be anybody's. Pollock once stayed there. They might have belonged to Pollock.'

'Statistically unlikely,' said Kirk.

'But they might have,' said Lenny.

'Or they might have belonged to some Belgian pornographer called René,' I said. 'Or Nancy Spungen.'

'Fuck you talking about?' said Lenny, and he went quiet for a bit. Me and Kirk winked at each other and he caught us. Then he started in about his night with Koons, and then we laughed, and then he fucked off.

'So how's your show going?' he asks me now. It's something to say.

'Fine.'

'Where's the gallery?'

'Bethnal Green.'

'What's it called?'

'The Doodlebug.'

'And it's all ready?'

'Yeah. Nearly. I'm just finishing the self-portrait.'

He stops in his tracks. 'Self-portrait?' he says. 'You finally got round to a self-portrait? That's amazing. How is it? Happy?'

'Happy's not the word,' I say, and start reading my travelcard. 'Happy's not the word,' and start folding it up, cos I really want to belt him in the mouth, give him a big healthy smack in his smug, handsome gob. 'And how's your work going,' I ask, 'how's the piece?' and the travelcard's the size of a stamp.

'It's coming along,' he says.

'You've got it all worked out, have you?'

'I think so. It's hard to tell. It may be something, or it may be nothing at all. I don't really want to talk about it. Not yet.'

'Well, fine,' I say, missing out the rest.

Well, fine, Lenny, then don't talk about it. Don't debase your shitty little self. I don't want to know anyway. I only asked cos I couldn't think of anything else to say. I only still know you cos I've known you for so long.

'And how's Eleni?' he says.

'Eleni's beautiful,' I say, cos she is, and cos he knows she is, and cos he's stuck with Brenda. Comical-looking Brenda who had him strapped to the banister well before he was Mr Bobby fucking Dazzler. Mental Brenda who threatens she'll stab herself in the neck if he ever attempts to leave her. 'Yeah,' I say, 'Eleni's beautiful.'

'Great,' he says. 'And your mum and dad? Still trying to sell the house?'

'No,' I say, 'they've given up. They can't get rid of it.'

'That's a drag.'

Fuck off, Lenny. 'Yeah,' I say, 'it is. But they're fine about it. They've decided to change things round a bit instead.'

A cab drives past and Lenny waves it down. 'I think I'm gonna take this,' he says.

'Oh,' I say, 'where're you going?'

'I'm meeting Jopling in Soho.'

'Oh.'

'I'm gonna show him some sketches I've made for the piece.'

'Oh.'

'Where're you going?'

'I'm going to Earl's Court to see Bianca.'

'Who's Bianca?'

The taxi's got the window down and Lenny's shouted, 'Soho,' at the driver.

'She's my therapist,' I say.

'Since when?'

'Since July.'

'You never told me that.'

'Well, you haven't really been around, Lenny.'

'Well . . . great, good luck er . . .' and he hovers in the doorway. He makes a move towards me, as though he might hug me, and then he makes a sort of sideways move, as though he might not hug me. He throws out his hand, but it's sort of the wrong way up, and I try to shake it but he does something funny with his thumbs and his knuckles and I try to join in but it all goes to pot.

'See ya,' he shouts as he bends himself into the cab. 'I'll call you.'

'Say hello to Jay.'

'I will.'

The taxi pulls away. I watch it as it scuttles up the road like a shifty cockroach. I can see Lenny sitting forward, bossing the driver.

Bianca makes me a cup of tea and lights the candles. She puts a sheet over the parrot and settles herself on her sofa. There are two sofas. I settle myself on my sofa. I stir my tea and take a look at myself in the back of the spoon. That wasn't a very good idea, as it turns out.

'So,' she begins, 'so how is everything? How are you and Eleni?'

'I've just been walking round the Tate with Lenny,' I say.

'Aahhh,' she says. Bianca is a sixty-year-old arthritic Austrian lady who smiles more than she should. 'Aahhh,' she says again and picks up her mug of algae, or whatever the fuck it is. 'Lenny.'

'Lenny,' I repeat.

'So he's back from New York?'

'Got back last week.'

'Lenny,' she says again, and drifts off into a reverie, taking small sips of her foul concoction.

'Lenny Snook,' I say, and fiddle with my lip.

'I see, I see.' She fixes me with her stare. 'And you have been crying, have you not?'

2

57 NORRIS AVENUE, BLACKPOOL

'Hector,' yells my mum, 'do you want some chicken?'

I've been vegetarian for years, she knows I have. Never slipped once, she knows that too. So what she thinks she's doing offering me chicken I can't tell you. She's been offering me chicken for nearly twenty years and she'll go on offering me chicken for another twenty, as though one day I might turn around and say oh go on then, and tuck in. I'm sick of it.

'Did you hear me?'

Yes I heard you, Mum. 'Mum, it's meat. Chicken's meat.'

'But it's not a cow,' she says, appearing in the doorway of the lounge.

'What kind of logic's that?' I say, pouring out the other half of my beer.

'Ooh, you and your long words,' she says, almost coquettishly, and flings her oven glove at me. 'Mushrooms. You'll eat mushrooms, won't you?'

'Yes, why wouldn't I eat mushrooms?'

'Well, I don't know what you're like,' she says, and lets it hang in the air, like she means so much more. 'It's always changing with you. One minute it's "Yes I will have a biscuit" the next it's "No, no, I don't eat biscuits." You're drinking, and then you're not. You'll have sugar in your tea, next time you won't. I don't know if you eat mushrooms or not.'

'Mushrooms are fine.'

'What?' says my dad, who's sat in the corner watching the rugby.

'Nothing, Dad. I just said that mushrooms are fine.'

'Mushrooms are what?'

'Fine, Dad,' I say, and he frowns and tucks in his chin. He gets back to the game, turning up the volume.

'Cos I can do you a mushroom risotto if you like.'

'That sounds lovely, Mum.'

'And will Eleni have that as well?'

'Yeah, that'll be nice.'

'Does she not want chicken?'

'No, Mum.'

'But she's not vegetarian,' she says, scrunching up her eyes, 'is she?' She knows damn well she's not, which, for some reason, she gets a kick out of.

'No, Mum, she's not. But she doesn't eat much meat and she doesn't like chicken.'

'Doesn't like chicken?'

'No.'

'I thought everyone liked chicken. I mean I can understand avoiding it if you're set against it, like you are, but if you're allowed it and then just not liking it, well . . . I can't imagine.'

'Well, there you go, Mum.'

'Do they not have chickens in Greece?'

'Of course they have chickens in Greece.'

'Well, I don't know,' says Mum, 'I've never been to Greece, have I?' She looks over at my dad and raises her voice. 'Never been out of the sodding country.'

'Well, there you go, Mum.' And suddenly I'm watching the rugby as well, even though I can't stand it ever since I got that stud in my head at school.

'Does she want some sausage?'

'Mum!' I finally do it. I've only been here four hours and already I've snapped at her.

17

'Ooh, you've changed,' she says, snatches back her oven glove and strides off back to the kitchen muttering, 'I'll do you both your rotten risotto, then,' as she goes.

Sparky, my parents' asthmatic, neurotic Yorkshire terrier, emerges from beneath the bureau and takes up two minutes yelping and squeaking like the sorry fucked-up mess of fluff that he is. He takes up a position on my left shoulder and stares at me with his awful leaking, rheumy brown eyes. I can smell his rank terrier breath coming at me in short stinking bursts. Ridiculous fucking specimen.

I take two big swigs on my beer and look at my dad. He's in profile to me. It seems like he's always been in profile to me. He's allergic to the settee, he says, based on nothing, and so his nose is permanently clogged, his mouth permanently open with his tongue lolling out on his lower lip. He's down on his knees by the television.

'What are you doing, Dad?' I say, and flick Sparky off my shoulder onto the floor.

'Eh?' He's not sure whether I've just said something to him or if something somewhere just made a noise. He doesn't even look at me at first, he looks towards the bookcase, like a book might have fallen down, but there are no books. We call it the bookcase but it's filled up with little ceramic grenadiers and photographs in frames. It's got fuck-all to do with books.

'Dad,' I shout, 'it's me,' and he looks over. 'I said what's that you're doing?'

He pushes himself up and sits on the edge of his chair. He smiles and shakes his head. I love my dad. 'Oh, it's a bloody nuisance, Hector,' he says, and he's looking down at what he's got in his hands.

'What is it?' I say.

He gives out a little laugh, smiles and shakes his head again. 'Oh, it's a silly bloody hearing aid thing they've given me.' He holds it up so I can see. 'It's got this Velcro on it and it's supposed to stick to the telly, but I'm buggered if I can get it to fasten.' He goes back onto his knees and starts giving it another go. He's stuck one piece of Velcro to the edge of the speaker and he's trying to make the other piece, attached to the aid, cling on. He's having no luck. The less luck he has, the more he tries to hold it there. And the more it drops off the more he shakes his head and sighs. I love my dad.

'Here, let's have a look,' I say, and I move onto the corner of the settee so I can see what's going on.

'It's so I can hear the television better without having it up too loud for your mum.'

I take it from him and he sits back down. I get on my knees and try to see if I can manage it. After a few attempts I hold both pieces of Velcro up to the light. 'Dad,' I say, 'you've got the same two bits here.'

'What?' he says.

'These two pieces of Velcro; they're the same sort.'

'What do you mean?'

'Well, Velcro, Dad. You know Velcro? You know how it works?'

'I can't say I do, if I'm honest with you.'

And suddenly I feel strange. I feel sad. Really sad. I don't know why at first. 'Well, it's like hooks and eyes.'

'Aye?'

'Or like male and female in electrics.'

'Is it?' and he leans in close for a demonstration. I hold up both pieces against the screen so he can see.

'You've got little hooks,' I say, 'and you've got little eyes. Little loops. Now what you've got here is just a lot of little loops.'

'I see.'

'You've got no hooks.'

'Well, that's what they've given me.'

'Well, it won't work like this.'

'There's been a cock-up,' he says. He takes the two pieces back and tries to stick them together, giving up almost straight away to show me that he's understood. 'Well, that's no good,' he says, 'just giving us loops.'

Then I realize why I feel so sad. My dad, who could build you a car, or rewire a house or plumb up your whole kitchen, doesn't know how Velcro works.

Through the ceiling I hear footsteps and it must be Eleni getting up. She's been asleep for nearly three hours, and she had a nap on the train. She didn't sleep last night, though. Nightmares. Her mother walled into the nave of a church. Just a pair of eyes peeping through a slit in the bricks, apparently. Eleni with a candle. And then it starts to rain. She woke up in a sweat. It was a cold night, but she woke up in a sweat. She got up at one point and I could hear her playing Gershwin on the piano. We only just made the train, she was so wiped out. I love Eleni. I loved the journey. She made me laugh for the first half-hour and then she put her head on my shoulder and slept till Warrington.

'I think Eleni's emerging,' shouts my mother. I can hear lots of hot fat sizzling, taps running, the clatter of plates and pans. I decide to go through to the kitchen.

It's a nice kitchen. Small, but uncluttered and functional. My mum has got it together in the kitchen. I have only vague memories of ever seeing anything stacked on the draining board. It seemed that everything was always washed up and put away back in its cupboard even before the food was served.

'That's lucky,' says my mum, 'cos this risotto's nearly ready.'

'It smells nice.'

'I've got some parsley. Do you want parsley on it, or shall I not bother?'

'Don't bother, Mum.'

We hear the toilet flush and then footsteps on the stairs. The door's pushed open and Eleni's rubbing her eyes. Her hair's all messed up and her dress is creased.

'Well well,' says my mother, 'look who's here.' She says it with wry, forgiving affection. She wants some chat and she can chat to Eleni and they make each other laugh. She loves Eleni. She hated Sheba, but she loves Eleni. Even though Eleni's Greek and struggles with her accent, they can blabber away for whole nights. 'We don't see you both enough,' said my mum on the phone the other night, so we cleared the weekend and jumped on the train.

'Did you have a sleep? Did you have a little nap, lass?' says Mum, going at her with a big spoon spotted with steaming rice.

Eleni blinks her eyes, looks around and smiles. 'Oh, hello,' she says, as though she's only just woken up that very moment. Sheba used to get up in a foul temper. Sheba never woke up and said, 'Oh, hello.' I used to dread her going to sleep.

'Hello, madam, wakey wakey,' says Mum.

I walk over to Eleni and put my arms around her. I kiss her on the top of the head. Her body's all warm and she smells of sleep. I want to fuck her.

Here's how we met: in 2004 I was living in flat 65, Pomfret House, Box Street, Bow. Eleni Marianos lived in number 67. I would often hear her piano through the door. We'd pass in the hall sometimes and say hello and blush and shuffle and drop things. In number 66 lived Mr Godfrey Bolton, an elderly, shifty-looking fella who, faced with the threat of a prison sentence regarding a violent attack upon a racehorse, one day saw fit to hang himself. The chair, falling against a candle that Mr Bolton had put on the bedside table (to illuminate his brief note?), caused a small fire to break out. Detecting the fire at an early stage, I burst out of my door, only to be met by Eleni Marianos bursting out of hers. Where-upon, with little discussion, we set about bursting through Mr Bolton's. Having put out the fire with my dressing gown (leaving me naked), we stood back and discovered our neighbour suspended from the ceiling by an equestrian bridle. Eight months later we decided to buy his flat and, since by then we were in love, knock it through at both ends to form one big flat. Some of our friends thought all this a little creepy, and said so behind our backs.

'Photo Finish' said Godfrey Bolton's note, and there was a small cross that might have been a kiss or a crucifix, it wasn't clear. 'Photo Finish', signed 'God Bolton'.

The four of us sat down with our various meals and watched a baffling sequence of soaps back to back. Mum tried to fill me and Eleni in as to what was going on in each one, but the more she explained the more we missed what was going on in the one we were watching, to the point where even Mum became confused and kept fiddling with the volume, as though that would make things clearer. My dad just sat there, taking it all in, tutting and shaking his head at the goings-on on the screen, as though he'd never known such debauchery. Eventually it got to half nine and he announced that he'd taken his tablet and was going upstairs to watch a documentary about Rasputin. Sparky followed.

'Do you not watch much telly back in London?' says Mum.

Me and Eleni are curled up on the settee. I've got my hand down the back of her skirt but we're hidden. 'Not really, Mum, no,' I say.

'Me and your dad do nothing else.'

'Are you watching this?' I say, nodding at *Celebrity Fit Club*.

'This?' she says, sniffing. 'I'm not bothered about this. They'll still be fat in a month.'

'There's a programme on Channel 4 about Tracey Emin,' I say. Eleni pushes her arse back against my thighs and purrs like she might go to sleep.

'Ooh, not her,' says Mum.

'We don't have to watch it,' I say, 'I've seen it before but Eleni's not seen it.'

Mum gives in. It's the mention of Eleni that does it. She loves Eleni. 'Turn it over,' she says. 'I'll watch owt.'

I pick up the remote and Tracey Emin's sat up on her settee smoking and drinking saying 'Fuck this' and 'Fuck that', ranting on about her abortion. And then she's trotting through some park, feeding squirrels, saying how we all need something small to look after. I steal a glance at Mum and she's just gazing blankly at the screen as though she's watching a magic act and trying to work out how they've done it. Eventually she pipes up. 'Good God,' she says, 'what's she like?'

'I know, Mum, she's a nut,' though I don't really mean it.

'Do you know her?' says Mum.

'I've met her a few times.'

'Well, I don't know,' says Mum.

Eleni pushes herself up on one elbow. 'Are you all right there, Connie? You want to lie on the couch?' She hasn't quite picked up that we call it a settee.

'No, no, love. You're all right on there. You two nestle up. I'm fine where I am.'

Eleni settles back into my arms. I stroke the fringe out of her eyes, look down at her, smile and kiss her on the nose. She smiles back and squeezes her eyes together like a cat. I want to go to bed soon and fuck her, quietly; the way we always have to whenever we come back to Blackpool for a few days.

Tracey's pointing a video camera around her flat and it's a right fucking dump. I look over to Mum. Her eyebrows are up and she's chewing on her knuckles.

'They want to be doing a documentary on you, Hector. You do better stuff than this.'

'I expect they will, Mum.'

'Well, I should think so. I mean, at least you can paint. Look at her. Look at them drawings. They look like they've been done by a half-baked monkey.'

'It's concept, Connie,' says Eleni, and because of her accent it doesn't sound pretentious. It sounds like she was born to utter things like 'It's concept, Connie', like she has no choice, like she should never say anything else. I love Eleni.

'What do you mean?' says Mum, not taking her eyes from the screen.

Eleni props herself up again. 'Well, she's being honest. She's making an effort to be as honest as she can be. And she is calling that art.'

'Well, what do you think about that, Hector?' says Mum, and I know that she's really referring to my paintings and how that's what she thinks of as art. But it's the same as the conversation about chicken. We've been having it for twenty years. She knows very well that I'm happy to call all sorts of things art, even to the detriment of my own paintings. It's that bit she doesn't like. She wants me to stand up for what I do; she wants a passionate hero, affirming his patch; and that's all well and good, but the fact is I'm totally open-minded on the subject. If Marc Quinn wants to freeze his own blood in the shape of his head, or Jake and Dinos want to stick dicks onto kids' chins, then it's all fine by me.

'I like her, Mum,' I say, as Tracey's talking about pulling a foetus out of her pants, 'I think art *should* be honest.'

'Well, I'm going to bed,' she says, 'I think she's a bloody fruitcake.'

She goes into the kitchen and rattles a few things around, turns off the lights, delivers a careful list of instructions about how to turn off the gas fire and how we're not to unplug the fish tank, and shuffles off out the door, nodding back to the telly. 'She's dirty,' she says, 'she's a dirty bloody lunatic, that lass. I'm lost.'

Me and Eleni watch the rest of it and when it's over we unplug everything but the fish tank and start kissing. I've had a few beers and all I want to do is kiss her for hours. We can hear my dad snoring upstairs and we undress as much as we dare and fuck, right there on the cream settee that my dad, based on nothing, is allergic to.

The next morning, Sunday, we're awoken by the sound of hammering. Not like someone's hanging a picture or putting a nail into the floorboards, but intermittent, heavy, laboured hammering, and the sound of falling masonry, as though my dad's knocking down the fireplace. I pull on a sweater and yesterday's underpants and wander downstairs to investigate. And there's my dad, stripped to the waist, huge grey sledge-hammer, knocking down the fireplace.

'What are you doing, Dad?' I say.

'What?' he says, looking at the television.

'What are you doing?'

He swings around and sees me. 'I'm knocking down the fireplace,' he says and runs the back of his hand across his brow. We're both stripped to the waist: him from the neck down and me from the feet up. Sparky's tucked away behind the curtain on the window ledge, choking on the dust and shaking like he's developed a chronic case of doggy Parkinson's overnight.

I remember when this fireplace was built, sometime back in the seventies, back when Mum and Dad were still aware of trends and still supple enough to follow them. Irregular slabs of purbeck stone and polished grey slate. I remember the plans laid out on the dining-room table and this bloated Italian bloke who stank of pork pointing at them with a translucent yellow screwdriver. Mum and Dad nodding and asking questions. Mum wanted a trapezium over the flue, Dad wasn't so keen. And now here he is: rid of it at last. He's spread a dustsheet out over the carpet and he's up to his ankles in broken rock and plaster. He puts down the hammer, wipes his hands on a towel and slumps into his chair. Jiggered, as he would say.

'Bloody hell, Dad. What you doing that for?'

'We've decided it's to come down,' says Dad, nodding at Mum, who's sat in the conservatory scanning the colour supplements.

'Bloody hell,' I say again. 'Fucking hell' is what I'm thinking, but 'Bloody hell' is what I'm saying cos I don't swear at home. It's not what we do. The air's gone mad with dust. Sparky's spasms are making the windows rattle.

Mum looks up and smiles. 'Well, look who's here,' she says, puts down her magazine and pushes herself up out of her little wicker chair.

'What do you think, then?' she says, putting her hand over her mouth, like a schoolgirl who's just sprayed something rude on the wall. She's chuckling.

'You're knocking down the fireplace?'

'We've decided it's old fashioned.'

Dad's got his head down and he's preoccupied with breathing.

'Shouldn't you be getting someone in to do this?' I say.

'Oh, your dad's strong,' she says, 'he's knocking on but he's still got some energy left. Haven't you, Derek?'

And Dad looks up, all red in the face, mouth open, fist to his chest. 'Eh?'

'I was just saying to Hector, you might be seventy-eight but you've still got it in you.'

'Oh aye,' he says, 'I'm not beat yet.'

I worry about this.

'Do you want some breakfast?'

'In a minute.'

'Bacon?'

'Don't start, Mum.'

'Is Eleni getting up?' and she's all frisky, like she's excited just to say her name.

'I think so, yes. The hammering woke us both up.'

Mum scampers over and takes me in her arms. She smells all clean. I return the embrace. 'Oh, and I do love you, Hector. I'm so glad you've come up to see us. I do love you.' She's got me in a clinch and I can barely move. 'Don't we, Derek? Don't we love him?'

'Oh aye,' Dad says, and grips onto his sweating purple head, staring at the floor. 'Always did.'

'I love you too, Mum,' I say, 'I love you both.'

'And we love Eleni. She's smashing, is Eleni. You can have right nice natural conversations with Eleni.'

Right nice natural conversations are important to Mum. She never had right nice natural conversations with Sheba. I had right nice natural conversations with Sheba, at first. And then . . .

'What do you think?' says Mum, nodding towards Dad's demolition. 'Do you think we're mad?' She hugs me again and I hold my breath cos I don't want her to smell last night's beer on me.

Eleni's put on her best clothes and we eat our toast and beans in the conservatory. That's what Mum calls it: The Conservatory. Basically it's a little extension built onto the back of the house overlooking the small lawn and rockery. Mum's filled it up with plants. They're everywhere, climbing up the walls, twisted around the brass light fittings. Mum's good with plants. And whenever she mentions me and my painting and says, 'Eee, I don't know where you get it all from,' I always credit it to her and how she's so good with plants and how that's a sort of art in itself. I don't say this as a platitude. I mean it. I'm useless with plants. Eleni's useless with plants as well. They die. Perhaps it's the fumes. Or perhaps it's just that we're useless.

'I was just reading this, Eleni,' says Mum, pointing with her big bitten finger to the newspaper.

'What's that, Connie?' says Eleni.

'About some woman called Frida Kahlo,' says Mum, rhyming it with callow.

'Ah yes,' says Eleni, smiling, beautiful, uncomplicated in her enthusiasm for whatever Mum is about to profess.

'Madonna's got a lot of her paintings, it says here.'

'Ah yes,' says Eleni, awaiting Mum's point.

'It says here that she was Mexican.'

'Yes,' says Eleni, realizing that there may not be a point after all. Or perhaps it's just me who realizes this.

'She was knocked over by a bus,' says Mum, stroking her chin like she's a man with whiskers, 'like Beryl next door.'

'What?' I say.

'Beryl Short next door.'

'What about her?'

'Beryl was knocked over by a bus. She'd gone all giddy on medication and just stepped out. She told me she thought she was stepping out to take a little paddle.'

'Eh?'

'A little paddle in the sea. But she wasn't. She was in the middle of Waterloo Road.'

Eleni and me look at each other and smile. I take a sip of my tea. Mum takes a sip of hers. And she's off again . . .

'Now you see she was very personal with what she painted.' Oh, so she has got a point after all. 'She believed in honesty . . .' here it comes, 'but the difference with her and that lass last night, that Tracey . . . what's she called, Hector?'

'Tracey Emin.'

'Aye, Tracey Emin. The difference between her and this Mexican lass is that with her – Frida Kahlo – you might want to hang some of this on your walls. I mean, I wouldn't, but some folk do. Madonna does,' and then, 'for example,' and she looks up and lowers her specs and she's finished. Eleni's on the spot.

'Well, Connie,' says Eleni, mopping up her bean juice with her last triangle of toast, 'all art does not have to be hanging on walls.'

'Well, I know that,' says Mum, 'I know that you can have statues and . . . and er . . .' She's stuck on statues and she's taken off her specs and she's searching her brain for something else that you don't have to hang on walls, finally relaxing and digging up '. . . sculptures.' I take another sip of my tea. 'Sculptures and all that. I know that.' Eleni's nodding, Mum's kicked off her slippers at the heel and she's waggling them on her toes. 'But when it comes to the likes of that lass last night, that Tracey Emin, well, you can't put what she does on a wall, can you?'

'Well, some of it you can,' says Eleni, 'her drawings, whatever. But if you don't want to, then that's fine. Art is whatever you want it to be.'

'Well, I don't want it to be that.'

'And that's OK,' says Eleni, and bites down on her toast. She sniffs the air. 'It smells so beautiful in here, Connie.'

'Thank you,' says Mum, and looks back down at the paper. She's not finished with us yet. Dad's in the lounge watching the build-up to the Belgian Grand Prix, which is doing nothing to abate Sparky's wretched convulsions. Mum clears her throat. I suspect she's just getting started.

'There's a painting of hers here called – ' and she straightens her specs and leans in – '*The Suicide of Dorothy Hale*, painted by Frida Kahlo in 1938.' Mum's sounding a bit academic now, which is weird. She carries on: 'Shows a young lass who's flung herself from a building.' She holds the paper up to her face. 'The Hampshire House building. Shows her falling and shows her fallen. There's blood on the frame, it says here. Ex-Ziegfeld showgirl . . . Dorothy Hale.' Mum looks up and pulls off a pantomime shiver. She lowers her specs, frowns, looks at us both. 'Ooh, imagine that: throwing yourself off a building. Can you imagine throwing yourself off a building, Eleni?'

'No,' says Eleni.

'Can you, Hector?' says Mum.

'No, Mum,' I say.

'Ooh, neither can I. I can imagine taking a lot of pills, or sticking your head in an oven, but I can't see throwing myself off some big building.'

All this is a bit of a revelation. I'm a bit shocked. I don't know why she just came out with such a thing. I steal a glance at Eleni. She's just looking at the floor. We sit in silence for a while. I mean it's not really silence cos Dad's got the telly up loud and there's a lot of cars screaming around Spa-Francorchamps, but it feels like silence, and given what's just been announced, it is.

And next thing you know . . . 'I mean it'd be like me throwing myself off Blackpool Tower. Imagine that. I mean I've never been up the Tower.

Lived here forty-five years and never been up the Tower. I mean I can imagine taking pills and all that, but throwing myself off the Tower? Give over.' She smoothes out the paper on her lap and cranes her neck to read more. Eleni bites into her toast and suddenly I'm irritated by the sound of her chewing. What's going on? Why's Mum talking about throwing herself off the Tower? And why am I irritated by the sound of Eleni chewing her toast?

I look at Mum. She's scanning the article like it's a big fancy puzzle but she's not giving up. Her lips are moving a bit and I see her make an 'F' and then I see her make a 'K'. And then 'Frida Kahlo', silently, to herself.

It won't have gone over her head, all this. Next time it comes up she'll remember exactly who Frida Kahlo is. She's sat there now reading about her, and you can be sure it's all going in. Ever since I started to do well in the art world, ever since they started writing about me in whatever magazines she could get her hands on in Preston, then she's taken an interest. She's never once said, 'Get yourself a proper job,' or 'I think you should be careful.' No, she's just enjoyed my fame and made an effort to understand. She's got an opinion about it all, has Mum. She thinks Jake and Dinos are really seriously poorly, and possibly danger-ous. Not dangerous in the way a critic might call them dangerous but like Mum calls them dangerous. Like maybe the police should get involved. Sarah Lucas is butch and rude. Damien Hirst's dirty and cruel. Rachel Whiteread's got some good ideas but it's all a bit dull once you've got the gist of it. She likes Gillian Wearing cos she's pretty and looks a bit like Eleni, but she didn't like that transsexual caper. And all them policemen idling about would have been put to better use out on the streets catching folk. Catching Jake and Dinos for a start. And as for Gilbert and George, well . . . now they *should* get a proper job.

I clear away the plates and carry them through to the kitchen. I hear Mum and Eleni start up again and I think Mum's asking her whether or not she thinks Madonna is a slag. She doesn't say slag of course, but that's what she's getting at. I can hear Eleni smiling and shifting position, getting comfortable, 'Well . . .' she begins, 'well . . .' I love Eleni. She seems immune to those parts of my mum that drive me off my nut. Good luck to her. I'm off to take a bath.

'Is the immersion heater on, Dad?'

He shouts 'What?' and I repeat myself and he says that it is, but to turn it off cos it's burning money, and I climb the stairs, wishing I could smoke a cigarette.

Above the bath, pride of place, is a small drawing of a budgerigar on old yellowed paper. It sits in an ornate gilded frame behind well-dusted glass. It's lying on its back, dead. But it doesn't look dead cos it's been hung the wrong way, so it looks like it's all right. I did it when I was eight. It used to hang on my Aunty Pat's parlour wall until Pat went mad and died five years back. By then I hadn't seen Pat for twelve years and Mum didn't think to tell me until after she was buried. I'd liked to have attended her funeral. I've never been to a funeral. Oh yes, little dead Bob used to hang on big dead Aunty Pat's parlour wall. I say hang, but in those days it was just tacked to the lilac wallpaper with a couple of drawing pins, curling up at the edges. It was the wrong way up then as well. It means everything. As I lie back in the glittering suds, I look at it for the fifty thousandth time. It's still good. It really is. I was only eight and it was done with one of those fat multicoloured biros, but somehow, somewhere in that aching eight-year-old brain, I'd managed to look at Pat's budgie, little Bob, and somehow comprehend a way of scratching him onto the paper so that you could tell that it was Bob, and not just any old dead budgie. It was this drawing that set me off. The attendant awe that it evoked amongst my elders galvanized my confidence, and supplied the necessary fillip to propel me towards a life of art. 'A life of art'. That's what I have. And all these visits home seem like some sort of gentle archaeological dig. And there is my Troy, behind that well-dusted glass, in that ornate gilded frame. Little Bob. Who'd have thought.

Aunty Pat used to do up her hair in a tall yellow beehive. It looked like ice cream. One dull day when I was six we were all on the beach having a picnic and she got a bee in it, a fat black bee in her tall yellow beehive, burrowing towards her scalp, smashed on lacquer, and Aunty Pat shrieking and shaking, standing up and falling over, Mum pinning her down and Dad going in there with a lolly stick. I was sucking on a Mivvy, not sure what to think, cos it was exciting and funny, but at the same time, awful and frightening, and she might get stung on the head, and what will that do? Will it kill her? Will it make her hair fall off? Will she turn into a bee? She's screaming like she's having unanaesthetized surgery as Dad coaxes it out on the end of the stick, the bee lapping up the vanilla.

All that happened right here, in the shadow of the Gaiety Bar, and I ask Mum if she remembers and she smiles and says she does and we tell Eleni the story. Eleni smiles and holds onto my hand. Her hand feels warm and I can feel her pulse on the pad of her thumb. In my other hand I'm carrying the video camera, just in case. Just in case something happens. Just in case the Tower topples over, or a clown goes mental and runs amok amongst the seaweed and seagull feathers. For there are sea-gulls. And, let me say it now, I remain passionate about the seagulls. I love the sound and the white, and the whole seagull thing. There are kids swinging from a musty rope beneath the pier. Folk out, walking their dogs. Old men with metal detectors looking for Atlantis and old threepenny bits. Drunken screams from the Pleasure Beach. It's dusk and the sun's going down. Mid-September. We talk a little about the sea and Mum asks Eleni if it's as nice as the sea in Crete. Eleni says that it is, and she means it. If Mum had asked me, I would have said that it is, and I would have meant it, cos I love Eleni and we agree about these things. And we mean it. Mum starts telling more stories about when I was little: falling off donkeys, swallowing sand, poking at dead seagulls. Mum looks out towards Central Pier, feasting on her cardboard dish of whelks, seeing ghosts. The tide's going out, the sun's going down and Blackpool's lighting up. I love Blackpool when it's lighting up. I love it when it's lit up and I love it when it's dark. All the times in between. I love Blackpool. I love the way it makes an effort.

'Ooh, when you were little, Hector,' says Mum, 'when you were little.'

We walk along in silence. Mum gazing down at her feet in the sand. Me and Eleni watching a passing tram, done out in bright multi-coloured bulbs to look like a Mississippi showboat.

And then . . . 'So when are you two going to have some kids?' says Mum, right out of the evening blue, as though it's monumental, like we're really getting it all out in the open now, like it's time to get down to things. Real things. Eleni squeezes my hand.

'One day, Mum,' I say, 'I suppose,' cos it's not monumental. In fact it's the opposite of monumental: it's routine. Mum asks, 'So when are you two going to have some kids?' about twice a week, sometimes more, and I always say the same thing: 'One day, Mum,' I always say, and always add, 'I suppose,' and that's usually the end of it. Sometimes Mum loses herself in a reverie about how bonny these kids will be and how much she'll cosset them and feed them and buy them Jaffa Cakes and bears and tiny shoes. 'Oh, go on,' she'll say, 'have some,' and that's usually the end of it. But today, this Sunday evening, it's not. It's just the start of it. Eleni squeezes my hand.

'Well, I'm late, Connie,' she says.

'Late?' says Mum.

'Four days late.' I let go of her hand. 'With my period.'

I love Eleni. I love my Mum. My Mum loves Eleni. Eleni loves my Mum, and both of them love me, so that's all fine, but Eleni's eagerness to please has just put on its gloves and I feel like saying 'Calm down' or 'Give it a rest' but I don't say anything cos Mum gets in the way of all that by stopping in her tracks and bellowing 'ARE YOU!?' in capital letters. With exclamation and question marks. Me and Eleni also stop in our tracks and we're all facing each other.

'Four days?' says Mum. 'Are you, pet?'

'Yes,' says Eleni. She looks at Mum and smiles. Mum looks at Eleni and smiles. And then both of them look at me and suddenly I'm aware that I'm not smiling. So I do, cos anything less would be wrong. Mum looks down at Eleni's buttoned-up coat, at her belly somewhere beneath her buttoned-up coat, through the cloth into her belly, right through into her womb, and so on. And when she's done with this penetration, this tunnelling through space and matter, she starts tunnelling through time and suddenly I can see her holding this thing, this nothing really, feeding this nothing really, buying it Jaffa Cakes and bears and tiny shoes, like it's something, a real thing, a soul, a poppet, a living breathing miniature of her and Dad and all that went before. Eleni looks down at it too. At this lateness, at this four days late, nothing for certain, nothing really, nothing-at-all kind of thing and she smiles and nods. For some reason I find myself turning on the camera. For want of anything else to do I aim it at Mum.

'Ooh, give over,' says Mum, blushing and smoothing down her hair. She hates it when I turn on the camera, and that's why I do it: to stop her. To diffuse this giddiness at Eleni's late period.

'What do you think, Mum?' I say, willing her to move on and hide. But she doesn't move on, she doesn't hide, oh no, in fact, quite the opposite, she looks me in the eye, straight down the lens.

'What do you think, Connie?' says Eleni, and Mum smoothes her hair, gathers her thoughts and tells her, tells us, tells the camera . . .

But first let me tell you what I think. Is Eleni pregnant? I doubt it. Do I want Eleni to be pregnant? I don't know. I really don't know. Do I want a child, children? Ask me something else. Ask me an easier question.

Ask me why Théodore Géricault shaved his head to complete *The Raft of the Medusa*. Ask me why a day on Venus lasts longer than a year on Venus. But a child? A baby, a toddler, an adolescent, an adult, half me, half Eleni? You see, artists aren't very good at all that. Artists are a little perturbed by all that kind of thing. Biological creation. They're suspicious. They imagine that it might hinder all their small plastic creations. They're afraid that biological creation won't be creative. They're afraid of the banal and the mundane. They live in fear of the shit and the puke, of the fatigue, the duty and the loss of control, the immensity of failure and the clash of wills. That's what artists are afraid of. I know – I am an artist. I'm Hector Kipling.

Mum takes a deep breath. 'I think it's lovely.' She's off. 'I think if you and Eleni had a baby . . .' She pauses. 'Is this all right?' she says. 'Is this what you want?' like suddenly she's an actress. The hair gets smoother and the eyes look out to sea.

'My father was an alcoholic cocky illiterate philanderer who left my mother when I was eight.' (That's news to me, but I must say I quite like it.) 'And then, on my eleventh birthday, my mother started complaining about pains in her feet.'

I know about this bit, but she's always told me that she never knew her father. I feel a painting coming on.

'By Christmas she was in the ground. I was an orphan.' She pauses to drag a tear across her cheek with her thick crimson knuckle. I shall never forget it. 'And so on, and so on. And then, to jump ahead a few years, I met your dad at a dance. Well, I'll tell you what, Hector . . . Eleni, darling: I didn't know much about love, I honestly didn't. But I knew what I liked – as you say in the art world – I knew he was for me.'

O Jesus Christ in Heaven Above, I Beseech Thee. No, seriously, I really do.

Her eyes are looking more and more like the vinegar-sodden whelks that she's just wolfed down. And so it goes:

'Well, there you go, we were married within a year. He was thirty-two, I was twenty-six.' Another salty pause. 'Three years later we had you. I had you. You, Hector,' and she points right down the lens and pouts, a bit like Posh Spice used to until she was told to pack it in and smile a bit more. 'And that was all we wanted. All that we could have wished for.'

You know what I think's going on here? Mum, the camera, all this? I'll tell you right now. It's Tracey fucking Emin, that's what it is. Somehow that programme last night – Tracey shuffling around King's Cross talking about her abortion – it's got into Mum, that style, that approach, the candour, the tone of the confessional. Here she is giving it all up and away, and I'm thinking: 'We're on the beach in Blackpool, Eleni's four days late, I've got my camera out and my mum's coming on like Tracey Emin. Giving it large. She's gone all White Cube on us. She's gone all concept. Mum! My mum. Mum as confessional Art Star.'

Mum continues: 'And I used to look at you in your pretty little cot and think that one day, one wonderful day, you'll have kids. It felt like . . . when you have a child . . . you don't just have that child, you have the children of that child, and the children of those children, and so on and so on . . . and it made me so happy that I cried. You in the cot trying to say Mama – although Dada seemed to come easier to you – trying to say all sorts of things. And then one day, out of the sudden blue, you were eight and you drew that budgie.'

She gazes out to sea and walks ahead a little, rubbing her palms together like she's on Channel 4 or summat, like she's a seasoned professional, like she's been up half the night messing with the draft of all this. I follow her. A seagull lands and starts pecking at a crab. Mum throws it a handful of nut crumbs. 'We all need something small to look after,' I expect her to say, but she doesn't. She's got her own thoughts, her own ideas, and here they come:

'And I know that me and your dad couldn't draw the bloody curtains, but you can. You can draw it all and make it look real and strange and lost. And I know that we're useless. That I'm useless, but I did make you and you can make other things, and if you went on and made a baby then I think that would be lovely.' We're back where we started with everything being lovely, which is more like Mum and I relax. I turn off the camera and wish she knew that I was smoking again. 'Was that all right?' she says and I say, 'Yes,' and, 'Great,' and, 'Definitely,' and, 'Amazing, Mum.' We set off back for home and talk of other things like candy floss and donkey shit and fuck knows what. Whatever it is it's got nothing to do with babies from then on. But it has really.

That night we all went back and congratulated Dad on painting the garage floor green.

'It looks a bit like we've got grass in the garage,' he says.

'You know what, Dad,' I say, 'you're right. It does.'

We ordered a Chinese takeaway. At half-past eight I took control of the television and made everybody watch a documentary about Edwin Hubble.

'Look at that,' says Mum, pointing at a nebula cluster, 'it looks like an eye.'

'The eye of God,' says Dad, though he doesn't mean it cos he doesn't believe in God. Neither does Mum. At least I don't think they do. They've never mentioned Him. My whole life, not one mention of Him. Until now.

Anyway, Mum needn't have bothered looking through Eleni's buttoned-up coat into her womb, cos that night, after Mum and Dad had scuttled off to bed, we fucked on the cream settee again, and Eleni's four-days-late bit all came flooding out. We didn't stop when the blood started to pour over the cream settee, we persevered and mumbled things like 'Yes' and 'Oh God' and 'Fuck!' Cos sex is like that, and that's how we like it.

'Mum,' I say the following morning as she's struggling to open the milk, 'there's blood on the settee.'

'Eh?'

'I said there's blood on the settee.'

She stops trying to open the milk and puts it down. 'How do you mean?'

'How do you mean, "How do you mean"?'

'How do you mean there's blood on the settee?'

'I mean there's blood on the settee.'

'How?'

'I had a nosebleed,' I hear myself say. I hadn't meant to say that. I'd been all set to tell the truth. Me and Eleni have talked it over and we've agreed that I should just tell the truth. Eleni's hiding upstairs.

'You had a nosebleed?'

'Last night.' This is pathetic. There's too much blood for a nosebleed, too much of it for it to have come from my nose. Who am I? Cyrano de fucking Bergerac?

'A nosebleed?'

'Yes.'

'You had a nosebleed?'

'No.'

'What?'

'No.'

'What?'

'No, I didn't have a nosebleed.'

'Hector, what are you talking about?'

'I don't know.'

'Are you sleepwalking again?'

'No, Mum. I'm just saying that I didn't have a nosebleed.'

'But you just said you did.'

'I know.'

'You said there was blood on the settee.'

'There is.'

'How do you mean?'

'How do you mean, "How do you mean"?'

Mum turns through three hundred and sixty degrees.

'She's not late anymore.'

'Who?'

'Eleni.'

'What do you mean she's not late? Where is she? What are you talking about?'

'She's not four days late anymore, Mum.'

There. I've said it. I fucking said it. I got it out. Fuck I'm modern. What a modern little fucker I am. I told her. She gets it. She's got it. It's got. It's done.

Mum picks up the milk, pushes past me, walks through to the lounge and stands there looking down at the cushions, all sad. I stand in the doorway wondering if she's thinking what I thought, what Eleni thought: I wonder if she's thinking the shape of the stain looks a bit like Africa. I wonder this. And I wonder what to say. And I wonder how she feels. And I wonder where Dad is. And I wonder why she picked up the milk.

Suddenly, out of nowhere, Sparky's on the scene, jumping up onto the settee and getting to work. Giddy as fuck, lapping it up. Oh, Sparky, you idiot. You idiotic little twat. Most idiotic of all the beasts.

In conclusion, let me say this: I wish – I really do, I really wish – that he wasn't doing that right now.

On the train home there is no great sense of regret. We had never planned to have a baby. In fact, it is important to mention that Eleni hadn't taken a test, seen a doctor or pissed on a strip of plastic. She was simply late. She's been late before, and no doubt she'll be late again. One day, of course, we'll all be late.

The late Hector Kipling.

'Ladies and gentlemen, what am I bid? We start at twelve million.'

3

We're back at home and Eleni's sat at the piano, staring at the TV. She goes through a series of diminished chords interspersed with ninths and sevenths and concludes it all with a C sharp seventh and an F sharp minor. Not that I'd know all this unless she told me what she was doing as she was doing it, which she does, calling out all the letters and numbers as she moves her body from side to side, her fingers flickering across the keyboard, hair in her eyes, fag in her mouth. Sometimes she takes it out and does it all with the fag between two knuckles, like producing glorious music is the easiest trick in the world. She's making me smile with how much she wants me to understand. I do the same for her with my painting sometimes, calling out the colours and the brushes. At times like these I think we're perfect. At times like these I think she thinks the same; imagine that.

'Put your fingers there,' she says, 'put your left hand here, and your right hand here. Now press them all down together at the same time,' and she takes my fingers in hers and settles each on its respective key. She squeezes my wrist and gives me the rhythm. 'That's called E flat diminished,' she says, 'and your left hand is playing two E flats an octave apart. Now just look at the screen and keep pressing them down. I'll do the pedals.'

I do as I'm told. There's a woman on the TV making a cup of tea. She pulls out the teabag, spoons in the sugar, pours in the milk and then, for no apparent reason, hurls the whole lot across the room. It cuts to a shot of the tea snaking across the linoleum, disappearing beneath the

41

fridge. Eleni rearranges my fingers and sets me off again. Brittle diminisheds repeat over and over as the woman pulls onto her head a yellow polythene bag with 'C'est Ça!' written on it. Then F diminished over and over again, and then I'm moved to a C ninth and we can see the shape of the woman's face through the polythene. 'And now F,' says Eleni, shifting me out of the way and doing it herself.

'What's this film about?' I say.

'It's about a man and a woman,' says Eleni, playing off key now and again, a bit like Les Dawson, but a lot more chilling than Les. 'One night at the start of the film they run over a cat and kill it. The man has been drinking and his response to the death of the cat is so . . . musketeer . . .'

'Musketeer?'

'What is that word you told me that means carefree, like a soldier?'

'Cavalier,' I say. I love Eleni.

'Yes, the man is so cavalier that the woman punches him in the face with the cat. They separate after that night and the rest of the film is about how they both cope with the separation. He drinks more than ever and sleeps on prostitutes and she is trying to learn French from a tape because she has become totally obsessed with a waiter who can only say, "Here is your bill. Service is not included." She also tries to kill herself a lot – as we see,' says Eleni, as the woman cuts into the bag with a pair of scissors. 'It's called *Dead Space*. It's a comedy.'

Later that day it's time for Eleni to indulge me a little by helping me to manoeuvre my life's work from the flat down into the street. I'm struggling with the winch. I'm stripped to the waist, sweat pouring off my chest, lowering a painting down into the street. Eleni's standing by the truck with her arms aloft, waiting to receive my painting of a big green face dangling in mid-air, big as a cathedral door, swaddled in bubble wrap, the big ugly face peeping through. Big ugly eyes staring out towards the canal, swaying in the breeze. It must seem quite a spectacle to that old dear who's stopped in her tracks to take it all in. Shopping by her side. Little dog sniffing at a lolly wrapper. Perhaps she's noticed that it's me hanging out there. Perhaps she's registered the big green ugly face and then looked up at me, and seen that it's my face. And I don't know why but it makes me feel very proud in a way, even if it's proud only in front of this crooked little pensioner down in the street. It's a quiet street and hardly anyone ever comes along. She's just stood there, looking up. In awe. I think I can say in awe. Either that or she's simple and she doesn't know where she is.

'Two more feet,' yells Eleni, 'two more feet and I got it.'

I've agreed with Myers, who runs the Doodlebug Gallery in Bethnal Green, that I'll take care of the transport and we've hired a little truck. I'm not even sure that it's going to fit, but Eleni says that even if it hangs over the edges, as long as it's covered and well secured then everything will be good. That's how she says it: 'Everything will be good,' her thick Cretan accent making it all sound easy as pie.

I begin to shake with the effort and the winch groans. Looking down I can see that Eleni has just about got her fingertips to the edge of the frame. She's shifting her new blue shoes across the pavement as she prepares to find her balance. The old woman's still stalled in her tracks, dog still sniffing the lolly wrapper, nose right in there, lapping up the raspberry.

'Here it comes,' I shout.

'Here I am,' she replies and steadies it at both corners, though she's too tiny to span the full width. It's the largest piece I've ever produced and fuck knows why I've said to Myers that I'll transport it myself. He should have offered some help if you ask me, but he didn't and I'm beginning to think that he's a bit of a chancer.

The old woman snags the leash on her dog and moves off. 'Come on, Reggie,' she says, and hobbles past Eleni, ducking her head, and Eleni smiles at her and says that we're sorry. And I think how I'm not, but I know that Eleni is, and how she means it, and how I love her, and how

I thank the stars for the day Godfrey Bolton rigged up that bridle from the rafters. 'I've got it,' she yells, 'it's with me now.' I give the winch a few more turns until she's eased it over towards the window of the old print works opposite and settled it against their wall.

There's a red Volkswagen Beetle coming up the road. It's got black spots painted all over it to look like a ladybird. Just as Eleni's cleaning off her hands and looking up to see if I'm coming down, a motorbike tears round the corner, leaning over on its side, the way Dad used to show me when he brought out his old photos of him at the TT Races. The ladybird swerves but it's no use: the motorbike panics and goes right through the middle of my face. Eleni falls back against the truck, and as quick as he's down the rider's back on his feet, skipping up and down to show he's all right. 'God, that was weird,' I can hear him say, 'that was fucking weird.' He takes off his helmet and he looks at his bike, smoking, still purring, right there, in the middle of my fat oily bubble-wrapped mouth. The canvas is in shreds.

I look down and think about jumping, but I don't. How could I think about jumping when I have a girl like Eleni? She's trying to grab hold of the biker to calm him down. He's in a right state. 'God, that was weird,' he keeps saying, over and over again. And then he collapses and I rush to the phone and call for an ambulance.

When I was with Sheba we lived in a small brown flat overlooking Leicester Square. I remember one night lying there on the floor, stoned on skunk, drunk on Tennessee sour mash. Sheba was out somewhere. I didn't know where. Probably fucking some fucking teenager. Down in the Square there were three buskers. One bloke was singing 'King of the Swingers' through a little practice amp, turned right up. Another bloke, in a long drape of burgundy velvet and a maroon dickie bow, was spouting something from *Turandot*. And in the middle of them both was a Bolivian guitar combo, going at it like they've just slaughtered a gram in the toilets of the Equinox. On top of all this you've got the hysteric jangle of the fair and a premiere of the new Bond film at the Empire and the theme music blasting out of twenty-foot speakers. Five fire engines screaming around Piccadilly. Next thing you know the little pastoral gimmick outside the Swiss Centre kicked in with its silly black bells, chiming out 'Molly Malone', though what that's got to do with Switzerland fuck knows. Anyway, I was lying there on the floor, listening to all this, and I thought, 'Fuck it. My life's out of control.' And it was. It definitely was. So the next morning, since Sheba still hadn't shown up, I packed a few things together and set off walking across the Square. I didn't get very far. I booked into the Hampshire between Garfunkel's and the Odeon. I took a two hundred and forty-nine pound a night room and stayed there for two weeks. When I finally got it together to phone Sheba to tell her it was over she was already gone. She'd moved in with some diabetic skateboarder who didn't mind her sleeping disorder, her compulsive masturbatory spasms and her filthy fucking bras flung all over the floor of his Clapham squat. Fine.

Here's a funny thing: Shakespeare stands in the middle of Leicester Square, flanked by four ugly fish spouting dirty water. He's resting his chin on his fist and gawping at a little statue of Charlie Chaplin. One night I was staggering through the Square, and someone had pushed a custard pie into Chaplin's bronze gob. There are some real artists out there. Real ones. Just pissing their lives away.

Eleni has my head in her lap and she's calling me things like 'baby' and 'angel' and kissing my hands and stroking the hair out of my eyes, which are crimson, I'm sure, and sore and glassy with tears. It took me three months to paint that ugly green face, God knows how many hours staring into the mirror looking like that shot in *The Shining* where Jack Nicholson's finally lost it – the one that goes on for about a minute and nothing's moving, not one hair, and you're thinking, 'Fuck, he's finally lost it.'

Eleni's kissing my hands, stroking the hair out of my eyes and calling me things like 'baby' and 'angel'.

For the second time in a week I'm in tears over a painting.

I saw Bianca earlier. I've seen Bianca every Monday for the past three months, since July. Ever since Lenny was shortlisted. Ever since Lenny accepted his shortlisting. Ever since they shortlisted Lenny and Lenny couldn't rouse himself to decline, that's how long I've been seeing Bianca. Not that there's a connection. Oh no, there's no connection. So what if I started seeing Bianca the day after he broke the news? So what if Bianca knows his middle name and the name of his mother's dog? There's no connection. So what if Bianca's scabby parrot squawks 'Lenny!' every time he sees me?

Anyway, like I say, I saw her earlier. She asked me if I wanted a herbal tea or a proper tea, and I said, 'All proper tea is theft,' and we got into a conversation about Communism, wit, Freud and beards. She told me that pogonophobia is a fear of beards and I told her about how Cuban intelligence once foiled a CIA plot to devise a powder to be smuggled into Castro's boots that would make his beard fall off. She smiled. It was the first time I'd seen her smile. She's quite pretty when she smiles.

THE PILLARS OF HERCULES, SOHO, LONDON

'So then she scrambles off into the bathroom and comes out with a broken bottle.'

'Shampoo bottle?' says Kirk.

'No!' says Lenny. 'A glass bottle,' and lifts his hand up into a claw, which me and Kirk take to represent glass. 'A broken fucking glass bottle,' says Lenny, 'and she's brandishing it in my face.'

I'm sitting in the Pillars of Hercules with Lenny Snook and Kirk Church.

'And she's screaming and screaming, "Kill me, Kill me," over and over.'

'With the bottle?' says Kirk.

'Eh?'

'Did she mean with the bottle?'

'Eh?'

'Kill her with the bottle?'

'I don't know,' says Lenny, 'I suppose so. It's not the point.'

'So,' I say, 'she's coming at you with this bottle . . . Carry on.'

'So I get down on my knees and I put my hands together.'

'Like you're praying?' says Kirk.

'Yeah, like I'm on my knees praying. Like I'm trying, like I'm really fucking, you know, trying to neuter the situation. I mean . . . fucking hell.'

'And?' I say.

'She says we should go to relationship counselling.'

'Brenda says that?'

'That's what she says, bottle in hand, me on my knees, making out that I'm praying.'

'So are you?'

'What?'

'Will you?'

'Will I fuck. I want out of it. It's over.' He runs his hand across his scalp. 'There's nothing to say. You can't make shit not shit by talking about it. I don't want fucking relationship counselling. I don't want this relationship to be fucking counselled. I want it to be cancelled!' he shouts, 'I want relationship cancelling!' And he bangs his fist down on the table and the table wobbles and looks scared like it's all the table's fault.

Kirk's saying nothing. Kirk's quite a quiet fella and he's seriously uncomfortable with things like passion and fists and shouting in pubs when everyone can hear. Lenny's not like that. Lenny and Kirk are very different. Kirk's got a thing about the right way of making tea. Lenny's all fist.

'I want this giant blue glove to drop from the sky and stamp it all out.'

'Like in *Yellow Submarine*,' says Kirk.

'Eh?'

'Like in *Yellow Submarine*, when the Blue Glove wipes out Pepperland.'

'Does it?' says Lenny.step

'Yeah,' says Kirk, 'it does. Big Blue Glove.'

'Well . . .'

'It's in your psyche somewhere, is that,' and then, 'obviously.'

Lenny looks a bit put out by this information. 'Anyway, what I'm saying is . . . what was I saying?'

'You were saying how you want an end to it,' I say, 'and then you stole an image from *Yellow Submarine*.'

'What do you mean I stole it?'

'All right, you appropriated it.'

'What's with all this stealing shit?' He's gone a bit sweaty.

'What stealing shit?' I say.

'All these snide jibes about stealing you've been coming out with recently.'

'When?'

'The night I came back from New York, just now.'

'I'm nipping to the toilet,' says Kirk, and does.

I light up a cigarette. Lenny lights up a cigarette. Copying me.

'So?' says Lenny.

'So what?'

'So, Hec, I've known you since you were seventeen and summat's going on.'

'Lenny,' I say, 'I've known you since you were seventeen and you're getting paranoid.' He takes it no further, and we both sit there staring at the ashtray.

Here's how we met: 10 December 1980, the day after news reached Blackpool that Lennon had been shot. I'm having a fag on the beach, humming 'Mother', looking out to sea, cos that's what artists do when they need to think. The sun is sinking and the tide's on its way out for the night. I gaze at the waves giving up the fight, filthy brown waves, like old tea and dosser's flob. I gaze at the horizon and think about New York. I think about Liverpool and how bullets must feel. I think about Spaniards and spanners and Edgar Allan Poe getting a kicking. And then I get back to the waves, the icy waves, and I see something white and square floating on the surface. And then no. Not floating. Appearing. The tide has gone and there's something white on the beach. An old washing machine. I wait for a long time and then I walk over to it. The beach is deserted. It's starting to rain and I open the door. Inside the washing machine is an apple. I examine the apple, look around, and take a bite.

The next day a photograph of me, standing by the washing machine, biting the apple, is delivered to my parents' house. There's a phone number, written in white, on a black plastic joke-shop moustache. That's how I met Lenny.

Kirk staggers back from the toilet and does a little drum riff on the table. 'So,' he says, 'it's over?'

'What?' says Lenny.

'You and Brenda. Sounds like you're saying it's over.' He looks a bit strange, like he might have been crying. 'You were saying you want an end to it.'

'Exactly,' says Lenny, 'I want an end to it. I want the tide to rush in and out, and the beach all smooth, and all these disappointing moats and castles washed out of existence.' Interesting. He continues, 'I want my heart running down the street in funny red slippers, squirting water from a plastic flower on its lapel.' I try to imagine such a thing. 'I want a heart with a lapel.' He's clawing at his stool. 'Is that wrong? Is it wrong to want that?'

I sneak a quick look around the bar. Everyone else seems to be having normal conversations.

A minute goes by. Lenny's staring at the clock like it's gonna draw a gun on him. And then: 'It's an easy thing to bring horror into a room,' he says. 'I could cut my throat open with this glass right now.'

'Go on, then,' says Kirk.

'But you'd have a task to get happiness in as fast.'

'What if that girl over there,' says Kirk, waving his pint at some little piece of jailbait in the corner, 'walked up to you and said she's in love with you and needs to take you down into the bog for a blow job?' Kirk got here early and he's a couple of pints up on us.

'Like I say,' says Lenny, 'it's an easy thing to bring horror into a room.'

'Her coming up to you and telling you she's in love is one thing,' I say, sucking on my fag, being careful not to offend Kirk, 'and asking you down to the bog for a blow job's another.'

'Exactly,' says Lenny. And the three of us sit there wondering what I mean by that, and what Lenny means by saying 'exactly', and what Kirk means by saying nothing but nodding and taking another swig of his pint. Men can be a bit sad sometimes. Especially when they're hunched up around a pub table saying things behind their girlfriends' backs. I say girlfriends cos none of us are married. We're all in our forties and unmarried.

Lenny's with Brenda Barker, who's a potter. He's been with Potty Brenda for six years and she frightens him. Two things in particular frighten him. The first is her proclivity for hurling knives. The second is the accuracy of her aim. There's a small wound on his shoulder right now. He's hiding it, but I can see it every time the collar of his shirt comes down.

Kirk used to go out with an agoraphobic called Audrey. Or I should say that he used to stay in with an agoraphobic called Audrey. She left him last year for a writer called Gordon. They'd met in counselling. Gordon wasn't agoraphobic but he wasn't too keen on going outside cos he was scared that flies would lay eggs in his ears. I think that's what Kirk said. That was five years ago and ever since then Kirk's been painting pictures of cutlery. Kirk's been painting a lot of cutlery and getting nowhere. He used to paint kettles but gave that up cos it was sending him mental. Me and Snook are always telling him to look beyond the kitchen, but he won't have it. As for me, well . . . I'm Hector Kipling, aren't I?

I'm Hector Kipling. It's my real name. Hector Derek Kipling if you want it all. Fuck knows what Mum was thinking. She said it came to her in a dream, but Dad's convinced it's the name of some old boyfriend. Sounds like a cartoon dog. Pompous little dachshund or summat. Anyway, I paint big heads. A bit like Chuck Close paints big heads but not so real as his; more saturated and skewed, more grotesque I suppose. Think Otto Dix. I paint the sort of big heads that Otto might have painted if he'd ever got round to painting big heads. And because these big heads are so big they tend to go for about £20,000 a shot. And they do go. They've been going for about five years now and so I'm not short of a bob or two.

But something happened the other day after that guy ran his bike through my canvas. I sat up all night, smoking, staring at a big white canvas propped up against the wall, on which I was gonna paint another big head. 'Fuck it,' I thought, 'once and for all, just fuck it. I'm through with big heads. It's over. It's time to move on.' That motorbike smashing through the middle of my gob was a sign. A symbol, if you like. It was the first time I'd attempted a self-portrait and it was only cos Myers was on my back, but it was obviously wide of the mark and that bike bursting through it was no accident. It was an omen. Or is an omen. Whatever. Oh yes, things are gonna change. Big Head's dead, long live . . . Well, I haven't decided yet, but it'll be fabulous and important and new and . . . I think it'll be big.

'So what you gonna do?' says Lenny.

'I don't know,' I say, 'but I think it'll be big.'

'Right.'

'Well, I mean, I've got the canvas now.'

'You could give that to me,' says Kirk, fingering a pimple on his temple, 'I could do a big spoon.'

Me and Lenny look at him.

'Maybe that's my problem. Maybe all this cutlery's just too fucking small.'

That's not your problem, Kirk.

'You could give it to me,' says Lenny, 'I had an idea to do something big a while back.'

'But you don't paint,' says Kirk, still fingering that pimple.

'I'm not talking about painting. I had this idea to take a big canvas . . . How big's yours, Hec?'

'Fifteen foot by eight,' I say.

'Yeah, as big as that. I had this idea to blag some veins from the hospital – I got my hands on some of Brenda's after her varicose surgery – and weave them into a canvas. I'd have to run it past health and safety but, y'know . . .'

I quite like it but he's not getting my canvas.

'I don't know,' I say, gazing at the ceiling, ignoring them, 'but it'll come to me. Summat'll come to me.' And we all sit in a bit of silence again like it might come to me in a minute. But it doesn't, and I didn't expect it to. I don't know why it all went so quiet. They should have known that I wasn't talking about that very minute.

Kirk's rubbing his head and looking a bit odd and Lenny asks him if he's all right and Kirk takes a swig of his pint, swallows, takes a deep breath, takes another swig, finishes it, takes another deep breath, puts his head in his hands and starts crying. Me and Lenny look at each other. And just like Kirk's no good with fists and passion and shouting in pubs, Lenny's no good with deep breaths and crying. Neither am I come to that, but I'm better than Lenny so I touch Kirk's dirty little cuff and I ask him what's the matter.

'Nothing,' he says, and wipes his face, and he must have had some ash on his fingers cos there's a black streak running from the corner of his eye to his mouth. Either that or he's wearing mascara.

'Come on, Kirk, there must be summat,' I say, 'what you crying for?'

'I've just had too much,' he says.

'Too much of what?' says Lenny. 'Too much of life?' He says it with a surprising sincerity and I feel quite touched on Kirk's behalf.

'No,' says Kirk, 'I mean just too much to drink.'

Neither of us believe him and we both sit there staring at him like he might say more, but he doesn't. He just stares at the froth on my pint like he's counting the bubbles. He takes out a pencil and starts to doodle a fork on Lenny's pack of Camel Lights. I look at Kirk's odd little face. He's quite ugly in a way. Chubby little face. But he's quite beautiful as well, in a way. I look at him now and I'm reminded of something Paul Gauguin once said. He said, 'The ugly may be beautiful, the pretty, never.' And I look at Kirk's damp fat face with the black streak of ash running from the corner of his eye to his mouth. 'How true,' I think. I'd never understood it before now, but how true. And suddenly I get it into my brain that I want to paint his head all big and . . . 'No! No! Stop it!' I think. 'No more big ugly heads, even if it is Kirk all sad and confused with something he's not telling us. No more big heads!'

'I might have a brain tumour,' he says, shading in the prongs of his fork, 'I've had a scan, an MRI, and I've got to wait for the results but my doctor's worried.' There's a pause, and then, 'Pessimistic,' he says. His eyes look like they've been laminated. There's some blokes over at the bar watching snooker, making jokes at the barmaid about balls and pockets. One of them says something and another pushes him and he falls off his stool and everyone looks and it's all gone a bit strange.

Like Lenny says: it's an easy thing to bring horror into a room.

I'm lying in my bed. It's the middle of the night and I'm staring into space. I keep staring into space for a long time until I suddenly get the feeling that space is staring back and I shut my eyes and stare at that, whatever that is. The back of the eyelids, I suppose. But it's not just the back of the eyelids when you shut your eyes, is it? It's something else. What is it? I don't know, but it scares the shit out of me sometimes. It's scaring the shit out of me right now cos I'm seeing things that I'm not even thinking of. Ever have that happen? Like you're witnessing some projection that you had no hand in? Insane tableaux: hundreds of iron dwarves riding a carousel, or masks made of lemon peel floating in a lake of mercury and pepper. Ever had that? Sometimes, of course, I just see big heads and I suppose that Kirk just sees mounds of cutlery, huge open graves of cutlery. Fuck knows what Lenny sees, or what Mum and Dad see, or what Eleni sees.

Eleni's sleeping. We came to bed at midnight, got all excited that we both had no clothes on – even after three years we still get excited that we both have no clothes on – and started kissing. My body started to feel very different to how it felt in the day and she lowered the sheet and licked my hips. But she's asleep now and I'm awake with my eyes closed and I can see Tutankhamen pedalling his bike out to sea. And I wonder what that means. I open my eyes for a few minutes and wonder why I'm seeing such a thing. And then I think about it, and somehow, it seems to me that I know exactly what it means. Well, I have my suspicions, let me put it that way.

The first time I came to London was to see a dead body. I was six. It was the only time I ever visited London with my parents. It took five hours by car. Me and Dad shared the driving. Him in the front, me in the back with a nice plastic steering wheel suckered onto the seat.

Dad wanted to see his chariot, Mum wanted to see his mask. I wanted to see his mummy. I wanted to see the corpse. The swaddled and crusted corpse.

But we didn't. We never saw it. The queue around the British Museum was so impossibly long we couldn't face it. Well, *I* could face it, but Dad's corns were playing up so that was that. We took a train to Hampton Court instead. Dad sat and had a pot of tea and me and Mum got lost in the maze. And then we went home. I was miserable, really miserable, and sulked, and wouldn't talk cos I'd really wanted to see that dead body. And I'm miserable now as I think about it, and I'm sulking now. But I'll talk now, cos I think there's something to say about all that and it has to do with me, my Aunty Pat, Big Heads and Kirk's tumour.

My Aunty Pat wasn't really my Aunty Pat she was my mum's mum's sister so I suppose that made her my Grand-Aunty Pat, but that made her sound a bit grand so we just called her plain Aunty Pat. So my Aunty Pat went mad and died. I have no idea how you might define this madness, but after it rained you couldn't keep her from running outside with a towel to dry the road. Perhaps it was some form of hydrophobia. Perhaps she was rabid. But I doubt it; there wasn't much rabies where she lived. I hadn't seen her for twelve years, but when she finally went under I wasn't told until two weeks after the funeral. Mum explained to me that since I hadn't seen, nor spoken to, Aunty Pat for twelve years, as far as I was concerned she might as well have been dead for twelve years. But of course she hadn't and I could have seen her at any time, though I didn't, and now I can't, so you're wrong, Mum, it's not the same thing at all. And she was the only aunty, or grand-aunty, I ever had, and it's the only death we've had in the family, the only death in my lifetime, and I missed out on it. All my grandparents died before I was born, so I missed out on that as well. None of my friends have ever died and no one I know or knew has ever died, so I missed out on that as well, and I missed out on seeing Tutankhamen and now he's pedalling out to sea on his bike. I didn't even know he had a bike.

Eventually, of course, three years ago, I did get to see some death. I got to see Godfrey Bolton's corpse hanging from the rafters and I was naked and I fell in love with Eleni Marianos right there beneath Godfrey Bolton's swinging grey feet and that's when I started painting big heads. Godfrey Bolton's big dead head. No one knew it was Bolton cos I didn't paint it from life, obviously, he was dead, and the coroner hustled him away. The eyes were open and the mouth was open, and although he was grey and green and God knows what other colours, everyone thought he was just a bit intense. I called it *God Bolton*, and with me being from Lancashire everyone just thought it was some intense bloke from Bolton; as though it was a comment upon the town. But it wasn't. It was Godfrey Bolton and he was dead, and it was beautiful, and Saatchi bought it, and suddenly I was famous. Interviewed, photographed. So what should we make of all that? Well, let me tell you something else.

New York, December, 1980. A jewelled forest of candles outside the Dakota Building. Millions upon millions of people all over the world, grief-stricken, incredulous, stunned. Me too. Oh yes, me too! But was I sorry for Yoko? Was I aching for little Sean and Yoko? No. I was sorry for myself. I was aching for myself. I was jealous of Yoko and little Sean. Jealous of Sean's and Yoko's grief, of the dignity, the nobility, the gravitas it bestowed upon them. And that's never gone away. I envy them to this day. I envy their famous and tragic history and I'm sulking cos some part of me wants it. I want that history. I want that gravitas. I want the texture of death. I want people to know and feel sorry for me and comfort me and say things like 'How awful' and 'We can't imagine'. I want that. I want that awful intense and serious unhappiness, cos then I might feel better, and then I might be happy.

Which brings us to Kirk Church and his tumour.

We had to carry Kirk home from the Pillars of Hercules. He couldn't even stand by the end of it all. Lenny had his shoulders and I had his feet and we lugged him across Soho Square, along Carlisle Street, across Wardour and down D'Arblay to Berwick Street where he lives with his collection of boxed scorpions and a cat called Bacon. And cutlery. A ridiculous amount of cutlery. Like it's some sort of mental problem he has. We carried him up the stairs and dropped him on the bed and then he went and shat himself. He was muttering, 'I'm sorry, I'm so sorry,' over and over as we worked on him with a flannel. But he wasn't saying it to us cos he was asleep and dreaming. Lenny didn't want to go home. Lenny couldn't go home. Lenny was scared to go home cos he's splitting up with Brenda Barker, and Brenda Barker throws knives and plates, and rips up floorboards, and then throws floorboards, so we agreed that Lenny would stay the night and that I'd go home to Eleni, cos I love Eleni and that's what's right with my life. But I'll tell you what's wrong with my life. I'll tell you the problem with my life. The fucking problem with my life is its lack of death. And now Kirk might be dying and I might get what I want, although, of course, I don't want to get what I want cos I don't want Kirk to die. Anyway, for now, while Kirk's still alive, all the attention's on him. Everyone's sorry for Kirk, everyone's rooting for Kirk, not for me. And it's only when he's dead that I'll get my share and I'm lying here in my bed and Tutankhamen's pedalling his bike out to sea.

Mum called the next morning. She said it's fine about the blood on the settee cos they never really liked it anyway, and it's old, and my dad, based on nothing, is allergic to it, and it's gone. They've taken it to the dump and they're looking for a new one.

'Why didn't you wait till you've got a new one before you chucked out the old one?' I said.

'Cos we're mad,' she said and giggled.

'But what will you sit on?'

'The chairs,' she said, and I couldn't argue with that.

She asked how her lovely Eleni is and I told her she's fine and how she's really sorry about the blood. Mum said not to worry cos now it's at the dump. She'd seen an advert in the paper and she's off to take a look but Dad's not going with her cos his guts are playing him up and he's in bed with a fever and a book about shelving.

'Go easy,' I said.

She asked me what I meant.

'Just go easy,' I said, 'with all that stuff you're doing to the house. You're both knocking on and you should be paying someone to do all that.'

'Nay,' she said, 'we're not paying folk to do what we can do ourselves. What's the point of that?'

I could see lots of points to that because I paint big heads and people buy them and I'm lazy and I'd pay someone to brush my teeth if there was such a thing. 'Oh well,' I said instead, 'I suppose so.'

She said goodbye and then rattled on for another ten minutes about how it's a good job that I don't eat meat because the French are feeding shit to their cows. She didn't say shit, of course. Dung, is what she said. Dung. I love Mum. I love the way she makes an effort.

4

J. SHEEKEY'S, ST MARTIN'S COURT, LONDON

I'm prodding at my tuna and crafting elaborate contours with the barley. I'm attempting a little barley head and squeezing the blood from my tuna to render the lips. Eleni's got the fisherman's pie but she's not playing with it, she's eating it, like everything's all right, like everything's as usual, as though last night's epiphany never happened. But then again, she was asleep and I've said nothing so she's entitled to eat her fisherman's pie. And now I'm beginning to shake. I am, I'm definitely shaking.

'What's the matter?' says Eleni. 'You're shaking.'

'Oh, nothing,' I say, looking for a dribble of soy sauce to work into the shadow beneath the nose.

'What's that?' she says, looking at my barley face. 'A face?'

'Yep,' I say, and grit my teeth, cos I hate people who say things like 'yep' and 'nope', and 'poss' and 'gotcha'. But I say 'yep' and grit my teeth. Not my real teeth; the teeth in my brain. I'll tell you about the teeth in my brain later.

'Is something bothering you?' says Eleni.

'Nope.'

'I think something is bothering for you.' Her accent, or her grammar or her inflection, makes it sound like a question or an accusation or a reprimand. First it was the nibbling on her toast in Blackpool that got to me, and now it's her accent. I love Eleni. I love her accent. What's going on?

'Well, maybe something is bothering me,' I say, and I think that my

59

accent, my dull, Blackpudlian mumble, must make it sound like a confession or a rejection or an ultimatum.

Eleni puts down her fork and strokes my neck. I put down my fork next to hers and cover her hand with mine and press, like I love her. Like I love her for stroking my neck when I'm being such a moody prick. I stare at my fork. I stare at both our forks there on the crisp white cloth. And I think of Kirk and my heart fills with petrol.

I tell her the story of Kirk's revelation and the journey home and the stairs and the bed and the shit and the dream and how Lenny couldn't face Brenda, and how Dad couldn't face Tutankhamen's queue, and how I could, and wanted to, and would have loved to, but didn't, cos Dad couldn't. And I tell her about Bob, the dead budgie, and Pat, the dead aunty, and Yoko and Bolton and Kirk's pessimistic doctor, and wouldn't it have been stimulating if that biker had died when he went crashing through my head? Wouldn't that have been fine? Wouldn't that have been a story? We didn't know him. What the fuck do we care? It might have helped the situation. Eleni frowns at the word 'situation'. Or maybe it's just the rest of it that she's frowning at. Yeah, now I think about it, it's got nothing to do with the word 'situation', she's frowning cos I've just revealed some horrendous and Satanic depravity, and I sit there thinking, 'Maybe she wants to call the police, or an ambulance, or . . . Fuck, I don't know, maybe I need the fire brigade. I need something, I know that, I need someone.' And Eleni strokes my neck again and I realize that I need Eleni. Then I realize I have Eleni, and calm down a bit and stop shaking. And I love her accent and I love her nibbling. Fucking hell, Hector, get a grip. You're losing it.

'I see,' says Eleni. I think she does see. I really think she does. 'I understand what you're saying.'

'But is that sick?' I say. 'Is all that perverse?'

'No,' she says, picking up her fork and loading her mouth with a ball of monkfish. 'No, I don't think it is perverse. I think it is an honesty of you and brave.'

Maybe I love her cos her language is so simple, which makes her thoughts seem so simple. Each word to her is a foreign word, so each word comes out with a balloon tied to the corner and the effect is wisdom. The effect is wisdom when maybe the reality is just limitation. No, Hector, that isn't true. She knows what she's saying. She chooses her words like a native. Perhaps more carefully than a native, so she's right and she's wise and it isn't perverse. Except it is. Cos something, some shitty dark thing inside me, wants Kirk dead. It wants Kirk on a slab and me in tears and a black suit saying what devastation all this has wrought. I'm a monster and I should be nailed to the side of a mountain. I'm a ghoul and a freak and someone should notify the tabloids.

The waitress takes our plates away. 'Kirk wanted my canvas to paint a big spoon.'

She smiles.

I smile.

We're both smiling.

It's beautiful. I think.

We're not being cruel. Kirk's a wonderful human being. I love Kirk. Kirk deserves the earth. But his paintings of cutlery are really quite crap. Is that wrong to say that? Should we tell him? Is the essence of friend-ship to tell a friend when you think he's squandering his life painting kitchen utensils? Or is it to encourage him, cos maybe it's you who's ignorant and perhaps the world just isn't ready for a ten-foot spoon. I don't know. Actually, didn't Claes Oldenburg already do a ten-foot spoon? He did a ten-foot dead match and a big burger and some lollies. I'm sure he did a ten-foot spoon. Who would have thought it, eh, Kirk? But there you go. It's been done.

We talk around it all for a little while, occasionally interrupted by the waitress saying 'thank you' as she fills up our glasses and empties our ashtray.

'Perhaps you should investigate the body,' says Eleni, all serious and Greek. 'Perhaps you should explore tableaux.'

Only Eleni Marianos could say 'perhaps you should explore tableaux' and not come over as bonkers.

'Perhaps you should experiment with narrative.'

Ditto.

'What do you mean?' I say, buttering my olive bread. Jay Jopling's just walked in with Sam Taylor Wood.

'If you want to examine it to be something more lateral then you should exploit fable.'

'Mmmm.' I'm not sure what she's talking about now. Examine something more lateral? Did I say anything about examining something more lateral? I don't think so. The word lateral never came into it as far as I can remember. Jopling's just had a glass of beer spilt over him by some actress he was shaking hands with. It's a funny old spectacle, cos he's obviously excited to be saying hello to her, and at the same time he's pissed off at the ale on his Nicole Farhi.

'You understand what I mean?'

I'm dragged back to the matter in hand by the inflection of a question. What is she saying?

'What? What are you saying?'

'Do you understand what I mean?'

'What do you mean by fable?'

She embarks upon a protracted and confusing speech about Greek mythology, citing Goya, Picasso and Malcolm Morley. Malcolm Morley? Malcolm fucking Morley? I listen as though she's on to something. But the truth is I don't think she is. She's not on to something. She's floundering. She doesn't understand. She just doesn't get it. She's Greek and her solution is to paint something Greek. 'Paint the Harpies,' she's saying, 'paint the Furies and the Fates,' stuff like that. She's wide of the mark. She's very fucking wide of the mark. 'Neo-classicism is the way ahead,' is what she's saying and it's fucking awful, a fucking disaster, cos I sit there feeling the love beginning to slip. I don't want the love to slip. Not with Eleni. Please God don't let the love slip with Eleni. Not like it slipped before. Not like it slipped with Sheba. Why is she saying all this? Stop her saying all this. Put an end to this ill-informed inventory of mythological freaks. Stop her suggesting that neo-classicism is the way ahead, cos it's not. It's definitely not. Not even close, Eleni. Why are you being so stupid? Why are you being so unlovable? Why is the love slipping? Please, God, please. Die or something, but don't do this. Die, right here at the table, face down in your sorbet, but don't get it all so wrong.

I ask for the bill and smile at the waitress. She's French with unruly black hair and magenta nail polish, and I watch her as she glides towards the till.

We walk home along the river, in the rain, which is supposed to be romantic, but it's not. It's foul and wet and stinks of pigeon. We hardly speak. I hardly speak. Now and then Eleni points out a building or a puddle or a dog or a boat. She asks me where I think the wind comes from and I mumble, 'I dunno,' and stare at my boots. She rambles on about how, when she was a child, she thought that the wind was caused by trees and that's why they shook so much in a storm. 'And the more they shook the windier it became.'

'Hmm,' I say. 'Hmm.'

She talks about meteors and astronauts, about stars and time and life on other planets. 'Hmm, yeah,' I say, and then, 'I suppose.' But what about death on other planets, Eleni? Ever think about that one? And then I close my eyes and see how far I can walk without hurting myself. 'Shut up, Hector,' I think, 'shut the fuck up. Ever think about that one, you twat?'

As we slump through the door the phone's ringing. It's midnight. I pick it up, hoping for something. I don't know what.

'Hello?' I say, and shrug off my coat.

'Hello,' says the voice. I watch as my coat leaks a puddle across the wood.

'Hello, sir,' I say, changing my tone.

'Sir' is Eleni's father. His name is Yiorgos. I don't mess about with Yiorgos. I'm very polite with Yiorgos. Yiorgos is a big man. Yiorgos is as big as three men and he's suspicious of me. So he should be. Perhaps if *he* died . . .

'How are you doing, Yiorgos?'

'Is Eleni with you?' OK, Yiorgos, I'll assume you're fine.

'Eleni's always with me.'

'Can I speak to her?' I can hear him sniff, and then a small grunt. 'Please' wouldn't hurt, Yiorgos.

'Of course, Yiorgos, I'll call her.' See how polite, craven and dull I am with him? That's the story of me and Yiorgos. I hold the phone against my chest. 'Eleni!' I shout. There's an echo. Eleni comes through from the bedroom towelling her hair. 'Your dad,' I shout. She runs across the room and takes the phone from me. I turn and set off walking towards my canvas in the far corner. My big white empty fucking canvas. I think about pissing on it.

Eleni whistles me and holds up two fingers, like a child miming a gun, and moves them back and forth in front of her lips. I light a fag, take twelve big strides across the room and slip it into her mouth. 'Thank you,' she says, and 'Papa?'

A cloud. It seems as though a cloud has just seeped into her eyes. I lie down on the floor and light my own fag. I'm just glad to be out of the rain. Glad to be home. I lie back on the floor and stretch out my arms and legs. I think of da Vinci and raise my head to look at Eleni. My chin doubles. I'm sorry, Eleni. I'm sorry I'm not good enough. I'm sorry I'm so feeble. I am. I mean it.

She's wearing a blue T-shirt with 'God Shave The Queen' written across the front in yellow letters. She pushes a marble around the floor with her foot. 'Oh my God!' she says, and then, 'Papa, no, no. Oh my God.' She loses control of the marble and it rolls towards my head. I look inside. I stare into the bleeding helix of green and yellow. How do they do that? Could that be done big? Could a giant marble be made? A marble the size of a man? How do they do that? I bet Claes Oldenburg knows how. I bet Claes Oldenburg's already thought of it.

'Oh, Papa, don't cry,' says Eleni, and then the rest is in Greek. I've not really made an effort with the Greek. I can say a few things, read a few things, but when they start speaking, well, I've not quite got that far. 'No, no, no,' she's saying. Is Yiorgos crying? Yiorgos? Huge Yiorgos? Crying? I try to imagine such a thing. I picture his hard black whiskers made soft by tears. I picture his lips all bubbled with spit. The sound of him. The smell of him. His immense leather fingers pinching the bridge of his quarried nose. What's going on? Eleni pulls on her cigarette and it's almost gone. What's going on here? It's all Greek to me.

At half-past midnight Eleni puts down the phone like she's putting a small animal to sleep.

'My mother has been badly burned,' she says.

'Oh my God,' I say, raising myself up. 'How?'

'There was a fire in the kitchen,' she says, 'Alexis tried to put it out with water.' Alexis is her stupid brother. 'She has been burning with a boiling fat. And then she fell into the fire.'

'How bad?'

'Bad.'

'Oh my God,' I say. 'Oh my God.'

I'm not sure what it is, but I don't think that I trust myself. I really don't trust these Oh my Gods. I stare at my canvas.

I like Eleni's mother, Sofia. I don't just like her; I love Sofia. I think I can say that I love Sofia. She looks like Eleni. I've seen photographs of her when she was young. It's Eleni. Sofia always holds me tight; really tight; beautiful amber arms full around me. Face against my chest, eyes closed. Turquoise eyes. Like she's listening to my heart and blessing the saints of my nativity. Like she's protecting me from big old scary Yiorgos who watches all this and breathes and grinds his feet into the tiles of his taverna. Sofia always holds me, and it feels a lot like love. Eleni's happy and that's what Sofia sees. I don't know what Yiorgos sees. Perhaps he sees the blackened pips buried in the core of me. Clever Yiorgos. Wise old Yiorgos. I'm sorry, sir. I'll do better sir. Try harder. Sorry, Yiorgos. Sorry, Sofia. Sorry that you're burned. Sorry that your daughter's crying. Sorry that I'm all fucked up and jealous of her; jealous of her burned mother. My mother's fine. She's looking for a new settee, Yiorgos, cos I fucked your daughter on the old one and made her bleed. And I know that you want a grandson, you've made that clear. But I'll tell you what: you don't want one like me, do you? Oh no, sir. I know you don't want a grandson that in any way resembles me. Sorry, sir. See how big he is? See how much he's crying? Strange isn't it, when big men cry. Strange when anyone cries.

'What you gonna do?' I say.

'I don't know. Papa says we'll see how she is tomorrow.'

'Do you want to go?'

'Do you want me to go?'

'No,' I say, and then, 'Yes,' and then, 'I mean, do whatever you need to do love.'

Eleni reaches for my fags and takes a long time taking one out. She clicks and fails with the lighter. Clicks and fails, clicks and fails, as though she's never used a lighter before. 'I think maybe you need anyway some space,' she says as she finally gets it going.

'I've got space,' I say, sweeping my hand around the room. 'How much more space could I have?'

'But I am in it,' says Eleni, and stares at the floor.

'But I want you to be in it.'

'You have a lot of pressure. The exhibition, the broken painting. The new self-portrait.' She stares at the empty canvas over in the corner of the room.

'Eleni, this isn't about me and my pressure. It's about whether you need to be with your mother.'

'We'll see.' And she walks off into the bedroom. I follow her.

'What's the matter, love?'

'I'm getting on your nerves.'

'You're not.'

'Yes.' She pulls back the blue sheets and climbs onto the bed.

'You're not getting on my nerves.'

'You've been impatient of me.' She pulls the sheets over her head. She's gone. She's disappeared.

'Impatient *with* you.'

'Yes, *with* me,' she says, appearing for a second. And then. 'No.' I sit on the edge of the bed and stroke what I think is her shoulder. 'I know, Hector, I can feel it.'

'Eleni, love,' I say, 'I'm sorry about your mum . . .'

I can hear her sobbing beneath the sheets. I gather her up. A tiny blue bundle. I hold her tight, tight enough to break her. How simple it would be right now to break her, to love her so hard she snaps. To crush her. It's an easy thing to bring horror into a room.

'I've just been tense,' I say.

'With me.'

'No, no, not with you. I've got a lot on my plate.'

'Your plate?' she says. It's not sarcastic. It's perplexed. Confused by the idiom.

'No, no,' I say, and ease her beautiful Greek face from the sheets. 'It's got nothing to do with plates. It's Kirk and . . . and I don't know . . . I'm just all messed up.'

Brilliant, this. Quite fucking brilliant the way I've just made it all about me. Like her mother's just fine. Like it's really me who's splattered with hot fat. Like it's really me who should be smothered in bandages. Eleni burrows back beneath the covers and I can hear her breathing. I sit for a long time and listen.

I walk out into the studio and look at the canvas. There it is, all giant and white, like the fucking Antarctic. Like I should just stick a fucking flag into the middle of it. I feel like I'm in a film about a struggling artist who keeps getting up at all hours of the night to look at his big, blank, empty canvas. And in a way I am. Except that I'm not struggling. I'm Hector Kipling. I might be getting up at all hours of the night to look at my big, blank, empty canvas, but I am not fucking struggling.

I climb into bed. Eleni's almost asleep, I can hear her breathing on the edge of a dream. I touch her thighs. I want to fuck her. She eases me away. Gentle, slow. Almost not at all. I really can't blame her. Her mother's unconscious in a Cretan bed smeared with Vaseline, what am I thinking of? I roll over, push my face into the pillow, listen to my heartbeat for an hour and then fall asleep. I dream. I remember dreaming. I dream of fucking Sofia, Eleni's scalded mother, in a strange bath. We're tiny and naked, in a strange bath filled up to the top with cold green, mild green, Fairy Liquid.

Monday's come round again and I'm with Bianca. We're sat about five feet apart and she gently pushes over the tissues with her foot, her toes on the box, like she's touching a landmine.

'So,' she says, 'what's going on?'

I look her in the eyes. She has these deep-set coral eyes.

'I don't know where to begin,' I say.

'Well,' she says, 'that's a beginning in itself.' When she listens she strokes her neck.

I begin to talk. She listens. She strokes her neck.

'Up to the age of twenty-four,' I say, 'I'd never had a bird shit on me. Then, one day, when I was twenty-four, I was shat on twice, the same day, by two different birds. Once by a pigeon outside Euston Station, the second time in Blackpool by a seagull hovering over the Pleasure Beach.'

'I see,' she says, her long fingers caressing her throat.

'So,' I say, 'what do you suppose that means?'

Archie March, for his solo exhibition at the Whitechapel Gallery and his poignant contribution to *Assassin* at Moderna Museet, Stockholm in which he displayed a perceptive and uncompromising dedication to exploring the borders of the subconscious.

Kim Large, for her inventive portrayals of domestic alienation, utilizing materials both unexpected and difficult, as seen at the Musée d'Art Moderne de la Ville de Paris.

Elvira Snow, for the presentation of her work at the Van Abbemuseum, Eindhoven; and for her solo exhibition at the Lisson Gallery, London, and for her contribution to several group shows, including *Aggggghhhh* at the Stedelijk Museum, Amsterdam, and *My Daddy Gone Crazy* at the Ikon Gallery, Birmingham.

Lenny Snook, for his outstanding solo exhibition, *Berserkr*, at the Walker Art Center, Minneapolis, and for his contribution to the Carnegie International, Pittsburgh.

Archie March. Just five years out of St Martins and he's covered a football pitch in Berlin with hexagonal black and white football leather. On the centre spot sits a ball. The ball is made of mud and grass. And that's it. *Football Crazy*, he calls it. He's going to have photos of it at the Tate and maybe a scale model. He's going to have a dartboard of bone and pork. There will be a glass pool table with glass balls and glass cues. There will be a kinetic sculpture of blue boxing gloves boxing skulls, and an entire wall of leopardskin cricket pads. A looped tape will chant 'He's strange, he's weird, he wears a goatee beard, Archie March, Archie March!' The whole thing will be called *Sports Illustrated*, and everyone in the know expects it to win. It's all about being accessible; bringing the opposing worlds of sport and art into a harmonious unity. Art for the common man. And funny and deep, I suppose, or so I'm told.

Kim Large fills baths with paint and lines them up in six rows of three. Eighteen baths plumbed up to run paint from the taps and the plugs open so it empties at exactly the same rate as it fills. In Tokyo she did it with white paint, in New York, black. For the prize she's going to use eighteen different colours. She calls the baths 'fountains' as a homage to Duchamp. And that's about it. Sometimes she does it with sinks and once, in Amsterdam, she did it with toilets, filling and flushing, filling and flushing. I like it. She never makes any claims as to what it all means other than it looks quite beautiful, and I like that. And I like her. In fact I quite fancy her. She's twenty-eight and looks a lot like Ingrid Bergman. Eleni knows that I quite fancy her cos I told her and I know that she's cool about that kind of thing. I love Eleni. I don't love Kim Large, but I do quite fancy her and I like her painty baths and I wish that I'd thought of it cos it's silly and pretty and smelly and odd.

Elvira Snow does something strange. A few years ago she set up a series of two-way mirrors and, in a notice at the entrance to the gallery, guaranteed that she was behind them, taking notes about you. Two months later the notes were published and that was all part of it. For the prize, so I hear, the room will be filled with cameras and microphones. Elvira guarantees she'll be sat at home, conscientiously watching. She's done this before at the Whitechapel, but this time, to make it a little more interesting for her audience, she'll be screening the fruits of the Whitechapel exhibition as part of her Turner presentation, so that the viewer will be able to sample a version of what they will become; fully aware that at Elvira's next show they will be the stars. I'm not sure about this. Is she taking the piss? It's all a bit Dixon's shop window if you ask me. Maybe if she had a camera trained on her at home, watching, then at least the voyeurism would be reciprocal. But as it is Elvira's nowhere to be seen, which is typical of Elvira. She's a bit of a ghoul and I don't think Elvira Snow is her real name. Kirk claims that he knows someone who went to school with her in Newcastle and says that she's really called Linda Clitheroe. And she drinks too much Campari, when everyone else is downing mojitos. And when she drinks too much Campari she gets opinionated, and her opinions stink. She's the sort of artist who says things like 'Drawing is dead' and 'Painting is dead' and sculpture, sculpture's dead as well. Well, you know what I say to Elvira? I say pretentious voyeuristic piss-taking conceptual installation is dead. But I don't really mean it cos it's obviously not, cos Elvira's doing it and it's up for the Prize. And I quite like it. At least I would like it if she followed my advice and put herself in there, cos as it is it smacks of *Candid Camera*, and that's not art is it? Is it? I don't know. It depends who says it I suppose. And it depends where it happens. In his second manifesto of Surrealism André Breton stated that the simplest surrealist act was to run into a crowded street with a loaded gun and open fire at random. Well, André me old son, it happens. It happens every few months these days, it seems. But is it art? Do we call it art? No, André, we don't call it art. We call it mass murder and madness, or sometimes war. We don't call it art cos the perpetrators are never artists, nor do they ever claim to be artists. Perhaps if an artist did it. Perhaps if it was done by an artist, in a gallery, maybe then we would call it art. And maybe not, because society has standards. Society sets itself limits. Sometimes it doesn't feel that way but it does. Doesn't it?

And then there's Lenny Snook. Leonard Raymond Snook. The oldest of the bunch. Eighteen years out of Goldsmiths and only now making an impact. For most of his twenties he employed his ideas about art to subvert what he referred to as 'the modern manners of society'. These pieces were conceived and implemented in conjunction with his colleague, compatriot, and fellow traveller, Hector Kipling. Hector Derek Kipling. During the nineties – at the expense of Kipling's promising painting career – they lurched around London signing mundane and overlooked features which were, to their eyes, silent, yet vital, motifs of daily life. At least that's how they chose to define their actions in an

71

open letter to *Farmer's Weekly* in the spring of 1993. (*Farmer's Weekly* chose not to publish the letter.) With money gleaned from a compensation settlement following Snook's father being torn apart at a Scottish air show, they commissioned a series of polished copper plaques upon which were engraved the titles of the piece – *Dry Riser Inlet*, for example – and their names, 'Snook and Kipling', or sometimes 'Kipling and Snook' – the billing was erratic and, according to rumour, often a spur to acrimony.

They signed puddles and weeds, pub trapdoors and bus lanes. Later they signed buildings and roads. In 1998 they planned to sign London until their friend Kirk Church recalled to their attention the artist Piero Manzoni, an Italian who died the same year Kipling, Snook and Church were born. Piero Manzoni, much to the consternation of Kipling and Snook, had already signed the planet Earth. At this point Snook and Kipling put an end to all their signing nonsense, and went their separate ways. Kipling returned to his painting and, in the autumn of 2004, painted the acclaimed *God Bolton*, for which he won the BP Portrait Award. Meanwhile, Snook began to investigate conceptual, sometimes kinetic, installations. He impressed the critics with his one-man show at the Walker Art Center, Minneapolis, where he displayed a limousine filled with blood, a deep white hole dug in the gallery floor and a Royal Scots Guard's sentry box inhabited by a real, edible, cooked, slightly burned, seven-foot pork-and-sage sausage. (A new one was cooked every day.)

At the Carnegie International, Pittsburgh, he sectioned off a large white space with sepia glass and subjected the public to a robotic green coffin and a robotic black pram chasing each other around the room with a precise and consistent distance of fifteen feet between them.

Hector Kipling – whose painting career was beginning to wane – was, allegedly, affronted by the exhibition of the pram piece, claiming that the concept had emerged from a quip he had made to Mr Snook during a meal at Yo Sushi! when, excited by the robotic drinks trolley,

Kipling had declared: 'Wouldn't it be funny if you did that with a coffin and a pram?'

Kipling concedes that it was not his idea to paint the coffin green – to lend it the appearance of a predatory alligator – nor to title the piece *Domesticated Goose Chase*. In fact he claims that no further comment was passed upon his rather 'offhand' declaration. Both he and Snook counted up their coloured plates and went halves on the bill. Outside it was a bright and sunny day and the two friends walked to Hyde Park where they fed pickled ginger to some ducks.

One year later, Leonard Raymond Snook was shortlisted for the Turner Prize.

BOX ST, BOW, LONDON

Eleni's on the phone to her dad, Yiorgos. Yiorgos's crying again. I'm playing with my hair trying to get it to look human. This terrible, clogged black hair I have. Like a chimp's. I'm playing with my hair and trying to smoke without hands. My eyes flood with tears and I begin to choke.

'O Thee mou,' says Eleni, 'kaimeni I mama.'

I should just get it all shaved off. I should just get it shaved right down to a number three, or even a two. A one. I should just get it shaved.

'Baba, ine endaksi, Baba, Baba.'

I should just get it shaved, but Eleni says that it suits me long. She's wrong. She's so wrong.

THE BOBO CAT CAFE, SOHO, LONDON

The Bobo Cat Cafe is not a cafe at all, it's a bar. There are no tables, no menus, no food, save for a few crude ashtrays filled with small damp nuts. The Bobo Cat Cafe's carpet has cancer. A dark and artless base-ment bar on Bateman Street, midway between Frith and Dean. A room with no room. Kirk's leaning against a peeling black pillar, papered with old postage stamps. He's wearing his usual blue parka. Lenny's propped up against a mess of red pipes, in his red leather coat, jacket, his ox-blood Birkenstocks crossed at the ankles and his pint held up as though he might put it down at any moment and clap. What would he be clapping? Well, not this bloke on the stage for a start. Not this fucking gimp. There's a bloke up on the stage with a green baseball cap, bronze specs and a dirty moustache. Dirty Moustache I'll call him. In his hand he caresses a scruffy brown notebook. He leans into the micro-phone. Close. Close so that his lips touch.

'Infra red / Infra sound,' he whispers, 'Infra penny / Infra pound!' and then he stops, steps back, pleased with himself, and turns the page. There arc two pink-eyed blow monkeys in the corner, nodding at each other and clapping. Everyone turns to look at them. Dirty Moustache leans in again and shields his eyes against the light. A small salute to the Bobo Cat squalor. He looks ill. He looks lost. He looks like a benign, effeminate Stalin. 'Here's another one,' he announces. 'Another quickie.'

Eleni didn't fancy a poetry reading. She's stayed at home to look through some old photographs. But Lenny thought it'd be a good idea if we got Kirk out of the house – out of the hovel – and so here we are. *A Party Poetical Broadcast*, they've called it. *Poetically Incorrect* would have been more apposite.

'This one,' announces Dirty Moustache, 'is called "Tide and Time Wait For Norman".'

There was this woman on before who did twelve poems about cows. Cow this, cow that. Cows in trouble, cows in debt. Cows with wigs, and blisters and boss eyes and socks. I don't know why we've come. I really don't. For Kirk? I don't think so, Lenny. I really fucking doubt it, Len.

The news is bad and Kirk has to go into hospital. Lenny's decided to pay for him to have it done private cos he's not a total cunt. I'm not a total cunt either and I don't really want him to die.

'And so I wandered around the streets,' whispers Dirty Moustache, finishing off, 'in a sarcastic dressing gown.' He's squinting at the page. 'The Global Village Idiot / The Small Talk of the Town'.

Silence.

He closes his book, jumps down from the stage and trots off to the toilet, where he belongs. A small patter of applause, like passing rain on a plastic roof.

Lenny and Kirk are in a huddle. I don't know what they're talking about, I've zoned out, I just catch snatches of it:

'She said, "I always carry two umbrellas in case I lose one," ' says Kirk. 'I said, "You might as well carry eleven, in case you lose ten." '

I stay out of it.

There's a girl sitting on the stairs smoking a joint and peeling off an old poster with painted purple nails. I can't keep my eyes off her. She's wearing a little black dress and about twenty bracelets. Her hair's all messed up, all black and in her eyes. Looks as though it's been cut with a knife. Ten rings. A tattoo of a black crow on her white shoulder. Scuffed black boots. Maroon lips. She must be in her early twenties. She looks at no one. No one looks at her, apart from me. I can't believe that the whole room isn't looking at her. What's the matter with everyone? Can't they see her? She was there when we came in. We had to step around her. She didn't look up. All this time she's spoken to no one, just sat there smoking her joint and peeling off the poster with her purple nails. I can't keep my eyes off her.

'How much of yourself do you think you could eat before you pass out?' says Lenny. He says it to Kirk and sniffs. I think they've done about half a gram each.

'I dunno,' says Kirk, 'I suppose it depends on where you start.'

'The order?' says Lenny.

'Yeah,' says Kirk.

'Yeah,' says Lenny.

'I mean fingers,' says Kirk, 'fingers seem like an obvious start.'

'Yeah,' says Lenny, 'the fingers.'

'Exactly,' says Kirk.

Now there's some other clown up on the stage taking us through his oeuvre. He's been introduced as German Bernard and he's drunk and small and sodden with sweat. In between poems he emits quiet, liquid groans through a closed mouth, squinting at each new page as though he's never seen it before. It's all whores and beer, like he's read too much Bukowski and can't quite get over it. 'She dropped his dick in the ashtray / He shat out of his armpits / Manson in a Nastassia Kinski mask / A bulldog sodomizing Thatcher / Two flies French-kissing by the cabbage.' That kind of thing.

I look over at the girl. She's finished peeling and now she's straightening up her rings. She grinds out the joint with her boot and kicks it across the floor.

'Soap, piss, mint and tea,' says German Bernard, 'I fry her up two eggs and carve my name on her knee.'

She unties her boots and then ties them up again. By her side there's a small blue bag. She goes into it and pulls out a phone. She's frowning, staring at the display, going at the buttons like she's playing a GameBoy. I reach into my pocket and turn on my own phone. There's no logic to this, but I do it all the same.

'It'd be like peeling a banana, and finding a sausage,' says Kirk.

'It'd be like leaning down to blow out a candle, and the candle blows out you,' says Lenny.

'The sound of a gnat landing on a horse,' says German Bernard, and turns the page.

She puts the phone to her ear and listens. Nothing. She takes it down and goes at it again. She shakes it and puts it back to her ear. She looks up and lets her eyes wander around the room. It's the first time I really see her eyes. It's the first time I've really seen anyone's eyes. They move around the room like searchlights and I stand there, sucking in my cheeks and gut, waiting for them to land on me. It feels like a clock ticking, or a bomb in a film you can see counting down. 'Seventeen, sixteen, fifteen,' I'm thinking, 'fourteen, thirteen, twelve,' in glowing liquid crystal.

'Hec,' shouts Lenny.

'Eh?' I say, glancing over and glancing back.

'Art strike,' says Lenny. 'What do you think?'

'What you on about?' I say and she's nearly onto me.

'Artists striking.'

'About what?'

'About nothing,' says Lenny, 'Just striking for the sake of it. Art as strike. Strike as art. Art strike.'

She looks at Lenny. Settles on Lenny. Lenny's so wired and agitated that her gaze is arrested. On fucking Lenny. I turn to face him. I pull a fag from my pack and light it with affected grace, showing her my fat arty fingers, showing her I'm an artist. Blowing out the smoke. Showing her the way I do it. That's if she's even looking. Fuck you, Lenny. Fuck you for making me look away. Fuck you for making her look at you. Fuck you for being so tall and bald and thin and handsome. If I speak she'll look at me. If I speak and look more interesting than him, then she'll notice.

'What do you mean?' I say, not being more interesting than Lenny.

'We organize every artist on the planet to go on strike as a communal, collaborative, conceptual piece.'

'And strike about what?' I'm not getting it.

'About nothing!'

'About nothing,' says Kirk, 'and that's the point.'

'That's the piece,' says Lenny.

'Give me that joint,' I say, and Lenny hands it to me. I look over. She's looking! Her eyes are mainly on Lenny, but for a second she looks at me, and in that second, because I'm looking at her, and because

Lenny's not, she smiles, half smiles, quarter smiles, but it's a smile, it's a definite smile, starting at the mouth, the closed maroon mouth, and passing through the eyes, the bottle-green eyes. I think they're green. I think it's bottle. It's the Bobo Cat Cafe, for fuck's sake, and I'm bleary with smoke and up to my forehead in lager. I'm about fifteen feet away and there's definitely something coming from the stairs.

'Who'll give a shit?' I say, turning back to Lenny, confident, content, careful not to blow it.

'Everyone'll give a shit,' says Lenny, 'we don't just get living artists to strike, we get the dead ones as well. We do it through the galleries, every fucking gallery in every fucking city, every fucking town and village. We get schools, community centres, hospitals, old people's homes, asylums, prisons to take down their art. We get all art stopped. We get advertising executives to cut it out, we take down the billboards, dismantle public sculptures, cover the nation's statues.'

'Christo could do that,' says Kirk.

'No, he fucking couldn't, Kirk. Christo'll be on strike as well.'

'Blind everybody,' says Kirk.

'No, not blind everybody,' says Lenny, 'keep it realistic, Kirk, not blind everybody.'

'Sorry,' says Kirk, and takes a sip of his pint.

I can feel her eyes burning into me. Even if they're not, I can feel them. Even if they're burning into Lenny, I can feel them. She smiled. It was a definite smile. I take another toke on the joint.

'Yeah,' I say, 'but you know what they did when the bin men went on strike? When the fire brigade and the cemetery workers went on strike?'

'What?' says Lenny, and I have him. I have him, cos he's not thought of this one. He's not thought of this one and now I'll have her looking at me.

'They sent in the troops,' I say, 'got the fucking army involved.'

'Right,' says Lenny.

'Right,' says Kirk.

'So,' I say. 'So suppose, like you're saying, artists go out on strike and the fucking troops are sent in. You've got the Royal Infantry doing installations, the TA hacking into cows and whining on about their chlamydia. You've got the Fifth Battalion painting spoons, Kirk,' and I smile at Kirk cos he might be dying. 'Sherpas and Gurkhas doing Zen rock gardens.'

There's a round of applause and the compère steps back onto the stage. 'Cool stuff,' he's saying, 'cool lines, brother.'

I look around for the girl. She's gone. I crouch to see if I can see her at the top of the stairs but it's no good, she's fucked off. What the fuck, what the fuck, and then: 'Ladies and gentlemen, welcome onto the stage our next poet, Rosa Flood.' A few hands are put together.

Rosa Flood jumps up onto the stage. My boots tighten around my feet.

She's the girl I've been staring at all night. She takes a swig of her vodka and lights up a fag. Fucking hell, she's beautiful. She takes the microphone from its stand and slumps down against the curtain. She has no notebook. The room goes silent. Someone laughs. I look over, indignant. She holds the microphone close to her lips so that we can all hear her smoking.

'Well, look at me . . .' She sounds American. 'Look at me stretched out upon this enamel slab / In a fabulous room / Imperfectly spliced / Like a smothered fish / My pipes / My bones / And every balloon of deep blue meat . . . removed / And my entire body filled / With puddles / And coughs / And old teeth / Well look at me / In the morning after that night we always talk about / Just look at me.'

'I'm looking, sweetheart,' shouts someone in the crowd.

I see myself out of body. In one hand a pint, halfway to my mouth. In the other a fag, halfway to my mouth. Neither one of them about to get there. She lies down on her side and curls up in a ball. I look at

Lenny. Lenny's got his mouth open, a bit like my dad. Kirk's rubbing his vein and staring into the mirror on the pillar.

'Fear of memory, memory of fear / That's what I think's going on here / Without you / No blood / Just sweat / And tears / Fear of memory / Memory of fear / That's what I think's going on here.'

'Oh, baby,' says Lenny, 'she's a fox.' I disregard him. I love Eleni. I've loved Eleni for three years. I do, I love her. I love her, but fucking hell. And then Rosa Flood disappears behind the curtain, 'Very dark,' she says. Sounds like she's from New York. 'Very fuckin' dark back here.' No one says anything. We can all hear her smoking. A little drunken laughter like she's playing with a fly back there. I finally put the pint to my mouth. Take it away. Down. Hold it there. Fag. Up. In. Draw. Out. Down. Hold it there. Waiting. Waiting. Finally:

'And then,' he said,
'I hate to shoot you down
Whilst you're still trying to glue on your wings
But it's time to talk about the state of things.'
Death's door was open
And banging in the wind
'Time to talk about importance
About disappointing performance
About the leech
About the maze and the mouse
Time to break into your back with this axe in my mouth.'
He lit a match and blew it out
Put it down on the table, and frowned
As though he were about to quote from the Bible
And he did.
'Jesus Christ,' he said,
'Don't you know anything?
It's like pushing a deathbed through a ghost train.'

He didn't explain what that meant
But I knew it wasn't a caress
'I know this . . .' I said,
And set loose a mongrel inside my head
To retrieve what I knew.
It dropped an old shoe at my feet.
'Love is the space between the hands as you pray.
Love is what hurts
When it's taken away.
The incipient chord
Of the chorus of betrayal.'
'You're like a dream,' he said,
'You never come true,
You're always in bed.'
His head was full of me
Nowhere.
And so I shared a pain in his shoulder
With death.
And instead of his love
I had settled for his restlessness.
For a spinning top
In my scarlet cot.
And for God,
In a bottle.
Or as you say . . .
A clock.
This is not a true story,
Until you think it is.

There's a small commotion backstage. The dirty mustard curtains are
tugged and punched, a foot comes through, a hand comes through, it's
a bit like Morecambe and Wise, and then the microphone's unplugged.

Silence.

The silence in my head. A howling kind of silence.

Lenny lets out a whoop, and crashes his hands together, over and over, till the whole room concurs and whoops and crashes with him.

In my head, silence. A howling-wind-down-a-black-back-alley kind of silence.

Kirk's been whispering to himself in the mirror on the pillar and suddenly he comes to, thinking the whole room's applauding his desperate incantation, his resolute formula, obliviously whispered into the mirror. He looks up and bows.

In my head, silence. Like a solar wind.

Rosa Flood. Rosa Flood.

Eleni Marianos was born on 20 March 1969, vernal equinox, the day John and Yoko married and flew off to Amsterdam to spend the week in bed together. On 20 March 2004, I spent a week in bed with Eleni Marianos. Now and then we ran a hot bath and slept in each other's arms. We turned off all the lights, lit candles and floated them on the water. Candles floating on the water and a blue rubber earth, and an alligator wearing flippers, and two yellow boats we used as ashtrays.

I love Eleni. I love Eleni Marianos.

On 1 May 2004, in Matala, Crete, we tied ourselves together at the wrist and leapt sixty feet from a cliff into the Aegean Sea.

On 5 November 2004, Eleni created a firework display on the kitchen table and set light to an egg.

On 31 December 2004, we broke into Blackpool Pleasure Beach and, at midnight, waltzed and then fucked in the Hall of Mirrors.

I love Eleni. I love Eleni Marianos.

We had to stay for another half-hour before Sam Delaney came on. Sam Delaney's a mate of Lenny's, which is why we came here in the first place. Sam Delaney was mad as fuck and limped around the stage shouting lengthy poems about pyramids and petrol. They weren't very good, riddled with imbecilic rhymes like 'Saturn' and 'slattern', or 'chorus' and 'Horus'. He was so drunk that most of it was like listening to a sleep-talker through a hotel wall. Still, Lenny liked it, or said he did. Kirk spent most of it in the bog and when he came out he couldn't shut up and talked for ten minutes without breathing; still going on about the Art Strike as though I hadn't already taken it as far as it could go. Delaney came down off the stage, said, 'Hello,' too close, and stayed there, swaying like a tree. At one point I gave him a light and he kissed me on the cheek. It was the kiss of a drunk.

Rosa Flood, meanwhile, had disappeared. She never emerged from behind the curtains. I imagined her round the back, squeezing herself out of some window, falling onto a heap of bottles, finishing her joint and singing a slurred dirge to a dirty grid. What a girl.

Lenny and Delaney are enthusing about going on somewhere but I have to get back to Eleni. Kirk has burnt himself out and is up to his neck in a steaming depression so I offer to walk him home.

He walks looking at the pavement, not speaking, flinching whenever anybody passes him. At one point I put my arm around him cos I think it's better than saying something, but he shrugs me off, so perhaps I should just say something. But what is there to say to someone facing death? Not definite death, but possible death. 'It's touch and go,' says his doctor. I hate this walk with Kirk all bowed and silent. I should say something. I should apply myself, concentrate and find the words. Just really concentrate here.

As he's putting his key in the door I say, 'Goodnight, Kirk.'

'Goodnight,' he says and climbs the stairs.

Well, at least I said something.

I walk to Oxford Street and climb on the number 8. It's freezing and it starts to rain and it's the ugliest bus I've ever seen, rattling down the ugliest streets, in the ugliest city, in the ugliest country, in the ugliest of all possible worlds. My skin feels like cardboard. My tongue is a slug. My heart is a clod of iced mud. My head is all filled up with its own brain and nothing else. And my brain is all filled up with Rosa's eyes and Rosa's arse, so get yourself fuck off up to your bed, Kirk. Hide yourself beneath your tear-sodden, sexless sheets, Kirk, and leave me alone with this phantom in a skirt. Leave me alone with that smile from the stairs. Leave me alone with her lips on the microphone. Leave me alone with her eyes and her arse and her spoken word.

'Love is the space between the hands as you pray,' she said. 'It's like pushing a deathbed through a ghost train.'

Well, that's exactly what it was like, Kirk, walking you home through the Soho night. What a girl.

By the time I get in Eleni's already asleep. There's a note pinned to the canvas: 'Hope your night was a good night. I love you.'

Sheba once wrote me a note saying 'Hope you had a good night' but it didn't say 'I love you' and she didn't hope that I'd had a good night, and when I crept into the bed she put on the light and sat up and my guts formed a fist.

I love Eleni. I love Eleni Marianos.

She's pinned the note to my canvas cos it's the one place she can be certain I'll look.

'Love is what hurts when it's taken away.'

I pour out half a tin of black and go at it with my biggest brush. I pull over the stepladder and make two converging vertical lines down the canvas, like two tram lines disappearing into the distance.

And that's it. I creep into bed. The light stays off and Eleni stays asleep.

5

GROVE ROAD, BETHNAL GREEN, LONDON

This is where Rachel Whiteread, back in 1993, erected *House*, a solid concrete cast of the interior of a three-storey house. The locals complained and said that real, empty, hollow houses should be developed on the site and Rachel's house was pulled down.

One night I drove past and there was some bloke on the roof of Rachel's house, snoring in his sleeping bag. There are some real artists out there.

Anyway, *House* is gone. I'm driving down Grove Road on my way to the Doodlebug Gallery to meet up with Myers and discuss what we can do about the missing painting. The show opens in six days, next Tuesday, and the catalogue's promising five new paintings, including a self-portrait. There's an exclamation mark after the self-portrait bit, like it's a big deal, which it is, or it was, or it might be again.

Myers had called me in some fucking funk about how he'd sold the whole show on this self-portrait.

'Joe,' I said – he's called Joe – 'you'll get your self-portrait.'

'But we've only got six days,' said Myers.

'Joe,' I said, 'you'll get your self-portrait.'

'Cos I've sold the whole show on—'

'Joe,' I said, 'I'll give you your self-portrait.'

On Grove Road I get stuck at the lights ready to turn right onto Roman Road. I remember the times me and Lenny used to write on traffic lights with Magic Markers. At first we wrote 'Go' on the red light, 'Sleep Now' on the amber light, and 'Stop' on the green light. Later we moved on to 'I'm In Pain' on the red, 'Help Me!' on the amber, and 'Fuck Off Then!' on the green. We stopped after a while. The police asked us to knock all that kind of thing on the head.

My phone rings and it's Mum. I fiddle the earpiece into my lug and struggle to clip the wire onto my lapel.

'Mum, how are you?'

'Have I got you on your mobile?'

'Yeah, that's the number you dialled.'

'Ooh, I don't like speaking to you on your mobile. Are you driving?'

'Yes, Mum.'

'Ooh, I don't like speaking to you when you're driving. Are you in the car?'

'Yes, Mum, I'm driving, and funnily enough the car is the thing that I'm driving.'

'Ooh, I worry about you driving and speaking.'

'But it's OK, Mum,' I say, 'I've got my earpiece in. They've got these earpieces now and I can just speak and steer and change gear and scratch my arse and everything.'

'There's no need for that, Hector.'

Mum sounds strange. There's no play in her voice.

'Mum, what's the matter?'

'What?' she says. 'What do you mean?'

'You sound on edge.'

'On edge?'

'A bit stressed.'

'Stressed?'

'Tense.'

'Tense?'

God, fucking Christ, is nothing simple?

'You sound nervous,' I say, 'you sound like you've just committed a murder or something.'

'I feel like I have.'

I hear a siren behind me. 'Somebody's life gone wrong,' I think. Ever since I was five, that's what I've always thought when I hear a siren.

'I might as well have committed a murder.'

'Why, Mum, what have you done?'

'I've bought a settee,' she says, and then sighs.

'But the old one was blood-stained and I thought you wanted to buy a settee.'

'We did want to buy a settee.'

'So why has buying a settee made you feel like you've committed a murder?' I've pulled up outside the Bethnal Green Museum of Childhood and I'm watching a child running, screaming, from some bloke dressed in a Cheshire Cat suit.

'We didn't want to buy a settee like this,' says Mum. 'It's hideous, Hector. I've gone and bought a hideous seven-foot settee.'

'So take it back,' I say.

'I can't take it back,' says Mum, 'it's second hand, I bought it out of the *Evening Gazette*.'

The Cheshire Cat's taken off his head and the kid's screaming more than ever.

'You mean you didn't even see it?'

'Of course I saw it! I drove round to the house and saw it. Your dad couldn't be bothered. "Do what you want, Connie," he said. So I did. I went round and saw it.'

'So why did you buy it?'

'Because I'm not right in the head,' says Mum. 'Because I should be locked up.'

'What does Dad say?'

'He's upstairs crying.' Then Mum begins to cry. Is everyone crying now? 'He came home from bowls, saw what I'd bought, shouted at me, threw the newspaper at me, went down the pub and now he's lying face down on the bed in the spare room, crying.'

It's not like Dad to go down the pub. Dad's never been the sort of dad who goes down the pub.

'Mum, it's . . .' I say, 'it's only a settee.'

'It cost eight hundred and forty pounds.'

'Eight hundred and forty pounds! Bloody hell, Mum! Eight hundred and forty pounds for a second-hand settee out of the paper? What's it made out of? Mink?'

'It's seven feet long, it's a nasty beigey, browny colour, it stinks of cigarette smoke. Every time you sit on it there's a sickening puff of smoke comes out of it, and you know what your dad's like about smoking.'

I scuttle around my seven pockets for a fag.

'You've still given it up, haven't you, Hector?'

'Yes, Mum,' I say, holding the mouthpiece away from my lips as I light one up.

'Big lump of a thing it is. It's too high. It's too bloody high. When I sit on it my feet don't touch the floor, they just dangle there.'

I picture my mother's little freckled feet dangling in her little Littlewood's slippers, and I fill up.

'I look like one of them folk in a film where everybody's been shrunk – my feet just dangling there.'

'Listen, Mum,' I say, 'just get rid of it.'

'How can we just get rid of it?' She lets out a horrible, heartbreaking sigh. 'How on earth can we just get rid of it?'

'Just chuck it out, I'll give you the money,' I say, 'I'll send you a cheque.'

'No.'

'Or cash. I'll send you eight hundred and forty pounds cash.'

'No you bloody won't!'

'Why not?'

'I'm not having you pay for my faults.'

I make a mental note to report this sentence to Bianca.

'Why not?' I say.

'Hector, you know that your dad won't have you doing that. You know what he's like with money.'

'Exactly. I know exactly what he's like with money, and that's why I'm offering.'

'He'll say no.'

'But, Mum, he'll get ill. Remember when he lost his wallet?'

'Eh?' says Mum.

'When he lost his wallet on the bus. His blood pressure burst through the roof. And that was only sixty pounds. Dr Bernstein had to put him on those tablets he's still on eighteen months later.'

'I know.'

'And now he's upstairs crying.'

'I know.'

'So let me pay.'

'No!' she barks, and hangs up on me. Mum's hung up on me.

So is everyone just fucking mad now? Is everyone just totally fucking mad and out of their heads now then?

I call back, but the phone just rings and rings.

I park the car under some crumbling grey viaduct off the Cambridge Heath Road. I see an old advert for Mazola cooking fat and think of Eleni's mother, all blistered and sleeping. Her squeezy amber flesh gone all shiny and crisp, or damp, or black, or whatever it is that happens when you get splattered with boiling fat and fall into the fire.

The Doodlebug Gallery is a new space pioneered by Joe 'The Eyes' Myers. Up until eight months ago it housed a squad of Geordie canoe-builders. It's an enormous cave of a space with painted purple bricks and neon strip lighting, and the ceiling's well away from the floor and that's why we're here. Six of my older paintings are already up. Heads of strangers mostly, apart from one of Aunty Pat I did from a bleached photograph I found down the back of the cooker. Four of my more recent paintings are leaning against the walls waiting to be hung.

Number one I've called *Dad*, cos it's a painting of Dad. A very big Dad. An eleven-foot Dad. I copied it from a Polaroid I took last Christmas. Big jolly Dad, laughing at the Queen.

Number two I've called *Mum*, cos it's a painting of Mum. A very big Mum. An eleven-foot Mum. I painted it from some sketches I made last March. Tense-looking Mum, scared to move in case I draw her blurred.

Number three I've called *Eleni*, cos it's a painting of Eleni. A very big Eleni. An eleven-foot Eleni. She sat for me at all hours of the day and night. A beautiful Eleni, cos I couldn't see how to paint her any other way.

Number four I've called *Lenny*, cos it's a painting of Lenny. A very big Lenny. An eleven-foot Lenny. Lenny doesn't know I've painted it, cos I haven't told him, cos I think the end result might piss him off a bit. I painted it from memory and so he looks like how he used to, back in the days before he looked how he looks now, which is just the same. Handsome. Conceited. Swollen with hubris. Eyes half closed, looking down.

I give the frame a little kick.

'So what are we gonna do about this?' says Myers, gesturing to an alcove. 'I sold this show on a self-portrait in the alcove.'

'I don't know, Joe,' I say, 'I'll come up with something.'

'Hector,' says Myers, 'you keep saying this. You keep saying that you'll come up with something. But it took you three months to complete the self-portrait and now it's in pieces and now we've only got six days.'

'It's not my fault it's in pieces, Joe.'

'I didn't say it was, but we're fucked with having an empty alcove.'

'A motorbike smashed right through the middle of it.'

'I know.'

'So it's not my fault.'

'I know that.'

'So it's not my fucking fault, Joe.'

'All I'm saying is, how are you gonna do it?'

'And all I'm saying, Joe, is chill out, you'll get it.'

We both stand there looking at the alcove, imagining what it is that he's going to get.

I don't like Myers. It's been eighteen months now and I don't like him. I may even hate him. Really hate him. Hate as it's defined in the dictionary.

Here's how we met: I was standing in the Waddington Gallery on Cork Street, trying to make some sense of a particularly slapdash example of Dubuffet's 'L'Art Brut', wishing that I could do that. Wishing that I could just paint like I didn't give a flying fuck about what anybody thinks.

A hand appeared on my shoulder.

'Hector,' said Myers, 'Hector Kipling.'

Strange-looking fella. Almost a hunchback. Cheap grey wig. Eyes like fused fairy lights. We shook hands and he regaled me with his credentials. He told me I was a genius.

'Thank you,' I said.

'You certainly are,' he said and palmed the wig into the nape of his neck. He stank of cigars. 'I was at the Serpentine last year, and I was transfixed by your *God Bolton*.'

'Thank you,' I said.

'I was standing there utterly transported, when who should appear at my side but Jay Jopling.'

'Ah,' I said.

'You know Jay?' he said.

'I've come across him,' I said.

' "Do you like Kipling?" said Jay. "I don't know," I said . . .' – here Myers put a hand on my arm – ' "I don't know," I said, "I've never Kippled." ' He threw back his chin, which was sharp and pockmarked, and laughed.

That's how I met Joe 'The Eyes' Myers.

'I mean,' says Myers, 'what are we talking about here? How badly damaged is the original?'

'It's in shreds, Joe, and covered in petrol.'

'Well, couldn't you just stitch it back together?'

'Stitch it back together?'

'You know, sort of like a Fontana-type thing.'

'What are you talking about, you fucking retard.'

Myers sighs and looks hopelessly around the room. Suddenly he brightens and holds up a big fat, nicotine-soaked finger. 'Otherwise,' he says, 'we could put up that one of Lenny Snook and say that that's you.'

'What?' I say.

'Put up the picture of Lenny and say that that's it – that's your self-portrait.'

'And how the fuck would that work?' I say, genuinely confused.

'Well, not that many people know what you look like.'

'I look nothing like Lenny Snook.'

'If you shaved your head.'

'Joe, I look nothing like Lenny fucking Snook!'

'But who knows what you look like?'

'I don't know,' I shout. I start pacing the room like I'm dealing with someone a bit backward. 'I've no idea of who or how many people know what I look like, the point is I look nothing like Lenny Snook, and plenty of people know what Lenny Snook looks like, and anyway what the fuck are you talking about? It's not a self-portrait, it's Lenny fucking Snook, I'm not putting up a painting of Lenny fucking Snook and calling it a self-portrait. What the fuck are you talking about, Joe?'

'It was just an idea, Hector,' says Myers, 'now calm down.'

I'm pacing the floor between Big Mum and Big Dad, and then I feel like I'm gonna collapse and I pace over to Big Eleni, and cos I can't stop with this pacing I pace over to Big Lenny and I don't know what it is within me that stops me from kicking his mouth through to the back of his head.

'How is Lenny?' says Myers.

But then again, perhaps it's Myers I should be kicking.

'What?'

'Lenny. Have you seen him? Isn't he back from New York?'

'Oh yes,' I say, 'he's back all right.'

'So has he told you what he's doing for the Prize?'

I lean on the wall and stare at the bricks. 'Can I smoke in here?'

'Of course,' says Myers, 'smoke away.'

Smoke away. That's exactly what I'll do. Exactly what I've always done.

'Has he discussed it with you?'

'No, Joe,' I say, 'no, he hasn't discussed it with me.'

'Only I heard from Searle, who'd been speaking to Jopling, that it was something to do with a sofa.'

'What?' I say.

'Something to do with a sofa, an old settee, a settee filled with . . . or not filled with . . . more encased in . . . or imbued with . . . err imbued . . . yes err . . . I don't know, it sounded a bit complicated. Ring a bell?'

'No, Joe,' I say. 'It rings no bells at all.'

Early evening. I've had to set up an emergency meeting with Bianca. She's teaching me to imagine my hands getting warm and to breathe through one nostril, whilst closing the other nostril with one of my warm fingers.

'As though your hands are filling with up with warm blood,' she says.

'Whose blood?' I say.

'With your own blood,' she says and frowns. 'Coming down your arms and into the veins of your hands.'

If I was standing up right now I'd be falling down, but, since

I'm sitting, I make do with lurching a bit to the left and leaning on a cushion.

'Lie down if you like. Lie down on the sofa,' she says. 'Feel the blood in your hands,' she says, 'and tighten your anus.'

BOX STREET, BOW, LONDON

It's Thursday afternoon. Outside it's starting to rain again. There's a pigeon on the ledge looking at me through the window like he's seen me somewhere before and he's trying to remember my name. In the far corner of the room stands Eleni's piano. There's a blue vase of purple tulips, a green bottle of water, a rubber snake, a painted egg, a glass ashtray in the shape of a heart and a smouldering fag. She's playing one note over and over again; one of the black keys, way down towards the bottom. Now and again she plays another note, a white key, but only once, and then she's back to the black key over and over, three-second intervals, sometimes twenty times in a row. She's gazing at the TV. Sometimes she picks up the remote and rewinds it. Sometimes she pauses it. She's pausing it now. There's a man in a rowing boat in the middle of the night, sobbing like a child and pointing a gun at the moon.

I'm lying on the floor at the base of the canvas. Two long black converging lines; each about eight feet long. I push myself up on my elbows, spread out my feet and look at my legs. Black jeans.

'Fear of Memory / Memory of Fear / That's what I think's going on here.'

Rosa Flood. There's a name for you.

'So what do you think you're gonna do?' I shout.

She closes the lid and the tulips wobble. She turns off the video and crushes out her fag in the ashtray.

'I don't know,' she says, 'I'm finding it hard to know what to do.'

I put a hand on the top of her head and begin to stroke her hair. The piano's well polished and I can see her reflected in the top, smiling at me, but with her eyebrows pointing up. Two converging lines. A smile like a sigh. Or a sigh like a smile. Her head feels warm and I run my fingers through her hair to the tangles at the end. She must have stopped brushing it.

We haven't talked all day, but now we're talking it feels like I can't believe we're not talking all the time, over and over, about the same thing. The one thing.

'What do you think I should do?'

'I really don't know, Eleni. What does your dad think you should do?'

'I don't know, he tells me that I should do whatever I feel I should do.'

'And so what do you feel you should do?'

'I don't know. What should I do?'

'Do you think you should go home?'

'I don't know. I suppose so.'

I stop stroking her hair and begin to stroke her neck right down to the collar bone, pausing to feel her pulse.

Beyond the pulse there's a silence.

There's a hundred different things I could say, and in Eleni's warm head I'm sure there are a hundred more. Neither of us mentions any of them.

Silence. A sort of silence. Just the sound of my fingers on her neck and a dog in the street, barking my life story to a puddle.

Overcome by the silence she stands up, runs across the room, puts on her coat and goes out, slamming the door.

Now we're sitting in the church on Beecham Street, staring at the altar. When I followed her in I found her lighting a candle and curtsying to the font.

Silence.

I've never known such silence with Eleni.

Me and Eleni have always talked. Always.

It's a dim, frosty, cheerless old church with a low wooden ceiling and the stations of the cross, shoddily executed, on seven sooty little windows. There's a moth, doing the rounds, very taken with Eleni's solitary candle. We have the place to ourselves. Eleni's got her eyes closed. She might even be asleep.

The door opens and a man walks in. He dips his fingers in the font, genuflects and takes a seat near the front. He looks familiar. Silence. A sort of silence. The sound of hammering coming from the cellar and the throb of a helicopter, and a drill, and a fire engine. Someone's life gone wrong. Someone's life on fire. The man looks round. Tall, lopsided, foppish-looking fella. I feel like I'm looking at this man the way the pigeon on the window ledge was looking at me. Suddenly it comes to me: he's the man who asked me for the time in the toilets at the Tate, the man who said, 'I've seen your stuff.' He stands up, walks down the aisle backwards and goes out the door, slamming it behind him. Is everyone slamming doors now, then? A sort of silence. You could hear a pig drop.

Me and Eleni have had a talk. I wrapped her up in my coat and walked her back home. There was still a lot of silence, save for the rattle of bottles from the brewery and someone, somewhere, playing 'Eidelweiss' on an accordion. We've decided that she should go home. It's been four days since the accident and her mother's condition is beset by complications. Her brother, who I think we can say is not really handling the situation, has disappeared. Yiorgos, due to an inflamed ulcer and chronic lack of sleep, is raving and sobbing, his taverna's losing money and his shingles have come back. We've also decided that I should not go with her. In fact the question was never raised. But I think we can say, by the very fact of its omission from our discussion, that the question has been decided.

I'll miss her.

I love her.

Eleni's asleep. We drank a lot of wine deciding she should go home. It's only half-past eleven and I am not asleep. I'm up. In fact I'm up the stepladder, wobbling around from the wine that I drank before and the wine I'm drinking now. The canvas is coming along; it's now completely black. Two converging black lines against a black sky. I don't know why I think it's sky. The way it looks right now it could be anything black. It could be the belly of a fly, the darkness of the throat, an acre of burned flesh. But it's not. It's the sky.

The two black lines stand out because they're dry. Then I go over them with red, so now there are two rust lines against a black sky.

Can you tell what it is yet?

It looks so fucking voluptuous that I want to take off my clothes and do a filthy loud bellyflop right into the middle of it. Just as I'm seriously contemplating actually doing such a thing, Lenny calls. He asks me if Kirk was all right when we left the Bobo Cat and I tell him that Kirk was just fine and how I'd looked after him and how Lenny isn't to worry cos Kirk's just fine. I ask him how he is, and he says he's fine, and I ask him how the piece is going, and he says it's going fine, but he may have to move out of the house, away from Brenda, to really crack it. I tell him that he's welcome to work at my place, and he says thanks and he may take me up on that. I ask him if I'm allowed to know what the piece is yet and he says he still doesn't want to talk about it. Then I ask him how he got on the other night with mental Delaney and he says fine.

'Where did you go?' I say.

'Oh, we went to Helen's bar,' says Lenny.

'Good?' I say.

'Oh, you know. You know what it's like in Helen's.'

'Yeah,' I say.

'I'll tell you what, though,' he says, 'remember that girl at the club who got up and did the poems?'

I look at my canvas. Two converging red lines against a black sky. 'Rosa Flood?' I say.

'Yeah that's it, Rosa,' says Lenny.

'What about her?' I say.

'Well, she was in Helen's. She's out to fucking lunch.'

I climb down the steps and put my foot right into the paint tin and I can't get it out. Like I've been studying Stan Laurel all my life.

'So you had a laugh, yeah?'

'Yeah, we had a laugh, it was a good night, you should have been there.'

'Yeah, well, I was walking Kirk home,' I say.

'Yeah,' says Lenny, 'and he's fine, yeah?'

'He's fine,' I say, 'like I said – I looked after him.'

'And how's Eleni's mum?'

'Not good. Eleni's going back to Crete.'

'That's good,' he says, like he's not taking it in.

We talk for a while about Brenda and how it's definitely it this time, how she's definitely not getting another chance, how it's definitely the end, definitely. We talk about his mum, who's in a home, and how Lenny really doesn't have a problem with that, and how anybody would be as deranged as his mum if they'd had their partner torn apart by a burning helicopter. I don't argue with that. And then he asks me how my mum and dad are.

'Oh, they're all over the place,' I say, and I tell him the whole thing about the settee. Every time I say settee I stress both syllables. 'They've bought this set-tee,' I say, 'this ugly set-tee.'

Lenny laughs.

'It's no joke,' I say, 'You know what my mum and dad are like, Lenny.'

'Sorry,' says Lenny.

'And so what about this piece?' I say. 'Are you gonna tell me or what?'

Silence.

'Or what?' says Lenny.

More silence.

'I hear it's about a settee. I hear that it's got something to do with a set-tee.'

'Where did you hear that?'

'Well, Lenny, that's not the point.'

'So what is your point?'

I spit on the floor. I dip my brush into the thick rich fudge of black and climb back up the stepladder.

'Lenny, I've offered to let you stay here to finish whatever the fuck it is that you're up to, but it's gonna get a bit messy if you're staying here, finishing whatever the fuck it is that you're up to, if you don't tell me what the fuck it is. What you gonna do? Put up screens?'

'Well, what if it's conceptual?' he says. 'What if I don't need to put up screens?'

'Well, is it conceptual?'

'Sort of.'

'Right,' I say, 'so it's a sort of conceptual set-tee type of thing that we've got going on here?'

'Hector!' he snaps.

'Don't snap at me, Lenny.'

'Well, why are you being so pushy about this?'

'Why are you being so evasive?'

'Why are you being so bellicose?'

'Why are you using such big words?'

'Why are you behaving like a five-year-old?'

'Cos you're behaving like a three-year-old.'

'Oh, for fuck's sake, listen to yourself.'

'Listen to *yourself*.'

Then his doorbell rings and he says he has to go cos that's someone at the door.

'So let Brenda get it,' I say.

'Brenda's not here,' he says, 'she's in Glasgow at some pottery festival.'

'Well, go and get it,' I say, 'and then come back.'

'But I think it's Rosa,' he says.

I stare at my brush and feel like eating it. I fall off the ladder and smash my head against the radiator and my knee against the edge of my easel. I roll around the floor for a few seconds and then make a considered decision to press my face into the pat of black paint piled up on my palette. Good idea. The paint feels cool against my skin. I raise myself up, catching my breath.

'Hector?' says Lenny. 'Hector? Are you all right?'

I just hang up.

Is everyone hanging up these days?

6

OLYMPUS DESK, HEATHROW AIRPORT

At the airport there's a billboard showing a young couple holding hands against a sunset. The caption says 'What's wrong with looking at the world through rose-tinted spectacles?' Somebody's spraypainted out the word 'spectacles' and written 'testicles'. There are two blokes in yellow jackets taking it down. Next to that is a billboard of a man grinning at his watch as though he can't get over that it's quarter past four. 'All the Time in the World' it says, and behind him there's a big blue world and a few of the other planets, as though he's an astrophysicist or something.

Eleni's talking Greek to the woman behind the desk. I'm biting my nails and flicking them on the floor, feeling a bit sad to see them lying there, gone from me, on the dirty airport floor.

We watch her suitcase disappear into a rubber hole and I take her by the hand.

It was a horrible drive out here. Eleni put on the tape of her score so far. She despises every single note of it. This morning she telephoned the production company and told them to look elsewhere. When they started to whinge about contracts and deadlines she screamed at them that her mother was dying and how dare they pressure her to come up with a soundtrack for a comedy about death. They said something about her fee and she tore the phone out of the wall and threw it against my big black canvas with two converging red lines. I shuffled off to the toilet to piss and think. I've never heard Eleni shout before. Then she cried. I've never seen her cry either, apart from the last few days. God, Eleni, I'm sorry about life. How dare it. How dare it make a woman like you cry.

We buy me some socks in Sock Shop and some toothpaste for Eleni and a few magazines and a Big Ben snow globe to give to her mum.

'I'll go straight through,' she says.

'OK,' I say.

'I hate to say goodbye in airports.'

I walk her to the departures lounge and put my arms around her. We kiss for a while and she starts to cry. I sniff, though I don't really need to. We kiss a bit more and then I hug her again. Behind her is another billboard showing a woman with a diamond clenched in her eye socket, like a monocle. Her lips are apart like it's supposed to be erotic, but it just looks like she's saying 'Err . . .'

We're standing apart now. Our arms are outstretched but our hands are still touching.

'Hector,' she says, 'I will miss you.'

'Well, maybe I'll come out soon,' I say.

'Well, maybe I won't be gone that long.'

'Eleni, don't say that.'

'Why?'

'Well, cos that's a terrible thing to say.'

Eleni lets go of my hand and frowns. 'I meant that it might not take long for her to recover.'

'I know,' I say.

'No!' snaps Eleni. 'You thought that I meant it might not take long for her to die.'

'No,' I say, appalled, 'I meant that it won't take long for it all to be OK, for her to recover.'

'So why is it a terrible thing to say?' she says, bashing her bag against my bad knee.

'I don't know,' I say. I say, 'I don't really know,' and say very little else. Nothing else at all.

Eleni looks at me for a long time. Eleni's never looked at me like this.

Silence. Airport silence.

'Hector, do you want my mother to die?'

Silence. Solar wind.

I pull her to me and press her head against my chest. 'Eleni, I can't believe you're saying this.' I press her tighter against my chest and look down. Her face is all crushed by my hands and she looks a bit ridiculous, her lips pushed out, like a fish.

'Yes, you can,' she says. 'What you can't believe is your answer.'

She pulls away and I let her. I let her cos there must be something inside me that wants that to be the last thing she says to me before she goes.

Eleni puts her rucksack into the X-ray and I wonder if she'll turn around. Should I turn around? Should I turn to walk away and then turn around? Or should I just turn the once and have done with it? And if I do turn around, will Eleni turn around at the same time? Or will she already have turned around and then be turned back again? Or will she be just about to turn around when I turn back? Or will neither of us turn around?

I turn around.

She's gone.

I turn around.

My skin feels all wrong. The air around my skin feels all wrong. The space between the clouds in the sky over the building surrounding the air around my skin feels all wrong. I don't want Eleni's mother to die. How could that be the last thing she said to me?

I set off limping across the concourse. Right above the main doors I see two more enormous billboards. The first shows a black, rather sinister car poised in the centre of a spider's web. The web's up in some tree. There's a spider on its way over. Big fat serious spider. 'When the moment arrives,' it says, in big fat serious letters, 'you'll need a vehicle you can rely on.' It's no joke.

Next to this is the second billboard. There's a good-looking bald man lying down on a white settee in nothing but a pair of scanty white underpants. It's in black and white and the soft edge of his belly button's been given a bit of a shine. There's a bottle of mineral water by his thigh. He appears to be very relaxed, lying back, with his hands behind his head. The man is obviously content. The man, as it happens, is Leonard Raymond Snook, and he's got his specs on. 'Sometimes You Need Some Clarity' it says.

I'm not sure. I'm not sure what I think about all this. I'm really in two minds about all this. I really am. I'm not sure whether to run out and buy the water, the underpants, or the fucking settee.

I get onto the M4, move out into the fast lane and put my foot down. I think of my mum's slippers at the sewing machine, pressing the pedal to the floor, the needle going up and down in a blur. I straighten my leg and push all the weight of my fat onto the accelerator, 80-85-90-95. And then I take it off.

After ten giddy minutes of abandon and resolve, it turns out that there's a long tailback coming up to the Hogarth roundabout, and everything has come to a standstill. So there you go, Hector. You can't even be fucking reckless. Pathetic. You'd be rubbish in a film.

What's so fucking special about Hogarth that he gets a roundabout named after him?

I'm sitting here in the traffic staring straight ahead. Cold blue eyes I've got, like cheap cufflinks. In the car in front there's a small boy waving at me from the back window. He's fucked if he thinks I'm gonna wave back. He doesn't know who he's waving at. Someone should tell him who he's waving at. But then there's hope for the little fella cos suddenly he produces a gun and aims it straight at me for a long time. Then, in a flash of brilliance, he shoots me. Once, twice, three times. And because I just stay fixed, staring at him, impassive, he goes on shooting me, pulling the trigger and blowing across the barrel, pulling and blowing, as many as fifteen times. My brain bursts out from the back of my head, my skull cracks in two and my eyes fall into the ashtray. Now there's a kid who knows what he's doing.

I don't want Eleni's mother to die. She's got it all wrong. What does she take me for? Why would I want Sofia to die? Where would that get me? If Sofia died all the attention would be on Eleni, everyone would be rooting for Eleni. I'm sure I could play it up for Lenny and Kirk, I'm sure I could squeeze some mileage out of it, cos I love Sofia and Sofia loves me and I think I could pick it up and run with the situation, but for fuck's sake, Eleni, what do you take me for? A cripple?

He's still shooting me, I notice. Good on him. Ever since he grew out of that waving stage I've grown quite fond of him – good luck to the little fucker.

Did Lenny think I wasn't going to find out? Did he think that he could just loll around in his underpants on a white settee and make no mention of it? Does he imagine that I lead such a cloistered life that I might never come to witness such a thing? I mean it was thirty foot across, fifteen foot high. The pants alone were the size of a small marquee. Are we blind? And then there was his head. His big bald handsome head, just like the one leaning against the wall of the Doodlebug. Except this head – the head on the billboard – didn't look like the head in the Doodlebug. This head – the head on the billboard – looked like a man inspired, whereas my head – the head in the Doodlebug – looks like a constipated pedant. But you know what they say – and in this case they say two things – first, they say that 'the camera never lies', and then they say that 'a picture paints a thousand words'. Sometimes those thousand words are the same word. And sometimes

– like now, stuck on the A4, being shot at by a shrunken assassin – that word is 'idiot'.

The phone rings and it's Mum.

'Have I got you on your mobile?' she says.

'Mum,' I say, 'what is it in your brain that dials the number for my mobile and then makes you ask whether or not you've got me on my mobile?'

'Ooh, Hector love, don't. Don't start having a go at me.'

'Mum,' I say, 'I'm not having a go at you, I'm asking how you are. The last time I spoke to you, you hung up on me.'

'Well, I'm sorry. I didn't know where I was.'

'You didn't know where you were?'

'Or what I was doing.'

'Mum, what's going on?'

'Hector,' she says, 'Hector,' she says again, 'Hector, your dad's in a right state.'

'About the settee?' I say.

'Yes about the settee.'

'Why, what's it done now?'

'It's done nothing,' she says, 'it's just sat there like a . . . it's like sitting on a million old fags.'

'So what's happening with Dad?' I say.

'Your dad's taken his teeth out and he's spending four, five hours a day in the bath. He's not spoken one word to me, apart from the other night when he knocked a fly out of the air with the *Gazette* and shouted, "You see? You see?" '

The traffic starts to move a bit. The little boy is now shooting his mother and I've made it up into second gear.

'He'll get over it,' I say.

Mum lets out a loud shriek. I hold the phone away from my ear. It's not like Mum to let out a loud shriek.

'You've no idea, Hector,' says Mum. 'Yesterday he kicked lovely little Sparky a good fifteen feet across the kitchen. I had to take him to the vet. Your dad's all sweaty in the night. Never still and sweating. I wake up in the morning and I feel like we've slept at the bottom of a river.'

'And how are you, Mum?' I say, moving up into third.

'I'm a mess, Hector,' she says. 'I've done this to him. Me. It's me who's done it to him, me, buying that huge ugly stinking settee. Eight hundred and forty pounds! Eight hundred and forty pounds for a giant upholstered dog end.'

I love Mum. I love the way she makes an effort.

'Mum, let me pay for it,' I say, 'I know you and Dad are against it and I understand why you're against it, but it's only eight hundred and forty pounds. I can make eight hundred and forty pounds by wiping my arse on an old scrap of burlap.'

'There's no need for that, Hector,' says Mum.

And she's right – there isn't.

She's sorry to hear that Eleni's gone away, and she's sorry to hear about Eleni's mother. She's never met Eleni's mother, nor Eleni's father. Nor has my dad ever met Eleni's mother and father. Of course they haven't. Mum and Dad live in Blackpool and Sofia and Yiorgos live in a tiny village in Crete. And even if they did meet, what the fuck would they talk about? Turkish oppression? The litter in Preston?

She asks me how things are going with the show, and the traffic slows down again.

'It's all going fine,' I say.

'Tuesday, isn't it?'

'Yes.'

'And you're showing the paintings of me and your dad?'

'Yes.'

'And you're showing your self-portrait?' she says, a little bit excited.

'Yes,' I say.

'And how's Lenny getting along with the Prize? Not gone to his head, has it?'

'No, Mum,' I say, 'it's not gone to his head at all.'

'Not long to go now, is it? When is it?'

'It opens on the ninth. Couple of weeks.'

'Not long to go, then.'

'No, Mum, not long to go.'

'Eee, I wish his dad was alive to see it. How's his mum? Still in the home?'

'Yes, Mum, still in the home.'

The traffic slows right down and I'm back into first, creeping along.

There's a police car and three ambulances. Everyone's got their heads craned to see. Up ahead there's a green florist's van upside down. Inside there's a man – the florist, presumably – bleeding his mind all over the steering wheel and two delicate hands that won't let go. There's a gold and bloody ring on his finger, one of those Irish rings with two tiny hands holding a tiny crowned heart.

'And how's Kirk?' says Mum.

I take a deep breath and look into the florist's eyes. 'Kirk's not too good, Mum.'

'Why, what's the matter with him?'

His head's all broken over the wheel and he's looking out to the side. Right into my eyes. 'He's got a brain tumour,' I say.

'No, don't say that, Hector.'

'He has, Mum,' I say, my voice getting a bit shaky, 'he's got a brain tumour.'

The florist's eyes follow me as I creep past.

'Oh my God! Little Kirk.'

'I know, Mum, it's horrible.'

'Oh, Hector,' says Mum, all gentle, 'you sound all upset, love.'

'I am, Mum, I am. I don't know what to do,' I say, pulling away from the wreckage. 'Listen, Mum, I'm gonna go, I've got to go, I don't want to talk right now,' and my voice trails off into a whisper.

'Oh, Hector. Hector pet.'

I hang up.

It doesn't seem right for a grown man to do a thing like that to his mother.

I can still see the bleeding florist in my wing mirror. Head like a sack of dog meat. 'There's a man,' I think, moving up into third, 'who's sold his last flower.'

I put on the radio and there's Fats Domino singing 'Lulu's Back In Town'. I whistle along.

7

Eleni's been gone for three days now and we haven't spoken. I've tried calling her but I have to call the hardware store in the village square cos Yiorgos's taverna doesn't have a phone. I've called six times but it's either engaged or I can't get a connection. I don't know if Eleni's tried to call me but there was a message on the answerphone last night that was just a lot of static, so that might have been her. I'd been out for a walk cos it's strange to pass through all this room with her gone. The flat is so empty and the ceilings are so high. Sitting there in the dark, full moon outside, listening to all that static, it felt like sitting in the Mir space station, like a dead machine drifting through nothing.

I've just had four slices of toast and a jar of pickled beetroot with a small clod of horseradish on the side. And then I drank the juice from the beetroot. I haven't had toast and beetroot for three years. Not since before Eleni. It's still not bad.

Yesterday I stayed in all day and pulled the armchair up to the painting. I watched it for four hours, like I was watching a film. At one point I stood up and spent three minutes turning it round. Then I sat down, watched it for an hour and then spent four minutes turning it back, pausing for two minutes to see what it looked like on its side, in landscape.

But today I'm not gonna do that. I nearly did that. I did it for half an hour as I was scoffing my beetroot, but today I'm not gonna do that, because that sort of behaviour seems to suggest that I might have some sort of mental-health problem, and I don't want that. God knows I don't want some sort of mental-health problem. Not on top of everything else.

So I'm up on the roof, smoking a fag, thinking about everything else and thinking about what, therefore, I should do today. I've brought up my phone and a can of beer. I swig the beer, smoke the fag and lie back in the deckchair looking out over the rooftops of Bow. It's pissing down but that doesn't matter. I call it rain-bathing. It's just good to be out of the house.

First I should call Mum and see how Dad is. No, first I should think seriously about going back to Blackpool and sorting things out. No, I should call Mum and see how Dad is, and then think about going back to Blackpool and sorting things out. If Dad's coming out of it then there's no need for me to go back. But if there's no improvement then I should definitely go back and help them get rid of that settee. And if they don't let me give them the money for it I'll lash it to the back of a horse and tow it around the streets ringing a big rusty bell till some cunt buys the fucker.

No, no, first I should call Kirk and see how he's getting on. I should apologize for the other night; for being such a useless, embalmed mute. No, first I should just go round and see Kirk. If I ask him on the phone if he wants me to come round he'll say no, and so I should just go round there anyway, leaving him no choice. I should ask him if he wants to stay in the flat with me and promise to be there every second of the day and night, waiting on him hand and foot.

No, no, no, first I should try to get through to Eleni again. Perhaps she can't get through, or perhaps her mother's dead and she can't get it together to call me, given what was said when we parted. Perhaps Sofia's dead and Yiorgos has crumbled. Perhaps Eleni's too busy piecing Yiorgos back together to worry about me. Perhaps she's just left me. But I should call her anyway, whatever. Whatever the circumstances I should just keep trying, every second of the day and night.

No, no, no, no. First I should just swig this beer and smoke this fag and let everything sink in a bit more.

So that's what I do. Then I go and get another beer and light another fag and lie back in the rain, letting everything sink in a bit more.

An hour goes by.

Another beer and ten more fags.

The sky is tangled and wet, like an old man's beard. The rain is iced and black and up there in the clouds I can see bottles and cushions, knuckles and buttocks. Up there in the clouds I can see Lenny Snook, slumped down in his pants, nipples like bullet wounds. 'Sometimes You Need Some Clarity,' it says.

First I should call Lenny.

No, first I should go and get another beer, and then I'll call Lenny. See how he's doing. See what he's been up to. See what's going on. See what's going on with Brenda. See what's going on with Rosa. See what happened when she called round the other night. That's what I should do, I should call Lenny and see what's going on with Lenny.

Fuck Mum and Dad and their ugly settee.

Fuck Eleni and her dying mother.

Fuck Kirk and his dying self.

Fuck this weather and just lying here letting it all sink in.

I should just call Lenny. See what Lenny's up to.

Just as I start dialling, the phone rings in my hand.

'Hector, I've sorted it all out. I've spoken to Lapping,' says Myers.

'Who's Lapping?'

'Alfred Lapping. The collector who bought *God Bolton* from Saatchi.'

'Ah,' I say. There's a flash of lightning.

'Lapping's willing to loan it out for the show.'

'Why are we gonna show *God Bolton*?'

'Because it'll sit nicely in the alcove and it hasn't been on public display for over two years and it'll be a bigger draw than any self-portrait.'

There's a beautiful roll and then a whip-crack of thunder.

'What?' says Myers.

'I didn't say anything.'

'So what do you think?' and I can picture him on the other end of the phone, skipping around his office.

'But, Joe,' I say, 'I've nearly finished the self-portrait.'

'Hector, you've only been working on it for four days. The show opens tomorrow night. How can it be nearly finished?'

'In fact I think it is finished.'

'I'm coming round,' says Myers.

'Don't do that,' I say.

'Hector, Lapping is serious about this loan. Now if you're saying that you have the self-portrait finished and the show opens tomorrow, then I need to see it. I'm on my way round.'

'Don't do that, Joe,' I say, but the phone is full of rain and the line goes dead.

One doesn't say the line dies. One says the line goes dead. Funny that.

'Hector Kipling didn't die. Hector Kipling went dead. Ladies and gentlemen, what am I bid? We start at twenty million.'

It's three o'clock and I'm sat at the piano. Eleni hasn't phoned. I haven't phoned Eleni. Nor have I phoned Mum, or Kirk, or Lenny. And nor, for that matter, have any of them phoned me. Mum's probably got her head in the oven, Kirk's probably dead, and Lenny's either getting stabbed by Brenda or fucking Rosa. Or fucking Rosa and then being discovered by Brenda – and then getting stabbed. Whatever, it's no excuse for not phoning me.

I don't know what Eleni's doing. I can't believe I haven't tried to call her again.

I'm playing an E flat diminished, the way Eleni taught me. I switch on the video and wind forward at random. I light another cigarette and then press Play. There's a woman – the same woman who put the polythene bag on her head – lying on a bed, surrounded by green candles, masturbating with a ginger wig pressed between her legs.

I pick out notes at random and somehow it seems to fit.

The doorbell rings and somehow that fits too. It rings again.

I run across the room, struggle with the ladders and throw a huge sheet over the painting.

The doorbell rings again.

I run back to the piano and pause the video.

The doorbell rings again.

I run over to the intercom, big strides, like a sprinter, and skid on a marble. I go flying. My head smashes against the ground and I hold onto my elbow. If I hadn't had four beers I'd be in agony.

The doorbell rings again; this time for a long time, on and on till it sounds like a fire drill.

I pick up the phone and Myers' face appears on the screen. Horrible face it is. All fat from cake and pork, big blowsy nose like a wrestler's knuckle. 'Hector?' he says.

'All right, Joe! All right! Stop ringing the fucking bell.'

He steps back into the street. He doesn't know I can see him. He puts his hands down his trousers and sorts it all out.

I'm standing on my threshold waiting for the lift to fail. I can hear the groaning of the cables and a buzz and then a clank as the doors settle and ease apart. And here's Joe 'The Eyes' Myers. Horrible face it is. One eye lower than the other two.

'Right,' he says, striding into the room, 'I don't have long. Where is it?' He knocks the tip of his umbrella three times on the floor like he's been watching *My Fair Lady* all afternoon.

'Do you want a drink, Joe?' I say, backing towards the kitchen.

'I'll have a beer,' he snaps, 'do you have a beer?'

'Do you want a glass?'

'No, no, I don't have time for a glass. Where is it?' He looks over at the big white sheet. 'Is this it?'

'Yeah,' I shout, 'but wait till I get the beers. OK?'

I settle myself in the kitchen, but I can see him through the hatch. Joe sits down in the armchair. He scans the white sheet as though he's reading his obituary. After a while I weave back into the room with two cans.

'Hector,' says Myers, 'are you drunk?'

'Of course I'm drunk, Joe, of course I'm fucking drunk. What do you take me for? An invalid?'

'Right then,' says Myers, snapping open his beer, 'let's see it,' and he jabs his can in the direction of the sheet so that a bit spills onto his trousers.

I walk over to the hem of the sheet, put down my beer, light a fag. 'Joe,' I say, 'Mr Myers, this might not be what you might not be – might be – might not be what you might be expecting.'

'Get on with it,' he says, taking a big swig.

I take the corner and, calling out something that must sound like 'Da da da da Daaa!!', pull and run with the sheet across the room like a feisty gymnast at the opening of the Olympic Games.

Silence.

Myers leans back in the armchair and looks at the big black canvas with two converging red lines.

Silence.

I fold the white sheet over my arm.

Silence.

'What is this?' says Myers.

'It's my—'

'What the fuck is this?' says Myers.

'Well, Joe, it's my—'

'What the FUCK is this, Hector?'

'That, Joe,' I say, '. . . is me.'

'Hector, this is dog shit.'

'No, Joe, it's something new.'

'Yeah it's some new dog shit,' says Joe, 'only distinguishable from old dog shit cos it's still wet.'

'No, Joe, it's me.'

'Exactly.'

'No, it's me. What you see before you is me.'

'Hector, you're drunk out of your mind. What happened? In between me phoning and me arriving you did this?'

'No, Joe,' I say furrowing my brow, 'this has taken me . . . days.'

Myers puts his beer on the table and pushes himself up. 'Right, well that settles it. I'm calling Lapping right now and getting *God Bolton* over there by tomorrow.'

'But, Joe, Joe,' I say, 'this is my self-portrait.'

'Hector, that is not a self-portrait. That is strange minimalist . . . discharge.'

'Joe, this is not minimalist.'

'Then what is it? Figurative? Impressionistic? Pre-fucking-Raphaelite?'

The pause on the video clicks onto play and suddenly there's the woman with the ginger toupee between her legs.

'Oh my God!' says Myers.

I throw down the sheet and stagger towards the screen. I hit stop. 'It's not porn, Joe. That's not porn and that,' sweeping my arm out, 'is not minimalism.' I feel like Peter O'Toole. 'Far from it.'

'Hector, I don't care.'

I move towards him like Bela Lugosi – like Peter O'Toole playing Bela Lugosi.

'Back off, Hector, back off.'

'You know what minimalism is, Joe?' I scream, as he trots towards the door and then out down the stairs. 'A true minimalist does nothing and gives it no title. Minimalism, Joe, means not even drawing attention to its non-existence. The true minimalist, Joe, doesn't even arse himself to get born.'

'Hector, you are drunk, and *God Bolton* is going into the alcove.'

'Fine, Joe,' I scream down the stairwell. 'Don't fall, Joe. I'd hate for you to fall and crack your head open on the steps. I'd hate to have to clean that up, Joe. I'd hate to have to pick up your brain with a tissue. A small tissue, Joe. A fucking baby wipe, Joe. I'd hate to spend an hour trying to find your brain with a fucking baby wipe, Joe!'

He totters down the stairs and slams the door.

It's the season of hanging up and slamming doors. And crying. It's the season of crying as well.

I sit upside down in the armchair and pick up Joe's beer. I drink it, spilling it down my neck and ears, and cry.

A plane flies over, very low and loud, like it might crash into the City. But it doesn't. I just thought for a few delightful seconds there that it might, but it didn't. Maybe next time.

The phone rings. It's Lenny.

'Hector, what the fuck's going on with you?'

I hang up. I'm hanging up, Lenny, that's what the fuck's going on with me. It rings again. I let it. The machine clicks on. 'I'm sorry that I can't crumble to the bone right now, but if you leave a massage after the tomb, I'll crawl on your back.'

And then it's Lenny: 'Fuck does all that mean? What's going on? Have you lost it?' There's a pause and then a little cough. 'I spoke to Kirk this morning and if you want to talk to someone who's really lost it, talk to Kirk. At least he has an excuse, man. He says that the other night you said nothing and just left him. Fuck's going on, Hector? I know you can hear all this. I don't know if you're listening, but I know you can hear it, so call me back, or crawl on my back, whatever. Hector, you is well out of order.'

You is? What the fuck's all that about? *You is*? He's forty-three, he's from Blackpool. *You is*?

I'm lying on the wooden floor, looking up at the ceiling. Last year I painted the ceiling white. I had to rig up a twenty-five-foot scaffold and do it on my back with Eleni pushing me along every now and then, with the paint running down my brush and forearms, like Michelangelo, except that I wasn't painting God. Although, in a way, I did paint God. I painted a large black spot, four foot in diameter, right above the place where Godfrey Bolton hanged himself. As I look at it now, it looks a lot like a hole. I could drag the table from the kitchen, balance the stepladder on the table, climb right up to the top, get a grip on the edges and heave myself in. So that's what I do. What I mean is I drag the table through from the kitchen, balance the stepladder on the table, climb right to the top, but I don't get a grip on the edges of the hole and I don't heave myself in. Of course I don't. Because it's not a hole. It's a black spot that I've painted on the ceiling. And so when I come to the bit where I'm trying to get a grip on the edges to heave myself in, I scratch my hands against the ceiling, lose my balance on the ladder, the ladder falls off the table, the table flips over and I drop through space and land on my back on one of the legs. It really hurts. It doesn't matter that I've had four beers and most of Myers' beer and quite a lot of the other one I took out for myself, which is actually five beers, or nearer five and a half or . . . What I'm saying is that it doesn't matter that I've got practically six pints sloshing around inside me – this time it really hurts.

I shouldn't really be driving in this state. I woke up with a hangover. I'd only slept for about an hour. Maybe it wasn't so much a hangover as a towering migraine of the spine where I smashed my back on the table leg. The point is I've been driving this car around with a dustbinful of booze inside me and now I'm trying to dump it in the Chinatown car park. I find a space and go in and out of first and reverse so many times that I might have to stop and rest my wrist.

I don't know if Kirk's gonna be in but I've taken the risk, and if he isn't then I'll just sit on a bench in Soho Square and make up names for all the pigeons. It wouldn't be the first time.

On the way I buy a half of Jack Daniel's and some Nurofen. Soho's full of newsreaders and quiz-show hosts, and smells of onions and petrol. On Frith Street two chefs are fighting. One of them has a ladle.

At first Kirk tells me just to go away. He's got his round head out of the window, the fat of his cheeks hanging down with the force of gravity.

Kirk's head. The head that may kill him. To be killed by your own head. What hell there must be in that head of his. That head shouting at me to go away.

'Kirk, I've driven all this way to see you, now come down and open the door.'

'I'm busy,' he shouts, 'I'm working.'

'So you can work with me in the room. You've worked with me in the room lots of times.'

'No.'

'You used to say that it helped you to work with someone in the room – with me in the room.'

Kirk's head disappears, but the window stays open. Maybe he'll throw down the keys.

An old man called Alfie taps me on the shoulder. I know that he's called Alfie cos Alfie's been tapping me on the shoulder for the past five years. He never remembers from one time to the next but I do and I know he's called Alfie cos he always says so.

'Excuse me, sir,' says Alfie, 'my name's Alfie.'

'Hello, Alfie,' I say.

'Hello, sir,' he says. He's small and hunched. One of his eyes is blackened and I notice a raisin in his beard. 'I was roller-skating down the Mall just now and . . . well, to cut a long story short, I was involved in a collision with Her Majesty's Household Cavalry and one of my wheels came off – I lost one of my wheels.' He looks down at the ground and sighs. 'So what I'm asking is . . . I wonder if you could spare me a pound towards the cost of a new wheel.'

'And where are your skates now?' I say.

'They're in a vault in Whitehall.'

This is fairly standard stuff for Alfie. It's never money for a cup of tea or a fag. One time it was a quid for some banjo polish and another to buy some talc to freshen up his Arthur Schopenhauer glove puppet which had become sticky from overuse.

'But, Alfie,' I say, 'I always give you a pound and you always go off and get pissed and then I always bump into you later in the day and you always spit at me and call me a Bolshevik cunt.'

'Ah no, sir,' he says, 'not me, sir. You're thinking of Alfie Bass.'

'No, Alfie, not Alfie Bass, Alfie, you, Alfie whatever you're called.' I hand him his coin. 'I'm subsidizing my own abuse here.'

'Ah, well, sir,' he says, smiling like a smutty wizard, 'isn't that the way of things?' And off he goes, whistling 'From A Jack To A King' through his scabbed black lips.

I think about Eleni. Eleni in tears. Sobbing on her mother's dead breast.

Suddenly Kirk's big bunch of keys – one for every door in his life, and a novelty bronze scorpion – smashes down onto my head. It really, really fucking hurts.

The first time I ever visited Kirk in his flat I couldn't believe how dark it was, and then he drew back the curtains and switched on all the lights and somehow the room got darker. It's a frightening little space. If you can call it space.

Here's how we met: 18 September 1997. Me and Lenny Snook are edging around the Royal Academy's 'Sensation' exhibition, quiet and gutted cos we're not in it. We join a small queue to view Marcus Harvey's painting of Myra Hindley.

'She's a piece of cultural ornamentation, like a bowl of fruit,' said Marcus Harvey.

'Why not just hang a bucket of sewer water?' said the *Sun*.

'These people who are queuing to see it are as bad as Myra Hindley herself,' said the mother of murdered Keith Bennett.

So me and Lenny are queuing to see this thing when, suddenly, a big, burly, bearded bloke appears out of nowhere and starts smearing blue ink all over the killer's face. There's a small scuffle and in an attempt to wrench the painting from the wall a stout, unassuming little man is accidentally elbowed in the head by a security guard and knocked to the floor. Taking sympathy on the little fella, me and Lenny pick him up and escort him outside where we all smoke a couple of cigarettes. There's a crowd of protesters holding placards. 'When we said Myra Hindley should be hung,' screams one of them, 'we didn't mean at the Royal Academy.' Forty minutes later we re-enter the gallery and queue up once more to get a good look at the defaced painting. Our new friend, Kirk Church, steps forward to admire Harvey's control of the little hand and is suddenly struck on the back of the head by an egg. Five more eggs are lobbed at the painting and a second man is arrested. 'I think it's brilliant!' said Winnie Johnson, mother of murdered Bennett. 'I think what's happened is brilliant!' but she wasn't talking about Kirk.

'Kirk, so how are you?'

'I'm having the time of my life, Hec, the time of my life.'

He's peering down into the grill, seeing if his cheese has started to bubble. I take off my coat and hang it on a nail. It slumps to the ground.

'So,' he says, 'you drove all the way here?'

'Yeah,' I say.

'And what are you? Pissed out of your head?'

'Does it show?'

Kirk stares at me for a long time and I keep very still as though the question isn't rhetorical.

'No,' says Kirk, and peers back into the grill.

Kirk's cat, Bacon, pads in to see what's going on. He already looks a bit disgusted. He looks me in the eye, shrugs, wanders over to his bowl and sniffs at his clump of mashed fish.

Kirk turns off the grill.

'What's that,' I say, 'cheese on toast?'

'Yes,' says Kirk.

Silence.

'Can I take my shoes off?' I say.

'When in Japan,' says Kirk.

I sit down and take off my shoes. I waggle my toes.

Silence.

Someone outside is screaming 'Margaret! Margaret!' over and over.

Silence.

Soho silence.

This kitchen is the scariest room in the flat. There are only three rooms in the flat but the kitchen is by far the scariest. The bathroom is scary cos it's full of scorpions mounted behind glass, and the sink is full of scissors. The living/sitting/bedroom is scary cos that's where Kirk keeps all his clothes and his paintings of cutlery. But the kitchen is the scariest of the three rooms, cos that's where Kirk keeps all his cutlery. Kirk could win awards for how much cutlery he keeps in one room. First comes the cutlery drawer which is – fair enough – packed with cutlery. Then come all the other drawers which are also – a bit worrying – packed with cutlery. Then come the cupboards. The doors of the cupboards won't close properly cos they're so stuffed with cutlery. And then there's the table and the draining board and the tops of cupboards and the floor. Knives, forks and spoons, wherever you look, wherever you don't, stolen from parties, cafes, bars, restaurants, hotels, aeroplanes, home. Stolen from all over the world. From any incident which involved the use of a knife, fork or a spoon. Bread knives, butter knives, fish knives, fruit knives. Big forks, little forks, meat forks, toasting forks. Tea-spoons, soup spoons, dessert spoons, coke spoons. He's fucking mad as a gibbon's bum, but I love him cos he's Kirk and he wouldn't be Kirk if he didn't have the scariest kitchen in London. Lenny loves him as well, and I love Lenny and Lenny loves me and Kirk loves us both, and it is – it's love. The real thing. And Kirk wouldn't be Kirk if he wasn't peering into the grill pissed off with me that I've turned up drunk to try and make him feel a little bit better than he does about his potential, and utterly plausible, imminent death. That's what I love about him.

In the living room, Kirk bites into his toast. He hasn't shaved and his whiskers have gone yellow with piccalilli. Kirk's sat on the bed, I'm sat on the floor.

I look at the ashtray. 'Is that a joint?' I say, shifting towards it.

'Yeah,' says Kirk.

'May I?'

'Be my guest.'

I pluck it out and light it. I offer it to Kirk but he just holds up his piccalilli toast in refusal.

Silence.

I take three big drags and put it out.

Silence.

I should have thought about all this on the way here. I did think about all this on the way here. Well, not all of it – some of it. I even practised a few sentences out loud but none of them amounted to anything more than a platitude: 'Kirk, everything's going to be all right, you know', 'Kirk, just try not to dwell upon it', 'Kirk, you know how much everyone thinks about you'.

I sit here now, on Kirk's blue wooden floor, looking quite calm, but in my head there're a trillion molecules thrashing it out, each thinking they know best; beating themselves against the folds of my brain, and my brain – or the little fella sat on top of my brain – or perhaps it's a woman – asking all these molecules to keep it down a bit, and don't they know that people are trying to get some sleep? My belly's a snowball, my heart's filled with cabbage and my bowels are burning up on re-entry. I should have thought about all this. I did think about all this, I think. I thought I did. But then maybe it wasn't this; maybe it was something else. Yes, in fact now I think about it, I think I was thinking about something else.

There's so much to say, but somehow that first sentence seems crucial. Why can't I be one of those carefree people? One of those passionate people? The sort of person who seems to enjoy their own personality? Why do I feel like my head's filled with civil servants sat at little black tables, reading, signing, stamping, forwarding and filing every fucking thought?

I go off looking for that first sentence. I'll find it if it kills me.

Meanwhile the joint's barged into my brain and started throwing chairs around.

'How's the toast?' I say.

And Kirk says, 'Good.'

'Piccalilli,' I say.

'Heinz,' says Kirk.

Bacon leaps up onto the window ledge and stares down an earwig. I ponder Bacon's beautiful green eyes. Indignant, incredulous. Infinitely patient. We could all learn a thing or two from Bacon.

'Kirk,' I say, 'I'm really sorry if I'm not handling all this very well. I mean, y'know, we never did this at school.'

'Nor did I,' says Kirk and licks the crumbs off his plate.

'Kirk, I'm sorry. All this has sent me on a bit of a funny one.'

'Yeah,' says Kirk.

'I feel . . . I feel . . . well, I don't know, Kirk, I don't know what I feel, it's . . . it's . . .'

'Hector,' says Kirk, 'are we just gonna talk about you?'

'No!' I squeak, appalled. 'We're not gonna talk about me at all. This is not about me. It's about you. We're gonna talk about you.'

'Yeah?' says Kirk and lights up the joint. 'So what are we gonna say about me?'

'Well . . .' I say, and panic. The molecules overpower the civil servants and stamp on their specs. The little man – or woman – sat on top of my brain has fallen off and got themselves wedged somewhere in my neck. There're also six and a half thousand old teeth bouncing around inside my skull, against the bone. 'Well . . .'

'Well what, Hector? Well what?'

The time has come.

'Well, I don't know, Kirk, what if you die? How does that make you feel?'

There, I said it. It's about the only thing there is to say and I can't believe it's taken this long to squeeze it out. Kirk appreciates it. Kirk's no fool. Kirk lies back on the bed and puts out the joint in what's left of the piccalilli. There's a small hiss and a plume of yellow smoke.

Silence.

Upstairs someone is learning the penny whistle.

Next door they're watching a Tarzan movie, by the sound of things.

I can hear Bacon's claws on the windowsill.

Silence.

'It makes me feel useless,' says Kirk, 'it makes me feel that I've meant nothing at all.'

I nod. Silence. 'But you're not useless, Kirk.' Silence. Bacon's claws and the blink of the earwig.

'It makes me wonder whether I was ever meant to mean anything.'

I nod. A slow nod. Hardly a nod at all. 'I know, Kirk, I know. I can imagine.'

'I fade off to sleep at night and imagine it may be for the last time. I think about whether that's a sad thing or a matter of general indifference.'

'It's a sad thing, Kirk.'

'I think about my paintings . . . and I feel like lugging them all down to the river and throwing them in. And then I think why bother?'

I raise my eyebrows, rather beautifully, I imagine.

'Why dignify them with such ceremony?' he says.

Kirk puts his hands over his eyes and embarks upon a sequence of tiny noises. I think he's crying. He might not be crying, he might be laughing. I doubt it, given what's just been said, but what the fuck do I know? Perhaps he's just taking the piss. What should I say? Should I say nothing? If I say nothing then what should I not say? And if I say something?

'Kirk,' I say, 'don't you dare throw your paintings into the river.'

The next thing I know Kirk's tossed a teaspoon at me and it hits me on the nose.

'Kiiirrrk,' I whine, 'why d'you do that?'

He sits up and I can hardly see his eyes for water. Well, that settles it: he's crying.

You know what? I'm sick of all this crying. Sick of everybody, every fucker, just fucking crying all the time. Whatever happened to repression? That's what I'd like to know. Whatever happened to bottling it all up?

'Hector!' he shouts. 'What's the matter with you?'

I freeze. I'm not used to Kirk shouting at me, and I'm not used to Kirk asking me what's the matter with me. It's a hell of a question – a hell of an answer.

'Nothing's the matter with me, Kirk. What do you mean?'

'Why have you come round here?'

'I don't know!'

'You don't know?'

'Yes!'

'Yes, you don't know?'

'No!'

'What, yes you do know?'

'Yes!'

'So what the fuck's going on with you?' shouts Kirk, and Bacon makes a swipe at the earwig. Gets it first time. Gone.

'Eleni's mother's dead!' I shout, and then clear my throat.

'What?' says Kirk.

'Sofia, Eleni's mother, she's dead.'

'She's dead?'

I say the next bit much more quietly. Almost a whisper. 'Well, she's not dead, I mean . . . she's not dead. I mean she's dying. Really dying. May very well die. In fact she might as well be dead. She's lost consciousness, is what I mean . . . and . . . may never regain it . . . so . . .'

Kirk looks at me for a long time, much longer than friends usually look at each other without saying anything. I know that he's looking at me and therefore I don't look at him. In the silence I work out what he's going to say. He's either going to say, 'Hector, I'm so sorry, that's tragic, come here, let me hug you.' Or he's going to say, 'Hector, do you want Eleni's mother to die?'

He's still staring at me. I light a fag.

'You've seen Lenny's billboard, haven't you?'

I didn't expect him to say that.

'What?' I say.

'You've seen Lenny's billboard, his water ad.'

I stand up. 'Oh, it's for water, is it?'

Kirk leans back. 'What did you think it was for?'

'I don't know.' I hold up my hands. 'Tampons?'

Kirk shrugs and starts to finger his temple.

'So where did you see it?' I ask.

'I haven't seen it, Lenny told me about it.'

I can't believe it. I cannot fucking believe it. 'He told you about it? When?'

'The other night. The night he stayed the night.'

'And why hasn't he told me?'

'I don't know, Hec.'

'And has he told you what he's doing for the Prize?'

'Yes.'

I turn on the spot and try to pace the room. I don't get very far. 'So what is it?

'Well, it's the coffin–pram thing – *Domesticated Goose Chase* – and the limo filled with blood and the sausage sentry box.'

'I know all that. I know he's showing all that, but he's doing something new. Has he told you about this new thing, is what I'm asking? This settee thing, is what I'm asking.'

'Yes, he's told me about that as well.'

'And why hasn't he told me?'

Silence.

I lie down on my back, wrists towards Jupiter.

'He says he doesn't want to.'

I sit up. Fuck Jupiter. 'Oh, does he? He doesn't want to? Why doesn't he want to?'

Kirk sits up and lights a cigarette. I pull my coat over with my foot, reach into the pocket, pull out the bottle and take a swig of the whiskey.

'Hector, please don't drink any more.'

'Why doesn't he want to tell me?'

'Hector, you're going to pass out. Put the bottle away.'

'Why doesn't he want to tell me?' I screw the top back onto the bottle.

'Cos he says that if he tells you, you'll start interfering.'

'Interfering?'

'That you'll start making suggestions.'

'Suggestions?' I unscrew the cap.

'And then you'll start claiming that it was your idea all along.'

'What?' I take another swig.

'He just wants to do it alone so that you can't accuse him of anything.'

'Is this what he said?'

'More or less. Hector, put the bottle away.'

My mobile rings. It's Bianca.

'Hector, you missed your appointment.'

I nearly crush the hand-piece in my fist. 'Shit! Is it Monday?'

'What?' says Kirk.

'Nothing,' I say.

'It's every Monday, Hector,' says Bianca.

'But is it Monday now?'

'Yes, Hector.' She sounds a little bit cross and a little bit gentle. A little bit tired and a little bit intrigued.

'And what time is it.'

'It's six o'clock. Your appointment was at five twenty.'

'Then I've still got ten minutes.'

'But where are you?'

'On the phone. We'll do it on the phone.'

I ask Kirk if I can use the toilet and even though I don't need to go I pull down my trousers and sit on the toilet. It feels good talking to Bianca like this, with my trousers pulled down – sitting on the toilet.

I'm driving up to Lenny's place.

No one thought it was a good idea. Kirk tried to hide my car keys and Bianca begged me to just go to bed and see her first thing in the morning. Bianca thought that my main objection to Lenny's billboard was a question of scale. She compared Rosa Flood to a landmine and Eleni's mother to heartburn. I asked her what she meant by this and she said that sadness is sometimes little more than trapped wind and had I made a serious attempt to burp myself? (I don't think Bianca's very good. I'm paying her fifty pounds a session to flounder. I'm paying her a quid a minute just to switch off the lights and do all her stabbing in the dark.)

I turn onto Delancey and get onto Parkway.

I think about calling him before I get there and take out my phone. Tiny winking envelope. I press all the buttons I've learned to press and pick up the message. It's from Eleni.

'Hector? Hector? I don't know why I call your name, I know you can't hear me. But it is nice to call your name anyway. It's Eleni. Why haven't you called me? It's Monday, about half-past six your time – maybe you're coming back from Bianca. I left a message last night, but here they tell me that no one has called for me. My mother is very sick, Hector. I think I must stay. I will stay. My father is poorly, as you would say. Poorly with worry. I know that you can't come out yet. I know that you have your show tomorrow. I am ringing to say good luck with the show tomorrow. I hope that you are not cross with me. I am not cross with you, by the way. Please call me, please. I love you. I'll try to call you at the flat. I love you . . . bye . . . bye . . .'

And the line goes dead.

So dead.

My skull fills up like an old porcelain cistern.

I love Eleni. I love Eleni Marianos.

I pull up and park outside Lenny's house. Perhaps Brenda's back and she's holding his head down in the dishwater. Perhaps he's masturbating over a photo of Walt Disney. Perhaps Rosa Flood's crayoning pentagrams onto the gusset of her knickers and quoting Aleister Crowley with a mouthful of newborn locusts. Who knows what the hell's going on in there. Perhaps I should call him – let him know I'm here. No. Fuck calling him. Why let him know I'm here? I'll just walk up to his shiny green door and ring the fucking bell. Then he'll know I'm here.

I walk up to his shiny green door and ring the fucking bell. His camera clicks on and Lenny says, 'Yes?'

I say, 'What do you mean, "Yes?", you can see who it is, it's me.'

The lock clicks and the door gives way.

As I climb the stairs I can hear Schubert's Symphony Number Five blasting out from Lenny's Bang and fucking Olufsen. I pull out the bottle and take a swig. I hear Lenny shout, 'I'm on the top floor,' as though that's some kind of achievement.

At the top of the first landing there's an enormous framed photograph of Lenny with David Hockney. They're both stood somewhere in the Hollywood hills with a couple of silly dachshunds and two takeaway tortillas.

'Right at the top. All the way to the top, man,' shouts Lenny.

'I'm coming,' I shout, struggling for breath.

The house smells of jasmine and ratatouille. I can see one of Brenda's big bowls on the kitchen table and one of her vases filled with hyacinths.

I light a fag. 'I'm coming, Len,' I shout.

On the second landing there's a Lennon lithograph of Yoko snuggling into a cosy white bag. The Schubert's making it all sound as though life's just fine. Like life's all about eating Brie-and-cornichon baguettes on Hampstead Heath and feeling a bit sad cos you've noticed a crisp bag blowing across the lily pond.

Lenny's alone in the top room. He's sat at his desk surrounded by something like thirty or forty tealights. He's drawing a line with a ruler. There's a Fiona Rae on one wall and on another there's a photo of Lenny, Marc Quinn and Gavin Turk with their arms wrapped around Gary Kemp. Lenny swivels round in his seat. 'Mr Kipling,' he says, in that stupid way he's been saying for seventeen years, like he can't get over that I've got the same name as someone who makes cheap little cakes.

'Mr Snook,' I say and plonk myself down in his armchair. I sit very still. Looking around. There's a huge white settee in the room.

Lenny moved down to London in 1981 to attend the Chelsea School of Art. From there he moved on to Goldsmiths. I also moved down to London in 1981. I spent three years at Camberwell School of Art. From there I moved to the Slade. We had every reason to go our separate ways. But we didn't. We didn't go our separate ways. We saw each other three or four times a week and eventually shared a flat together. The flat was khaki and unseasonably damp and smelled of baked tomatoes. We shared it with a percussionist called Randolph Rosenberg who has since lost a leg and taken up a career in coin magic.

'Kirk called,' says Lenny, 'and said you were on your way.' He's got a pencil in his hand; he puts it in and out of his mouth like it's a cigar.

'Right,' I say, glancing at the white settee.

'Says you've had a few.'

'Oh yes,' I nod, 'oh yes,' and I nod again, and the room turns into some kind of giant tombola drum. 'Oh yes, I've had a few.'

'Hector,' says Lenny. He stands up. 'Hector, is something the matter?'

Brilliant, Lenny. What a fucking genius you are. What a monster of intuition you fucking are. What a master of signals.

'Something the matter?'

'What's the matter, Hec?'

I sit up in the chair. I look at the big white settee with a white wooden window frame fitted into the backrest so that you can see straight through. The window has magenta curtains. There's a space between the front and the back and a medium-sized cactus sitting on a ledge.

'Nice settee,' I say.

Lenny looks over at it, like he's seeing it for the first time. Behind him, on the wall, are several drawings of settees, windows, cactuses.

'Is that it?' I say.

'Is that what?' says Lenny.

'The piece,' I say, 'the big holy secret.'

Lenny puts down his pencil and picks up the ruler. 'Not all of it, no.'

'What's the cactus about?'

He's chewing on the ruler with his sharp white teeth. 'I'm not gonna use the cactus, I'm taking the cactus out.'

'Yeah,' I say, 'I would.'

Lenny stands up and starts to pace. He picks up my pack of cigarettes and takes one – stealing my cancer. 'Help yourself,' I say. He does. 'Can I sit on it?'

'What?'

'Can I sit on your fancy settee?'

Lenny thinks about it.

'People are gonna want to sit on it,' I say, 'unless you're gonna rope it off. Are you gonna rope it off?'

'No.'

'Then people are gonna want to sit on it.' And I get up and I sit on it. I lean back – not on the window, just to the left of it. Lenny's behind me. I lean down and peer at him through the little window. 'So why have you put a little window into the back of a white settee?' I say it nicely, inquisitive, interested. Like I really want to know.

Lenny lights the fag and fidgets like he really doesn't want to tell me.

'I mean, I'm trying to see it but it's not exactly jumping out at me.'

'It's not—'

'Not exactly jumping.'

Lenny shuffles over to the door and blows out his smoke against the wall. Schubert's getting irritated.

'Hector, it isn't finished. I don't really want to explain it all till it's finished.'

'Does that mean you can't?'

'No, it means I won't. Not till it's finished.'

I cross my legs. 'What's left to do?'

'Hec!' snaps Lenny. 'I don't come round to your place and tell you how to mix your colours.'

'That's cos you wouldn't have a clue.'

He paces back to his desk and sits down. I sit up. The walls are blue and spinning under dirty water.

'So what's it called?' I say.

133

'It doesn't have a title yet.'

'What about . . .' I take off my shoes and stretch out. 'What about . . . Err . . . what about . . . *Sometimes You Need Some Clarity*? What about that?'

Lenny picks up his stupid specs and puts them on. He looks me in the eye, like the specs harbour some ancient and forgotten power. 'Is that what all this is about?' he says. 'I can't believe all this is about that.'

'What's "all this"?' I say.

'This!' shouts Lenny. 'You coming round here, clotted with drink, insulting me.'

'How have I insulted you, Lenny?'

He turns away and gets back to drawing his line. 'This is really boring.'

'Lenny, how have I insulted you?'

'Let it go.'

'Was it just now when I said you couldn't mix paint?'

He turns back and brandishes his pencil. 'Your whole attitude is insulting, Hector. You don't turn up on somebody's doorstep, twenty miles out of your skull, and then start laying into them.'

'Who says?'

'Fuck off, Hector.' He stands up again and paces to the other side of the room. Once again I'm compelled to look at him through the little window in the back of his magnificent white settee.

'OK, so I did a water ad, big fucking deal. I did a water campaign.'

'Campaign?' I say and rub my cuff across the pane as though I've misheard him.

'Yeah, yeah, campaign, and yeah I'm sure that you think I've made a fat scarlet arse of myself, and that's fine, that's fine, Hec, but really . . . really it's none of your fucking business, is it?'

I push myself up and sit forward, each hand on its respective knee. One of his candles flickers out. 'What did you say when Tracey Emin did the Bombay Sapphire ad?'

'I don't know, Hector,' says Lenny, 'it was a long time ago. Remind me. What did I say?'

I crane my neck to face him. 'You said, "Silly fucking tart," you said, "Silly mental tart, what a sell out," that's what you said.'

'All right, all right, Hector, so I'm a silly fucking tart and I've sold out. I'm helping a bunch of people sell bottles of water, but like I say it's none of your business. Why does it bother you so much?'

'It doesn't bother me at all.'

He paces back to the window. Schubert's coming to his senses. Lenny turns it off.

Silence.

'I needed the money,' he says, arms in the air. 'I needed the fucking cash, y'know? I mean . . . y'know, it's not easy. It's hard to sell a hole in a gallery floor, it's hard to sell burst balloons and a seven-foot sausage. I'm not a painter. People don't really buy ideas.'

'They'll buy this, though, won't they?' I say, patting the dazzling white cushion.

'Hopefully,' says Lenny, 'hopefully, yeah.'

'And they bought *Domesticated Goose Chase*, didn't they?'

'Yeah, so?'

'And how much did that go for?'

'You know how much it went for.'

'Remind me.'

'A hundred and fifty thousand.'

'That's right, a hundred and fifty thousand.'

'Hector, we're not going over all that again.'

'Who says?'

Lenny puts out his cigarette in a pink ashtray. 'All right. All fucking right, Hector, let's go over it all again. Let's exhume that old stiff. Let's get out our tweezers and pick away at what's left of the meat. So what's your point?'

I curl up in a ball. 'Calm down, Lenny.'

'I've been telling you for years to do a self-portrait, and then you do one. Do I accuse you of nicking my idea? No.'

'It's not the same.'

'It's exactly the same. If you thought that a coffin chasing a pram around a gallery was such a great idea then why didn't you do it?'

'Cos . . .' I say, 'cos it's not such a great idea.'

'Then what's your fucking point?' bawls Lenny, towering over me, huge and bald, fists clenched, towering over me with his sharp white teeth.

I start to cry. I'm curled up in a ball and starting to cry. 'Don't, Lenny, don't. Give me a fucking break.'

'What's the matter with you, Hector? You're fucking mad.'

'Lenny, Lenny, stop, just stop.'

He bends down, close to my face. Too close to my face. His breath smells of mint and smoke. 'You're losing it, Hector. Whatever "it" means to you.'

'My dad's dying.'

Silence.

'What?' Lenny straightens up.

'My dad's dying.' I unfurl from my ball. 'By now he might even be dead.'

'Hector, what are you talking about?'

'My dad! I'm talking about my dad, you heartless fucker. My dad's on his fucking deathbed and you're just screaming at me.'

Lenny sits down beside me. He lifts me up and cradles me in his arms. He rocks me and clears the hair from my eyes.

Silence.

I wish he hadn't turned the Schubert off.

Through the wall I can hear Cilla Black saying, 'Well, well, well, chuck.' She goes on to say something else but Lenny has his hand over my ear and I can't tell what it is.

I can't tell you what happened next, cos what happened next is I lost consciousness. So there you go – I was wrong – I can tell you, I just told you – I lost consciousness – that's what happened next.

In the morning I woke up in a pool of blood. Lenny had scribbled a note saying, 'Good luck tonight Hec. See you there. Sorry about your dad. I love you. Lenny.' There was blood in my hair and all down the side of my neck. There was blood on my woollen arms and blood all over the cushions. Blood and beer and whiskey and toast. All over me, and Lenny's settee. It must be the season of bloody settees.

Except, of course, it wasn't blood. It took me a few minutes to realize. It was fucking beetroot. I'd thrown up beer and beetroot and whiskey and toast, all over Lenny's piece. He must have woken up, written his note, and left before it happened, cos I'm sure he would have mentioned it. I'm sure he wouldn't have left me lying there to choke on my own vomit.

I went downstairs and fetched a bucket of suds and a sponge. I managed to break down the lumps and the general viscosity of it but there was no hope of sponging out the general bright redness of it. In fact the harder I sponged the redder it got. Lenny's white windowed settee with a vomit stain in the shape of . . . in the shape of – I don't know, is it me, or is that vomit stain in the shape of Africa?

I'm back at home. I called Eleni from Lenny's but the old fella in the hardware store said she wasn't around. I think he was saying that Eleni and Yiorgos were staying at the hospital in Matala, although he might have been saying that he hoped Italians liked Mahler, I don't know, it was a bad connection.

I searched Lenny's house for any signs of Rosa but all I found were Brenda's things. I tried on one of her sweaters and a pair of her jeans. The sweater looked a bit effeminate but the jeans were quite snug. I looked around for a clock but they didn't seem to own one. I walked home along the canal and by the time I arrived back at Box Street it was five o'clock.

Now it's six o'clock and the show opens at eight. I've had a bath and changed my clothes and I'm stood in front of the mirror trying to get my hair to look like it wasn't cut by a blind three-year-old. Perhaps I could make it to a barber before the show. I'm wearing a black suit with a lemon shirt. Black shoes, grey socks. Perhaps I should put Brenda's jeans back on.

In fact that's what I'll do.

So now I've got on Brenda's jeans and a black polo neck with a green hoop around the chest. I'll wear my horrible Crombie and maybe even my homburg hat. It's a few years since I've worn my homburg.

My guts are full of lava. I feel like I've swallowed twenty fried eggs and a hot bicycle chain. I can't face eating but I know that I should so I open a tin of tomato soup and soak it up with two pieces of pitta bread and a bowl of puckered olives. I think of Eleni and consider giving her another try. By the time I finish the soup I've decided against it. I decide to call Mum instead.

It rings for a long, long time. I nearly give up. In the end Dad answers.

'Dad!' I yell. 'How are you?'

'Oh, not too grand, Hector lad, not too grand.' He doesn't sound too grand. He sounds frail.

'What's the matter?'

'Well, I don't know, I'm all giddy and dizzy and . . . I don't know, I'm not right, Hector.'

'Well, what's going on, Dad? How's Mum?'

'Your mother's gone out for a walk. She's gone out in her wellies but it's not raining, and she's put on her sunglasses but it's not sunny either. I'm worried sick about her.'

I pick up a cigarette and smoke it cold. 'Well, maybe she's just prepared.'

'Prepared for what?' says Dad. 'Yesterday she went out, saying she was going to get her hair done, and then she comes back with a photo of herself riding on the Big One.'

'On the rollercoaster?'

'Aye, the Big One.'

'What the hell's she doing on the Big One?'

'She's got this photo of herself printed the side of a tea mug, mouth wide open, screaming, hair all over the shop. She looked like Ken Dodd.'

This is not good news. Mum's seventy-two and bad with her nerves. She won't let Dad drive faster than thirty, even on the motorway. What the fuck's she doing riding the Big One?

'Dad, listen, what the hell's going on with this settee?'

'Don't keep saying hell, Hector.'

'Well, what's going on?'

'Bugger all's going on with the settee. I've put it out in the garage. I've got the car parked out in the street all spattered wi' bird doings.'

I walk over to the loading doors. 'Well, what are you gonna do about it?'

'I've taken a hose to it.'

'I mean the settee.'

'Well, maybe I should take a hose to that. We've put it back in the paper, original price, but no bugger's phoned.'

There's a man by the canal carrying a bucket.

'Dad, let me buy it.'

'Why would you buy it?'

'Because I need a settee.'

'Nay, Hector, you've got a settee. You've got that nice blue settee.'

'Just let me buy it, Dad.'

'Don't be soft, Derek . . .'

'Hector.'

'Eh?'

'My name's Hector, Dad. You're Derek.'

A small silence.

'Aye, well don't be soft, Hector, I'm not having you wasting your money as well.'

The man with the bucket takes off his shoes and socks and dangles his feet in the water.

'But I wouldn't be wasting it, Dad. Lenny needs a settee.'

'I thought you said you did.'

'Well, I meant for Lenny. Lenny needs a settee.'

'Well, he doesn't need this one. No one in their right mind would want an atrocity like this.'

Tall, lopsided, foppish-looking fella with a bucket, dangling his feet in the canal.

'But it's for an art piece, Dad.'

'Herpes?'

'An art piece,' I shout, 'Lenny needs to make it into a piece of art.'

'He'll have a bloody job.'

'He's doing a sculpture.'

'Hector,' says Dad, like he's talking to a simpleton, 'it's a settee.'

'I know, Dad.'

Silence. I hear Dad sigh and sit down.

'I don't want to talk about it, Hector, it sets my heart off pounding. I've had to sit down.'

I can hear him breathing and then I'm sure I hear his eyes close.

The other phone rings.

'Hector, are you on that mobile?' says Dad.

'Yes, Dad.'

'You're at home and you're phoning me on your mobile?'

'Yes.'

I can hear him shaking his head. 'You think money grows on trees?'

'No, I—'

'You think money grows on trees?' he says again like a kind of Lancastrian Robert De Niro.

'Well, it sort of does, Dad.'

Dad gasps. 'I'm putting the phone down,' he says, 'it's costing me is this. Go and answer your other phone. Bye.'

'Dad, it's my show tonight.'

But he's gone.

It's Myers on the phone worried about where I am and how *God Bolton* looks magnificent in the alcove, but how the wine hasn't turned up and the heating's packed in.

That tall fella with the bucket's still there. He's scooping up wads of slime from the canal and putting them into the bucket which is already full of something, I can't tell what. He stands up and goes on his way. Tall lopsided foppish-looking fella. The bloke from the toilets in the Tate. The bloke from the church. He gets around.

I open the fridge and stare at the beers; all lined up like little bombs. The soup's made me feel worse and all I can think of is that a beer might make it better. I wish Eleni were here. I wish Eleni were here to make it better. Whatever 'it' is. Perhaps I should just listen to Bianca. Perhaps I should just try to burp myself.

8

THE DOODLEBUG GALLERY, BETHNAL GREEN, LONDON

Myers was right: *God Bolton* does look magnificent in the alcove. In fact it all looks magnificent. I got here just before eight and rearranged all the lights and now it all looks as spectacular as I ever imagined. I'm good. Fucking hell I'm good. I've got it. I've got it in abundance. I might even be a genius. (I didn't touch the beers but I did smoke half a joint; but even so, it all looks incredible – I think.) Twelve paintings, each one eleven foot by eight. Each one a madly colourful and hysterical big head. Twenty-four enormous eyes staring down and out and across the old canoe factory. Fifteen spotlights, a plinth of Tibetan butter candles and the complementary amber glow of the sodium street lamp. It's been open half an hour and there must be about thirty people here. I say here – I mean in the gallery. I'm not actually in the main gallery. I'm in another room. A much smaller room, a tiny room. A cupboard. I'm standing in a small cupboard peeping through a crack in the door.

Most of them I don't know. I can see Myers stood in the middle of it all, beaming, sweating, filling up everyone's glasses. I can see Kirk at the far end frozen in front of *God Bolton*; rubbing at his head with a fag between his fingers, frozen. Jenny Saville's all in black and she's got her face right up to *Mum* squinting. Gillian Wearing's talking to Georgina Starr about *Dad* and Matthew Collings is polishing his specs by the door. Lenny's not here yet and Kirk looks a bit at sea. I should come out of this cupboard. I should find a way of walking out of this cupboard that won't look like Hector Kipling just walked out of a cupboard at his own show. Myers keeps glancing over and frowning. He's come out in an egg-yellow suit and a pair of sandals. He looks an arse.

I push the door open a little bit more, slowly, like it could be a draught. I can see Gilbert and George in green and copper worsted staring at a brick. Paul Smith's here, Kathy Burke, Dinos Chapman, David Baddiel's over in one corner chatting to Stuart Pearson Wright. Suddenly I see Bianca. Bianca's knocking back the wine, staring at *Lenny*. What the fuck's Bianca doing here? I didn't invite Bianca. I told her about it, of course, but I didn't fucking invite her. And why's she knocking back the wine in front of *Lenny*? And why's she nodding slightly? I'm sure she's nodding slightly. I need to piss. I need to crap. I need to vomit again. Tomato soup and dry puckered olives.

The huge iron door opens and in walks Jay Jopling with Sam Taylor Wood. Then it's mental Delaney. He holds the door open and shouts something down the stairs. He must be shouting down to Lenny. Jay and Sam head over to *Aunty Pat*, greeting Myers on the way. Sam says something about the yellow suit and Myers stands back, holding out his arms like a Restoration fop. I look back to the door. Delaney's still holding it open.

There's a mirror on the back of this cupboard and I keep catching a glimpse of myself. I look a fool.

Lenny doesn't know I've painted him. Lenny's not expecting to be confronted by his own head. When Kirk saw it he was beset by an attack of gawping. Five minutes he spent in front of it, jaw loose, eyes in shock.

There's a little knock on the cupboard door.

'Hector,' whispers Myers, 'come out of there.'

'How can I?' I whisper back. 'I'm in a cupboard.'

'Exactly, Hector. Come out of the fucking cupboard. Everyone's asking where you are. I can't tell them you're in the cupboard.'

Delaney gives up on holding open the gallery door and wanders off to get a drink.

'Tell them I'm sick.'

'Hector, they all know that you're sick. They're all aware of that. It's no excuse not to come out here and talk to them.'

'Create a diversion,' I say.

'What?' says Myers.

'Create a diversion and I'll come out.'

'What do you mean, create a diversion? This is the opening of your show, not some fucking war movie.'

'Well, it feels like a war movie, Joe.'

'Hector, come out!' snaps Myers. 'I'm talking to a fucking cupboard. People are starting to look!'

'Joe, you're wearing a yellow suit, you look like a fucking budgie, that's why people are looking.'

The big factory door eases open and Lenny walks in. He's wearing his specs, a turquoise tracksuit, Chinese slippers and a yarmulke (he's not Jewish). He holds the door ajar for a few seconds and then a girl squeezes through, pushing her white-ringed fingers through her messy black hair. A tattoo of a crow on her shoulder. Black dress. Bottle-green eyes. Rosa Flood accepts a glass of red wine and downs it in one.

I really need to get to the toilet. I think about pissing myself. I mean that I actually consider pissing myself as an option at this juncture. Like a scuba diver. I begin to imagine how it might feel. Warm at first, no doubt, and whilst it was still warm I could step out of the cupboard and lay myself out on the floor, gazing at the ceiling, feeling it get cold. Listening as they all start to smell it. Maybe I'll hum something. Something soft. A snatch of Elgar. Just lying there in the middle of them all, sodden crotch, stinking of piss, humming a snatch of Elgar or Grieg or whistling – maybe I should whistle. Then you'd have your self-portrait, Joe. I could call it *Piss Whistle*.

Lenny strolls over to Kirk who's still transfixed by Bolton's big dead head. They hug and Lenny introduces Rosa. Kirk bows and kisses her hand. Rosa pulls off a tough little curtsy. Stiletto boots, bloody lips.

What the fuck am I doing in this cupboard?

There's no intimacy between Lenny and Rosa. I mean they're not holding hands or tickling each other's rumps, so for now I'm er . . . mollified, yeah, that's the word. They stand well apart and at no time, since they walked in, have their bodies been within a foot of each other.

Bianca's moved over to *Mum* and she's rummaging in her handbag. I'm convinced she's gonna pull out a notepad, but it turns out it's only her specs. She's all in blue with her hair washed and dragged back from her brow, like an ageing ballerina. Her specs are bold and tinted, like Sophia Loren's. What the fuck's she doing here?

It's only a matter of time before Lenny sees *Lenny*. Kirk looks like he's delaying the moment. Rosa touches Bolton's mouth, lights a fag and shuffles off in the direction of the toilet. Kirk's showing Lenny his veins.

I'm looking in the mirror and I can barely see myself, but the little I do see is clenched and orange.

Suddenly the door of my cupboard is swung open and the light floods in. Gilbert has his fist around the handle, and George is sipping a glass of champagne. 'Is this part of the show?' says George, raising an eyebrow.

Afraid that they might think I'm encroaching on their whole living sculpture thing I blurt out, 'No!' I steady myself against the sides and hold onto my hat. 'No, no, George,' I stammer, 'this is just me hiding in a cupboard. It's not art – it's my life.'

Gilbert doesn't look convinced and takes a step back, the better to appraise the composition of me – Hector Kipling – cowering there in my homburg and Crombie in this shoddy plywood cupboard. I'm balanced on a pile of old canoe receipts trying to keep my footing. The cupboard's rocking. Suddenly, sensing the fatuity of my situation, I step out and close the door behind me.

'So, Gilbert,' I say, 'so, George, how the hell are you both?' and I tip my hat like a gent.

'We're capital,' says George.

'*Va bene*,' says Gilbert. 'How are you?'

'Now that you're out of the closet,' says George.

I laugh. 'Ha ha!' I laugh a little bit more and blanch or blush; I'm not sure which. 'What do you think?' I say.

'About what?' says George, eyeing up the cupboard.

'The show,' says Gilbert, 'I think he means the show.'

'Oh, the show,' says George.

I nod.

'It's terrifying, Hector. Utterly terrifying. I've soiled my briefs.'

Coming from George I take it as a compliment.

Gilbert sniggers and drains his champagne. 'Our glasses are empty!' he says.

'They possess a negative fullness,' says George and turns his back in search of another. Gilbert follows close behind, and I'm left alone by the cupboard.

I'm not too sure how many people witnessed all this. Jenny Saville, definitely. Gillian and Georgina, definitely (they're whispering behind their hands). Jay, maybe, Sam, maybe. I'm pretty certain Bianca spotted it – she did a double-take worthy of Cary Grant – so there goes my next fifty quid. Lenny and Kirk, thankfully, didn't spot it; they're still in a huddle with their backs to me. And Rosa, thank Holy God in Heaven and all his saints, Rosa is still in the bog.

'Were you in that cupboard just now?' It's Matthew Collings in a big hairy coat.

'Yes, Matthew!' I snap. 'So what? It's all part of it.'

Matthew looks around and wrinkles up his nose. 'I thought you were going to be showing a self-portrait.'

'This is it, Matt,' I say, nodding at the cupboard.

'Right . . . right . . . so it's a kind of er . . .'

'It's a kind of "short fat Northern bloke crouched in a cupboard bidding goodbye to his marble collection" sort of thing.'

'Right,' says Matthew and fiddles with his hair.

'It's a sort of "René? You know that you thought therefore you were?

146

Well, I think therefore I might be as well, so could you order an extra pie?" sort of thing.' And I push past him and head for Bianca.

I see Lenny move his hands in a way that I take to be an impression of me. He still hasn't seen his big shining head cos it's hidden round the corner. And once I've finished explaining that to him I'll get round to tackling the issue of the red vomit on his white window settee. Where's Bianca?

'Great stuff, Hector,' says David Baddiel.

'Thanks, Dave,' I say, push past, and move in.

'Bianca!'

Bianca turns and smiles. 'Hector, sweetheart, this is all so wonderful!' She makes a move either to kiss or hug me but I'm horrified and reel back.

'Bianca, what are you doing here?'

'I've never seen your work,' she says, fag in hand, 'I thought it would be helpful to see your work.'

'Helpful to whom?'

'Helpful for both of us,' and her face lights up as she clasps her hands together.

'Well, it's not really helpful to me right now. You could have come in the daytime or something, not to the fucking opening. Aren't there rules about this sort of thing?'

'Rules?'

'Ethical codes, codes of ethics, whatever you call them.'

'No, Hector. All rules must be personal – we've talked about this. What are you so afraid of?'

'Bianca, Lenny's here!'

'I know, I saw him. He looks half dead.'

'Not the painting, the bloke.'

'Oh.'

'And Rosa, Rosa's here.'

'Rosa?'

'Rosa Flood. The girl I told you about. The girl from the poetry thing.'

'Ah,' says Bianca, relishing the moment, '"Death's door was open / And banging in the wind."'

'Exactly!' I feel like bungling Bianca up into my arms and rustling her back to the cupboard for a private session.

'Well, charming,' she says, 'now you can introduce me to all these people.'

'But, Bianca, I don't want to introduce you to all these people. I want to do the opposite of introduce you to all these people – I want you to leave. Now.'

'That painting of your mother is adorable. She obviously loves you very much. And your father . . .' She looks up into Dad's baggy blue eyes and presses her fists to her bosom.

'This is a walking fucking nightmare, Bianca!'

I see Jay Jopling whisper something to Lenny and then leave.

'This is worse than any bad dream I've ever told you about.'

'Hector, Hector, relax,' says Bianca, stroking my arm.

'Relax? Bianca, you might as well have brought your fucking parrot!'

'Gustav,' she says, and smiles.

'I'll see you next Monday, now go home, I've got to talk to Lenny.'

She looks slightly hurt and I can't really cope with it. I've not been at this caper long enough to know who to talk to when you feel that you might have hurt your therapist. Maybe I need two therapists. The second one to talk to me about my relationship with the first. And so on.

I go over to Lenny and Kirk, who look like they're talking about their feet.

'Lenny!' I say. 'Kirk!'

'Hector!' says Lenny.

'Hector!' says Kirk.

148

'Where the fuck have you been?' says Lenny, but he's smiling and doesn't seem to expect a serious answer. Well, that's a relief.

'Sobering up?' says Kirk.

'Yeah,' I say, rubbing at my eyes, 'a bit hungover.'

'Mmm,' says Kirk.

'Yeah, sorry. How are you, Kirk?' Kirk shrugs. 'Sorry about last night. Both of you: really, really sorry about last night.'

The two of them exchange a glance and smile. Not nasty smiles; two gentle, forgiving smiles. I love Lenny. I love Kirk.

'That's all right, Hec,' says Lenny, pulling my hat down so that my ears stick out. 'Any news about your dad?'

'Er . . . yeah . . . yeah,' I say, 'I er . . . spoke to him this afternoon.'

'You spoke to him?' beams Lenny. 'So he can speak?'

'Why, what's the matter with your dad?' says Kirk, scrunching up his veiny brow.

'Oh, he's been a bit off colour,' I say and lift a glass of wine from a passing flunky.

Lenny straightens up and adjusts his yarmulke. 'You said last night that he was on his deathbed.'

I bring my lips together to say whatever it is that I might possibly say in this moment, but my lips are having some trouble picking up a signal.

'You told me,' pipes up Kirk, 'that it was Eleni's mother who was on her deathbed.'

Kirk looks at Lenny. Lenny looks at Kirk.

'Eleni's mother is on her deathbed!' I snap.

'But not your dad?' says Lenny, watching my mouth.

'Yes, my dad! My dad as well, probably, now can we not talk about all this?'

'He's probably told his mum that I'm on my deathbed,' says Kirk.

'No, I didn't.'

Silence.

I can see Bianca over by *Eleni* watching the three of us. As Lenny and Kirk turn back to reappraise *God Bolton* I make a two-handed gesture at her designed to imply 'Why the fuck are you still here, I thought I told you to go?' But she just smiles and makes a two-handed gesture of her own, designed to imply 'So this is Eleni, isn't she adorable?'

'Where's Rosa?' says Lenny, and Kirk shrugs.

'Rosa?' I hear myself say. 'Who's Rosa?'

'I told you about her,' says Lenny, 'Rosa Flood – the girl from the Bobo Cat. The American girl.'

'Oh her,' I say.

'Oh her!' says Lenny. 'Like you can't remember.'

'Like your tongue wasn't hanging out,' says Kirk.

'What?' I say, feigning outrage.

'Oh yeah, her,' says Lenny, not letting it drop.

'Well, hang on, hang on there, sonny, you're the one who's with her, you're the one wearing her on your fucking arm.'

'Fuck you talking about?'

'Bit young for you, isn't she, Lenny?'

'What do you mean?' says Lenny.

'You know,' I say.

Lenny breaks out into a big grin. Sharp white teeth. 'I'm not fucking her, Hector. Christ, she's like twenty-one or something.'

'I didn't say you were, did I? Did I say you were?'

'You implied it.'

'Did not.'

'Well, what's she a bit young for?'

'Er . . .' I mutter, '. . . her age? I meant she was a bit young for her age.'

'That doesn't even make sense,' says Lenny.

'Who's a bit young for her age? Who are you talking about?' says someone else. Lenny didn't say it, and Kirk didn't say it. My skull is aglow. I turn around.

'He was talking about you, Rosa,' says Lenny, and I nearly throw my drink over him, but I don't cos that wouldn't really help the situation right now. She's right at my side and she smells of jasmine and musk. Sky black hair and impossible eyes, sullen, crucified.

'What were you saying about me?' She puts her hand on her hip and sniffs.

'I wasn't saying anything about you,' I stutter. 'Er . . .' and the circumstances of my whole life – and several past ones – gallop through my brain. 'I meant that I thought you were amazing the other night.'

She looks to Lenny for advice. Lenny just smiles and swigs at his bottle.

'The other night at the poetry thing,' I continue, like a kite out of control, 'I thought your poems were . . .' Silence. 'Beautiful.'

'Thank you,' she says and bows her head. I might have defused the situation. Oh God, please let me have defused the situation. 'That's very sweet of you.'

Sweet! She called me sweet. Or she said that something I said was very sweet. Whatever, it's not a total disaster.

I can still see Bianca. God, I think she's drunk. She's plucking at David Baddiel's chin as though she's got a problem with his beard.

'Hector Kipling,' says Lenny, 'Rosa Flood.'

I hold out my hand. Rosa steps back and puts her glass on the floor.

'Oh my God,' she says. 'Oh myyyyy Gaaahhhd! You're Hector Kipling?' she says and her lips fill up with teeth, and at one point a tongue. Whatever, she's smiling. Laughing, even. 'Oh my Gaahhd!'

Things are looking up.

'You painted all this?'

I look around. 'Yes,' I mutter.

She puts out her hand and I take it in mine. I'm not sure what to do. Since Kirk has already kissed her on the back of the hand I decide against it and look into the possibilities of kissing her somewhere else. But it's no good, anywhere other than the back of her hand would be either over zealous or indecent. I seize the moment and kiss her on the back of the hand and bow, just like Kirk bowed.

She laughs in my face. 'Jesus, you guys are so fuckin' English!'

I pull away and straighten up. 'I'm sorry,' I say.

'Don't be sorry,' she says, 'I'm totally fucking honoured. You are a total fucking genius.'

I want this moment to last for ever. And when forever's over and done with I'd like it to last for whatever they can come up with next that's better than forever.

'Well, I wouldn't say that,' says Lenny.

Cunt.

'You are a god!' says Rosa.

Rosa Flood just called me a god! What a girl.

'A god?' splutters Kirk, spraying his beer.

'Which one?' says Lenny.

'Horus,' says Kirk, 'the Egyptian bird god.'

'Well, he's got the beak for it.'

I will kill them both. Sometime in the near future when I get them both together in more suitable conditions I will slowly and messily kill them both. I scratch at my forehead holding my hand across my nose.

'Ganesh,' says Kirk, 'the elephant God,' and doubles over.

Rosa laughs too. Perfect laughing teeth. She can hardly light her joint for laughing.

Kirk – I hope you die. I hope your tumour bursts open all over your fucking pillow tonight. I hope the surgeon's wife leaves him that morning and he hits the sodium pentathol.

'Did you see the one of you?' says Rosa.

Lenny shakes his head and looks at me. 'The one of me?'

Oh fucking fantastic.

'The one of you. This guy is so on it. It's fuckin' perfect. Come see it,' and she takes him by the hand and leads him across the room. They don't walk side by side; Rosa's well ahead leading him on, like a child pulling a great Dane (or should that be a Mexican hairless?). Kirk tugs at my sleeve but I ignore him.

It's not a great painting. If I had to position it in the league of the twelve paintings here I'd place it about number ten. But then I painted it from memory. It might even be read as a departure. And it's not that I've diminished Lenny in any way. I never set out to insult him. I've made the head a little shinier than it is and one of his eyes is not quite like the other, a bit skew-whiff, a bit boss and puzzled. He's wearing a dog collar, like a vicar's dog collar, and he's sat back, leaning his head against some old purple silk gazing down at the viewer as though they've just snotted on his shoe. I never set out to piss off Lenny. And I never set out to hide it from him. He was away in Amsterdam at the time and when he came back I never found the moment to mention it to him. I knew that one day the moment would arrive, of course I did, but I'd deal with it then.

I've never seen Lenny so still. I've never seen anyone so still (the dead florist in the van maybe). He's stood about four feet away, swallowing, grinding, taking it all in.

Kirk's looking at it like a plasterer confronted by a damp patch.

Silence.

And then: 'When did you do this, Hector?' says Lenny.

'When you were away,' I say.

'You never told me you did this.'

'Isn't it incredible?' says Rosa.

Another unspeakable silence. Endless fucking chatter, coughing, laughing. Everybody's shoes on the factory floor.

'Why am I wearing a dog collar?' says Lenny.

'Cos I was gonna paint a vicar,' I say, 'but then I painted you.'

Lenny thinks about this. I think we all think about this. I know I do.

'So what ... er ...' says Rosa, 'you start with the clothes?'

'Does he fuck start with the clothes,' says Lenny.

'Did this time,' I mutter, and drain my glass.

'I look weird,' he says, and twizzles his finger in the direction of his painted eyes.

'You look like a Nazi,' says Kirk.

Cheers, Kirk.

'He looks beautiful,' says Rosa.

'An emasculated Nazi,' says Kirk.

I panic and pull round in front of them with my back to the painting, 'Kirk, he does not look like a Nazi.'

'I look dead,' says Lenny.

'No!'

'What's with all that purple silk? I look like I'm lying in a coffin.'

'Ha!' I say. 'A coffin?'

'Yeah, that's what it is, that's exactly what it is,' says Rosa. 'It's beautiful.'

'You've never painted me,' says Kirk.

Lenny turns. 'Why would you want him to?'

'I don't want him to.'

'Paint me,' says Rosa and takes hold of my hand.

'I'd love to,' I say.

'Oh Christ,' says Kirk and gives Lenny a look.

Lenny looks away, like he's seen enough. He takes a drag on his cigarette, exhales into my face and asks Rosa if she has the wrap. She goes into her pockets and hands it over. He invites Kirk off to the bog, leaving me alone with Rosa. Strange chess, Lenny mate, strange chess.

'What was all that about?' says Rosa.

'No idea,' I say, 'I think he's losing it. It's the pressure.'

'Of what?'

'Hasn't he told you? He's up for the Turner Prize.'

'Oh yeah, he mentioned that. So is that some big deal?'

'No,' I say, 'not really. But he thinks it is.'

She takes out another cigarette and offers me one. She pulls out a battered old Zippo and ignites it with a flick of her knuckle. As I light up I catch her eye and even think about winking. In fact maybe I do wink. Who's to say?

'Would you really paint me?' she says.

I look into her eyes. It feels like I have the right to look into her eyes; after all, I'm an artist. I'm a major artist making a major decision. I can see myself in them, tiny and bloated. 'Yes,' I say, 'I'll paint you.' She smiles and squeezes my hand. I squeeze back and then she lets it go.

We walk over to *Aunty Pat*. The smell of Rosa is making me blink.

'Who's that?'

'It's my Aunty Pat.'

We're almost touching and I imagine that at least eighty per cent of the people here must think we're together. I imagine that we live together and that she's smart and strange and wild and funny and the sex is great and sometimes I cook for her and sometimes she dances around the bedroom in nothing but a wet orange sarong.

'That is my favourite so far.' She says it quietly, almost a whisper, sincerely, almost in awe.

'Thank you,' I say, almost not pompous.

My phone rings.

'Hello?'

'Hector?'

'Hello?'

'Hector, it's Eleni.'

I hold it away from my ear and look at the buttons. All those buttons. Numbers, arrows, stars, letters. 'OK' it says on the big round button. 'OK' in green capital letters. No, no, no it is not OK. It's the opposite of fucking OK. 'Off' it says in red. My thumb shifts across the keypad like a metronome.

Err . . . I turn it off.

I know that's a monstrous thing to do, but that's what I do. That's the choice I make. I turn it off and put it back in my pocket.

'Who was that?' says Rosa, not really interested.

'A dead line,' I say.

Silence.

Marc Quinn comes through the door and then some ugly actor with a pretty girlfriend.

'I feel lost in her eyes,' says Rosa, gazing up at Aunty Pat. 'I feel buried alive by those eyes. She's too beautiful.'

'Yes.'

'And her hair, has she really got hair like that?'

'Yes, she had hair like that. She's dead now,' and I run my hands across my eyes.

'Oh, I'm sorry,' says Rosa.

'No it's OK,' I say, sniffing 'it was a few years ago. It was quick. God bless her.'

Rosa steps way back, almost to the other side of the gallery, to get a better view.

Why did I do that to Eleni? For fuck's sake, Hector! You haven't spoken to her for four days. You have no idea what's going on, how she is. She may be in tiny pieces. Her mother may be dead. Her father may be dead. She might even be dying herself. You didn't just hang up; you hung up and then turned it off. Turned her off. Flicked her out of existence like a light switch. For fuck's sake! Turn it back on. Turn it back on right this minute, you fucking robot.

'And who's this?' says Rosa, moving over to the next painting.

'Erm . . .' I say.

'*Eleni*,' says Rosa, peering at the label. 'Who's Eleni?'

All the blood in my body is summoned to my head. My feet turn blue. 'She's er . . . she's my sister.'

'Your sister?'

'Yep. She's a . . . a dentist.'

'A dentist?'

'Yeah, teeth,' I say, and point at my teeth.

'She doesn't really look like you,' says Rosa.

'Well – ' and I hold up my hands – 'who does?' and I laugh like I've just come out with something really quite magnificent.

Suddenly there's a whiff of patchouli and a little tanned hand on my arm.

'Hector, I have to go,' says Bianca.

'Oh,' I say, 'Bianca, do you?'

'I do, dear, but I think it's all amazing, it's all so . . . fucking . . . amazing.'

Christ, how many has she had?

'And you are . . .?' says Bianca, holding out her hand to Rosa.

'Rosa,' smiles Rosa, curtsying and shaking her hand, half expecting Bianca to kiss it.

I wouldn't be surprised.

'Ah, yes, Rosa. I see. I'm Bianca.'

'My osteopath,' I say.

'Osteopath?' says Rosa, and frowns. I think the Americans must have different words for all these jobs I'm plucking out of the air.

Bianca smiles and squeezes up her shoulders. 'Yes, that's right, I straighten him out,' and she winks at me.

'Rosa, Bianca. Bianca, Rosa. Well, see you, Bianca. See you on Monday,' and I kiss her on the cheek, pushing her towards the door with my lips. We hug. We've never hugged before and it feels disgraceful.

'Goodnight,' calls Bianca over my shoulder.

'Goodnight,' calls Rosa.

After a brief scuffle and a volley of platitudes I see her off.

Matt Collings is watching my every move as though it's all one complex piece of performance art – I think he's impressed. Stuart Pearson Wright's explaining to Jenny Saville the genesis of his cane. Gilbert and George are doing something strange with each other's fingers.

I wander back to Rosa, smiling at my people. It's filling up nicely. Rosa just stands there gazing at *Eleni*. I draw alongside and stare at

Eleni too. We stand in silence for a long time. Well, look at this, just look at this: Hector Kipling and Rosa Flood gazing at Eleni Marianos.

'You know what?' says Rosa. 'I don't like this one as much as the others.'

I look deep into Eleni's eyes. 'Oh?' I say. 'Why not?'

'I dunno.'

I see Lenny and Kirk emerge from the bog.

'I think . . .' says Rosa and fiddles with her rings, 'I think it's that all the others are so powerful and jarring cos they're kinda grotesque, but this one has no adrenalin, no thunder and lightning. It's just beautiful, so it kinda lacks something.'

I look deep into Eleni's burnt-bronze eyes. Life's a terrible thing. 'The ugly may be beautiful, the pretty never,' I say.

'What?' she says.

'Paul Gauguin,' I say.

'Ah,' she says.

Silence.

For some reason all this has given me an erection. The feeling that I have just betrayed Eleni so horribly, so completely – first by turning off the phone, and then by denying her identity – the feeling that I have mortally insulted her soul, the feeling that I'm in the pay of the devil, has given way to a dark and lurid arousal. How can that be? I look deep into Eleni's eyes. 'Yes,' I say, 'you're right; I have a problem painting beauty.'

Silence. I concentrate on swallowing. I wish everyone else would just leave now. After all, I feel that I may be about to say something.

I swallow and turn to look at Rosa. 'Perhaps I shouldn't paint you after all.'

What a guy!

Rosa smiles and looks down. This is obviously not the first compliment she's ever received. Her familiarity with such foppery is apparent from the precision of her skill in accepting it. She smiles, bows her skull and stares at the floor, offering up her mind without the burden of the eyes, making herself all the more beautiful. There is nothing more beautiful on this earth than casual guilt feigning considered innocence. Or is that just me?

'Oy oy,' says Lenny, 'what are you two looking so coy about?'

Rosa straightens up.

I take a swig of my wine but forget to take the cigarette from my mouth and the result is just silly.

'Has he proposed to you?' says Kirk.

'Or merely made a proposition?' says Lenny.

I really wish these two had stayed away a bit longer than they did. Another five years would have done it.

'Fuck off,' says Rosa, 'you think a man and a woman are incapable of communicating with each other without loosening each other's pants?'

'Yes,' says Lenny and clinks Kirk's bottle.

'Oh, hello, Eleni!' says Kirk, looking up into Eleni's eyes.

'Oh yeah, hello, Eleni,' says Lenny. And then he looks down at my legs and cocks his head. 'Are those Brenda's jeans?'

'What?' I say.

'Are you wearing Brenda's jeans?'

Kirk looks at my legs.

'What?' I say.

'You're wearing Brenda's jeans.'

'No I'm not,' I say.

'Who's Brenda?' says Rosa.

If I'm honest, I'm not really enjoying myself.

'They look like Brenda's jeans,' says Lenny.

'Well, they're not.'

'Who's Brenda?'

Lenny lifts up my sweater. 'That's Brenda's belt!'

'I know,' I say.

'Why are you wearing Brenda's belt?'

'To hold up Brenda's jeans.'

'So you are wearing Brenda's jeans?'

'Oh yes,' I say.

If ever there was a perfect moment for an asteroid to collide with Western Europe, now is the time.

Lenny stares at me.

'He's probably got her knickers on as well,' says Kirk.

'Who the fuck's Brenda?' says Rosa.

Suddenly, behind us, there's a commotion and we all turn to look. It's fine by me. Matthew Collings is down on the floor holding onto his head. That's fine by me. Myers is pelting across the room in his yellow suit looking like an animatronic fucking omelette and the tall lopsided foppish-looking fella from the canal is rushing towards *God Bolton* with a bucket full of something horrid.

'Fuck,' says Lenny.

'Fuck,' says Kirk.

'Fuck,' says Rosa.

They all say it at the same time. In fact a lot of people say it. Maybe everyone says it. I know I do.

'Fuck!' I say.

I'd like to tell you that it all happens in slow motion, but it doesn't. It's all over in a flash. In fact there is a flash. There's a dim, hypnotic, sad little flash as the bucket spins, catches the spotlight and smashes into God Bolton's throttled blue throat.

Oh dear.

I'm outside now. And I'm running. Oh yes. You might even say that I'm in pursuit. It's frosty and calm, almost pastoral in a brooding, industrial kind of way. Still. Silent, save for the sound of Tall Lopsided's boots slapping against the cobbles. Tall Lopsided's legs getting away from my short tubby ones. As he disappears into the dark, headed for Vallance Road,

I swing out wide on the corner of Tent Street. I hear a snatch of Nina Simone, it gets a little louder, louder still – what is that song? – and then suddenly a huge silver Volvo appears in front of my thighs. I bounce up nicely against the windscreen and land with a thud on the greasy grey pavement. What a mess. Someone's thrown away a vegetable samosa and half a bottle of Lucozade. Bus tickets rocking in the breeze. The Volvo hasn't stopped. I can hear him changing up a gear. Someone has tried to chalk the *Mona Lisa* on the wall. My spine feels like a buckled slinky. There's a copy of *Razzle* flapping about in a doorway. 'LIVE, 30 second wank GUARANTEED!! 09090 44 79 79.'

Oh dear.

9

When Rosa said, 'Paint me,' I saw no canvas nor palettes. I saw only my brush on her flesh. I saw her legs apart so that I could get into the corners.

Myers had tried to rugby-tackle Tall Lopsided as he sprinted across the room towards the door, but Mental Delaney had got the wrong end of the stick and rugby-tackled Myers, who crashed to the ground with a bold yellow 'Ooof!' For a few seconds no one moved. Most people stared at *God Bolton*, monitoring the progress of the dark and noxious fluid as it made its way down his collar into the bevels of the frame. Collings was still on the ground, but even he couldn't resist the thrill of how it would turn out. I looked at Lenny and then at Kirk. Lenny and Kirk looked at me. It no longer seemed to matter that I'd painted Lenny like a dead, emasculated Nazi reclining snottily in his coffin. It no longer seemed to matter that I was wearing Brenda's jeans. I looked at Rosa. Rosa looked at me. The most bizarre thing I could have said right then was 'Wait here' but that's exactly what I said, and then paused for a moment, balancing on one leg, feeling a bit like Batman. And off I went, thundering down the stairs, alone, frightened, fractured, scuffed, incredulous, my mask a bit skew-whiff and my cape caught on the banister.

Lying there on the pavement amongst the grids and litter I was beset by an overwhelming and relentless sense of déjà vu. Abundant and tireless.

There was nothing vague about it, nothing fleeting. The images were crystal and endured for well over fifteen minutes. The effect of all this was that during those fifteen minutes I fancied that I was capable of – if not madly accomplished at – seeing into the future. For fifteen minutes of my life I was able to anticipate and then witness the ensuing few seconds of my existence with alarming accuracy. It was as though the anticipation and the fulfilment of each shattered incident existed at one and the same time. For instance, it was inevitable that a small bird would land, mess around with half a bagel and then alight, scared off by the slamming of a distant door. As I stared at the wheels of a milk float I heard the flapping of wings. And there was the bagel, midway between the samosa and the copy of *Razzle.* I lay there on the kerb and wondered if anything was broken. Nothing hurt, but I wondered if anything was broken. Maybe everything was broken. Maybe I was finished. Maybe all this seeing into the future meant that I was finished. Maybe one is only permitted to see into the future when one has no further investment in it. Maybe one would eventually tire of seeing the future and beg to see the past instead, as a treat, on a Sunday: three hours of the past for a whole week of the future. Every Sunday, every week, for evermore.

Apparently, the whole exhibition fell apart after the attack on *God Bolton.* The stink of the dripping manure saw off the first batch. Only the most curious remained. Someone, who shall remain nameless, had commented on how, somehow, the resonance of the room had been enlivened by the passion of assault. Eventually the appearance of the police rendered the whole affair rather unsavoury, leaving only the intimates, the alcoholic, the dedicated and the dedicated alcoholic intimates. I am told that Myers gave my number to the police since I was the only one who had arsed themselves to attempt apprehension of the attacker and, for all Myers knew, might even have succeeded. But I'd been gone for an hour by then and nobody knew the outcome. Some feared that I had caught up with the attacker only to be attacked in return. Others feared that I had caught up with the attacker, attacked him and then suffered a subsequent arrest. Others, namely Matt Collings, wondered if I wasn't in fact in cahoots with the attacker and the whole thing was just another part of the show. Whilst still others thought it likely that I hadn't even got close to the attacker and was therefore merely sobbing into my hat, like a big fat baby, on the steps of the canal. Who knew? And would they ever know? Who knows? The whole thing was a nice little mystery for them all.

Lenny and Kirk had bid goodbye to Rosa at the gallery entrance. They planned to take a cab round to Box Street to see if I was there, but failing that they were off into town to try and salvage the evening. Rosa, since she lived just around the corner, declined the offer of a lift and said she would walk.

Stilettos on cobbles, that was the first thing I heard. Of course it came as no surprise.

At first I couldn't open my eyes. I could feel her hand on my forehead, pushing back my hair. Her cold rings, the sound of her bracelets. When I did open my eyes it felt like they'd been rolled in petrol. The night was sticky with gum. Each blink was the slamming of a door.

Calling an ambulance didn't seem to occur to her. Instead she opted for dragging me down the street, me on all fours, all threes in fact since she had hold of one of my hands, smiling down at me, offering me encouragement. What can I say? It worked. This is the street where Rosa lives: La Via Della Rosa.

She eased me onto her white settee and covered my bleeding brow with a white flannel. She knelt down on the white boards and whispered, asking me how I felt. I really had no fucking idea about all that kind of thing and so gave her no answer. My eyes were open and I knew that I wasn't in a coma, but I might have been. I knew that I wasn't dreaming, but I was hardly awake. I knew that I wasn't dead, but I was assured that my life was over. Her eyes were close to mine. Someone, somewhere, was learning to play the tom-toms. She took a long look into every corner of me – it lasted for years. Eventually she smiled as though she'd just reached the punchline of a weak joke. Her own eyes were a brilliant crocodile green, spattered with black, like tiny gunshot. It was around then that my ability to foresee the approaching seconds abated. Up till now I had felt as though my body was suspended on broad jets of air, but suddenly the supply was winding down, so slowly, so gently, soft white fingers twisting the taps. I was here. I was here, wherever it was. I was in the white room, bleeding on the white settee. The white flannel, the white taste, the white walls, Rosa's small white face peering through her sweaty black hair. The white shelf above the white grate was populated by white horses, balls, pebbles and skulls. Rat skulls, rabbit skulls, cat skulls, otters, birds, badgers, bats. Maybe even the skull of a pig. All white and dry and filled with old flies. Fly skulls. The skulls of dust. The telephone was white. The candles, the chairs were white. My Little White Death.

She brought me through a cup of something she called tea, though it was filled with bits of stick and strange black pods. I burned my lip on the first sip and put it down on the floor.

'What the fuck happened to you?'

Here she was, close up. Not an atom out of place. She wore a white T-shirt that covered her thighs. Purple toenails. Tattoo of a cartoon bomb on the bulb of her anklebone.

I told her about the pursuit, the car, the dried-out samosa and how, right up until now, I'd been able to see into the future. She said that that was either a shame or a blessing. I asked her what she meant but she only bowed her head and sipped at her tea. In turn, at my request, she filled me in on the events following my departure from the gallery.

'Horse shit?'

'That's what most people thought. I mean it was definitely shit but there was some difference of opinion as to the species. And then it started to smoke a little and there was this smell. There may have been some kind of acid in there along with the horse shit, the whole thing was kinda melting.'

'Melting?'

'Kinda, yeah. Smoking and melting.'

'Can it be saved?'

'Well, that guy in the yellow suit who was running the show asked if there was a painter in the house, and your friend Kirk stepped up and suggested warm soapy water and kitchen roll.'

I sighed.

Well, there I was on Rosa Flood's white settee. Sighing and bleeding.

'Do you have a cigarette?' I said and she went into the pocket of her jacket and pulled out a packet of Dunhills. After helping herself she handed me her Zippo and I lit one. I turned the Zippo over in my hand. There was a crude engraving on one side: 'To Rosa. Smoke yourself to the bone and chain. Charlie C. – An Old Flame'.

I didn't like that. I didn't like that one bit.

'I guess this is all kinda strange.'

'Er . . .' I said, 'er . . . yeah. You could say that.'

She took a long drag of her cigarette, almost finishing it in one. 'So what was all that about, man, that guy flinging that pail of horse shit all over your painting?'

I'd fallen into a kind of daze, even though the Kodo drummers were rehearsing in my heart.

'I mean, why did he do that?'

'I have no idea,' I said, but wished to God that I did, cos the last thing I wanted right then was for the conversation to dry up.

'I mean, do you know him?'

I told her about having seen him twice before. I told her about the sighting in Tate Modern, but I didn't mention the toilets or the crying.

And I told her about the church but I didn't mention Eleni, and when she asked me what I was doing in a church I muttered something about Thomas Hardy and Westminster Abbey, giving the impression that I was well read and that the whole thing took place in Westminster Abbey.

She went on to tell me some story about how Thomas Hardy's heart was eaten by the family cat. 'His body was cremated and his ashes entombed in Poets' Corner, but his heart, so they say, was to be buried in the family plot. But, on the day, it was left out on the kitchen table and the fuckin' cat ate it. Yeah, man, you should paint that kinda shit. And Walter Raleigh's widow, she carried his head around in a bag for the rest of her life. You should paint that as well.'

'You seem to know a lot about English history.'

'Two things is hardly a lot.'

'I suppose not.'

She was struck by a new thought and clapped her hands together, bouncing on her rump and squealing, like a skittish child. 'Or Rasputin under the ice, struggling to get his hands free.'

Well at least she wasn't suggesting Greek myths.

'Yeah?' I said.

'Or the bedroom of the Unabomber. Or the aftermath of some random shooting. You should move out of just painting heads. You should be painting what Goya would be painting if Goya was still painting. Did you know that by the time Goya was forty-seven, six of his seven children were dead? You should paint like Goya! Or you could paint some guy who's thrown himself off a skyscraper, call it King Kong.'

Was she just coked out of her mind or what? Or was this just her?

'Like what happened to my friend Charlie?'

'What?' I said, horrified.

'My friend Charlie,' she said, 'threw himself off some skyscraper and signed his suicide note "King Kong".'

'Charlie C?' I said and raised, or tried to raise, my eyebrows.

'Oh, you read my Zippo. Yeah, Charlie C.'

'Why did he do that?' I asked, appalled.

'Cos he was crazy. His name was Charlie Conga, and we all used to call him King Conga, and then just Kong, and I guess it all kinda went to his head somehow, and next thing you know he's taking the elevator up to the top floor, mashed on ketamine, and he smashes a window and bang, splat. Charlie Smoothie, right there on Fifth Avenue. It was only for reasons of taste that they didn't just haul out the shovels. You see what I'm saying? You should be painting this kinda shit, man.'

'I will,' I said, and you know what? I really think I will. I liked this girl. Fuck, I really liked this girl.

'I mean after you've painted me. If the offer's still open.'

'It's still open,' I said. Rather smoothly, as I remember.

'I'm glad,' she said, and peeled off one of her eyelashes, dropped it on the floor and flicked it across the room.

'So is Charlie C,' I said, 'Charlie Conga, the guy you were talking about in all those poems the other night?'

Rosa stood up and stubbed out her fag in the eye socket of what I took to be the skull of a kitten. 'Shit no, I never wrote no poem for Charlie,' and she sat back down, laughing, covering her beautiful white teeth with her beautiful white hand.

'So who were they for?'

Rosa turned her head and stared at the candles like she had no intention of answering.

Silence.

The sound of a tear appearing in the corner of her eye.

'They were for some fuckin' asswipe.'

'Ah,' I said, not unfamiliar with MTV.

'Some fuckin' jerk who ran off with some fuckin' stripper at my twenty-first.'

'You had a stripper at your twenty-first?'

Rosa scowled at me. 'No, fucker, she wasn't working; she was just there. And then they left. I should have killed him. I thought about it.

I mean it, I seriously thought about killing him. I counted the ways. I had a gun. I was gonna go with the gun. I was just gonna shoot him in the back.'

'Yeah?' I said, and nodded, casually, like this was the sort of conversation I had every day.

'Yeah, shoot him in the back. Since he'd already stabbed me in mine.' She lit another cigarette on Kong's Zippo. 'That's when I came over here. I met this English guy in New York. A dancer. He invited me over to London to stay with him. And then we got married.'

'You're married?'

She smiled, relishing my dismay. 'Yeah sure. Only so I could get my papers. He's gay.' She smiled again at my poorly concealed relief. We gazed at each other for a long time. Two pairs of eyes, charged in the candlelight. Two warm brains, softly electrocuted. Eleni was already betrayed.

'So how about you?' she said, still looking me in the eye. 'You seeing anyone?'

'No,' I said. And then I said it again: 'No,' I said. And then: 'Not at the moment.'

Indecent silence.

Understandably concerned that one of us might say something to scotch the moment she took me by the hand and lifted me to my feet. The clink of her bracelets and the smell of musk beneath the wax.

The bedroom was as black as the living room had been white. The walls, floor and ceiling, all blacker than any black I had ever encountered. A black clock on a black desk. A black chest on a black rug. Black curtains on a black rod. Black books on a black bookshelf. There was a television in one corner, painted black, and on top of the black television a black Madonna cradling a black Christ. Black candles on black china plates. Two black guitars and a black tambourine. She lowered me onto the black bed and rested my head upon the black pillow. She took off my top, eased down Brenda's jeans and nestled down beside me.

Before I had time to implement the fine points of my will, her hands were finding mine and she curled her body around my back like a cat. Like a warm black cat. Like a warm and disastrous cat; The Cat That Ate Thomas Hardy's Heart. That cat.

Fade to black.

It's dawn now, and I'm stretched out in the bath gazing at my penis. The water is filled with shining white bubbles and my penis is in there somewhere, bobbing on the surface, like butter wouldn't melt.

I've never been the sort of man to give it a name, nor imagine that it's something other than me, with eyes and a mouth and a mind of its own. I've always steered clear of those cartoons that suggest such a thing, and I call it a penis, not a dick or a cock or a knob or a tool, I call it a penis. My penis and its balls. What a mess. What a fucking mess. All men have had these moments, lying back in the bath, in times of sexual crisis. All men have looked at their penises like this. And perhaps women look at their breasts in this way or sometimes their vaginas if it's a shallow bath. Comforting to know that practically everyone on the planet has at some time lain back in a bath of some sort, in a time of sexual crisis and damned their genitalia. You could publish a book. Books.

'Fucking parasite,' I say, 'fucking leech.'

I imagine that there's nothing there. No penis, no balls, no hair. Not that there's a vagina there. Not that I'm lying back in the bath imagining that I've got a vagina. Nor am I lying back in the bath considering castration. No, it's simpler than that. I mean that there's just nothing there. The legs meet and there's just a smooth patch of skin, like the inside of the elbow or the back of the knee. Smooth, hairless, harmless. It doesn't even have a name. There's no arsehole and no urethra, because we don't need to shit or piss. We don't need to shit or piss because we don't need to eat or drink. No need to reproduce. We are not born. One day we just appear and continue to keep up appearances forever – we never die. It never rains and there is no disease, decay or even doubt. Since we have fewer organs we are much smaller creatures. But we still have a brain. But a splendid brain. We need to be neither soothed nor hugged nor made to laugh. And everything just looks and sounds as nice as it could ever look or sound. And no one ever lies. And there is no such thing as love.

I lean back my head on the rolled-up towel, put my hands together and pray that I might spend eternity in this bath. No genitals, no hunger no sickness, no longing. Just me and the bubbles and it never gets cold.

My phone is still switched off and sits on the edge of the bath like a black box of pain. I take it up in my hands and go through the stored numbers – forty in all. Not even enough to take up the phone's memory. But all of them owed a call. I access the voicemail. 'Welcome to Orange Answerphone. You have nine new messages . . .'

One day I'll learn not to feel this way. One day I'll have learned to pour milk over this agony. One day the next thing I do won't be the wrong thing to do.

The next thing I do: I hold the phone under the water. I have it by its throat. I hold it down by my fat hip and watch it give up its bubbles. It slips from my grasp like soap and clatters against the white enamel. The light goes out.

Silence.

I lean back my head and gaze out the window. After weeks and weeks of grey the sky has cleared to blue. I don't know where I am. All I can see is the backs of houses and a few low roofs. There's a woman on one of the roofs learning to walk the tightrope. She's not very good and keeps falling onto a pile of old mattresses. I seem to be facing east. A mellow sun hits the mirrors and in turn the bathwater which ripples and swells across the flaking paint of the ceiling. The water's getting cold. I bring the phone up into the air and toss it onto the towel. I half expect it to flap.

There's a Chinese dressing gown draped across the sink and I try to put it on. After splitting the stitching under the arms and wrestling with the knotted blue belt I take it off and make do with one of the towels. There's a mirror on the door of the medicine cabinet and when I look into it there's a face. Not a face I recognize. Not a face I like. Not really a face at all. I need to lie down. I really need to lie down on this scarlet floor. I stare deep into my own eyes and think of all those tiny things that scrabble about our bodies. I see them as a mob of drunken revellers. I see them as the disenchanted citizens of a Utopian society. I see them as busy and ravenous little shuttles from their mother ship Lucifer. Multiple millions of them, industrious, feeding, excitable and abandoned in every crevice, knob and socket of my body. It makes me feel less alone. I look away from the mirror and up to the ceiling. There's an ugly little spider navigating the broken bulb.

Idea For a Piece: Fill polished copper wombs with spiders. A hundred and twenty wombs all over the gallery floor. Twelve thousand spiders in all. Allow them to get about. And if they get up the punters' trousers, well fuck 'em. They shouldn't have come to the show in the first place. Call it *Fuck You. You Shouldn't Have Come To The Show In The First Place.*

The creepy little fella starts on his way down. His spittle thread glinting in the sun. I'm put in mind of Robert the Bruce. I'm sat in a chalk cave, in a kilt, with a burning red beard and a planished brooch. But I don't feel like taking up arms against the English. I don't even feel like rousing myself from the cave. I'm just anxious that the little twat might land on my towel. But then, in the next moment, sensing my meat turn to vegetable, maybe I do want to take up arms against the English.

'O England, My England . . . You and me. Outside. Now!'

I bid goodbye to the bathroom and walk into the black bedroom. Rosa's lying on her front, covers kicked off, naked, still. One hand is tucked beneath her thighs and the other lolls on her head. Between her fingers and in her hair a cigarette has burnt itself out. A two-inch worm of ash curled across her scalp. I blow and some of her hair comes away. She needs looking after. She has a little bald patch. One day she'll kill herself. I kiss her on the cheek and bless the silence.

She made an awful lot of noise last night. And at one point hurt me quite badly.

I tiptoe out of the room and spend the next five minutes trying to button up Brenda's jeans. I scribble a short note and leave it by the kettle (the kitchen is entirely blue):

> Rosa, thanks for finding, helping, saving me last night.
> Whichever one it was, (perhaps it was all three), thank you.
> Please don't think that I have crept out, (although I obviously
> have), but if I was silent it was only to allow you to sleep. It is
> unthinkable for us not to see each other again so, my beautiful
> poet, if I may retire into prose, here is my number: 0208 . . .
> etc.

I steal out of the front door with all the stealth I can muster given my age, state and girth. I close the door behind me and draw a deep breath, relieved to have pulled off such a shabby exit with such nimble aplomb. I am, therefore, a little vexed, to say the least, when I stumble over a small army of bottles, left out on the landing, and suddenly find myself rolling down the stairs, bouncing on my shoulders and shins, watching my homburg hat beat me by a few seconds to the hard green tiles of the second floor. A few of the bottles come along for the ride and I'll be a monkey's uncle if one of them doesn't split itself in three on my forehead just before my nose hits the skirting board. Lying here at the bottom of the stairs, with small drops of blood pattering down onto the green tiles, I begin to remember something of the night before. I had been dragged into this house on my hands and knees, and now it looks like my departure will be equally discreditable.

Here I am, look. Here I am. I'm squeezed into a phone box on the corner of the Roman Road, and Mum's all over the place. Mum's in little pieces that won't fit together.

'Well, where are you?'

'I'm in a phone box, Mum.'

'I didn't think they had phone boxes in London any more.'

'Well, they do, Mum, and I'm in one.'

I'm surrounded by twenty girls all with their knockers and pants askew. It's like trying to talk to your mother from the inside of Hugh Heffner's head.

'Hector, love, come home, your father's broken out in sores.'

'Eight hundred and forty pounds, Mum; I'm sending it to you right now.'

'Don't you dare, Hector.'

'Mum! Mum, remember when I had all those warts on my fingers and you bought them off me, 25p each? Well, it worked, didn't it? The next day they were gone.'

'What's that got to do with anything?'

'Well, Mum, I'm offering you eight hundred and forty pounds for Dad's sores. I'm sending a cheque.'

'We'll rip it up.'

'What am I gonna do if I come home? There's nothing I can say to Dad that's gonna make him feel better about you blowing that much money. All I can do is replace the money. Mum, please let me give it to you.'

Mum sounds like she's crying but she's trying to hide it from me. 'Just come home, Hector love. I need a hug. How did the show go?'

'It went fine, Mum. Don't cry.'

'I'm not.'

'You are.'

'I'm not crying, Hector, I just need a hug from my son. Your dad needs a hug from his son.'

'If I come home will you let me give you the money.'

'No.'

'Well, I'm not coming home.'

What kind of son am I? What kind of horned and scaly ice-cold fish monster am I? Why don't I just get on the train right now? It's only three hours and my mum needs a hug. My dad needs a hug. What kind of dung beetle am I? I can hear whispering coming from my skin.

'Mum, what's that noise?'

'What? Sorry I can't hear you?'

'I said what's that horrible noise?'

'Oh, that's your father upstairs with his head in a bucket.'

My credit clicks to zero. 'Mum, my money's running out.'

'Come home, Hector.'

'I will, Mum, I've just got to sort a few things out. I need to sort out what's going on with Eleni. Do a bit of paperwork, have a few meetings.' I hear Dad again, upstairs on the bed, having eight hundred and forty quid ripped from the lining of his stomach. 'I'll call you later.'

'Hector?'

'Yes, Mum?'

'I just wish—'

The line goes dead.

I step out of the phone box and look up to the sky. The blue is now powdered with clouds and the skin on my face thinks it might rain. I have a fiver in my pocket and I could get it changed in Tony's Caff and call Mum back, but I don't. I don't. I walk up the Roman Road, clutching my eye, and think about heading home. But I'm not sure if I can face home. I'm not sure if I can cope with the look home's gonna give me.

It seemed unreasonable to try and call Eleni from a phone box, and besides I should listen to her messages before I speak to her. I take my mobile from my pocket but it's still dripping. No amount of button-pressing will get it to light. I throw it into a skip. There's an old settee in the skip. 'He who looks for signs will find them everywhere.' Book of whoever, chapter something, verse I dunno. I resolve to go home.

I'm approaching the corner of Box Street. In spite of the bath I feel filthier than ever. I'm hobbling down the street, a headache in each foot. I turn the corner and see the gables of my building. The gables see me. I stare at the floor. The floor stares back. I close my eyes. My eyes close me.

There's someone sat on the step by the front door. From this distance it might be Lenny. It makes sense, and I think of what I can say to him when he asks what happened to his settee.

'What can I say?' I'll say. 'I threw up on it.'

What can I say?

But as I draw closer I see that it's not Lenny. The posture's all wrong; the clothes, the sentiment, the shoes, the hair, the tears.

I think about turning round but feel too weary for such giddiness. In between realizing that it's not Lenny and then realizing who it is, there are a good thirty seconds when I have no idea who it is. A stranger, a dosser, my father, a ghost.

I suppose my boots are the first thing he sees of me. He lifts up his head, all sticky and damp, and pulls a handkerchief from his pocket. He wipes his mouth, dabs his eyes and blows his nose. There are griffins on his tie and wolves on his cufflinks, he's wearing brogues and red silk socks. Brylcreem. Rolex. All in all he's turned up pretty sharp.

'Hello, Hector,' says Tall Lopsided.

'Hello there,' I say.

He pulls himself to his feet and he's taller than I ever thought. Taller than Lenny.

'I'm so sorry, I'm so, so sorry,' and he lumbers towards me. I take a step back and then, in the next moment, partly to stop him falling over and partly to absorb the spectacular grief, I allow him into my arms. He tucks his head onto my chest. I push my hat back from my brow and look at the sky, 'I can't take any more,' I say, 'I really can't,' I say to the sky.

'Tough,' says the sky.

'I'm so sorry, I'm really so sorry,' whimpers Tall Lopsided.

I ask him his name.

'Freddie Monger.'

'Freddie Monger?'

'Yes.' He's convulsed with sobbing.

'It's all right,' I say, 'I swear it's all right.'

'I'm so, so, so, so sorry,' says Freddie Monger. And you know what? I really think he means it.

10

He's staring at the painting; two red lines, converging, like they're supposed to. Freddie Monger must be in his early thirties and not a bad-looking fella by common standards. But in both his dress and his manner there is something peculiar, perhaps anachronistic. His jaw is triangular, bold and meticulously razored. The sort of man who shaves twice a day. The sort of man who sets aside the time. His movements are slow and he smells of expensive cologne. As he leans back in my big blue chair he brings his hand up to his skull. Those eyebrows might be plucked. That ring might be a ruby.

'Would you like a drink?'

'Thank you, that would be a tonic.'

'A tonic?'

'What?'

'You want a tonic?'

'No, no, I mean that a drink would be a tonic.'

Fuck, he's posh. Even his cigarettes are taken from a silver case. His voice – now he's stopped blubbing – is brittle and commanding.

'Right, I see. A beer's all right, then?'

'Thank you.' He lights his cigarette with a slim jewelled Cartier lighter.

'Glass?'

'Please.'

I catch sight of myself scampering across the room with a ridiculous gait. I feel like I've invited David Niven round for cocktails.

'This is a spectacular space,' he says, blowing out his smoke in a long well-bred plume. 'What's the history? Some kind of warehouse?'

'Yes, yes' – I've gone a bit posh – 'well, it was a furniture depot. Then it was broken up into flats. This floor used to be three separate flats.'

'I see. And you and your girlfriend knocked them through.'

I hand him his glass and take a seat on the settee. 'How do you know about my girlfriend?'

He takes a long swig of his beer, balloons his cheeks, breathes and then gets back to his fag. Somehow he makes the whole thing look like he's just partaken of an oyster. 'I saw you with her. Remember?'

'Right,' I say. I take a fag from my crumpled box, light it with a match and slug on my can. 'That's right. I saw you that day in the church.'

'What were you doing in a church?'

What is this? Why am I sat here, in my own home, being interrogated by a stranger? He was the one who threw horse shit all over my painting. Shouldn't I be interrogating him? Shouldn't I be on the phone to Scotland Yard? And why am I saying Scotland Yard and not just the cops? There's something about this bloke. He's made me come over all Graham Greene.

'What was I doing in a church?'

'Yes.'

'Eleni's Catholic. Eleni, that's my girlfriend. Her mother was dying.'

'And is she still dying?'

I glance over at the red eye of the answer machine winking away in its dark corner. 'I don't know,' I say, and we both get on with our smoking. His fingernails are as crisp as seashells.

I ponder the pros and cons of asking him what he was doing in the church, but somehow feel that this is not the way forward. Is there a way forward?

'So,' I say, at last, 'I expect you feel like talking.'

'Actually, Hector, it's the last thing I feel like doing, but I suppose I must.'

'Well . . .' I say and shrug.

'I know, I know.'

'I mean, otherwise, I'm not sure what we're both doing here.'

'I know, I know,' and he grips the bridge of his nose; not like it delivers any comfort, but like he's read too much Proust – which, judging by his posture, he probably has.

'So why did you do it?'

Silence.

He's breathing down his nose, eyes closed. I get the feeling that he's about to either answer, or vomit.

'Actually, we've met before,' he says at last.

'I know,' I say, sitting forward with my can, 'in the toilets at the Tate.'

'I mean before that,' he says, 'years ago.'

'Have we?'

'Oh yes. Quite a number of years ago.'

'How many years ago?' I don't like this.

'Quite a number.'

I feel cold all of a sudden. He's obviously about to tell me something momentous. Of course he might just be nuts and about to tell me something utterly banal, but there's something about his eyes, something about the way he moves his fingers.

'Quite a number,' he says again and I take another swig of my can.

'What number's that, then?'

'Oh, quite a number, quite a number.'

I've met some peculiar people in my time but this guy's making a surprise new entry in the top three. Why does my stomach feel like it's full of ash and jam? What's he gonna tell me? That he's my brother? That he fucked my mother? That he's death himself, in a Mayfair blazer, and that that Volvo last night really did slam a lid on it all? Then what of Rosa? Is this what is known, in certain circles, as purgatory?

'Where did we meet?'

'We met here.'

'Here?'

'On the stairs. You were struggling up the stairs with your shopping. You had a bag of oranges. The bag split.'

'Did it?'

'It did. A dozen oranges rolled down the stairwell. I helped you pick them up.'

'Right.' I have no memory of any of this.

'Remember?'

'No.'

'Oh.'

And we both get back to our smoking and drinking. Monger pours out the rest of his beer into the glass and gets to work on it. He slips off one well-polished brogue, kicking at the heel with the toe of the other.

'So,' I say, 'what has all that got to do with anything? Why have you been following me?'

'Do you think I've been following you?'

I think about this. 'Well . . . yes . . . in a way . . . you have, haven't you?'

'I suppose so,' he says, and stares at the black spot on the ceiling. 'What's that?' he says.

'It's a black spot,' I say and stare at it too.

'I see.' He looks around the room as though he's measuring it for a carpet. 'So,' he says, 'a furniture depot. I must say, it's perfect for you.'

'Look, Mr Monger . . .' I stand up.

'Freddie.'

'Freddie. Look, Freddie . . .' I find myself pacing the room. 'Look, Freddie, I'm getting a bit creeped out now. I invited you in cos I felt that we both understood that you had some explaining to do. But so far . . .' and I pause here and stride back to the table for my beer, 'so far . . . you haven't explained anything.'

'I suppose not,' says Freddie and assesses his chin. Perhaps it's time for another shave. I finish my beer and conclude with a long and ill-bred belch.

'So?' I say.

'So what?'

'So what's the story, Freddie, man?'

'Well . . .' says Freddie.

I put up my hand. 'Hold it right there. I'm getting another beer, you want one?'

He looks into his glass and then raises his head. He smiles. It's the first time I've seen him smile. 'That would be most agreeable.'

I stride off to the kitchen and open up the fridge. There are only two beers left and I get that end-of-the-party feeling. Something inside me tells me that I'm gonna need more than one more beer. I open up the freezer. There's some vodka in there.

'Here you go,' I say, snapping the ring pull and filling his glass.

'Capital,' he says.

'So, Freddie,' I light yet another fag, 'what's the story?'

'Ask me what I was doing on these stairs all those years ago.'

'Well, Freddie,' I say, raising my can, 'what were you doing on these stairs all those years ago?' My tone is cartoon and flippant, as though his answer holds no interest at all.

'I was visiting my father,' says Freddie.

'Were you?' I quip and take another swig. I'm not sure how long I can keep this up. I know – somehow I know – that he has the upper hand.

'I was visiting my father,' and he stares up at the ceiling.

'OK . . .' I say, still not getting it.

'Oh yes. You see, I've been in this room before.'

I follow his gaze up to the black spot.

Two men, two total strangers, staring at a black spot on a white ceiling.

Silence.

He lets out a little chuckle. Or is it a shiver? No, I think I can say it's a chuckle.

What the fuck.

'Oh my God!' I say.

'With me now?' says Freddie.

'Oh my God!' I say again.

'With me now?'

'Godfrey Bolton was your father?'

'I've been in this room before.'

'Christ!'

'Yes, it's not the first time that I've been in this room.'

Still staring at the spot, I begin to shake. The big black spot will swallow us whole. The wailing spot. Or maybe not. Maybe that's just me being dramatic. It wouldn't be the first time.

'Godfrey Bolton was your father?' I say again. A silence follows and I consider repeating the sentence a third time whilst my brain collates the minutiae of the implications.

'Exactly.'

'So that's why you threw horse shit all over him.'

'Exactly,' says Freddie, and straightens his tie, as though he's just captured my remaining rook.

I think about all this. The next question, the obvious one, is mine: 'Why did you throw horse shit all over my painting of your father?'

'Your painting of my *dead* father.'

'Well . . .'

Freddie Monger sits up in my nice blue chair and crosses his legs. I take a good long swig. Christ, I wish life was easier than this. I wish that life did not resemble some shifty and faithless old friend as much as it does.

'Your question is why did I throw horse shit all over your painting of my father's suicide?'

I wish he hadn't put it quite like that, but I really can't argue with the detail and so answer: 'Er . . . yeah, I suppose that's my question.'

He crushes his cigarette into the ashtray, dusts his knees and fiddles with his cufflinks, the way posh people always do when they're about to embark upon a story.

'Well, it goes like this,' begins Freddie, obviously acquainted with the formalities of the preliminaries. His tone is measured. He holds his cigarette between the fleshy uppers of his fingers with his thumb pressed against the filter. Now and then he lends it a light tap into the ashtray, one long finger teasing the burning tip like he's playing a new musical instrument.

'I was raised by my father, my mother having died in the agony of my delivery, though it had never been his desire to raise me, neither with nor without her. He had feared me from the very beginning. From the very conception. He feared that I would scatter their love, that I would cleave them apart like a small axe. And then at last, or rather at the first, I did. So you see to him I represented nothing more, or is it less, than an instrument of murder. He might as well have been obliged to raise a cancer in a Petri dish.' He takes a breath so deep that I'm not sure if there's enough left for me. I am, you see, taking a few deep breaths of my own. 'So . . .' he continues, eyes closed, 'that takes care of the first sixteen years of my life, save to say that on twelve occasions, between the ages of fourteen and sixteen, I was forced to parade around my father's bedroom in a selection of my dead mother's dresses, whereupon I was drunkenly, narcotically and savagely violated. On precisely twelve occasions I was buggered and fellated and whipped and burned. He had named me Freddie, the same as my mother, and I couldn't help but wonder, therefore, if this indecency had been constructed in my infancy.'

He lets all this hang in the air for a moment as he tops up his glass with beer. I feel that I should say something. In fact I'm certain that I should say something. But my brain is in spasm. And what would I say?

'Oh, I'm sorry.' Is that what I should say? Or: 'What a palaver, Freddie, that must have been beastly for you.' I have no idea what to say. What the hell is he telling me? I've never had anyone, let alone a stranger, sit before me and report such spectacular atrocities. And with such considered and eloquent bravado. I say nothing. Instead I drain my can and wish I was walking on the beach with Eleni and Mum. Monger leans back into his chair and stares at the black spot on the ceiling.

'My father – Godfrey to you, though it was a name he adopted in later life – was a very successful breeder and trainer of horses. He ran a thriving stud farm on the outskirts of Rickmansworth. My mother had been an heiress of sorts. That is to say that she inherited her father's debts. Her own mother had also died in childbirth. Wonderful symmetry, isn't there?'

I am so irrevocably adrift in the world of Freddie Monger that it takes me some time to awaken to the fact that the man himself has actually addressed me with a question, albeit rhetorical. Or is it? From the other side of the coffee table he fixes me with his gaze. His eyes are a kind of bleached indigo. His mouth is twisted into a sinister rictus. What a face! What a ruined and desperate face, all of a sudden. And yet there is something else in it. The word 'arch' springs to mind. 'Sorry, what?'

'Are you listening to me?' He dispels the rancour of an Edwardian bully.

'Yes of course I'm l-listening to you. How on earth could I not be l-listening to you?'

'I said wonderful symmetry, isn't there?'

'Wonderful,' I say, and then, 'so your mother was raised by her father . . . er . . . also?'

'You see, my mother was a species of fallen angel, whereas my father was something of a demon in ascendancy.'

'I see.'

Monger plucks another cigarette from his case. He offers me one. I show him the one I'm already slaughtering.

'Rich girl in penury, scoundrel in bloom. That sort of thing. Anyway, I won't bore you with much more.'

'Really, I'm not bored. I'm just a little . . .' and I pause, afraid that I might conclude with some word anomalous to my dialect, such as 'fascinated' or 'intrigued', but after some thought, some dread, I manage to exhume ' . . . discombobulated.'

He smiles – that buckled smile – suitably placated. 'Anyway,' he says, 'to cut to the chase, one night, two nights after my sixteenth birthday, my father, Godfrey Bolton, as you know him, placed a bit in my mouth, tied me to a stable door and hammered nails into the soles of my feet.'

Right, that's it, I want him out of here. I don't want to be listening to all this.

'I think it was what has come to be known as child abuse.'

'He hammered nails into the soles of your feet?' I manage to squeak. 'What, like Christ?'

Monger chuckles to himself and shakes his head, 'No, no. Not at all. Not at all like Christ. Like a horse. Like a pitiful horse. What I'm saying is, he shoed me.'

'He nailed horseshoes onto you?' I think of the horseshoes that used to hang over Mum and Dad's demolished fireplace.

'Precisely.' He brings the palms of his hands together in an attitude of relish. He's not stopping now. 'I was left in the stable overnight. Around dawn I regained consciousness and was able to free myself. I galloped off across the fields and never saw him again.' Monger stands up. 'May I use your toilet?'

I can barely speak. 'Er . . . yes . . . yes . . . over there, the door with the number three on it.'

'Thank you,' and he limps off.

I have to say here, in my defence, that there was a certain degree of dubiety regarding what Monger had just told me. The tale was so horrific, so decorous and lurid, that I couldn't help but think that he was just a total fucking mental case who'd read too many Gothic horror novels. I had never before come across anyone so abused, and not only abused, ritually abused. Do such things go on? I try to imagine my dad shoeing me. It was never going to happen. I put out my fag and immediately light up another. I can hear him whistling as he pisses. This has gone far enough. I want him out of here.

The toilet flushes and he emerges, doing up his fly and tightening his belt. His voice echoes across the distance as he staggers back to his seat. 'That day I came to see him, the day I assisted you with your spilt oranges, I'd finally tracked him down. I'd read about his impending trial in the *Evening Standard*. Godfrey was his father's name; Bolton, my mother's maiden name. In fact it was me, unbeknownst to him, who had put up the bail. You see I'd made a little money of my own by then.' He taps the side of his nose with his finger and sits back down. 'A keen mind abhors faintness and lassitude.'

I don't know what lassitude means. What does lassitude mean? And why does a keen mind abhor it?

'Anyway, he wasn't in. I knocked and knocked. I waited on the stairwell for several hours, but he never appeared. It crossed my mind that he might have jumped bail for fear of having to justify his depravity at trial. Did you read about the trial, by any chance? I'm sure that you did.'

'Yes,' I say, my voice atremble, 'yes, he'd done something weird to a horse.'

'He'd cut out a horse's tongue, and violated its privates. Some sort of vendetta on a botched con. Whatever . . .'

Oh yeah, whatever. Maybe I should have phoned Scotland Yard after all. He's fiddling with his cufflinks again.

'I have some small dealings with collectors of art.'

'Yes?'

'Yes, yes, I er . . .' he pauses and brings a finger to his lips, 'mix in circles. Anyway, the point is that one day I found myself in Hyde Park.

The next thing you know, I've wandered into the Serpentine Gallery. It was about eighteen months after my father's suicide and . . . well . . . perhaps I shall finish there. You can imagine what I was confronted with, Hector.'

It's the first time he's used my name since I met him on the front step. I'm lodged in the corner of the settee, curled up like an egg. I wish Bianca was here. I can barely speak, but I do: 'Your dad?'

'Quite. An enormous rendition – rather splendid, if I may say so – of my father, in repose. Finished. Eyes agog in mortal terror. The way I had always wished them.'

'Thank you,' I say.

'I had only stood him bail so that I might have a chance of getting to him before he was incarcerated beyond my resolve. And then it was too late. You, however, had been privileged to gain access to his final torment. And to torment me – or so it seemed at the time – had preserved this memento mori in the name of profit. I came back the next day with my bucket, but alas, the exhibition had closed.'

Suddenly, the telephone rings; I'm delivered to my senses and somehow remember that I'm located on a planet where telephones exist.

'Aren't you going to get that?' says Monger.

'No . . . no . . . I don't think I can . . . should . . . will. The machine's on.'

Monger replaces his shoe. 'Ah yes,' he says with a certain amount of what he, I'm sure, would call ennui, 'the machine is always on.' And with this he puts his face into his hands and presses till his fingers turn pink. I think he's crying again. Oh great.

'I am not here, and neither are you. This machine, however, is, and may be able to assist us in one day being in the same place at the same time. So leave it a message. That is its purpose.'

Monger looks up, his cheeks wet.

Meanwhile – it's Mum:

'Hector, I don't understand what you're talking about most of the time.' (Pause) 'In fact any of the time. Are you drinking again? It's Mum. Your father's in hospital. They took him in this morning. He couldn't catch his breath and they've had to put a mask on him. I've just got back and he's stable, but they're worried about how he might respond when he wakes up again.' Pause. A little crying and then a sniff. 'Hector, I'd say maybe you should send that money – I know you're only trying to help but . . . you know your dad; it doesn't matter how much money you make . . . he'd still see it as the Kiplings losing out and . . .' breaths, 'and that's what we are: we're the Kipling family.' More breaths. 'Silly bloody family it is, but . . . but it's – ' out and out sobbing – 'it's all my fault. I feel that it's all my fault. And . . .' Unbearable silence. 'Hector, it's your mum, your dad's in hospital. I'm going.'

I'm holding back my tears. Mum sounds like she's drowning in hers. And Monger, Freddie fucking mental Monger, is curled up in the chair leaking through his knuckles.

God, I love life.

Eleni's dressing gown hangs on the back of the bathroom door. I'm sat down waiting for the piss to come, staring at it. Eleni's dressing gown is a soft clean cotton apricot, made in Portugal. I can smell it from here. It smells of Persil and Comfort. Rosa's dressing gown smelt of musk and sweat and blood and smoke. The ruddy Chinese silk was smudged here and there by scuffed umber fag burns. The hem, frayed and bitten. Collar in tatters. Last night is dripping from the ceiling. Drip, drip, drip. Tripperty-trap, tripperty-trap. Rosa slapped me in the face and told me to keep quiet. She eased her fist into my mouth. I tried to kiss but could only bite. Her nails felt like ten little beaks. Here comes the piss. Here comes the love. I know, of course, that it's not love, but that's what I've been taught to call it. Whenever I have felt incapable of squeezing this muddy hurricane from my brain, I have always called it love and had done with it. It is all I know of love. There is this word infatuation, but it hardly behoves me to pull out the dictionary at this juncture.

Infatuation is only the lobby of the gallery of love – as I have been taught to call it. I love my father and I love my mother. But what has this love to do with the love that is now flooding my intestines? We need two different words. More than two. We need a hundred-page glossary. Two thousand different words, three definitions apiece, six thousand strains of this thing. This thing. This thing dripping from this pen, dripping from this ceiling, as I drip into this pan.

Dad is in hospital and I am making no moves to pack a bag. Let that be my definition.

This is – I think, maybe, I don't know – the first germ of love that blooms inside before you begin to talk about it. Soon you might mention the word to a friend. You won't say that this is love, only that it feels like love, but by then it's too late, the word is out of the bag and soon you'll be running it past her. Past the woman herself. I'll say it again: Dad is in hospital and I am making no moves to pack a bag. I toss my fag into the water and it fizzes and fades like a silly life.

Monger is still sobbing. In fact so much of him seems made of water that I feel I could just absorb him with a large towel.

'Hector, I'm sorry,' he blubbers. 'There was no need to take out my anger on your painting. It's a magnificent painting. And now it's ruined. I have ruined a part of your life.'

I drop onto the settee. 'I'm sure it's not ruined. It was only horse shit and acid.'

'If there's anything I can do. If there's *anything* I can do.'

I pour out the rest of his beer and bring it to his lips like a suckling mother. He sniffs and sups. He sniffs again – a big bubbly sniff – and pulls out his handkerchief. Eventually he's restored to a place of equilibrium.

'You must think me a fool,' he says.

'Fool isn't one of the words I've been considering.'

He smiles and wipes his eyes on his cuff. 'Do you have any more beer?'

'I have some vodka. Would you like a vodka? I'd like a vodka,' I say. 'I'll go and get the vodka.'

In the kitchen I take a good swig from the bottle and pour out two glasses. I drink both of them and pour out two more.

Settled back in our seats, he tells me of his feelings leading up to and during the attack, and even laughs at the slapstick of Myers and Delaney. I tell him about my pursuit and the Volvo and how I saw him run back for his wallet. I stop there. I tell him nothing of Rosa, though God knows I'm tempted. God knows I need to tell someone. If he wasn't here I'd be telling it to the wall, to the floor, to the lamp in the corner, to the freckles on my knuckles and the scab on my shin. I think about calling Bianca but she's probably sleeping it off. Instead I tell Monger about the attack on Marcus Harvey's *Myra*, and about Kirk getting it in the back of the neck with a flying egg. I tell him about the mad Chinese on Emin's bed, Napoleon's troops shooting the nose off the Sphinx and how they pissed all over Duchamp's *Fountain*. I make a joke about sewing up a Fontana but by then I think I've lost him and a polite smile dwindles to a cipher.

'You have a lot on your mind,' he says, apropos of nothing.

'What?'

'I can tell. Your mind is split in twelve.'

'Twelve?'

'Twelve.'

'Why twelve?'

'It's a nice word. I like the sound of it and I like the look of it upon a page.'

I think about twelve.

12.

He may have a point.

'Why is your poor mother so distressed?'

'Because she's my mother.'

'Ah,' he says, 'and is that an indictment of you or of her?'

'Of both of us, I suppose.'

'But of course that's not the real answer.'

'But of course,' I say, as though that's the end of it.

'You feel in some way to blame.'

'To blame for what?'

'You tell me.'

'Why should I?' I say.

He says nothing, but stares up at the ceiling.

Silence.

I tell him the whole story. Every last, lost fucking detail. I've poured out a few more glasses, dimmed the lights, and the memory of his father's florid abominations are beginning to fade. He sits forward and listens, playing with his ring, asking questions now and then. When I reach the end he sits back, reshapes his hair and smiles.

'What are you smiling about?' I say.

'I'm smiling because it's perfect,' says Monger.

'What's perfect?'

He stands and begins to hobble around the room, lowering and raising his voice according to his distance from me – which is, sometimes, considerable.

'It's very simple, Hector. Here's how I make my recompense. You give me the eight hundred and forty pounds—'

'What?'

'Wait. Listen. Hear me out. You give me the eight hundred and forty pounds. I take the train up to Blackpool, reply to their advert in the local newspaper, go round there, buy the bloody thing and take it off their hands straight away. What the hell, I'll offer them nine hundred. That way they'll make a profit. Wouldn't a profit be enough to escort your father from intensive care?'

I really can't argue with this. Like he says, it's perfect.

'You'll do this for me?'

'Hector,' he says, trotting over and kneeling at my feet. (A bit over the top, this trotting and kneeling business, but he does.) 'Hector, it's the least I can do,' and he puts his hand on mine. His eyes are wide and glad and the pad of his thumb rubs against my wrist. 'I owe you, sir.'

'Sir?' I say pulling my hand away and leaning back.

'I owe you, Hector Kipling. What better way to repay the debt of my folly?'

All this poshness is giving me a headache. I'm not being flippant in saying that, I mean it. The bloke is giving me a fucking migraine with his fol de rols and his la di das.

'OK,' I say, 'OK, if you're up for it.'

'I'm most certainly up for it. You give me that money and I'll take a cab to King's Cross right now.'

'Euston.'

'A cab to Euston right now.'

'But I don't have the money.'

'Where's the nearest hole in the wall?'

'I can't take nine hundred pounds out of a hole in the wall! And besides how do I know that you won't just run off with the fucking money? You throw horse shit all over my painting, run away, turn up at my flat, ask me to hand over nine hundred quid and point you in the direction of a train station?'

He makes another grab for my hand and captures it. 'I know, I know. Of course. No need, no need. Listen, I'll do it. I'll write a cheque to them and you pay me upon delivery of the sofa. How does that sound?'

'Well, that makes more sense.'

The telephone rings. I let it.

'Shouldn't you get that?'

'No.'

'It might be your mother.'

'Exactly.'

The machine clicks on.

'Hector? Hector, it's Eleni. Where are you? Why are you not return-ing my calls? I have been phoning and phoning. I have left messages on your mobile and messages at home. Where are you? What is going on? Where were you last night? I rang three times . . .'

She's crying. She's definitely crying.

'I rang three times Hector. At midnight, at two and at five. Have you listened to these messages? How can you not be calling me? I'm tired of leaving messages. I'm tired of saying it all. They say my mother may not make it. Hector, where are you?'

She's wailing. She's definitely wailing.

Odd. I've never heard Eleni wail. Monger is lighting a cigarette and folding up his handkerchief. All the time he is watching my face. All the time my face is breaking out in horrible boils of despair and disgust.

'I don't know what to say, or do, or think, Hector. I don't know whether to worry about you or be angry with you. I rang Lenny. He says that something happened at the show. That you ran out. You haven't called Lenny either. I spoke to your mother, and your father is in hos-pital. You haven't spoken to them. Hector, where are you? Why did you hang up on me last night? Hector, I am worried, so worried about you. I cannot believe that you have not answered my messages . . .'

There's a long silence as the storm of tears turns into a light drizzle.

Bleep.

Silence.

Monger clears his throat.

Silence.

The phone rings again.

'I'm afraid I'm not here, and neither are you. This machine, how-ever, is . . .'

I didn't expect the answering machine to fly into so many pieces. I thought it might just crack a little. I mean, I only hit it with the stepladders. Twice. Twice with the stepladders and then again with a chair. And then I go back for the stepladders. The red light's still flashing and I half expect the voice to carry on speaking, like Ian Holm's head in *Alien*, his wires and fuses still fizzing, a warm blue smoke snaking from his ragged neck. I deliver one more blow. As both myself and the ladders buckle at the hinges, the volume dial flies across the room and comes to rest, at last, beneath Eleni's piano. The red light glows brighter than ever and then fades to black like a soused coal.

Monger sits there perfectly still, utterly composed, as though I've just stood up to draw the curtains. He picks up the bottle of vodka and pours out the last two glasses.

My brain is a bonfire.

'Have you tried St John's wort?'

'What?' I snap, throwing the ladders at my painting. A sizeable gash appears in the bottom left-hand corner. We both look at it.

Monger leans forward and offers me my glass. I take it.

'I said can you call me a taxi?'

'I'm sorry.'

'If the phone is still intact,' he says, and we both look over at the phone.

'Yeah,' I say, draining my glass, 'the phone's still OK. I'm sorry . . . erm . . . I'm really sorry. I've just got a few problems right now . . . as you can see.' I begin to cough.

'Well,' says Monger, 'I really don't want to become one of them, Hector. No, no. In fact, quite the opposite.' He checks the laces on his brogues. 'So if you'll give me your parents' phone number and anything else I should know, I shan't inconvenience you any further.' He stands up and smoothes himself down.

He's so tall. I wouldn't like to be that tall. Tall enough to make people stare. Tall like a freak. If he put on some weight, and wrestled a bit more life into that face of his, he could be a real, bona fide monster.

'OK,' I say, 'OK,' trying to calm myself down, trying to remember which muscles monitor breathing in and which ones look after the breathing-out bit. 'OK, well, if that's what you wanna do. If that's . . .' I'm shaking, 'if that's what you're offering to do, I er . . . I suppose that would be great. Excuse me, this is all a little strange.'

'Of course it is, Hector. Good God, we'd both be perfect fools if we didn't acknowledge all this as being a little strange.'

'Yeah, well . . .'

'So if you'd call me that cab.'

I call him that cab and write out Mum and Dad's number on a page from my sketch pad. I write down the name of the newspaper, the *Evening Gazette*, Mum and Dad's address, how to change trains in Preston and how not to give the game away if Mum mentions anything about how she wishes her son dressed a bit more like him. Monger smiles and puts the piece of paper into his wallet – vermilion lizard skin, cards all gold – asks me if I would like to see a picture of his kids and then pulls out a photograph of two juvenile goats. He throws back his head in snorted posh laughter. I almost smile and walk him to the door. He makes a move to hug me and I try to avoid it but his wingspan is so broad that I have no choice but to succumb to his embrace. I feel like a doll in the arms of a desperate child. It's a first.

Alone.

Silence.

The telephone rings again. I let it. Ring, ring. Drip, drip. Ring, ring. Drip, drip. The silence when it stops aches more than the silence it broke.

Fuck's sake, Hector. Call Mum. Call Eleni. Call Lenny. Call Bianca. Call Kirk. Call an ambulance. Call a hearse. Call Myers. Call time. Call a fly or a nosebleed. Call the Samaritans or a horse. Call Benson and Hedges. Call Gilbert and George.

I wish I could call Rosa. I want to call Rosa. My bowels are telling me to call Rosa. My passion is to call Rosa. My rage is to call Rosa. My heart, my throat, my tongue, my thighs, my flesh, my pipes, are all screaming at me to call Rosa. Well, they can all shut the fuck up cos I didn't get her number.

I put on my Crombie and take a long vodka walk down to the shops. I buy a tin of Heinz macaroni cheese, a tin of Heinz meat-free ravioli, a tin of Heinz tomato soup, a loaf of suffocated bread, a tub of Flora, a packet of crisps, some chewing gum, sixty Camel Lights, four cans of lager and some nail clippers. In the newsagent's I buy the *Evening Standard* so that I can add to my Brian Sewell collage. I buy a mint Aero, a packet of Nurofen and a birthday card.

Having clipped my nails and digested the soup, the ravioli, the crisps, the bread and two of the beers I lie down on the bed to sleep.

Brown and blue seagulls chattering in a plywood sky. Blackpool Tower on fire in a high and howling wind.

11

I'm on a bench in Golden Square watching the pigeons. That one's called Duggie and the one with the missing toe and half an eye is Mr Osgood who's flown in from the Midlands to see how the other half live. So far he's impressed. He's left a wife and kids on the ledge of a small chemist's in Wolverhampton. He's already been down Trafalgar Square, where he was welcomed into the throng like a prodigal friend. At one point his ebullition had reached such giddy heights that he thought 'Why not? Fuck it!' and perched on the head of a Norwegian albino whose obsequious new wife caught it all on camera. 'Fame!' thought Mr Osgood. 'I'm gonna live forever – or at least for a few months – on some polished pine mantelpiece in Oslo.' That's what he thought.

I'm waiting for Kirk. I've rung his bell five times now.

I woke up at four in the morning. I felt – if I may be so artless (or is it artful?) – like shit. Like mindless, heartless, stinking shit. The stuff itself. The consistency, the colour, the contours, the aroma. Brian Sewell would hate all this. But I'm sorry, Brian me old son, that's how I felt, how I still feel, and no amount of Tchaikovsky or Bizet will tell it any better.

Mr Osgood has found a discarded box of Dunkin' Donuts and is fighting with Duggie – in a mad frenzy of pecking – over the hundreds-and-thousands scattered by the railings.

I'm not sure why I've come to see Kirk. I haven't returned any phone calls. I should be in Blackpool. I should be in Crete. I should be round at Lenny's with a mop and some bleach.

But then I don't need to be in Blackpool, cos Monger's on the train with a cheque for nine hundred quid and the answer to all our problems. Well, the answer to Mum and Dad's problems. I still have a few problems in storage.

I should be in Crete. I should be holding Eleni's beautiful Greek head in my monstrous Lancastrian hands. But what am I gonna do in Crete? Sit there by Sofia's sad bed and watch her slip slowly and silently (or would it be noisily?) away into some other dimension. What would I do? Learn something?

It starts to rain and I sit there feeling like I'm in a film. I think it's a film, or is it an opera? Whatever it is, I think it's French. Everyone has gone. The pigeons have gone. It's just me, the trees, the plants and the rain. Drip drip. I stare at my fingers for an hour. Maybe two.

'Well, what happened to your mobile phone?'
  'I dropped it in someone's bath.'
  'Whose bath?'
  'My bath, Mum, I mean my bath.'
  'You said in someone's.'
  'Why would I be in someone else's bath?'
  'You tell me.'

It's still raining. Hailing in fact. It looks like it may never stop. I might as well be in a bath right now. The wind is driving sharp bullets of hail into the phone box. If you can call it a box.

'How's Dad?'
  'Why haven't you called?'
  'I only just got the message, Mum.'
  'You should have called anyway.'
  'Mum, it's all gonna be all right, you know.'
  'And why have you only just got the message?'
  'Cos I only just got home, and my mobile is dead.'
  'Aye, cos you dropped it in someone's bath.'

'My bath.'

I don't like this. I don't like any of this one bit.

'So in between getting the message that your father's in hospital, and phoning me, you had a bath?'

'Mum!'

'Whose bath was it?'

'Mum! How's Dad?'

'Some lass's bath?'

I'm stunned. How do mothers know everything? What is it? Do they work in teams? Is she in contact with a network of mothers from East London, all stood on street corners and ladders muttering into walkie-talkies? There's a flash of lightning. Do they control the weather?

'No, Mum! No, not some lass's bath. Forget the bath, it was a slip of the tongue.'

'Well, that's what happens if you've got a slippery tongue.'

'Mum, how's Dad?'

'He's just sleeping. He's got chest problems and they want to keep him asleep. He's all white.'

Oh Christ, don't say that. There's a deafening punch of thunder, like Jupiter just burst. 'But is he gonna be all right?'

'How the bloody hell do I know, Hector? Ask a doctor. Ask God!' And that's it. She's held out till now, but I can hear the tears collecting in her throat. 'I wish it was me. I do, I wish it was me. It should be me lying there in a bed. Lying there dead.'

'Mum, Dad's not dead.'

'No, but I should be. What have I done? What have I done to him?'

I can see her with her hands over her eyes. She can't speak now for crying. I'm going to say something now. I'm gonna find the words. I'm gonna make it all all right again, and I'll be a magnificent son and the next time I see her she'll hug me and kiss me, and so will Dad, for being their little hero.

'Mum, I promise you, things are gonna work out.'

'Hector, you don't know what you're talking about. You're talking like you're soft in the head. You won't even come home. You haven't once offered to come home.'

'Mum, is the settee still for sale in the *Evening Gazette*?'

Nothing but crying.

'Mum, if the settee's still in the paper, it'll be all right. Someone'll come along and buy it, I'm sure. Why don't you take yourself off to the hospital and tell him that someone's bought the settee?'

'Because he's unconscious!' Oh my God, that was a very loud scream. Not the sort of scream you'd associate with a lovely mum like Mum. More like Elizabeth Taylor in *Who's Afraid of Virginia Woolf?*.

The time's getting close to say that perfect thing.

'Hey, hey, Mum, calm down, calm down. Have them wake him up. Why not have them wake him up enough to tell him that the settee's been sold?'

'Cos it hasn't been sold!'

Jesus fucking Christ, that one hurt my ear. My guts are full of riot police.

'Well, just tell him it is, Mum!' Now I'm shouting.

She hangs up.

I ring straight back. No answer. I try again. No answer.

Another flash of lightning. Another crack of thunder. Hail like hot coals.

I try again. This time she picks up and gets right down to it.

'Hector, what happened on the night of your show?'

'What do you mean what happened?'

'I spoke to Eleni . . .' She lets it hang in the air. And it really does hang. It hangs magnificently.

'And?'

'You haven't spoken to Eleni once since she went to Greece.'

'It's the Cretan phone system, Mum.'

'She said that someone had damaged one of your paintings.'

'Oh that,' I say, a little relieved that she's not back onto the bath incident. 'Yeah, some bloke threw something at *God Bolton*, but it'll be fine.'

'So then I rang Lenny and he said that you'd disappeared.'

'Er, yeah. I suppose I did.'

'So where have you been? And who's the lass whose bath you were in?'

'Mum, have I mentioned a lass?'

'No, but you've mentioned a bath.'

I take the deepest breath I think I've ever taken.

'Mum, you are so not on the right track here.'

'Why haven't you phoned Eleni?'

'I told you, it's the—'

'Her mother is dying.'

'Mum! I know that! Don't you think I don't know that?'

'So what with not calling me, whose husband's on his deathbed, and not calling Eleni, whose mother's on her deathbed, what is it that you've been up to that's more important?'

I might as well be in a small, smoky room, with an old Anglepoise lamp shining in my face.

'Up to?' I stutter.

'There's a lass.'

'Mum, there's not a lass.'

'There is, there's a lass.'

'Not a lass.'

'A lass.'

'Mum, this is getting surreal now.'

'Don't use your big words on me.'

'You know what surreal means, Mum. We've talked about it a million times. Salvador Dalí, that mad Spanish fella.'

'Ooh, don't talk to me about him. This is no time to be talking to me about him. He once did a number two in the corner of his studio and painted it.'

She's been reading the colour supplements again.

'Yeah. And why shouldn't he?'

'Listen, Hector,' she barks, really meaning business, 'let me tell you one thing – you are not going to do a big number two in the corner of this family and paint it. I'm sick of it. I'm sick of all this art. Why can't things just be normal? What's wrong with just seeing things the way we see them? Isn't that enough?'

'Mum, we've been over this. You know it's—'

'Now you'd better come home and explain yourself.' She's hissing. I've never heard Mum hiss. 'You'd better ring Eleni and explain yourself – if you can. You'd better get rid of this trollop with the bath and sort out what's important.'

'Mum, there is no trollop.'

'Of course there's a trollop.'

'Why does there have to be a trollop?'

'A mother knows these things.'

I double over, and then squat in the phone box. 'How do mothers know these things?' I snap, genuinely curious.

'So there *is* a trollop!'

'She's not a trollop.'

'Oh my God!'

'She's American.'

'Oh no, my God!'

'She's American and she's really—'

The line goes dead.

Well, that went well.

Idea For a Piece: Record all conversations with Mum from now on. Transfer them to Dictaphone tapes. A hundred Dictaphone machines on the gallery floor, full volume, all playing Mum. Call it *Love.*

I walk back to the bench, sit down in the weather, and weep for fifteen minutes.

I walk, through the hail, to the newsagent on Beak Street and buy three more phone cards. In the next half hour I call back at least ten times. There is no answer.

Let me say this: I know a lot of things. I read and talk and listen and watch and I know a lot of things. But I don't know this: I don't know what to do.

Rosa's not a trollop. Rosa's a poet. How am I gonna tell Mum that Rosa's a poet? How am I gonna tell Mum that Rosa's hand around my throat, squeezing the sorry life out of me, as a million other sorry lives were pumped out of me, is worth all this duplicity? How am I gonna say all that to Mum? Well, I'm not, am I? I'm obviously not.

What am I gonna say? That I love this woman? And wait till she meets her? Wait till Mum meets Rosa? Mum wouldn't like Rosa. Mum loves Eleni. Mum would detest Rosa. And why does it all matter? Christ, I need to see Bianca. I really need to see Bianca.

'Hello? Bianca?'

'Hector?'

'I'm in a phone box in Soho.'

'It's Bianca.'

'Bianca, I know, I just called you.'

'Hector, your show was magnificent. You are such a talent. Those faces!'

'Bianca, listen.'

'And Eleni, that glorious painting of Eleni. That was my favourite.'

'Bianca, I want to speak to you about Rosa.'

'Oh no, Hector. That girl I met? She's not well.'

What the fuck's she talking about? 'How do you know she's not well?'

'A therapist knows these things.'

'Mum!'

'What?'

'Bianca!'

'Did you just call me Mum?'

'No!' I want to die. I want lightning to strike me in the groin. Right here, right now.

'I need to talk about this girl.'

'I'll say one thing, Hector. You should forget about her—'

I hang up and march out of the Square towards Piccadilly. The pavement rushes past like I'm on a bicycle.

I can't forget about her. I want to forget about her. I so want to forget about her. But if forgetting is just not happening, then how the fuck do you forget? By thinking about forgetting? But thinking about the thing you want to forget only enforces the . . . Oh, I don't fucking know! Yes, yes. I'll forget her. But I may be gone some time. If you want me, I'll be down the pub.

BOX STREET, BOW, LONDON

I'm lying on top of Eleni's piano, plucking the hair out of my eyebrows. Soon there will be nothing left.

I've managed to put Rosa out of my mind. No, really, I have. The night was a dreamless sleep and when I woke up I woke up suddenly and leapt straight out of bed. I felt a little raw and blistered for the first half hour, but then I took a shower and even sang a little George Formby ditty, 'With My Little Stick Of Blackpool Rock'. I've hardly thought about her at all. I had a breakfast of orange juice and toast, and I've decided to cut back on the booze. Maybe even stop altogether. In fact yes – stop altogether. No more fucking booze. No more fags. Well, less fags. Let's not go mad. No more booze and less fags. And try to eat some vegetables. Maybe take some vitamin supplements. Do some push-ups.

Call Eleni. Call Mum. Maybe fly out to see Eleni. There's nothing stopping me flying out to be with Eleni. But what if Dad gets worse? What if Mum's stopped picking up the phone and Monger can't get through? Or what if Monger's just some top-quality fruitcake and just went home the other day? Or what if he does buy the fucking settee and it makes no difference? What if Dad's beyond help? Christ, what if he dies? I don't want Dad to die. I don't want anyone to die. Really, I don't. All that stuff I said before, I didn't mean it. I can't fly off to Crete with my father in hospital. I should go home to Blackpool. There's nothing stopping me. I could call a cab right now. Why not? But what if Eleni's mother dies and I'm in Blackpool? I don't want Sofia to die. I don't want anyone to die. I only want Rosa to die. To die in my head, or my heart or my gut or my groin, or wherever the fuck it is that she's set out her stall. But it's all right. She's on her way out. She's fading. I've hardly been thinking about her. I'm not thinking about her. And even if I do find myself thinking about her I've developed a discipline of simply punching myself in the head three times and screaming 'Get out!' Which seems to be working.

I might just sit down on the sofa with a cup of apple-and-ginger tea, and read a book. Here we go. Someone recommended Paul Auster's *Leviathan* so I bought it a few weeks ago and now I'm plumping up the cushions and boiling the kettle. I haven't had a fag yet. I'm doing really well. I've been up for two hours and I haven't had a fag. So I suppose that it's all right to have one now. Yeah, I'll just have one now, whilst I'm waiting for the kettle to boil.

Fuck, I feel a bit dodgy now. That tea and those three fags have turned my guts into a swamp. I might just have to lie down. Whatever. At least I'm not thinking about Rosa. She hasn't come into my head once. Thank Christ for that, because it was really starting to worry me that I was obsessing about her so much. Much better now. Now that she's only hanging around in the wings. When I was obsessing about her she was right there, centre stage, beautifully lit. But now she's hardly there at all. Soon she'll be gone and I'll lock the stage door behind her.

Soon she'll be out of here and I can get on with the day. In fact I think she is gone. Almost gone. Maybe she's completely gone. Yeah, yeah, you know what? I think she's completely gone.

Leviathan, chapter one: 'Six days ago, a man blew himself up by the side of a road in northern Wisconsin.'

Oh Christ.

I'll put on some music. I'll have a fag and put on some music. I think there's a couple of beers in the fridge. It's early but it might take away this gut ache. This is not a good day to give up the booze. I'm doing myself no favours, giving up the booze today. I put on some Gregorian chànts and lie back on the sofa. There we go. Better now. I stare at the black spot on the ceiling. I close my eyes and wonder how Monger's getting on. I've become quite accomplished at spotting when lucid thought turns into dream, and it's turning right now. One minute I can see Monger ringing Mum and Dad's bell, sniffing the plants in the porch. I can see Mum opening the door and inviting him in. I can see him stopping to look at the watercolours in the hallway and complimenting Mum on her hairdo. But then Monger floats up to the ceiling and can't get down. Mum goes and gets the broom. She ushers him along the ceiling but when he reaches the stairs he flips over onto his front and slides up to the top floor. The landing ceiling's too high for her to get at him with the broom, but it's OK cos Dad comes out of the bedroom and starts firing at him with a tiny bow and arrow until he hits home. Monger bursts and falls to the floor. Mum collects the debris in a bucket and fries it up with some onions. They both sit there in front of *You've Been Framed*, forking bits of rubber Monger into their green, purple-toothed mouths. But this is not a dream. It might have been a dream, had the doorbell not rung.

Well, everyone else has had a good cry, why not Lenny? I never thought I'd live to see the day, but there he is, slumped in the chair, wet bald head, like a buoy in a storm. Who'd have thought.

'I'll kill her. I will fucking kill her.'

'Who will you kill?'

'Who do you think? Brenda.'

'Lenny mate, calm down, calm down. What's happened? What did she do? Just tell me so I can help.'

'She's . . . she . . .'

There's a long thread of snot hanging down between his left thumb and the floor.

'She what?'

'She's destroyed the piece.'

'The piece?'

'I got home after your show the other night and she's chucked something all over my settee piece, blood or something, she's slashed the cushions and smashed the window. She's a fucking head case. She's totally fucking out of her mind, Hec.'

I take a long drag on my cigarette and blow out three blue rings. Well, well. There goes one problem.

'Why's she gone and done that?' I say.

'Cos she's seriously, dangerously fucking insane, I'm telling you.'

'But there must be a reason.'

Lenny straightens up and his beautiful face is so sodden with tears and snot, I take Eleni's tissues from the piano and hand him one.

'She thinks that I've been fucking Rosa.'

I catch my breath. My brain sprouts whiskers and I catch it again. 'Rosa?'

'Yeah.'

'B-but . . . how does she know about Rosa?'

'She doesn't know about Rosa. There's nothing to know. Rosa was round my house the other night and she . . . she came round so that we could go to your show together and she said she had to get changed. She had a bag with her and she had to get changed. And somewhere along the way a bra's been left behind. So . . . so Brenda comes home and finds this bra.'

A bra? I didn't see any bra. I scoured that house for things like bras. I didn't see a bra. Did I? Maybe I did see a bra but thought it was Brenda's. Obviously Brenda's more attuned to these things. Obviously Brenda knows a foreign bra when she comes across one.

'A bra?'

'Rosa's fucking bra. So I try to explain and she' – he's really breaking up now – 'and she disappears upstairs. I can hear her screaming and thrashing. And then I hear her footsteps . . .' Sob, sob, sob. Come on, Lenny, come on. Get on with it. I need to know all this. 'I hear her footsteps on the stairs, and then I hear the front door slam. I go upstairs, right up to the top floor. And there's my piece. There's my fucking piece in fucking tatters. Fucking ruined. Stained, slashed, smashed, fucking destroyed. Completely fucking decimated. I'm not going back. I'm never gonna go back.' And he lies down on the floor and curls up into a ball. A big, tall, bald, sobbing ball. Who would have thought.

I blow out some more smoke rings. I have one question.

'So did you?'

'Did I what?'

'Did you fuck Rosa or not?'

'No!' snaps Lenny. 'Listen to what I'm saying. She just had to get changed. She went into the bedroom to change. I stayed downstairs. Don't you start, I've been through all this with Brenda. She just got changed and somehow left a bra behind. I don't fucking know. How do you explain that to your bird and expect her to believe it?'

'Well, I suppose . . .' What is it that I suppose? I'm not really thinking straight. I know he needs advice, but I'm not sure that I have any. 'Well, I suppose . . . er . . . I suppose that it is a little bit suspicious having a girl round at the house in the first place.'

Lenny picks himself up from the floor and comes at me.

I've known Lenny for twenty-six years and he's never come at me. But here he is, coming at me.

'Lenny, man, what the fuck!'

He starts slapping me about the head with the slabs of his palms. Well at least he's not punching me.

'Lenny, man, what the fuck? Fuck's all this about?' I manage to squeal.

'You're no fucking help! You've never been any fucking help! You've never been ANY fucking help! All you think about is you!' And he keeps on slapping me about the face. Fuck, I don't need this.

'Lenny, Lenny, Lenny,' I say, in between blows.

'You don't give a shit about anyone, you twisted fucking get! All you wanna know is whether or not I fucked Rosa, and you only wanna know that cos you wanna fuck her, you don't give a shit about me, or Brenda, or the piece, or any-fucking-thing else!'

He may have a point there.

'Lenny, that's so not true!'

'All you care about is your fucking self!'

'Lenny, Lenny, please.' I've got my arms up and I deliver a few slaps of my own until the whole rumpus dwindles into a melee before tailing off into a debacle. Fuck, I'm tired of all these words. Why don't I just paint all this? 'Lenny, come on, calm down, I haven't said anything.'

'It's fucking ruined. The show opens in a week and it's totally fuck-ing annihilated. Ripped to fucking shreds.' And he collapses back onto the floor into a ball. An almost perfect ball. Difficult, when you're so tall. Still, he pulls it off.

Idea For a Piece: A black bucket of tears. Real tears. Collect the tears of loved ones. Make loved ones cry enough to fill a bucket. A big black tear-filled bucket in the middle of a white room. Call it *Autumn*.

She's out there somewhere, thinking. What is she thinking? Rosa, are you thinking what I'm thinking? And what is it? What is this thing we're thinking? Or is it just me? Are you thinking of other things? Did it all mean nothing? What did it all mean?

'So then Kirk starts wiping it down with a cloth.'

'A wet cloth?'

'Yeah, a cloth dipped in turpentine.'

'Idiot.'

Lenny's sat on Eleni's piano stool, hitting notes now and again. We're sharing that last beer.

I tell him about being hit by the car and make up some story about being taken to the hospital by some passing coppers; quite an elaborate story. I give the coppers names and features. I describe the doctor and how I quite fancied one of the nurses. Oh yeah, that's right, I'm pathetic.

'So what are you gonna do?' I say.

'About the piece?'

'Yeah.'

'Well, I'm gonna have to start again – if there's time – or just forget the whole thing.' He starts to cry again and I put my arm around him. He feels huge. I've never held Lenny before. I'm not sure what to do. When I've held crying girls (and I've held plenty), I've kissed their brows and cheeks, I've squeezed their hands and stroked their hair. I can't be doing any of this with Lenny so I just rock him a little, but that just feels silly and so I stop. 'Can I stay here for the night?'

'You can stay here as long as you want, Len.'

I tell him about Monger, and Monger's story. In an attempt to present some consolation I tell him about Monger's plan to buy back the settee and that maybe he could bring it back to London, and how the settee might be a possible replacement for the one that Brenda destroyed.

'But you said that it was fucked. I thought the whole point of your dad being in hospital was that this settee was totally fucking ugly.'

'The ugly may be beautiful, the—'

'The pretty never. When are you gonna stop saying that?'

'When it stops being true. And anyway, my mum and dad's idea of what's ugly may not be the same as ours. Maybe it'll be a fantastic settee.'

'We'll see,' says Lenny and releases himself from my embrace. He stands up and pulls on his jacket.

'Where're you going?'

'I have to go down to the Tate to sort things out. *Domesticated Goose Chase* is arriving from Amsterdam. That's if Brenda hasn't intercepted it.'

'Here, take a set of keys,' and I hand him mine.

'Thanks, Hec,' and he smiles at me. A beautiful smile. 'Sorry for hitting you.' What a beautiful man he is, this friend of mine, this Lenny Snook. What a gentle soul. And what a twat sometimes. But not now, not now. God bless him.

I heat up some sardines and boil some broccoli. There are a few cherry tomatoes from last week but they've gone a bit soft. No matter, I bung them on the plate with a smear of mustard. Some kind of peace has descended.

I take a page of sheet music and begin to make a list of the things I should say to Eleni. This has gone on long enough and I'm about to ring her, but I can't afford to be an idiot about it. I number the issues, one to ten:

1. *How's your mother? (Sympathize in proportion to the severity of the answer.)*
2. *How's your father? (Assure her that he's a very strong man, and will always be there for her.)*
3. *How are you feeling? (Assure her that I'm quite a strong man, and will always try to be there for her.)*
4. *Explain about Monger's attack. (Keep it simple.)*
5. *Tell her about Dad. (But don't compare it to her mother.)*

6. *Explain my lack of contact. (Blame the Cretan phone system.)*
7. *Say that I mean to come out any time now. (I just have to wait to see how Dad is.)*
8. *Tell her I miss her. (I do. I really do.)*
9. *Tell her Lenny's moving in for a while. (But that he'll be gone if she needs to come back.)*
10. *Ask her if she wants to add anything. (I'll listen and apply myself to the best of my ability.)*

I stare at the page and then, after some careful consideration, obliterate the list with a fit of heavy grey squirls. My stomach is filled with dead butterflies and my left thigh is beginning to fizz.

The telephone rings. I'll just have to play it by ear. If it's Eleni, my love, at last, I shall just speak from the heart, for the heart is no fool. Except, of course, for those times when it is the biggest of all fools. Whatever. I pick up the phone.

'Hector?'

'Yes?'

'Hey, Hector, it's Rosa.'

'Rosa!' I say, nearly falling off my chair. And then I say it again, 'Rosa!'

'Hey, what are you up to?'

'Erm . . .' I look around the room. For what, I don't know. 'Nothing much. Just making a shopping list.'

'How ya doin', angel?'

'I'm doing fine, chuck.'

She calls me angel, I call her chuck. Such is the language of love. Well not love, but you know what I mean.

'Yeah?'

'Yeah. Er . . . how are you?'

'Oh, I'm just hanging out. You know . . . I just bought a new little frog skull, so I'm painting it green.'

'That's nice.' What a girl.

213

'Have I caught you at a bad time?' says Rosa.

'No, it's a good time. A very good time.'

'I just called to say thank you for your sweet note and . . . and . . .'

'De rien.'

'What?'

'I said "de rien".'

'What?'

Fuck, this is going terribly. 'It means "that's nothing" in French, "not at all" . . . well not "not at all", that's "pas de tout", which means the same thing. It means "don't mention it".' Fuck, this is all so fucked.

'Well, listen,' says Rosa, 'I think maybe we need to talk.'

'Oh yeah, we should talk.'

'I mean – like you said in your note – it's unthinkable that we won't see each other again.'

'Unthinkable,' I say.

'Yeah. So . . . you wanna meet up?'

'Oh yeah.'

'You wanna meet up right now?'

'Oh yeah,' I say.

'Yeah?' she says, a little excited.

'Yeah, yeah,' I say, a little excited myself.

'OK, why don't I come round in like an hour?'

'Round?'

'Lenny told me you live in my part of town.'

'You've spoken to Lenny?'

'The other night at the show, he said that you lived nearby.'

'Oh yeah, nearby.'

She asks me where I live and I give her the address. She says that she'll be over in an hour and I see no way of contesting such an announcement and say 'Fine' and 'Great' and put down the phone. She'll be over in an hour.

'Fine. Great!' I say to the ceiling, 'Over in an hour.'

'Fine,' says the ceiling.

'Great,' says the door.

I light a cigarette, and smoke it as fast as any cigarette has ever been smoked. I light another one and try to get the time down. I dunno, it's close, you'd need a stopwatch. I pace up and down the room, and then around the room hugging the corners, a mad rabble of possibilities all barking out their bids as my brain turns into the floor of the Tokyo Stock Exchange.

There's nothing in the room to imply the presence of Eleni. I mean there are a hundred things, but nothing overtly feminine that might give the game away to a stranger. We were never one of those couples who populate their home with photos of themselves. That's one of the things I loved about her. I mean love about her. I only mean loved, in the past tense, meaning when I first met her. One of the things I loved about her when I first met her. And still do. I still do love her, really love her, for not wanting to populate our home with photos of ourselves. There's her piano, of course, but that could be mine. There's her coat on the back of the front door but I can put that into the bedroom.

Christ, the bedroom! The bedroom's full of Eleni. Her clothes, her shoes, her hats and bangles. Her books are all in Greek. Her collection of owls and cows all lined up on the purple shelves. There's a photo of Yiorgos and Sofia on the wall by the window, and on the wall above the bed there's a charcoal sketch, naked and alive, her eyes wide and rich with trust. I drew it two hours after our first kiss. I pace around the room, bouncing off the walls like a lost bluebottle. Fucking hell, Hector lad, what are you doing? Don't do it. Don't bring Rosa into this bedroom. Don't fuck Rosa Flood. Do not bring Rosa Flood into this room and fuck her.

'Fuck her in the kitchen,' says the ceiling.

'Fuck her on top of the piano,' says the door.

In the bathroom I pile all Eleni's soaps and creams into an old rucksack. There's no way I'll be able to keep Rosa out of the bathroom. I can lock the bedroom and say it's a dump room, tell her that the settee's a sofa bed, but how the fuck am I gonna keep her out of the bathroom? Combs, tweezers, ducks, sponges, perfumes, tampons, lipsticks, toothbrush. All of them into the bag. It's a disgraceful obliteration.

I can't do this. When she rings on the bell I'll go down to meet her. I'll say I've got the builders in, I'll say there's been a small fire and maybe we should just go for a coffee. I just can't do this to Eleni. I mean I've already done it, but that was a one off. A lapse of will. Think about it, Hector. Just fucking think about it, you piece of dried-out old crap. Eleni's mother is dying. Really, really dying. Not dying like people die in films or in books. Dying in real life. Proper dying. Eleni's watching her fade. Eleni's holding Sofia's cooling blue hand and I'm fucking some whacked-out American child poet. No, no, no. There is no way that this can continue. There is no way on God's earth that I will allow this treason to continue.

'And forty Camel Lights,' I say, placing the basket on the counter. I've got three bottles of Rioja in there as well. 'In fact, make that sixty.'

'I only have them in tens,' says Sergio, the old, silver-haired Italian rake.

'Whatever, give me six. It all goes down the same hole – as my father used to say.'

'Same hole,' he repeats as he raises one grubby grey eyebrow, making it sound rather ribald.

Used to say? What am I talking about? He still says it. He's not dead. 'All goes down the same hole,' he says, has always said, will always say. He's probably saying it right now as some nurse spoons Angel Delight and gravy down his lovely freckled neck.

I'm having difficulty standing in one spot. My thigh is fizzing again and my legs seem hell-bent on walking. They haven't discussed this with me, but they seem to have made their own decision. Fair enough. Who am I to dictate the will of my lower half? I pace over to the bread display and look at the bread for a long time. I'm not sure what I'm looking at? What is bread? And what are these? What are these things in jars? Herrings, it says on the label, but what, or who, are herrings? And why?

'Is that all?'

I turn around. 'What?'

'The wine and sixty Camel Lights? Is that all?'

'Er . . .'

'Yes?'

'And some of those,' I mumble, pointing at the condoms behind him.

His face breaks open in a broad bright smile, all gold teeth and basil. 'Avanti!' he yells.

'What?'

'It is the name of the condom.'

'Yes, that one.'

'*Andare avanti! Andare avanti!*' he shouts as he tosses them into my bag with great gusto. 'It means for you in English, I think, how you say – go for it, my old son!' and he winks at me like an old pantomime pirate.

'Ah yes,' I say, for I seem to remember Eddie Waring yelling such a thing when they held the grand final of *It's An International Knockout* in Blackpool, when I was a kid.

I pay in a hurry and beat a retreat to the door. 'Go for it!' he screams after me as I run out onto the street, appalled. 'Go for it, my old son!!'

As I reach the corner of Box Street I see a dirty red truck pulling up outside my door. Two men jump out, open up the back, and begin to manoeuvre a huge beige battered and ugly settee onto the pavement. It's difficult not to think of childbirth. I'm Hector Kipling and I have this voice in my head screaming, 'Push! Push! Push!'

'What's going on?' says Rosa, who is suddenly behind me.

'Oh!' I squeak. 'Oh my God, you made me jump.'

'Hello, soldier,' she says and kisses me on the cheek, giggling. She smells wonderful.

'Hello, er . . .' She's wearing a tan leather flight jacket, a Russian hat, black tights with a tartan skirt and heavy, unlaced combat boots. 'Hello, er . . . Scottish . . . Cossack, pilot, punk.'

She giggles again and takes my hand in hers which is speckled with green paint, presumably from painting her new frog skull. What a girl.

The two men from the truck are gasping for breath and ringing on my doorbell.

'So what's going on?' she asks me again.

'Oh, it's a long, long story.'

'It's a long, long fucking couch.'

'Settee,' I say.

'Huh?'

'It's not a couch. It's a settee. In Blackpool we call it a settee.'

She frowns, intrigued. 'Blackpool?'

'That's where I'm from. A small town in the north-west of England. It's called Blackpool.'

She stops in her tracks and lets go of my hand. 'Wow,' says Rosa, almost bouncing, 'Black-pool. I love that. Black Pool. That sounds like such a sacred site.'

'Oh yeah,' I say, as one of the men at my door is overcome with a fit of coughs. 'Oh yeah, it's a real sight.'

'Cool,' she says, and regains my hand.

This is not pleasurable. How could this ever be pleasurable? This is the opposite of fucking pleasurable. This is . . . How could anyone find having burning hot candle wax dripped onto the flesh of their belly pleasurable? It's fucking agony, and I wish it would stop. But I don't want to tell her to stop cos the last time I told her to stop I got belted in the mouth. She wears an average of three rings on each finger, so another belt in the mouth is not something I can afford to provoke. God, Mum was right, this lousy settee does stink. No wonder Dad's in hospital. I might well be joining him by the end of the night.

I stare at her navel, and then at the crow on her shoulder, and then at her breasts. I think I'm still inside her but, quite honestly, it's difficult to tell with so many other nerve endings crackling and spitting.

Avanti!

'You fucker!' she drawls, and brings the flame up close to my left nipple. 'You pathetic little fucker,' and tries to light it like a wick.

'Ooowwww!'

'You like that?' she says, bouncing in my lap. 'You fucking like that, man?'

This is worse than the other night. I don't want this. I'm not sure that I'm up for all this. Oh shit, my nipple's on fire. She's poured lighter fluid onto my chest and my tit's gone up in flames like some dessert in a posh restaurant.

'Fuck, Rosa! Aggghhhh! For fuck's sake! Blow it out! Blow it out!'

'OK, baby,' she whispers, suddenly gentle, 'OK, my angel,' and with this she reaches down and pours half a can of Stella over my scorched chest. I'm beginning to regret that I ever invited her in. 'How's that?' she says, lowering her head and lapping up the ale. 'That nice? That nice, baby?'

'No!' I scream.

'No?'

'No, Rosa, no that is not fucking nice! It bloody kills!'

She cracks me across the face with the back of her hand, grips my throat, spits in my eye and scrapes her nails across my scalded flesh. And that's when I come. Oh yes. That's when the core of my soul spasms and snaps, spilling out its filthy pips.

Well, there you go.

Funny old business.

It's getting dark and she's asleep in my arms, eyes closed and tucked away behind her damp black fringe. She smells of Eden. Everything about her is forbidden and my heart is swollen with ache. The dust, confused. The ashtray, full of us. Empty glasses, empty cans. Underwear and bottles on the sticky wooden floor. The cartoon bomb on the bulb of her ankle bone. The blisters on my nipple. The silence of a grave dug in space. What the fuck was Mum thinking of when she bought this settee? This obese beige settee, now drifting out to sea.

I suppose it was reckless of me to fall asleep. Lenny had said that he wouldn't be back till eight and it was about six when me and Rosa were done with our organs of increase. I thought that I might be able to close my eyes for a quarter of an hour, keeping it lucid, just to take the edge off my fatigue; after all I would need my wits about me to manoeuvre Rosa out of the flat without it looking like her departure was imperative. I could tell her that I have to speak to my mum and needed privacy. But no, that would be flawed and might well lead her into the bedroom and burden me with the farce of a fictitious phone call. I could, of course, just tell her the truth, that Lenny was due back. But then that's no good either. She might be suspicious about why we couldn't just be open with Lenny and announce our coupling with pride and glee. I could tell her that I had to be somewhere and leave with her. Yeah, that's what I'll do; I have to be at a private dinner, and if she wants a lift home, then that would be a pleasure. Perfect.

Except of course that it isn't perfect. It would have been perfect, but it's not, cos I didn't sleep for a quarter of an hour, I slept for two hours. I might have slept for three hours had I not been awoken by the key in the door and the clunk and thud of Lenny's Docs crossing the floor.

Clunk, thud. Clunk, thud. And then silence. I can feel him behind us. I can hear his breath and his stomach. It sounds like he's carrying some shopping cos I can hear the faint rustle of polythene as it rests against his leg. I might even be able to hear his heart. Or is that mine? I keep my eyes closed and my mouth open. I breathe through my nose. My torso stinks of Stella and petrol. No one moves. Rosa's still asleep. About a minute goes by. I think it's a minute, it's hard to tell when it's the worst minute of your life. It's the worst minute of my life, and yet, I want it to last forever, cos I have very little desire to embark upon the next minute. The next minute is only seconds away. The next minute – the next twenty, thirty – will be about as awful as minutes can get. Who's gonna break it? Who's gonna cross the line? What is there to say? There's nothing to say. It's all there. There's no use in Lenny asking us what's going on. There's no use in me explaining, justifying, denying the circumstances. It's all there in three dimensions. I might as well sleep. Maybe he'll go away.

Silence.

How long's he gonna just stand there? What's going through his big bald head? Perhaps he's assessing the settee, weighing up its possibilities. Well, maybe me and Rosa should never wake up. Then he can just lug the whole thing down to the Tate: me and Rosa, naked, on a monstrous beige settee. That'd be fine by me. I'd be quite happy to sleep till mid-November. I'd be quite happy if Saatchi bought us and put us on permanent display on the South Bank. Happy to sleep for ever. After all, before Lenny walked through the door it was a perfect moment. Why alter one detail? The mark of a great artist is knowing when to stop. The same might be said of life. We should all be allowed to choose when to stop. The problem is that when the moment is perfect we never do choose to stop, just in case things get more perfect. We only ever choose to stop when things are far from perfect, and stopping then is easy. But that sort of stopping leaves a bad taste in the heart. Whatever. I have the option to wake up from this sham, to untangle myself from Rosa's embrace, and throw open the loading doors. I have the option not to acknowledge one more thing, not to utter one more word. To implement the courage to summon up my cowardice. To sway on the ledge and swallow, before plummeting four floors to the hard and bloody cobbles of Box Street. I wonder how that might feel?

Silence.

Is he just stood there behind the settee gawping at Rosa's mad, damp

221

body? I'll fucking kill him. Is that what he's doing? Taking it all in, whilst he's got the chance? Get your fucking eyes off her you cheap bald opportunistic, thief! Give us some fucking privacy! He might even have his cock out, for all I know. Jesus, what a hideous thought. For all I know he might even be gawping at my body, with his cock out. I wouldn't put it past him. Why doesn't he move or speak? If this goes on for much longer he'll be hearing from my solicitor.

Silence.

Suddenly Lenny's phone rings. I hear him bend at the waist as he puts down the bags.

'Hello?'

In my arms, Rosa is stirring.

'Huh?' she says, her eyes half open, her hand on my inner thigh.

'Eleni?' says Lenny.

I open my eyes and turn my head. Lenny is towering over the back of the settee with the phone to his ear. Behind the blue lenses his eyes are fixed on my eyes. His ear, however is in Crete.

'How are you?'

Nothing but eyes.

'What?' says Rosa.

'Shhh,' I say, and she looks up at Lenny. Now he's staring at both of us, shifting his contempt from one to the other.

'No,' he says, 'no, sweetheart, I still haven't heard from him, I'm afraid. I told you, I haven't seen him since the show.'

Rosa reaches down for her T-shirt and drapes it across our hips.

'Eleni?' says Lenny. 'Eleni?' He takes the phone from his ear and looks at it. He frowns and presses a button. 'Eleni?' He looks at it again, presses another button and slips it back into his pocket. His eyes return. Beneath the T-shirt Rosa moves her hand up my thigh. I don't know why, and I wish she wouldn't.

Lenny lifts his eyebrows towards what used to be his hairline and puckers up his lips. Oh well. Here we go.

'Hi, Lenny,' says Rosa.

'Hi, Rosa,' says Lenny.

'How did it go?' I say.

'How did what go?' says Lenny.

'How did it go down at the Tate?'

Lenny's mouth changes shape. It's not a smile, but it belongs to the same family. It would be a smile, were it not for his eyes.

'Fine,' he says, 'it went fine, Hec,' and he returns his gaze to Rosa. Rosa's got her hand around my balls and she's squeezing. I have no fucking understanding of why she's doing that. 'That was Eleni,' says Lenny.

'So I gathered.'

'Who's Eleni?' says Rosa, spreading her fingers. 'Isn't that your sister, the dentist?'

Lenny looks ashamed of me. I really wish that he wouldn't. But then again, I'd have no respect for him if he didn't.

He turns and walks away. He unpacks his shopping, squatting in front of the open fridge, filling up the shelves with dried tomatoes, greasy olives, free-range eggs and banana cheesecake. He tosses two packets of wheat-free fettuccini onto the draining board and spills a bag of clementines into the fruit bowl.

I can't think of anything to say. What can I say? What can anybody say? Lenny looks set on milking the silence, and Rosa is simply bewildered, her fist around my balls, trying to get the hang of things.

Lenny kneels by the phone and unpacks a new answering machine. He mucks about with the wires and plugs as Rosa shifts her hand up and down, up and down.

'You bought a new answering machine?' I say.

'Yeah,' says Lenny.

'Thanks,' I say.

'Well, we'll be needing one,' he says. 'If I'm gonna be staying here, I'm gonna need an answering machine.'

'Yeah,' I say, 'yeah.'

Lenny fiddles with a few buttons and then leans in close to the microphone. 'Hello, this is Hector, Lenny and El . . . Lector and Henny,

223

shit!' and he presses a few more buttons and starts again. 'Hello, this is Lenny Snook and Hector Kipling, neither of us can take your call right now, so if you leave a message after the tone, we'll get back to you. Bye.' There's a click and then a bleep. The machine repeats it back to him and he straightens up. 'You never know who's gonna call,' says Lenny, smiling at us both. 'You never know a lot of things.'

'We never know anything,' says Rosa. 'We know nothing. Nothing at all.'

Well, I'll go along with that. I make a grunt of assent.

I'll tell you what, though, I can no longer conceal this erection. And yet I must. And yet it seems impossible. What the fuck is she doing with those fingers? Where are they going now? My God! Is that legal?

Lenny lingers a while, saying nothing. I'm counting backwards from a million to zero. When that doesn't work I turn onto my front.

'Well,' says Lenny, realizing that all the main points have probably been covered, 'I'll be off, then.'

'You don't have to,' I say.

'Yeah, whatever, Hec,' he says and makes his way to the door. 'Oh, by the way, Kirk went into hospital this morning.'

'No!' says Rosa.

'No!' I say.

'Yeah,' says Lenny, and starts to pick at his teeth. 'I found him collapsed in his flat. He'd been there for two days.' His eyes fill with tears. So do Rosa's. Mine, for some reason, do not. Why don't mine? 'Yeah, so now he's in hospital.'

'Oh fuck,' I say.

'Just thought you might like to know. Oh yeah, and your mum called again. Wants you to call her. And Eleni. That was Eleni just now. Your sister. The dentist.' And with this he opens the door and then slams it behind him.

Rosa lifts her thigh up to my belly and snuggles her face into my neck. 'Weird job,' she whispers, 'pulling teeth all day. Tiny fragments of the skull just peeping through.'

'Yeah,' I whisper and offer her my thumb to kiss; anything to prevent her from elaborating.

I gave Rosa a lift home and took myself off to my dinner party, which was back at my place. Two boiled eggs and banana cheesecake. The wine flows and the company is delightful – it's Mum:

'Ever so smart he was, ever so smart. Lovely smell. You don't often see men like that in Lancashire.'

'Well, that's fantastic news, Mum.'

'I made him a ham sandwich and he had a little frolic with Sparky – Sparky adored him – and listen to this, he said it was a very rare piece and worth much more than what we were asking. I said, "Give over," he says, "No, no, I'll feel like I'm cheating you if I don't give you more for it," and he writes out a cheque for nine hundred pounds. Nine hundred pounds, Hector! Can you believe it?'

'I can't believe it, Mum. That's amazing, I mean, you made a profit! Have you told Dad?'

'Oh aye, I was straight on the phone to the hospital the minute the fella left. I mean he took it right there and then. He had a van out the front with a horsebox hitched to the back of it. We called in Barry from next door to give him a hand. I got straight on the phone to the hospital. I just got back from there now. He's a lot, lot better. They say he can come home tomorrow.'

'Mum, this is all just brilliant. I can't believe it's all turned out so well. You sound all happy again.' I've got a big smile on my face, spooning in a mouthful of egg. Dad's not dead. Dad's not gonna die. What a magnificent son I am. If only they knew. If only I could tell them. One day, maybe, one day they'll know. I'm smiling. Jesus, look at the breadth of this smile.

'So what's going on with this American lass?' says Mum, suddenly sombre.

There goes the smile. Bye.

'Nothing, Mum, nothing's going on with her.'

'Hector, you told me only yesterday that you was in a bath with her.'

'I never said I was in a bath with her.'

'You said you was in her bath.'

'Whatever.'

'You was in her bath and there's nothing going on with her? How do you make that out?'

'It's over, Mum.'

'It's never over, Hector. You behave like that and it's never over. Never! Do you hear?'

'Yes, Mum.'

'Have you spoken to Eleni?'

'Yes, Mum,' I lie. I'm not really lying cos I'm gonna call her right after this. I really am, that was always the plan.

'And what have you said?'

'Her mother's a lot better. She's gonna stay out there for a little while and I've said I'll go over. I mean now that Dad's feeling better it'll be all right to go and see her.'

'Well, you do that. You fly out there and you look after her. I can't believe that you've risked losing that girl.'

'I won't lose her, Mum.'

'How do you know? You'll lose her if you don't change your ways. You'll lose her if she finds out about all this.'

'She won't find out about all this.'

'And you'll lose her if you keep secrets from her. Secrets don't like to be locked up. They're like rats, they'll bite you if you back them into a corner.'

I tried to call Eleni. I tried every ten minutes for an hour. No luck. I tried to get the operator to put me through. No luck. About half-past ten Lenny returned with two suitcases, a large box of tools, wood, paint, panes of glass and a long tube of rolled-up plans. He laid it all out in front of the enormous ugly beige settee and said, 'So I can do what I want to this, then?'

'Absolutely,' I said, and smiled.

After that he wouldn't talk to me, not another word. He wouldn't even look at me. He was behaving like a silly, bald child, stomping around, banging cupboard doors, cooking up his pasta and totally ignoring me. I sat and watched him shovel it down. I asked if there was any left over but he just carried on eating. He'd made just the right amount for himself. Fucking hell! You'd think he'd caught me in the arms of his mother.

ST THOMAS'S HOSPITAL, LONDON

All these tubes and wires. The blips and bleeps and clips and nozzles. The clinical minimalism of the fabrics and the machines. The frosted mask. The way the tape pulls at the skin. The flowers are starting to wilt and everything's on wheels. The sum of all that must be inserted and drawn in the final throes. Please don't let me die in a hospital. More to the point, please don't let Kirk die in a hospital. Not in this hospital. I really don't want my friend Kirk, whom I love intensely, to finish his life right here, right in front of me. And then it occurs to me that this would be preferable to finishing his life without me, or in the company of another, say. If he's going to go, then better he goes in front of me. At least I'll report his end with the appropriate ceremony. Of course I'm not happy about such thoughts but what can I do? I'm not happy anyway and thoughts just do as they please. Thank God I didn't see Dad like this.

This morning I was woken by the sound of laboured sawing. By the time I emerged from my room Lenny had already cut a perfect square into the back of the settee and was busy filing down the dovetails for the window frame. There was a faint whiff of sweat and putty.

He kept his head down whilst I buttered my toast and prepared a coffee. When I asked him if he wanted one he looked over and shook his head. Oh well, it was a start.

I took the phone into the bedroom and tried Eleni again. Nothing but static and formal electronic Greek.

It was only when I asked him about Kirk that Lenny relented and mumbled the name of the hospital and the number of the ward. I asked him how he was and he said, 'Unconscious.'

'And what do the doctors say?'

'They don't know. He was almost dead when they brought him in. He'd had nothing to eat or drink for two days, and they don't know.'

'But do they think he'll—'

'They don't fucking know!' he screamed, and I couldn't think of any more questions.

I put on my Crombie and then my hat. I walked to the door, thought better of the hat, threw it into the bedroom, and set out for the hospital.

Two nurses turn up with a trolley of towels and bedpans. One of them asks me what happened to my face and I say that I took a few blows whilst apprehending a mugger.

'Poor you,' she says.

'Yeah, well,' I say, 'they'd made off with some old lady's handbag.'

She smiles and sighs. Her eyebrows are a model of concern. The other one just gets on with the pillows. They pull the screens around and ask if I'd care to wait in the corridor.

I'm out in the car park smoking a fag. I keep pulling my shirt away from my burning nipple. Now and then I put my hand inside and waft my fingers back and forth, and then I blow on it, but it does no good.

I have Rosa's number written on a scrap of paper. Originally she wrote it on my hip, in blood, but I worried that it might rub off in the night so I wrote it out on the back of a receipt. I'm looking at it now and feeling in my pockets to work out how much change I have. She looked into my eyes last night, just before she got out of the car, held my face in her hands, fixed me with her stare and whispered, 'I love you.'

'I love you too,' I said.

I'm thinking of calling her. I speak the numbers out loud. Long and solemn vowels, like it's a fucking psalm. I whisper her name over and over. Somewhere in the distance I can hear someone screaming. That's what scares me most about hospitals: you can always hear someone screaming. There's the rattle of tools, the clang of the vending machines, the drone of the boiler room, and always, always, in some distant bed, the shriek of a departing coward let down by his faith.

An ambulance flies through the gates, screeches to a halt and a flock of doctors race out to meet it. There's some sort of human being broken into pieces beneath a dark wet blanket. Man, woman, boy, girl, it's difficult to tell. It's not the blood that disturbs me, nor even the flashes of blue. It's the occasional bulbs of soft wet pink, shining through the black. It's these glistening bubbles of cherry blossom that make me throw up all over my shoes. I wish I'd never looked. I wish all that had been withheld from me. I'd really rather not have to go through what's left of my life knowing that all this can be reduced to that. To remains.

I have no friends. Squatting here in the car park, this is what I realize. Everyone has gone. There is only Rosa now to smile at me. But then Rosa doesn't know anything about me. Nor I of her. I have lost them all. I have been found despicable in the eyes of my loved ones. If I was as famous as Lenny all this would be in the papers. They'd have paparazzi in the bushes. Eleni would have been tracked down by some sweating hack with a phrase book and a Dictaphone. There'd be pictures of Kirk, smuggled out by the nurses, pictures of Dad, pictures of Mum, an artist's impression of the big beige settee and what went on, and how, and why. And then, in their columns, they'd discuss what might be wrong with me and what was to be done. And I'd buy every single one of them, cos I'd really like to know. But I'm not as famous as Lenny, so I'll just have to get by. I'll just have to work it out on my own.

I make my way back to the ward and the nurses tell me that whilst I was gone Kirk woke up momentarily; the first time since he was brought in. I sit at his side for an hour. I try to speak to him – the doctors say that it's helpful if I speak to him – but what am I gonna say? Tell him what's been happening? Tell him what he's been missing? Fuck, he's better off in a coma. I try to remind him of some old times but his eyes are shut tight and don't even flicker, so I stop and just stare at the floor. No use in my being here. No use at all. Tick, tick. Tick, tick.

'Hi, Rosa?'

   'Hector? How's it going? What you up to?'

I'm actually on my hands and knees, halfway under the bed, cos I'm not supposed to be using my phone on the ward, and I don't want Kirk to hear me, just in case he's having a crafty semi-conscious listen.

   'I'm down at the hospital looking after Kirk.'

   'Oh my God, how is the poor little guy?'

   'He's unconscious. But anyway, listen, I thought maybe I could come over later. I mean Kirk's mum's gonna be here in an hour and then Lenny's gonna visit him tonight. So I . . . er . . . I just wondered what you were doing and er . . .'

   'I'd rather come over to your place. I feel happy at your place. I love it there.'

It's the sound of her voice. I love that as much as I've ever loved anything. I've never heard a voice like hers.

   'Shall I come round about seven?' she says. 'How's seven?'

   'Seven's good,' I say.

   'OK, angel, I'll be right there. Do you need anything?'

   'I need you,' I say, and immediately wish that I hadn't.

   'Aw, little angel,' she giggles, 'you are such a fucking angel.'

I'm just putting my coat on and making for the door when I become aware of Kirk's head shifting slightly on the pillow. When I look over it's still again. I wait a few seconds and I'm just about to leave when Kirk's blue eyes spasm and flutter, and eventually, a small liquid gash appears between the lids.

   'Mum?' he whispers.

   'No. It's Hector.'

231

'Lenny?'

'No, Kirk. Hector. It's Hector.'

'The doctor?'

'No,' I say almost losing my patience, 'it's me. It's Hector.'

'Hector?'

'Kirk?'

'Hector?'

'Kirk, are you awake?'

'Am I?'

I kneel down and take his hand. 'Kirk, mate. You're awake. It's gonna be all right.'

'Where am I?'

'You're in hospital. You're being taken good care of. I'm here, Kirk. I'm taking good care of you.'

His eyes struggle to move around the room. At last they come to rest upon my face. 'What's happening?'

'You're recovering,' I say, 'that's what's happening. You're getting better.' I squeeze his hand so tight that he has to move his arm to shake me off.

'I don't think so,' he says, and a tiny puff of laughter escapes from his lips. 'I really don't think so. I think we can tot up the scores now.'

'Eh?'

'You won't believe how big it all is.'

'What's very big?'

He closes his eyes and stretches his jaw. His tongue is all white, his breath smells of ink. '*It* is very big. The thing you don't know about.'

I feel a little indignant, and shift on the stool. 'What's the thing I don't know about Kirk?'

'Exactly,' croaks Kirk. 'Good question. Best question.'

'Kirk, you're not making sense.'

'No, Hec, that's you who's not making sense.' And he smiles and leans his head to one side.

A nurse marches up and takes his pulse. She smells of bleach and methane. She writes at length in a little blue notebook, stops, pauses to think and then writes a little more. And then off she goes. Perhaps she's a poet.

'Kirk,' I say, laying my palm upon his brow, 'have you seen something?'

Silence.

'Kirk, tell me what it is. What do you know?'

'I know that all the lines collapse to the base, and all the shapes fly off to the sides . . .'

'What?'

Silence. The sound of his dry tongue, peeling away from the gums.

'And words . . . mean nothing at all . . . so forget it.'

'Kirk . . .'

'There are sparks . . .' he mumbles, 'concealed in the heart of the cream.'

That's what he said. That's what he left me with. Cheers, Kirk, that's cleared that up, then.

BOX STREET, BOW, LONDON

By the time I walk through the front door Lenny's just putting the finishing touches to the window. He's polishing the panes with a blue cloth, breathing on the glass and coaxing out the grease into an immaculate sheen. The frame has been painted beige to match the upholstery. In the meantime he's punched ten thousand black hairs into the flesh of the fabric giving the whole thing an element of a constricted life. I must say, it's looking good.

'How's it going?' I say.

'Fine,' he says, 'in fact you've arrived at the perfect time. I need you to give me a hand.' And with this he moves to one end of the settee and beckons me to take the other. 'Let's put it over by that wall and stand it on one end.'

'OK,' I say, just so fucking pleased that I might just have my friend back.

We lug the beast over to the opposite wall and stand it on its end. It's then that I notice the bathroom door leaning up against the wall.

'So how is he?' says Lenny.

'He woke up for a few minutes.'

Lenny's face breaks open into a smile. 'Yeah? Did he say anything?'

'Well, he was kind of rambling.' I take another look at the door.

'I'll go down there. Is his mum with him?'

'Yeah. Er . . . what are you doing with the bathroom door?'

He walks over to it and runs his hand down one of the panels. 'It's OK, I'll put it back on. I wanted to try something.'

'What?'

The telephone rings.

'Aren't you gonna get that?'

'Er . . . I er . . .'

'It might be Eleni,' he says and glares right into the centre of me, right into the heart of the cream. 'I think you should take it, don't you?'

'Take what?'

'The call, bonehead.'

'Hah! *You're* calling *me* a bonehead?'

'Hector, pick up the fucking phone!'

'You're the bonehead.'

Lenny races across the room and picks up the phone. 'Hello? Yeah, it's Lenny. Yeah, he's here, hang on.' I walk over and he passes me the phone. 'It's your mum.'

For a while I don't say anything, but just hold it to my ear and listen to her crying. Lenny's pulled out a Stanley knife and he's cutting away the fabric from the base of the settee.

'Mum?'

'Hhhhecctooor.'

'Mum, what is it, Mum? Is it Dad? How's Dad?'

'Hhhhecctoooor.' Gasping. Gasping.

Is it Dad? Is this the phone call I've spent my whole life dreading? Oh well, it was always going to happen. One of these days the phone was always going to ring and it would be either Mum or Dad and they'd utter the name of the other in the same sentence as 'dead'. She can't bring herself under control. I can hear her sniffing and trying to catch her breath. Oh my God, it must be Dad.

'Mum, it's not Dad, is it?'

'Hector, we've been burgled.'

'What?'

'We've been robbed!' she screams.

'Mum, Mum,' I say, 'take it easy, what's happened? Tell me what's happened.'

She can barely speak for the torrent of tears. 'I went to fetch your dad from the hospital and –' drip, drip ' – by the time we got back we'd been robbed . . . It was that man, Hector. It must have been that man.'

'What man?'

'That man who bought the settee.'

My blood turns to frost. 'How do you know? What's gone?'

'When he gave me the cheque I put it into the safe behind the Lowry picture.'

'You did that in front of him?'

'No, he asked if he could use the toilet, but by the time he came back I was still struggling to hang the picture back up, and he saw it, he saw where we keep everything, and that's what's gone.'

'So what's gone?'

'Everything! I was settling your dad down into his chair and he asked if he could see the cheque. I went to the safe and it was completely empty. All our savings. Fifteen thousand pounds! He's stolen fifteen thousand pounds from us.'

'Oh my God! Mum! Oh my God!'

'Your dad's gone straight back to the hospital. He went straight back in the same ambulance that brought him home. And Sparky's run off again. I don't blame him. I feel like doing the same.'

Lenny's carrying the bathroom door over to the settee and leaning it against the base. It's too small but I get the idea. He's doing some kind of human settee with a window and a door sort of thing. Lenny rests for a minute and looks over, aware that something's wrong.

Mum's taking hundreds of tiny involuntary breaths. There's an agonizing squeak in the back of the throat and half a pint of spit. It sounds like it might never stop.

'Mum, I'll send you the money.'

'Hector, it's fifteen thousand pounds. It's everything we have in the world.'

'I can get double that for a new painting. It'll take me two or three weeks to do a new painting and I'll just send you the money. It's all right, Mum, really it's all right. Have you called the police?'

'Yes, but the cheque's gone as well and I can't remember his name, the name on the cheque.'

'Monger?'

'Eh?'

'Was his name Monger?'

'No. What are you talking about? Why are you asking if his name was Monger? Where do you get that from?'

Fuck, why don't I just come clean? Why don't I just tell her the whole story? 'Or Bolton? Was it Bolton?'

'Hector, what are you talking about? Why are you just calling out names at random?'

'Well, was it? Was it Bolton? Think, Mum.'

'No, it wasn't bloody Bolton. It was something like Parker or Parsons, but neither of those. Partridge, something like Partridge, but it wasn't Partridge either. Where do you get Monger and Bolton from? What are you talking about, Hector?'

Lenny's laid the door flat on the floor and he's going at the insides of the settee with a screwdriver. Now and then he looks over and frowns.

'Mum,' I say, suddenly resolute, 'I'll be on the first train in the morning. I'm coming home, Mum. Listen to what I'm saying, I'm coming home.'

'Well, it's about bloody time.'

Lenny's crouched down with his body half inside the settee. He's put down the screwdriver and he's struggling to untangle something from the springs and threads. Suddenly he reels back with his hand over his mouth. He reaches in and pulls out a small bundle. On the other end of the line, Mum's convulsing.

'I'll be right there, Mum. I'll come home, and then I'll paint this painting. Mr Myers can sell it and I'll replace everything that's been stolen. Really, it's all gonna be fine. Mum. Mum, please don't cry. It breaks my heart to hear you like this.'

Lenny's poking at the bundle with the screwdriver, slowly unwrapping it. The more he unwraps it the tighter he holds his hand over his face.

'Hang on, Mum,' I say, fearing the worst.

'What?'

'Just give me a second.'

I walk over and arrive at the scene, just as Lenny is turning over the last fold. I stop in my tracks and Lenny retreats to the other side of the room, whimpering behind his hands.

Sparky. Sparky, me old mate. What the fuck are you doing in there? What the fuck are you doing down in London, all black and chapped and stinking and dead? What's your story? What's your fucking story, Sparky?

13

Mum and Lenny have taken themselves off to their respective hospitals. I eased Sparky's carcass into a black bin liner and walked him down to the canal. I'd always imagined a tiny grave in Mum and Dad's back garden, pebble for a headstone, never the Grand Union Canal with its old trikes and mattresses. I'm lying on the floor looking at the spot on the ceiling. What's going on? Dad's in hospital, Kirk's in hospital, Sofia's in hospital, I'm having an affair with a sado-masochistic Brooklyn poet, and some stranger who threw horse shit all over my painting of his dead father has robbed my parents and sent me the corpse of their dog hidden in the base of a hideous settee. I don't know, is it me, am I exaggerating, or has my life just turned into some sort of drunken collaboration between Feydeau and Dante?

Any moment now Rosa will ring the bell and I'll be dragged in even deeper. I wish I could sleep for ten million years.

In my dream they're all in the same hospital. Well, actually a tent. A military hospital tent pitched in some trench. The black sky is brilliant with flares and tracer fire. Dad's bed is shoved up one end and his face is pressed into the pillow so that I can only see the back of his sobbing head. Kirk's sat up and quoting Poe to his hands. His hair could do with a comb. Sofia's all raw and red on a crisp white bed, like a monstrous piece of sushi. Two small flames flicker in the sockets of her eyes. It's a windy night and the walls of the tent are punched back and forth, back and forth for ten million years. What a palaver.

I love the shape of my fingers as they grip the charcoal. I love the feeling of my hand as it brushes across the page. I have to be careful not to become preoccupied with this elegance as I draw her. But it has always been the case. Eleni says the same thing about her hands when she plays the piano. When the beauty is flowing through you it's difficult not to sit back a little and watch the extremities work their magic. I'm finishing off her eyes. From across the room and from the page, she's staring straight through me. My hand leaves the page, pauses, and begins a sequence of bold, broad strokes, as I get to work on her hair. I have no idea why I can do this. Or rather, I have no idea why everyone can't do this. Only this makes me happy. Every time I take up my charcoal or my brushes, I kiss each stick, each brush. I kiss the pad, the canvas, the tubes, the tubs, the palette, the turps, the rags and the ladders. And then I kiss myself. Each hand. Each finger in turn. And then a peck for the thumbs. If I could kiss my eyes I would. Instead I kiss my palm and lay it upon each lid. I am ready to begin and it scares the shit out of me. What if it has gone? What if the gift has fled? Sometimes I have to rush to the toilet before I can proceed. Sometimes I throw up and sometimes I just sit there, paralysed, unvisited. It's about trust. It is not me who can do this. It is another. And others must never be trusted. I despise this compulsion. And yet only this makes me happy. Only this. How I hate it.

'Why don't you do all of me?' she says.

'All of you?'

'I could just undress and then you could draw the whole damned thing.'

'The whole damned thing?'

'The whole goddamned thing. Whaddya think, soldier?'

I must have swallowed with such gusto that she took it as a yes, because now she's standing up and beginning to undress. 'So what do you say?'

I feel like I'm in some terrible seventies soft-core porn film –

Confessions of a Randy Dauber, or something like that. She's down to her underwear and before I can loosen my jaw enough to say leave the underwear on, the underwear's off and Rosa Flood's spreadeagled on my floor.

'Do me from this angle,' she says, and saucy trombone music kicks in. We're in the smoky basement of my brain, brushes on the snare, two kazoos and a battered sax.

'OK,' I say and turn over the page. Though foreshortening was never my strong point.

She never questioned the explicit presence of Eleni's chattels in the bedroom. But then there wasn't really time. She emptied out a bottle of turpentine across my pelvis and came at me with a palette knife. Confident that she couldn't possibly break my skin with a palette knife, I came over all cocky and croaked, 'Go on then, slit my fucking throat.' And that's when, much to my chagrin, she managed to slit my throat a little. What a girl. She then grabbed a fistful of my hair, wrestled me into the bathroom and proceeded to shave my head with my beard trimmer and a Gillette razor. Too drunk and terrified to protest, I sat on the edge of the bath and groaned as she massaged my nicked dome with half a bottle of Body Shop baby oil. And then it was back to the bedroom for a prolonged bout of unhappy-slapping and something she must have read about after Googling 'Gomorrah'. By the time we fell asleep the sheets emitted a pungent stink of sweat, turps, semen, ash, lemon juice, ginger, excrement and blood. At some point we heard Lenny come home and took great care to censor the ferocity of our throes. Though at one point I screamed, 'Fuck, Rosa, what are you gonna do with that?' and, to be honest, it would really surprise me if, at some future date, he claimed not to have heard it.

I woke up at eleven, put the bed sheets onto a long spin cycle and lit seven jasmine joss sticks. I stood in front of the bathroom mirror between half past and quarter to, picking at scabs and realizing that I didn't have the right shape of head to carry this off. There was a small trough at the crown that I feared might gather water in a storm, and that birds might settle and take sup at the expense of my dignity. I despaired, to say the least. By noon Rosa regained consciousness and I made us both a nice pot of peppermint tea. There was a note by the kettle:

> *Hector, what the fuck are you doing? I sat up all night with Kirk. He didn't wake up once. Meanwhile . . . what the fuck are you doing? I don't think I can stay here, considering. What the fuck are you doing? Shouldn't you be in Crete? Shouldn't you be in Blackpool? Shouldn't you be down St Thomas's? What the fuck are you doing? I've gone out for a long walk and a think, cos I don't understand what the fuck you're doing! Lenny. Who loves you – up to a point.*

Up to a point.

Rosa's in the bath. I can hear the tiny splashes and frolic of Rosa in the bath. I can smell it all from here. I can smell her eyes, her nails and the freckles on her neck. I can smell the suds and the tiles. The toothbrush, the towels, the talc and the oils.

I've pulled the ladders into the very centre of the room and I'm sat at the very top, hugging my knees, staring through the window. Things are going to change. From now on, things will never be the same. Not that they ever were. For suddenly it's clear. I have the option to say no to all this. I can climb down from this ladder right now. I can confront Rosa and send her on her way. I can put twenty thousand pounds into Mum and Dad's bank account within the hour. I could be at Heathrow by three. I could spend tonight beneath the stars with my Eleni in my arms. Sofia will recover, Dad will recover and they'll go into Kirk's head with their needles and their knives and scrape out all the dark. Monger will be arrested, Lenny will win the Prize and by next July there'll be a rosy-nosed baby squawking like a damp bird in the softly mad middle of a glorious summer night. And all I have to do is come down from this ladder. It's the New Dawn of a Golden Age. Fuck, you know what? I think I might have given up smoking. Just now, sat atop this stepladder, just about to climb down.

I can hear a taxi out in the street. So much for Lenny's long walk. He probably walked as far as Mile End Tube and just couldn't face the Hogarthian squalor. 'I'm too tall for the Tube,' he always says. One time he even claimed to be too famous for the Tube. Yeah, Lenny, of course you are. Bless. Artists in taxis. Artists in Groucho's. Artists in the dark corners of empty VIP rooms, sipping their tequilas, whispering about anatomy and cash.

Outside the front door I hear the groan and fizz of the lift.

Artists in lifts, instead of taking the stairs.

I don't care if he wants to take me on, have it all out. I won't argue with him. No. I feel like a new monk, all bald at the top of this ladder. I'm glowing. I'm radiating an extreme and magnificent monkness. And Lenny's gonna pick up on that. After all, he's a sensitive chap. He's gonna stride in here all ready to strap me to the rack of his indignation, but I won't be having any of it. Yes, I've done wrong. Yes, I've been led astray. But all this is as nothing to the right I will now do. All this pales in the light of this fresh and epiphanic resolution.

One last fag. Before the lift opens I'll have lit just one last fag. I'll smoke it in front of him. I'll ask him to prepare a ceremonial ashtray, with Stella and pepper, as an end to all bitterness. We'll sit and watch the final plume rise to the ceiling and lovingly speculate upon the moment when one can say, with surety, that it has finally passed away.

I slide it from the packet and roll it around in my fingers. I examine it closely. The speckled filter, the millimetre seam, the ochre leaves squeezed into the barrel, the word 'Camel' and the word 'Light'. I gaze at the flame, violet and lemon, passing into amber and grey. I take it in and, at long last, the smoke, it seems, has little resonance with the shape of my ghost.

The clang of the lift. His Docs on the tiles. His key in the lock. My lofty sublimation. My transcendent otherness. My arse on the wood, ten feet off the ground. I don't care. I really don't care. I will forgive him.

'Eleni!' I shout. 'Eleni.' My mortification is so fantastically spectacular that the stepladder is suddenly incapable of maintaining the perpendicular and I find myself flailing through space into some biblical abyss and smash my skull on the sharp edge of Eleni's piano.

'Hello, Hector,' she says, nonplussed at my shabby descent, as though she expected nothing less. Her face is ravaged by tears. The word 'erosion' springs to mind.

'Eleni,' I groan, cupping my head, 'what are you doing here?'

She drops her bags and collapses to the ground. Her hair completely covers her face, hanging down, brushing against the boards. She looks like she's just been picked off by a sniper. I'd say that she'd passed out were it not for the fact that her fingers are clawing at the wood – her nails chewed down to the wrists. I suspect she doesn't like my new haircut.

It wasn't like I expected. Like everything else in life it failed to live up to expectations. When Eleni finally announced that her mother was dead I felt like my brain (or my heart – what *is* the difference?) sent out dishevelled and ill-equipped search parties in a quest for a shard of emotion. As it went, Eleni presented her predicament and I responded with a specific degree of equanimity that might well be read, by some, as a kind of inhuman indifference. I don't know, I'm still trying to work it all out. All I can say for now is that I lit another fag.

Sofia, extinguished by fire, had struggled, in vain, with the cheerless shadow. Yiorgos had drunk himself into the last corner of his taverna and shrunk to the size of a seed. Meanwhile Eleni had wept the length and breadth of Crete, dismantled and scattered, whispering to her shoes, spitting at insects and praying on her knees to the cruel and idiotic Aegean Sea. All this as I had busied myself, back home, scaling the twin faces of cowardice and lust. Well done, Hector. Nicely done.

'Where have you been? Why haven't you called me? Why did you never call me?' She's back on her feet. Actually that's not quite accurate. She's back on her knees. But I interpret it as being back on her feet, considering.

'I've been in hospital!' I plead. 'I've only just got back from the hospital!'

'What?' she whimpers, through a fat bubble of tears.

'When the lunatic attacked my painting I was knocked down by a car. I chased him from the gallery and I was hit by a car . . . a Volvo, and I've been in hospital ever since.'

Eleni wipes at her face with her exquisite little hands. I love Eleni. I love her more than breath. Eleni would never set fire to my nipples.

'Eleni . . . Eleni, angel, I'm so sorry.' I hold her in my arms, rocking her.

'Oh, Hector,' she wails, 'Mama is dead. My mother is dead.'

Yes, well that's obviously terrible news. Horrible news. No, I mean it, really, really, the most awful, atrocious, abominable and tragic news. But all I can think of right now is that just a few feet away – just a few minutes away – Rosa Flood is naked, tattooed and recumbent in my bath. Our bath. My and Eleni's bath. Oh Good God! Oh Jesus Fucking Costello! I take a deep sniff of Eleni's hair. It smells of aeroplanes and luggage. It smells of Bibles and morphine. It smells of distance, lentils, Chianti and death.

'Why have you come back?' I say. The moment it leaves my lips I know that it's the wrong thing to say.

'I had to come back for some documents and keepsakes. And to see you,' whispers Eleni, 'I have to fly straight back tomorrow. I need to be there for my father. He's very lost. I just need to pick up a few . . . Hector, Hector, please . . .' she sobs, 'Hector, please come out with me. I need you. Hector, please come back with me.'

'Of course,' I say, and kiss her scalp. 'Of course I'll come back with you.'

'Oh, Hector,' she moans, 'oh, Hector.'

'Eleni,' I whisper, 'Eleni, Eleni, Eleni.'

She looks up at me. 'What happened?' She sniffs and wipes at her eyes. 'What happened to your hair? You've shaved off all your hair.'

'They did it at the hospital.'

'Why?'

Good question. 'Er . . . they thought they were going to have to operate, but at the last minute I perked up a bit and so . . . they er . . . apologized. Gave me it in a bag. Y'know, like they do with gallstones.' What the fuck am I talking about?

I don't know what's going on with Rosa. Maybe she's asleep. Maybe she's heard everything and is just keeping still and silent. I don't know. I have no idea. Let me announce it now, once and for all: I, Hector Kipling, have not one fucking idea about how to proceed.

'And what is this?' says Eleni, clocking the butchered settee.

'It's Lenny's new piece. Lenny's left Brenda and I've told him he can stay here till he sorts it all out.'

She gazes through her tears at the whiskered flesh settee and frowns. 'It looks like skin, hairy skin.'

'I think that's the idea. Naked Settee. There are ten million stories in the Naked Settee, and this has been one of them.'

'What?'

'*Naked City*, it was an old American TV show.' She just gawps at me, askance. 'Forget it, it was a bad joke.' I suppose this is no time to be cracking bad jokes.

She walks over and examines it a little more closely. 'Why does it have a window?'

'You tell me.'

She puts her hands up to her face and resumes her grief, hopeless and small.

'Eleni, don't,' I whisper, walking over and taking her back into my arms. 'Please don't.'

'It reminds me of my mother,' she sobs and I can feel her tears soaking through my shirt and onto my breasts. I don't really understand how Lenny's horrible settee reminds her of her mother. What does she mean? Was she a hairy woman?

'What do you mean?'

'I can't explain. Everything is reminding me of my mother. She was naked when she died, I don't want to see this thing.'

'Listen, I don't want to see this thing. And I very much doubt that the Turner judges or the Great British public will want to see this thing, but we're all lumbered with it.'

'She was naked and burned and the hospital was so hollow and cold. There were people screaming in every room.'

Reminded of my own recent experiences, I blurt out, a little indelicately perhaps, 'Oh! Oh, yeah, Kirk's in hospital as well!'

'Kirk?'

'And Dad! So is my dad.' Sensing that I might be sounding inappropriately buoyant, I add, '. . . as it happens.'

She pulls away from me and looks up, deep into my eyes in such a baffling manner that I am not sure whether she is issuing consolation or revulsion. It seems to go on for hours. At last she looks away and asks, 'Why is your father in hospital?'

I tell her the whole tale of the settee and Monger, and the burglary and Sparky's murder, and she seems to soften a little, though she still seems a mite suspicious about some of the holes in the story, regarding how I was able to stage-manage this whole conceit, involving numerous phone calls, when I had just told her, no less than five minutes ago, that I had only just been discharged from hospital, where they had shaved my head and let me take the hair home in a bag. And who can blame her for suspecting that this whole picaresque fable is nothing other than the desperate ravings of an emotionally challenged halfwit? Not me, for one. What a girl.

At the conclusion of my exemplum she utters not one word, but lights a cigarette, gathers up her bags, kicks the hairy settee with unnerving ferocity, and shuffles off in the direction of our bedroom.

In the wasteland between my throat and my groin, all hell has broken loose. I'm lying on the floor staring at my fatuous red and black canvas. I begin to wonder how I might get my hands on a flamethrower. Eleni's still in the bedroom, presumably changing out of her clothes. Fuck knows what Rosa's up to. I haven't heard one squeak. My life has become a ticking bomb. I suppose that one's life is always a ticking bomb, nestled in the breast, but my bomb has never ticked as loud as this. Tin fists and jackboots down Blackpool's gravel promenade. I can see no way out of this, and it's making me tremble. It's really quite upsetting, all this trembling business. Trembling and sweating, I begin to sneeze, just as I'm beginning to imagine how, precisely, the axe might fall – for fall it must.

'Hector, what is this?' says Eleni, emerging from the bedroom in her clean peach pyjamas.

'What's what?'

She's carrying a red rucksack. She marches over and lays it at my feet. 'This,' she says, and frowns.

'I don't know,' I say, 'what is it?'

'Hector, I don't like this.'

'What don't you like?'

She fluffs open the shiny nylon edges of the bag, revealing bottles and tubes. 'Hector, all my things are in this bag. I find this bag in the bedroom cupboard and all my things from the bathroom are in here.'

I want to vomit.

'Are they?'

She grips the bag at its base and upends it. 'Hector, why is all this in a bag?'

'Because er . . .' I say. 'Because er . . .' I reach out to her. I try to smother her in my arms. 'Eleni, Eleni, I'm so sorry about your mother.'

'You've put all my things . . . all my things from the bathroom into a rucksack. Why have you done that, Hector?'

'Because I was packing. I was packing, ready to come out and see you, and . . . I thought you might want some of this stuff, so . . .'

'And why are there no sheets on the bed?'

I hug her even tighter. 'Because I was in the middle of changing them.'

'But why is the mattress all stained? There's blood on the mattress.'

'Because I was hit by a fucking Volvo, remember?' This is shouted into her ear. It is the most ridiculous sentence of my life thus far.

She pulls away, violently away, and strides off to the other side of the room. She slumps down in the chair and curls up into a ball. I decide not to follow.

Silence.

'So you've stopped doing big heads?' says Eleni, and I assume she's talking about the new painting.

'I'm thinking about it,' I say. 'I'm thinking about stopping the big heads.' I look over. Her back is turned to the painting. She's not talking about the painting. She's sat up in the chair with my sketch pad open on her lap.

'Who is this?' she says.

'I've no idea,' I say. 'It's just a study from a photo in a magazine.'

'A pornographic magazine?'

Oh, if only my confession were that simple.

'No, it looks like that, doesn't it? I know. No, it's from some art magazine. I was just studying form.'

She looks closer and begins to shake a little. 'If this is from a magazine, then why is the corner of this chair in the picture?'

248

'Er . . .'

'Hector,' her voice is breaking up, 'Hector, who is this?'

'I've told you,' I say, rising through the octaves, 'I have no idea. The er . . . chair is there to suggest a sense of scale. To lend it . . . depth, er . . . perspective.'

She stands up and runs across the room. 'I'm going to be sick!' she declares, her hand over her mouth.

'Eleni,' I call after her, 'Eleni, I'm telling you the truth,' though I don't know why I bother, cos she's on her way to the bathroom, and in about three seconds the sham of the remark will be exposed by fact. I follow close behind.

At first she doesn't even notice. She runs directly to the toilet and collapses onto her knees. I put my arms around her waist and hold on tight as she empties her stomach into the pan. Awful, bestial, liquid convulsions, one after the other, four in all, and then she keeps her head down, awaiting the fifth. Her abdomen spasms beneath my fingers and I turn my head to look at Rosa. Now there's a painting. The mistress of all masterpieces. Fuck Rembrandt, Vermeer, Velázquez, Leonardo, fuck 'em all. Rosa's face in this moment. What new, cruel species of smile is this? She makes the enigma of *La Gioconda* look like Lucille Ball. I can't believe I'm here, living in this century, residing at this address, kneeling on this floor, holding onto these hips, staring into those eyes, suffering the punches of this worthless heart. I can't believe it. I really can't. But there you go, I'm stuck with it. I press my head against Eleni's shoulder and vomit down her back.

It's all going very well.

Idea For a Piece: Large white gallery furnished to resemble a hospital ward. Six empty beds. On the seventh bed lies the artist of the piece, dying. Catheters and masks. Books and flowers. Grapes and machines. The glowing green blip of a monitor. The bleached floor. The finished meal. A solitary bluebottle, let loose. Footless slippers. Rings removed. The artist dying. Really dying. Call it *About Time*.

I'm out on the street with Eleni. Will this rain never stop? The taxi is waiting, its diesel purr echoing against the cobbles.

'Eleni, don't go!'

'Of course I must go!'

'No, no, you absolutely must not. Not now.'

'How can I stay?'

'In a million ways!'

'There is not one way I can stay!'

'You have to let me explain.'

'No, Hector, you have to let me explain. You have taken everything that was having a past, and everything that was having a future, and you have screwed them up into the ball and kicked this ball through a sewer so it has turned into nothing. You have treated me without respect, you have abused everything that we ever had. Well, I hope that you have now what you were looking for, for all this time. I hope now that you can paint, Hector. I hope now that you can paint with the passion, as much as anyone has ever painted. As long as you're sure that my mother is enough for you.'

'What do you mean, am I sure that your mother is enough for me? What does that mean?'

'I mean is my dead mother enough death for you, Hector? Is it? Or which one will you be wanting to be next? Kirk? Your father? Then will that be enough? Or me? What about me?'

'Eleni, how can you say such things?'

'I open my mouth and move my tongue! Because it is true.'

'It is not true.'

'You don't even believe yourself when you say that.'

'Eleni, this is awful. This is the most awful moment of my life.'

'Then go and fucking paint!'

'Stop!'

'I'm going.'

'Just don't get into this taxi!'

'All there is left for me is to get into this taxi!'

'Eleni, come back inside!'

'Hector, goodbye!'

And she throws her bags into the taxi. I hold open the door.

'Eleni, I love you!'

'No, Hector, you do not love me! Love resists!'

'Eleni!'

'You have not resisted!' She ducks into the car and sits back.

'Where to, darling?' says the driver.

'Hell!' screams Eleni. Really screams. Screams like I have never heard her scream. And I have never heard her scream. Not once. 'Hell!' she screams again. Really, really screams. The driver fiddles with his meter.

'Eleni!' I plead.

'Just drive!' she barks. She slams the door and her grief is swallowed by the glass. I feel like she's shut herself up in some gas chamber. Or shut herself out. Maybe it's me, who must now inhale this poison. He lets off the handbrake and shifts it into first. I watch as his little brown shoes dance upon the pedals, and the next thing you know the whole package eases off. The back of Eleni's head – her beautiful Greek head – shrinking with the distance.

I watch it go.

Her go.

The humped taxi, like a fat black orthopaedic shoe, slides away. The orange indicator. The wide left turn. The puff of the exhaust. And then . . .

Nothing.

And only that which was there before.

Silence.

*

In the lift on the way back up, my heart is in my mouth, hanging out over my lips. I poke at it with my thumb. My tongue can't bear the taste. My brain can't bear the stink. I take a breath and spit it out. I watch it on the floor and crush it with my boot. The lift's bell rings. Here I am, on the fourth floor, and in I go. Now here's a most splendid conversation:

'Rosa,' I croak, leaning my head on the bathroom door. 'Rosa, please, say something.'

Silence.

'Rosa, let me explain.'

Silence. A turn of the knob. The squeak of the hinges.

'Rosa, really, let me explain.'

The rug scuffing up on the base of the door.

'Rosa?'

My feet across the threshold.

'Rosa?'

Silence. The silence of an empty bath and the last hundred bubbles, bursting against the enamel.

'Rosa?' I shout, out into the room, out into space, 'Rosa? Where are you?'

She is nowhere. Nowhere that I know.

I drift out into the hall and cock my ear to the stairwell. The distant patter of dirty combat boots on stone. The clunk of a Zippo. The twisting of a lock and the slamming of a door.

Idea For a Piece: The main door of the gallery, slammed shut over and over. Ten o'clock till six o'clock, six days a week, twenty-six weeks, over and over, again and again, every ten seconds, opened and then slammed, opened and then slammed. The artist dressed in blue. The door painted white. Call it *Communicating At An Unknown Rate.*

14

The last time I sat on this train, Eleni slept in my lap. I remember how I wanted everyone who passed to see her. To see how pretty she was in sleep. How happy and safe. How happy with me. I smiled at people just to attract their attention, just so they would notice her. I'm not smiling at anyone now, quite the opposite. In fact my radiant contempt must be affecting business at the buffet. No one wants to pass me twice. Can't blame them. I wouldn't want to pass me. On the other hand there is nothing I would rather do than pass me. At least then I could leave myself behind. Board another train. Go somewhere better. Be someone else. Perhaps that's what Monger has perfected. Perhaps he is someone else every few days. What bliss. To lead a thousand lives in the space of one – and then to make a bit of money on the back of it. What's his game, then?

There was no discourse between Eleni and Rosa. Rosa remained in the bath and Eleni ran into the bedroom. While she packed a couple of bags, I stood in the doorway, scratching my head, unable to utter one word – and the idea of putting two words alongside each other was completely beyond my comprehension. Hence, I was silent. Not one part of me made the smallest sound. Not even my heart, which had stopped and hardened into glass. And even when it shattered, deep inside my breast, and rained down on my bones, even then there was silence. Eleni's dresses fell into the suitcase like secret parachutes. Even her shoes made no sound. She packed away old diaries, documents, statements, certificates, a rosary, sunglasses, two toy owls and her favourite cow. All of them silent as they found their place in the hush of her luggage. I felt as though my head were underwater. Under Rosa's water. Which in turn made no sound. She was obviously not about to step out. And for that I was thankful.

If this was chess I'd simply lay my king on its side and shake the hand of my opponent. But it's not, and I can't, and I'm not even sure if my opponent has a hand. I believe he has a fist, but his fist is bloodless. His fist is made of diamonds and tar.

We're pulling into Warrington. I snap open another lager. I watch an ant as he crawls across my ticket. I flick him into oblivion.

There's seagull crap all over Dad's blue Mazda. I ring the bell and peer through the frosted glass for a shape in the hallway. Nothing. I ring again, a silly and erratic sequence of rings that I've been doing ever since I was tall enough to reach the bell. I don't have a set of keys. Never did. There's a Kentucky Chicken box in Mum's shrubbery and a parcel in the porch. I should have phoned to tell her what time my train got in. But I didn't, and now I'm locked out. But that's all right. I'm too drunk to bother much. In fact I might just be drunk enough to climb on top of the garage and squeeze in through the window of the spare room. Yeah, now I think about it, I'm definitely drunk enough to climb on top of the garage and squeeze in through the window of the spare room. Just let me lie down for a few minutes. Let me just lie here on the floor of the porch for a few minutes and snore beneath this boorish watercolour of Tintern Abbey. There's fly paper hanging from the lantern. A moth trapped in the letterbox. One of Sparky's old stools, drying on the lino. Damien would love this space. He could call it *Porch*. He could fill it with seawater and pills, call it *The Logic of Fossils in the Comical and Rococo Arsehole of a Long Distance Lorry Driver Called Balzac*. I don't know. I'm past caring, I really am. I sleep. I dream. In my dream I'm asleep, and in that sleep I dream, etc. My brain is dipped in lager and cheese, and when Mum wakes me up I wish that she hadn't. She wakes me with her foot.

'Hello, Mum.'

'Hector!' she yells, boggle-eyed, scandalized. 'What on earth are you up to?'

'What?'

'What on earth's going on?'

'Nothing's going on, Mum,' I say, 'what do you mean what am I up to? I said I'd come home today and I have. Here I am. I was locked out and I fell asleep in the porch. What's the big deal? What do you mean what's going on?'

'I mean why's your thingy out?'

'My thingy?'

'Your thingy's out,' she says and nods at my groin.

I look down. I'm wearing a pair of black button-up Levi's and all the buttons are undone. My green and yellow pants are peeled down to my thighs and sure enough, there it is, my thingy. My poor confused fucking thingy, basking in the dusk. That's it. That's definitely it. No more drinking.

As I help her unpack the shopping there's a long interrogation regarding my bald head and the bruises on my face. I manage to justify more or less everything and then it's back to my thingy in the porch. This I cannot justify. 'I must have been dreaming,' I say.

'About what?' says Mum.

'I have no idea.'

We can visit Dad at seven o'clock. Until then me and Mum sit in opposite chairs wolfing down plates of paella and lettuce. The paella's full of peas and they roll off my fork till I'm left with nothing but peas. Thirty, forty, perfectly spheroid, perfectly green, chemically shiny, stupidly salty, ignorant peas.

Idea For a Piece: Ten trillion peas packing out the Turbine Hall of Tate Modern. Er . . . that's it. *Peas In Our Time.*

'I thought you were going to go and see Eleni,' says Mum.

'I was going to see Eleni, I was, but then you rang and told me about Dad. How can I go and see Eleni when Dad's lying in hospital?'

'Have you heard from her?'

I take a breath. I've spent most of the journey preparing for this conversation. I've been over and over every option. Finally, exhausted by the demands of duplicity and the relentless maintenance of my deceit, I've resolved to tell the truth. Every last detail. Well, not everything. There's no need for me to go into too much detail regarding Rosa. I don't have to talk about ropes and knives and flambéed nipples. In fact I should just leave Rosa out of it for now. But I'll tell her everything else. I'll tell her that Eleni came home, but I won't explain the circumstances of her departure. But then Mum will want to know about her departure. Well, if I leave out the bit about Eleni actually coming home then I won't have to get into the whole departure thing. And anyway if I tell her about Eleni coming home then I'll have to explain why and that means telling Mum that Sofia's dead, and I'm not sure that I'm up to that right now. Not right after the paella.

'Well?'

'What?'

'I said have you heard from Eleni?'

'No.' There we go. Nicely handled.

Mum clears away the plates and shuffles off into the kitchen, her slippers barely leaving the carpet. 'Sparky's still not turned up,' she mutters as she banks the corner out of sight.

'He will,' I shout. Though I don't know why, cos he obviously won't.

*

Dad is stoned out of his mind. I don't know what they've given him but he looks like William Burroughs, propped up on his pillows, drawling on about the hospital food. Christ, he even sounds like Burroughs.

'And then they brought me some meringue, but I couldn't eat it and it was covered in pins and the wool wouldn't . . . it was singing that song. It was singing that song again.'

'Right, Dad.'

And he starts to whistle, but his mouth's all dry and white and all that comes out are toneless little puffs of breath. 'So what is that?' he says.

'I dunno.'

'Derek,' says Mum, placing her hand upon his, 'don't keep going on. You'll tire yourself out.'

He glances over with these new reptilian eyes and stares at Mum's hairdo. 'There's Sparky,' he says.

'Dad,' I interrupt, as Mum looks to the ceiling, 'Dad, listen, my exhibition went really well. You know that I had that show opening? Well it went really, really well. I've got lots of commissions. I've written a letter to Michael Parkinson, asking if I can paint him. The National Portrait Gallery have shown an interest in that one. Should get a lot of money for that one. I'll do it for you, Dad. I know how much you like Michael Parkinson.' He's looking at me, but he's staring straight through me. 'And guess what, here's the best part, you know that painting I did of you? Remember when I painted you? Well, it was in the show the other night and someone wants to buy it. And you know how much they want to buy it for, Dad? Eh?'

No response.

'For forty thousand pounds, Dad. Forty thousand pounds. And I thought that since it's of you, then some of that should come your way. In fact all of it should go to you. What do you think of that then, Dad? How do you fancy forty thousand pounds?'

Of course there's not a word of truth in any of this. His pyjama buttons are undone and there's a long strip of taped bandage cleaving his blue-and-mustard torso.

'What do you say, Dad?'

Dad looks at me as though I'm speaking Aramaic and turns to Mum. 'Who is this?' he asks her. 'Is it Mr Chorley? Is it Baldy Chorley, that bingo caller?'

'No,' says Mum, 'it's Hector. Hector, your son. He's had a haircut.'

'Remember when he wa' having a doo-dah wi' that Mrs Slatt and he kept fixing it for her to win? It wa' in the *Gazette*, 'bout three years back. He wa' buggering about wi' the balls, reading out whatever numbers came into his head, which were always the numbers where Slatt was sat. Remember that?'

'It's not Mr Chorley,' says Mum, 'it's our Hector.' She wipes his nose tube with her tissue. 'Derek, it's our Hector. Listen to what he's saying. Did you hear what he just said?'

No response.

'It's me, Dad. It's Hector. I was just saying, remember that painting I did of you? Well, someone's buying it.'

'Ey up,' says Dad, craning his neck to see behind me, 'there goes that chair again, off out the door.' He rests his head back on the pillow. 'It's a rum do,' he says and closes his eyes.

It was a beautiful thing. When we arrived home Mum made us both a cup of tea, set them down on the coffee table and then asked if I would draw her, like I did when I was little. And so I did. And you know what? It's the finest drawing I've ever done, by far. She lolled back in her chair and sipped at her tea. As I unpacked my charcoals and pads she began to weep. I worked fast, scratching at the paper, describing mad, erratic loops and lines, sometimes from the wrist, other times from the elbow. When I tackled her hairdo, it came straight from the shoulder and maybe my lower back. I wet my thumb with spit and smudged every shadow, one by one, starting with the jaw, ending with the relief of the fringe on the brow. Mum wept the whole way through.

'You know what this is about, Hector?'

'What what is about?' I said, breaking up another stick.

'It's all about that settee. All this would never have happened if I hadn't bought that bloody settee.'

'Well, you did, Mum, and that's that. There's no point in regretting what's done. Where's that gonna get you?' I sharpened the charcoal with my teeth and returned to the eyes, reworking the lashes.

'Do you know why I bought that settee, Hector?'

'No, Mum.'

'I bought it cos I'm not right in the head. I bought it cos something outside of me told me to buy it.'

I stopped drawing. For the first time I noticed the tick of the clock on the wall. 'What do you mean,' I said, 'something outside yourself?'

'I don't know,' she said and wiped at her cheeks with a scrap of pink tissue. 'Like a voice. Like someone else's voice was urging me to say yes and write out a cheque. Not my voice. A man's voice. The voice of a man. I knew I didn't like the bloody thing. I knew that your dad would hate it. I knew it was too much money, but there was this fella, in my head, whispering, "Buy it, Connie, buy it, Connie. You know you want to." And so I did, and I believed that I wanted to. Maybe it was because it reminded me of my grandmother. She had a settee a bit like that. Next thing you know, I've got my chequebook out and I'm booking a van. I don't know, Hector,' she said, 'does all that sound queer?'

'No, Mum,' I said, 'I understand.' I worked on her nostrils.

'I don't want to go mad, Hector,' said Mum, her face on her lap. 'I don't want to lose my mind.'

'I know, Mum,' I said, 'I know what you mean. Neither do I.'

This is my old bedroom. I mean it's nothing like my old bedroom as it's been my parents' since I left home. The wallpaper's changed, the carpet's changed, the curtains, the light fittings, the door handles, the door. I'd hardly recognize it were it not for the consistency of shape. It's the shape that comes flooding back, like a smell. On the shelf above the mantel-piece there's a framed photograph of my grandmother. The one feature that has never changed. Ever since I was born – and presumably long before – this small tinted photograph of Mum's mum in bloom. She's sitting on a bench in the garden of some stately hospice. She's wearing a yellow cardigan and her ginger hair is all blown to one side. She's smiling and nothing about the photograph suggests that three days later she will be dead. In the past I've turned this photograph to the wall, but not tonight. Not tonight Emily. Emily Lane, that was her name. I like that. I've always liked that. I like the way it sounds when it's spoken out loud. I like the way it feels in the mouth. It's a sensual thing.

I undress and lie back on the bed. My breast is scabbed and seared. I think of Sofia. Poor, burned Sofia. I think of her. How could I not, at a time like this?

So. She is gone. She has faded away to nothing in the space of a few days. Never to return. And what does it mean? How does it feel, Hector? What is your understanding of this? Can you feel it? Is there any part of your soul that can feel it, or is the loss merely somatic? Does any part of you register the shift? No? Well, then think about it. If not one part of you registers the shift then you're not thinking about it enough, or rather, you're thinking about it plenty, but the quality of thought is hardly incisive. Then make that incision. Dig deep. Dirty your hands. Dirty the whole caboodle. Don't fear the dirt, Hector. Not now. Not now, mate. The dirt is all you have.

All right, let me come at this from another angle. After all, this is it, Hector. This is death, this is really it – the real thing. At last, someone died. Now come on, get it together. This kind of thing is not to be sniffed at. Come at it from another angle, creep up on it from behind. Put your-self in Eleni's place. The woman who bore me, the woman who fed me, bathed me, gave me suck. Gone. How would I feel? I turn out the light and lie there in the dark. How would I feel? Gone. Once and for all.

Silence.

A passing car.

Silence.

Fuck, I'm hungry.

Silence.

I sneeze. I sneeze again and quite enjoy it.

Hmmm. So let's think about this. Sofia. Beautiful Sofia. Dead. Dead. The end. Well, er . . . now let's see. Let me just think about this. It feels er . . . Well, it feels . . . or should I say, I feel? Yeah, that's better. I feel. I feel er . . . Sofia, Eleni's mother is absolutely dead, totally finished and done with and I feel er . . . what? What do I feel? Er . . . I feel . . .

Shit! What's wrong with me? Shouldn't I be flailing around the mattress in a fit of impulsive despair? I'm not flailing at all. I'm dead still. And what's this? What the fuck is this? Is that a smile. Is that the ghost of a smile creeping across my lips? Oh my God I think it is!

Silence.

I smoke a fag out of the window. The night is full of ice, and all these vapours pouring from my lips, creeping through my teeth, serve only to remind me that nothing is real. Nothing will ever be real. Nor was it real in the first place. I think of Descartes, but not for long. In fact I only think of how to spell his name and something I once read about how he shut himself up in some oven to have a right good think about things. I mull it over for a while and wonder if such a thing might help. After a minute or so I abandon the idea. After all, I'm five foot nine, and weigh fifteen stone; I'd be lucky to get one leg into Mum's old Neff.

I awake in the middle of the night and scribble something in my sketchpad. In the morning I read it back. I dreamt of a pig. An enormous pig. Forty foot tall, resting on its haunches. The pig told me a poem. Here is that poem in full, verbatim, unexpurgated:

I am a joint of meat,
Not veal, nor beef, nor lamb.
My tail is short and sweet,
I oink – therefore I'm ham.

I make no apologies for this. I am not the author. Blame the pig. Or praise the pig. Whatever. I am not familiar with your tastes.

The next day we sit with Dad for two hours, but he's asleep the whole time. The nurse happens by every now and then and has a little chat with us. Eventually she introduces us to the doctor, Mr Poliakov, who was also, presumably, the surgeon, since he refers to the operation in the first person. I think he's boasting a bit and take a consuming dislike to him. But then I've always disliked doctors. Something to do with their mania to save life at all costs. Things should never be that simple. Basically, Poliakov's a bit worried about Dad. He's not doing as well as the other blokes on the ward and his blood pressure is still alarmingly high. They've administered him some pills to thin things out, but so far, well . . . 'We'll just have to wait and see,' says Poliakov, before strolling over to the other side of the room, consulting his notes.

It's difficult to think of things to say. Mum's sat upright in her chair on the other side of the bed. What is there to say? How can we possibly discuss anything other than the crisis set before us? And yet how can we possibly discuss the crisis set before us? We sit there for another hour. It is the longest silence of my life. The sort of silence that might be broken at any moment. The sort of silence that may shift, but never does. That sort of silence. The worst kind, believe me – I know about silence.

Dad's face is as white as a plate. His hands are on the edge of blue, that blue that's on the edge of grey. That grey that's on the edge of green. That green that will soon give way to brown and all manner of blacks. For the first time in my life, I hold his hand. I don't know what it feels like. I think of Rosa. God knows why, but I do. I wonder where she is, what she's thinking. At one point I find myself wondering what she's wearing. Something blue, perhaps. I look around the ward and feel sicker than the lot of them.

If I don't have a cigarette soon I'm going to explode all over this car. Mum's curled up in the passenger seat going through a box of tissues. There seems to be no end to the tears in her head. I wonder if it's possible to die from crying. Not that I'm in any danger of that. I keep my dry eyes on the road.

'Do you want the radio on?' I say.

'Do I hell as like want the radio on,' says Mum.

'Righto,' I say and pass her another tissue, as though she can't do it for herself.

Silence.

'Mum,' I say, 'he'll be all right, you know. Nothing's gonna happen to him.'

'We don't know that, Hector,' says Mum. 'Don't be an idiot. Your dad's getting old. I'm getting old. In fact there's no getting about it, we're old, the pair of us. We might go at any time. You have to start preparing for that.' She sounds a little cross with me. I wish she didn't cos it makes me feel like running the car off the road into some shop window.

'And how do I do that?' I protest. 'How do you prepare yourself for something like that?'

Mum stares off to her left. 'By accepting it as a real possibility. Not just by saying that everything's gonna be all right all the time.' She can't look me in the eye. 'Cos it might not be. There's no good reason to say that it will be. You just have to give it some thought.'

'I do, Mum,' I say, 'I do give it some thought.'

Jesus, Mum! Jesus monkey-legs-Costello, do I give it some thought.

She goes into the glove compartment looking for more tissues, but it's empty save for a small torch and an old Liza Minnelli cassette.

'I'm sorry,' she sniffles, 'I'm ever so sorry.'

'What are you sorry for?'

'I'm sorry for leaving you alone.'

'What do you mean, leaving me alone?'

She's got her hand over her face and the tears are running down her wrist. 'I never gave you a brother or a sister. I'm sorry.'

'Mum,' I say, finding it difficult to carry on driving.

'I'm sorry that there'll only be you when we're gone.'

'Mum, stop talking like this. You're still here, Dad's still here.' The road is turning into a billion scarlet crystals.

'I'd like to have held a little grandkiddy before I . . . to have seen some part of me and . . . but I suppose that's not going to . . .'

I pull over to the kerb and hit the brakes. 'Mum,' I say, putting my arms around her, 'stop it. Please stop it. Today's a day just like any other day. Yeah, Dad's a bit sick right now, but he's had an operation, and I know he doesn't look too bright, but who does after something like that? And you will hold a little grandson or daughter. Both! Three of each! Eleni'll come back from Greece, her mother will be fine, everything'll be fine. Just give us a bit of time. Give yourself a bit of time. Give Dad a bit of time.'

Mum opens the window and dries her chin. 'Why have we stopped? Take us home.'

We don't say much more. Two miles pass in silence. Halfway through the third mile, pulled up at the traffic lights, Mum turns to me and belts me across the head with the wide, flat slab of her hand. She struggles with the door and runs off down the street, ducking into some alley. I've never seen Mum run before. Not even when I was little. Mum was never a runner. But she's running now. There she goes, tiny little steps, bent at the waist, her handbag flying out behind her. Christ, she can shift, can the lass. Look at her go. I can't find it within myself to follow. Maybe she longs for me to follow, to take her in my arms and promise never to go. Or maybe she wants to be alone. In which case I'm a good son, cos that's the way I leave her.

The lights have turned green but I've forgotten how to drive the car. You might as well ask me to drive the space shuttle. All I can see is dials and pedals. None of it means anything. A mob of horns break out behind me. A couple of cars get it together to pull wide of me and pass, but the remaining six, stranded back at red, let loose their fury with a sequence of klaxons and curses. This is the new music. Music to make your skull glow. I step out of the car and walk to the car behind. The driver winds down his window relishing the prospect of a good old-fashioned exchange of accusation and slander, but I'm having none of it. I'm sick of it. I'm sick of only words. Like Kirk said, 'Words mean nothing at all.' I step back and balance precariously on one leg, whilst thrusting the other into the cabin of my accuser. My foot connects with his head and his dentures fly out onto the passenger seat.

I've never kicked anyone in the head before. Nor slapped, nor punched. I have gone through life without ever committing one single act of violence upon the body of another. Until now. I can't say I regret it. I can't say I didn't enjoy it. I did enjoy it. I dare say that I enjoyed it in inverse proportion to how much he didn't enjoy it. Or maybe he did. Who's to say what monsters are left roaming the streets these days.

'I've forgotten how to drive, OK?' My face is right up to the open window. 'My dad just died, my mother just ran off down some alley and I've forgotten how to drive, OK?'

'I'm sorry,' says the man, holding onto his jaw.

'My dad is fucking dead!' I scream. 'Dead!' The whole street can hear. I feel reborn. Pedestrians are stopping in their tracks. 'Have you any idea how that feels?'

He shakes his head and mutters, 'No.'

'Have any of you?' Now I'm addressing the entire street. 'Have any of you any idea how that feels?' I find myself waiting for an answer since the question, I suddenly realize, is not strictly rhetorical. Silence. Good.

'Well, it feels like having all the shit that you've ever shat stuffed back up your arse in one sitting!' This one is announced to the whole town. Unfortunately, much to my er . . . chagrin – I believe that's the word – it is also announced to Mum, who is standing on the corner of the alley, wondering why I haven't followed her. She's struggling for breath, leaning against the wall. She pauses a moment to take it all in and makes off again, back down the alley.

I look at the driver and think about spitting, but I don't. After all, I'm not a savage.

Pedestrians start to move along, drama over, slightly dejected, as though they were expecting more. The driver winds up his window and replaces his dentures. I stride off back to the car, fighting the burning agony of my exertion. Trying, with every atom of my might, not to hold onto the groin that I've just torn asunder.

I've been back at home for an hour and Mum still hasn't shown up. The house is freezing. All over the floor there are photographs of Dad. I've spread them out into some sort of emotionally chronological order. About fifty, sixty Dads, all gazing out from the lounge carpet.

The phone rings.

Such is the silence of home that my guts are sent into a sudden fist.

Ring, ring. Ring, ring. Just like when I was a boy.

Mum and Dad still favour a phone with a dial and when it rings it rings exactly like phones used to ring. The way they should always ring. For some reason they keep it out in the hallway on a little wicker table, with nowhere to sit.

Maybe it's Mum.

I hope it's not Mum.

I don't want Mum to phone.

I want Mum to ring the doorbell.

I don't want a scenario whereby Mum is sobbing in some phone box on the edge of the M6. I want her here, safe inside. Safe in my arms, cos then I'll find the words. I've given it a lot of thought and I think I know what to say now. I think it's all gonna be all right. In fact I'm sure it is.

'Hello? Mum?'

'Hector?'

'Dad?'

'Hector?'

'Dad! What are you—'

'No, Hector, it's me. It's Lenny.'

'Lenny!' I shout, as though I haven't heard from him in over a decade. 'Lenny, mate, how are you?'

'Yeah, good.'

This is obviously not true, since he sounds like he's speaking from the bottom of a mineshaft, up to his neck in water.

'What is it, Len? What's the matter? Is it Brenda?'

'No, it's not Brenda, er . . .' The line goes dead.

'Hello? Lenny?'

'Yeah, I'm still here.'

'Right, cos I thought that the line had gone dead.'

'No, I'm still here.'

'So what is it?'

'Hector, listen . . . are you listening?'

Oh God, I don't like the sound of this. Why is he asking me if I'm listening? Of course I'm fucking listening. What does he think I'm doing? 'Yeah, Len, of course I'm listening.'

Fearing that I may be about to fall to it, I lie down on the floor. Fuck it's cold.

'Hector,' whispers Lenny, 'Kirk's dead.'

Silence. Absolute. The collision of dust. The breath of mites. The sound of nothing bumping into never.

At last I say, 'What?' as one does on reception of bad news, thus urging the messenger to revisit the agony of the report.

'Kirk died this morning.'

'Kirk died?'

'Yeah. He's dead, Hec. His mum phoned me about an hour ago. I'd have called you straight away but I haven't stopped crying.' He pauses and I can hear that he's off again. And you know what? I think I might be about to join him. I think this might be it. I think this might be the Big One. I thought that Sofia might have been the Big One, but then I hardly knew her, and when it came to the crunch it turned out that she wasn't the Big One at all. But this is different. This is Kirk. Little Kirk Church with his bonkers blue face.

'Oh my God!' I say. It's something to say.

'I know, Hec,' says Lenny, 'I can't get my head round it.'

'Neither can I.'

'It's like going back thirty-one years.'

'Thirty-one years?'

'Come on, Hec, what happened thirty-one years ago?'

'I really don't know, Lenny, what happened thirty-one years ago?'

'It's thirty-one years since my dad died.'

Bastard! Oh, he had to bring that up, didn't he? Had to get that little dig in. Had to take the first tentative steps towards the subjugation of my grief. Christ, I can't believe that he's gone for it so early in the game. Like a goal scored from the centre spot. I can't fucking believe it. The audacity of the man. There should be laws against this kind of thing.

'Oh my God!' I say again, until I can work out the next thing to say. It's not easy. You think this sort of thing is easy? No, it's not easy. In fact I know what I'll do. I'll just cry. The tears are there awaiting instruction; the lump in the throat, the fever behind the eyes, the build-up of snot. Snot and spit of the finest quality, saved up for just such an eventuality. Here goes, I'll show him. I'll show him who's who and what's what when it comes to suffering. Just like when his dad died! Hah! I'll show the fucker a thing or two. Here goes. Boo hoo. Boo hoo.

'Hector, lad. Hector, don't.'

'Why not? What do you expect me to do? You expect me not to cry?

Lenny, you've just told me that our best friend's dead. What do you fuckin' expect? You expect me not to cry? Huh? You expect me not to cry? Is that what you expect?' I might be laying it on a bit thick here. I'm sounding like Harvey Keitel.

'Hector, this is awful. Really fucking awful. I don't know what to say. I erm . . . I can't really speak right now. I just thought that I should let you know . . . and . . .'

'And I appreciate that.' Big sniff.

'I really don't know what there is to say. I feel like you and me have so much to say to each other at the moment, and we're not saying it. Or you're not saying it. And something like this . . . well . . . I don't know. It feels like the world just turned into a gas planet and . . . Listen, let's talk when you get back, OK?' His sobs have reached the pitch of wailing. I therefore work on an acoustic beyond wailing. Some might call it shrieking. Controlled shrieking I'd say, but shrieking nonetheless. This is how it goes:

'OK, Lenny. OK,' shriek, followed by a long moan, 'OK, let's just think about all this. Oh my God! Oh my God, Lenny!' Implausibly protracted whimpering. 'Listen, I have to go. I can't do this. Not on top of everything else. Not with Sofia and Dad and Mum and . . .' Almost a howl.

'How's your dad?' he squeaks through a blocked nose.

I open up my jaw and make a sound so racked and primeval that there is nothing for it but to hang up the phone and collapse into the nap of the carpet. After all, Kirk is dead and, no matter what I might have led you to believe, my universe is coming apart at the seams. At least I think it is. I mean, it must be. It should be. No, it is. Of course it is. What do you take me for? I mean, come on, Kirk is dead. My friend, my beautiful friend. I mean, come on. You think I don't feel something like that? You think this kind of thing doesn't go through me like hot needles? I'm not messing about here. This is the Big One. Oh yes, this is the real thing, and I'm in hell. I'm sure Lenny is also in hell, but not the kind of hell that I'm in. No, Lenny's hell, terrible though I'm sure it is, at least has cushions, and fags, and toilets, and beds. My hell has none of these. My hell is like the surface of Pluto. Not a blanket in sight. In fact, no sight. Only ice. Nothing but ice. That's the kind of hell I've got, Lenny. So what do you think of that?

Somewhere around midnight Mum came home. I'd raided Dad's supply of lagers that he keeps under the stairs. In fact I drank them under the stairs, chatting away to the laundry basket and a packet of seeds.

I was awoken by the incessant punching of the bell. She pushed past me and made her way upstairs to attend to her toilet. A son does not interrupt his mother when she's attending to her toilet. And fast on the heels of her ablutions came bed. I never stood a chance.

For a long time I sat outside the bedroom door and eavesdropped on her sobbing. I pressed my ear up against the painted wood until it dwindled to nothing. The air felt hungry for more, so I curled up on the landing and cried my heart out. Cried it all the way out. Cried it right down the stairs and off out the door, up the hill and down, on its way to the beach and, inevitably, out to sea. All the way to Ireland, across and over the hills to Blacksod Bay and on and across, all the way to America.

Oh God, Rosa. What are you thinking?

I've taken off all my clothes and I'm curled up in the bath, staring at Bob the budgie. Little dead Bob. It's impossible not to think of Kirk.

But I don't know what to think. Maybe it's not about thinking. Maybe thinking shouldn't come into it. But how can one not think at a time like this? What am I supposed to do? Not think? I'm thinking. I'm trying to think.

No one likes to be awoken by a phone ringing in the middle of the night. Worse still, a phone that rings and rings, stops, and then rings again.

Stops and rings, over and over. No one likes that sort of thing. No one that I know. I know I don't.

Mum must have taken a sleeping pill or two, cos when I finally emerge from my bedroom, there she is on all fours at the top of the landing, trying to lift her head to negotiate the stairs.

'It's all right, Mum,' I whisper, turning her around and pointing her in the direction of her bed. 'You go back to sleep. I'll get it.'

'Id'lll bi ve hopisal . . . hopistal . . .' she mumbles, a rope of drool between her lips and the knuckle of her left thumb.

'No, no, Mum. It's probably some drunk with the wrong number.'

'Id'lll bi abow y' da . . . bow . . . Deri.'

Christ, what's she taken?

'Mum, go back to bed,' I whisper, and I give her rump a little push with my knee. Off she goes, banging her head on the doorframe.

The phone stops just as I reach the bottom of the stairs. What a deformed sort of silence: the silence between alarms. It's difficult to breathe in such a silence. Impossible to move the eyes. Impossible to move. I squat in the hallway, naked and shivering. I can hear a can in the front yard, clattering against the rockery. My teeth are clenched. I think I might be stuck like this for life.

When the phone rings again I almost pass out. Up in Mum's room I hear a vase crash to the floor.

'Hello?'

Silence.

'Hello?'

Silence.

'Hello? Who is this?'

The line isn't dead. The line is alive. I can hear a siren in the distance and a soft breath. I can hear the creaking of plastic. Maybe a stomach.

'Hello? Who is this?'

More silence.

Well, I suppose the good news is that it's not the hospital.

'Eleni? Eleni, is that you?' I hear the barking of a dog. 'Eleni, say something.'

Silence.

Something tells me that it's not Eleni. 'Listen, you've been ringing this number for the past quarter of an hour. The least you can do is say something. Who is this?'

The line goes dead.

I hear Mum up on the landing, collapsing onto her face as her elbows give way.

'Mum, it's not the hospital. It's just someone messing about. It's definitely not the hospital. Now go back to bed.'

I hear her pivot on her knees and, once more, her head smacks against the doorframe.

My teeth alternate between clenched and chattering. I'm hugging myself up into a tight ball and turning blue. What now? Aren't things difficult enough right now? What now? Who now? I sit there for another five minutes before it occurs to me that it really might be just some drunk with the wrong number. Or some drunk with the right number. What do I know? I don't know anything about Mum and Dad's friends.

I must have polished off a couple more lagers cos when I wake up, my nose pressed against my shoulder and my neck folded in two, I see a couple of cans lying on their side. I was dreaming about Lenny until the phone rang again. I was dreaming that he was lost at sea on top of a bouncy castle. He had one of those contraptions you see in old war films where you have to blow down some funnel to speak to the panicking captain. His brow was pearled with milky sweat.

I pick up the phone. 'Hello?'

'Er . . . ergggggggghhhhhhh . . . ah . . . ahhhh . . . eerrrrrrggghhh.'

'Lenny?'

Silence.

'Lenny, is that you?'

Silence.

Suddenly alerted to something going on at the top of the stairs I look over my left shoulder. I wish that I hadn't.

Mum's naked and sliding down the stairs on her belly, one stair at a time, arms stretched out in front of her, like she's body surfing – which I suppose she is in a way. In fact there's no 'in a way' about it – Mum's body surfing down the stairs on her big fat naked belly, totally stoned, no idea where she is, no idea who she is, no idea who I am, in fact no idea about anything as she arrives at the bottom and concertinas against the banister, her bum pushed up against the wallpaper. An unprecedented spectacle, I dare say. But then what do I know? I left home twenty-five years ago.

'Lenny? Lenny, listen, if that's you then you're doing this at a very bad time.'

'Oogggghhhhhaaaaaaaghhhha ha ha ha ha gggggghhhhh!'

Shit. I don't like the sound of that. I don't care who it is; I don't like the sound of that.

I put my hand over the mouthpiece. 'Mum? Mum, you all right?'

Her nostrils start to snore.

Another ton of silence comes in through the front door.

'Who is this? Please, please tell me who this is. If you're just someone trying to—'

'Hector!'

Shit, they know my name.

'Hector.'

'Monger?'

Silence.

'Monger, is that you?'

He offers up a small laugh, and then a sniff, and then: 'Hector, my dear, you know perfectly well who it is.'

This is going to be difficult. Even when I thought that Monger had appeared in my life as a figure of salvation it was difficult to stomach the unction of his tone, but now that he's revealing himself as some sort of nemesis then I don't know how long I can hold out. 'Monger, what's going on? What have you done? What are you doing? Why are you doing this to me?'

'Kicking strangers in the head,' says Monger. 'Kicking strangers in the head and driving away. Not good, Hector. Not good.'

Oh Christ, he's here. He's still here in Blackpool. My life is turning into an urban myth. Next I'm gonna find out he's speaking from the upstairs extension.

Take control, Hector! Yeah, I will. Go on, then. All right, give me a fucking chance. You've got to take control. I know. Don't you think I know? Yeah. Yeah, I've got to take control.

'You murdered Sparky!' I scream, sounding a bit like Bonnie Langford.

'Who's Sparky?'

'The dog! Our dog! You murdered our fucking dog!'

'Hector, calm down, sir.'

'You murdered our dog, you robbed my fucking parents – my dad's in fucking hospital – you fucking . . . psycho! What's going on? What do you want? What have I done? What do you want?'

'Blood,' says Monger, and leaves it at that.

'Blood?' I squeal, and then clear my throat. 'Did you just say blood?'

'What do you think I said?'

'I'm going to the police.'

'Hector,' he whispers (I imagine him with his head tilted forward, showing me only his brain and eyes), 'if you go anywhere near a policeman I will kill you. I will murder you very slowly, with things you didn't realize you could be murdered with.'

I can scarcely breathe. It's a first. No one has ever threatened my life before. It feels rather exciting. Like I'm really living.

Idea For a Piece: A murderer sat in an armchair in the middle of the gallery. On his lap, a set of kitchen knives. No bars, no guards, just you and the untethered killer. Call it *You Pays Your Money, You Takes Your Chances*.

'You don't scare me,' I say, glancing at Mum's sleeping face. 'You think you scare me? You don't scare me.'

'You don't believe me?' whispers Monger. 'You think I'm not up to it? Look at your rat of a dog. You think I'm joking? You think my father committed suicide? You think that my father possessed the mathematical agility to construct a knot like that? Think about it, Hector. You think my father possessed the industry to persevere with such a knot? Hell, he could have just swallowed pills if he was going to do it himself. Oh yes. Oh most certainly yes, Mr Kipling, a noose like that takes craft. Or should I say art? You go to the police, Hector, and I will kill you slower than anyone has ever been killed before. I will go into *The Guinness Book of World Records* with how slowly I will kill you.'

Silence.

There is nothing to say. I mean, really, what can you say to someone when they announce something like that?

15

BOX STREET, BOW, LONDON

On the train back the next day I saw off the morning's hangover with endless vodkas. I tried to read the papers but I'd forgotten how to read. I tore every picture to pulp with a sharp blue biro. No one was spared. England smashed past the window. Sheep on its hills. Dogs in all its filthy alleys. Factories and fields. Oblivion. Wet, green, black and brick-red oblivion.

The morning had been a kind of midnight. Hopeless misery as me and Mum prepared a breakfast that neither of us could face; and prepared is hardly the word. Mum kept leaning against the washing machine baring her teeth and clenching her eyes. Now and then she stuck out her tongue like a Maori and stared straight through me, hands up in the air, fingers spread. My own behaviour was not much better. As the beans came to the boil I carried the pan through to the lounge and poured them into the fish tank. Now there was a death for you. Death by hot beans. Not the sort of thing you see every day.

Idea For a Piece: A ton of hot baked beans suspended in a glass box high above the gallery floor. The show runs six days a week for two months. At a random hour on any one of twelve unspecified days the beans spill down onto the punters' heads. Call it *You Pays Your Money, You Takes Your Chances II.*

There was no way I could justify my return to London without telling Mum about Sofia and Kirk. So tell her I did. And what a charming half-hour that was. Mum plucked away at her tights till there were more holes than tight. Events were reported in a voice about two thousand octaves higher than my normal register – which, by the way, is rather deep; much deeper than you might expect from a man of my sensitivity.

'Threes,' said Mum.

'Threes?' I said.

'Deaths come in threes.'

'Mum,' I said, and pulled off a little snore, 'come on. You know that's just an old wives' tale.'

'Well, that's just what I am,' she scowled, 'an old wife!' She took off her slippers and hurled them at the window.

Oh my God. What if she's going the way of Aunty Pat? The last thing Pat did, before they came round with the buckled jacket, was order a taxi. She put all her stuff into the boot: old letters, photographs, bed sheets, toiletries, a change of clothing and a jar of sugared almonds.

'Where to, love?' said the driver.

'1922,' said Aunty Pat, 'and can we stop at an off-licence on the way?'

Mum sat back in her chair and fell asleep. I woke her up when the cab arrived and she went all soppy, hooping her arms around my neck and telling me to be careful, as though I were Jason about to tackle the clashing rocks. Which, in a way, I suppose I was.

'Now you go and find Eleni,' she said. 'Hug her half to death,' (curious choice of phrase), 'tell her I'm thinking about her. And hug Kirk's mum from me. I've never met her, but just tell her that your mum sends her a hug. And Lenny – hug Lenny for me.'

'I will, Mum,' I said, though that seemed like an awful lot of hugely implausible hugs. 'And look, Mum, look . . .' and I gave her the biggest hug I've ever given her. The biggest hug any son has ever given any mum, ever.

As the train approached Euston I thought about throwing myself out of the door. But just as we passed the Roundhouse, we slowed down

277

suddenly and the worst that could have happened was a sprained ankle. And I didn't want that. Not on top of everything else.

Having sat here on top of the stepladders for five hours, doing nothing, thinking nothing, being nothing, I think it's safe to say that my brain is in shock. It's a curious phenomenon, one's brain being in shock. It feels like your entire soul has queued for weeks to find a space near your eye sockets. There are scraps of soul behind the nose, at the back of the throat, marauding across the tongue and buried deep within the ears. But for the most part the finest seats are around the eyes. At times like these all you can do is breathe, and swallow now and then. Your human-ity is reduced to involuntary spasms. I think you could say that I'm in a bad way. Sat atop these ladders, snapping brushes, burning money, whistling 'Misty', chewing on old cherries that should have been thrown out a fortnight ago.

I climb down from the ladder and push it over onto the wooden floor, relishing the sound. A sound that makes sense. I walk into the kitchen and smash a few things. I visit the bedroom drawers and rip up a few things. I lean against a leg of Eleni's piano and smoke until my tongue is hot. And then I put my face into my hands and laugh like a lunatic in bloom, which is fine. There's something uniquely gratifying about put-ting your face into your hands and laughing like a lunatic in bloom.

The phone rings. I pick it up. It's Myers. I put it down. Easy. I'd like to put him down.

I'm going to call Eleni. Any moment now, I'm going to call Eleni. I love Eleni. Eleni is the only woman I have ever loved. The only human being for whom I would hurl my body upon the blast of a grenade (I acknowledge that such an eventuality is hypothetical and ultimately unlikely, but it's the principle that counts).

The phone rings again. Lenny's prosaic message, and then: 'Hector, Joe Myers here. Was that you just now? Did you hang up on me? I've been leaving messages for days and days, Hector. I spoke to Lenny Snook and erm . . . well, he told me that you had some problems back home. Erm . . . well, listen, I don't want to bother you if you've got a lot of stuff on your proverbial plate but I've got Alfred Lapping from the Doodlebug breathing down my neck and, well, listen . . . Lenny intimated that you might have some information regarding what happened at the show last Tuesday, and so on. I mean, regarding the identity of the assailant. He seemed to think that you might have spoken to him. So erm . . . Anyway, what I've done is, I've given the police your phone number and address. I hope that's all right. It's just that Lapping needs to make an insurance claim so . . . Well, listen, Hector, just give me a call. It's Joe Myers and—'

Bleep.

I spend the next hour stood on my head. Very enjoyable. I wake up with bleeding feet, having toppled over at some point and smashed straight through the glass coffee table. I wrap them in towels and pluck away at my left eyebrow. Ten more hairs and it will be completely gone.

You know what I can't bear? I can't bear the indifference. Or is it the disappointment I can't bear? I'd expected so much more than this. I mean I've cried for Kirk, I've cried for Sofia; endless, endless hours of unabandoned sobbing. But eventually the sobbing abates and then you're met with a baffling lull. An indefinable, hollow stoicism that you learn, in time – in not very much time – to refer to as acceptance. And before you know it, it's as though nothing has happened. There persists an all-pervading sense of incredulity, but this can hardly be logged as an emotion. In fact quite the opposite. In the midst of this open-mouthed disbelief, emotion is found wanting. You wonder why you're not tearing out your veins at their source, but really you know. Ultimately you know the answer to this: it's because, really – really, deep down, deep as it gets – you don't really care. Not really. Not like you're supposed to care. Not like people used to care.

The doorbell rings. I ease open one of the loading doors and look down. There's a police car in the street. The doorbell rings again, a copper looks up and sees me there, standing in the open loading doors looking down.

'Go away!' I mouth, waving my hands.

'Mr Kipling?' shouts the copper, his head tilted so far back that his cap falls off.

I raise my voice a little. 'I don't know anything! If you're here to ask me if I know something then the answer's no. I don't know anything about anything, no matter what you've been told.'

'It's about the assault on your painting, Mr Kipling,' says the copper, his hand on his radio.

'Go away!' I shout, scanning the street for any sign of Monger. 'Please go away. I don't know. I have no information to give you. Please, please, I'm very busy.'

'Just a few questions,' says the policeman.

'No!' I scream. 'No questions. Now fuck off!'

I close the door and take a step back. One step hardly seems enough, so I take a few more. I take so many steps back that I end up by the front door. What I should really do is keep going. I should wait for the police to drive away and then keep on stepping back. I should be outside. I should be walking the streets, not pacing this room. In the street there are certain laws by which I must abide. In here there are none. In here anything seems possible. In here the most heinous activities might pass unprosecuted. It distresses me to discover myself thinking in such terms. But what can I do? How can I not? The brain is not playful. Not really. The brain is committed to a rigid system with which no other organ can compete. The brain has its agenda and colludes with the fingers to see that demands are met. Eyes, on a leash. Liver, fuelled. Heart, whipped. Cock, primed. I should be outside. I should definitely make my way out into the street.

It looks like Lenny's settee might be finished. He's fitted a new door to the base and painted it red with '206' in black on it – the number of his childhood house. He's built up a hidden wedge beneath the supporting arm so that the whole thing stands on its end, erect, seven feet high. The window, the curtains, the follicles, the slapped-on coat of varnish. Huge fleshy settee. Who lives in a house like this? I walk over and pause before the door, my fingers on the handle. The whole thing stands and falls on what is behind this door. My love for Lenny depends on what happens next.

I open the door.

Nothing.

Nothing at all.

Just the hollow shell of an expurgated settee.

I step inside and close the door behind me.

It's a peculiar feeling, stood here inside this settee. The settee that put my dad in hospital, the settee that has driven my mother to the edge of sanity. The settee bought and delivered by a man who has threatened to kill me.

I slump down in one corner and gaze at the light creeping in through the window. I might just love it in here. There is no reason to leave. I close my eyes and dive. I close my eyes and examine every nook. Immaculate silence. Elegantly sightless. Oh yes. I gaze out into the wilderness. Creamy black. I focus on a solitary molecule and step inside. Inside it is warm, in a small kind of way. Small warmth. My brain beats. I don't want to admit it. It's the last thing I want to admit. But you know what, Lenny? Fuck, I'll tell you what, Lenny: I think it's a masterpiece.

I'm awoken by the phone. The machine clicks on and then clicks off again. Eleni. It must have been Eleni. Or Rosa, it might have been Rosa. Or Mum, or Monger. Any of them. Anyone else would have left a message. I turn over, push my shoulder blades against the door, and stretch out my legs into the recess of the backrest. This is where I live now.

I spent the first six years of my life overlooking a busy road and so am accustomed to heavy traffic. In fact I would go so far as to say that

I am inordinately fond of the rumble of passing engines. Maybe these sounds, at an early age, made their way into my dreams, and never woke me. It's everything else that wakes me. The smallest of sounds may wake me. I am often woken by my own breath, for example. By the dripping of a tap, or the yawning of some buried pipe. The hum of life wakes me. The opening of a door wakes me. The sound of voices wakes me. The sound of one of my best friends giggling with some girl, when my other best friend has just died, wakes me. The sound of boots on wood and drunken shushes wakes me.

'What are you doing?' I hear him whisper. 'Come in, for fuck's sake what's the big deal?'

'I should go,' whispers Rosa, 'this whole thing is so fucked.'

'Come in!'

'No, I wanna go. Let me go!' And I hear a brief scuffle. I hear two bodies in opposition. Her heels sliding across the boards, a punch, a squeal, two voices laughing and then her arse down on the floor. One of them sneezes. Her buttocks sliding across the polished pine. Black tights snagged on a nail. Bracelets and boots. The voices getting louder in their attempts to keep it down.

'Where is he?'

'He's in Blackpool.'

'How do you know he won't come back?'

'Because he won't. Because he'd have told me if he was coming back.'

'I should phone him.'

'Yeah, go on, do that. Phone him.'

'Lenny, I don't think I should be here. I don't know what I'm doing here.'

'You're doing this,' I hear Lenny say, and then . . . silence.

To Rosa's credit I can hear her heels scuffing around and then a lunge and then a slap. To her discredit the slap seems to make her laugh and then silence once more.

This silence is the worst of all. Of all silences mentioned heretofore, this silence is the worst of all.

'Hey,' squeals Rosa, 'you put a door on the bottom of the couch!'

'Yeah,' says Lenny, like he's split the fucking atom.

'Why'd you put a door on it? That looks kinda dumb.'

'Why's it dumb?' says Lenny, a little perturbed. I'm tempted to step out and answer at length.

'I don't know. I mean the whole thing looks like skin, like with all the hairs and stuff, but then it's got a fucking window and a door, man, I dunno, I just don't get what it's supposed to be.'

'It's whatever you want it to be.'

'Right, yeah, that's the bromide of the cop-out. What do you want it to be? That should be the point.' What a girl.

'I want it to engage you in a dialogue about home and soul. It's a kind of exoskeletal sanctum sanctorum. A suburban carapace.'

'A what?' sniggers Rosa.

'A parody of domestic synergy.'

'But it's just basically, fucking ugly.'

'Ah,' whispers Lenny, and then, 'the ugly may be beautiful, the pretty, never.'

'I've heard that before.'

'Paul Gauguin.'

It was difficult enough holding down the puke after all that suburban carapace crap, but now my entire upper body, and a good half of the lower, is consumed by foaming bile.

'Look,' continues Lenny, 'I'll show you.'

In the time between realizing that he is about to open the door, and the door actually opening, my eyes dart about in their sockets like giddy bingo balls, looking for a place to hide, as though I were the size of a fly and such a thing might just be possible.

And suddenly, there I am, cowering in the one corner of this one-cornered atrocity, my bloody feet wrapped in bloody towels, my bloody scalp, shoulders, chest and back, and every other bloody part, cracked and blistered and swollen and bruised, exposed and illuminated by the dying light of the East End sun.

'Evening,' I say, doffing a hat I wish I had.

Rosa in shock.

Lenny in shock.

But neither of them in anywhere close to the kind of shock that I'm in.

'I'd ask you in,' I say, 'but I've got nothing to offer you.'

'Hector!' says Rosa.

'Nothing at all, I'm afraid.'

'Hector,' says Lenny, one part accusatory, two parts accused, 'you're back.'

'Oh yes,' I say, shifting not one muscle, 'I'm back. Hi, Rosa.'

'Hi.' There's a new expression on her face. Fuck, is there no end to this girl's talents?

I wink and return my attention to Lenny. 'I expect your next question is what the fuck am I doing in here.'

'Er . . .'

He's wearing a long magnolia mackintosh, a plum baseball cap and a pink checked shirt that looks unnervingly like gingham.

'Well, I'll tell you what I'm doing in here . . .' and I start to cry. I cry and cry and cry. Of course I do. What better way to combat his ignorant levity? What better way to stab him in the heart, other than actually stabbing him in the heart? Which remains an option.

'Hector, Hector,' coos Rosa, kneeling down and cradling my head in her lap. 'Angel, my angel,' and she places her palm upon my brow. Her soothing palm, save for her nails and the kick of her rings. I'm too confused to stop crying. If I stop crying I'm gonna have to start talking. But talking is out of the question. There is nothing to say. All I have to express is being expressed right now; sobbing into Rosa's lap, her fingers across my scalp, Lenny silenced and removed from the centre of that thing we call attention.

'How's your dad?' says Lenny, attempting to drum up some tears of his own.

'Oh, you know,' I manage to sniffle, 'really not well. I believe the word is moribund.'

'Oh God,' whispers Lenny and puts his hand to his chest. 'Oh God, Hec, I'm sorry.'

Why does he have to be so fucking nice?

I raise myself up on one elbow and pursue the matter: 'All the other blokes on the ward are packing their cases to go home and Dad . . . well . . .' I drag my forearm across my nose, 'he's . . .' long pause whilst Rosa plants a hundred kisses on my cheeks and ears, 'I don't know, Lenny . . . what can I say . . . he's just not doing well, that's all I can say . . . in answer to your question.' I bow my head, lower my eyes and then, at last, close them.

'Hector,' whispers Rosa, 'you should be in bed, baby. Come to bed.'

My God, I wish she hadn't said that. I was just beginning to hate her and then she goes and says a thing like that. She runs her hands up and down my back and whispers, 'There, there, it's all gonna be all right, sweet one.'

No woman has ever called me sweet one. Only Rosa could call me sweet one.

'Come on, let me put you into bed.' She hooks her elbows under my armpits and begins to lift me from the hollow of the settee.

'Hector,' says Lenny, as I'm dragged across the floor in the direction of the bedroom, 'we'll talk in the morning, OK?'

'OK,' I manage to utter, baffled as to how I might subvert the protraction of this preposterous spectacle. 'OK, I'll see you in the morning.' I even manage a little wave. My feet are seen to cross the threshold, linger for a while, and then disappear out of sight as the door is kicked shut.

We make no mention of what was going on with Lenny just now. We make no mention of anything. She undresses me and then herself. Kirk's death has had no apparent effect on Rosa's er . . . ardour. She still pinches my scabby coral nipples between her fingertips, like she's crushing nits, and bites my inner thighs until they bleed. She still pulls my hair and presses her thumb into my thorax. Still nuts me with each thrust and tries to put out my eyes as she comes.

Anyway, enough of this pornography. Tomorrow is another day. Tomorrow is the seventh: the worst day of my entire life. Apart from the eighth – which was almost as bad as the ninth.

16

Rosa's white face on Eleni's favourite pillow. Rosa's pale lids. Her veins filled with milk, and all the blood rushed to her lips. The smell of her on the slashed mattress. Soft breath and softer swallows. Her feet against my calves. The slightest shift. Her buttocks against my swollen belly. I feel sick, and sorry. Sick in all sorts of ways; sorry in just one.

Eleni is not sleeping. With no idea of where in the world she is at this moment, I only know that she is awake and raw and rent asunder. I'd say that it breaks my heart, were it not for the fact that the idiom has always disappointed. The heart, after all, is a pump, and a broken pump no longer pumps. Alas, this is scarcely the case. If only the heart really did break in moments like this; then the game would be up and we might all take our ease. But no; rather the heart is renewed, made vital, and pumps all the more, heralding not the end, but a new and appalling beginning.

But no matter; such things may be overlooked.

My desire for Rosa, far from being in abeyance, is now doglike in terms of its gormless devotion. This battered and bloody mattress has become the floor of heaven. Her tongue is in my mouth. Not something I like to think about. But if thought can be suppressed in such moments, and one's instinct for abandonment brought to the fore, then the benefits are often manifold. Her tongue is eating away at my mouth, counting my teeth with the tip. In the name of playfulness I try to push her out and there follows a peculiar scuffle of lips. The next thing you know it feels so nice that we begin to flail and wheeze like a pair of hysterical, unmedicated mental patients. Such is love.

Lenny's stripped to the waist with his head inside the settee. I'm barefoot in my dressing gown and make it into the kitchen without him noticing. Rosa fancies an egg and I'm headed for the fridge to see if I've got one. I doubt it: I've always been disgusted by eggs, so unless Lenny bought some, she's gonna have to settle for some Marmite on a lump of hard ciabatta.

I open up the fridge. Nothing but beer and old cheese. I must say, if I was on my own, then I might be tempted, but it's hardly quality fayre when one has a young lady over to stay. I fill the kettle and open the hatch. Lenny's put on a CD of Mozart's *Requiem* (cheery), and he's got his khaki Maharishi buttocks thrust up into the air, swaying to the er . . . rhythm. Now and then his head appears, shining with sweat, his brow ravaged by stress. The show opens the day after tomorrow and he's obviously got the Tate barking up his arse to get the thing delivered by tomorrow evening. He climbs inside and closes the door.

I mix up a coffee and stroll through. I detest this piece of music. It's twats like Mozart who turned death into something to worry about. Death is not so grand as this. Death is a short, shifty-looking fella, hobbling down the street in a cheap green jacket. He should never be set to music. At least not this kind of music. Something on a piccolo perhaps. Or a kazoo and ukulele.

Lenny emerges from his piece and jumps to find me there, sitting in the blue chair, cross-eyed with confusion, sweaty with terror, damp with arrogance.

'Oh! Morning,' he says.

'Morning,' I say right back at him, 'though it's technically afternoon.'

He looks at his watch. 'Shit! I've got them coming round tomorrow night to haul this off.'

I look at it, this thing that they're coming to haul off. I don't know. I really don't know. Why don't they just lug it down to the canal?

'Got a fag?' says Lenny.

'Yeah,' I say and light one for him.

'So,' he says, leaning back.

'So,' I reply, slinging my legs over the arm of the chair.

'Is she sleeping?'

'Yeah.'

Silence.

'Where did you get that dressing gown?'

I look down at myself. I'm wearing a rather ornate robe with peacocks and humming birds gliding up the arms and back. The hem is trimmed with gold silk and there's a fancy HK monogram right over the heart.

'Eleni bought it for me in Spitalfields,' I say. ' "Classic Robes".'

There's a brief hiatus of coughs and sniffs at the mention of Eleni. Lenny pulls on his fag and decides to pursue things.

'Why's it got a hood?'

'You know what, Len,' I say, rent by these platitudes, 'I can't answer that question. But I'll say this: I'm happy that it does cos I think it has the effect of making my head look smaller, or my neck more slender. Either way, these are things that bother me when I'm kitted out in hoodless attire. OK?'

'Are you all right?' says Lenny.

'I'm fucking fantastic, Len,' I say and hold my cigarette above my shoulder like Lauren Bacall in a Classic Robe.

To think we used to be friends. To think that there was a time when we were never at a loss for words, when conversation would flow like a glittering Niagara. To think that we once excited each other. And look at us now, caught up in a scrum of mumbled chestnuts.

We sit here, wallowing in the polarity of our circumstances and blow out smoke instead of words.

Silence. Oh my tiny little God; such a silence.

'So when's Kirk's funeral?'

'Don't know yet.'

'Where's it gonna be?'

'Cardiff, I expect.'

More silence. Not much of one, but enough to mention that there is one.

I'm sat on the window ledge moving my hand around my face, squeezing at the eyes, the bridge of the nose, fingering the lips, all that kind of thing. A little show. The expected display.

'So,' I begin, 'how are you feeling?'

Lenny stretches out on the floor and stares at the ceiling for years, mortified that his answer might be trivial. At last he manages to line up a few words, cunningly disguised as sentiment: 'I suppose that something like this gives rise to the conception of a faith of some sort.'

Huh? What the fuck does that mean?

'What do you mean?' I say, all polite, though I really want to knock out his teeth with a chisel.

'Well, it's like when my father died . . .'

Oh shit, here we go; boo fucking hoo.

'When you're young – I mean when you're little – there's this idea that's seeded in your imagination; this idea of death. But for a long time it's only hypothetical. It's like saying that you, or someone you know, might be struck by lightning. It's unlikely, they say, but it must always be borne in mind as a possibility . . .'

I yawn.

'And then, one day, that lightning does strike. And once it's struck you find yourself living in fear of the weather. Do you know what I'm saying?'

'Yeah, yeah,' I enthuse, following up my yawn with another.

'What I'm saying is that when someone intimate dies, then you have no choice but to assemble a list of possibilities as to what that means. I mean . . .' he says, and takes his earned pause, 'I mean it feels unacceptable, idle, to settle for the initial and instinctual response—'

'What's your point?' I say.

'What?'

'I said, what's your point?'

His face hardens into brick. 'What the fuck are you saying that for? What the fuck are you talking about? I'm making my point. I'm right in the middle of making my point!'

'OK, carry on.'

He paces around the room. 'I can't believe you just interrupted me like that.'

'Sorry, sorry, carry on.'

He clears his throat. 'For fuck's sake, Hector!'

'I'm really sorry, Lenny,' I lie, 'please, please carry on. You were just saying that it feels unacceptable, idle, to settle for the initial and instinctual response. So what response is that, then?'

He glares at me.

'No, no, really, that's a real question: what's the initial and instinctual response?'

Silence.

Lenny sits back down and caresses his scalp. 'The initial response,' he says, 'the conditioned response is to abandon hope.'

'Abandon hope,' I mutter, in affirmation. I maybe even nod my head.

'But there's so much time and space in which to question this; you find yourself lying in bed, constructing all manner of outlandish scenarios.'

'Do you?' I say.

'Yeah,' says Lenny.

'What sort of scenarios?'

'Well, it starts with a negation of that initial instinct; that banishing of hope. So then you begin to stimulate hope . . .'

I yawn again. I don't mean to. I really don't mean to this time, but it's stuffy in here and I'm still in my gorgeous dressing gown.

'You undergo a sudden onset of illumination and rationality. It comes down to this: if your instinct – the instinct of futility – is wrong, then the alternatives are imbued with some sort of optimism.'

'Optimism?'

'Yeah, optimism. And that's sort of what this piece is about, yeah?' he says and nods at the big settee. 'I mean, for example, what if all these reports of the supernatural are valid? Or what if it's only language that defines an end, when the truth is that there's no such thing as an end. You know what I'm talking about.'

Do I, Lenny? Do I really? I don't fucking think so, mate.

'I'm talking about the transformation of energy. I'm talking about materialism versus spiritualism. Just because we have insufficient mental resources to comprehend some kind of soulful continuity, it doesn't necessarily imply that such a scenario is implausible.'

Silence.

'For example,' he adds.

Silence.

'So,' I say at last, asking the only question that – in my opinion – needs to be asked, 'where's Kirk now?'

Lenny stares at the floor, basking in the conferred privilege of owning the answer to such a question. 'Here,' he says.

'Here?' I say.

'Right here.'

'Right,' I say, 'and so, like . . . I dunno . . . can he like, hear us and stuff?'

'He doesn't need to hear us. He hears everything. Knows everything. Hearing us – this conversation right now – is small fry to the likes of Kirk. The dead – dead Kirk – see beyond this moment. The dead see the consequences, as well as the history, of this moment. And actually, "see" is the wrong word. I'd say that "know" is the word, but that's not really the word either. In fact, of course, there isn't a word.'

'OK,' I say and light another fag.

'He's with us right now. He really is.'

'OK,' I say, 'really, I'm not arguing with you.'

Silence. A distant drill and the odd seagull over the canal.

'You're smoking a lot,' says Lenny.

'Yeah,' I say, 'I know,' and take a long drag.

Silence.

Silence. Mozart. The small noise of my thumbnail against the filter and the ash landing on the dirty blue saucer.

'So what's going on with you and Rosa?' says Lenny.

I see. So it's come to this. Well, I suppose it was inevitable. Dear me. Oh dear, oh dear, oh dear. That it has come to this.

I laugh. I actually throw my head back in laughter. 'What do you think's going on?'

'What about Eleni?'

'Lenny, do you really expect some kind of informed answer to that?'

He shrugs his shoulders. 'I dunno. I mean—'

'Come on, Lenny, it's not exactly complicated is it? Eleni's away and I'm fucking someone else. What is it that you need to know? Which part don't you understand? I think it's called an affair. It's a common phenomenon. Read books, watch films. Take a look at the *Daily Mirror* now and again.'

He looks at me, disgusted. Appalled, I presume, by the chilly pragmatism of my response.

'Don't fucking look at me like that,' I snap. 'What was going on last night?'

'Nothing was going on last night.'

'What was she doing coming back here with you?'

'Ask her.'

'I'm asking you.'

'And I'm saying ask her.'

'Why? Are there different answers?'

'No, there's only one answer. The answer is: nothing.'

'Nothing?' I bleat, bringing my hands to my head.

'Nothing,' he says again.

'Nothing?' I repeat.

'Nothing at all.'

'Nothing at all?'

'Nothing at all.'

'Nothing? Nothing at all? Really? Nothing at all?'

'Hector!' he bawls.

'Lenny!!' I bawl back.

Silence.

From the bedroom comes a little cough.

'I'm going for a piss,' announces Lenny, and strides off across the room.

'Good,' I call after him, 'that'll do you the world of good.'

I fucking hate him. I used to fucking love him, and now I fucking hate him. And I fucking hate her. Now that she's squeezed every last atom of spunk out of me, I fucking hate her as well. I may even hate everybody. Everything. What was going on last night? Why those silences? Only mouths stoppered up with kissing are capable of such protracted silences. Lenny and Rosa kissing. I can't get the image out of my mind. And yet, maybe I've got it all wrong. There remains the possibility that I've just jumped to – nay, leapt upon and devoured – conclusions. I feel sick the length and breadth of my colon. I am no longer in a position of control. I have fled the cockpit. I am hanging from the wing, naked and frozen, buffeted by the wind. And I'll tell you another thing: here comes a loop-the-loop.

Here comes Rosa in Eleni's favourite T-shirt, scratching at her fanny. Hair like an electrocuted puppy, eyes all puffy, and all the more beautiful for looking so perfectly adrift. Here comes Rosa, and there goes the cistern, the sound of Lenny's zip, footsteps, footsteps. The feet of my loved ones, headed this way.

'What happened to my eggs?' says Rosa.

'There are no eggs. Do you fancy a beer?'

'Yeah, sure.'

'Good, I'll go get us all a beer.'

'Thanks.'

As I trot across the room, thrilled that things are progressing, Lenny emerges from the toilet, seeing to his buckle.

'What's going on?'

'I'm getting us all a beer. You want one?'

Lenny frowns. 'A beer? No. I bought some cranberry juice the other day. I'll have a cranberry juice.'

Fucking geek.

The sun's pouring in through the windows, flooding the walls and floor with a horrible yellow glue.

Silence.

The clink of glasses on the wooden floor and then me: 'So,' I say, 'here we all are.'

They smile. Lenny's slumped in the blue chair and Rosa's squatting by the fireplace. Impossible to ignore the shadow at the top of her thighs.

'Fag, anyone?' I say, trying to keep things cordial.

'No,' says Lenny.

'Yeah,' says Rosa and reaches over (I'm leaning back on the Naked Settee).

'Cheers,' says Rosa.

'Cheers,' I say back.

I take a swig of my beer. Rosa takes a swig of hers. Drag on my fag. Drag on hers.

Lenny sips his cranberry and stares at his piece.

'So,' I say, and allow it to echo against the walls.

Silence. Sick of all this silence.

'So what?' says Rosa.

My brain scans an octillion different replies and, after a little consideration, comes up with: 'So, Kirk's dead, and here we are; all in our own little chapels of rest.'

'What?' says Lenny.

'Chapels of rest,' I repeat.

'What?' says Rosa, swigging and dragging.

I take a big swig of my own. 'Well, let's face it,' I say, 'none of us really give a fuck, do we?'

Silence.

The question hangs in the air like a starved vulture.

Silence.

Lenny reaches over and lifts a cigarette from my packet. Rosa watches him do it. So do I.

'Do we?' I say. 'I mean, if we're honest, deep down, right down there in the shafts.'

Rosa looks at Lenny. Lenny looks at Rosa. Both of them look at me.

'What the fuck are you saying?' says Lenny, saying something at last.

'I'm saying that you came through that door, last night, giggling your tits off. Meanwhile Kirk's in some fridge with a little brown luggage label tied to his toe, that's what I'm saying. I'm simply saying that life's allowed to go on.' I pause and smile. Nice one. 'I'm saying that it makes us all feel special.' My smile broadens into teeth. 'A little more important, a little more attractive.'

Silence.

Fat walloping silence.

They're both staring at me. Agog. Beautifully agog. I see no reason not to go on.

'I'm saying that we should all just be honest about this. I'm saying that we should forgo the pantomime . . .'

'Pantomime?' says Lenny, sitting forward, fingers forming fists.

'. . . forgo the pantomime and come right out with it. Well, listen,' I say, and rise to my feet with my hands in the air, 'I'll be the first one to voice it. I'll be the instigator of the truth. I'll say it right now, once and for all, for better or worse, come rain or shine, in sickness and in health; I'll say it right now, hand on my heart. Here goes . . .'

'Hector,' says Rosa, as though she might leap up and soothe me. She doesn't. She just sits there and says it again. 'Hector,' she says. But it's not enough. It's not nearly enough.

'Shut it!' I say. 'Not now. I'm about to say it. I am about to speak the truth. For once in my life I am about to speak the truth. Here goes. Here goes . . .'

I spread my feet and arms into a small star shape. I tilt back my head to expose my throat and then: 'I'm glad! I am glad. So glad and so fucking happy. So glad and happy that Kirk Church, one of my best friends, is dead. Glad that he's gone. Glad that Sofia is dead. Glad that we're all dying. Glad that we all can. Glad that we must. Glad that we should. Glad that that's the way of things. Glad that you're both looking at me like I just took a Stanley knife to the throat of a baby. Glad! Glad, glad, glad!! Fucking happy. So totally fucking happy! So . . . so, so much . . .' I'm losing the thread, come on now, Hec, concentrate, 'I am a monster!' I yell, scaring myself, 'I am the most perfect of monsters. Kirk's dead!' I scream, and then: 'Ha ha ha ha ha ha ha ha!!!'

Ho, ho, ho. The look on their faces. You wouldn't need a knife to cut the atmosphere, you could slice it in two with the foot of an elephant. This is living. This is it! This is fucking *it*! My God! What ecstasy! What immaculate fucking rapture!

And I'm not finished yet: 'Eleni's mother is dead. Ha! My father is on his deathbed. Ha! And if you two collapsed right now, right here, in front of me, then you know what? Ha! Ha ha ha ha ha ha ah ah ah haha hhah ha ha ha!!!' I begin to spin around the room like some coked-up dervish. 'Ha ha ha a ha ggghg aha gha hhaaa hgh haagggggh!!!!! Ha hha ha hahahhhhhggggh!'

After a few botched tackles, Lenny finally hits home and wrestles me to the ground. I manage to plant a small fist on the surface of his scalp but he counters with a smarting slap to my cheek. I pull away and stagger to my feet. Rosa comes in low and blasts me up against the wall. 'Thief!' I scream. 'Fucking thief!' I scream.

'What?' yells Lenny. 'You talking to me?'

'Yeah,' I scream, really scream, 'I'm talking to you, you fucking pickpocket, you fucking sneak thief fucking grave-robber. What else do you want from me? Take it all! Steal the lot. If I jumped out of that window right now, you'd jump out after me, and still make it to the ground before me.' My eyes are nothing but hot salt.

'What the fuck are you talking about, Hector?' He slaps me again.

Rosa's got her fingers around my throat and she's squeezing me blue. Which, given the circumstances, seems a bit unnecessary. What a girl!

'Go on! Come on!' I croak, 'Come on you vicious, parasitic cunts, kill me. Come on, do it!' I take a deep breath and then: 'Kiiilllllllll meeeeeeeeee!!'

Lenny pushes Rosa away. She falls back against the settee and springs forward on her hands and knees, eyes like absinthe, hissing like a cat, which scares me a bit. Lenny takes my head in his long, soft hands, and dashes my skull against the skirting board.

Silence.

Black. Or white. I can't remember.

But silence.

Perfect.

Sublime.

I remember that.

*

Idea For a Piece: A grave. A real grave. My grave. A little mound of earth and grass in the middle of the National Gallery. A headstone, a candle, a flower. Something tasteful. An orchid, a lily, or even a poppy. *The Late Hector Kipling.*

17

Monger's not dressed like Monger, and I'm not dressed like me. He's wearing a hooded parka and combat boots. The hood's up and his gloved hands are thrust deep into his pockets. I'm still in my dressing gown. Hood down. Classic Robe. He's turning onto Lackerty Road. I'm on the corner of Baxter and Platt. As soon as he's out of sight I set off in pursuit, months of gum and grease on the soles of my bleeding feet. It's been almost an hour now, but I think I've finally tracked him down. He's going into his pocket for keys. He's struggling with the lock. Hood pulled back. Fag in his lips, making him squint. The door opens and in he goes, slamming it behind him.

It was the police who woke me up. Lenny and Rosa were standing off to one side, the image of innocence, whilst a young constable administered to me with smelling salts. Apparently my exhortations had been so loud and maniacal that a neighbour had seen fit to call in the cops. I made a statement, referring to my recent bereavements and made no mention of Lenny's assault. The constable offered his sympathy and even held my hand as I sipped a glass of hot ginger tea. All the while Lenny and Rosa presided over the scene, silent, dispassionate, like *American* fucking *Gothic*.

Soon after the police left Lenny and Rosa were helping each other into their coats, shamed by my hysterics, shameless in their togetherness.

'We're going out,' said Lenny.

'Where are you going?' I asked.

'I just need to get out of here for a while,' said Rosa, and off they went.

I flung open the loading doors and watched them as they took off down the street. They weren't holding hands, but it looked like they might. Once they rounded the corner they would fall into each other's arms and kiss like there were a million tomorrows. That's why I screamed. 'I'll kill you both! I will fucking kill you both! You think I won't kill you? Well, let me tell you this: I will fucking kill you!'

Then I saw the cop car, still parked there on the kerb, the young constable looking at me, mumbling into his radio.

'Thank you,' I called to him and waved, suddenly calm. 'Thanks for your help. Thank you.'

And that's when I spotted Monger, skulking in some doorway, spotting the cop, lighting a fag and making off towards the corner.

Great. Oh great. Oh just so fucking superbly fucking great.

I'm sat here, in the caff opposite Monger's flat, writing a letter to Eleni. There's a pile of eleven crumpled pages at my feet, and I'm not having much luck with the twelfth:

> Dear Eleni,
>
> I feel the need to write to you since I believe that you are owed some kind of explanation as to what was going on the other night. That girl in the bath was not . . .

Was not . . . Was not . . . er . . .

Was not what? Not a girl? Not in the bath? Not human? Not important? I stab at the page with my pen and screw it up like the rest. My coffee arrives and I begin to count the bubbles. I think of Kirk and how he used to blow on his pint. I take a sip, scald my lip, and think of Sofia. And then Eleni. My poor poor Eleni. My angel Eleni. My one true . . . Oh fuck, what a load of bollocks.

I flood my coffee with sugar and examine the spoon. I gaze at my face in the back of it and think of Kirk. But what do I think? Do I think of his face? The way he moved? His choice of clothes? The things he said? The way his eyes crinkled up when he . . . I don't know. All I can say is that I think of Kirk. Fat lot of good it is to Kirk, all this thinking of him. They say that a soul is sustained in the memories of those they leave behind. But what kind of a life is that? A life of yesterdays. A life of not actually being there. No new stories, no new jokes. No prospects, no hope. In other words: Death. I place the spoon on the saucer and watch it dry. It doesn't take long.

My body, it seems, is no longer my own. My brain and bones are beset by parasites, and my bowels are being devoured by something huge and ticklish; six furry legs, two million eyes, needle-sharp teeth and an outer shell of blister and scab. I shall soon be hollow. And once I'm hollow, then pain can move in. Real pain can move in and put its feet up on the ledges of my spine. Can't wait.

'Another coffee, sir?'

'Why not?'

And off he goes. Can't wait.

Now that I know where Monger lives I should just call the police. I don't know why I'm sat here in this pink caff, dealing with it all by myself. But what can I do? What proof do I have? And besides, better that it's me watching him than him watching me.

I haven't really stopped shaking since he told me he was going to kill me. I'm not sure that I want to stop shaking. There's something gratifying about the knowledge that someone cares enough about you to want to kill you. It's like Lenny was saying about how death is only abstract. But there's nothing abstract about Monger. On the contrary, Monger is magnificently real. If only we could do this with cancer: hide out in some cafe across the road and follow it to see where it goes.

I fall to my knees and hang my head down into my lap. I wish I could see myself from ten feet away. I think I'd quite like to paint it.

'Another coffee, sir?'

'No, thank you,' I say, raising my eyes, 'no thank you very much, I don't think I should. Do you? I mean, really?'

'So do you want the bill?'

'Oh yes,' I say, 'the bill.'

'Well, it's six coffees. That's five pounds forty.' He looks at my feet.

I begin to go through my pockets, but then I remember I'm wearing a dressing gown and that I only have two pockets to go through and both of them are empty, save for the odd tissue. I should have lobbed a few bob into my hood as I left the flat, but Monger was making his move and there was no time for thoughts of financing the pursuit.

'Er . . .' I say, 'I er . . . don't really . . .' And that's when I see him again. The door opens and out he comes, all dressed in black and cream, like the Monger of old. Tie pin, cufflinks, handkerchief, spats. Spats! He takes a left and heads off towards Platt Street.

'Can I pay you later?' I say to the clod in the apron.

'Later?' he says, palms askance.

'Like tomorrow?'

'Tomorrow?'

I hesitate. And then: 'Oh never mind.'

'Never mind?'

'Yeah,' I say, 'never you mind.' I stand and push past him on my way to the door.

'Five pounds forty!' he shouts, obviously not understanding my suggestion of a deferred payment.

'Right,' I mutter and stumble out onto the street.

Monger's climbing into a taxi and I look around for a taxi of my own so that I can yell, 'Follow that taxi!' But this, alas, isn't Manhattan and I'm left in the middle of the street with some blue-faced waiter

swearing at me, screaming something about care in the community and
Baroness Thatcher.

I let it go.

I haven't climbed a wall since I was in my teens. And I'm not really
climbing a wall right now. I'm climbing a drainpipe, but my feet are on
the wall. My poor bleeding feet. The belt of my gown has come undone,
exposing my belly to the October winds. I don't know what makes me
think I'm up to this, but here I am, about to break into private property. I really don't know what it is – perhaps it's the season. I'm about
twenty-five feet up in the air, the sort of height that's gonna kill you if
you have to come down from it in a hurry. It occurs to me that the
higher I climb, the more unstable the drainpipe's gonna be – the more
unstable I'm gonna be. There's a small extension on the building below
and as I draw level with the roof of this extension I panic and attempt
a leap. Messy and uncalculated. I catch my breath, fling out my arms
and, like an Alsatian impersonating a kitten, smash into the side of the
roof, all paws and snout. But no matter; I'm not dead. I'm still up in
the air. I'm still safe, dangling there at a fatal altitude.

I lower myself into Monger's bathroom from the window, via the
sink, and onto the floor. I take a few minutes to grimace and wheeze and
growl and whine, attending to the sundry agonies of my flesh. Only my
arse is intact. My feet, my hands, my elbows, knees, knuckles, nipples,
thighs, groin, face and neck are burning and bleeding with such ferocity that I can't believe they pass unheard in the flat below. I have so many
pains I don't know where to begin. And so I join them all up into one
big pain. But the one big pain is more than I can take and I think I might
pass out, so I pester them all back to their respective corners and resolve
to monitor their intensities in a formal and alphabetical order. Since, as
I mentioned, my arse is intact, I meditate first upon the pain in my balls.
Jesus Harold Christ! I wonder if Monger's got some morphine kicking
about. I wouldn't put it past him.

For a while I toy with the idea of running a lukewarm bath, just to bathe some of these wounds and offset infection, but taking a bath, however brief, in the flat of a lunatic who is hell bent on killing me would be madness. But isn't this madness anyway, just being here? Why the fuck did I think that this was a sensible idea? I know that I need to nail this fruitcake and remove him from the board. I need to leave no space between arrest and imprisonment. And then I need to flee the country. But, fucking hell, this is total insanity. At school they never taught us what to do when your life is threatened by an irrational and sinister dandy. Or maybe they did. Maybe I was just off sick that day.

Were it not for a toothbrush, toothpaste, a bottle of Listerine and a scattered display of shaving gear, you might assume there was no one living here. There's a bar of Imperial Leather soap by the bath and a toilet roll on top of the cistern, but apart from that, nothing to report.

The kitchen is another matter. The kitchen stinks. The walls are damp and scorched and the floor's as filthy as a market pavement. A mob of flies patrol the one bare light bulb, to and fro, as though they've found their answer. On the work surfaces a hundred or so other flies lie still and brittle. Others, some of them only half dead, languish in the mould of an old salad, or tremble on the creased green skin of a forgotten coffee. I linger in the doorway, look at my feet and, having seen enough, decide to go no further.

The living room, for me at least, has no precedent. The first thing I notice – for how could I not? – is the cacophonous ticking of some fifteen to twenty battered junk-shop clocks. The clocks are dispersed, with no apparent method, throughout the room, on various surfaces, and half a dozen of them are strewn across the floor. The largest clock is about a foot and a half tall and sits on top of an old mahogany wardrobe. It is the only clock that tells anything approaching the correct time. The rest are buckled and grazed, missing faces or hands, or sometimes both; but all of them, no matter what their condition, are vibrant and ticking. The sound is appalling. In the middle of the room sits a threadbare scarlet sofa bed that hasn't been put away and a dozen bottles scattered either side. The wooden floor is stuck with a discordant collage of rugs and wrappers. There is a black butcher's bicycle, and a blue bubblegum machine. There is a birdcage filled with billiard balls and nails, and over by the fireplace, a small dead tree. Two grimy windows, caked with pigeon shit and soot, offer up only a hint of the buildings opposite. The stench is crippling.

In another corner stands a full-length mirror and just to the left of that, two long clothes rails hung with cellophane-wrapped shirts and blazers. Along the bottom of the rails a dozen pairs of expensive shoes are lined up in neat rows. Leaned up against the adjacent wall are eight clean umbrellas, six canes, a basket of fine hats and a small Moroccan box filled with collar studs, cufflinks, tie pins, watch straps, signet rings, playing cards and dice. It is the only part of the flat that bears any relation to the man I met. Elsewhere there is such a rich jumble of arcane ephemera that I find it difficult to know where to begin. With the stuffed mice in the fireplace? With the red fire bucket filled with dentures and bells? With the fingernails on the mantelpiece, or the rocking horse with the rotting plastic saddle and the eye sockets filled with fag ash and sand? It is the home of a chronic sociopath and my tongue and gums are as dry as a Victorian flannel.

Another corner of the room is festooned with magician's silks and tinsel bunting. There are twenty-five to thirty canvases stacked against the wall, and a work in progress clamped into an antique easel. The work in progress (if you can call it progress – or work, for that matter) is a disastrous soup of rust and pink paste, trying to pass itself off as a representation of the human face. A smear of burnt sienna which, since it cleaves the face in two, I take to be the nose, is highlighted with what looks like wax and vicious flecks of schoolroom chalk. The mouth is an idle crimson gash, and the gas-blue swirls, which must be the eyes, bob and frolic beneath an angry amber brow. It makes Dubuffet look like Raphael.

Upon investigation, the other canvases are equally abominable. It looks as though they were painted by a child, or a robot, or a monkey; or some kind of robotic monkey child. Were it not for the noose I might have missed the point altogether. But since there is a noose – an infantile umber line and loop, cross hatched with jagged, unmixed lampblack acrylic – the point is inescapable. Since there is this noose in every last one of these diabolical stabs at portraiture, I am left in no doubt whatsoever regarding Monger's subject matter. For they are surely, are they not, painfully misbegotten renderings of his late, purportedly murdered father, Mr Godfrey Bolton. And you know what? No one could really blame me if I just squatted down and shat right here on one of the numerous ticking clocks that populate this filthy wooden floor.

Instead I collapse back upon the sofa bed and stare up at the ceiling. I won't even begin to describe the ceiling. Suffice it to say that there have been times – and even within recent living memory – when I have felt considerably better than I do in this moment. Is this it, then? Is this what I am dealing with? The envy and rancour of a failed artist? I use the term loosely. I mean most failed artists are usually some kind of artist to begin with. Kirk, for example. At least Kirk's ill-judged cutlery pictures were halfway there in terms of hyper-realism, when it came to representing knives, forks and spoons. At least you were left in no doubt as to the intention. He was simply misguided in his belief that anyone might be remotely interested in such insular interpretations of domestic flotsam. But with Monger it really is a titanic struggle to apply the epithet of artist in the first place, before you can even begin to broach any discussions about the application of the word failed. Indeed when it comes to Monger, the word failed seems to suffice in every respect; so why concern oneself with any mention of the word artist, which is clearly wide of the mark, no matter how you look at it? What a fuck-up the man is. What a forty-eight-carat fuck-up on every level. And his bed stinks of piss.

Fearing that I might pass out with the pain of my wounds and the turmoil of my spirit, I raise myself up from the bed and for some reason attempt, for the first time ever, the lotus position. A ridiculous idea, of course, and one which I can safely say will never be revisited for as long as I live. As I'm attempting to wrestle my left heel out of the pillow of my right thigh in an attempt to forgo the early stages of a thrombotic seizure, my eyes are suddenly drawn to a curious item, partly concealed by one of the lengths of frayed hemp that pass for curtains in Monger's Boschian dungeon. At the end of the row of fancy shoes there is a small battered blue suitcase, with two stickers in the upper left-hand corner, boasting of bygone excursions to the Trough of Boland and the Keswick Motor Museum. Recognizing it immediately, I attempt, and then fail, to swallow. The suitcase belongs to Mum. In the first moment of realization I wonder why on earth Monger would have bothered to snaffle Mum's tatty valise. I mean isn't it enough for him to make off with Mum and Dad's fifteen thousand pounds in cash and Sparky's scabrous cadaver?

And then, in the next moment it hits me. Oh, how it hits me. Of course, of course. I walk over to the case and squat down on the sticky floor. After a few fumbled seconds of resistance, the clasp finally succumbs and I take the lid between my fingertips and lift it away from the base. And there they are: fifteen identical, slipshod portraits of Her Majesty Queen Elizabeth the fucking Second. Fifteen neatly bundled bricks of fifty-quid notes squeezed between the burgundy nylon pleats of Mum's forgotten travel bag. If Quentin Tarantino ever saw fit to set a film in the North of England, wherein a twee clique of Lancastrian pensioners pulled off some spectacular and lucrative crack deal, then it might very well look something like this. I take a few deep breaths. 'Sometimes people forget to breathe,' said Bianca the other day. Well, Bianca, let me tell you, chuck, right now I'm not one of those people. I'm breathing. Oh yeah, I'm breathing all right. I may even pass out with how much I'm breathing.

Call the police. I look around for a phone. Call the police as soon as you find the phone. Isn't this all the evidence you need? The cops can haul him in, and then whilst they're holding him, Mum can identify him as the man who . . . Oh bollocks, this is all so fucked! Does any of this match up? Let me think about it again. Let me just stand here, rooted to the spot, and go over all this again. Is this any kind of evidence? I begin to cry. I don't know. Is this any kind of evidence? How am I gonna prove that he took the money? I know fuck all about the law. Aren't they gonna want solid evidence? What if I point the finger at Monger but they have no right to hold him? What's he gonna do to me then? What's he gonna do to me anyway? And what the fuck am I doing here, stood in the middle of his fucking flat, when he might come home at any second? I need to reason with him, that's what I need to do. Maybe I should leave him a note. A note! Ha! What am I thinking of? I need to call in the fucking military, not go leaving him notes.

My body has turned to ice. I can't swallow. I don't think that I will ever be able to swallow again.

I've found the phone under a pile of old towels and I'm shaking so much that the earpiece is banging against my head. At the other end it just rings and rings. Lenny must have forgotten to switch on the answer machine cos there's no end to this ringing. I try his mobile and go straight through to the voicemail, which is no good at all. I hang up and try another tack.

'Hello?'

'Mum, it's me, it's Hector. What's the news?'

'Oh, Hector,' she sighs, 'Hector love, where have you been? I've been ringing and ringing. Where are you?'

'It doesn't matter where I am, Mum, I'm asking you what's the news?'

'Oh my God, you're round at the trollop's house!'

'Mum, I'm not round at the trollop's house. I'm asking you what the news is.'

'There is no news,' she barks. 'He's still out for the count, there is no bloody news!'

I look around the room for a cigarette and find a fat cigar. What the hell, it seems a little inappropriate, but I light it anyway. 'Listen, Mum, I don't really have the time to have a big old chat right now, I just need you to do something for me.'

'Have you spoken to Eleni?'

'Mum, I need you to put down the phone and then dial 1471 and phone me back with the number. Can you do that for me, Mum?'

'Why? Where are you?'

'I'll explain later.'

'You're at her house.'

'Why would I . . . Mum, if I was at her house . . . I mean why would I be asking you to do this?'

'The trollop's house!' she screams down the receiver. 'The trollop! The trollop!'

'Mum, will you stop calling her the trollop?'

'Why, what do you want me to call her?'

I actually pause to consider this. After giving it some thought, trollop seems just fine.

'Mum, please just do what I'm asking you to do. Please!'

'Eleni's mother's dead and you're off out in the night playing silly buggers. I can't believe I've raised such a heartless, conniving, bloody—'

'Mum!' I bawl and take a big hit on my cigar.

'Now you listen here, Hector. Don't you dare scream at me. Don't you dare scream at your mother like that!'

I hang up.

Not good, not good. Not at all good-son behaviour, I know, but I don't really have the time.

I press a few more buttons.

'Myers?'

'Hector? Hector, what on earth is going on?'

'I'll tell you later. I'll explain everything later. Now listen . . .'

Myers does as he's told, calls back and I write the number on the back of my hand.

'So what's all this about?' says Myers.

'Er . . .' I say, and hang up.

Out in the hallway I hear a door open and slam downstairs, which is a shame cos I wasn't really planning on leaving these premises the same way that I entered them. Nevertheless, given this slamming of doors, I tighten the belt on my gown, stub out the cigar and scramble off in the direction of the bathroom, leaving myself no time to collect the case of money.

I haven't wet myself since I was six – apart from twice when I was seven, three times when I was eleven and once in my teens after a pint of tequila, but I was unconscious each time – so this is a first. I'm still. Dead still. As terrified as I've ever been in my whole life. What if it's him? What if he finds me here? And how can he not find me here? Why the fuck did I light that cigar? I can hardly breathe. My murder may be only minutes away. Not only my death for fuck's sake, but my fucking murder. I can hardly breathe for the excitement. How will he do it? With a knife? With a hammer? An axe? Oh God in Heaven! I collapse onto the toilet and let it all out. Once the water has settled I curtail my breathing and listen.

Footsteps on the stairwell.

This is it, this is it: The Real Thing. These are most certainly my final moments. My very last minute on the face of this planet. And what has it all meant? What is revealed? Is anything put into perspective? Is anything resolved? No! No! Nothing at all; I am to die as I have lived: trembling, craven and confused. At this rate I won't even earn a grave. I may even be robbed of my death. I'll just be missing. Missing sbeneath the floorboards or dissected, boiled and distributed in small pieces the length and breadth of the country, or maybe just flushed down the khazi. Not good.

I leap up from the toilet. For fuck's sake, Hector, you have to at least try and make an escape. I put my foot on the sink and raise myself up onto the window ledge, Monger's telephone number bleeding across the back of my sweating hand. Another door slams and then silence. A door opens and then more steps. I'm far enough out of the window for him to give me a small push and that would be it. My robe is caught up on the taps and I have no choice but to jettison the fucking thing. I slither out of the small opening and land on the roof, naked and torn. Naked as the day I was born. But let us not speak of the day I was born. Not so late in the day that I'm about to die.

The leap from the drainpipe to the ledge was a small feat compared to the suicidal recklessness of the leap from the ledge to the pipe. In fact it seems totally impossible. If this were a film and I were the hero then I might just make it, but it's not a film and if I were to attempt such a thing then I'd just be a fat naked corpse spreadeagled across a huddle of bottles and bins.

Idea For a Piece: Just a fat naked corpse spreadeagled across a huddle of bottles and bins.

I hear the front door open and a light comes on in the hall. It's only a matter of time before he smells the cigar, finds my dressing gown in the sink and starts nosing around.

The night is setting in. I have surely seen the last of the sky. I crouch against the wall, trembling in my final dusk. I think I may be about to pray. Pray! Me! Ha! 'Our father,' I whisper and think of Dad, 'who art in hospital, Derek be thy name.' Impossible! Impossible to pray at a time like this. I bring down my hands and hold on to my battered penis.

'Hello?' I hear him shout. 'Who's there?'

Silence.

Oh my God, I think I'm getting a hard on.

The telephone rings and I hear him pick it up. 'Hello? Who's that?' Pause. 'Yes, I know you are. And I'm asking you who you are.'

Someone's peeping at me from behind a lace curtain on the other side of the street. I keep my hands over my groin. Perhaps they'll call the police. Is that a good thing? I squat, staring back, trying to work out if that's a good thing.

'Connie Kipling?' bellows Monger.

Oh, nice one, Mum.

'How did you get this number?'

Before it's too late I scramble to my feet, swivelling my head in search of new solutions. It seems that I have the option to make it onto another roof nearby. It's still gonna have to be a mighty life-or-death Hollywood-style leap but it's a better option than the drainpipe.

I hear Monger yelling at Mum and then the phone slammed down. Just as the bathroom light comes on I take a deep breath and leap. I fly through the October night in slow motion, teeth bared, tail up, eyes agape. David Attenborough would have been proud.

I hid in the bushes, squatted on my haunches, bloody feet in the wet soil, half-tempted to forage for ants. My breath billowed into small damp clouds and I pretended to be a dragon. I picked up a twig and pretended to smoke. Calm. Calm. Nice and calm. Well at least I was alive – if you can call this life. Alive, and with a reasonable chance of seeing the morning. At least I wasn't a headless torso, oh no, not really – it only felt that way. The sky flew off into outer space and it began to rain. I sheltered there for a long time, tented by the sooty leaves. What I really needed was a drink. But where was I gonna get a drink in this state?

Idea For a Joke: Bald, bleeding, naked savage walks into a bar and orders a double whisky. 'Sorry, sir,' says the barman, 'I'm going to have to call the police.' Er . . . that's it. Big laugh, round of applause.

The windows at Box Street are quickened by candle flame. I can hear strains of Haydn oozing through the open loading doors, warming up the rain. It's almost as though Eleni were back home. If only, if only. The moon is up and full and must surely be shining across the wooden floor. I bet they're at it. Oh yes, that's what they'll be doing; no doubt about it. Eating each other alive, sucking on each other's bits, licking each other to the bone. Meanwhile I'm down here in the street in a stinking tartan blanket that I found in the boot of some burnt-out car.

Ringing on the bell is, of course, out of the question. What am I gonna do, disturb them? Alert them? Give them time to reposition, reconvene into an appearance of platonic decorum? Oh no. I've come too far for that kind of thing. That's what they're banking on. I know what's happened: they've come back with a cosh and a sack of Valium, but I'm not there. Lenny's seen my keys on top of the piano and taken it as an all clear to shimmy out of his togs and give Rosa a good seeing to. Little does he know that she'll suck his eyes from their sockets. Little does he know that she'll be tipping gunpowder into the blind eye of his cock and launching it, with a blowtorch, toward the far hills of Neptune.

There's a discreet, hardly noticeable, little manhole on the towpath of the canal that can easily be lifted with a suitable lever, and there on the ledge is a spare set of keys. It was Eleni's idea. Most people would just leave a set with one of the neighbours, but not Eleni. For Eleni, it was akin to buried treasure. For Eleni, even finding herself locked out of her home was turned into some quaint adventure. She loved the romance of the quest. Perhaps she'll come to love it again. Perhaps. After all: I love Eleni.

I don't take the lift, but tiptoe up the stairs, crafty as you like. Nice to be inside. Though nice is not the word. The key is so beautifully silent as it slips into the lock, like threading a needle. Already I can hear my worst fears confirmed. Their sweetly strangled sobs, their pathetic oohs and ghastly ahhs, creeping out beneath the door and onto the stairwell. What a pair of treacherous automatons. I mean, her I can forgive, I suppose, she owes me nothing, but Lenny . . .

Once through the door, I realize that these strains of mangled betrayal are not emanating from the bedroom. Rather, the groans and sighs are rising from the settee; the Naked Settee. Lenny has laid it back on its feet and I am able to spy him naked and writhing through the silly little window. And now that I listen properly, it's Lenny who's making all the noise. Doesn't sound like she's having such a good time. In fact she's making no sound at all. That's not like her – but then maybe Lenny's just not like me.

Haydn's gone all silent and cheeky, like a half-drunk sprite.

I crouch down and approach the back of the settee on all fours. Fucking thief! Fucking fucked-up fucking thief! I'll surprise them. I'll give them the shock of their fucking lives. I throw off my blanket and pad across the floor like a bloated mog. Lenny groaning. For fuck's sake, man, get a fucking grip. I creep right up to the little window and peer in. What a sight! What a fucking disgraceful fucking apparition: Lenny's sweaty head, Lenny's purple mug contorted in rapture. The get. The unholy fucking get. I twist my head but I can't see her. I can see her thighs wrapped round his hips, but her face eludes me. I raise myself up on one elbow to get a better view. It looks like they might be coming to the end. Lenny's hardly moving now, his groans are receding and his eyes are stilled. I give a little knock on the window. He looks over. I smile and wave. No response. I smile and wave again. No response. He just stares straight through me, cold, unblinking.

I think I can say that he's no longer my best friend. He's not even my worst friend. He's no friend at all. In fact he's my enemy. I want to destroy him. I want to see him in pieces. I rise to my feet and look down at the two of them, and, as quickly as I rise, I fall. I fall back onto the floor, totally appalled, totally unconscious. I didn't expect to see that.

Odd, given the circumstances, that my dream should have been such a pleasant dream. But it was. Utterly pleasant. Me and Aunty Pat combing the beach for shells and me finding a pearl. Simple as that.

No history and no consequence. Me and Aunty Pat, by the sea, on a warm spring afternoon. Odd, given the circumstances.

I have no idea of the time, but I awake with only one thought in my head: 'So she doesn't really love me after all. She said that she loved me, but she never really loved me at all.' That's the thought. Sad, isn't it? But it's all right, cos I never really loved her either. After all, I love Eleni. I never stopped loving Eleni. Not for one second.

I'm gonna have to stand up again in a minute and deal with reality. I've never been particularly adept at dealing with reality, even when the reality in question was comparatively benign. So how in hell am I gonna deal with this sort of reality? And furthermore, is this reality? Is it possible?

Haydn's on a loop, the same old surges and lulls, over and over. I have to stand up now. I have to stand up, if only to turn off this incessant flightiness. One more note and I shall lose my mind.

Click. Silence.

Any moment now I'm going to turn round and confront the Goyaesque atrocity that awaits me in the middle of my living room. Living room! Ha! What an expression.

I love you, Eleni Marianos. I love you, my angel. I never loved her. Never. Nor him, come to that. Never. It means nothing to me. It means nothing to me that he is lying on top of her, naked, her hands across his buttocks and what's left of her lips buried into what's left of his shoulder. It touches me not at all. Her eyes never seduced me. Not really, my love. Her bright green eyes – one turned to mud and the other on the floor – or is that the small marble you rolled around beneath your pretty foot that night you received the call about your mother? I really don't know, Eleni. It's hard to tell from here. And look at Lenny. Just look at the old fool: the spit of Wallis's *Chatterton*. Trust Lenny Snook to end up the spit of Wallis's *Chatterton*. The sweet lanky fool. And do you remember, Eleni? Do you remember when we made love on my parents' settee, and you bled and you bled? And in the morning I had to confess to my mother that there was blood on the settee. Funny the way things have turned out. Just look at all this blood, Eleni. Look at all this fucking blood, love. How am I gonna explain this one to Mum? Come to that, how am I gonna explain this one to anybody? Well, listen, Eleni, my one true love, my goddess, my sun, listen, it's been nice talking to you again, but as I draw closer to this tableau I'm afraid that I'm overcome by the need to retch and faint. So goodnight, my sweet one, I must leave you now. I must purge what's left of my guts and collapse, artlessly, to the floor. Sorry. So very, very sorry. Goodnight, and God bless.

I didn't call the police. I covered up their bodies with an old tarpaulin. I sat in the dark and chatted to every face that floated in and out the door. There were many. I stared at my painting for hours. Somewhere around 4 a.m. I got it together to call Monger. No reply.

I lit a dozen joss sticks to veil the smell. I ran a bath and tried to drown myself, but panicked every time I ran out of breath; just like when I was little and Mum tried to rinse my hair.

I stared into space for a thousand years and tried to come up with at least one lucid thought. In the final months of the thousandth year I gave up and bathed my wounds, peeling off one nipple, only to find another one beneath.

I'm drunk on all this death. Drunk to the extinction of thought. Drunk to the point where there are only eyes and breath. I have no opinion. No feeling. My heart is dipped in chloroform. I cannot paint. I do not know how to paint. I never did.

I should call the police. But what is there to say to the police, really? 'Yes, officer, why don't you come on over and take a look at the mutilated bodies of my best friend and lover? I don't mean, sir, that my best friend is my lover – far from it – I mean the dead bodies of my best friend and my lover . . . or rather my ex-lover, who is . . . or should I say was . . . his lover now, since . . . Oh, never mind. Anyway, sir, whilst you've got your notebook out, mulling over that line of inquiry, do you recall when I screamed from my window and swore that I would kill them both? Remember that, officer? Did your constable get all that down? Yes? Good. Well, you'll never guess what, but . . .' No, it's never going to work. Is all that ever going to work? No, it is not.

Lenny had such beautiful shoulders, and I can't believe that Monger mistook them for mine. How many shots must he have fired to contort them into such a terrifying jelly of bone and tendon? Anyway, let us not dwell upon the gore. The gore is not important. The important thing is the extinction. The important thing is the new non-existence of Lenny Snook – my oldest friend. The important thing is the absence of . . . Well, never mind all that. I collapse down, and then, in the next moment, collapse up. I bare my teeth to the sky and stretch the flesh of my face till I think it might tear. Fuck it hurts, to stretch the flesh of my face till I think it might tear.

I open the fridge, assess Lenny's stash, and proceed to make up a nice plate of boiled ham, pork pies, chicken wings, chorizo, Scotch egg and anchovies. Waving a cheery goodbye to nearly twenty years of vegetarianism, I wolf down the whole lot and wipe my mouth on a crusted pink tea towel. Then I'm sick. And then I'm sick again. I finish off a bottle of three-month-old Blue Nun and smoke whatever I manage to find in Rosa's pockets, at the bottom of the bin, or on the floor beneath the bed. And then I'm sick again. I play Dylan's 'Ballad Of A Thin Man', over and over on the stereo, jacked up full blast, until I poke at my ears with the tip of my fat little finger and contemplate the spots of blood thereon. One of Rosa's green eyes has rolled up against the leg of the piano stool, and I lie on my side for about three-quarters of an hour, gazing deep into its dead dark pupil, quoting Georges Bataille.

I take myself off to bed. If you can call it a bed any longer. The mattress is so torn, so rank and haunted, the pillows so perverted, the sheets so desperately forlorn, it makes Emin's *Bed* look like the cradle of a newborn sylph. The little sleep I manage is peopled with hags and vicious bees. I wake up every fifteen minutes, kick off the sheets and spit at the walls. At one point I awake to find the clock in my mouth.

In the morning the mattress is awash with turps, bleach and chocolate milk. My head has overnight been transformed into a shovel factory. I walk over to the full-length mirror and begin to scream the words, 'Giraffe ink, giraffe ink,' over and over, until, at last, it begins to mean something. It is about then that I hear the slamming of the door.

18

TATE BRITAIN, PIMLICO, LONDON

I'm not sure what Lenny had in mind when he came up with this *Hole in the Gallery Floor* business. Nor did I ever understand the rapture of the critics when they saw fit to hail it as seminal and significant. I mean, for the love of God, what does it signify? Right now, of course, ten feet down, it feels a lot like a grave. My grave – which is nice. But then the entire room, up above, feels like a grave. But then graves are nothing special. In fact, as we have witnessed from the rituals of the Neanderthal, there is little in life so simple as a grave. Any child with a bucket and spade and the carcass of a crab is more than capable of rising to the occasion.

At first I'd toyed with the idea of gathering up the corpses and squeezing them into the base of the hairy settee, lugging the whole lot down here and seeing what the critics made of that. But, alas, the practicalities of transporting the macabre package over to Pimlico and setting it out in a suitable manner proved to be beyond me. Then I had a better idea. And so here I am.

I made it over to the Tate just before it closed and, at the last minute, scrambled through the barriers that separated the Turner pieces from the other galleries. I've been here all night. At one point I made great sport with the beam of the security guard's torch, concealing myself in one of the recesses of the hole. But after two or three tremulous calls of 'Hello, is there anybody there?' the guard gave up, and I snuggled in, rested my bald head into the crown of my soft homburg, and managed to pull off a few beautiful hours of uninterrupted sleep.

The lights were switched on about four hours ago and I've heard some mumbled discussions about the definitive composition and last-minute adjustments. At one point I discerned a few choice sentences concerning the difficulties they were having regarding their attempts to contact Lenny Snook and the deferred arrival of his promised piece. (Apparently it is not without precedent. In 1995 Damien Hirst was three weeks late with the installation of *Mother and Child Divided*. And that was the year Damien won. So the signs, or so it would seem, are propitious for old Lenny.) I particularly relished the perplexed tones when it came to a debate about the meaning of a brief French quotation that had appeared on the gallery walls overnight, apparently written in blood.

'There's no mention of this in the programme,' announced a voice which I understood to belong to a rather shrill and bossy woman who everyone addressed as 'Miss Cookham'. Miss Cookham went on to stress that it had never been agreed that Snook might be permitted to deface the gallery's walls. After all, wasn't it enough that he had gouged a ten-foot hole in the gallery floor? At one point I heard Miss Cookham calling out to ascertain if there was anyone nearby who spoke French, and then, since there was not, she ordered some lackey to unlock the bookshop and bring to her, with haste, a copy of André Breton's *Second Manifesto of Surrealism*.

'Strange,' she said, and I think she lit a cigarette. 'Very odd indeed.'

It's becoming unbearably hot and noxious down here. All along the walls there are snaking lengths of coiled and colourful wires, stripped sockets, junction boxes, halogen lamps and a large pipe that runs, half buried, across the dust and rubble floor. I presumed it had all been put there, by Lenny, for effect, to lay bare the viscera of the gallery, or some such nonsense. But ever since the lights were switched on up in the gallery, the pipe has been getting hotter and hotter, and since I just scalded myself by leaning my wrist on it, I'm having to wedge myself up

321

in one corner. But then that only brings my head closer to the halogen lamps, which is causing my hat and scalp to boil and steam. Therefore I take off my coat and hat and struggle to cover up the pipe. The air has become increasingly difficult to breathe, and I feel stifled by the heat and the stink of iodine. Up above I hear a generator lurch into life, and then the first slow trickles of Kim Large's paint baths, as they begin to fill and drain. Then it's Archie March's kinetic boxing-glove gadgets, beating the crap out of twenty-two Bakelite skulls. And then, if I'm not mistaken, the banal whirr and chug of a green coffin in pursuit of a black Victorian pram. And if I listen very carefully I'm sure I can make out the muffled clamour of two thousand British painters – everyone from Gainsborough to Hockney, from Constable to Bacon – not turning, but rather writhing in their respective graves. And so I salute them, and turn a little in mine. In fact I have to turn anyway, regardless of deference to my forebears, since I'm suffering the most agonizing fucking cramps of my stupid, cramp-ridden life.

Here's what's bothering me: is it legitimate to mourn the death of Sparky more than I mourn the death of Sofia? After all, I never loved Sofia. I may well have stated, somewhere back in time, that I loved Sofia. I may well have said that I loved Sofia, merely because she was the mother of the woman I loved. But, in truth, I never loved Sofia. And perhaps I never loved Eleni. And perhaps I never loved. But, you see, Sparky was family. I know that he was only a scabby, blistered, half-blind Yorkshire terrier, but he was the fourth Kipling, in the same way that George Martin was the fifth Beatle. Sparky was a rock. Sparky was the foundation stone of . . . Oh I don't know, he was a dog! Just a dog, and half the time he made me want to kick him down the Promenade, but he also made me smile. And now all that panted enthusiasm has passed into another realm. Or perhaps it has just been curtailed. Perhaps it was only of the moment. No matter. Farewell, Sparky old fella. Farewell.

There was a tricky little moment just now when I heard footsteps up above, and as they grew closer and closer to the hole I had to remove my hat and coat from the pipe and fold my fat bulk back into the recess. I understand that there was some concern regarding a smell of burning emanating from the hole. At the last minute I realized that my T-shirt and jeans which I had draped over the lamps were beginning to scorch and smoulder, and so just before the voices appeared at the top of the hole I managed to whip the clothes away and bundle them into my lap. I'm sat here now like a rare hirsute meatball in just my underpants and socks. My feet are sodden and choked and so the socks come off. And then, since my life is surely over, I decide that there is no point standing or rather crouching on ceremony and off come the pants. What a spectacle. As the great Breton also said, 'Beauty must be convulsive, or not at all.' I think we would have got on, I really do.

Outside his immediate family and friends, the world will not really suffer the loss of Kirk Sidney Church. I'm sure that his mother and father are presently inconsolable, and will continue to be so for the next few months or so, but after that I'm sure that some form of consolation will be tolerated and even welcomed. After all, he only returned to his parental home twice a year, and phoned only once a month, so they can hardly really justify any profound feelings of loss. Not really. In my opinion – for what it's worth. He had nothing of any true merit to offer the world, no particular talent. The two people who knew anything about him and kept regular and convivial company with him towards the end are now obsolete and defunct: one dead, the other barely alive. To think, since he will live on only in the memories of the nearly dead, or alternatively, live on only in the brain of a creature such as me, it is as though he might never have been born. So, therefore, ladies and gentlemen, that was Kirk Sidney Church. What can I say? He was kind sometimes. Funny sometimes. Insightful and cynical. His paintings were truly awful and his flat stank of Pledge and egg. He was too shy and ugly ever to sustain the affection of a good woman. He spent his evenings in tears and, in his final days, was beset by the compulsion to dwell upon these few small details. So perhaps there is this to be said for him: that he died happy – satisfied that it was not the way he had lived.

Rosa was a stranger. Rosa is still a stranger. Stranger now than ever. Rosa was the last woman I ever kissed. Rosa was the first woman I wanted to die in front of. Not for. I didn't want to die for her, I just wanted to die in front of her, or behind, or just to the side of. What the fuck, the point is that I would gladly have died for Eleni, to save Eleni. Whereas with Rosa, I would gladly have died to stimulate her, to excite her, or merely to entertain her. I think there is a difference. Did I love her? No fucking idea. All questions of love are now buried in the earth. If only I . . . etc. It's a pity that she had to leave so horribly: with a bullet, or three, smashing half her face into a bloody pulp. But let us not dwell upon this. The gore is not the point. The point is that she will never again call me 'angel', that is the point. The point is that she's dead and in no position to love, or not love, me. And so I let it go. I let all that kind of thinking go. The tide's coming in and rising, and I let all that kind of thing blow away in the wind.

There is no mistaking the persistent clunk and hum of *Domesticated Goose Chase*. There had always been a design fault in the motor driving the wheels of the pram. Lenny had muffled the noise of the coffin by installing a compact wad of cotton, but the drone of the pram he had never managed to overcome. Ideally – as I always maintained – the piece should have gone about its business in a haunting silence. The extraneous noises had always exasperated Lenny and he felt thwarted by his failure to master the problem. I think of him now, as I listen to the clumsy murmur of the axle. I think of him now with his bald head in his hands, confounded by the shortcoming. Gritting his perfect teeth and muttering, 'Fuck,' and 'Fuck,' once again, 'Fuck, fuck,' for minutes on end, tormented and surly, and the problem unresolved.

I'd known Lenny Snook since we were both seventeen, and he was going bald even then. But Lenny being Lenny it had never been a problem cos he had the head for it and it suited him, cos he was a handsome fucker. He was handsome in middle age and I imagined he'd be a handsome pensioner. Bald and handsome. All the more handsome for being bald. All the more bald for being handsome. Whatever that means. It was a pain in the arse. But all he is now, as I forecast long ago, is an Exquisite Corpse.

My fear is that he died despising me, cursing me and damning the day he had ever set his eyes upon me. But then that says little about Lenny and everything about me. Perhaps I should come up with a finer and more noble fear. For instance: my fear is that Lenny's wounds caused his death to be an extended and unfathomably painful trial, and that at the end he wept and begged for his lost father. Or that he screamed in medieval agony as he prayed for the tormented soul of his awkward and buckled mother. Ah yes, that sounds a little better. That, then, is my fear: that he died in a spirit of familial anguish and not, as I may have previously suggested, pissed off by the petulance and childish pedantry of his very great friend – The Late Hector Kipling.

I was still in bed when I heard the slamming of the door at Box Street. There was enough time for me to scurry into my pants and squirrel myself away behind the dense velvet curtains. Then, at last, the door to the main room was flung open, and in walked Monger carrying a duffel bag and holding a delicate pink handkerchief over his nose and mouth. He was wearing a panama hat and a pair of peculiar Harold Lloyd-style spectacles. I caught my breath, clenched my fists and tried, with all my might, not to move. In fact I had a serious talk with every last cell, the length and breadth of my body, about not moving, but it amounted to nothing. I was trembling behind the curtain, monitoring his every move. He put down the bag and, after testing the air, folded up the handkerchief and arranged it carefully in the breast pocket of his blazer. It was then that I noticed he was sporting a cheap false moustache. Next he limped over to the settee and lifted the sheet from Lenny and Rosa; the better to appraise his handiwork. He was only a silhouette, but

I imagined him smiling. After a few moments of rapt contemplation he replaced the sheet and smoothed it down at all four corners. After that he settled himself into the big blue armchair. He reached deep into his pocket and took out a cigarette case, his jewelled Cartier lighter and a gun. He tipped his hat over his eyes, sparked up a fag and began scratching at his thigh, which went on for some time. Before long, with the help of a few swigs from his hip flask, he fell asleep.

Silence.

Pathetic, if you ask me. Pathetic murderer behaviour.

The gun, the weight of it, the temperature, felt strange in my hand. I suppose that was to be expected, since I had never before held a real gun. As a child I had run amok with many toy guns of all shapes and sizes, and as I stood there keeping careful watch over the sleeping Monger I was reminded of a time when I had frightened Mum in the kitchen, firing at her repeatedly, shouting at her, over and over, 'There you go, there you go, Mum. How do you like that, you punk? Eh? How do you like that?' Mum, as I remember, had been a little discombobulated by this zealous display of homicidal play-acting, and had backed herself up against the sink, calling out for Dad to come and take me off her hands. Nonplussed by her giddy supplications, I had continued to threaten her with my silver plastic Smith & Wesson, 'Come on, then, lady. Make your first move! Who do you think's gonna come off the worse, me or you?'

I curled my sweating finger around the trigger and thought about shooting Monger right there and then. Wouldn't it be easier if I did it whilst he was sleeping? I don't know. I realized that I had to think very carefully about all this. After all, it's not the sort of decision you want to make in a hurry – like buying a house or proposing marriage.

I pulled the sheet away from Lenny and Rosa and looked at them both, all dead and wet. And dry, in a way. Dry in many ways. In fact, hardly wet at all.

As I replaced the sheet, Rosa's dead left arm dropped, her knuckles rapping on the bloody wooden floor. Upon hearing this, Monger's eyes sprang open like a sinister and suspicious automaton – or a kind of natty cyborg, if you like. Whatever, I had awoken the beast and I really wanted to go to the toilet all of a sudden.

Silence.

Frozen.

And then, at last: 'Ah, Hector,' he said, and reached for his gun.

'Ah, Monger,' I said, showing him the strange and fatal machine that I held in my quivering hand.

Monger repositioned himself, smiled and straightened his tie. He removed his spectacles and threw them across the room. I watched them skid across the floor and come to rest by the leg of Eleni's piano stool, shunting Rosa's bloody green eye towards the bedroom door.

I was about ten feet away. I lifted the gun and pointed it at the centre of his face. I wasn't sure if I should be cocking it, or whether that was just something they do in cowboy films. I was pointing it at his face and, judging by his expression, was reasonably assured that no cocking was required.

He straightened his cufflinks and cleared his throat. 'Hector, you really are the most awful nuisance.'

I came very close to pulling the trigger right there and then, if only in protest at his dreary verbosity.

'Says you,' I snapped back, rather petulantly, given the circumstances.

'You are aware, are you not, that you look an utter fool standing there with a gun in your hand?'

'Well, it's your gun, Monger, and I've got it. So who's the fool – eh?'

'Still you, I'm afraid.'

'Why are you doing this to me?'

'Why not, Hector?'

'You murdered Lenny and Rosa, you nut! Look at them! You killed them!'

'Ah yes,' he whispered and tilted his hat to shadow his eyes, 'sorry about that, old boy. It was rather remiss of me, I know. But you see I caught a glimpse of the balding pate, thought it was you and saw no reason not to muck right in. I must say that I'm a little ashamed to have slain the great Lenny Snook. He was really quite a talent. How will history ever forgive me?'

'Quite a talent? Lenny Snook, quite a talent?'

'Well, a deal better than you, let us say.'

'You know nothing.'

'Well, I know what I like, as they say.'

'Who gives a flying fuck what you like? I've seen your paintings, Monger. And I'll tell you what, in my time I've seen many things. I've seen shit smeared on top of shit, literally, in a gallery in Tokyo, I saw literal shit smeared on top of literal shit, but even that wasn't as shit as the shit that I saw in your house, not even close.'

'Oh, so it was you.'

'What was me?'

'You, round at my flat.'

'You know it was.'

'Yes, and I had a charming tête-à-tête with your ridiculous mother.'

'Monger, I am so close to shooting you right now that I really wouldn't push it.'

'Yes, she really is quite an unfathomable idiot.'

'I want the money back! I want all that money back! And the case. I want Mum's little travel bag back as well!'

'I told her that I had happened upon you fornicating with a tattooed and gothic harlot whose language would shame the coalface. Well, you can imagine how well she took that. I think perhaps that you should call her. She was slurring a little. I wouldn't be surprised if her head wasn't in the oven by nightfall.'

'I er . . .' I said, and swallowed, 'I er . . . think I may be about to shoot you now.'

'Go ahead,' said Monger, wafting his fag in the air, 'go ahead and shoot me. I could do with a little excitement.'

There was no fear in his voice. His eyes were shining and his teeth were brilliant white, as though I'd just asked him what he fancied from the bar. Beneath my finger I could feel the cool metal of the softly bevelled trigger.

'Why have you done all this? Why are we stood here like this? Why am I about to kill you?' I said.

'Hector, calm right down. You are not . . . you are simply not about to kill me.'

'But I really think that I might be. I really think that I am about to kill you. Fucking hell, you psycho, you invertebrate fucking bivalve, I really think that I may be about to pull this trigger!' I closed one eye and corrected my aim to connect with the middle of his forehead.

'Hector, you just haven't thought any of this through,' and he blew out two perfect rings. Then he closed his eyes and ran the tip of his little finger across one lid.

'I'm about to kill you! I swear on . . .' I couldn't think of a life left to swear upon. 'I swear on . . .'

'You're a disgrace, Hector. I will destroy you,' said Monger, chin up in the air, 'I will fucking annihilate you, you sad, impotent specimen. You are no more capable of pulling that trigger than—'

And that's about the moment when I pulled the trigger and watched his head turn into a special effect. His hat span across the room like a posh Frisbee and his hair flew up into a ridiculous quiff. My painting behind him was splattered with . . . Oh, need I go on? I'm sure you can imagine.

An hour crept by. I think it was an hour. I hardly recognized it. Bearing no resemblance to any of the numerous other hours of my acquaintance, I hardly recognized a single second of it. I believe that I slept, though it was barely sleep, and come to that it was barely me.

Upon waking I rummaged through his duffel bag and found a trove of ammunition. Through a process of trial and error – learning how to load and reload – I shot up the entire flat. The mirror got it, the bed got it, my painting got it, and, just for good measure, Monger got it as well, over and over, over and over. In the end I threw down the gun and beat my head against the keys of the piano until even music was destroyed. Before I passed out I caught sight of my painting, rent by ladders, bullets and the shrapnel of Monger's skull. A self-portrait at last.

Now I'm perspiring at such an alarming rate, I'm beginning to steam. And once again I am thrown into a flap that I will be discovered before I have the opportunity to fully explain why it is that I'm here in Lenny's hole in the floor of the Tate. But no matter, the moment is almost upon us, and no matter what, I sincerely believe that they will warm to my cause once my point is finally made. After all, the room above is filling up and fairly rings with the trill of lyric banality and the clash of crystal. I must say that I never imagined my life ending this way. But then I never imagined all those other lives ending in the way that they did. But what does that really tell us about anything, other than that my imagination is not up to scratch? I always thought that death would unpick me slowly, meticulously, over a long period of time; first subjecting me to one ailment, just to put me in the mood, and then, as the years shuffled by, it would gleefully augment my suffering, little by little, with each succeeding malady spread on top of the other, much like a glaze, until, at last, there existed a dense impasto of crippling afflictions that would finally suffocate the subject, rendering it muddy, lifeless and without form. And that was the best that I could have hoped for. You see, I suppose I always found it near impossible to really delight in the rich tints and manifold textures of life, since they always seemed to me to be casually flattened by the lacklustre tones of the final account.

And so here I am, at last, scaling the walls of my dead friend's deep and admired hole, naked and sweating, fumbling for finger holds with one hand whilst clutching a loaded gun in the other. Who would ever have thought that it could come to this? My bare feet are quarrelling with their bleeding toes and I sear one side of my scrotum on the rage of a lamp. Just as I am about to poke my head above the trench my brain is assailed with the dizzy clamour of the mob of critics. I'm not sure if that is the correct collective noun when one is speaking of a gathering of critics – what else should it be? An ostentation, as in peacocks? Or a murder, as in crows? Perhaps a pride, an envy, a gluttony, or even a sloth. I believe that it is Brian Sewell who first comes to the aid of the baffled Miss Cookham, assisting with the translation of the offending French slogan daubed upon the wall, in what seems commonly agreed to be blood.

'Why it's perfectly straightforward, Becky,' declares Sewell, with sixty-three plums pushed into his mouth: ' "L'acte Surréaliste le plus simple est de marcher dans une rue peuplée avec un revolver chargé, et de tirer au hasard." It's Breton at his most asinine. It means, the simplest – or one might say the ultimate – act of Surrealism is to walk into a crowded street with a loaded revolver, and open fire at random. That's what it says, but then Breton was a charlatan of the highest order. An utter quack.' He's sounding unnervingly like Monger. 'I mean, quite honestly, I fail to see what point Snook is making here. I find it not only tiresome, but extremely jejune, and, I might add, cretinous to boot. I mean, for goodness' sake, André Breton, this was a man who—'

And that, at last is it, I believe. That is my cue. That is when I make my move. A fleshy, unfathomable behemoth scrambling up and out of the dirt with a gun in its fist, eyes like cheap cufflinks. The first shot was understandably wide of the mark, ricocheting off the ambulant pram and shattering the back window of Lenny's blood-filled limousine, thus flooding the gallery floor with ninety gallons of bubbling pigs' blood. Although, in truth, it never was real pigs' blood, as Lenny had always claimed, but only a sort of synthetic blood, a sticky, sweet and rather too pink substance, much used in the movies, which went by the charming name of Kensington Gore. But then, you see, that is hardly the issue. Indeed that was only the start of it. For with the next shot, or twelve, the gathered pack of now howling traducers were brought to their knees and invited to savour some real pigs' blood – some authentic Kensington Gore.

19

WANDSWORTH PRISON, LONDON

I understand that it is customary, on occasions such as these, for the perpetrator of the atrocity to have the good grace to turn the gun upon himself. Apparently, in ninety-nine per cent of cases, the befuddled culprit is so discomfited by the severity of their gesture that they seek solace in the kiss of the very same bullet. Alas, in the event, it seems that I was found lacking with regards to this requirement. In the event, I'm afraid, the compulsion to play by the rules, and do the decent thing, evaded me. To be honest, I never even considered it.

I'd love to be able to tell you that I won, but I didn't – I lost. I lost spectacularly; in fact I came in last. Still, not bad, to be last – which was in fact fifth – when I wasn't even nominated. Archie March won, even though most of his idle gimmicks were ravaged in the fallout. You might think it a little indelicate that they should have even considered the question of winners and losers after such an abomination. But, at the end of the day, art is business, and that business is primarily show business, and the first principle of show business is that the show must go on. So the show went on. Archie March showed up on the night in a black tux with a black beret and a black sable armband and dedicated the accolade to the dead and the prize money to the families of the dead. As you might imagine there were a number of outspoken opportunists and diehard Breton enthusiasts, posturing in the pages of the broadsheets, saying that I should have won, but, as you might imagine, they were roasted and vilified as nihilistic ghouls, cut from the same cloth as the handful of diabolic reprobates who hailed 9/11 as a masterpiece of postmodern deconstructionist installation. The red-tops indulged themselves in an orgy of punning with headlines which ranged from the obvious and asinine 'Art Attack!', 'Artbreaker!' and 'Artless Swine!' to the more sophisticated 'A Turner For The Worst', 'A Brush With Death' and, gloriously, my personal favourite, 'I Don't Know Much About Mass Murder, But I Know What I Like!'

Newsnight cobbled together a nice little special on me and heli-coptered in Damien and Tracey, who, on the whole, felt that I had taken things a little bit too far, and that the well-mined and ubiquitous motif of death had finally reached its zenith. Jake and Dinos put in an appearance on *Question Time*, stating that the ultimate role of art was to illuminate the eternal dilemma of mortality without actually ramming it down the spectator's throat. They found my statement to lean too weightily, too indecently, on the literal, and would have found it more compelling if I had merely implied the notion of indiscriminate slaughter rather than actually slaughtered people indiscriminately. In a self-aggrandizing coda to their condescension, they took the opportu-nity to speculate that my barbarism represented an all-consuming final curtain to the theatre of the YBAs, and that they should henceforth be referred to as MABAs: Middle-Aged British Artists.

My ceiling is twenty feet lower than my old ceiling and there is no piano. But there is no grey so grey that the trained and cultured eye cannot throw out a good length of rope and heave up a thick tough fudge of blue. And often, therefore, these walls are far, far bluer than all those bleached and hoary skies of recent memory. Even the mice are a kind of lavender. Even the spiders.

I have finally stopped painting big heads. In fact, I have finally stopped painting altogether. Oh yes. You see, for the first two months they allowed me a few lousy brushes and a meagre selection of acrylics, but consequent to a psychiatric evaluation of my output it was decided that I shouldn't even be in the same room as a pencil, which is a shame, because I was right all along. Because death, you see, was the answer. I'll say it again: Death was the answer.

When my life was starved of death it was not really what you would call a life. Since my life sought justification through representation, it was imperative that this representation should be consummate by way of being omniscient. As long as the ultimate desolation remained in the shadows then all my attempts to capture and illuminate the profound were damned to the shallows. Consequently, when my life was beset by, not one, but multiple bereavements, then the process blossomed in the glow of a glad and orgasmic ignition. What I'm trying to say is that one cannot interpret the curves and drops of existence until one has skidded a little on the ice and gravel of annihilation. Is that clear? Good. Then let us proceed.

Bianca comes to see me every fortnight, as a friend, free of charge; though our conversations are much the same as our conversations of old that used to retail at about a pound a minute, two syllables per second, or thereabouts. Of course my issues, if that's what we must call them, are a little more complex; and whereas we used to look forward to a day when we might terminate the treatment, we now have a tacit understanding that any kind of conclusion lies far in the distance. (And that the word terminate has, of late, taken on a very different meaning.) She's the one friend that I have left, since the remainder of my friends, who aren't actually dead, now see fit to shun my company (which isn't very difficult for them, obviously, since my company is rather easy to shun these days, and looks set to continue being the case for the next thirty years or so).

As to why I did what I did, Bianca is still working on it. I sometimes wonder if she regrets ever having met me. And then, other times, I believe she spends her evenings lining up her lucky stars and slipping them all a tenner. After all, I'm Hector Kipling. And what self-respecting Kleinian psychoanalyst could ask for anything more? She started off by grilling me as to whether or not, if at any point, I might have heard some sort of voice, or voices, in my head. Imperative voices, she called them. I said no, and she took my hand in hers and told me that it was nothing to be ashamed of, and that I would, in fact, be in very good company should I concede this to be the case. She told me that Pythagoras had had them, Socrates had had them, St Augustine, Galileo and Hildegard of Bingen, whoever he was. I asked her if she meant Hildegard of Ogden and she scolded me for being flippant, and scorned my tendency to resort to infantile comedy in the face of mature tragedy. I asked her if there was such a thing as immature tragedy and she poked me in the middle of my third eye and said, 'There you go again!'

Apparently Galileo heard the voice of his dead daughter, whereas Socrates was often advised as to the best way round to his mate's house. We talked about Van Gogh, Rothko and Munch, and Bianca posited that my breakdown might very well date back to that day at Tate Modern with Lenny when I broke down and wept before the Munch painting. We talked about Breton and Manson, about Lee Harvey Oswald and Mark Chapman, and then about Jake and Dinos Chapman. Then I began to sneeze a lot and had to lie flat on my back and chant something in Tagalog or Urdu, I'm not sure which. We talked about God and which one, and what sort, and what we think he or she, them or it might be up to these days. I assured her that I'd made a few half-cocked attempts at praying in the prison chapel, begging Jesus and his dad to deliver me from evil, to forgive me my trespasses, and please not to make any rash decisions concerning the fate of my mortal soul, that kind of thing. Bianca disregarded such talk and told me not to dwell upon grim themes of retribution: tridents, fire and the eternal gnashing of teeth, and how the Church of England's official line is, of late, that hell is just black nothing as opposed to the white wonderful something of heaven. Even the Vatican has recently seen fit to knock all that purgatory palaver on the head. She discouraged my visits to the chapel, opining that all organized religions are merely the fossils of enlightenment, and that any prolonged contemplation of the violent renderings of Christ's wounds could well set us back a few sessions. She went on to talk about Buddha, a short fat bald bloke, much like myself. Sedentary, contemplative and celibate, much like myself. The next week she brought in a small orange book and quoted from it at length: 'Whatever joy there is in this world / All comes from desiring others to be happy / Whatever suffering there is in this world / All comes from desiring myself to be happy.'

'But I didn't gun down those critics out of any desire for my own happiness,' I protested.

She leaned in and gazed deep into my eyes, 'Really? Think about it, Hector, dear. Think about it.'

I thought about it. 'No,' I said, 'look at me. Do I look happy?'

'A little,' she said. She smiled, raised up my hands, brought them up to her lips and kissed each one in turn. 'Buddha said: "What you are is what you have been. What you will be, is what you do now." '

But later that night I found myself masturbating over a vision of Bianca and Rosa getting off with each other in a spotlit bubble bath in the middle of the Sahara, so I think I still have some way to go before I can think about tucking into a nice bowl of pad thai in the splendid glades of Nirvana. The closest I'll ever get to Nirvana is by putting a bullet into my haunted, unkempt head, if you get my drift. But there I go again with the jokes. But then again you can't make a Hamlet without cracking a few gags. But, as I say, there I go again. Fuck, life drags. Sometimes I find myself wishing that I did hear voices in my head, rather than all this high-pitched silence. At least then I might have someone to talk to. At least then I might suffer a little conversation with someone other than Solomon Otto Sudweeks.

Solomon Otto Sudweeks is my terrifying cellmate. The first thing I can tell you about him is something that you already know: he has an idiotic name. He told me that if he had been born a girl then they were going to call him Trinity, which would have been even more idiotic. He bears a striking resemblance to Zero Mostel (who also had an idiotic name), though he's a deal fatter than Mostel and sports a kind of Tsar Nicholas moustache that went out of fashion sometime early in the last century, in a basement in Ekaterinburg. He sweats like a warm Emmental and is an habitual sleepwalker, though he never gets very far, obviously. Oh, and I should also mention that he hates me, which, given his proclivity for homicide is a bit of a worry, to say the least. He was dealt an unconditional life sentence about six years ago for butchering a clown who'd scared the wits out of his daughter at a party in Whitechapel. He then, a little confused and inconsistent, to say the least, proceeded to smother his daughter and dismember his wife with an antique Caribbean machete. He's bounced my head off the walls of the cell two or three times, and, on one occasion tried to drown me in mouthwash, but on the whole the wardens don't seem to be overly concerned about such trifles. I get the feeling that they think I deserve it. And perhaps I do. I say perhaps, because even though I can boast a bigger body count than Solomon, I'm not really what you would call a hardened criminal. Not really. I just had some kind of a conniption fit, as Bianca would say. Or a reet funny do, as Mum would say.

Er . . . would have said. As Mum would have said.

That's right – poor old Mum is dead.

Oh, and Dad, by the way, I should mention – Dad is dead as well.

It was a terrible business. Really quite awful. As you can well imagine.

As the news broke the following morning, on the lurid bulletins of *GMTV*, Dad was apparently sufficiently conscious to absorb the shock and the shame, and within three brief minutes his heart broke. Really broke. I mean like a clock might break. And at twelve minutes past eight, it stopped. He didn't even make it through the weather, which, just for the record, forecast high winds, thick cloud and heavy rain throughout the North-West and down into the Midlands.

Mum, meanwhile, slept on until noon, in a haze of Vicadin and Safeway's gin, deaf to the endless ringing of the phone. It was a journalist from the *Daily Telegraph* who first broke the news concerning the rumpus at the Tate. And then a Dr Dennis Bannister from the Victoria Hospital who delivered the final blow with a slow and whispered description of how, at the end, Dad had curled up into a trembling foetal ball and for the next half hour, uttered only one word, and one word alone, over and over: 'Connie, Connie, Connie.'

It was about twenty past one, therefore, when Connie Mary Kipling, in nothing but her bra and a pair of her husband's blue jockey shorts, climbed the sea wall, just north of Squire's Gate, and screamed and screamed into the bluster of the building squall, before surrendering herself to the tea-brown, high-tide foam of the Irish Sea. A little after sundown her bloated cadaver was washed ashore about four hundred yards south of Lytham's white windmill. Mum had always been rather partial to Lytham's white windmill, and would often take me there as a child, to fly my Aristocat kite. Thomas O'Malley and a scrum of kittens, smiling on high, or swooping out towards the dunes.

Given my volatile state of mind in those first few days, I was offered no report of all this until the following Tuesday, when, for fear of me hearing it from some other source, an avuncular vicar named Boris Crossland ushered me into a small blue room and recounted the events with – to be honest – a very lilting turn of phrase and meticulous attention to the finer details. When pressed he revealed to me that he had once, many years ago, taken the role of Poggio in the Bispham Amateur Dramatic Society's shoestring production of *'Tis Pity She's A Whore*. I thanked him for his well-modulated account and he took me in his arms and spoke of God's mercy and his baffling proclivity for forgiveness, and then, pleased with how well all that had gone, launched into a hushed rendition of a few apposite lines from *The Tempest*:

> Our revels now are ended. These our actors,
> As I foretold you, were all spirits and
> Are melted into air, into thin air:

> And, like the baseless fabric of this vision,
> The cloud-capp'd towers, the gorgeous palaces,
> The solemn temples, the great globe itself,
> Yea, all which it inherit, shall dissolve
> And, like this insubstantial pageant faded,
> Leave not a rack behind. We are such stuff
> As dreams are made on, and our little life
> Is rounded with a sleep.

When it was over I disentangled myself from his sincere embrace, rose to my feet and applauded heartily. He appeared wonderfully proud and fulfilled, and I swear that I glimpsed the first bubble of a tear in his eye. And then, the door of the small blue room was thrown open, and a blowsy-faced Glaswegian in a black uniform and cap wrenched me by the arm and marched me off to a much darker room. And that is where I spent the next week and a half, weeping and squeaking till my bed sheets were so sodden and salty, it was as though they had been fetched fresh out of the sea – which in a way, they were.

At my trial I made a little noise about how the bodies discovered in Box Street were not of my doing, but then, since I realized and then acknowledged that I had indeed dispatched Frederick Monger, and that Lenny and Rosa might still be alive were it not for my intrepid stupidity, it all seemed a rather moot point, and I elected to let it go. And so, therefore, it is on record for all time that I am named as the assassin of Lenny Snook and Rosa Flood. Furthermore, since the inquest into the case of Godfrey Bolton's suicide was reopened and found to be replete with all sorts of anomalies, then I am also, for the record, the convicted slayer of that twisted old horse-fucker.

My wake shall surely be an intimate affair: Boris Crossland and Bianca Schulz, sharing a plate of ham and a half bottle of flat Hooch, quoting Faust and bickering about Jung, Gomorrah and the dissolution of the monasteries. What a send-off.

And here I am. A warm worm, in aviary earth. Solomon is asleep and snoring like a hollow donkey. No doubt he'll be up and about in a minute or two, off on one of his nocturnal rambles to the door and back. The best that I can hope for is that he doesn't pause by the bed, as is often the case, and piss all over my pillow before I can steer my head beyond the trajectory of his merry cascade. That is the best that I can hope for. Though you might as well remove the word hope from all dictionaries, since it has little meaning anymore. Pandora's Box has been hosed down with bleach, dismantled plane by plane, nail by nail and tossed upon a well-built bonfire, the ashes scattered into space. That, to belabour my point, is the fate of hope in the life of Hector Kipling. The Late Hector Kipling, as I am known around here – if only to myself.

I never found out what happened to Eleni. As far as I understand she knows nothing of the pandemonium that broke upon the heels of her departure. It may be that some friend – some other friend, not mentioned here – has, in the meantime, made contact with her and supplied her with a report of my form and condition. But it may also be the case that she boarded an aeroplane that night and, having cultivated an understandable distaste for the British as a race, and therefore any manifestation of the British press, is completely ignorant of my transgression. All through the period of my arrest, remand and subsequent trial I heard nothing. Nor did I make any attempt to contact her and furnish her with the glad tidings of my predicament. After all, why bother? Where would that have got me? Indeed, it is some comfort to feel that there is at least one living soul, somewhere, far out there in the surviving world, who might just – just possibly – retain the last vestiges of something resembling love for me – albeit soiled and buckled. At the very least it is something for what is left of me to hang onto. It sustains as a welcome balm to the vilification of the media and the manifold hostility of my fellow countrymen. But then, who can blame them? They do not know me. And then, even if they did, really, who can blame them?

If I am honest with myself, I doubt that I shall ever see or hear from Eleni again. After all there is little hope that she could ever forgive me for my insouciance regarding the passing of her mother; let alone my squalid liaison with Rosa; let alone the unfortunate blip of a well-publicized mass murder. And therefore, if that is indeed the case, and that she is gone from my life for evermore, then it is as though she too were dead. After all, it feels exactly the same. To conceive of her somewhere, in a land far from here, going about the concerns of her daily life, is no different than if I were to imagine the continuing carefree existence of Kirk or Lenny, or Mum and Dad – or Sparky, for that matter. The point is, she has been removed from my life, if not from her own. And thus, she is just another victim of my wicked infirmity. Yet one more innocent and hapless soul to have died by my hands. Sometimes, of course, I dream about her, and sincerely believe her to be alive. But then do I not dream of all my dead loved ones in an identical manner? So what comfort am I to take from such illusion? And besides, more often than not, in my dreams of Eleni, she is quite dead. And so it goes on. And so goodbye, Eleni. Farewell and adieu. Which pains me to say. For you see, I think about her till all thinking hurts. Like a wrecking ball's punch to the belly of my brain. I think about her more than I think about anything or anyone else. I think about her to the point of being utterly baffled as to the meaning of the word think. Till think rhymes with clink, and thought rhymes with caught. Thinking with sinking. Wedding bells with prison cells. First kiss with only this. And love let loose with hangman's noose.

I lie on my back and pull faces at the ceiling. After a while I notice that one of my blackened molars is loose. After five excruciating minutes I hold it between my fingertips and press it against my nostrils to see how it smells. Not too bad. I summon up a gob of bloody flob, toss it to the back of my tongue and swallow. I return my attention to the ceiling and resume pulling faces. Oh, if only they would indulge me with a blunt black pastel, or even a brick of chalk and a sunlit wall. Then I might begin to write some of this down.

picador.com

blog
videos
interviews
extracts

Still Water Saints

Alex Espinoza was born in Tijuana, Mexico, the youngest of eleven children. At the age of two, he migrated to southern California with his family and grew up in the city of La Puente, a suburb of Los Angeles. Earning a BA from the University of California at Riverside with honours, Espinoza went on to receive an MFA from UC Irvine, where he was the editor of the university's literary magazine. He now teaches creative writing at UC Riverside. *Still Water Saints* is his first novel.

Still Water Saints

A Novel

Alex Espinoza

PICADOR

First published 2007 by Random House, an imprint of
The Random House Publishing Group, a division of
Random House, Inc., New York

First published in Great Britain 2007 by Picador

This edition published 2013 by Picador
an imprint of Pan Macmillan, a division of Macmillan Publishers Limited
Pan Macmillan, 20 New Wharf Road, London N1 9RR
Basingstoke and Oxford
Associated companies throughout the world
www.panmacmillan.com

ISBN 978-1-4472-4830-9

Visit **www.picador.com** to read more about all our books
and to buy them. You will also find features, author interviews and
news of any author events, and you can sign up for e-newsletters
so that you're always first to hear about our new releases.

Para mi padre, Federico Espinoza (1923–1989).
Your hands and heart shaped me.
I have not forgotten.

Feast of the Epiphany of Our Lord & Día de los Reyes

Magi and Kings of Africa, Arabia, and the East

Patrons of travelers.

She could walk on water.

She roamed the banks of the Santa Ana, among the long green stalks, chanting to the moon, to the gods of Night and Shadow. She rose and stepped onto the river, her footsteps gently rippling the surface.

She summoned the spirits of the dead. They whispered their secrets to her, and she scribbled their messages on scraps of paper and in the margins of her phone book:

Tell Ramón the locket fell on the floor between the bed and the nightstand.

I'm all right. It's like Disneyland up here, only without rides.

I don't miss my ears because they were too big.

She fought the Devil. Every night he came to her, his head crowned with horns, his skin covered in scales. He cursed and called her names. She beat him back with her bare hands and sent him running, his cloven feet tapping against the tile of her kitchen floor.

She was a Bruja. A Santa. A Divina. A Medium, Prophet, and Healer. Able to pass through walls and read minds, to pull tumors from ailing bodies, to uncross hexes and spells, to raise the dead, and to stop time. When doctors failed, when priests and praying were not enough, the people of Agua Mansa came to the Botánica Oshún, to Perla. The shop sold amulets and stones, rosaries and candles. They bought charms to change their luck, teas to ease unsettled nerves, and estampas of saints, the worn plastic cards they carried in their purses or wallets for protection.

As thanks the customers brought her booklets of coupons and long strips of lottery tickets. They gave her fresh bouquets of roses and carnations. They showed her pictures of aunts and uncles she had helped see through heart surgeries and hip replacements. They brought in the children

she had saved from drug addictions and prison sentences. They told her of the abusive husbands and gambling wives she had chased away for good. Men often grew uneasy in her presence. The women always opened up.

"I think I have bilis," Gilda Mejía said, walking up to the register where Perla stood. "Look." She stuck out her tongue. "It's all yellow. Plus my stomach's upset."

"What happened?"

"Where do I start?" Gilda rested her hands on the glass countertop. She rented an apartment over at the Agua Mansa Palms. Her brother and his new wife had moved in a few weeks ago, after he lost his job. The couple was making it hard for Gilda to relax when she came home from work because they were always in the living room watching television with the volume turned all the way up.

"You think they'd turn it down, but no. They're not deaf. And his wife. I can't stand her. The way she talks to my brother. And she's cheating on him. I see the way she looks at that guy from 312. There's something going on there." It was too crowded for three people in a one-bedroom apartment, she explained. Her brother and his wife fought well into the night, making it hard for her to sleep. She was irritable all the time, and her nerves felt ready to snap at any moment.

Simonillo was perfect to cure strong cases of bilis, to relieve tension and stress. Perla stepped away from the register and walked over to the packets of herbs that hung from pegs on the left wall of the botánica.

"I want you to make a tea with this," she said, handing the bag to Gilda. "Drink it on an empty stomach. It's bitter, so suck on a sugar cube or put some honey in it."

"Okay," Gilda said, handing over money for the herbs. "I just want to be better."

Perla took a blue seven-day candle from the shelves behind the register. She pointed to the picture of Our Lady of Regla on the glass candleholder. The Virgin, holding the infant Jesus, floated on a bed of clouds high above a cathedral. "Light this veladora before going to bed. Keep it lit all night while you sleep."

After Gilda left, Miriam Orozco's van pulled up. She got out, but her husband stayed in the car.

"Hi, Miriam. How can I help you?" Perla said.

"It's not me this time." She pointed to the van. "It's him. He's embarrassed to talk to you."

"Embarrassed? Why embarrassed?"

Miriam shrugged her shoulders. "Men. You know how they're like. Big babies."

Perla walked out into the parking lot. The car door was locked. "Talk to me, Jorge," she shouted and knocked on the window.

He rolled it down. "Hi," he said, resting his elbow on the door.

"What are you embarrassed about? Miriam says you don't want to come in."

Miriam stood behind Perla, jiggling the car's keys. "Tell her. Don't act dumb." She crossed her arms and sighed.

But Jorge stayed quiet.

Miriam said, "Here's what happened: Jorge went to a doctor who said he has depression. The pills the doctor gave him made his mouth dry. Jorge, tell her! You've missed work." Miriam walked over and leaned against the van's hood, watching Jorge through the windshield spotted with mud. "He doesn't touch me anymore."

"The doctor," Jorge said, raking his hair with his fingers. "He says I'm going through a midlife crisis. Menopause for men. Is that for real? I cry a lot. I'm no fun to be around. I can't look at my wife in that way. When we're in bed. Together. You know?"

"Come with me," Perla told Miriam. Back inside the botánica, Perla asked her, "Has he been eating anything strange?"

"No," she said.

The oils, bath salts, and scents were kept on the shelves next to the herbs and teas. Perla picked up a bottle of "Love Musk" cologne. "Has he been drinking?" She took a prayer card of Saint Job from the plastic rack on the counter.

"No," Miriam said. "He's been sober now for fifteen years."

"I'm only making sure. Have you been putting a lot of pressure on him? To do things? Around the house? Are you fighting over money?"

"No. Everything's good. Except for this."

They walked back out to the van together, and Miriam got in. Perla

handed the bag to Jorge and said, "This is a cologne I want you to wear. It'll help you with your love problem. There's an estampa. Job." She showed him the picture on the card. "He's the patron of depressed people. Pray one rosary to him. And I want you to keep taking those pills the doctor gave you. Even if they make your mouth dry."

"He's bad at following directions," Miriam said. "I'll make sure he does, though."

"Good," Perla said. "If he's not better, have him go see the doctor again. If still nothing, bring him back here."

Miriam started the car, took the rosary wrapped around the rearview mirror, and handed it to Jorge. "Hold this," she said as they pulled away.

Perla helped a man whose daughter was fighting hard to kick a drug habit. Someone else needed luck in starting up a new restaurant. An old woman Perla recognized but whose name escaped her memory brought in her grandson because the boy was wetting his bed.

"He's thirteen," the old woman said. "Too old to be peeing in bed. I think he needs a limpia."

"I don't wanna do this," the boy protested. He crossed his arms and glared at Perla. "It's stupid."

The old woman tugged at his shirt. "Stop it, Tony."

Perla took the sign that read BACK IN A FEW MINUTES and taped it to the door. She led the boy and his grandmother behind the counter and through the curtain that separated the front of the store from the back.

The small kitchenette, with the mini-refrigerator and microwave Darío had given Perla when he left her the store, occupied much of the cramped stockroom. The rest of the space housed three bookshelves about six feet tall on which Perla kept her back stock. The narrow hallway separating the kitchenette and shelves from the bathroom and utility closet was where she held private consultations.

Perla worked slowly to gather the items, trying to remember what Darío had taught her. "Limpias are delicate because you're cleansing a body and chasing away evil spirits," he had said. "So it's important to concentrate." He had used a cigar, feathers, and an egg. He had chanted and whispered, rocking back and forth on his heels.

She covered the floor with a sheet and stood the boy in the middle. She

coughed when she took a puff from the cigar, then blew the smoke around his body, letting it drift and settle around his head. After beating the air around him with a gray plume she pulled from her feather duster, Perla told Tony to close his eyes. She took an egg from the refrigerator and rubbed it over his body and face.

"This is lame, Grandma," the boy said, then opened his eyes. "Can we go?"

Perla turned to the boy's grandmother. "There."

The old woman pointed to the egg. "Aren't you supposed to break it and look inside?"

"Oh," Perla said. "Yes." She cracked the egg and poured it into a Styrofoam cup.

"Tony," said the boy's grandmother, pointing. "See that red swirl? Inside the yolk? That's what was doing it. That there."

The boy looked. "Yeah, right."

His grandmother pinched Tony's arm, leaving two red marks on his skin. "We'll see what you say when it starts working."

Perla covered the cup with plastic wrap she kept on the shelf above the kitchenette's sink. "Throw this out before you get home."

"Why?" Tony said.

"Because if we don't," the old woman said, "the spirits will stay with you. So we have to get rid of it to lose them. Right?" She looked at Perla.

"Yes."

"So we're just gonna, like, throw that egg out the window of a moving car?" Tony asked. "What if it hits somebody?"

"Would you rather we not? Would you rather the spirits follow us? Keep making you pee in bed? All your friends will find out and make fun of you, Tony. And that girl you like. You want her to know?"

The boy blushed. "No."

"All right then," the old woman said. She took some money from her purse and handed it to Perla.

Perla walked them outside and found a group of customers waiting for her in the parking lot. She sold a "Quit Gossiping" candle to a high school girl and a jar of "Adam and Eve" love oil to a man who rode up on a ten-speed bike. Then Rosa Cabrera came in with her four-year-old daughter,

Danielle. Rosa was one of Perla's favorite customers. She had been in high school when her mother had first brought her to the store. Now, she was in her late twenties, married, and taking classes to become a hair stylist.

Danielle's hair was pulled back in two pigtails that glistened wet. She wore faded denim overalls and a red-and-yellow-checkered undershirt. She held out three wild clovers to Perla.

"We came from the park," Rosa said. "When I told her we were coming to visit you, she picked them."

Perla stepped around the counter and bent down to hug Danielle. She took the clovers and gave her a kiss on the cheek. "They're pretty," Perla said. "Thank you."

She put them in a mug and set them next to the statue of Santa Bárbara to the right of the front door. The statue stood on a square pedestal, holding a gold scepter in one hand, a chalice in the other. Long curls of her brown hair rested in folds on her shoulders. Perla turned to Danielle and pointed at the saint. "I think she'll like them, too, no?"

The girl smiled and pressed her face against her mother's thigh.

"I need something to keep me calm. To help me focus. I have a big test coming up." Rosa pointed to the incense sticks by the herbs and teas. "Can I get cinnamon?"

Perla took the pack, then walked over to the register to ring her up. "How's school?"

"Good. Just a lot of things to memorize, you know?" She sighed, unzipping her purse. "Who knew studying cosmetology would be so hard?"

"It's worth it, though." Perla put the incense in a paper bag and handed it to Rosa. "You'll see."

"I hope so." She took Danielle's hand, and they turned toward the door. "We'll come by your house tomorrow. After my test. I'll let you know how it went."

Hayley Garrett burst through the door, nearly knocking Rosa and Danielle down.

"Envy," Hayley said, tucking back strands of blond hair and shoving her keys in her back pocket. "Someone has that envy thing for me. What you told this one man last time I was in here."

"Envidia?" Perla asked. "The Evil Eye?"

"That's what I mean. I was in the bathroom at work, in one of the stalls. I overheard this girl, Iris Camacho, tell someone else she hated skinny white girls. She said my name. She said 'I want 'em all to go away. They're so stupid.' Something like that. I didn't catch the rest because somebody flushed."

Perla thought a moment. "How have you been feeling? Tired? Anxious?"

"Well, I always feel that way."

"Has your period come on time?"

"Yeah." The girl smirked.

"Stomach feeling okay? No heartburn?"

"Nope," Hayley said. "I've been too freaked out to eat. Working two jobs is a lot. I lost ten pounds. Everything fits me baggy." She laughed. "This Evil Eye, isn't it like a curse? Maybe she cursed me, and that's why I'm not eating. That possible?"

Perla said, "Well, yes."

"Yeah. I think that's what she did. She cursed me." Hayley paused, then laughed again. "Maybe it's a blessing. I'm starting to look good."

"Losing weight quickly like that could do bad things to your body and your system."

Hayley touched her stomach. "Well, I guess it's not worth it then. All right, all right. What do I do?"

The white wood chips of the cuasia rattled inside the plastic bag when Perla reached for it on the peg and handed it to Hayley. Cuasia, Perla explained, worked to strengthen the body and restore balance.

"I want you to soak these wood chips," Perla said. "Use one teaspoon of the chips for each cup of cold water. Steep this for twelve hours, then strain it. Drink one cup in the morning on an empty stomach and a second cup at night. Understand?"

The girl nodded.

Perla also sold her a bottle of "Repel Evil" bath salts and a "Hex Removing" veladora. "Here," she said. "Bathe with the 'Repel Evil' salts in the morning before work. It'll protect you from the girl's envidia. Light the candle at night when you're alone."

Hayley ran her finger across the pictures on the front of the candle.

"Horseshoes," Perla said. "Rabbit's feet. Crosses. Lucky symbols. Positivity."

"I hope this works," Hayley said. "Even though I might gain back all that weight I lost."

*   *   *

It was time to close. Perla began where she always did, dusting the figure of San Antonio, who stood guard on the wooden table by the front window. She took a bottle of ammonia and, using a crumpled-up sheet of newspaper, wiped down the window's glass. She straightened the statues displayed on the right-hand wall and made sure they all faced forward. She organized the shelves of soaps and oils, bath salts, and incense sticks. Some of the pegs on the wall were empty, so she grabbed some herbs from the back to fill in the gaps. She rearranged the gems and crystals, the books and decks of Tarot cards, the amulets and pendants, the rosaries and crucifixes inside the glass case where the register sat. She took inventory in her binder—noting which candles were low, what packets of incense sticks had sold, what herbs and teas she was missing—and set the list next to the phone. *I'll place an order first thing tomorrow morning.*

She locked the door, then closed out the register, separating her starting fund for tomorrow and recounting it before putting it back into the drawer. She took the rest of the money and placed it in a metal cash box. Tucking the box under her arm, Perla walked to the broom closet next to the bathroom. The closet was cramped, only wide enough for one bucket and two mops. She bent down to hide the box under a loose floorboard, then pushed the bucket over the spot.

She filled a glass bowl with tap water from the sink in the kitchenette and returned to the front of the store. Perla looked at all the stones—lapis, limestone, tourmaline—inside the display case. Removing a piece of quartz, she let her fingers slide across the edge and brought it up to her nose. It carried the scent of something fossilized, of ancient oceans and extinct fishes. Quartz helped with concentration, with memory and enlightenment and insight. Perla rubbed the stone three times over each eye and pressed it against the middle of her forehead, leaving it there for a minute to see if she sensed its energy, before dropping it into the water. The stone tapped the edges of the bowl as she carried it toward the statue of Santa Bárbara and set it on the floor beside Danielle's flowers.

She took more statues from the shelves—Our Lady of Guadalupe, the

Buddha, San Simón, Vishnu—and arranged them around Santa Bárbara. She grabbed one of the fold-up chairs she kept near the door, placed it before them, and sat down. She focused hard on the statues' faces. She wanted them to say something. She wanted to witness them move or bleed from the palms of their hands and the soles of their feet. But nothing happened.

She imagined the botánica's counters and walls as outstretched arms, beaded with amulets and ankhs and silver medallions, those arms then becoming her own, gathering her customers in. She thought about wisdom that stretched on and on, beyond the sky, beyond that and into death. She closed her eyes, tried to see it, to tap it. But nothing came.

Perla could not do what they said or believed, could not float through walls and utter strange words, could not speak with the spirits of the dead. She never could, and she knew she never would.

But Darío had said she had el don, the gift. It was strong in her. He had said so. And there were times she had even believed him.

         *   *   *

The iron security gate unfolded like the bellows of an accordion as Perla pulled it along the rail in front of the door. She snapped the padlock shut, turned around the corner of the building, and headed home. Her house was close, just across the empty lot next to the shopping center. Wild sage and scrub grew beside the worn path that cut through the field. Boys sometimes rode their bikes there, doing tricks and wheelies as they bumped over mounds and breaks, falling down, laughing and scraping their knees, their faces coated with grime. Their tires left thin tracks that looped around the salt cedar trees, around the soiled mattresses and old washers and sinks that were dumped here.

People told of a curse on these grounds, of a group of monks traveling through Agua Mansa in the days when California was still a part of Mexico, back before states were shapes on a map. They said a tribe of Indians massacred the monks; they skinned them and scattered their body parts around the lot for the crows. Still others said Mexican settlers had been lynched from the branches of the cedars by Anglos who stole their land for the railroads. Seeing a piece of stone, Perla wondered about the monks and those men dangling from branches. *A tooth? Part of a toe?* Empty soda cans and wrappers were caught under boulders and discarded car parts. *What would*

the monks think about having a tire for a headstone, a couch for a marker? She thought of her husband, Guillermo, of his tombstone, of the thick green lawns of the cemetery where he was buried.

When she reached her house and stepped inside, the air was warm and silent. Perla put her purse down on the rocking chair near the front door and went around, pushing the lace curtains back and cracking open the windows. She breathed in the scent of wood smoke from someone's fireplace down the street, a smell that reminded her of her father toasting garbanzo beans. She went into the kitchen and looked for something to eat.

Dinner was a bowl of instant oatmeal with two slices of toast, which she took out to the patio. The night was cold, and the steam from the oatmeal rose up and fogged her glasses as she spooned it in her mouth. Police sirens wailed down the street, and dogs answered, their cries lonely and beautiful. She looked up, and in the flashing lights saw a set of glowing red eyes.

Perla flicked on the porch light. It was an opossum, its fur dingy and gray, the tips and insides of its ears bright pink. It stood motionless, behind the trunk of the organ pipe cactus, staring at her. It climbed to the top of the fence, making a low, faint jingle as it moved. Perla looked again; a small brass bell was tied to a piece of red yarn knotted around the opossum's tail. She took her spoon and threw it. When it hit the bottom of the fence, the animal darted, the clatter of the bell frantic. The opossum disappeared behind the branches of the avocado tree and down the other side of the fence into the empty lot, the ringing growing fainter and fainter.

From under the kitchen sink, behind the pile of cloths and old sponges she could never bring herself to throw away, was a bottle of rum. She poured some into a cup and took a drink. Then another. The warmth calmed her nerves.

She imagined the ghosts of the dead monks and the lynched men rising up from the ground, awakened by her thoughts. Curls of gray smoke at first, they slowly took human form. They walked in a straight line. One in front of the other. A slow procession following the opossum's tracks through the lot and back home.

She took another drink and closed her eyes. That animal. It was a messenger. It was letting her know. Something was out there. It was coming.

She sat down and waited for it.

Release

Blanca, my sister, stands in front of the mirror, rocking her hips to a song on the radio, puckering her lips and blowing kisses at herself. She tosses me a bottle of nail polish, bright red with silver bits swirling around inside. When I put it on her nightstand, Blanca says to take it, that she bought it for me. The color's too bright, I tell her. She laughs.

Pulling me off her bed, Blanca walks me over to the mirror, tells me to look at my reflection, at my pretty green eyes. Pictures of some of her boyfriends are taped along the edge of the mirror. I look past those photos to the red pimples on my face, the dark and blotchy skin, and the rolls around my belly stretching out my shirt, my jeans, the elastic band around my underwear. My body's out of control.

Blanca wants to go to school to be a makeup artist and hair stylist, so she's always trying to pretty me up, always trying to put lipstick and mascara on me. She takes clips from the drawer to fasten my hair. There's something about the way my sister moves, the way her fingers pass over my face, the way her body hums. She glides. It's like she's underwater. When I remove the hair clips, Blanca gets upset, wants to know what's with me. She doesn't get me. Says that I mope too much and that I should learn to be more confident. But it's hard to be confident when you weigh as much as I do. When your body's so big that even breathing's hard.

My mother comes into the room, holding the car keys. We're going to the botánica to buy more of the tea I've been drinking to control my ap-

petite. Blanca shakes her head and asks if the tea's even working. I just lost five pounds, and my mother reminds her of this.

My sister rolls her eyes.

In the car, my mother lights a cigarette. She says I shouldn't pay any attention to Blanca. That five pounds is five pounds, and I shouldn't let her attitude discourage me. My mother's recently cut her hair short and bleached it because she started seeing too much gray. It's spiked on top, and she thinks this makes her look edgy. She's decked out in gold and silver anklets and a toe ring that she never takes off.

My great-grandfather used to call my mother "Gorda" because she was chubby when she was a young girl. He would pinch her cheeks and stomach. It was embarrassing, and it wasn't until after my mother gave birth to me and started exercising that she lost the weight. And it's because of her "victory over obesity" that my mother's decided to help me win my battle.

She says that, in many ways, I'm lucky that my weight's mostly around my belly because stretch marks there are easy to deal with, that you can take the sap from an aloe vera stem and rub it on them and, over time, they'll disappear. But her weight was all in her thighs, where the stretch marks almost never go away.

As we drive down the street, my mother goes on and on about self-esteem and self-perception, about men not wanting to marry fat women, and I find my mind wandering, tuning out her voice. I catch a glimpse of myself in the sideview mirror. The words *objects are closer than they appear* are stenciled along the bottom of the glass, and when I lean my head out the window, the words are tattooed across my forehead.

I began gaining weight a few years ago. It hit me fast. My mother blamed herself for not taking better care of me and regulating my diet. She decided that this summer was our chance. We needed to do something before it was too late. We needed a plan of attack. So my problem became her project. The strategy was to have me exercise from her stack of old workout tapes, the same ones that had helped her lose weight, and to begin drinking the tea we got from the botánica.

She's been going there for years to consult Perla, the owner, on everything from nerves and migraines to picking lucky lottery numbers and the whole business with my father. I was one and Blanca three when she kicked

him out for gambling her life's savings away. The first place she ran to after she did that was the botánica. Perla told her what saint to petition for help in finding a husband, but aside from a few boyfriends here and there who drank or cried too much, she's never really found a man.

Since my summer vacation started, I exercise once a day for at least an hour. I drink the tea twice—once in the morning in place of breakfast and again in the afternoon. I eat a very light lunch and dinner, mainly vegetables, skinless chicken breasts, and fish. She knows I hate all this, that I feel it's not working and that we're wasting our time and money. The other day I asked her why she didn't just take me to a doctor. She said doctors don't know anything about this. Doctors would look at me and say I was fine. They'd stick me in a room, put me on a scale, poke me, give me a clean bill, and she'd be left owing all the money. No way, she said. Who needs that? We can beat this, she said. The workout tapes are the best, she said. And she believes in old Perla, her bitter teas, her store crowded with saints and Buddhas, jars of powders and vials of oils to seduce lovers and attract good fortune.

Five pounds, my mother says as we pull up to the botánica, and she stabs her cigarette butt into the ashtray. She spreads her fingers out, wiggles them. Five pounds.

*   *   *

The botánica's air is stuffy, as if no one's opened the windows in years. It smells like a bottle of vitamins. When I was younger, Perla had display racks and bookcases in the middle of the store. Once a man in crutches came in. He couldn't make his way around the place, and she had to move some of the chairs so that he could get to the counter. I tried not to stare at him.

Perla greets me from behind the counter. She puts her glasses on and stands there looking at me for a minute like she doesn't know who I am. Sometimes I imagine what she must have looked like when she was younger, if she was the kind of girl who had a lot of boyfriends. Even though she's older, her arms are trim and lean, and they remind me of those of a British grandmother I saw once on television who was training to swim across the English Channel.

"Where's your mamá?" she asks.

I point and say she's smoking and can't come in but that she says hello.

She congratulates me when I tell her I lost five pounds. She says it's a start, a great start, and that by drinking the tea and doing my exercises, I'll probably lose more.

As she gives me the tea and I reach out to pay, the bill falls out of my hand. I bend down to pick it up and knock over a rack of prayer cards. Perla laughs when she sees me gathering them. "Don't worry," she says. "I'll get it."

She waves goodbye and tells me to say hello to my mother.

I close the door behind me and walk to the car where my mother waits.

           •   •   •

The whole business with the job wasn't my idea. A few weeks ago my mother told me about the part-time cashier's position at Las Glorias Market. Her friend Cecilia, who is a supervisor there, had mentioned that they needed to fill the spot quickly. The exercise tapes and the tea were good, my mother thought, but what I really needed was to be on my feet, moving around more.

"It's great pay," she'd said. "They have contests and raffles for employees. Cruises and getaways to resorts in the desert."

I wasn't into the idea. I imagined myself in one of those green smocks the employees at Las Glorias wear. Pulled tight over my stomach, my body squeezed in the cashier's booth. I shook my head and told her I couldn't do it. That I had no experience.

"You're smart," she said. "They'll train."

She kept pressuring me until I gave in and went down to fill out the application and schedule an interview with Cecilia. They gave me a math test where I had to show that I could count back change and figure out percentages without using a calculator. I got all the problems right, and that same day I was told the job was mine.

The cashier's booth where Cecilia and I spent this past week training was too small for both of us, so she had me stand on the outside instead of right next to her. When I told her I was sorry she said, "We'll manage," smiling, but avoiding eye contact.

My training period is over today. Before the start of my shift, Cecilia

walks me out to the front of the market, and we sit on a bench next to the twenty-five-cent merry-go-round. It's real hot, and the sunlight stings through my black pants. I wish I could wear shorts and sandals, something light and thin. Nothing dark and thick like what I always have to.

Cecilia reaches into her pocket and gives me a red star to pin on my apron. "Red is after you finish your training," she says. "On your year anniversary, you get a green one."

She points to two gold ones pinned on her apron. "Each of these represents five years I been with the company."

I ask if she ever gets sick of the whole thing.

She rubs her hands against her jeans. She wears a man's flannel shirt two sizes too large with the sleeves rolled up. A mother walks over to the merry-go-round, puts her daughter on one of the horses, and feeds a coin into the slot. The horses bob slowly up and down to the song "My Favorite Things."

"I've got a good job here," Cecilia says. "A steady paycheck. Good people to work with. Why would I leave?"

Cecilia assigns Miguel Angel to bag for me. I've never talked to him, but I'd seen him on my first day, sitting in his car out in the parking lot with the stereo blaring music. He's not much to look at, and his face is dotted with acne scars the size of thumbprints. Both his ears are pierced, and they made him take the hoops out and cover the holes with bandages.

"Hey," he says when he gets to my station.

I try to ignore him.

"Rosa." He squints at my nametag. "I'm Miguel Angel."

I shake his hand.

He points to the star. "What's that for?"

"After your training, they give you one."

"Sweet. Congratulations."

"Thanks. Didn't they give you a star?" I ask, eyeing his apron.

"No. Guess I'm a special case."

When my shift ends, I walk to the break room and collect my things. Just this morning management had put out a box to raffle off a trip to the Bahamas, and it's already filled to the top with folded pieces of paper. I take a pencil and fill out an entry form. I imagine myself thin. In a tangerine bikini. On a beach with a radio next to me, my skin shiny with lotion.

"Have you ever been there?" a voice asks from behind. I turn to see Miguel Angel standing by the bathroom door. He winks at me.

I shake my head.

He sits down on some cases of diet soda. "Could I ask you a question, Rosa?"

I shrug, folding the form up and pushing in into the box with the rest.

"What's your last name?"

"Why?"

"Just curious."

I point to my time card.

He squints. "Rodríguez. Cool," he says. "I'm Miguel Angel Cabrera."

I tell him I have to go, that my mom's waiting for me outside.

"Okay," he says. "Te watcho."

"Yeah," I say. "Later."

When I get home, I hang my apron on the coat rack near our front door, the red points of my star getting caught in one of Blanca's knit caps. I change into sweats and stand in front of the television, exercising to my mother's workout tapes.

The woman on the tape wears tights and bends and stretches and tells me to breathe, to feel my muscles working, to push and pull and lift and move, her voice keeping with the beat of the music playing in the background. When we reach the end, she sits down Indian-style on a black mat and raises both hands over her head. "Breathe in," she says. "Then out. Relax. Exhale. Exhale. And exhale."

The video stops and pops out of the VCR. I turn the television off and sit on the couch, toweling my face, breathing so hard and heavy my chest hurts. I can't even think about getting back up right now.

*   *   *

Every Saturday at noon, a mariachi band performs in the market's parking lot. They set up next to a cart that sells slices of fresh mangoes and cucumbers powdered with chili.

Miguel Angel is assigned to bag for me again.

"Hey, it was cool bagging for you yesterday," he says. "We make a good team."

I nod and continue ringing up my customer.

"Do you like this kind of music, Rosa?" He points at the lot with his chin.

"I don't know," I say.

He gives the customer her groceries and puts his hands on the counter. There's no one at my check stand. We watch the band through the store windows, the musicians in their tight gold pants and matching jackets with embroidered designs, their hats as big as buckets.

"You don't know?" he says.

"I don't know it that well," I say. He winks, flashes a smile. I smile back.

"Got a smile. Got a smile." He claps his hands. "I knew I could. Cumbia. Do you like cumbia?"

"I don't know that either." A group of people has gathered around the band, and some dance to the music.

"I got this tradition going," he says. "See, every Saturday night I listen to music in my apartment. By myself. I open the windows and crank some tunes."

"That sounds fun."

At about two, Cecilia has us take our breaks. We sit on the benches in front of the market just as the mariachi band is getting ready to leave, putting the violins and trumpets in their cases and snapping them shut.

"How old are you?" he asks.

"Sixteen."

"Do you got a boyfriend?"

"No."

"Really?"

"Really."

"That surprises me. You're way pretty."

I think about my wide thighs that remind me of tree trunks, my blouse stretched out so far that the buttons look like they're about to come undone. I think about Blanca. Always wanting to do my makeup and nails. "You should think about going to beauty school with me," she'd said as she clipped my hair up the other day when we were in her room. "We could open up a salon. Be in business together. 'Rodríguez and Sister Salon.' What do you say?"

"Maybe," I'd said. "Who knows what I'll end up doing with this life."

"Why are you so quiet for?" Miguel Angel asks, looking over at me.

"Just because."

"Hey, you should come over to my place next Saturday, and I can teach you about cumbia music."

I cross my arms. "Why?"

"It'll enrich your life."

"My life's pretty rich already," I say.

"You're missing out, girl."

"I'm sure a guy like you can find someone more exciting to spend a Saturday night with."

"What's that mean? What's with the attitude? Maybe I wanna hang out with you."

"Why?"

"Don't be that way." He laughs, his smile smoothing out his acne scars so that they dissolve into his skin. "It'll be fun. Come over next Saturday." He taps me on the shoulder with his knuckle. When he stops, I find myself hoping he'll do it again.

"Maybe."

"Maybe? Come on, Rosa. Just for a while. I promise I won't do nothing. If I do, you know where I work."

"Depends," I say. "On how I'm feeling."

"We'll play it by ear then."

"What do you want with me?"

"What do you mean? Hey, I'm cool here. Okay? I just wanna hang out."

"I don't know."

"Think about it," he says. "Consider yourself invited."

"I will. Thanks."

I look at my watch and realize our break's nearly over. We get up and walk back inside, the automatic doors sliding shut behind us, the air conditioner cooling our skin.

*   *   *

We clean the house Saturday mornings. We each have a section: Blanca gets the kitchen and one of the bathrooms; I get the living room and the second bathroom; my mother supervises, does the vacuuming, and mops the kitchen and dining room floors.

At work today, Miguel Angel will want to know if I'm going to listen to music at his place. I haven't seen him all week.

"What do I tell this guy?" I ask Blanca. She's scrubbing the stovetop with a scouring pad, her hair wrapped in a bandanna.

"What do you mean what do you tell him? You go."

"Keep it low." I peek my head down the hall, listening to my mother vacuuming.

"Is he cute?" Blanca straightens and looks over at me.

"I don't know. I guess."

"Does he go to your school?"

"He's older."

"How much older?"

"I think he's about twenty-five."

"You tramp," she says, laughing. "Go for it."

After I've showered and dressed for work, Blanca comes into my room and sits on my bed. "Let me see your hand, fool," she tells me.

"Why?"

"Sit. I'm doing your nails."

She starts by smoothing out the tips of my fingernails with a file, bringing my hands up to her face, scraping away the dirt underneath, blowing on each one before buffing it. Once that's finished, she uses the end of the file to push back my cuticles. Reaching for the bottle of polish, she shakes it a few times and paints each nail, using long and even strokes.

"Just make sure he sees your hands," she says after she's done. "He'll go crazy over this color. What are you gonna tell Mom?"

"That I'm working a long shift."

"Good one," Blanca says.

He was assigned to stock today so he didn't bag for me, but we were scheduled off at the same time. After our shifts end, we head over to his place.

He lives in an apartment building called the Agua Mansa Palms in a part of the city known as the Zoo because all the streets are named for animals—Antelope, Buffalo, Coyote. His place is on the second floor, away from the street. From the living room window, I look down onto a narrow alley where green and blue trash cans with numbers painted on their sides are lined up against the wall. He pours a soda for me into a plastic tumbler with the image of a cartoon dog, rubbed away from too much washing.

"Sorry I don't got a better glass," he says.

"It's all good. Have you lived here long?"

"Naw. Only a few months." The stereo sits on the floor. He walks over and turns it on. "I won't turn it up too loud. I don't want the people downstairs to get pissed. Listen, okay?"

"Okay." I finish my soda, and he gets me another.

The bass line travels along the floor, and I feel it through the soles of my work shoes. Accordions blend with trumpets, trombones, and a woman's high-pitched voice.

"Were you serious when you said you never heard this music before?" He walks over to the kitchen and returns with a beer in one hand, a soda in the other.

"Well, no. I've heard it. I'm just not familiar with it."

"What do you mean?" He takes a sip of his beer.

"It's not my style."

"What do you mean it's not your style?"

"It's just not." I put my hand up to my face, pretend to examine my nails. "All that music just sounds too much alike to me anyway."

"Don't say that. Listen, this is cumbia. Those guys in the parking lot, they play mariachi. Big difference."

"I get it," I say, nodding. "I think I get it."

"Check it out, let me play you some more of my favorites."

About a half-hour later, I decide to leave. "This was fun," I say. "I should go, though."

"So soon? But there's more I want you to hear."

"Sorry. I have to go."

"Did I at least get you interested in cumbia?"

"A little," I say. "I can see myself getting to like it. Learning more about it."

"Cool," he says. "Let me give you a ride." He reaches for his keys and sunglasses.

"I'll walk."

"Don't be dumb. You've been on your feet all day. Plus it's still pretty hot out there."

I have him drop me off on the corner, so my mom doesn't see us. "Thanks for the ride."

"No problem. Wait," he says as I reach for the handle. "What you said back at the apartment, did you mean it?"

"What part?"

"The part about wanting to learn more about cumbias."

"Maybe." I get out of the car and shut the door.

He leans across the seat, rolls the passenger-side window down, and looks up at me, his arm sticking to the back of the hot vinyl car seat. "Maybe this is something we can do every Saturday after work. You can come over, and we can listen to cumbias. I can teach you about them."

"Why are you all eager to teach me this?" I sigh, pretending to examine my nails again.

"Because I think you're missing out on something meaningful."

"Not even," I say.

He slides his sunglasses down the bridge of his nose, and it excites me. I see my face in the car's window. My features look distorted. My cheeks narrow out and when I smile, the bright sunlight does something to my lips and they pucker out, soft and full and exotic.

"It's all in Spanish," I say. "I don't understand most of what they're saying anyways."

"You don't gotta listen to the words. Just the music. Come on. You can see I'm a perfect gentleman. Didn't try nothing today."

"Fine. But don't think I don't know how to take care of myself." I put my hand on my hip.

"I know you do. I'm not dumb. I'll see you at work." He pulls away from the curb, his Renault speeding off down my street.

When I walk in the house, my mother asks how work was.

"Same," I say. "The customers were rude. The break room was boiling because the air-conditioning vents broke down, so I went into the cooler."

At dinner she reminds me to do my exercises before bed.

I tell her, "What do you think I've been doing every night?" I look over at Blanca, roll my eyes, and she laughs.

"What's with you? Rosa, I'm trying to help you here," my mother says.

"Is that what you call it?" I say, thinking of the way I'd looked in the car's window today.

She puts her fork down and stares at me. "Just look at yourself. Look at that body. Do you want to go on living like that?"

"Mother, stop," Blanca tells her. "It's baby fat."

"What do you know?" she says to Blanca. "Stay out of this. Baby fat, my ass."

Later that night, after I've exercised and showered, Blanca comes into my room. I sit on the floor in my nightgown, and she climbs on my bed. She takes a few strands of my wet hair and braids them together.

"What got into you?" she says.

"I don't know," I say. "I was just tired."

"I saw you guys parked at the corner."

"You did?"

"Yeah. He's cute. He reminds me of Jacob."

Jacob, whose picture is one of those she has taped to her dresser's mirror, is a Jewish guy Blanca dated for six months until he moved with his family to Florida. On their last night together, she lit some candles, snuck him into her room, and they made out until the sun came up. They still write to each other, and Blanca plans on visiting him sometime next year. She doesn't know how she'll get there, but she will, she tells me. She will.

"What's this guy's name anyway?" she asks.

"Miguel Angel."

"Nice. Did he notice the nails?"

"No."

"Shit."

I turn to face her. "I'm hanging out with him again next Saturday, though."

She smiles. "He's so into you."

"You think so?"

"Yup. I know so."

Later that night, I lie in bed with my hair wet, my pillow dampening and smelling of conditioner. I picture Miguel Angel and me sitting on his couch, making out, touching each other all over the place. I slip my underwear off and let my finger feel the moisture gathering between my legs before I slide it in, let it tickle the walls inside. Turning my face toward the pillow, I pant into it, imagine him on top of me, in me. I tense up just before I release and my body, my whole body, melts into the mattress.

· · ·

On the second Saturday, he tries to get me to dance with him.

He stands in front of me, his feet bare and shuffling across the hardwood floor. "Come on, Rosa."

"I don't know how to dance."

"You promised," he shouts over the music. "You told me on Wednesday that you'd dance with me today. Take off your shoes."

"I never promised you anything."

"Stop being shy. Come on." His hands beckon me.

I kick my shoes off, pull down my socks, and stand. The hardwood floor creaks under my feet.

He squeezes my hands. "You're afraid. You're trembling."

"I'm fine."

"Do you want some water or something?"

"I'm fine. Really." I let go of his hands. "I don't think I'm ready to learn this yet."

"Come on."

"I'm not good. I've got no rhythm."

"Close your eyes."

"No, I don't—"

"Just do it. Don't be afraid."

I do it, and I feel his hands press against my hips and move them back and forth. Slowly first, then quickly. The whole apartment shakes to the vibration of the music. The sound waves travel through me, right down to my muscles, my bones, breaking things up, making my skin lose its grip on my body.

"Feel that?" he says. "Feel that?"

"Yeah."

His body presses against mine. "Let it in, Rosa." He leans in and whispers it to me. "Let it in."

We take quick steps around his living room, sometimes tripping on each other, laughing as we do.

"You're pretty good," he says.

"You're just saying that." After a while, I sit down on the couch and try to catch my breath.

"Here." He hands me a glass of water. "Are you feeling okay?"

"I'm okay," I say, panting.

"Are you sure?"

"I'm fine."

"Do you need something to eat?"

"What?" I turn to look up at him.

"Do you need something to eat?"

"Nobody ever asks me that."

"Oh," he says. "I get it. Sorry."

"I wasn't always like this," I say. "I used to be thin."

"Oh yeah? Well, I wasn't always this nice. I used to get into all kinds of trouble." He sits on the couch and fans my face with his hand. "Couldn't stay out of it."

He drives me home again and parks near the same spot on the corner. Before I step out, he leans over and gives me a light kiss on the cheek.

"Next Saturday?" he says, putting the car in gear.

"Yeah."

"Good. I'll teach you to salsa."

*   *   *

On the third Saturday, we mostly talk over the music. He serves me carrots and chopped cucumbers with ranch dressing on a paper plate.

"Eat. Don't matter if you're heavy, Rosa. You gotta eat."

This morning I'd filled my thermos with some of the tea to take to work. I'd planned on drinking it during my break, but it had been too busy, and Cecilia never gave me one. I brought the thermos up with me to his apartment.

"I have to drink this first," I say, unscrewing the cap.

"What is it?"

"It's this tea to help me lose weight."

He leans over and puts his nose next to the opening. "Stinks like cat piss."

"It does." I pour the whole thing into a cup that he gives me.

"Wait," he says. "You're really gonna drink that?"

"I have to."

"You don't have to." Reaching across the table, Miguel Angel takes the cup. He pinches his nose, raises it to his mouth, and swallows the tea in three giant gulps. "I took that one for you. Now you owe me another dance."

"You didn't have to."

"I wanted to."

"I hate this. I hate myself."

"What do you mean?"

"Look at me." My hands slap my thighs. "Just look."

"I'm looking."

"And?"

"And nothing."

"I'm fat," I say.

"So you are. So what. You've got plenty to feel good about."

"Like what?"

"For one, you've got a family. More than I've ever had."

"What do you mean?"

"It's only been me and my dad. I don't talk to him a lot. Kicked me out when I started getting into trouble." He pauses and takes a deep breath. "Broke into a sporting goods store with a buddy. Did my time. I was in jail for five years. My dad never came to see me. Guess he always hoped I'd turn out different. It feels like shit coming out and having no one there to meet you, you know?"

"I'm sorry," I say.

"It's okay. I got used to it. Had this crazy guy from Oklahoma City named Tucker for a cellmate. Guy was a real trip. But jail's a bad place no matter what. A straight-up bad place."

"But you're out now," I say. "You're free."

"Yeah. Have a job at the market. A parole officer who checks up on me." His eyes scan the apartment: its bare walls, its curtainless windows, its dripping sink in the kitchen. "I'm real free now."

*   *   *

Perla had a small ice chest with fruit bars that she sold for fifty cents when I was a little girl. I can still see the faded spot in the linoleum where it stood.

"The grape ones were your favorites. Turning your tongue so dark purple it almost looked black." Perla watches me stare at the empty spot as she gets another box of the tea.

"They were so good. Especially during the summer," I say. "On days like this." I'm running low on tea again. My mother was going to drive me, but I told her it would be better if I walked, that I could burn extra calories.

Perla gives me my tea and as I head out the door, I turn back around. "Why don't I feel this tea is working?" My question catches her by surprise.

"You lost five pounds, didn't you?"

"I gained some of it back. Then I lost another eight."

"Some people are like that. Their weight fluctuates."

"What do I do?"

"What you're doing now. Just keep drinking your tea. Eat right. Exercise. Focus. Do everything you can to keep the weight off."

"It's frustrating. I'm losing it. But it doesn't feel like it's enough."

"I know. But I've helped other women lose weight with this. Remember that it takes time. You'll see. You'll start to notice yourself change."

"It doesn't make sense to me. Maybe I was meant to be this way."

"You haven't been doing this very long. You have to be patient."

"Why am I doing this?"

"Many reasons," she says. "Health. Self-esteem. Happiness. Your family doesn't want to see you hurting."

My eyes fall on the spot on the floor again. I remember the cooler's hum, the old box of baking soda underneath the fruit pops, the smell of damp cardboard. "I'm not," I say. "I'm not hurting."

She's quiet for a long time. She steps forward. Reaching across the counter, she takes the box of tea back. "If you think you don't need this, tell me." She points to the shelves and candles, the herbs and incense sticks. "Tell me, Rosita."

"I don't," I say in a low voice. "I don't need this right now."

"Fine." She opens the register and pulls out the bill I paid with. She folds it in half and presses it in my hand. "But come back to me when you do need this. You. No one else. I'll be here. Waiting."

*   *   *

"I want to talk to you about this new friend of yours." My mother comes up to me in the kitchen as I drink the last of my tea. It's early Friday morning, and I'm scheduled to be in at eleven. Blanca's standing against the kitchen counter reading the newspaper, taking bites from a piece of toast.

"What new friend?" I ask.

"This Miguel Angel guy," she says.

"What about him?"

"Yeah, what about him?" Blanca says.

"Cecilia called me earlier," my mother says. "She talked to me about him. Says she's been seeing you two leaving together after your shifts on Saturday. Is that true?"

"Yeah. It's fine. We're just friends."

"Friends? Well, did you know your friend is on parole?"

"Parole!" Blanca shouts. "Get out of here. No way."

My mother turns to her. "Blanca, please." She shakes her head.

"Yeah. So he's on parole," I say. "So what?"

"So what? Tell me," my mother says. "What do you think he wants with you?"

"Let it go, Mom," I tell her. "Are you driving me to work or not?"

"Men like him are always up to something. You better watch it," she responds.

"You're thinking that just because I'm fat a guy can't like me, right? That a guy like him can't find me attractive?"

"I didn't say that. But just take a moment. Look at yourself."

"I'm over that, Mom. He taught me how to dance. That's all." I walk over to the sink and pour what's left of my tea down the drain.

"He's bad news, Rosa," she says.

"So what if he is. I don't care. I don't need any of this."

"Fine," she says. "It's your life. Mess it up. Live however you want."

I walk out the front door. From inside I hear Blanca shouting, "Go on. You go to that man." She's clapping and cheering, her bare feet slapping against the kitchen floor.

*   *   *

I get all the way to his street before I realize I'm dressed in my green apron and hat with the market's logo on the front. The city's repaving his block, and I make my way down the sidewalk, smeared in spots with black streaks of asphalt. Miguel Angel doesn't work on Fridays. He isn't home when I get there, so I sit out on the front stoop and wait. About an hour later I see him strolling up.

"Hey," he says.

"What's up?"

"What are you doing here? Didn't expect to see you till tomorrow."

"Are you pissed I came? I can go."

"Not pissed. Just surprised. What's happening?"

"My mom."

"Your mom?"

"Cecilia called and told her you're on parole. Thinks you're a bad element. Doesn't want me seeing you."

"Maybe your mom's right." He looks out across the street.

"Maybe people should stop telling me what to do."

"What's wrong with that? Shows they care for you."

"Shows they think I'm not smart enough to do things for myself. That I'm helpless and should be grateful for every bit of good attention I get because I'm so fat."

"No one's saying that. You're thinking it."

"What? So now you know what I'm thinking?"

"Don't get pissed at me. I'm on your side, remember?"

I untie my apron and toss in on the ground. "I didn't mean to get mad."

"It's cool. I understand. No worries."

"You've been a good friend. A good listener."

"It's the least I could do," he says. "Someone did the same for me when I was in jail."

"Yeah?"

"Yeah. This girl named Wendy." He walks over and sits next to me on the stoop. "A friend of Tucker's sister. We used to write to each other. I'd draw these sketches for her—birds, clouds, a cliff with trees I'd seen in a book.

Her letters helped me so much, you know? Helped me get by. I couldn't wait to get them. I thought about going to see her once I was out. To thank her in person."

"Why haven't you?"

"Don't know. Guess I'm chickenshit. Guess it's enough to know that there's someone out there that's got my letters. It's enough to know that my words and sketches, my thoughts, are out there roaming free without me. Floating around."

I try to imagine her, this Wendy. A housewife with a husband and kids. An ex-con's letters pressed between her mattresses. I see her taking them out and reading them when she's alone. I think about the thrill they give her. See her living with that feeling for the rest of the day as she bathes her kids and makes her husband dinner.

Around us everything's still, and the temperature's starting to rise. The sun beats down on us, and the cheap polyester of my uniform makes it feel ten degrees hotter. Torn scraps of paper and fast food wrappers are stuck to the melted asphalt out in the street. The smell reminds me of the field trip my fourth grade class took to the La Brea Tar Pits. A tour guide explained to us that prehistoric mammoths and birds wandered into the dark pools and got trapped there. The tar worked like quicksand. The more they struggled to free themselves, the deeper they were dragged in. These creatures died, and their bones lay buried for millions of years without anyone ever knowing they'd lived.

February 14

Feast of
Saint Valentine

Priest and Martyr

Patron of love, lovers, engaged couples,

happy marriages,

greeting card manufacturers,

and beekeepers.

Invoked against fainting, plague, and epilepsy.

Even though the bed was warm, the sheets soft against her skin, Perla forced herself up and got ready. She used a pail and clippers and cut the flowers from the backyard, laid each one out on the dining table, and arranged them there. A piece of twine held the stems, the bouquet wrapped in aluminum foil to keep it together and make it easier to carry. It was getting late, and she hurried. She wanted to stop off at San Salvador's first to light a candle before taking the flowers to the cemetery

When she arrived, the church was empty. She thought about Guillermo's funeral Mass—the people crowded inside to pay their respects, the heavy organ music, the mahogany wood of the coffin polished and gleaming under the church's lights.

Smoke stained the feet of the statue of Christ near the front entrance. Perla knelt before the statue, picked a flower from the bouquet, and placed it at the foot of the railing. She lit a candle and prayed an Our Father. From behind her came the sound of a door closing. She turned to see Father Madrid making his way down the aisle, and she rose to meet him.

Father Madrid was from Nicaragua. Once during a service he had told the congregants about the war he had lived through and how he had watched as his family was killed by the guerrillas who came and destroyed his village. He told how he fled, hiding inside a cave deep within the jungle, fearing for his life.

He smiled. "¿Cómo está, señora?"

"I'm good," Perla responded.

"How is everything over at the store? I tell many people here about you," he said. "I tell them to go see you for novenas and scapulars. I tell the mothers you sell the baptismal candles. Not to go to the indoor swap meet. I tell them your prices are better. I try to give you business."

"Thank you, Father."

"What pretty flowers you have there," he said. "Such a beautiful bouquet."

"They're for my parents and my husband. I'm going to the cemetery."

"Oh." He extended his arm and put his hand on her shoulder. "I didn't know you had lost your husband. I always see you alone. I just assumed he practiced another faith."

"No, he was Catholic," Perla said. "We were married in this church years ago."

"Yes? I imagine it looked different in those days."

"It was smaller. They remodeled it in the seventies. Did you know that?"

"I saw pictures. Was your husband's Mass held here?"

"Yes," Perla said. "And my parents' funerals, also."

"I see," he said. "I'm sorry for your losses. All of them. I'm glad to see you are still here."

"Yes. I'm still here."

"Remember that the church is yours. It's here for you." He pointed to the bouquet. "You want me to bless them?"

Perla offered up the flowers. Father Madrid raised his right hand and bent his index finger so that it touched his thumb. He whispered in Latin, and Perla caught words here and there that she recognized. When he finished, she thanked him and left.

                        *   *   *

The stone trail that curved past the cemetery gates was wet from the sprinklers. Across the lawn, plastic pinwheels and balloons twirled in the breeze. Bouquets of flowers sprouted up from vases buried in the soil.

Perla set her sweater on the ground and knelt. She took the scissors from inside her purse and trimmed around the edges of Guillermo's marker, removing tangled roots and dry blades of grass. She rose and walked to the curb with his vase. She filled it with water and went back to him. Nesting the bouquet in the vase, Perla wondered about all those other arrangements she'd left, the miniature Christmas trees, the birthday party hat she had secured to the stone with a strip of duct tape, and the cards and noisemakers. They were all probably lost in a heap of dried flowers, crunching and yellow,

among stuffed animals and Easter bunnies with stained fur and missing eyes.

She picked the sweater off the ground, shook away ants, and put it on. She tucked the scissors back inside her purse and walked across the lawn to her parents' markers. She arranged their flowers before tossing the aluminum foil in a trash can. She sat on a bench near a statue of Jesus. He stood on a tall pedestal, his outstretched arms receiving the souls of the dead gathered around him. The shadow of the figure's hand fell across Perla's face, his head resting on her lap.

◦   ◦   ◦

The Prospect Shopping Center was a narrow building whose white stucco exterior had flaked off in sections over the years. The bright blue trim running along the edges of the flat roof and the storefronts that faced Rancho Boulevard had faded away long ago. A sign at the edge of the parking lot stood perched on two rusted posts, and the neon bands spelling out the center's name zapped on every day at six in the evening. There were only three businesses in the strip mall—Best Donuts, Everything Ninety-Nine Cents, and the Botánica Oshún at the very end of the row.

Today a boy sat at a table in the parking lot. He was selling decorative balloons with stuffed animals floating inside, heart-shaped boxes of chocolates with white and pink ribbons, and arrangements of silk flowers. Inside Best Donuts, the owners had hung crepe hearts and silhouettes of small Cupids. Donuts with white frosting and red and pink sprinkles filled the pastry racks. Agua Mansa was drained of its blues and greens, of the yellows of school buses, of the rusted browns of trucks hauling gravel from the quarry in Colton. Everything today was red and pink.

She ordered a medium coffee and two donuts. Old Vithu counted the change back and folded the bills neatly for her, then went over to help someone else. His granddaughter Alice walked around the store with the phone pressed against her shoulder. She was speaking Cambodian, her words loud and fast, and giggling every now and again. She lit an incense stick and set it next to a gold Buddha statue sitting on top of the smoothie machine. Perla sat at the table nearest the door with her coffee and donuts; she had a few minutes to spare before it was time to open the botánica.

A radio played behind the counter. A woman's voice spoke softly. "My name is Deborah. I'm calling from Agua Mansa. I'd like to dedicate 'We've Only Just Begun' by the Carpenters," she said. "For my fiancé, Juan."

Perla sat there, taking small bites of her donuts and quick sips of coffee. Paper hearts swayed above her head, and faceless Cupids aimed their arrows at her.

∘   •   ∘

The botánica was always busy on Saint Valentine's Day. When she helped the young women who came to buy candles and love potions, it was hard not to feel jealous. Perla could hear the passion in their voices. They glowed. She thought hard, tried to recall if she had ever looked that way, if her voice had ever carried the same pitch, if she had glowed. At moments, she caught quick glimpses of herself in their reflections as they leaned over the glass and peered into the cases, tucking strands of their hair back, pointing with lacquered nails, some in suits and dark slacks, others in stirrup pants and baggy sweatshirts, pushing baby carriages. Throughout the day, the customers kept coming. They bought red velas and stones, amulets and oils, Kama Sutra candles and incense sticks. The day passed quickly, and when Perla stopped to rest, she saw that it was already late in the afternoon.

Alfonso walked in a little after five. "Buenas," he said, smiling. He held out a one-hundred-dollar bill. "Could you break this?"

"You're lucky I was busy." Perla took the register key out of her pocket and opened the drawer. "You can count it out if you want." She handed him a bundle of twenties held together with a paper clip.

"No. I trust you."

His store, Everything Ninety-Nine Cents, was larger than the botánica; it had six aisles, two cash registers, four shopping carts, and a stack of wire baskets for customers to use. A cooler stocked cans of soda and bars of ice cream. They sold bottles of hair spray, toilet bowl deodorizers, sponges, plastic picture frames, combs, bars of bath soap, quarts of motor oil, teddy bears, dolls, hammers, plungers, and rubber mallets. All of this and more for only ninety-nine cents.

Alfonso had taken over the store a few years ago when his father retired.

Perla liked having him as a neighbor. He ran an honest business and took care of maintenance around the shopping center. He made sure to call the landlord right away if any of the lights in the parking lot were out or if there were potholes that needed to be patched.

"What are you doing for Valentine's Day?" Perla asked him.

"We're going dancing. That's why I'm closing early. I want us to be at the club before eight, and I still need to go home and get handsome." He winked. "And you? Don't tell me you're just going to sit at home alone."

Perla laughed and closed the register's drawer. "I'm too old for dates. I haven't danced in years."

He smiled. "Don't give me that." He rested his elbows on the glass countertop. "Why don't you come? We can cumbia. Just us two."

"And how would your wife feel about that?"

Alfonso was married, and there were times his wife, Carmen, came and helped around their shop. Carmen was a college graduate with a degree in marketing. She would sit behind the counter and ring customers up or supervise the employees. She also kept track of the store's finances, recording losses and profits in a ledger they kept in their office.

"Maybe I want it to only be you and me," he said.

"Stop that. I'm old enough to be your aunt, tonto." Perla laughed again, and slapped his hand.

She turned and looked over in the direction of his truck. Perla saw herself wearing an elegant dress, a shawl draped over her shoulders. Not in a thick purple knitted sweater with crumpled napkins and bobby pins stuffed in the pockets, not in a pair of simple black pants and worn sneakers. Her hair would be styled and beautiful, not an uncombed mass of dyed brown hair. Her body would be thin. Like it had once been. *Hadn't it been that way?* Alfonso would hold the door to the truck open. The two of them would ride off, the chrome horns on the hood like arrows guiding them to a nightclub where women twirled around in ruffled skirts and men wore cowboy hats and boots and were always brave and handsome.

Perla looked down at her hands, her thinning skin, her jagged green veins, then at the gold band of her wedding ring. In the gleam, she heard Guillermo's voice again, felt him rubbing the small brown mole on her neck that he liked to kiss.

"Be good," she told Alfonso. "There'll be sobriety checkpoints. No drinking and driving."

"No, ma'am," he said and left.

His truck backed out and disappeared down Rancho. A few minutes later, Teresa Martínez walked in, her keys bunched up in her hand. She said, "I need some tea. It's my turn to be the patient."

Teresa had been her doctor since before Guillermo's death, before Teresa moved her practice out of Agua Mansa to a modern five-story building in Rialto less than two years ago. In the months after her husband died, Perla had suffered from insomnia and had fallen into a deep depression. One afternoon, Teresa showed up on her doorstep.

"I've never known you to miss an appointment," she'd said. She sat with Perla through the evening, listening to her reminisce about Guillermo and the life they'd shared.

"I hope I'm lucky enough to have what you did," Teresa had said. "Someone worth building something that strong with. Believe me, it would make my mom happy. She keeps pressuring me to get married and have kids. 'Settle down,' she says. 'You're thirty-seven. You should be thinking about a family. Look at your brothers and sisters. All of them have kids. But you? Your father and I want to see our baby a mother before we die.' What's wrong with having a career? I have choices. This isn't Mexico. This isn't the rancho anymore. I'm happy with my life. I'm a pretty successful doctor. My job demands a lot of focus. So what if I'm single?"

That was almost five years ago. Teresa was now forty-two and still not married.

"Guess what?" Teresa said today. "I met someone. This new doctor who works in the building. He's a pediatrician."

"That's good." Perla smiled.

"He's great," Teresa told her, taking a deep breath. "He's nice and funny and successful. You should have heard my mom on the phone when I told her. I think she's started planning the wedding already."

"It's not too late," Perla said, pointing to Teresa's stomach. "For babies."

"Oh, God." She set her keys down on the counter. "You sound like my mom. Craig and I, we've only been going out for three months. It's too soon for all of that. And my life's hectic as it is, what with work."

"Is that why you're stressed?"

"Yeah." Teresa sighed. "I have so much to do. It's hard keeping up. I never thought this change was going to be so drastic."

"You regret it? The move? This new building?"

"Sometimes I do. But I couldn't stay. It was time to move on. Besides, if I hadn't I probably wouldn't have met Craig."

Teresa bought a box of valeriana tea. "And you?" she asked. "Are you feeling okay? Everything still good?"

"Yes," Perla said. "I'm fine. I'm eating right. I'm walking."

"Good," Teresa said. "I know I have all these new patients, but I still want to take care of my oldest and dearest." Teresa reached into her pocket. She pulled out a business card. She took a pen from the cup by the register and wrote down a phone number.

"This is my new cell number," she said, handing the card to Perla. "You call me anytime. If there's an emergency or whatever. Doesn't matter what time. Keep it in a safe place."

Perla tucked it behind her ID card in her wallet.

"When will I see you?" Teresa asked, grabbing her keys.

"In May," Perla said. "My checkup is in May."

"Okay. If I don't come by before that, I'll see you in May." She leaned over the counter and kissed Perla on the cheek.

"Good luck with your boyfriend," Perla told her.

"Light a vela for me." She walked out the door, her fingers crossed.

Perla dressed the candle the way Darío had taught her. She reached for the screwdriver she kept in the coffee mug packed with pens near the register. She took the last red candle from the shelf and stabbed the screwdriver into the top, making a hole in the wax deep enough to pour in some rose and lavender oil. On a scrap of paper she wrote *Teresa* and *Craig*. She drew a heart around both names, placed the paper underneath the candle, and kept it lit while she balanced the register and closed up for the day.

Perla was in the middle of untangling some scapulars when she heard a soft tap. A young boy stood in front of the door, his hands pressed against the glass pane.

"Closed," she shouted.

But the boy stood there, nervously looking over his shoulder every now and again.

"Cerrado." Perla backed away slowly. She reached for the screwdriver—red shavings from the candle still stuck to the metal—and gripped the handle. "Closed," she said again. "Come back tomorrow. Mañana."

When a car pulled into the parking lot, he turned and ran off. The sides of his fists left impressions like a baby's footprints on the window glass. She waited for thirty minutes before leaving. The air outside was cold. She buttoned up her jacket and clutched her purse. When she looked back to make sure no one was following, Perla saw only the Virgen de Guadalupe painted on the wall of the botánica facing the empty lot, the bright orange flames around Our Lady's body fading to thin black lines in the vanishing February sun.

Relics

I didn't cry when my father died. Emphysema took his life. He was a two-pack-a-day smoker. In the end, it got so bad that he had to wheel around a tank to help him breathe. We'd sit out back together listening to Dodgers games on the radio, and he'd shove a ten-dollar bill in my hand, urge me to go down to the store for one last pack of menthols, one last drag. I almost went once. But the sight of that green tank beside him and the way his body would cave in and collapse every time he coughed stopped me. I couldn't contribute to his demise. He left us six months ago.

It was just after five this afternoon, and I was sitting in my office going through some last-minute things when my girlfriend Deborah called to tell me she was canceling our date for the night.

"Don't you want to know what's wrong?" she asked when I remained quiet.

"Okay," I said. "What's wrong?"

"You. Ever since your dad died, you've been off."

I sat back in my chair. "What do you mean? Off how?"

"The Juan Sandoval that I met last year was different. He used to take me to flea markets. He'd take me out dancing and to the movies. He wouldn't mope around in his robe all weekend. He exercised. You're quiet and sulky all the time now. When I try and get you to talk to me, you clam up."

"Okay. No more silent treatment. Let's talk. What do you want to hear?"

"I want to hear that you're hurting. That you miss him. That you *feel*

something. You didn't cry at his funeral. It's been six months, and you haven't."

"It's a guy thing, you know?" I explained, a little irritated, not understanding where any of this was coming from.

"No, I don't know. Look," she said, "there's no other way to put this, so I'm just going to say it: I think it's best that we back up, okay? Slow things down."

"What do you mean? Are you dumping me?"

"No. But you need some time alone right now. I've been giving this a lot of thought, and I've come to the conclusion that you have unresolved issues to work out."

"What does that mean? Don't tell me I've got 'unresolved issues.' I *know* what I'm feeling, okay? Right now, I'm feeling pissed at you."

"Don't be angry. I'm doing this because I care," she said. "I need to stay out of your hair for a while. I don't want to become a nag. I love you too much. You have to figure this out on your own. The last thing you need is me sticking around and further complicating this whole situation."

I calmed down. "Listen," I said, in my most rational-sounding voice. "I'm about to leave here. Meet me at home, and we can talk about this. I want to see you. I need to see you."

"You need space," Deborah said. "You need to be alone with yourself. I'll lay low for now." And she hung up.

I sat there with the receiver pressed against my ear until the line went dead. She's overreacting, I told myself. By the time I get home, there'll be a message on the recorder. She'll apologize. She'll laugh and say she wasn't thinking. She'll drive over, we'll hug and kiss and have sex. Everything will be fine. I grabbed my things and left the office.

I did love my father, very much. He was good to us. When I was a kid we built model airplanes and classic cars together. The cars were his favorites. Somewhere in my mother's attic, there's a box filled with '57 Chevys, T-Birds, and a 1964 Ford Mustang that we never got around to painting. He let me drive the station wagon down the street once when I was thirteen, my feet barely reaching the pedals. My senior year in college, he took me on a two-day camping trip in the mountains. We spent a good part of that trip roasting marshmallows and knocking back bottles of beer. I decided that

when it came time for me to get married, I would ask my father to be my best man.

When I get home, there are no messages. I sit down on the couch, reach for a pair of my girlfriend's sunglasses on the floor near my feet, and toss them aside. A month after we started dating, I suggested she bring some things over. She arrived with two duffel bags stuffed with blouses, blue jeans, nylons, running shoes, high heels, and a second alarm clock for "her side" of the bed. She filled the bathroom counter with jars of creams and moisturizers, a light-up hand mirror, and a box of tampons.

"Are you leaving anything at your place?" I'd said.

She laughed. "Sure. Plenty."

"You wouldn't know it."

A stack of fashion magazines sits on top of the coffee table near one of her house plants. In the sink, there are coffee mugs with red lipstick marks along the edges. Scattered about the floor of the bedroom are her balled-up socks, a pair of her panties, and an old college sweatshirt of mine that she likes to sleep in.

I haven't changed out of my suit when the phone rings, but it's only my mother.

"Juan? I just got off the phone with Deborah. She told me. How are you?"

"Jesus," I say. "She called and told you she broke up with me?"

"She's not breaking up with you," my mother reports. "She's just giving you space."

"Right. Space."

"You should come over. I made empanadas for the meeting today, but no one ate them."

Back when I was a kid, my mother helped found the Agua Mansa chapter of the official Elvis Presley fan club. The five members spend afternoons snacking on peanut butter and banana sandwiches and cookies. They sit around in a circle listening to his records and planning bake sales to help fund their trip to Graceland. The meeting was at my mother's house this month. There's music playing in the background. I make out Elvis singing "Jailhouse Rock."

"I have some food left," she continues. "Come over. Don't be alone. I'm going to watch *Love Me Tender*. Come watch it with me."

"What happened with everyone wanting to give me space? Look at me. Sitting around my apartment. Enjoying all this space."

"Don't be rude," my mother says. "Come over."

"I'm fine," I tell her. "Seriously. I just want to hang out here. I'm tired. I have a meeting tomorrow at work. And my girlfriend decided that I need to cry."

"Do you have food there?"

"There's something. I'll eat a sandwich."

"You're not that far. It won't take you long to drive over."

After five minutes of her pleas, I give in. "Only for a bit. A little Elvis goes a long way."

I change into my jeans and a T-shirt and head out the door.

.   ◦   ◦

We'd gone shopping for a birthday gift for my father the day my mother lost me in the department store. Somewhere down an aisle of racks crammed with dressy men's slacks and blazers, she turned to check the size of a shirt. I must have wandered off, must have seen something that caught my eye because what I remember next is looking up and not seeing my mother.

The place was a maze. I ran around looking for her, but the more I ran, the more lost I became. I bumped into displays, knocked things down. I ended up in the gardening section clear across the other side of the store. The shelves looked taller here, the aisles wider and threateningly lonely. A nun in a black habit stood by a group of wooden Adirondack chairs. As I approached her, she smiled. I stood there until she stopped considering the chairs in front of us and shifted her attention to me. She called me "young man" and kept asking if everything was okay. I looked down at my shoes, looked in the direction I came from.

"Are you lost?" she asked.

"No," I said. "My mom lets me do what I want."

"Is that so?" She raised an eyebrow. "Well, you look lost to me." She grabbed my arm. "Come on."

She said her name was Sister Raphael. As we walked down the aisles, she told me a story about Jesus getting separated from his parents in a temple. It was meant to make me feel better, but given that I wasn't Jesus and this

wasn't a temple, I gave up trying to understand her point. We made our way past bins full of flip-flops and slippers and through the maternity section. At the front where the check stands were stood a security guard who led us into an office.

"I'll leave you here," said the nun.

Inside the room, rows of black and white screens showed different sections of the store. One monitoring the entrance lobby blinked intermittently, distorting the images of the men and women walking through the automatic doors. Another showed the spot where my mother and I had just been. A camera panned to the other end of the department, and when it returned, a man in a motorized wheelchair maneuvered around the racks of slacks and shirts my mother had rummaged through.

When my mother burst into the room, she was frantic, tears welling up in her eyes. Tucked under her arm was a silly-looking ceramic bust of Elvis Presley. I pouted as we finished shopping, made up a lie about a strange-looking man lurking behind a display of ski jackets. I told her someone could have kidnapped me or that I could have been locked inside after closing and been stranded overnight. The store was out of the style of coat my father had been eyeing all year. Instead, we bought him a package of boxer shorts and a set of drill bits.

"Those are stupid presents," I said.

"Then you pick something else out. I'll pay, and we can say it's from you."

Up front near the register there was a display case with some inexpensive gold lighters.

"That," I said.

"You sure?"

I nodded.

"Bueno."

When we were standing in line, I pointed to the Elvis head. "Is that for you?" I asked.

She nodded.

"His ears are pointy," I said. "He looks like an elf."

"Ay tú," my mother said. "He looks like the King."

It was wrapped in a shopping bag. She'd placed it on the floor of the car

so it wouldn't roll around. All I wanted was to take a hammer or my shoe or my fist and smash that head into a million tiny pieces.

                              *   *   *

I'm standing in the kitchen watching my mother serve me empanadas on a plate. She's complaining that Mary Jane Polanco eats everything but hardly ever brings snacks to the meetings.

"So tell her something," I say.

"What do you mean? Have you *seen* Mary Jane?"

"Which one's Mary Jane?" I ask. "I have trouble keeping track of your friends."

"The hefty one."

"You mean the fat one?"

"Yes. Her. Well, they're all—"

"Fat?" I say again. "Yes, they are."

She stops what she's doing. "What's with you?"

I walk over to the table and sit in the chair my father always took. He would be there for hours—checking his stocks in the newspaper, squinting over strands of numbers, jotting down figures on the backs of envelopes and sale circulars, a lit cigarette dangling from his lips.

"You're being a brat," my mother says. "Relax."

I take my glasses off and clean them with a napkin. "My girlfriend left me today, Mom. She's gone. I'm alone. You're alone. She's alone. We're all alone."

"I didn't think you wanted to talk about it." She points to the top cabinet. "Get the television trays out. We'll miss the movie."

"How can we? It's on tape."

Deborah had found a set of four trays at a flea market one Sunday afternoon. They depict Elvis in the different stages of his career: young Elvis as he'd appeared on *The Ed Sullivan Show*; Elvis in skintight black leather; Elvis from the *Aloha from Hawaii* special; and chubby Elvis from the *Viva Las Vegas* concert. On each of them he's either snarling or pouting, his eyes seducing invisible fans.

"She'll flip," Deborah had said that day. "She'll absolutely flip." It was the first time she held my hand. She'd worn a pair of denim overalls and a hat to

keep the sun out of her eyes. We'd brought bottles of water and sliced celery sticks and carrots that we carried in a backpack in case we got hungry. Deborah bought a *Partridge Family* lunch pail that still had its thermos, and she found a *Six Million Dollar Man* action figure in a red jumpsuit just like the one Lee Majors wore in the opening credits of the show. We walked around the flea market imitating the sound Steve Austin's bionic legs made whenever he ran fast or jumped high.

"You know, Mom, I can't stay. I was busy at the office today. I'm worn out," I say, handing her the trays.

"What are you going to do? Sit up in that stuffy apartment all alone? Don't be dumb. Stay. Have an empanada."

"Space, Mom. Remember? According to everyone, I need space. Or maybe I need a hobby. Like you and your Elvis thing."

"This isn't a *thing*," she says.

"Then what is it exactly, Mom?"

"You don't understand."

"You're right," I say. "I don't. What I understand is that, right now, I'm irritated and I want to go home."

"Fine. Go," she says. "But take some empanadas." She places four of them in a plastic bag and hands them to me.

"I'll call you tomorrow," I say, taking the bag from her. "Enjoy your movie."

           o   o   o

After my mother's, I stop off at the Excelsior Liquor Store. Behind the clerk are rows of bottles of rum, gin, and tequila, but I'm here for vodka. There's a brand with crude Cyrillic letters that comes in two proofs. There's another one in a sleek blue bottle that looks like a vase. I stand there for a while debating. The clerk glares at me.

"Is this a stickup or what, bro?"

"No," I say, pointing from bottle to bottle. "I can't figure out what I need."

I have the cash to buy the expensive blue bottle but opt for one at the very end, the plastic bottle. It looks unassuming and potent. That's what I want tonight: something potent.

I mix screwdrivers using the orange juice Deborah bought last week. There isn't much left, and when I run out, I substitute some Tang. I drink and flip through the stations, switching between a program about the engineering feats of the Egyptians and a show about pets performing miraculous rescues, before settling on a countdown of the greatest love ballads of all time. They're only on number eighty. Somewhere between numbers fifty and forty, I feel the alcohol really kicking in. I stumble into my kitchen, fill another glass with Tang and the last of the vodka. I sit back down, tell myself I'll stay up until they get to our love song. But do we even *have* a love song? The last thing I remember hearing is Karen Carpenter singing, "We've Only Just Begun."

"That's it," I slur. And I pass out.

I wake up this morning, feeling my way to the shower. My head's splitting, and I'm nauseated. Deborah's lotions and bottles of nail polish fall as I reach over the counter for my watch and rings. My stomach is doing a serious number on me. Remembering my father's advice about eating bread to help cure a hangover, I grab the empanadas my mother gave me. I bite into a strawberry-filled one and drink a glass of water.

I arrive at work late and unprepared for my meeting. The office is decorated for Halloween. Small cardboard tombstones are arranged around the water cooler, fake cobwebs cling to the walls and the corners of windows and across computer screens, a skeleton wearing a silly top hat and bow tie is pinned to the back of a door.

"My proposal's going through some revisions, and we'll need to reschedule the meeting," I tell my assistant. "I'll be in here." I point to my office. "Revising." And I close my office door behind me. Between the throbbing headache and upset stomach, it's hard to concentrate on anything. I give up after a while and just sit at my desk, shuffling papers around, clicking random files on my computer. At around eleven-thirty, Deborah calls me.

"You're at work," is the first thing she says to me.

"Why wouldn't I be?" I say. "Where else would I be?"

"That was stupid of me to say."

"How was your night?" I ask.

"Lonely. I missed sleeping with your arm around my waist. Yours?"

"I went to see my mom. I made screwdrivers and watched a countdown of love ballads. I heard ours."

"We never had one, Juan."

"Oh. Come over, okay? This is stupid, Deb."

She lets out a long sigh and clears her throat.

"Jesus, this is impossible," I say. "What do you want me to do here?"

"Give this some time. Juan, this is all so much for me. We both need some distance."

"Bullshit!" I shout. "Distance. Distance from *what*?"

"I just think that us getting serious, your father dying, it all happened so quickly. You're still processing it, sorting through it. It's disconnected you. We need some space from each other right now."

"Then why'd you call?"

"Because I care."

"I worry," I say. "Worry you won't come back to me."

"Don't think that way."

"How long will this take?"

"I'm not sure, honey. We'll take it slow. We'll figure that out when we get to it. Hey, I'm not disappearing here. I'll be in touch."

She hangs up.

The room spins around me. The floor rocks. I get up slowly and leave the office early.

Back at the apartment, I go around looking at the things she left behind. There's a book she was reading with the corner of page 117 folded over. There are notes in the margins, and some passages are highlighted in yellow. I take a pair of her nylons and pull them over my knuckles, wrap them tightly around my hand.

We met at this place across the street from my office called Red's Tavern. I'd gone with a co-worker to grab a drink. She stood with a group of girls at the bar and kept turning around to look at me. She wore a blouse with the word *oui* written across her chest, and she was the only one among the group of five who was drinking beer.

I tapped her on the shoulder. "That means 'yes,' " I shouted, pointing to her blouse.

"Are you hitting on me?" She laughed.

"Oui," I responded.

"Good," she said. "Because you're cute."

"Oui?" I asked.

She laughed again. "What does a girl have to do to get a guy like you to ask her out?" She leaned forward, gripping her pint with both hands.

The beers I'd had were making me feel loose, confident. "Stand up on this," I said, slapping the counter. "And dance."

"That's it?" She handed her glass to her friend and used the stool I'd been sitting on to hop up on the bar. She strutted around to a song playing on the jukebox, her feet stepping between half-empty pints of beer and baskets full of pretzels and nuts. People around the bar cheered. She balled up napkins and tossed them at me. When a guy in a baseball hat made a lewd comment, she grabbed a handful of peanuts and hurled them at him. The whole room broke out in laughter.

"Never dare me," she said. "I'll always do it."

After our third date, I told her about my father. He'd been back in the hospital that week. "You can meet him once he's home again," I said. "Hospitals are odd meeting places. Too sterile."

"They're not odd to me."

She took him some balloons, a bouquet of flowers, and the latest issue of *Car and Driver*. They talked about hot rods, Deborah's love for spicy foods, and my father's desire to visit the Vatican someday. She told him how we'd met, how she'd danced for me at a crowded bar, and how, despite her bravado, she had actually been terrified.

They also talked about my mother. She was home that afternoon, cleaning and preparing for his homecoming. My father adjusted himself in his hospital bed, fiddled with the tubes leading into his nose.

"My wife can be a handful," he explained.

"Señor," Deborah said, "I met her last week. She's not bad."

"She means well. She loves her Elvis Presley."

"She showed me her collection of records and her scrapbook. Does it make you jealous?" Deborah teased.

He laughed, rocked his head slowly, the tubes tapping against my arm. "No. She's liked him ever since she was a teenager. But he's dead. Once I get to wherever he is, I'll make sure to let him know who really had her heart."

When Deborah went to grab a soda from the vending machine out in the hallway, my father beckoned me. Rolling the magazine up and tapping me on the shoulder with it, he urged me to lean in closer, much closer.

"Don't lose her, Juan," he said. "Whatever you do, don't. That girl's got vida."

"No, señor," I said. "I sure won't."

"And don't forget about your ma," he said, his eyes welling up. "In case I don't—"

"Ya," I said. "Don't think that way, hombre. You're going to be just fine." I turned to see Deborah standing in the doorway.

"I'm sorry. I didn't mean to walk in then," she said as we left the hospital.

"You didn't know," I responded.

One of my last memories of him is that day in the hospital. The way he'd smiled as Deborah recounted our first meeting, how he'd lifted his hand to show her how small I was when he taught me the difference between a good Cuban cigar and a bad one. How he went on and on about my mother and her love for all things Elvis. The way he looked at both of us as we stood over his bed. He nodded a lot, kept saying we were good. We were a good set.

░   ░   ░

Today the dead are set free. They wander. They follow, mimicking your movements. They knock over dishes, slide chairs across floors, crack mirrors, slam doors. They shift and morph. They take the forms of stray dogs and owls and moths beating their wings against porch lights. They become the dust kicked up by the Santa Ana winds. They become the wind itself. You breathe them in.

The Day of the Dead falls on a Saturday this year. I take my mother to the farmer's market held in the parking lot of my old high school. She buys a few dozen bouquets of orange and yellow marigolds and some bananas. From there I drive her to the Botánica Oshún to pick up the sugar skull she had ordered two weeks ago. When we walk into the store, the woman behind the counter reaches for a package near the register. She unwraps it slowly, revealing a white head made of confectioners' sugar. Bright red and green plastic jewels adorn the figure's forehead; others are set deep within its eye sockets. My mother examines the details, traces the skull's wide, eerie

grin. The woman tells us that no two ever come out the same. She sells my mother packets of herbs, a bundle of incense sticks she says help attract the spirits of the dead, and a box of six candles. The idols and saints watch us from the shelves, some smiling, others with blank expressions, waiting for their chance to perform miracles, to sweat holy oil, to cry tears of blood.

Back at her home, my mother gathers her Elvis paraphernalia—teddy bears, coffee mugs with his portrait on them, small black-and-white pictures, an alarm clock that wakes to the tune of "Hound Dog," lunch pails, commemorative plates that she ordered from the television, and the bust she bought that day in the department store. She clears off the surface of the dining table and matches up and groups her souvenirs together in a strange kind of order. The tin trays and a velvet portrait Deborah had also given to her are arranged near each other.

She's been doing this ever since I was a kid. Once when I was fourteen, I brought a girl I liked to our house. The altar stood there in the middle of the dining room like a gaudy piece of jewelry. Despite the pleas to my father to convince her to take it down or to at least move it to another room, the altar stood there.

"My mom," I said to this girl. "She's kind of into Elvis."

"Yeah. *Way* into him."

We spent the rest of the afternoon hardly talking, sitting at opposite ends of the couch watching music videos.

"Why'd you let her?" I'd asked my father after the girl left.

"I don't interfere with your mother and her Elvis thing. That's a whole other part of her life she keeps to herself," he'd said, stabbing a cigarette into the grass.

She scatters the marigolds across the floor and on top of the altar, arranging them among the mementos assembled over the years. She makes peanut butter and banana sandwiches and slices them into triangles. She arranges them on a platter near a black-and-white photo on a wire easel. The sugar skull goes next to Deborah's velvet portrait.

From her purse, she pulls out a bottle of aspirin, opens the cap, and pours the pills into her hands. She organizes them in small piles near the Elvis bust. She lights the incense and sprinkles the herbs around the floor near the altar. When it's all said and done, when all the candles are lit, all the

offerings positioned carefully, when the prayer to the dead is recited, my mother stops to admire her shrine.

Every inch of the table is covered. I pick up a tabloid magazine with a crude pencil sketch of Elvis just below the headline that reads: HE LIVES. I touch the small square of exposed wood, imagine us gathered around the table eating dinner. My father sits at one end, my mother at the other. I'm young again, my father still has all his hair, my mother is warm and beautiful.

"What are you doing?" she asks, taking the magazine from my hand.

I think about my father, our model T-Birds and airplanes, the ashtray I made for him in elementary school that had a mold of my hand. "Hold on," I say as I run down the hallway.

In my parents' bedroom, on top of their dresser, is a small cedar box. I find the gold lighter I picked out for him the day I got lost. I take that and a pair of his shoes and go back out to the living room.

"See? There's still some room here. Let's work some of Dad's things in." I rearrange the altar, making space.

"Wait," my mother says. "Don't."

"What do you mean 'don't'?"

"This is for Elvis. A shrine for Elvis."

"What about your husband?" I shout. "Your dead husband. What's with all this Elvis crap? Your husband died six months ago. You should be thinking of *him*." I point to the altar. "Not that."

It's not the sensation of her hand making contact with my skin. It's the sound the slap makes across the dining room that stuns me. She reaches for his shoes on the table. When she tries to snatch the lighter, I grab it and shove it in my pocket.

"Dead," I shout. "He's gone. And you're prancing around this place like some lovesick teenager. Grow up. It's embarrassing. It always has been. What are you thinking?"

My mother looks right at me. She wears the same expression I saw on her face that night when she knelt by my father's side as he took his last breath.

She says in a voice so low it's almost a whisper, "I'm thinking just how much he means to me. Just how much he's always meant."

"Who?"

But she doesn't answer. Cradling my father's shoes in her arms, my mother walks into the bedroom and slams the door.

I don't go straight home. I drive around town for hours. I bump over the railroad tracks running parallel to the 10. At Alta Vista I make a left and head down to Buffalo, passing the Agua Mansa Palms where a group of girls in baggy jackets huddle around a guy on a motorcycle and loud cumbia music blares from one of the apartments. I end up at the Excelsior Liquor Store again. This time I buy a six-pack of Rolling Rock and a carton of menthol cigarettes.

At the cemetery, an issue of *Auto Monthly* and a red hat with the words *Built Ford Tough* written across the front rest on my father's marker. I turn back, hoping to catch a glimpse of Deborah's car driving off, but there's nothing.

I arrange the carton of cigarettes and the six-pack next to the hat and magazine. I'm bad at this, I think. This arranging and rearranging. I try to envision my mother's altar, the way she grouped and organized her collectibles. But no matter how hard I try, no matter how many different ways I change things, none of this looks right to me. After a while, I give up and drive off.

I pull over next to an empty lot, put the car in park, and leave the engine running. There's a packet of ketchup Deborah had left in the cup holder one time when we were on our way home from picking up drive-thru. That night, she'd rested her foot on my dashboard and hummed a tune as we waited for our food. I trace the outline of the lighter in my pocket with my finger, recall the spark, the way the flame flickered and sputtered the first time my father used it.

At the intersection of Central and Descanso, I notice a billboard perched over the roof of a gas station. A figure wearing a white suit with shiny gold and silver buttons stands against a bright blue background. His head is down and tilting slightly to his right, completely obscuring his face. Both his arms are stretched out, his palms raised up toward the sky. The sign reads:

An Evening with the King
November 3rd
San Jacinto Indian Casino
Off I-10

*   *   *

The mountains off the 10 fold in and out of one another. The stereo is playing Elvis's "Burning Love," and we drive with the windows rolled all the way down. The wind kicks up dirt and gravel. When sand gets lodged in my eyes, I rub until I can see clearly, concentrating hard on the asphalt before us. My mother had still been angry with me when I phoned her. I felt bad about our fight and asked her to give me a chance to make it up. I mentioned the show and offered to take her. After all, I said, it's not every day a genuine Elvis Presley impersonator performs at an Indian casino near us.

Deborah called me earlier today saying she was coming over to pick up her things. I try hard to forget about it, forget that when I get back to the apartment later tonight, she'll be there walking out of my life.

At the casino, we sit next to a woman in leather sandals named Nora who tells us the impersonator we're about to see is really a man named Denny Jenks from Modesto. She's attended at least twenty of his performances, and she swears he's by far the best around. Nora tells my mother she's been to Graceland and visited Elvis's tomb. Hearing this, my mother smiles, and Nora takes her hand.

"No words," Nora says. "No words to describe it, honey."

There are candles lit at each table, and groups of people sit at attention waiting for the show to start. The disco globe above the room spins, casting specks of light across the dark walls. A woman up front faints before the music even begins.

Still holding hands, Nora and my mother rise in unison. They stand on their chairs, wave bar napkins, and crane their necks, looking past the rows of tables and benches, past the heads and through the mist at the figure in a powder blue jumpsuit who's just walked onstage. The spotlight falls on him. My mother and Nora scream, their faces turn red. They throw their heads back, fan themselves with the napkins they're holding.

Here's my mother, Evelyn. She's just lost her husband to emphysema.

Evelyn considers herself to be Elvis Presley's number one fan. She owns all his movies. She likes to play his records every night. Evelyn has a scrapbook with clippings she began collecting years ago when she was a girl in Mexico. It's something she's proud of and remembers taking to school one day, showing it to her friends Isela and Margarita. She didn't allow them to touch the pages. She turned them herself, smoothing out the creases and bubbles on the clippings with her palms.

Standing on a chair in an Indian casino, Evelyn's clutching the hand of a woman she's just met. Wearing a lavender poodle skirt that she pulled out from deep within her closet, Evelyn dances. Her skirt fans out, exposing the ruffled slip underneath. She wears a pair of black-and-white saddle shoes with bobby socks rolled all the way down to her ankles and an angora sweater with a furry collar. The two women close their eyes and dance. With each step, with each steady rocking of the hips, they give themselves over, releasing part of themselves, taking something new in.

Later that night, walking through the door of my apartment, I find Deborah in the bedroom. Her clothes are folded and arranged in small neat piles on the bed. Her blow dryer and alarm clock are on the floor near her high heels and tennis shoes, her socks and nylons.

My father's gold lighter taps against the loose change in my pocket. I hear his voice, feel him in the night air around us. *Vida. That girl's got vida*, he says over and over again, his voice so loud in my head now, so clear. I feel his breath on the back of my neck, his hands on my shoulders, pushing me toward her, guiding my steps. And he tells me, *This is it, mijito. ¿Entiendes? This is what we do. This is how we hold on.*

Feast of
Saint Gabriel the Archangel

Angel of the Annunciation

Patron of messengers,

diplomats, clergy, postal workers,

broadcasters, telegraphs, telephones, childbirth,

and stamp collectors.

There was no one inside the botánica. The rain was keeping the customers away. Perla lowered the volume of the television she kept on a chair behind the counter and walked over to the front window. The asphalt was slick and shiny. Parts of the street were flooded, and wide puddles had formed at the edge of the parking lot. Rain unsettled Agua Mansa. It's only a matter of time, the ones who remembered would say. The Santa Ana is too unpredictable. It will spill over the banks and flood the streets. People will be ripped away by the currents. The whole city will be washed away all over again.

Perla was one of them who remembered. So much rain had fallen that winter. She was nine and had gone with her mother and father to buy firewood from a man who sold it cheap. The wood was stacked in neat piles next to the man's shack. He smoked a pipe, the skin around his fingernails split like the wood he helped her father load onto their truck. Her father had brought a blanket to cover the logs so they would stay dry.

"Don't matter," the man had said, helping her father secure the blanket over the wood. "Water'll soak through."

"We're not going far," said her father.

The rain came down hard as they made their way back. It tapped loudly as it hit the pickup's hood. Crossing the La Cadena Bridge, Perla looked out the window, past the sheet of rain, and saw the río a few feet below. It was a mass of dark brown water, churning fast and violent. Her father stopped once they crossed the bridge, the firewood banging against one side of the pickup.

"¿Qué pasa?" Perla's mother asked.

He didn't respond. He stepped out and looked back at the bridge. Water

soaked his hair and his jacket, and Perla's mother shouted at him to get back inside.

Perla turned around, her knees pressing into the bucket seat, and looked through the cab's rear window at what her father was watching. The columns cracked and gave way, and the river swallowed the road behind them. A car traveling toward the river stopped; the driver got out and ran past her father, trampling through the mud to the edge of the bank.

Pieces of lumber floated in the water like splinters, mattresses like islands. A woman's head bobbed up and down, disappearing every now and again among the waves. There was a man with his arms around the branch of a tree, fighting hard to hold on.

Her mother pressed her hand over Perla's eyes and said, "No mires."

Still, Perla heard the man screaming, the loud rush of the water, the sound of things cracking, breaking off, and washing away.

The dead were found once the rains stopped, mud caked over their bodies, limbs twisted and caught among branches and the crushed roofs of houses.

"Unos cuantos minutos," her father said once they were back home, drying his face with a handkerchief. "We could have been on that bridge. This troque could have been our tumba." He knelt on the floor of the living room and blessed himself. Her mother prayed a rosario to La Virgen that night.

It was pouring now. As she stood there watching, a figure jumped over a puddle and crossed the parking lot with a jacket held over his head. When he walked in, the boy took the jacket off and draped it over the back of one of the chairs to dry. She stepped behind the counter and made sure the cash register's drawer was shut.

Perla said, "¿Qué buscas?"

"No." He shook his head. "I looking for nothing."

He wore a long-sleeved flannel shirt and light blue jeans with a big silver belt buckle shaped like a motorcycle. His hair was cut short around the sides and back, and gold hoops dangled from his earlobes. A thick silver necklace hung around his neck with a crucifix that tapped against the pearl snap buttons of his shirt. At first he said nothing, just smiled nervously at Perla and stood there holding a book and pens.

He spoke with an accent. Perla pointed to the sign taped near the shelf above the register. "Hablo Español. Si prefieres."

"No," he said again. He hesitated and furrowed his eyebrows before speaking. "I talk a little English. I need to do the practice." He showed her the book he was holding.

Perla took it and read the title: *1,001 Big Questions.*

"I am learning how to reading this book. See?" He opened it, flipped through the pages, found one with the corner folded over, and showed it to her. It read: Have you ever done something so shameful it caused you to resent yourself?

"I found the book by where I live. I know a lot of the English words." He spoke slowly. "But I want to learn more."

He knew chill. Chill out. Chillin' like a villain. Tight. Get over it. Relax. Whatever. Disability. Okay. Food stamps. Faggot. Laid-off. Library. Fuck no. What up, dog? Buy one, get one free. Dude. Casino. Bitch. Speak English. Cell phone. Tweeker. Emergency. I'm from California. I'm in the United States Marine Corps. Nice to see you. 411. She's a ho. Are you lost? Wetback. Bro. Who's your Daddy? Call the landlord.

"Are you from here?" she asked.

"No. Michoacán," he said. "I only been here since a few months."

His name was Rodrigo. He lived in one of the small duplexes on Galena Court, he told Perla. She avoided that area. Some of her customers lived there. They told of gang fights and drug deals, of ranflas that drove around at all hours with their music blaring from speakers that rattled windows, of a baby run over by a drunk driver one night last year.

"You talk English good," he said, taking the book from her. "You teach? You teach me more, yes? I learn it from you." Rodrigo pointed.

She smiled. "I'm not a teacher. I run my botánica. I'm a businesswoman. Take a night class. At the high school." She pointed out the window.

"I can't, okay." He touched the jacket to see if it had dried yet. His gold bracelet tapped against the chair's seat. "I only come in two time since today. First time I sit here. And you remind me of my Abuela Josefa from Michoacán. I sit quiet. Like I do in her kitchen when I was small. Second time was last month. I looked through the window, but you tell me you were closed. I come here because your store is nice. You help people all the time. All the time there's people in here. You are very smart and know things books have. I think this: She can talk in both Spanish and English. I can pay you for teaching me English."

"Hijo," she said, clasping her hands and walking back to the register. "No puedo."

"Please, okay? You talk to me in English so I can learn. Teach it to me. You?"

"I can't." She leaned against the counter. "I never went to college."

"Books. I seen you. Using and reading from them."

"They're not books like that. They can't help you that way." She went to the case where the books were and Rodrigo followed.

She took one and opened it. The page showed an illustration of the palm of a hand, its lines all labeled, intersecting and breaking apart, the swirls of the fingerprints curling like smoke.

"Look," she said. "These aren't the kinds of books you need." Perla pointed to the ones lining the wall near the register, the ones with her notes in the margins. "They're different. Different books."

He studied the hardback cover of the one before him. "What does that read?" He pointed to one word.

"Palm," she said. "It's a book about palm reading."

"Reading? Like reading words for learning?"

"No," she said. "It's another kind of reading."

He flinched and shoved his hands in his pockets when Perla reached out to take them. "It's fine," she said. "Show me your palms."

He stuck his left hand out and placed it, palm up, on the counter.

She rubbed it gently. "This book teaches you to study these lines." Perla traced them with her finger.

Rodrigo took one of the pens he carried and gave it to her. "Write it. Write it here," he said, pointing to his palm.

She pressed the tip of the pen softly into his skin. The liquid gel was gold, and it dripped out slowly, freckled with bits of glitter.

"I like this feeling," he said, blowing on the gel to harden it once she finished. "I like how you write. You write more words for me? On the paper?" Rodrigo handed her a sheet from the pad tucked under his arm.

She wrote a list of words. She didn't think, just let them come to her: rain, river, water, hill, mountain, car, speed, time, statues, store, shopping, center, nice, going, trees, home, bus, learn, remember.

He watched carefully. Her wrist and hand moved gracefully over the

page. The pen glided over the surface of the paper, the words shiny, the flecks of glitter sparkling under the store's light.

He shoved his hand back in his pocket when a customer walked in.

"I am going now," he said. "I learn. I learn these. And I come back here to see you. You teach me more." He grabbed his jacket and ran out the door.

* * *

It rained all night and through the next morning. It was still coming down hard in the afternoon when Rodrigo burst through the door. He stomped on the ground a few times before walking over to the counter. From his jacket pocket, he pulled out the notepad and gel pens. He put his book of questions near the countertop display of prayer cards.

"I read the words you gave me yesterday," Rodrigo said, taking his jacket off. He cupped his hands together and put them up to his lips, blowing puffs of air to warm them.

"Sit," she told him, pointing to the chair nearest to Santa Bárbara. The candles at the statue's feet were lit. "Put your hands over the candles."

Perla bent down, reached behind the shelf under the register, and disconnected the space heater she kept there. She walked around the counter and plugged it into the outlet behind Santa Bárbara. The metal coils glowed bright orange as she positioned it close to Rodrigo's wet pant legs. She made him té de canela, and they sat for a while, watching the rain pound the pavement.

"I come for more words," he said, finishing his té.

She looked over at the notepad, the bundle of pens, then at the boy. He shivered. His hair was soaked. She left him sitting there, warming himself, and walked over to the counter. Perla smoothed the sheets of paper out, took the gold gel pen, and tried to conjure up a list of helpful words. But nothing came. She reached out for his book and flipped through the pages. She stopped at one question and read it to herself:

Who are you, exactly?

She wrote without thinking:

Who am I? Ha. That's a good question. I'm someone who is wondering why she is answering this question asking her who she is. I'm no

one important. Just some vieja who lives alone in a house my husband and I bought when we got married years ago.

Who am I? Perla María Portillo. Seventy-two years of age. Born here in Agua Mansa, California, and I think I will be lucky enough (or unlucky depending on who you ask) to die here.

I am someone who is always trying to figure out who she is. When I was younger, I was a daughter. A best friend. A wife. An apprentice. Now I'm just Perla who runs the botánica.

Rodrigo rose and walked around the store. Perla put the pen down and watched him. He paced nervously, his hands gripping his elbows. He shivered, bit his fingernails, and looked around suspiciously.

"Te sientes—" she started to say, reaching out to touch him. "Are you okay?"

He nodded.

"Here." She handed him the notebook and pens. "What do you want with it?"

"For reading." He shrugged his shoulders, his voice low. "For keeping my mind away from bad things. From the bad things I think."

Rodrigo folded and unfolded the paper. He focused on the ground, his eyes resting on the tips of his cowboy boots.

"What bad things?" Perla asked.

"Just I am being silly."

Perla reached into the case. "Here," she said, handing him a book. "Take this."

He studied the bright colors on the cover and ran his hand over the title before flipping it open. There were pictures, and the pages were thick and glossy with gold-leafed edges.

"What does it say?"

"It's about saints. Their histories and their miracles."

"I will bring it back tomorrow," he said, moving to the door.

"You can stay awhile. Let the rain pass."

"I am good," he said. "I am needing to go."

"Okay," she said. "I'll see you tomorrow."

The rain stopped in the middle of the night, and the next day the sun came out. She could see clouds reflected in the puddles near the cars parked in front of the donut shop. It was as if the sky had shattered, the pieces scattered about the black asphalt. When Rodrigo showed up, his hair was messy and uncombed, and stubble was growing on his face.

"I forget the book," he said. "Sorry. I will bring it back tomorrow."

When she reached a hand out to touch him, the boy flinched.

"Could I make you some té?" she asked

"No. I am fine. I ate a McMuffin." He held the notepad out. "I bring only one of the pens," he said, reaching into his back pocket. "I forgot the rest, too." He sat in the same chair and closed his eyes.

"Do you want me to write you more words?" Perla asked. "Or should I answer one of the questions from your book?"

He didn't answer her. His head fell to one side, resting on his left shoulder. He began to snore quietly.

She thought about what he had said last time about thinking bad things. Maybe there was something going on at the duplexes that he was involved in. *Drugs? Gangs? Maybe he's an illegal. Maybe he's hiding out from La Migra.* She had heard about sweeps in the area. Border Patrol agents had shown up recently around Agua Mansa. Last month they'd raided Catalina's Laundry Services and Las Glorias' parking lot where the day laborers gathered waiting for work.

She reached for the book and flipped through it until she found a question: *What do you fear most?* She wrote:

Being forgotten.

The space heater's coils glowed red. Rodrigo was still, his legs stretched out before him. From behind, taped to the window, an image of a solemn-faced Jesus—his robe pulled back to reveal his Sacred Heart, thorns wrapping around it, piercing the flesh—watched over the boy. Perla flipped through the book again and decided to answer a different question: *What are you most ashamed of?* She wrote:

I am ashamed of the fact that I only agreed to do this job because it would get me out of the house. Guillermo spent all those years

working, leaving me alone in the afternoons. No kids. No nothing. I felt like I had no life. Like things could have turned out differently if I'd only married someone who could give me more.

I am ashamed that I'm still angry at my husband for not being able to give me a baby and that I had once thought about leaving him because of this.

I am ashamed of so many things. I am ashamed that I can't write them down here.

She stopped only when Rodrigo stirred. It was getting colder now that the sun was going down. There were blankets on a shelf in the utility closet. Spreading one out on the floor, Perla opened a can of "Serenidad" aerosol. She got on her knees, aimed the nozzle a few inches away from the surface, and, with a slow broad motion, sprayed a fine even mist over the blanket. She picked it up and walked out front with it.

Rodrigo was snoring loudly. She noticed for the first time the long and elegant slope of his nose, a small dent shaped like a horseshoe in the middle of his forehead, and the faded remnants of a cluster of acne. She conjured up images of his mother and his father. Here was somebody's son, she thought. Alone and invisible. If she could call or write her, Perla would tell Rodrigo's mother, *He's fine. Your baby's fine. I gave him some té. He's warm. And now he sleeps.*

It wasn't until she covered him that she noticed the marks. Small round welts dotted the backs of Rodrigo's hands. They looked tender and painful, so Perla was careful as she tucked his hands under the blanket.

The rest of the day customers shuffled in and out. Yet he slept there, completely undisturbed. Hasari Gupta, who owned the Excelsior Liquor Store, showed up with his wife, Lakshmi, to buy more packages of incense sticks and a statue of the goddess Ganesh.

"The baby broke the last one we bought. He's getting to be that age. With those busy little hands." Lakshmi laughed. "Touching here and there."

"Drunk?" Hasari asked, looking at the way Rodrigo's head hung over his left shoulder, his mouth an oval. "You want me to call the police?" He pointed to the phone.

"No," Perla told them. "He's a customer. Just very tired."

"Be careful," he said. "My brother was working at a Circle K in Fontana. Second night on the job and he got robbed. Guy came in pointing a gun at his head. Good that nobody was hurt. Now my brother, he is afraid all the time."

"You make sure he doesn't sleep too much," Lakshmi said, her purple sari billowing out, sweeping over Rodrigo's feet as they walked out the door. "He'll be up all night."

He slept through the ring of the cash register, the honking of a car alarm in the parking lot, and Alfonso coming in to break a fifty-dollar bill.

"¿Y ese?" he asked.

"Nada, tú. I know him."

"I'm right next door." Alfonso used a pen clipped to a pocket of his apron to point to his store. "If he gets crazy or anything happens, I'm here. Okay?"

"Ya," she said. "I'll be fine."

He stirred a little when Rosa Cabrera walked in, excited and out of breath, waving an envelope in the air. Rosa opened it and pulled out a certificate with her name on it. "Perla, look. I'm officially a licensed hair stylist. Can you believe I did it?"

"I can," Perla said. "You worked so hard. I'm happy for you." She slipped the form back in the envelope, then reached over to hug Rosa. "What are your plans now?"

"Well, first I'm going to start cutting hair from home. I'm going to save the money so that I can rent out a station at a salon. Miguel's taking me out to celebrate tonight. Just the two of us. We got a baby-sitter for Danielle. I can't believe I'm finally done," Rosa shouted, waving the envelope around and stomping her feet. From the chair, Rodrigo mumbled something in his sleep, and Rosa turned and saw him.

"Oh, sorry."

"It's okay," Perla said.

"Is he sick?"

"No. He just needs to rest."

"Does he live nearby?"

"Yes, I think so."

Rosa said, "Tell him. If he needs a haircut or a trim. Give him and your

other customers my address. I can do perms and highlights and colorings. All for real cheap."

"I'll tell them," Perla said.

She let him sleep while she balanced the day's records and counted her deposit. He only woke when Perla turned all the lights off and grabbed her purse.

"What time?" he said looking around, the shadows of the santos perched high above on the shelves watching them.

"Go home." Perla handed him the sheets of paper. "It's getting late."

"I sleep for a long time," he said, stretching and smoothing his hair back. "I wish I could sleep here all night. It's warm."

"Come back and see me, okay?" she said, thinking of the marks on his hands. "If you need anything."

"Yes," Rodrigo said. "Tomorrow."

He walked across the parking lot and down Rancho toward the Galena Court duplexes. He had stirred when Perla tucked the pouch of shells and stones into the left pocket of his jacket. She had been more careful when she slipped an estampa of El Santo Niño de Atocha into the right pocket. Watching his figure fade into the night, she thought of Elleguá, the patron Orisha of all roads, the opener of locked doors. Perla asked him to clear Rodrigo's path, to remove any of the boy's obstacles, to make him strong and wise. To help him find the way back to his mother and father, wherever or whoever they might be.

She closed the door and stepped out into the night. Perla buttoned up her sweater and tucked her purse under her arm, put gloves on to warm her hands. The air was thick with the smell of settling rainwater, of things washed clean.

*   *   *

He hadn't been back in over a week, and Perla found herself beginning to worry about him. *Something's not right,* she told herself. *I shouldn't have let him go that night.*

When she arrived at the botánica, she went straight to the reference books Darío had left. She opened them up and began her search. There were salves and ointments to diminish the appearances of deep scars and inci-

sions. Something using fresh papaya juice. Flax oil mixed with lime water. Peeled nopal paddles placed over burns, then wrapped in gauze. She used strips of paper to mark important references in the books. One by one, they filled the main counter, stacked three and four high.

She came across a picture in one of the first-aid books. It was an arm. On it was a lesion. *Healing cigarette burn,* the caption below the picture read. *Intentionally placed on the forearm of a two year-old toddler just three days earlier.*

Had someone done this to him?

Perla continued flipping through the books, her eyes scanning the pages. They caught something in the margins of one. It was Darío's handwriting. The pencil's lead had rubbed into the paper, and the words were blurred and fuzzy.

He'd know what to do. If Darío were here now, he'd know. He always knew.

His left leg was shorter than the right. Both his ears were pierced, and he wore scarves wrapped around his head and adorned his wrists with bracelets made of shark teeth. He pulled into town one day, driving a trailer with balding tires and a cracked front windshield. He parked it down by the río and washed his clothes and bathed in the water there. Soon they started seeing the trailer in the Prospect Shopping Center's parking lot, in front of the space left vacant by Lety's Flowers.

Merchandise arrived in boxes, and the man could be seen shuffling about, working furiously, hanging packets of herbs on the walls, assembling shelves and cases. Soon there were pictures in the window and on the door of the shop, images they recognized and prayed to—La Virgen María in a blue satin robe kissing a cross, San Judas holding a staff, San Miguel slaying a demon. A week later, handwritten signs printed on simple lined paper appeared stuck to light posts and telephone poles around the city:

SEÑOR DARÍO

CONSEJERO ESPIRITUAL Y CURANDERO

Leo las Cartas
Hago Limpias y Curaciones

Se Venden Todas Clases de Tés y Hierbas
Preparo Perfumes y Velas
Ayuda de Todas Clases de Problemas:

* Trabajo
* Alcoholismo
* Enfermedades Desconocidas
* Problemas de Amor y de Dinero

Botánica Oshún
Prospect Shopping Center, Agua Mansa

Nobody had ever seen anything like it around Agua Mansa. They said the name Oshún had something to do with Voodoo or witchcraft or deep dark magics and curses. Peacock feathers and amulets of animal bones and a statue of a hooded skeleton wearing a red robe and wielding a scythe could be seen through the window. They said if you stepped foot in the shop you would be hexed. No one went in the first few weeks it was opened.

Every Sunday they saw him at Mass, sitting up front, a cane tucked neatly between his legs, always the first in line to receive the Host, always first to shake the priest's hand. Perla's mother and some women at church looked at him as he passed, tipping his straw hat as he left San Salvador's.

A friend of her mother said, "I heard he's a brujo. That he reads cards and talks to the dead. Could it be true?"

"Pura mentira," the other woman standing with them added, glancing at Perla and her mother. "Te lava el coco."

"The Devil," the first woman added. "That's what he is—the Devil."

*   *   *

It was three in the afternoon. Perla was bored. She went into the kitchen and poked around inside the refrigerator, deciding what to cook her husband for dinner. Guillermo would be home from the plant in a few hours. She rummaged through the cupboards and saw that there was no more salt. She would need it, she figured. Looking at the clock above the range, she saw that there would not be enough time to take the bus to the market and be

back early enough to prepare things, so she put her shoes on and walked across the lot toward the shopping center.

Perla stopped in front of the botánica before heading into Tienda Arellano. There was a statue of San Antonio in the window. A halo of stars circled his head, and he wore a simple brown robe with a gold sash. Pinned to the robe were dollar bills.

Why is everyone so afraid? she thought. *San Antonio's in the window. There's crucifixes and pictures of Mary and Joseph by the door.*

Tienda Arellano was smaller than a grocery store, with only six aisles and a few shelves. They stocked some produce—tomatoes, avocados, iceberg lettuce, scallions—in wicker baskets along the floor. Old barrels by the front door stored pinto beans and rice customers scooped up with a liquid measuring cup. One cooler stocked sodas, eggs, and cheese, and gallons of milk and orange juice. She walked down the candy aisle toward the back where the condiments and spices were and took a can of salt. When she went to pay, Perla found Alfonso behind the register instead of his father. At the edge of the counter were a stack of textbooks, each covered in brown shopping bag paper. His name was written on one, "Chicano Power" and "Puro Aztlán" scrawled all over another. One had a pencil sketch of a peace sign just below the year, 1972.

The boy said, "Hi, Mrs. Portillo." His hair was long and wild, and it came down in bangs, covering his eyes.

"Hi, Alfonso. Where's your father?" Perla asked, giving him money for the salt.

"He went to drop my mom off," the boy said. He was tall and skinny with oversized feet and long arms and legs. His voice squeaked when he said, "She went shopping."

"Are you all alone in here?" she asked, taking her bag.

"First time," he said, smiling. Then he went back to reading one of his textbooks.

When she passed by the botánica, the door was open. It was empty inside. She looked at her watch. It was still early, and she didn't want to go back home just yet.

It was much cooler inside the shop. The shelves were bare, with only a few charms and amulets and scapulars of Our Lady of Mount Carmel and

Saint Jude. Nailed to the wall were pictures of San Ramón and the Holy Trinity, and the figure of a woman in a white dress with a star above her head emerging out of the sea, *Yemayá* written in black letters along the bottom. Incense sticks and bars of soap were grouped neatly on the counter near the front window where San Antonio stood. Some of the bookshelves were empty; others housed statues of saints and velas like those her mother lit. Silver medallas and rosary boxes and white Holy Communion candles were on the floor. Baptismal gowns hung from wire hooks on a string suspended over the counter.

The man came out from behind the curtain that covered the entrance to the stockroom. When his shorter leg hit the floor, his sandal made a soft slapping sound.

"¿En qué le ayudo?" he said, standing across from Perla.

She didn't say anything to him, just stood there cradling her bag of salt. "Oh," she said. "I'm only looking. That's all."

"You live around here?" he asked, looking at the bag in her hand.

"Across the field," Perla told him. "I was next door buying salt." She pointed at the bag. "I saw your store. I wanted to see what you sold."

"You've never been to a botánica before?"

"No," she said.

"I sell novenas and estampas. Religious articles. Rosaries and velas. Scapulars and statues of santos. Do you know what curanderos are?"

"Yes," Perla said. "Healers."

Her mother talked of the curanderas who lived in a shack at the foot of a mountain near their pueblo in Michoacán. They were two wise sisters, one blind and the other deaf. The deaf one was a curandera who healed with herbs and salves. The blind one divined the future using stones and chicken feet and feathers that she arranged in patterns on the ground of their hut.

"Well, I'm a curandero, too," he said. "I do limpias, and I know how to read palms and Tarot cards. People around here think I'm some evil brujo, right?"

She said nothing, remembering the suspicious whispers of her mother's friends.

He slapped his knee and laughed. "Not you, though. You're different. You're curious, aren't you?"

"Yes," Perla told him.

"And you believe."

"I guess," she said.

"Look around," Darío said, waving at Perla. "I'm still organizing things." He pointed to the piles of merchandise on the floor. "But browse."

A stone as big as a fist stood on a white plate behind the door. The stone had a necklace of red and black beads wrapped around it. Shells small as dimes were glued on its surface to form a face.

She pointed. "What's that?"

"Elegguá," he said. "Elegguá is old. Older than anything. One of the Orisha. Powerful African spirits. Elegguá is their messenger. He plays tricks on people. But he is also very strong. He protects your home from evil things."

"It's nice," she said. "Your store is nice. I'll come back in. Maybe tomorrow."

"I'm Darío," he said. "Here." He handed her an estampa of El Santo Niño de Atocha. "A gift. So that you will come back."

She said goodbye and walked home to prepare dinner.

Perla didn't go back for a few days. There was too much to do around the house: she needed to get rid of a bag of old clothes and shoes that the Salvation Army came by to pick up; there was washing and ironing to do; she helped her mother plant roses in her garden. She came home from her mother's, sat on the bed, and kicked off her sandals. The temperature had reached almost one hundred degrees, and she'd been working outside all morning. Perla poured herself a glass of water and lay on the bed, trying to nap because her head was hurting. When she pulled open her bedside table's drawer to look for the bottle of aspirin she kept there, Perla found the estampa of El Santo Niño.

She showered and dressed, then walked to the botánica. She was surprised to find a handful of people inside the shop, milling about, asking Darío questions, looking and pointing. He limped around behind the counter, asking a woman to describe her symptoms of anemia while bagging a Saint Joseph scapular for someone else.

"I thought maybe I scared you away," Darío shouted to Perla when he saw her.

"No," she shouted back. "I was just busy around my house."

She touched the merchandise this time—the stone Elegguá figure behind the door, the packets of powders and the bars of "Santísima Muerte" and "Suerte Pronto" and "Ama Me Siempre" soaps. She smelled the candles and the incense sticks, twined the scapulars and rosaries between her fingers.

She bought an estampa of San Ramón Nonato and a card with baby angels, some sleeping on clouds, others playing harps.

"What does the name mean?" she asked Darío after the other customers had gone and they were alone. "What does Oshún mean?"

He pointed to the stone face behind the door. "Like Elegguá, Oshún is an African spirit. The spirit of sweet water, of lakes and ríos. Of love and beauty and fertility. She loves dance and bells and fans and yellow flowers. She is the one you seek when you have money problems. She is beautiful and young just like my mother was when she left Cuba for Mexico. There she met my father, and they married. I was raised Católico, and when I was old enough she taught me Lucumí."

She said to Dario, "What is Lucumí?"

He leaned up against the counter and continued: "A religion. Some call it Santería. It came from Africa. In the Caribe, the monks tried to convert the slaves working in the sugarcanes to Christianity. When the slaves refused, they were beaten. They prayed in secret in the woods and worshipped their spirits by hiding them as santos so the monks would never know. They told themselves Oshún would be Nuestra Señora de la Caridad del Cobre." From a box, he took an estampa of Nuestra Señora and placed it in front of Perla. "Sometimes she's Saint Cecilia, sometimes someone else. My mamá showed me how to pray to Oshún and to see the other spirits in the santos at church. She made me promise not to tell anyone what she taught me, not even my father. We secretly made altars to Oshún and left her honey, canela, shrimp, and fresh water. We made boats from bright strips of paper and sent them out into the stream near our pueblo, just the two of us, the boats our offerings to Oshún. When I came here and saw the río, I named the botánica for her in honor of my mother."

He stopped talking and totaled up Perla's purchases. Darío used a pad and pencil to keep track of his sales until the register he had ordered arrived. He kept the money in a metal lockbox on a stool behind him. He totaled Perla's purchases and put them in a bag.

He looked at her and said, "The baby angels. On the card. The estampa of San Ramón. San Ramón you pray to for help with having babies, did you know?" He paused. He reached his hands out and touched Perla's head, her collarbone, her shoulders. "A baby," he repeated. "A baby. A baby. You want a baby."

The bag fell out of her hand onto the floor. Her knees weakened, and she gripped the counter.

"A baby," he said, his bracelet rattling. "You've been trying. Trying now for a long time." His eyelids fluttered. His face glistened with sweat. "Tell me, am I right?" He opened his eyes and looked at her. "Tell me the truth. It's the only way I can help you. And that's what you want: my help."

And it came as no surprise to Perla when she began to tell him everything—how they'd been married for fifteen years and had been trying to have a family, how they went to a doctor and found out Guillermo was sterile.

"He doesn't like talking about it," she said. "I'm getting older. And I don't think I'll ever be a mother."

She talked without stopping, without pausing to take a breath.

Darío pulled his hands away from her shoulders and said, "Tell your husband he should come in and see me. Tell him I've helped couples like you. Tell him I have teas and remedios we could try."

He walked around the counter and picked the bag off the floor. He handed it to Perla and said, "Go home. Come back here with him. We can try something."

That night, after they had dinner, she followed Guillermo into the garage. He turned the radio on and popped the hood of the Monte Carlo. He pulled the tab off a can of beer and threw it in the trash, then rested the beer on the roof of the car as he checked the oil.

He loosened the radiator cap and poured in antifreeze. "Car's temperature's running high," he said. "Don't want it overheating."

"I went to the botánica today," she said, leaning up against the washer.

"That crazy store?"

"The man there, he's nice."

"Is it true? What they say about him? Is he really a witch?" He looked up and shook his head.

"He's not. He's a curandero. A healer. He told me something. He touched my forehead and around my shoulders." She walked over to Guillermo and stood next to him. "He knew. He said he saw a baby."

Guillermo put the jug of antifreeze down and looked at her. "He saw a baby? What does that mean?"

"He said—" She paused. "He said he could help you. Us. He's helped other couples like us before. Have babies."

He took a long drink of his beer and tossed the empty tin can in the trash. "Those brujo types, they're just out to make some fast money. If a doctor couldn't help me, what makes you think his bull could?"

"We could try," she said.

"For what?" Guillermo shouted.

"We need to try everything."

"Is he going to put a spell on us?" Guillermo laughed. "Is he going to make me kill a goat and drink its blood? All that stuff doesn't mean anything." He waved his hand. "I'm not doing it."

"Please. We need to try everything."

"Hey, I'm fine here. We don't need to try anything. Why do we need kids?" he said. "I've gotten used to it just being us. We don't need any of that. We got the two of us."

"I want it," she shouted, hitting the car's fender with both hands. "I have nothing. I feel like I'm suffocating here. All day I'm alone."

He slammed the car's hood and walked back into the house. He went to bed that night without saying a word to her.

The next day, she found Darío helping an old man who was complaining about a pain in his elbow. There was another woman waiting to talk with him.

"My baby had a diaper rash," she told Perla. "The doctor gave me some cream, but the cream's been irritating his skin."

"My mom used to use sábila," Perla said. "On me. When I was a baby. Have you tried that?"

"Aloe?" the lady asked. "I didn't know you could use that."

Perla wrote everything down on a piece of paper for the lady. When she and the customer Darío had been helping left, Perla said to him, "My husband. He doesn't want to come in and see you."

"I thought he wouldn't." He laughed. "Most men don't like to. They don't

like admitting there's something wrong with them. Makes them feel weak. They get embarrassed."

"Is there something you could give *me?*" Perla asked. "To help him through me?"

"Something, maybe," he said. "What I really need is him. Here. He's the problem. Not you."

"I guess I wasn't meant to be a mother," Perla said, looking over at the statue of the Virgen María in the middle of the glass case.

"No, you weren't."

She looked up at him, confused.

"That customer. I saw how you helped her. Listened to what you said. You have el don, the gift of healing."

"We were just talking, and I told her what to do. It wasn't anything big. I don't have powers."

"It hides. Gets buried. I felt it the first time you came in. But power like yours, like mine, like the woman I learned from, it doesn't come without a price."

He walked around the counter and pulled his pant leg up. The skin of his left leg was shriveled and pale and scarred just above the ankle. "Polio," Darío said. "It shrunk my leg. It was my price. The woman I learned from, she was burned in a fire. Another man I knew, he was blind in one eye, but his gift of prophecy and his healing powers were strong. You"—he pointed to Perla, to her stomach—"you'll never have children. It's the price you pay. But you do have power. I saw it when you walked in. Shining blue around your whole body. Why don't you let me help you? Teach you to make it stronger? You could be my apprentice. Think about it," he said. "I know it sounds crazy. And I know it's not what you want."

"I want a family," she said, starting to cry. "Not power."

She grabbed her purse and ran from the store. At home, she sat cross-legged on the floor of the spare bedroom. She imagined it furnished with a crib and a rocking chair. The walls painted a pastel blue or rose. Lace curtains covering the windows. Picturebooks and stuffed animals and a wooden toy chest. Bottles warming in hot water on the stove. Guillermo pacing, rocking their baby in his arms. She cried all afternoon, alone in her house, frustrated and angry at Darío for saying what he did, at her husband for being so stubborn, for not being able to give her the family she deserved.

When Guillermo came home from the factory that evening, they walked to her parents' house for dinner. Guillermo joined her father in front of the television, while Perla went to the kitchen to help her mother. She was peeling potatoes. Long strands of her hair fell down one side of her face. She pushed them back with the palm of her hand and looked at Perla standing near the stove.

"Ahora te enseño," her mother said. "None of this is written down. So memorize it all. Because once I die, you'll be left. Then you'll give these recipes to your babies."

"I'm never going to have kids, Mamá. I'm getting old." She didn't say anything about Darío, what he'd told her. She still didn't know how much of it she believed.

"You still can," her mother said. "You're still young."

"I wasn't meant for it. I don't know what I was put here to do."

"¿De qué hablas?" Her mother stopped peeling and looked over at her daughter. She cleaned her hands on her apron and walked over, placing her hand on Perla's forehead. "Are you feeling okay?"

She thought about Darío, his hands passing over her face.

She went down the hallway into the bathroom and locked the door. She turned the faucet on, watched water spill out, filling the green porcelain sink. In the mirror she conjured up a different face looking back, a different reflection. Not one with skin starting to tire and arms and hands that would never hold a baby. She imagined herself young. Starting everything over again.

She sat at the edge of the tub and looked down at the floor, the shaggy bath mats, her sandals. When had this happened? When had she become this woman? Did she take a wrong turn somewhere? *I could walk away. Leave him.* The sound of the television came through the walls. Guillermo and her father were talking about the game. She heard her mother drop a pan in the kitchen.

Maybe he's right. Maybe I do have it. Maybe he can teach me. Maybe he should.

She gripped her knees and cried, her shoulders shaking, her head dizzy and light.

She walked home with Guillermo in silence. When he tried to take her hand, she refused to give it to him.

"What's with you?"

She said nothing. Passing the empty field, Perla looked past the trees and saw the wall of the botánica painted with graffiti.

"The man at the botánica offered me a job," she said to Guillermo.

"Doing what?"

"Helping around the store. He'll pay me."

"You don't need money. You don't need to work."

"What if I want to?"

They stopped in front of their house. He opened the door to the chain link fence, and they both stepped into the yard and walked to the porch steps.

"You don't need to. We have enough money."

"I'm not doing it for that," she said. "I'm doing it because I'm empty."

He fiddled with the house keys. The sun was setting. Burnt orange light spilled onto the sidewalk, erasing the cracks and chips in the concrete.

She took his keys and threw them across the lawn. "I want more. Something else to do besides sitting at home all day cooking and cleaning. If I can't have kids, I can have a job. I don't care what you want. I didn't have a say in any of it, of us not having kids. So you can't have a say in me getting a job."

He stayed quiet. He shrugged his shoulders. "Do what you want." He fetched the keys and went inside.

The next morning Guillermo said nothing when he left for work. He walked down the driveway, slammed the car door shut, and pulled out, the tires skidding as he drove away.

She dressed modestly—a green pleated skirt, a plain tan cotton blouse with red buttons, and a pair of low flats. Perla grabbed her purse and went to see Darío.

"Señor," she said, closing the door. "Where do we start?"

Darío smiled. "I think we begin at the beginning." He turned the television off and had her sit down in one of the chairs. He closed the front door, flipped the sign, and sat next to Perla. "I want to tell you about how I got started doing this."

He had been taught by a woman who lived in Mexico. "She was a Fidencista," Darío said. "They're disciples of El Niño Fidencio, Mexico's most famous curandero, a man many said was blessed by God himself. This

teacher of mine, her name was Agripina. When she was a child, she had been caught in a church fire and was the only one to survive. The flames burned one side of her face. Skin melted over her eye. It was hard to look at her. But that woman liked to joke around and laugh. She had the best sense of humor. Not serious at all. That fire, she said, gave her powers. Made her see things. Sicknesses and diseases. So she started helping people with remedios and petitions. She delivered many babies. Many of them were named for her."

He stopped and handed her a notepad and a pencil. "First," he said, "I will show you how this place is laid out, how I've decided to set everything."

Perla followed him around the store, jotting down the names of santos and herbs. Candles and crystals. Spirits and talismans. By the time they were finished, she had filled up seven sheets of paper. Her hand cramped up, and when a customer came in and asked for something to help with her loss of appetite, Perla was relieved.

"Now go home," he said. "Read those notes. We'll continue tomorrow."

She and Darío spent a good part of the next week arranging the store—stocking the candles and sorting through the piles of merchandise. Once the botánica was set up, Darío had her follow and observe him. She watched how he handled cases of empacho, susto, and low sex drive. Preparing for limpias, Darío had her gather the necessary items—the romero, the cigars and rum, the feather and the egg, which he said would absorb the malas vibras—and arrange them to his specifications.

Darío talked about santos like Jesús Malverde, San Simón, and La Santísima Muerte, ones she'd never heard the priests at church mention. He showed her astrology charts and books on palmistry and auras. She learned the tenets of Buddhism, Judaism, Hinduism, Voodoo, Candomblé, and the Lucumí of Darío's mother. He taught her about some of the other spirits—the many guises they assumed, the many roles they served. There was Changó the lord of lightning, thunder, drums, and dancing. Orunlá, the spirit of wisdom and divination. Oggún, who liked offerings of smoked fish and oak leaves. Obatalá, the wise father of all the spirits. Yemayá, the daughter of the seas, whose colors are sky blue and white. Elleguá, the energy of the universe, Elegguá who opens roads and possibilities.

The day the cash register arrived Darío made her learn to use it first.

"I don't like those things," he said. "You learn, then you teach it to me."

Guillermo hardly spoke to her that first week. He turned the other way in bed while she sat up and studied from her notes. In them there were treatments for anemia, gout, diabetes, and kidney stones. There were remedies for tapeworms, susto, and choque de nervios. She concentrated, memorizing her scribbles, sought patterns and connections, quizzing herself well into the night, her husband's snores keeping her company.

She came home one afternoon and found him in the bedroom, just sitting there.

"You get off early?" she asked, putting her stacks of books on the bedside table.

He said, "I lied. I said I wasn't feeling good."

"Are you hungry?"

"No." Guillermo took her hand in his and squeezed it. "I know it's too quiet in here for you," he said. "I can tell this work makes you happy. I'm glad to see you this way. I'm sorry I can't give you what you want."

Five years passed quickly, then one day Darío called from a phone booth to tell Perla he was leaving.

"I have to go," he said. "For good, Perlita."

"Why?"

"Because. When I came here, it wasn't to stay forever. It was just to open the store. To find someone to run it. Now I have to go again. Move to another town somewhere and start the whole thing over again. Perlita, I want you to take over the store."

"But how? I can't."

"You have to. Trust me, Perlita," he said. "I know what I'm doing."

⁎   ⁎   ⁎

Darío always knew what he was doing.

She reshelved the books. It had been so long now. And in that time, her parents had died. Guillermo had gone quietly in his sleep. Three years ago, Darío's daughter Sylvia had called. Her father's cancer had been too much, had ravaged his body. In his notebook he'd written, "Call my Perlita when I go. She was my favorite. My best pupil."

Perla remembered those early days when the store had first opened. She

remembered the piles of boxes and merchandise on the floor, remembered climbing the ladders and stocking things, getting the store ready, exactly to Darío's specifications.

It was still like that today. The only thing that had changed over the years was the amount of merchandise on the sales floor and in the stockroom. It had grown. There was more of everything. Cluttered and busy. But it was all still exactly where he'd wanted it to be.

None of it, she thought, telling Darío. *I haven't changed it. It's all still just like you told me.*

On the shelves nearest the door were the statues—the Divine Eyes, the Money Frogs, and clay Pancho Villa courage heads, white witches and black spirits of good luck, bronze Buddhas of good health and happy homes, Vishnu and elephant-headed Ganesh and Shiva the Destroyer with his many arms, the wood-carved Kachina dolls covered in feathers and beads, Santísima Muertes in red and black shrouds, Santa Teresa, San Simón sitting in his chair with his black suit and bolero hat, the Infant of Prague, Our Lady of San Juan, San Antonio, and the little Holy Spirit doves perched on terra-cotta tree branches.

Then there were the veladoras. The colored seven-day candles—blue for serenity, red for love, white to end curses, green to attract prosperity. There was Santa Bárbara, patrona of prisoners and invoked against evil; San Judas Tadeo of lost and desperate causes; La Virgen de Guadalupe, madre de México; El Santo Niño de Atocha, who keeps lawsuits away; Nuestra Señora de la Caridad del Cobre, patrona of Cuba, who protects travelers at sea; San Martín de Porres, the patron of African-Americans and the poor; San Martín Caballero, who draws customers to your business; La Mano Poderosa, the holy hand of the crucified Christ; and Las Siete Potencias Africanas—Elegguá, Orunlá, Obatalá, Oggún, Changó, Yemayá, Oshún in the guises of Catholic saints. There were the mystical spell velas—Ven Aquí, Indian Spirit, Justo Juez, King Solomon, Shut Up, Evil Away, Break-Up, Do As I Say, Trabajo, Víbora, Quédate, Road Opener. Below them were candles shaped like crosses and snakes, skulls and mummies.

Then there were the soaps and cleansing bath waters—Gemini, Conquer Everything, Black Horse, Fast Luck, Eres Mío, Cuauhtémoc, I Control

All, Quetzalcóatl, Si Puedo, San Simón, Bring Me Everything, Enemigo Retírate, I See Everything. There were glass vials of rose and tea and patchouli oils and aerosol sprays—Hex Removing, Mariposa, San Judas, Osiris. There were the Holy Helper and Good Spirit floor washes, and beside the strawberry-, frankincense-, vanilla-, and cinnamon-scented packs were the Lotería, Paul Bunyan, Mother of Clarity, and Mother Teresa incense sticks.

The herbs and teas hung on short metal pegs—anís de estrella, cuasia, huizache, boldo, manzanilla, valeriana, epazote, uña del gato for diaper rashes and body aches, cola de caballo for kidney stones and skin problems, damiana for hangovers and bed-wetting, yerba buena—spearmint—good for colic and uncontrollable flatulence, romero—rosemary—for rheumatism, canela—cinnamon—to reduce fever and aid indigestion.

There were the silver medallas stored in a plastic tackle box sitting on a shelf behind the register, Egyptian ankhs and pendants in wooden boxes lining the countertops near the booklets and novenas, the estampas and rabbit's feet, the Tarot cards and numerology charts. In the glass cases were satchels filled with stones and gems—quartz, hematite, coral, geode, pyrite, turquoise, jade. There were necklaces of cowrie shells, rosaries, scapulars, menorahs, and Stars of David.

She took it all in and concentrated, then walked over to the books she had shelved and rubbed her hands over their spines—*Interpreting Dreams, The Zodiac, Candle Magics and Rituals, Essential Yoga, Palmistry, The Mystery of the Tarot, La Santa Biblia Católica*. Perla grabbed one, not bothering to note its title, and flipped through the pages until her eyes rested on a particular passage:

> It is a universal truth that all manner of belief stems from an inherent human desire to know what occurs beyond our own plane of existence. With the help of the candles and stones, chants and offerings, the lines of communication between our world and the Other Side open up. These roads widen and expand, clearing a path where knowledge is shared in order to help us feel a part of a greater consciousness. Much like a mechanic who utilizes wrenches and other implements to aid him in his task of "fixing" whatever is broken, so

do the candles and amulets and deities described herein help to ful-
fill the task of alleviating and uncrossing, healing and enlightening.

She read the passage over and over. She read it to the audience of Buddha
and Shiva statues gathered next to the plastic display of prayer cards on the
counter. She whispered it to the Kachina dolls and the glass unicorn. They
offered up no insights. No knowledge. She imagined copying the passage
down in Rodrigo's notebook, imagined him reading it to himself, searching
for meaning in the words.

"What should I do now?" she said out loud, her words desperate. Then
she heard Darío, his voice in her head, clear and strong. *Feel it, Perlita,* he said.
All of it. Use it. This santo here for this. That yerba there for that. Don't waste any part.
All of it is precious and powerful. Like you, Perlita. Like you.

Asi Like Magic

I don't know how to dress for this. Everything I have is either too tight or too bright. Or too shiny and skimpy. My shoes are too high, too silver and gold and red, the straps that wrap around my ankles too flimsy. Everything about the way I dress is too much. I have nada to wear. Nothing fits right anymore.

The last time I worked with Beatrice she'd gone home early complaining of a headache. I was off the next day, and that was when she died. Something got clogged in her brain, a blood vessel popped. Y como nada my only friend up and died on me.

"We didn't think to call everyone," Steven, the front office manager, said to me when I got to the clínica. "I'm sorry. We're taking donations to get a wreath."

I gave him ten dollars.

"You can go home today if you're not up to working," he said. "Come back next week."

I left and went straight to the club. I knew Bibi would be there, balancing the books like she does every Friday morning and getting ready for the weekend shows.

"What do I wear?" I asked her. Bibi sat behind a desk, her face rubbed raw and pale without mascara and lipstick.

"Something somber. A dark gray or black dress," she said. "You can find one at the indoor swap meet in San Bernardino. They should be open right

now." She punched the adding machine's keys; a long receipt spilled over the edge of the desk like a waterfall. "Don't stress about it."

I didn't want to tell her I had no money to spend. That I'd been saving up for the operation. That I was more determined than ever to go through with it. She'd think it was stupid. What's the point? she'd say. Me with my wild ideas. It was a big step. And I was too young to make those kinds of decisions. It's been slow going because I don't get paid very much, but every month I've been putting away a little, saving the tips I get when the men toss dollar bills onstage while I dance. I keep the money in an envelope taped to the bottom of my nightstand. I have a lot. But it's still not enough.

So I left the club and took the bus home. I spent all of Saturday crying, unable to go out shopping for a dress. It's now almost ten on Sunday, and I've been going through my things all morning. The funeral's at noon.

The closet's almost empty. All my clothes are piled up on the bed. As I go through what's left, I find my black skirt, the first one I bought when I moved here to California, hiding behind a gold-sequined dress and a pair of imitation Guess jeans. I have a top. It's dark brown with a fur collar muy fluffy and warm. The blouse has shiny white buttons, but some have fallen off. It'll have to do. I'll use small safety pins to close up the gaps.

And shoes? I'll wear the low flats. The dark blue ones that almost look black. No one will be able to tell. You would have to squint to notice that they're not quite what they seem to be.

*   *   *

I needed to make more money. La Lola, who dances with me, said they posted new jobs every day at the unemployment office.

"Look for the little cork board," she'd told me as we dressed before the show one night. "They pin the cards there. But if you want something that'll pay you under the table, right outside there's a telephone booth where people stick flyers looking for all kinds of help. My sister got a job as a babysitter. One hundred bucks a week it pays. Cash."

I met Beatrice at the bus stop the day I went downtown to find some work. While I waited, I decided to do my nails. I'd bought this new color called "Temptation" and had just started to paint my pinky when Beatrice showed up, wearing a green smock and pants with white shoes.

"That's such a pretty color." She pulled out the most recent copy of *Tú* from her purse.

"Thank you. Got it at Las Glorias," I told her. "It's on sale right now. They have them in those plastic clearance bins in the cosmetics aisle."

"I like anything that's red. It's such a sweet color. So alive—you know?" She smiled.

I moved over so that she could sit on the bench. "I know what you mean."

"I'm Beatrice."

"Azúcar."

"Azúcar. I like that."

I'd already read the magazine Beatrice was holding. It had this recipe for an ointment to rid your thighs of cellulite. You could make it at home using olive oil and fresh lime juice. I'd made it and had been using the stuff every night even though my legs were trim from all the dancing and walking I do.

"Does it work? I need to lose some weight," Beatrice said, massaging her own thighs. "Just look at me. I've got to do something about my figure."

"I've seen some results. But when I'm done, I smell so much like a salad that it gets me thinking about food again."

We swapped beauty tips. She gave me a recipe for a hair conditioner made of egg and honey. I told her how every morning I apply a facial mask made from a sábila plant I was growing in a coffee can.

"Just slice a stem in half and massage the gel into your face," I explained. "Leave it there for a half-hour before rinsing it away with warm water, then pat your skin dry."

I'm not sure how long we waited there that first day. But it was nice to have someone to talk to and right away this girl seemed special to me. Call it intuition. She was taking the number 4 also, and when the bus pulled up to the curb, we boarded and took seats next to each other.

"Are you a nurse?" I asked.

"No. I work at the Clínica Mujer."

"The one on Alta Vista?"

"Yes. Are you a patient? You don't look familiar to me."

"No." I smiled. "I've never been in there."

I make a good woman. You would never know standing next to me in

line at the market or the bank. The hair's all mine, no wig here, no extensions. It took me years to grow it this long, and I'm proud of it. I can braid it, tease it, wear it curled up, or blow-dry it straight.

My eyelashes. So thick, and they flutter up and down like a bird's wings. My face is smooth, my cheeks so kissable that a man once stopped me on the street and said I had the complexion of an angel. That's because every night I rub creams and lotions into my skin, especially around my eyes to prevent wrinkles. I keep up on the latest beauty treatments the stars use. I buy the magazines, clip those articles out, and pin them to my dresser and next to the bathroom mirror. I follow them exactly like they're written, and it pays.

I've seen the way some women stare at me while I wait with them at the bus stop, the way they roll their eyes, hiding their mouths behind their hands and whispering in Spanish because they think I don't speak it. Until I snap back at them, and they shut up right away. It's because I do myself up, because I take the time to make myself look this good that they're jealous.

It's the way I walk in high heels, the way my legs look in nylons. It's my curves, too. So round and tight. It's all about confidence. The way I hold my shoulders, keep my back straight, never slouching, always crossing my legs, says to people that I know I'm a woman. A real chingona.

So, you see, it wasn't unusual that Beatrice didn't notice. I convince most people.

"What do you do there?" I asked. "At the clínica?"

"I just answer the phones and schedule patients. I've been there for a few years."

"You must really like it."

"I do. We give these women someplace safe to come," she said. "Sometimes it's hard because you see some sad things. Women strung out and pregnant or beaten up. The county comes and takes the babies away from them. Sticks them in foster homes where they end up getting abused. I wish I could save just one of those babies. Break that cycle." She sighed, shook her head. "And what do you do?"

"I dance," I said. "I'm a dancer. But I don't strip or nothing like that."

"Like cabaret? With music and costumes?"

"Yes," I told her.

"How glamorous." She looked down at her shoes, then over at my high heels. "I'd fall and break my neck if I ever had to dance around in those. Are you going to work now?"

"No."

"A rehearsal or something?"

"Actually, I'm on my way to the unemployment office. I need a second job. I'm saving up money for something big."

We traveled down the street, houses and intersections whizzing by real fast. The windows on the bus were amber and scratched up with graffiti, and I could see my reflection looking back at me, transparent, the branches of a tree melting into my hair, the letters of a street sign floating across my face.

La Beatrice, she took my hand and said, "I've got an idea. The clinic is looking for someone to come in mornings to clean up around the office. I know it might be beneath you compared to your dancing career. But it's something."

"True. It is a little menial. Nothing like the show." I went along. "It needs to be under the table, though. My other job can't find out."

"I can work it out with the office manager. Leave it to me. I'll put in a good word."

A few days after, once Beatrice had cleared everything with Steven, she gave me a tour of the clínica and got me ready to start. There was a checklist of things I had to do every morning, and when I completed them, Beatrice would sign off so that I could get paid.

We'd get to the clínica at seven, two hours before it opened. Beatrice had a set of keys to the front door and the supply cabinets. She always carried them with her, stuffed in the deep pockets of her smock. While she organized folders and scheduled appointments, I'd go around with my list. I'd empty the wastepaper baskets and polish the furniture. I'd collect the toys that were scattered around the floor in the waiting room and put them back in the buckets. I'd stack the magazines on the coffee table and make sure the floors were swept and mopped clean. I'd scrub the toilet and the sink the patients used.

Across the street is Tom's Original Burgers #2. We'd sneak over before the clínica opened, have a cup of coffee each, and split a blueberry muffin.

We gossiped about everything: our families, our futures, our dream husbands. When I'd tell her about my dancing, the costumes, the applause I'd get from the crowds, she'd sit there with elbows resting on the table, all wide-eyed and smiling.

In high school, she'd been in a play. A small part. Just a few lines. She rehearsed day and night for weeks in front of a mirror. For a while, she'd wanted to become an actress, but instead went to trade school and took classes in office management.

There were so many moments when I could have told her, so many times when we were on our knees reaching under the waiting room chairs for blocks or as I swept around the front desk where she shuffled papers and printed out reports. But I stayed quiet. On the morning I finally worked up the nerve to tell her, I walked into the clínica and found her sitting in the chair, her hand over her eyes. When Steven showed up at nine, she took off because she couldn't stand the headache. She wanted to lie down.

"I'll see you next time," she said, handing me the keys to the clínica. "Here. In case I can't make it in tomorrow morning."

Y fue todo.

                              •   ▫   ▫

I bought a bouquet of red roses from a woman on the corner. The flowers fall right in the middle of the pile on top of her casket when I toss them. I sit on one of the folding chairs and grip my knees, my eyes looking down at the grass.

"Te tengo algo que contar," I say. "Me llamaban Andrés Contreras. Nací niño. In Arizona. I never knew my father. He split when I was a kid. My mother, Josephine, raised me solita. When I was thirteen, I stole a pair of panties from the Junior Miss department at Sears. I wore them every day for a week, and it was the best feeling in the world. My mother found them stuffed in my drawer, underneath my T-shirts and tube socks. When she asked where they came from, I was honest. I told her I'd stolen them and that I wanted to be a Vegas showgirl. And my mother, she didn't care. She'd had her suspicions, she said. She grounded me for stealing. She then put her arms around me and said that life for someone like me would be hard."

I stop for a minute, let my breath catch up to my words.

"It has been hard. But, listen: I'm tough. Once when a boy at my middle school called me a sissy because I'd started plucking my eyebrows and filling them in with pencil, I punched him in the stomach so hard he fell over and cried. I carried rocks in my pockets, leather gloves with the fingers cut off just in case someone decided to pick on me. I came to California because there's nothing in Arizona. I took the job because I'm saving up money for the surgery. The doctors put you on hormones first and after that you can have the breast implants. You go through counseling to make sure you're ready for the operation. To become a woman. It's long, I know. And expensive. But I'll get there.

"I dance at La Chuparosa. I do Madonna, but only songs from her first two albums. Sometimes I catch myself getting sick of doing the same routine. Maybe I should try something different. What do you think?"

Only the wind answers me back. Stirring up leaves that get caught in my hair. I shake them out and walk down the path toward home.

· · ·

I've decided to be Pat Benatar tonight. La Lola thinks it's a mistake. Maybe it is. Tonight I'm just not thinking straight. It's hard enough for me to pull myself together to do a routine. But I have to. This time of the month is always good for money. It's always packed, and everyone's just gotten paid. The men come to the club to drink and tip big.

"Pat Benatar? What brought this on?" La Lola stands before the mirror in boxer shorts and a stuffed bra. She hasn't shaved her legs and stubble is starting to grow on them, the tips of the hairs like millions of tiny black needles. "You've only been doing Madonna forever. *For-ev-er!*" Her face is caked with foundation, filling in the deep creases around her cheeks and forehead.

"It's gotten muy tired," I say. "I want something different."

"Career suicide, Azúcar. Did you see the crowd out there? Pat's so second-rate. At least you could have chosen Stevie Nicks or Annie Lennox. But Pat?" She adjusts her red wig, straightens her fake tetas. "Please."

"And Cyndi Lauper isn't just an eighties babosa?" I shake my head.

"She's not Pat. That's for sure."

"What song are you doing?"

" 'She Bop.' " She pulls a pair of panties on and squeezes into her bright orange dress, taking three deep breaths before she has me zip her up.

" 'She Bop'?" I say. "Why are you doing that one and not 'Girls Just Want to Have Fun'? That's everyone's favorite."

"What do you know, *Pat*?" She smirks. The fishnets La Lola wears have tears she made with a razor blade, and she puts them on slowly, careful not to rip them more. She laces up her black boots. " 'She Bop' is better to dance to."

" 'She Bop' is about masturbation."

"Qué what?" She laughs. "It's *so* not."

"Haven't you listened to the words?"

"I lip-sync it, don't I?"

"But have you listened to the words? What they're saying?"

"I lip-sync it," she says again. "*Lip-sync* it. What do you think that means?"

"That you're not paying attention to the lyrics," I say. "You should pay attention to the words to help you pick up cues to work into your act." A few weeks ago, Bibi asked me to give La Lola pointers on how to finesse her performance. Bibi hadn't been happy with what she'd been seeing. As she put it, "That girl's a whole lot of attitude and nothing else. Too wrapped up in her own drama."

Lola asks, "What song are you doing?"

" 'Love Is a Battlefield,' " I say.

"Why *that* one?"

"Because I like the lyrics. And, in the video, a bunch of women get sick and tired of being ignored. They fight back."

La Lola rolls her eyes. "It's just a stupid video, Azúcar. Nothing more. It's all scripted. Make-believe. Así like magic."

"I know what it is."

"Then do your routine without the whole *mystique*. Get your head out of the clouds, mija. I know you just lost your friend, but it's time to get over it. Bibi wants you on. She's not gonna go for no tired washed-up acts." She gets up to take a smoke in the back alley before her performance.

I finish my makeup and put the black wig on, teasing it a few times until it's perfect. I put on the blue dress and tie torn strips of cloth to my waist.

After La Lola's Cyndi, the crowd is worked up, hooting and clapping, tipping like crazy. Bibi's always the MC, always dresses as Marilyn Monroe.

Tonight, she's in a black velvet dress and matching gloves with a blond wig. Bibi's voice is deep. She laughs loud and stomps around up there, ungraceful, scratching and grabbing her huevos, pretending to spit. After she announces my name, I walk onstage as the room dims. The crowd quiets down, their whistles and claps floating around me, mixing with the threads of smoke in the air.

It feels different. The lyrics to the song, the pace of the music, the way I have to position my feet when I spin. I miss a few steps here and there but cover it up by twirling and curling up my lip, pouting the way Pat did in the video. The crowd cheers.

I think of Beatrice.

＊　　　＊　　　＊

There's a botánica that sells velas and statues of santitos. It's the only one in all of Agua Mansa, and the same old lady has been there all the times I've walked by on my way to the discount store. I've never been, never had a need. But today, after buying two bottles of Aquanet and a packet of hairclips, I stop in there for a candle and a prayer card of Nuestra Señora de Guadalupe to help guide Beatrice on her journey to Heaven, which is where I assume she'll end up because she was so good, at least to me.

Only when I get in there and tell the old cura lady that my friend died and that I want to help guide her, she tells me, "Lighting a candle won't be enough for that."

"¿Qué más?" I ask her. "What do I do?"

"Pray a rosary," she tells me. "For nine days."

"Why nine days?"

"It's the number of days it takes their spirits to wander around before they move on."

"But why nine days?

"It's written that way."

"Where?" I ask her. My questions start to irritate her.

"It just is. Trust me. Are you willing to help your friend or not?"

"Sí," I say. "What happens if we don't do it in time?"

"After that it's too late," she says. "They stay stuck in Purgatory. Or here. Ghosts haunting houses and cemeteries. Not good for them. Not good at all."

"I don't know how to pray the rosary," I tell the cura lady. "What do I do?"

So she gives me this book to read, an instruction manual. With pictures even, and it tells me what each bead stands for. I have to buy a rosary since the only one I had I tossed into the crowd one night during my performance.

"Give me that one." I point to the cheapy plastic one with pale green beads that glow in the dark. I cup my hand around the box to make sure each bead lights up.

"There are more here," the cura lady says. In a case near the register are wooden rosarios and more expensive glass ones.

"Give me that one, too," I tell the lady, pointing to a red one with beads that shine like wet pomegranate seeds.

What I have to do first, she said, is light a white candle. Then I have to pray the rosario the same time every day for nine days straight. I use the glow-in-the-dark rosario since the more expensive one I bought only for my act. I thread it between my fingers, and the beads click against my nails. I open the book, and it's all laid out there for me, all very easy to follow, all of it drawn out like a blueprint with numbers and arrows.

I can't tell off the bat if I'm doing it right, if my words are meaningless, empty puffs of air bumping up against the ceiling because I've never really believed in any of this. God probably thinks I'm just playing the part for now to get something out of him.

*   *   *

I must have set the alarm clock to go off at the wrong time because it wakes me an hour and a half early. Instead of sleeping in, I decide to get up and dress and go to Tom's to have coffee and a muffin before Steven gets to the office.

I sit at the booth that Beatrice and I always took, the one that looks onto the front of the clínica. It's hard, but I try not to feel lonely without her. Eight days have passed already. The vela's halfway gone, and when it's lit, bits of black ash float around the melted wax. Today will be the last time I'll pray the rosario. I've memorized it by now, know the order of the prayers. I slip into it easily—closing my eyes, caressing the beads, my voice whispering, my mouth forming each word.

Burger and breakfast special prices are airbrushed into the windows in fat letters. I look between the legs of a backward "R" and see a woman peeking through the main door of the clínica. She's holding something wrapped in a towel. The baseball cap she wears is pulled down low, her hair in a ponytail. I can't see her face.

By the time I pay and make it across the street to the clínica, all that's left is the bundle sitting on top of the newspaper near the front door. I walk up slowly, bend down low to get a better look. Something moves. I reach a hand out, peel back a layer of cloth to see a baby rubbing its eyes with its own small fists. There's a blue bag near it, full of diapers, wipes, a canister of formula. There's also a note. The words are big and crooked and wobbly.

He's a boy, the note says. She apologizes for leaving him here like this. She just can't keep him. She's sorry for doing this. She hopes he'll understand someday. Toward the bottom of the note the writing becomes bigger, the letters shakier and harder to understand until they dissolve into wavy lines and strange shapes. I stop trying to make sense of it and put the note in my purse.

His face. So red. Eyes pressed between soft skin. They're not round. They're slits. His hand reaches up. Small fingers wrap around my own. Pick him up. I have to pick him up off the ground, or he'll cry, get sick because the concrete's cold, dirty. I scoop my hand under his head, place my arm under his legs, lift slowly, and bring him up to my chest. So light. Like holding a possibility. Did she rock him in her arms while he slept? But my arms. They can't move, feel like they'll break off the rest of my body, and he'll fall to the ground and shatter.

My back is to the entrance of the clínica. I stand at the top of the stairs looking down onto the street, the passing cars, a man pushing an empty shopping cart down the sidewalk.

I hear Beatrice's voice, *I wish I could save just one of those babies. Break that cycle.*

I hold him tighter, his cheek pressing against my shoulder.

I walk to the corner. Hop on the first bus that pulls up.

His pajamas are dirty. Only three diapers are in the bag. He'll need things. The discount store has this one aisle. There are diapers there, plastic spill-proof bottles, teething rings filled with water, bibs with pictures of bears and birds with musical notes drifting out from their beaks.

By the time I get to the shopping center, the stores are opening. It'll be hard to shop with the baby in my arms. Since I don't have a stroller and I'm afraid I'll drop him if I have my other arm full, I peek into the botánica and see the cura lady standing behind her counter, a notebook and a pencil in her hand.

"Seño," I tell her. "I need your help. I'm watching this baby for a friend, and I have to run next door to buy some things. Could I leave him here with you for a minute?"

I pass him gently over to her. "Andale." She waves me away. "He'll be safe here. Go do your shopping."

At the discount store, I start with the diapers. Then I buy a stuffed animal that squeaks every time you pick him up. And lotion and baby powder and a few T-shirts. By the time I'm done, my basket's full. The clerk who rings me up puts everything in one bag because I tell her I'm walking and will be carrying a baby.

"I know totally how it is," she says. "I got kids, too, and I take the bus."

"Oh," I say.

"How old is your baby?"

I guess. "Three weeks," I say to the cashier.

"Congratulations. I'll double-bag. Just to be safe." She winks. "For you."

"Thank you," I say.

Back at the botánica, the cura lady holds him in her arms. "Where's his mother?" she asks.

"She left the country." I put my bag down and reach for the baby. "She'll be back next week."

"Strange," she says, stepping away, picking up her booklet and pencil.

"It's not strange for someone to leave the country."

"Yes," she says. "But strange if you've just given birth." She points to the diaper bag. "And stranger that she wouldn't leave him much."

"She left some things."

"Not a lot. I peeked into it."

"You peeked?"

"He needed to be changed. What's going on with the mother?"

"She has problems, seño," I say, toda serious. "Big problems. Drugs. And lots of other things."

"Like what?" she asks. "What other things?"

"Her husband." I point to the baby. "The father. He used to beat her. Call her and the baby all these bad names. Told her if she ever left, didn't matter where, he'd find her. And he'd make her pay."

"Qué lástima," the cura lady says. She's quiet, then says, muy seria, "You have to take care of him." Plastic cards, each with a picture of a different saint on the front, are arranged in a small rack on the counter. The cura reaches for one and hands it over to me.

"This," she says. "Nuestra Señora de la Caridad del Cobre. She'll protect you both. You make sure nothing happens to him. You do whatever it takes to make sure he grows up safe, you hear me?"

In the picture, Nuestra Señora stands on the heads of baby angels with wings sprouting from their necks. She floats above an ocean where three men sit in a paddleboat looking up at her.

I stand in the doorway, looking back at this old cura lady, her hand gripping my arm, her bottom lip curled down, defiant and tough.

"You hear me?" she whispers. "Whatever it takes."

"I'll try."

                     *   *   *

He lies on my bed. Do I have to burp him? Will it make him sick if I don't? I reach back in my memory, try to picture the women sitting in the waiting room at the clínica rocking their babies, tucking their small heads under sweaters and blouses to breast-feed.

I had to bathe him in the sink because the bathtub's too big. I took all the dirty dishes out and let the water run, touching it with my elbow to make sure the temperature was just right. It was hard holding him in there. I was afraid to let go, afraid my arm would slip or get caught on something.

The formula. The formula was easy to make. You fill the bottle with warm water and pour a capful of the powder in, then screw the top on and

shake it. I sat with him on my bed, propped a pillow against my back. I didn't know if my angle was off, if I was holding his head too low, and I remembered reading in a magazine that if you were to hold a baby's head wrong while feeding, milk could fill his nose and he could drown. How was I going to do this? How was I going to save him from dying?

He sleeps now. He was fed. He rests. I'm thankful.

When the time comes, I recite the last rosario. The prayers tumble out quickly and with force and, when I reach the very end, I watch the room for signs, try to feel if the temperature drops, look over to see if the candle by the window goes out. But nada pasa.

The baby kicks at something. I look over at him. Who will he grow up to be? I see him. Fifteen or twenty years from now. Body all scarred in strange places and marked up with tattoos. A troublemaker. A bandido. Stealing cars and money. Leaving his own babies behind.

I ask Beatrice, "¿Qué le doy? There's no way I can do this. You know it. Just look at what a mess my life is. This was never part of my plan."

The light coming through the window falls differently on the floor and the furniture. Shadows are sharp and menacing.

I have to go. Back to the clínica. I have to.

·   ·   ·

I wait at Tom's with the baby. Wait until Steven's Honda pulls out of the parking lot and takes off down the street.

I'm sorry, Beatrice. For using the keys you trusted me with to do this. I fill his blue bag with wipes and tubes of creams for diaper rash, bibs and pacifiers and bottles of pills to help ease the pain in his gums when his teeth start coming in. In the waiting room, I take pamphlets: *When Your Child Has Colic, What Is SIDS?, A Balanced Baby.* The bag is packed full and heavy, but I keep cramming more in, fitting things here and there, folding and pushing down. I have to. I have to. For him. I throw the keys and the note that came with him in the dumpster behind the clínica.

·   ·   ·

Agua Mansa passes by us. I watch the avenues and streetlights, hoping to see my apartment, La Chuparosa, and the rooftop of the clínica one last time.

I took all that money. I went right for the envelope. I had taped it so good and strong to the bottom of the nightstand that chips of paint and varnish peeled off and flaked my hands and arms. I paced in the kitchen, planning my next move. I thought about all those shows. All those nights I rolled around onstage, bruising my knees and legs while I did my thing up there in my tight dresses and lace halter tops. Necklaces and earrings, boots and belt buckles, all of it making me sweat, weighing me down. All those mornings I scrubbed the toilets and mopped the clínica's floors, organized the waiting room only to come back the next day to find it all a mess again.

I imagined myself finished. Reunited with the woman I should have been.

And then I touched the soft spot on the back of his head.

The rocking of the bus has lulled him to sleep now. And I let my voice fill us up with dreams.

"Don't worry," I tell my baby. We merge onto the 10, leaving the city behind. "You'll have things—clothes, toys, your own soft crib to sleep in. I'll make sure of it. The money will be enough to last us for a while until I find another job. We'll settle down. Find a small place with a yard for you to run around in and trees for you to climb.

"I'll pick a birthday for you. I'll tell you how I met your father. How we fell in love. How we held hands while we talked about a future all romántico like I'd seen on the telenovelas. People will tell me we look alike while we stand in line at a department store waiting to take our family photo. They'll believe my made-up stories—the ten hours I spent in labor, how much you weighed, the first time you rolled over on your stomach.

"When you're older, you'll go away leaving me to dance around in our empty house with the memories of my youth—of when you were young—bouncing off the walls covered with pictures: you in elementary school; you in a baseball jersey and cap with your fist stuffed inside a worn mitt; both of us smiling in front of a faded blue background with fake painted clouds that look like swan feathers. But you'll come back one day when my body is old and bending. You'll find me there in my bed asleep with my long gray hair spread out across my pillow like a spider's web. I'll be waiting for you to wake me with a kiss. Like a fairy tale. Like magic.

"After I'm gone, you'll tell them about me, won't you, hijo? You'll tell

them about my dancing, the costumes I wore, the way I made the crowds cheer.

" 'She was a class act,' you'll tell everyone while you pass around my picture. 'A real lady.'

"They'll smile and see that I was and never doubt your word."

Feast of
Saint Bernardine of Siena

Franciscan Missionary Preacher

Patron of advertising, public relations, Italy, and
the diocese of San Bernardino, California.
Invoked against hoarseness, respiratory problems,
and compulsive gambling.

Three months had passed since Teresa had been to the botánica, so Perla brought along a box of valeriana tea to give to her. The receptionist in Teresa's office sat at her desk, writing on a piece of paper. She looked up, startled, when Perla tapped on the window that separated them.

"Appointment?" she said, handing over a clipboard.

Perla nodded. "Nine o'clock."

"Sign in and have a seat. You'll be called in shortly."

The waiting room was empty. From the window came the sound of the nurses and file clerks talking and gossiping. She had never gotten to know these new nurses very well. They always appeared to be in a hurry, rushing to get Perla into an examination room, jotting things down in her file quickly and without looking up. She missed the girls at the old clinic. She knew all their first names—Magali, Annette, Beatrice—and brought them lemons or avocados from her trees.

She didn't like this new office either. The building was too cold and impersonal. The old place was perfect. It was small and the waiting room felt more like a living room.

When the nurse called out her name and led Perla into the hallway, she saw on one wall the framed diplomas with Teresa's name, their embossed stamps, the fancy letters with thin swooping tails.

"Step on the scale," the nurse said. "Here, I'll take that." She reached for the small wire cart Perla had brought along with her.

Inside the examination room Perla sat on the table and removed her sweater.

"Don't talk or move. Uncross your legs." She took Perla's blood pressure. "What are you here for?" she asked, recording the results.

"A checkup," Perla said.

"Have their been any changes in your condition since your last visit?" She closed Perla's file and looked up.

"No," Perla said. "Nothing's changed. I feel the same."

Teresa would be in shortly, the nurse said before leaving. On the wall there was a poster with the words *The Respiratory System* written across the top in bold letters. In the diagram, plumes of air traveled down a tube labeled *trachea*. Strands of blue and red lines twisted and knotted around one another and fanned out to the arms and legs, the fingers and toes, the heart and brain.

At the botánica there were charts and books that showed how to read palms. One book contained an outline of the chakras of the human body and how and where they all lined up. Sitting there, Perla tried to remember. She envisioned a figure sitting in a lotus position. Indigo and violet and orange chakras like gems lined up and hidden behind the heart or floating just above the genitals. Perla was still gazing at the poster when Teresa walked into the room.

"Hi." She sat on the stool and wheeled herself over, her shoes skidding across the tiles. She looked over in the corner and pointed to the cart resting against the sink. "Is that yours?"

"Yes. I have some shopping to do on my way home. Heavy stuff. I don't want to carry it all back from the bus stop. How did the té work?"

"Good. It made me feel better. I'll need to get more."

"Here," Perla said, handing her the box she had brought.

"Oh, thank you so much, Perla." She set the box next to a glass jar of wooden tongue depressors on the counter. "How are things?" She opened Perla's file.

"Good," Perla said.

"Okay. Let's take a listen to your heart and lungs." Teresa walked over to her.

"How are you?" Perla asked. "How is everything with that doctor? What's his name?"

"Craig." Teresa smiled. "Very good. I'm taking him to meet my parents this weekend." Teresa pressed the stethoscope over Perla's heart. She listened carefully, squinting her eyes. She placed it on her back, slid it around, and instructed Perla to take deep breaths.

"Excellent," she said. "Everything sounds good and strong in there."

"You're nervous? About him meeting your parents?"

"A bit," Teresa said. "I wouldn't be surprised if they ask us if we've set a date for the wedding." She laughed.

She took her stethoscope off and placed it on the metal table, next to the thermometer. "It's been so long since I've brought a guy over, you know? I just want everything to go smoothly."

"It will," Perla said.

Teresa opened up Perla's file and scribbled something in a chart. "Your pressure's a little high, but that's normal. Just remember not to skip your medication. Stay away from salt and greasy food and alcohol. Watch what you eat."

"I know. I take good care of myself, Teresa. I eat right. I still walk every morning."

"I know you do," she said. "Just don't overdo it."

"All right."

Teresa sat down on the stool and rolled back over by the cart. "I sound like a broken record. If I do it's because I care. Especially about you. You've been my patient for years now. You're one of the few that came over with me from the clinic."

"What about everyone else?"

"Some stayed there. The others? HMOs. Shuffle patients around like cards." She rested the back of her head against the wall and sighed. "How's the botánica?"

"Fine," Perla said. "Nothing new." She wanted to mention Rodrigo. She wanted to ask Teresa about the marks, if there was anything to help heal cigarette burns. But she could see Teresa was tired. *She's got a lot on her mind, I'm sure,* Perla thought. *So much work, so many patients.* When she'd walked by the front office, Perla had seen files stacked on desks and cramming tall white bookcases. Office assistants were busy pulling and filing and refiling folders. Others clicked and typed on computers or scheduled appointments for patients who called on the phone. *Plus she's seeing the doctor now. Craig.*

"You seem distracted," Teresa said.

"What do you mean?"

Teresa stretched her legs out, and they touched the examination table. "Off. Your voice is off. I can tell. Far away."

"I'm just tired," Perla said.

"Do you think it could be work?"

"What do you mean?"

"Could be wearing you out. You've been running that place for, what, about thirty years now?"

"About," Perla said.

"Ever thought about getting someone to help you out around there?"

Perla said, "No."

"You should. That way you could take a vacation. Relax. Travel."

"I can't right now."

Teresa hesitated before speaking. "I'm sorry. I'm just saying. It's that, well, I don't want you working too hard." She got up and placed her hand on Perla's shoulder. Perla tried to look past Teresa's layers of clothing and skin and into her body where her chakras lay, glowing like embers, warm and tranquil, nourishing her soul and heart. *If I had a daughter, this would be her.*

Teresa said, squeezing Perla's shoulder, "I'm here to help. Look out for you."

"Are you worried about something?" Perla asked. "Did you see something in the tests we took last time?"

"No. I'm sorry. I didn't mean to scare you. You're in great shape for someone your age. You're alert and sharp. Your heart's as strong as a horse's. You've got lungs of iron, and your blood's rich. You'll probably outlive me. Take it easy. That's all I meant. Take it easy. Step away. Clear your mind."

❋   ❋   ❋

<h2 style="text-align:center">¡JESÚS SALVA!</h2>

LOST? CONFUSED? HE IS THE WAY.
THE TRUTH. THE LIGHT.
COME FIND HIM. IGLESIA DE DIOS. AGUA MANSA.
REPENT. FOR HE IS COMING SOON!!!

The sun had faded the words on the flyer taped to the light post in front of the medical building. There was a phone number and the church's address

and a map with black lines for streets. A quote from the Bible scrolled across the bottom. It was the Twenty-third Psalm, one Perla knew well. She always instructed her customers to say it when praying for a particularly serious petition to be granted or when confronting great danger. Perla turned away and recited it:

> *The Lord is my Shepherd; I shall not want.*
> *He maketh me to lie down in green pastures:*
> *He leadeth me beside the still waters—*

Just then the bus pulled up to the curb. The cart banged up the steps, and Perla set it against the handrail as she reached into her coin purse to pay the fare. She took a seat behind the driver, bracing the cart between her legs, running a list through her head of the things she needed: milk, a gallon of drinking water, a packet of dried chiles, bleach. *It's a good thing the prices at Las Glorias are low.* She looked at the cart and thought of Alfonso.

"I've got no other choice," he had told Perla when he announced he'd be packing up the business and moving to a new shopping center. "I'm in the red most of the month. My store's just not making it. They're taking my customers away."

Perla had asked, "They who?"

"Las Glorias. All modern and high-tech. I can't compete with them. They got everything cheaper. You can wire money to Mexico. Refinance your house. Get cable television. They even got this shuttle that goes and picks people up who can't drive. I can't do that. I'm dying here."

"It'll be fine. This will pass. Just wait—"

"No," he interrupted her. "We're moving. There's this new strip mall. Near the 215 in Grand Terrace. We can get in there for a little more than what we pay here. It's right off the freeway. By some new apartment complexes. It's perfect."

Perla rested her elbows on the glass counter. "Te me vas?" she'd asked.

"Yes. I have to."

"Did you tell your papá?"

"Yesterday. When I came back from checking out the new space. I took

pictures of it and sent them to him over the computer. He's sad. He was here when this shopping center opened. When this botánica was a flower shop. When Mr. Finch owned the donut place." Alfonso shook his head. "I think this is right. So does my dad."

"It'll be lonely here without you."

"I'm sorry. I can't stay. I have to compete with those places."

The day after, Alfonso started packing things and hauling them away. Over the next few weeks she watched as he filled the truck's cab with boxes and crates of supplies and merchandise. The last week, they had a sidewalk sale. They put up tables in front of the shop and sold some of the clearance merchandise at half price. There were candy dishes, marbles, decks of playing cards, plastic combs and hand mirrors, hairclips and packs of assorted socks.

"How much is this cart?" Perla asked, taking some plungers out of it and setting them near the curb.

"That's ours," Alfonso said. "But if you want it, it's yours. A going-away present. For my favorite neighbor." He showed her how to collapse it, how to lock the wheels to prevent the cart from rolling away.

The bigger things—the metal shelves and cases, the two Casio registers and the coolers—were going to be moved later in the month. By the end of May they'd be out completely, Alfonso had told her.

At Descanso and Meridian, the bus stopped to pick up a woman holding a little girl by the hand.

"Aquí, Yessica," the woman said as they took the aisle seats across from Perla.

The girl held a backpack with a picture of a mermaid. The mermaid sat on a rock underwater. Rings of coral adorned her fingers, and she wore a tiara made of scallop shells. She thought about the pouch she'd placed in Rodrigo's pocket that last night. He hadn't been back since. She tried hard to blink away the memory of those marks. The way he'd trembled when she reached out to touch him.

He knows where I'm at. Burns or not. I've got other customers. I've got other things to worry about. If he needs me, I'm right here. I'm not going anywhere. Alfonso is. But I'm not.

*   *   *

The banners flapped in the wind that came down from the passes, and the windshields of cars gleamed in the sun. The bus dropped her off on the corner of Valley and Pepper, and Perla made her way through the crosswalk, the cart trailing behind. She walked across the bridge over the freeway. The billboards along the westbound lanes of the I-10 hovered above a veil of exhaust. *Familia Medical: Para Tu Salud* read one showing a woman cradling a naked baby. A family of five wearing 3-D sunglasses posed together on one ad that read *Summer Fun Passes at Universal Studios, Hollywood.* A girl blew kisses at passing cars and semis. *I'm Reina,* was written above her head. *I'm at the Fantasy. Exit Pepper Avenue. South.* Next to the freeway a green road sign marked the miles to cities: Fontana, 10; Ontario, 17; Los Angeles, 53.

Inside Las Glorias, posters announcing sales on toilet paper and ground beef hung from the ceiling on transparent wires. Murals covered the walls: Pancho Villa riding a horse; Vicente Fernández singing to a woman in a red dress; Benito Juárez holding a scroll; an Aztec sun calendar; Indians in feathered headdresses climbing a pyramid; La Virgen de Guadalupe looking down onto the farmacia's counter. Near the last of the check stands, a man stood behind a glass window, speaking to a customer through a round hole. *Giros a México y Latinoamérica,* read the sign above him.

Perla bought some bolillo and two pieces of pan dulce from the racks beside the pastry cases. In the produce section, she picked up vegetables— cabbage and carrots, celery and squash to boil. Down the dairy aisle, she grabbed a half gallon of milk before heading to the household supplies for the bleach.

She walked up Aisle 14 where the veladoras were. They had expanded the section. There were so many now. She picked one up, the price "$1.25" stickered on its side. Perla did some calculating in her head as she pushed her cart to the check stand. *I could ask my wholesaler to cut me a break on the price. That way I could compete.*

She had finished putting all her groceries on the conveyor belt and was reaching for her wallet when she looked up and saw Rosa Cabrera behind the counter.

"You're working here again?" Perla asked.

"Yeah. Just temporary. For extra cash to save up for my station." Rosa punched some numbers on the register and passed the groceries over the

scanner's red lasers. "But don't worry. I'm still cutting hair from home. So come by, okay?"

A bag boy wheeled the cart back around and set it besides Perla. "I will."

Rosa flicked a switch near the phone, and the light above her check stand turned off. She placed a sign at the end of the conveyor belt. "You're my last customer. I have to go and pick Danielle up. A lady who works the night shift is watching her."

She took the phone and dialed a number. "I'm closing out," Rosa told someone on the other line, then hung up. She pulled out the register's drawer and said, "About a week ago one of the cashiers was going to the manager's office with her till when she was dragged into the bathroom and robbed. Now when we have a lot of money a security guard has to escort us." When he arrived, Rosa handed the security guard her till, then walked around the counter. "I'll see you soon," she said, hugging Perla.

"Okay. I'll see you."

The sun was higher now. Heat rose from the concrete. Perla pushed the cart across the parking lot toward Pepper, walking under the shade of the ash trees lining the street, the shadows of their leaves like ghost hands patting her arms and shoulders and face.

                ▪   •   ◦

Perla decided not to stop off at home before opening. She could place the milk and the vegetables in the mini-fridge at the botánica. Everything else would be fine.

The shopping center was quiet when she arrived. The moving van was gone, and so was Alfonso's car. Yesterday he and the men he had hired had worked all day without stopping. She cupped her hands around her eyes and looked in. The shelves were gone. The counter where the registers had been was pulled out. Only blond strips of wood from its foundation remained, dry caulk and glue drizzled over them.

The slip of paper fell on the ground when she pushed back the iron gate to get to the front door. Perla had stepped into the botánica and only noticed it when she turned to keep the door from hitting the cart. It was no bigger than a business card. Her name was written in block letters. She unfolded it and read the note:

Senora I come to looking for you but you are gone I come back soon. I am needing your help. I am afraid. The cops they wont help me and not even a church because I have feeling they will call the migra.

Please be here.
Rodrigo Zamora

She walked out into the parking lot and used the note to shield her eyes. Maybe she had just missed him. But there was no sign.

Aftershocks

I normally sleep in on Sundays, but when my husband, Darrell, woke up early this morning and went out for a run, I couldn't go back to bed. I've been sitting in my pajamas all morning, watching the news and sipping coffee, waiting for him to get back home. As I'm about to turn off the television and get dressed, the phone rings.

"How are you?" I hear my mother's voice ask.

"Fine," I tell her. "What's up? How are you?"

"Not good. It's your dad."

"Oh?"

"Your father." She sighs. "Cabezón. He hasn't been taking care of himself. Every time I try and remind him to make an appointment or watch his diet, all he does is get mad at me."

My father has diabetes. When it first developed, he was always thirsty. My mother complained that she couldn't sleep because he kept getting up in the middle of the night to go to the bathroom. He was tired all the time and became moody and irritable. He began losing weight.

She says he's been smoking and drinking despite his illness, despite the pamphlets from the doctor that she tries to get him to read. They explain in detail the complications that will develop if a person suffering from diabetes doesn't watch his diet or exercise daily.

He developed a cyst on his right heel that she noticed one morning when she bent down to pick the remote control off the floor. His bare feet

were hanging over the edge of the mattress. "It was about the size of a quarter," she says. "Now it's infected. Who knows how long he's had it?"

Gangrene has set in, and they'll be amputating his foot.

"No blood was flowing there," she explains. "No feeling. He didn't even know he had it. We caught it too late. They have to take care of it before the infection spreads."

I stay quiet. From where I sit in the kitchen, I can see a pair of Darrell's old sneakers near the front door. I try to imagine my father hopping around on one foot. Will he need a cane? Can he be fitted for a prosthetic?

"I need you to go down and see Perla at the botánica," my mother says. "Find out if there's anything I can give him. A tea or something, I don't know. He's not taking his pills, so find out if there's anything I can sneak in his food."

"If the doctors can't help, what makes you think something from there can?"

"I have to try, Nancy. Your father doesn't care. You know him."

Apparently my father's taking this whole thing in stride, his usual fashion when faced with tough news. He told my mom he was going to take all the shoes and socks that he owns and donate just the left ones, not the complete pairs, to the Salvation Army.

I imagine him slapping his hand on his thigh, saying to my mother, "Lorena, vieja, wouldn't that be too much? Just too much. One shoe. One red sock. One of each."

The last time I saw him was just over two years ago. He wasn't cracking jokes, though. He was angry, shouting at me and Darrell, shaking his fists at us.

*   *   *

Growing up, I was the troublemaker of the family. My kid brother, Jesse, and I are four years apart. As teenagers, we were the opposite of one another. I was loud and rebellious. Jesse was quiet and shy, perfectly content to stay at home with my parents on Saturday night instead of partying with his friends. I pissed my father off back then, questioned his authority and challenged his will. It wasn't deliberate. I didn't do it because I hated him. I was born with this defiant streak in me, something I could never suppress. I can

say that now. But what mattered to me when it came to my parents, especially my father, was that I got *my* way. Our arguments became a part of our relationship. It was the way we were wired, I suppose. He enforced and tried to dictate. I revolted and fought back. We argued and would go weeks, even months, without speaking while my mom would act as liaison between the two of us. Eventually we would come around and things would smooth themselves out just in time for another confrontation.

Like any good parent, he lectured and punished and threatened me. I stayed out past curfew and hung out with a group of "questionable" girls. I went through this punk rock phase where I wore green lipstick and safety pin earrings. My mother was always more tolerant.

"You take after him," I remember her saying once, after my father and I had gotten into an argument over a hickey on my neck. "Both of you are as stubborn as bulls. Always butting heads with one another."

After I graduated from high school, my father wanted me to attend a college nearby so that I could still live at home and he could "keep me on his radar." But I was eighteen and told him that wasn't going to be the case. That I would be leaving. After it was clear to him that I wasn't going to bend to his will, he said, "Fine. At least let me help. I don't want you living like some homeless person." He promised to pay part of my tuition and told me he'd be sending a check every month. He was proud of me, I could tell. Proud that I had made it all the way to college. We hugged and apologized to one another for all the arguments throughout the years. We promised to learn to understand each other. I packed my things, and he drove me all the way to Santa Barbara.

My senior year in college, I met Darrell. I was sitting out in the courtyard reading a magazine when he came up to me. He was tall and his shaved head shone smooth and waxy under the sun. He had the most beautiful black skin I'd ever seen. I dropped my magazine, and he bent down to pick it up.

"Nancy Pérez, right?" A pen jutted out from the side of his mouth.

"Yeah."

"We have Español," he said, in a heavy accent. "Soy Darrell."

I tried not to wince at his rough pronunciations. "Hi."

"Hola. Mucho gusto. Práctica," he said. "I try to practice as often as I can."

"It helps."

Our textbook was in his hand, the page turned to the lesson on the seasons and temperatures. "Can you help me translate this?" He sat down next to me on the bench and pointed to a sentence: A Juanita le gusta el verano.

Every day after class, we'd go to the library. I'd help him conjugate verbs, count, and recite the months of the year. As a way to practice rolling his R's, I would have him repeat the word "ferrocarril" over and over.

Our first real date was a week after we'd gotten our grades.

"Una A," he told me over the phone. "Let's celebrate."

María Candelaria with Dolores del Rio was playing at a small theater downtown. After the movie, we went for a walk along the beach. We took our shoes off and left them in his car. I don't really remember now how it happened. It just did. Somehow, we ended up sitting down on the beach, our bare feet burying into the sand, our toes wiggling up against each other's. His stroked my cheek, then he put his lips to mine and we kissed.

After long debates with my parents about graduation and the commencement ceremony, I decided not to walk. They had moved to Las Vegas that same year—into a master-planned community that had its own man-made lake complete with paddleboats and swans. Since my father had been diagnosed with diabetes just that year, I told them the last thing we needed was for them to hop in a car and drive all the way out to Santa Barbara. No, I said. What my father needed was rest.

"It's just a stupid ceremony," I said to them over the phone. "All that matters to me is that I get the damn piece of paper." I said I would save them the trip and go out there to spend a few weeks.

Darrell and I had been going out for about ten months. He wasn't going to walk either. His family was in Louisiana, and he had no money to fly back and spend the summer with them, so we were going to be with each other the whole time. I asked him if he wanted to come with me.

"I want them to meet you," I said.

"I'd like that. If it's cool with your folks."

A few days before, I called home. "Can I bring someone?" I asked my mom.

"Of course," she said. "Your father can't wait to see you. That's all he's been talking about for the past few weeks. His daughter, the college graduate."

We drove there in Darrell's car. When we were about an hour outside Santa Barbara, he said, "I've been having some real fun with you the last year, you know that?"

"Fun?" I turned to him. "Is that all it's been for you?"

"I didn't mean it's only been fun. I mean, well, it's been fun and really great."

I began to worry he was breaking up with me.

"I *hope* what we have is more than just *fun*," I said.

He cleared his throat and drummed his fingers against his leg.

"You're having more than just fun when you're in love with someone," I said and smiled.

"You in love with me?"

"Like you couldn't tell?"

He shrugged his shoulders, relaxed, and tried to play it nice and cool. "Maybe. Maybe not. Maybe I just wanted to hear you say it."

A few hours later, we stopped for gas at an AM/PM in Victorville. From the car, I watched as he stood in line with bottles of water, bags of Doritos, and soft serve ice cream drizzled with chocolate jimmies. He walked over and handed me the food. When the tank was full, Darrell came around the car to my side and opened the door. My fingertips were coated with fake nacho cheese when he kissed them.

"Mi amor." He said it perfectly, and it made me proud. From his pants pocket he produced a small box. Round oil stains coated the concrete but he still got down on one knee. A Youth Authority van full of boys with crew cuts and in baggy orange jumpsuits pulled up to the gas pump next to us. A guard in a uniform got out. "I'll be damned," he said and gave Darrell an approving nod.

He proposed in Spanish. The boys in the van slapped each other on the back and cheered. One of them said I was *fine*.

A woman knows these things. She knows it's right. When she sees a man, on his knees, the grime coating his legs, his skin, the scent of petroleum and popcorn on his clothes, she can't help it. She loses herself, thinks about that moment just before the doors to the church open as the wedding march begins and her relatives and gray-haired tías sit in the pews wearing funny hats, balls of tissue paper pressed against their noses. I saw Darrell

there and the desert behind him opened up, vast and wide and untamed and the sky was so purple. Everything stopped like it did that night at the beach when we first kissed. And all I could think of was how much I loved this man.

"What do you say?" For a minute, I could see the hesitation in his eyes, a moment when he questioned what he had done. "I bought the ring just before we left. Been carrying it this whole time. My brother said I was fucking nuts. It feels good. I almost chickened out back there, you know? Before you said you loved me."

Inside the store, the man in the uniform was at the counter. He said something to the attendant and the people behind him in line. Everyone looked over at us. A woman scooping relish onto her hot dog stopped. People leafing through magazines put them down and stood still.

Darrell held the ring up.

I closed my eyes and took a deep breath. "Sí," I said. "Sí."

When he slipped the ring on and kissed me, the people in the store cheered, the boys clapped and hooted, pressing their hands against the iron bars of the van's windows. The hot dog woman walked over to the car. "You're going to make a darling bride, sugar," she told me.

We drove through miles of flattened desert, and everything looked different the rest of the trip. I had graduated and would be starting a teaching credential program in the fall. Darrell had graduated with high honors. We were young and in love and engaged. I twirled the ring around on my finger, imagined my dress, Darrell's family flying in from Louisiana and meeting my relatives.

"We won't tell them right away," I said. "I mean, not the minute we walk through the door. We don't want to shock them."

"Sounds fine," he said. "You know them better than I do."

I took my engagement ring off and placed it back in the box.

It was after nine by the time we pulled up to the driveway of my parents' house. The front porch light came on, and my father stood in the doorway. Even though it was night, I could hear the hum of air conditioners up and down the block. My parents kissed and hugged me. When I introduced them to Darrell, my father said hello, then turned and went back into the house. My mother shook his hand and led us both into the living room.

When we sat down, I noticed how much weight my father had lost since the last time I saw him, how pale and gaunt his face appeared. He moved more slowly, staggering. When he walked into the kitchen, he almost tripped.

"Is that really you?" Darrell said, pointing to a high school picture of me hanging above the fireplace.

"Hard to believe, isn't it?" I smiled, feeling embarrassed. In the picture, one side of my hair was dyed red and the other blue.

"She got this crazy idea," my mother said. "She looked like a snow cone."

My father came back into the living room and sat in his recliner. "Your drive good?" he said to me.

"Fine."

"Good," he said. "That's good." His raised his voice and shot a glace at Darrell. "Is he your friend from school?"

"We took Spanish together," Darrell said. He leaned forward. "She was a real help. We studied together."

"I see," my father said. He looked over at me and at Darrell again. An awkward silence filled the room.

I was glad when my kid brother, Jesse, came downstairs. "Hey," he said to me. We hugged, and I introduced him to Darrell.

I reached out to touch the side of Jesse's head. Tattooed there was the number thirteen.

"Did that hurt?" I asked.

"Like hell," he said.

"And he doesn't think I know the reference," my father said. "But I do."

Jesse got up and walked over to the sliding glass door that led out to the backyard. My parents hadn't planted grass out there yet, and there were no trees. He turned the light on and went out.

"Pot," my father said. "It has something to do with pot."

"I hear some kids call it 420. Write it on their folders and get the numbers embroidered on jackets or write it on the bills of baseball caps with markers," Darrell said to him.

My father didn't respond. He just rocked in his recliner. After a while, he excused himself and went upstairs to sleep.

In the kitchen, my mother told me about his prognosis, how he needed to watch what he ate, how he needed to stop drinking and smoking.

"But your father," she said, shaking her head slowly. "None of that matters to him. Doesn't take care of himself at all. I get so frustrated sometimes. And he and Jesse are always fighting."

"It's him," Jesse muttered. "You should see the way he gets, Nancy. Soon as I'm old enough, I'm out of here."

"Quiet," my mother said to him. "This sickness, it's serious. The doctor said if he doesn't take care of himself, he could die."

I slept in the room my mother had designated as mine even though I had never actually lived in the house. All my things were there, though. From my old bed, I listened to the desert wind, blowing sand against the window. I heard the sound of the bathroom door opening. The fan went on. Without having seen who'd gone in, I knew it was my father. I crept down the stairs into the den. Darrell was sitting up on the roll-away cot that my mother had pulled out from the closet.

"Hey." He was in his pajamas and a T-shirt.

"You're not sleeping," I said.

"Too much wind." He got up and walked over to the glass door. "The whistling noise is keeping me up." I heard the hiss of the toilet upstairs. A few seconds later came the click of my parents' bedroom door closing.

"Let me ask you a question," Darrell said. "Is your dad okay with this?"

"What do you mean?"

"He was throwing me some shade. Didn't shake my hand. Didn't acknowledge me all that much. He okay with me?"

"Why wouldn't he be?"

"Don't know," he said. "How much you tell them about us? They know we're dating?"

I stayed quiet.

"Shit," he said and walked over to me. We sat down on the bed. "They don't know we've been dating? You didn't tell them?"

"They know," I said. "I just haven't *told* them."

"You embarrassed of me or something? You afraid they won't approve of me?"

"That's dumb," I said. "I'm not afraid. I love you. That's what counts. I'm not afraid of them."

I turned and went back to my bedroom.

It was eight-forty when I woke the next morning. Darrell was right. It

was time. I slipped on the engagement ring and went downstairs. My parents were sitting at the kitchen table. My father had his bottles of pills rowed up next to each other. Darrell sat next to him, and I went over to the refrigerator. I took a carton of orange juice and poured some into the glass in front of my mother, keeping the engagement ring in full view. She didn't notice.

I pointed to the pills. "Have you even been taking them?"

"What's this? Is everyone turning into my damn doctor?" My father slapped his hand on the table. Darrell's eyes fell to the floor.

"Can we have a few days of peace and calm before the two of you start?" my mother said. "Or do I need to put you both in boxing gloves all the time?"

"Sorry," I said. "Just looking out for you, Dad." I sat on the opposite end of the table from him, pressed both hands on the surface. After a short silence, I cleared my throat and said, "Here's the thing: Darrell and I have something to say."

Darrell shifted uncomfortably in his seat, then got up and walked over to the counter.

"He proposed." I looked over at Darrell. "Yesterday. On the way here. I said yes."

At first my father said nothing. He simply shook his head a few times and cleared his throat. "Well," he finally said. "That's something, isn't it?"

"I said yes," I said again. "I hope I have your blessing." I looked over at my mother, who remained quiet. She watched my father, then made the Sign of the Cross.

"I don't want to tell you what to do, Nancy," he said. "Because every time I've tried, you just ignore me anyway. Disrespect me. But, I don't like this. Don't like this one bit."

I walked over and held Darrell's hand. He was sweating.

"Octavio," my mother said. "Let's go upstairs."

"No," he said, pounding his fist on the table.

"I knew this was a bad idea," Darrell said to me in a low voice.

My father looked at him. "Then why'd you do it? Huh?" He then turned to me and said, "Is this what you've been doing in school? Going out with black boys? Having sex with them? Being a tramp?"

"Octavio," my mother said. "Con calma." She turned to Darrell. "My husband, he's sick. He's not racist or anything. His blood sugar level's off. That's it." She turned to my father. "Just take your stupid pills, and stop making an ass out of yourself."

My father clenched his fists. "Don't make excuses for me, Lorena."

"We should go," Darrell said. He told my father, "Look, señor, I can understand why you're upset. I mean, I can imagine. Nancy and me, we got something good here. We want to share it with you. And you," he said to my mother.

When he tried to get up, my father stumbled and held on to the wall. "Don't come in here trying to win me over. You're no good."

"What the hell is that supposed to mean?" I said.

My mother helped ease him back down into the chair. When she tried to place her hands on his shoulders, my father recoiled.

"Tell me," I said. I crossed my arms, widened my stance.

Darrell grabbed my arm. "Let it go," he whispered. "Come on."

"Let them do what they want," my mother pleaded. "You should be worrying about taking care of yourself. Not going out of your way to pick fights with her."

"Fine," I said to my father. "Be that way."

In the hallway, my mom tried to calm me down, tried to convince us to just let my father rest and think about the whole thing. "News like this, it's natural that it would upset him. He gets mood swings. Stay," she said. "I want you to. Just wait a while. He'll be better."

"Sorry, Mom," I said. "I knew this would happen. Doesn't matter what I do, it's never good enough. He always has to find something to hassle me about. I'm sick of this."

I kissed her, and we grabbed our bags and left.

On the drive back, I slid close to Darrell, put my head on his shoulder, and watched the cars traveling in the opposite direction. This was it, I thought. If my father wouldn't accept Darrell as my husband, if he wasn't going to give us his blessing, I would never speak to him again. What he needed, I felt, was for me to show him that this time the little games of tug-of-war we'd been playing since I was a girl weren't going to work. We were no longer living under the same roof. I didn't have to abide by his rules. I was

going to show him that this time he'd done it. He's pushed me too far, I told myself. All he wants is to make my life difficult, to make it so that we would never have a normal relationship where we both understood and loved and respected each other like we'd promised to do.

"Does he think I'm going to give in?" I said to Darrell. "Well, he's wrong. If he doesn't care about what makes me happy, I don't care about him. He's gone to me."

When we returned to Santa Barbara, we were married. I wore a white dress with spaghetti straps. Darrell wore a dark suit with a silver tie and a carnation pinned to his lapel. He looked so handsome. We said our wedding vows in Spanish, and Darrell was so proud of himself for not having mispronounced any of the words.

We stayed in Santa Barbara for another year while I earned my teaching credential. The only contact I had with my family during that time was the phone calls from my mother. She always made a point to call me when my father was around. She would say in a loud voice, "You sound *so good*, mija. So happy" or "Wonderful. It looks like things are coming together for both of you over there" when I told her Darrell and I bought a coffeepot that was on sale. Darrell had been interning for a local councilman "until something else popped up." That something else finally came when he was offered a job working for the city of San Bernardino.

"Where to?" he said. "That's your neck of the woods." He unfolded a map of the area on the floor of our apartment.

I sighed when I saw my hometown. "Here, I guess." I pointed to Agua Mansa.

I looked in the newspaper for a place. There was a small two-bedroom house with a detached garage for rent. Darrell and I took a drive down there one weekend and checked it out. We signed a lease and packed up everything we owned. Whatever didn't fit in our cars, we just donated or gave away.

         *   *   *

Agua Mansa had changed since I had left for college. The freeway had been widened, the mounds of dirt the tractors gathered pushed back and held up by tall concrete walls with engravings of speeding locomotives and mountains etched into their surfaces. An apartment building near the house I

grew up in burned down one night and in its place a Baptist church called the Holy Nazarene was built. On Descanso, a Salvadoran restaurant that sells pupusas now occupies a building that used to be a Taco Bell. Even though I recognized streets and locations, I had a hard time getting around. I got a job teaching second grade at Wyatt Elementary. Despite knowing exactly where it was, and even though I left early enough to give myself plenty of time, I took a wrong turn and got there a few minutes late, frazzled and embarrassed.

One of the few places that looks exactly the way it did when I was a kid is the Botánica Oshún. The botánica was the place my mother came to only when other measures had failed. She believes in the power of the unknown, in the intangible strength and magic of rocks and stones and amulets. There's a thing to be said, I remember her saying once, about something as unassuming as a lucky coin or a medalla someone wears around their neck, the way these things absorb the hopes and desires of the owner, the way they act to harness, to stockpile, so much life energy that even the simplest and most ordinary of articles can retain so much strength, can have the ability to make great and wonderful things happen.

"Sure," I had said. "Sure, Mom."

Today, women hover around the counter in polyester skirts, their faces shiny from the liquid foundation they dab onto their cheeks with cotton wedges. They peer at the talismans in the cases, pointing and muttering, wondering which is good to help a sick baby or a dying parent.

I take a seat by the window, drumming my fingers against the back of my chair.

"I'll be with you soon," Perla says to me as she walks over to a woman about my age in a pair of cotton stirrup pants and red sneakers.

"I'd appreciate that," I say. "I'm kind of in a rush."

The woman she's helping asks Perla, "And this will help with the rash? The doctor said it was from the diapers. I've started using the cloth ones."

"Make sure you put it on him every day," Perla tells her customer as she rings her up.

The woman pays and leaves. Perla tucks the twenty-dollar bill in the register and shuts it. "You're the Pérez girl, aren't you?" she says to me once we're alone.

"Yes," I say. "Nancy."

"How are your parents? Do they still live out there in Vegas?"

"Yes."

"I miss seeing your mother at Mass and in here. How is she?"

"Good," I say. "Except she doesn't like that there isn't one of these places out near her. At least not that she knows of."

"And your father? How's his diabetes?"

"Not good. My mom called this morning. He got a cyst that became infected. They're going to amputate his foot."

She sighs, shakes her head again.

"He's stubborn, you know. Hates taking his pills. My mom's afraid. So, she asked me to come by and talk with you. To see if there was something you could recommend. Some herbal remedy."

"Nopales," she says. She reaches for a small plastic sack and opens it up.

"Nopales?" I furrow my eyebrows. "That's it? Cactus?"

"Have her take a patty and remove the thorns." From the sack, she pulls out a few packages of instant horchata drink mix. "When she's removed the thorns and washed the patty, have her blend it until it turns to pulp. Mix that with some water and stir it with a spoon. She can use flavoring to make it taste better." She hands me a few of the packets of horchata powder. "Like horchata or tamarindo. Whatever he likes. It has to be sugar-free, though. Have him drink it daily."

"Okay. How much?" I take some money out of my pocket to pay for the packets.

She shakes her head. "It's nothing. I bought those for me. They were on sale. Buy two get one free. I have more."

"Thanks."

"And tell her to give him massages." She makes small circles with her hand in front of my face. "On his good foot. To keep his blood flowing."

"I'll tell her," I say, putting my sunglasses on.

*   *   *

It's early Monday morning. When I get out of the shower, Darrell says my mom called.

"They're getting ready to do this thing with your dad. What are you going to do?" He's reading a section of the newspaper and doesn't look at me when he talks.

"What do you mean?"

"I mean she says it's pretty serious. They're getting rid of his foot, but they think the infection's spreading. You should go."

I put my jacket on and lean up against the door frame.

"Well?" he says.

"Not until he apologizes."

He laughs, shakes his head. "Whatever."

"I know. You think it's stupid. You think I'm acting like a brat," I say. "Are you forgetting that I didn't have anyone to give me away at my own wedding? Are you forgetting how shitty, how completely shitty I felt after that whole incident?"

"Nope," he says. "I haven't forgotten. She says your dad says you owe him an apology."

"Oh, I see." I shake my head. "He insults the man I love, then expects me to apologize. That sounds fair."

"I'm not sure who's to blame for what," he says. "I can't wrap my head around any of this."

"That's easy," I say. "He made an ass out of himself in front of the man I love."

"This whole thing, it's not just about me." Darrell walks over to the sink and washes his hands. "The two of you have been at each other since you were a kid. I'm just saying you may have to be the one to give first if you ever want this relationship to work again. You may have to be the bigger person and go see him and let the apology slide."

I step away from the door frame and stand in the middle of the kitchen. "I don't want to give first," I say. "He made it clear: He doesn't care about me. About us. I don't care about him."

Darrell's silent. "'Course not," he says, drying his hands. "You ended the whole thing."

"Right."

"Man's not your father anymore. You're not his daughter."

"He did it to himself. He asked for it. Could have handled things differently. I don't care. I just don't."

"Yeah," Darrell says. He reaches for his car keys on the counter, near the packets of the horchata powder I got from the botánica yesterday. "I can see that."

He kisses me on the cheek and leaves for work.

I take the long way to school this morning, passing the car wash where my dad used to take our Chrysler. What Jesse and I liked the most was sitting inside with the windows rolled up. We'd watch as the automatic hoses sprayed water on the car. The bristles would descend from the ceiling. They'd pass over the car and swirls of white soap would drip down, coating the windows. I remember once looking through the wet glass, seeing my father standing at the end of the car wash, waving at Jesse and me as we sat there listening to the strong jets of water rinsing the soap and wax away.

Inside the classroom, my students are shuffling about, hanging their jackets in the coat closet, getting settled in their desks. I prepared a lesson on earthquakes for today, and I tell them we'll be having a mock earthquake drill.

I stand in front of my classroom, talking to them about plate tectonics, about the Ring of Fire, and pressure points. We talk about Richter scales and magnitudes and epicenters. We talk about the fault lines our school and homes rest on. I go over what to do after the shaking stops, how to shut off the gas, and the essentials every first-aid kit should have.

"Is California sinking?" April Lugo asks. "My mom says she wants to win the lottery before it happens, then move to Texas with my grandparents. But it can't sink before she wins the jackpot. She says it's not fair that old people always win it."

"It's moving," I tell April. "Not sinking. The piece we're on is drifting north."

My students look at me confused.

Lily Sánchez says, "My dad says when the Big One hits, California will become an island."

"Will people get hurt?" Jimmy Phuc asks.

"If they're not prepared they will. So, we must be ready. Have an earthquake kit. Wear heavy shoes in case there's broken glass on the floor. Expect aftershocks."

April asks, "Will people die?"

I think about my father lying on a bed in a hospital. I imagine him hopping around on his one good foot, urging me to dance with him like we used to when I was little, bracing himself against my mother and Jesse, trying not to fall over, as they lead him to the recliner where he likes to sit.

We end with the earthquake drill. I watch the clock near the door, shout "Now" when the second hand reaches the twelve. My students duck under their desks and lock their hands together behind their heads. Their faces are pressed against their knees.

"Everything around you is shaking," I shout to them. "Whatever you do, don't unlock yourselves. Stay in your position. Glass is falling to the ground and breaking. Bookshelves are toppling over. Stay put. Don't move. Stay right where you are."

I know that beneath us the ground is rumbling. Oceans of magma are hardening to form layers of rocks that the earth's restless temper will break apart. We float on giant plates that crash and buckle into one another, and straight roads bend into elbows, rivers rechannel, mountains sprout up. We separate, then collide and try to hold on to one another. Because we know it's only a matter of time before we're pulled apart again.

I turn off the lights and run around my classroom. A few students shout and giggle. Someone screams. I toss books on the floor, take coats and hats and throw them up in the air where they get caught on the light fixtures hanging above.

Tired and out of breath, I stomp on the ground and continue running up and down the aisles. I shout and throw a clipboard against the wall. I pound the tops of the desks, feeling the sting and vibration throughout the palms of my hands, running all the way up to my elbows, my shoulders, my neck.

"This is it," I shout, my hands turning red now, throbbing. "The Big One. It's here. This is it. This is it."

Feast of
San Juan Soldado

Martyr

Patron of illegal immigrants,

the poor, the helpless, and those unjustly accused.

Invoked against political and civic corruption.

Alfonso had been gone a few weeks now. Today the construction workers arrived. They unloaded sheets of drywall and pieces of lumber, tool-
boxes, sanders, drills, and band saws with sharp steel blades. Things
crashed and fell against the floor of the shop as they tore down walls and
rerouted the wiring. Hammers pounded, power tools turned off and on, the
voices of the men laughing, cracking jokes, cursing, made their way
through the wall and into the botánica where Perla stood watching. The few
customers that came in didn't seem to mind all that banging and noise. Still,
she turned the volume of the television up to cover it.

"Are you expanding?" a woman buying a Virgen de Guadalupe prayer
card and a can of Lucky Bingo aerosol spray asked.

"No," Perla said. "The store moved."

"Do you know what's coming in?"

"No."

"I hope it's a check-cashing place. One where I can pay my utilities."

That afternoon, the workers gathered up their tools and supplies. Metal
boxes and cans of plaster and paint rattled around the beds of their trucks as
the men pulled out of the parking lot and sped down the street.

Everything was quiet again after the last of them left. It was past four.
Outside the sun burned bright white against the trees, singeing the tips of
their leaves and turning their barks ash gray. Since she had come across Rodrigo's note, she had stayed late just in case he came by. The note was taped
to the register now. *He'll be back. If he really needs me, he'll show up. It can't be that
bad if he hasn't showed up since he left the note.*

She flipped the television to channel 34 and caught the last half of *Primera
Voz*. It ran a report about people disappearing along the border, women
coming home late at night from maquiladoras near Ciudad Juárez. They as-

sembled circuit boards for radios and computers, all for low wages, the report explained, only to end up mugged and raped in dark callejones, under blurred streetlights, their bodies dumped in shallow ravines. The camera showed a pair of legs dangling over the edge of a dirt mound, feet stuffed into white heels with gold clasps, the edge of a skirt torn and bloodied.

Más desapareciones en Tijuana, a voice said.

Images of a wall covered with pictures of boys and girls flashed across the screen: *Antonio Macías; Josefina Peña, hija; Olga de la Cruz, Su familia la busca.* Staples stitched their faces to street signs and wooden beams. *Babies ripped from the arms of their mothers to be sold on the black market,* the reporter mentioned. *Sex trade. Young girls sold into slavery. Satanic cults that practice cannibalism and human sacrifices.* A reenactment showed a sleek silver car, an arm with a gold wristwatch reaching out to grab a girl selling gum to tourists along the border. A hotel sign blinking off and on. There was a bedroom with bare white walls and a pair of hands passing over the girl's body. The images on the screen blurred and faded out slowly. Then hooded figures holding hands and chanting around a group of red candles passed before the screen. There was a pentagram drawn in white chalk on a floor and the number 666 written in blood on a woman's forehead.

Perla turned the television off once the program ended, then locked the front door. From the shelves behind the register, she took a candle of Juan Soldado and lit it. The image on his veladora was neither a drawing nor a painting, but a photograph. El soldadito's boyish face, his round eyes, looked back at Perla as she lit the vela and set it on a plate. Juan Castillo Morales had been a soldier stationed in Tijuana in 1938 when the body of eight-year-old Olga Camacho was discovered in an abandoned garage. She had been raped and killed. The police arrested five suspects, but, by morning, had fixed upon Morales as the murderer. He confessed, was tried, and was publicly executed by a firing squad. Soon after, doubts arose about his guilt. Word spread that corrupt generals and town officials were responsible, that the confession was false, and that Juan was innocent of the crime. People said blood oozed up from the soil of his grave and claimed to hear his voice crying out for justice. And so in death, Juan Morales became Juan Soldado, invoked against corruption and injustice, protector of ilegales, patron of the downtrodden and poor.

Perla looked at her register and shook her head. *I barely have enough for someone to buy something to eat.* She counted out her small deposit and

thought about Rosa at the market, the thick wads of bills in the slots of her register.

She locked up and started for home. Children played in the yard of a house across the street, swimming in an inflatable pool in the shade of a tamarisk tree. Instead of cutting through the lot, Perla took the sidewalk. On the corner, she tried to stretch her neck, tried to see past the telephone poles, past the plastic branches of the cell phone tower disguised as a tree where birds didn't nest, to the Italian cypresses near Galena Court.

No sign of him. I'm right here, she thought. *You need me? I'm right here. Not gone.*

        •   •   •

Rosa took a plastic chair and set it on top of the newspapers she'd spread out. She draped a white towel over Perla's shoulders and tucked it tightly under her collar.

"I'm spending too much money on dye," Perla said. "Maybe I should just stop doing it."

"I think you'd look fine with white hair." Rosa arranged her scissors and combs, and filled a spray bottle with water. "Like sophisticated."

"Sophisticated?" Perla laughed as she sat in the chair.

"That's the word my sister, Blanca, always used when we were younger. 'Rosa, look. Do your hair this way. You'll look so *sophisticated,*' she would say. Always trying to give me makeovers and do my nails." Rosa smiled. "God, I miss having her around."

"And your mother?" Perla asked. "Have you talked to her?"

Rosa sighed. "Every now and then. She's still mad at me. I can tell. All this time. Ever since Miguel, things between us have never been the same. The only reason she came to our wedding was because Blanca forced her. When the baby was born, she hardly ever stopped by. Blanca says it's because she's not ready to be a grandma yet. That she still sees herself as a young woman. She turned fifty-six last week. She's got this new boyfriend, Roy, who thinks he's a musician. Carries a guitar around everywhere. A real show-off. Smooth talker."

Rosa leaned over and pointed at Perla with a comb. "That's what you need, I think. A boyfriend. Someone to take you out, to drive you around town." On top of an overturned trash can sat a portable radio. Rosa turned

the volume up and adjusted the antenna. "A guy to take you dancing. That's what brought Miguel and me together, you know? Dancing."

"I'm not a girl anymore."

"Girl? You don't have to be. Look at my mom. Besides, it would be nice. So that you wouldn't be alone all the time." Rosa combed out strands of Perla's wet hair and began snipping off the tips. "I know you miss your husband."

"I forget," she said. "Sometimes I'll wake up in the middle of the night thinking I hear his snores. Or I'll feel the sheets being pulled away. All this time, and I'm still not used to it." Strands of hair tickled the back of Perla's neck.

Rosa stopped cutting when two police cars sped down the street. "Every day you see more and more of that around here," she said. "It's getting crazy. Did you hear about the break-in over on the next block?"

"No. When?"

"Last week. This girl Sandra and her husband. Their house was robbed. They were both there. Happened during the night while they slept. Could you imagine? They took their computer and television and stereo and everything. Good thing no one got hurt."

"They just walked in?"

"Through a window." Rosa stopped to add another load of laundry to the washing machine. "I'm telling you. The other morning we come out and find bottles of beer and Night Train in the yard. Over there." She pointed toward the street. "We're thinking about getting a dog. In case they ever try and rob us."

Around Rosa's garage, boxes with "Navidad," "Baby Clothes," and "Hats and Sweaters" written on their sides sat on the shelves. Trash bags full of crushed aluminum cans and plastic bottles waited for Miguel to haul them to the recycling center in Las Glorias' parking lot.

"You're lucky," Perla said. "You have Miguel and your daughter. You don't live alone like I do." Turning to the street, she imagined Guillermo jogging up and down the sidewalk the way he used to, each hand holding barbells, sweat covering his face. "He was old when he died, but Guillermo, he was very strong. He was my company."

"If you need anything, you come here," Rosa said. "If you hear a noise or someone breaking in, you jump out of your bed, and you run down the street over here to us. Don't matter what time or anything."

When she finished, Rosa plugged her blow dryer into an outlet, then combed and styled Perla's hair, fluffing it up to add volume. She brushed the clippings from her shoulders and back and behind her ears with a clean paintbrush. She untied the towel and walked Perla over to the full-length mirror nailed to the back door that led into their kitchen.

"Wait," Rosa said, reaching behind an overturned trash can. She held out an aluminum baseball bat. "Here. Take this."

"What? Why?"

"Protection," Rosa said. "For the night."

Perla took the bat and turned to look at herself in the mirror's reflection. She could see the street—the cars parked along the curb, the crooked wooden posts of a fence, thick iron bars over a window screen.

She held the bat tightly and widened her stance.

•   •   •

By mid-June, fireworks stands had gone up in the parking lots and fields around Agua Mansa. They had already started selling sparklers and rockets. People stood out in their front yards or in driveways lighting firecrackers, tossing them up into the trees or shoving them in empty soda cans.

Perla leaned the bat against the couch. She turned on the shower in the bathroom, then went into the bedroom. She removed her underwear and bra and stood looking at herself naked in front of the dresser. On it were pictures: her high school graduation photo; she and Guillermo at their wedding; the two of them standing in front of a boat when they took a trip out to Catalina Island a few years before he died. She tried to find remnants of herself in the face that looked back at her, smiling. She remembered being soft and tall and always laughing like her mother. She looked down at her hands. The brown spots dotting their backs appeared foreign, and she couldn't recall when they had first formed. Her arms were thin, so thin. *What had they looked like before?* Her breasts were flattened and wrinkled, and the skin by her knees and around the soles of her feet was dry and split like an elephant's.

She thought about Rosa's garage, about those boxes stuffed with old clothes and Christmas tree ornaments, about the dog they wanted to get. Maybe she could get one, too, or bars on the windows. She looked around the room. Was there anything they would want? This was all she had now.

Old photos. Couches covered with blankets and sheets to keep them clean. A television with two large knobs and wood-paneled doors to cover the screen. Lamps with heavy bases, their shades ruffled along the edges like old-fashioned petticoats.

After showering, she changed into her nightgown and walked out to the living room. She squeezed the bat over and over again, massaging the neck until it was warm.

She stood in the middle of the living room and widened her stance, bending her knees, bracing herself. The night air boomed and hissed from the fireworks her neighbors lit. Smoke drifted across the front window in thin ribbons. She pictured it: a figure standing a few feet away near the kitchen. He towered over her so high that his head scraped against the roof of the house, banging the chandelier, as he made his way across the room. He knocked over the desk, spilling sheets of white paper and pens. His long arm reached out. Smoke fingers wrapped around her neck, scratching her arms. Perla swung at the figure again and again, the bat cutting through the black mist of his body. The figure bled back into the walls and floors. The bat rolled across the floor and under the coffee table where a pair of Guillermo's shoes still sat, the laces neatly knotted.

⁎   ⁎   ⁎

The dollar bills pinned to the statue's robe weren't even real. It was play money from a game for children. The notes were green with fuzzy letters and numbers printed on fluorescent paper. Anyone standing in front of the display window that faced the parking lot could see that it was fake.

The statue had always been there. Darío had placed it there and pinned the ofrendas to Saint Anthony's robe.

"Take it out if you want," he'd said the day he left for good. "The window's due for a change."

But she had decided to leave him there even though the statue's robe was fading, the soft velvet so worn away that white netting could be seen in spots along the back.

She noticed the shards first, the way they sparkled on the concrete walkway. *One of the construction workers probably dropped something.*

She had her key in the lock and was turning the knob when she stopped

and saw a piece of glass jutting out from one side of the front window. Saint Anthony was gone. There was a rock on the floor beside the display table, which had been toppled over.

Perla didn't go inside. She turned around, walked through the lot, and went back to the house. She found the baseball bat, under the coffee table, grabbed it, and walked back to the botánica. She inched open the door, gripping the bat with both hands. Aside from the window and the things in it, everything looked fine. Nothing else was missing or broken. She went straight for the closet and removed the loose floorboard. The lockbox was there, the bills and rolls untouched.

After she put the money in the register, she took the broom and went outside to sweep up the glass. A truck pulled up and parked a few feet away. It was one of the construction workers. He stepped out, a leather tool belt draped over his left shoulder, black hair pulled back in a ponytail. He flicked a lit cigarette on the asphalt and ground it in with his boot sole. He took his sunglasses off and watched her.

"You all right?" he asked, pointing to the window. "Everything cool?"

Perla stayed quiet.

He pointed to the window again. "Ventana? That's how you say it, right? Somebody break? Quebró? Ventana?" he said again, pointing. "Policía come?"

"I speak English," she said.

"Oh. Were you robbed?" He walked up to the window. He looked at it, then picked up the rock. "Are you okay?"

"I'm fine. They only took my statue. It was here. In the window." She showed him the outline of the base. "Saint Anthony."

He wore a backward baseball cap. A patch of hair covered the tip of his chin, braided and thick as a root. *Domínguez* was written in marker across the thermos he toted. He said, "I got some extra sheets of plywood in the truck. Give me a sec, and I can patch it up for you."

He measured the window and the sheet of plywood. He made small marks like X's in the wood and cut it with a saw he pulled out of a toolbox. He pointed with his chin to the bat near the front door. "That your weapon?"

"Someone gave it to me," she said.

"You could do some damage with a bat like that." Sweat beads collected on his forehead, dampening his eyebrows. "If I were a crook I wouldn't mess

with you." He rose and said, "There. That should hold up for now. We'll wanna get it fixed soon. I'll call the landlord. Tell 'em what happened. We'll need to place an order for some glass."

He grabbed a pad and a pencil and took some measurements. Perla looked at the rock that he'd set on one of the chairs before putting up the plywood.

He said, "You want me to take that? I'll toss it for you."

"Thank you."

He put it in the front seat beside him and drove away.

She turned the fan on and stood there looking at the empty window, at the bent heads of the silver nails the construction worker had hammered. *A statue,* she thought. *Who would want a statue? Saint Anthony. Rodrigo? Did he come back? Did I miss him again?*

The note was still taped to the register. She stopped to light the candle of Juan Soldado again and placed it at the foot of the statue of Santa Bárbara.

She busied herself the rest of the day by rearranging the statues on the shelves. She brought out some incense sticks and candles and tried to arrange them in a different order, making sure they were all visibly priced, that each peg looked full and organized.

She closed early, locking up at three. The construction worker had taken down the SPACE FOR LEASE sign from the window of Alfonso's shop. In its place was a new sign:

COMING SOON

Stigmata

Body Piercing and Tattoos

Perla gripped the bat as she made her way home. She tried not to think about any of it. Alfonso. Rodrigo. If he would come back or not. The rock. The missing statue. Walking through the lot, she stepped cautiously to avoid killing any of the beetles that darted across the path. They dashed around in a panic, hiding under the leaves and shrubs below.

Taking Stock

I took my first hit of speed the same night I popped Nancy Pérez's cherry. My friend Beady's parents were away that weekend, and the party was his idea. He got this bug up his ass and started spreading the word around school that week. Had some flyers made in printing class and passed them out. Wild party at my pad, he told everyone. Keg and DJ. Party until everyone passes out or the neighbors call the cops. We called him Beady because his eyes were always low and red from smoking weed. You'd see him walking around campus with a bottle of Visine. Allergies, he'd tell the teachers.

His older brother, Ramón, got the keg. The DJ was this puny dude who called himself Chaos. Showed up with a milk crate full of records. Set up the turntables out on the patio, spinning and mixing all night. Everyone huddled around the keg, drinking beer from plastic cups. All the girls were dancing together, waving their arms in the air, hooting to the beat of the music, taking turns stepping into the circle they'd formed.

Nancy had it for me. Beady said she would hit him up for information.

"What's his deal?" she'd say. "Ask him if he thinks I'm cute. He seeing anyone?"

She wasn't my type, I won't lie. But she still looked fine in those tight denim skirts, the outline of her panties showing through. I intrigued her, she told Beady. I liked that. That I intrigued her.

So she's there at the party, sitting on a lawn chair with her friend when I

stroll up. And I can tell she's checking me out. I'm getting myself some beer, shooting it with Beady and this other fool, when I turn around and catch her eyeing me.

I go over and we get to bullshitting about school. Next thing I know we're both feeling good from the beer, and we end up in Beady's parents' bedroom. Music's thumping downstairs. I hear the girls dancing, clapping their hands, calling one another out. We're getting it going nice and heavy. She's letting me do everything. So I'm touching her here and there and she's moaning, saying, Oh yeah. Um. I like that there. She's taking my hands and putting them where she wants. We end up on each other. Going at it while the party's happening downstairs, and the DJ's flashing strobe light's turning the bedroom red then blue then white. Beady's parents watching us the whole time from framed pictures on the wall.

When we finished I told her, "I'll see you around."

"Yeah," she said. "Anytime. You know where I'm at."

After everyone split we got high. Ramón had this friend of his there, some dude from around San Bernardino named Smoky. The speed was cooked good and strong, he told us. Made fun of me and Beady when we said we'd never done none.

So we crouched around the coffee table. Empty blue cups tossed over the top. Bags of chips. Cigarette butts jammed into an ashtray shaped like a sombrero from the vacation Beady's parents took to Acapulco.

Here's what it felt like and why I'm still doing it. It felt electric. Like volts of energy making my blood boil, turning everything inside me on all at once. I punched a hole in the wall of Beady's bedroom. And I didn't feel no pain or nothing. I felt invincible. All this shit got pushed aside. I'm talking pushed way aside. I know I'm not doing it no justice. So there's no point in even trying to describe it except to say it's good. I came to life that night, and I didn't wanna die no time soon.

∗   ∗   ∗

Me and Beady rent a two-bedroom apartment at the Agua Mansa Palms. We got nothing. No furniture except for a couch with the stuffing coming out of the arm that Beady got from his aunt, and a freestanding lamp in the corner next to a wax plant I took from my mom's garage. The only thing we spent

money on was the television. Sleek black and real modern. Beady says it looks like we can contact the *Enterprise* with the remote because it's all high-tech. A twenty-seven-inch Panasonic with stereo sound. I got it on an employee discount from my job. I work in an electronics store. Selling television antennas and power strips, cable wires and connectors. Have to wear a nametag and vest. The pay sucks, and the only reason I stay is because I need the cash. That's why I'm real dependable. I'm never late. Never take longer than a thirty-minute break to eat. Never call in sick. This one time I was running a fever of one hundred and five. Dragged my ass out of bed to work a morning shift. Those are the best shifts because it's nice and slow and I check out the stock, eyeball the expensive cordless phones, computer printers, monitors, and keyboards. The closing shifts are when all the fat fucks come in, the couch potatoes looking for splitters to hook up their cable to their VCRs, buying remotes, bringing in their runts who run up and down the aisles making a mess out of all the merchandise, banging on the keyboards, using the typewriters and leaving stupid messages on the sheets of paper like "Bite Me" and "Juan Loves Deborah."

Beady and me, we got this scam going. We only do it on slow nights when my manager, Bill, does the paperwork. Bill usually goes in back about eight, a half-hour before we close. Stockroom's so small the manager's desk bumps up against the door. So he leaves it cracked open, just enough for me to see his bald head when I stand by the register.

The way it goes is Beady uses some of his money to buy something real cheap like a pack of batteries. Before he comes in, though, I put some shit aside, small and not so expensive, like three universal remotes and some printer cables. When he strolls up to pay for the batteries, I ring him up, make sure Bill hears me giving the total. Real quick I stick the stash in the bag, say thank you real loud, say, "I hope that works out for you. If you have any problems hooking that up, just give us a call." Pointing to my nametag, "I'm Shawn."

You don't need a receipt to get your cash back here. Just as long as nothing's opened and our tags are still on the boxes. So Beady goes in a few days later to return some of the stuff. He never takes back too much. We spread it out. Do it little by little. We got a good thing going, so we don't wanna blow it. We keep the return amounts low because too much will make man-

agement suspicious. Play it right and we could pull about two hundred bones a month.

Tonight we're coming back from scoring some from this Vietnamese kid we know who's our source. We're going to our pad to get high and stay up all night and watch pornos since I'm off tomorrow and Beady's gonna call in sick.

"I say fuck the forty-dollar shit," Beady goes. "Let's go for one of those printers. Or those Sony monitors you guys just got in."

"Not even," I say. "Only got three or four of those in. Management watches that." They've been getting all suspicious lately, making us empty out our pockets every night before we leave and anytime we step out of the store for a smoke.

"We could take one this month. One next month. Stockpile the shit." He laughs.

I roll the window down, watch the streetlights blur as we drive past. The way light bends and the trees fly by makes me think about time travel, the speed of light, the ghosts of dead stars up in the sky right now looking down on us and laughing. How we're all just moving, just passing through and nothing's ever meant to last.

I can't wait till we're at the pad sketching. Beady's tapping his hand on the steering wheel, and it starts to get me all edgy. He's not even paying attention to how slow we're going.

"Stop driving like a grandma," I go. "Fuckin' punch it, man. Let's go."

At an intersection, he guns the engine. When the light turns green, we take off, the tires skidding on the concrete. I imagine flames trailing behind us like in the cartoons.

When we get back to the apartment Beady tells me he invited this friend from his work.

"Her name's Daisy. You'll like her. Says she's got this supplier who cooks some real good shit out in Perris."

She's standing out in the hallway when we stroll up. Daisy's got this red windbreaker on, and she's wearing red Converse high-tops with black laces. Acid-wash jeans too baggy for her skinny ass. First look and I know already I'm not gonna be liking this scab because of the way her eyes move, all hypnotic like a cat's. I get this vibe. She's too low and mellow.

We get the music going and Daisy sits on the couch, talking real slow, like she's on downers. Beady hands her a beer. I get up and take one from the fridge and pace around the dining room. She takes sips of her beer and gossips with Beady about work. She never once eyes me, never once asks me about myself. That's another thing that bugs me about this scab. How she just comes in making herself all regal in my pad like she don't care one way or another that I'm there.

She's got a runt. Two-year-old named Xavier. Says, "My mom's got him. I told her I was having a girls' night out." She laughs. I can see a big black gap where a tooth should be. Her face is pockmarked. She's got speed bumps on her face that she's tried to cover with makeup and they're dusty tan, so it looks like she's slid marbles under her cheeks.

I throw my beer across the room and say, "Fuck this." The kitchen's full of dirty paper plates on top of the stove and all over the floor because Beady and me don't own real ones. Forks we get whenever we go grab fast food. Got a drawer full of ketchup and hot sauce packets from different restaurants, individually wrapped sets of plastic utensils, and straws. When I crouch over the counter to snort my lines, I sweep my hand across it and all those paper plates and utensils fall to the ground.

Right when the speed's starting to hit me and I'm getting pumped, Beady and Daisy get up off the couch and go into the kitchen to snort. I'm pacing around, listening to music. Beady comes around, turns the television on, and changes it to the Spice Channel. Two girls, one redhead and the other a blonde, are standing under a waterfall. They're naked and feeling each other up, rubbing nipples, their lips pouty and shiny.

"Don't get too crazy," he says. And he takes that skank into his bedroom. A few minutes later I hear moaning, Beady's headboard banging up against the wall. Then it's quiet. He walks out, naked, the tattoo of Jesus on his chest looking at me. Jesus' face is tanned, hair from Beady's chest poking out of his left eye. A mole right by his nose looks like snot.

"Hey," Beady goes to me. "Want some?" He grabs my arm.

The bedroom door's open, and I can see her leg, pale and skinny. Skin's sagging like it's dripping right off the bone.

"It's cool," I say, rubbing away some drip coming out of my nose from the speed.

He turns around and goes back to her. He leaves the door open. I can see him riding her, those ugly-ass legs of hers wrapped around his waist. She laughs, says something that sounds like my name. I reach for the remote, turn the volume up on the television hoping to drown it out.

*   *   *

The only reason Beady gets me to go with him to Daisy's a few days after is because he says her supplier out in Perris gave her a break on the speed so we could try it. He says if we like it, he'll hook us up.

"Daisy says his shit's good," Beady goes. "And it's cheaper than what we pay now."

"Don't matter," I tell him. "We'll be driving out to fucking cow country and spending money on gas anyways."

"It's all good."

"Bullshit."

When we get to her pad, the runt's there, too. Running around in nothing but a saggy diaper that's got pictures of blue bears prancing around rainbows on it. He stinks like a sewer.

"Here," Daisy says. She gives the runt an empty plastic soda bottle to play with. She's got the speed sitting on the coffee table between an ashtray and an oven mitt.

Beady takes it and says, "We're going another route." They decide they're going to shoot.

"What for?" I say. "Same shit. Different hole."

"It hits you faster," she says.

I'm keeping mine the same, I tell them. "Not getting me near needles."

"Rots your nose," she says.

Like your body's not already fucked up, I wanna say to her. Just look at you. Twenty-something, and you look like a corpse. Pale and sick skinny. Eyebrows nothing but sorry-ass drawings. Cheap dye job. Dime store, I think. The runt's playing in the kitchen, and I feel sorry for the bastard. This accident's his mom.

"I got this thing," I say. "Needles freak me out."

"Aw," she says. "You afraid, güero?" She walks over and sits next to me on the couch, runs her fingers through my sideburns, rubs the stubble that's growing on my head because I haven't shaved it in a few days. "Look at you.

All mysterious with those bright blue eyes." She gives me a long-ass look. "Those cords would look real good on the floor of my room, you know that?"

Beady laughs. Goes, "Stop throwing moves."

I snort my lines, hoping the speed'll rub away that picture. I watch the runt while Beady and Daisy get to cooking their shit. They're doing it in the kitchen while that kid's banging a blue block against a cabinet door. Runts. Sometimes I think they got this instinct. Like they know just when you're thinking about them. Like some telepathy. Some Aquaman sonar shit because just as I'm watching him there on the floor while a few feet away his mom's got a man's belt tied around her arm and Beady's about to stab her with a needle, the runt turns around and sees me eyeballing him. So he gets up and walks over.

He's handing me the block. It's dripping wet from his spit. He's making these noises and grunts that almost sound like words. Pointing. His hair's a mess. Looks like it hasn't been combed in weeks. Yellow stains on his cheeks and he's smelling even more. The diaper's so loose and sagging that when he starts pissing, it runs straight down the sides of his leg and onto the carpet and he's not saying or doing nothing except pissing and grunting, pissing and grunting. What a sorry-ass situation, I think. All-around sorry.

* * *

"Where's your piece?" I ask Beady. It's Tuesday night, and we're out for a drive.

Bill always schedules me to open with him on Tuesdays because it's when we get a shipment from the distribution center out in Industry. We get there at six in the morning and check in merchandise and stock shit. I got off at noon. When I came home, I crashed and didn't wake up until seven at night because I'd been spinning since we got back from Daisy's the day before.

Beady was in the living room watching television when I woke up. He was still in his overalls, his hands greasy from tire grime. He'd stopped to pick up food. On the kitchen counter there was a burrito wrapped in foil for me. A few minutes later he showered. We got dressed and decided to go out for a drive.

"She couldn't get her mom to watch the kid," he says, lowering the radio.

We're doing sixty-five up Rancho. We bounce over the railroad tracks and continue up, passing the freeway. On Valley we hang a left, heading toward Fontana.

We stop at a liquor store and get a twelve-pack of Bud Lights in the can and some smokes. Beady lights one up and hums to the Beastie Boys' "Girls" on the radio. When we pass the porn shop on Valley, Beady laughs and goes, "Hey, let's scope it out. Twenty-five-cent movie arcades."

"For what? Place is full of fags cruising and cops looking to bust."

We drive past the empty Kaiser Steel plant, past the tall smokestacks like burned-out birthday candles. Off the main road, we turn down some small street that's all dark. A few minutes later, we pull over and park in front of an abandoned warehouse next to these old railroad tracks.

He uses a brick to bust the window, and we climb in through there. The warehouse is one big room. Old wooden pallets are stacked up in the middle of the floor, and the front cabin of a tractor is over by the main doors of the place. Air's stuffy and smells like oil. We take a spot near the windows. The huge gravel pyramids from the factory across the street are lit up, and we watch cement mixers haul ass around them. It's warm, so Beady and me take our shirts off and lie there with our backs against a pile of crates, smoking and drinking beers, tossing the cans behind us.

"Daisy thinks you don't like her," he says.

I sip my beer, take a drag of my smoke.

He laughs. "What's your problem with her, man?" He gets up and walks over to the windows. Unzips his pants and takes a piss.

"Didn't say I had one."

I take long puffs, watching him shake his dick before zipping his pants back up. I can tell he's already got a good buzz going nice and strong inside that head of his. He's talking all slow, almost whispering. He sits back down. Me, I'm relaxing to the hum of the cement mixers across the street.

He says last night's speed made him feel like he was superhuman. "Like it was a love potion. We were going at it for hours, man." He flicks his cigarette butt.

"Better watch it with her," I say, wiping the sweat from my forehead and down the middle of my chest. "Could be using you."

"Don't worry." He takes another beer, cracks it open, and hands it to me.

"She's too smooth," I say. "Too fly for my taste. Watch your step with that one."

∗   ∗   ∗

I notice little things around the apartment at first—her socks tucked near the couch, a pair of heels in the hallway, a curling iron in the closet by the entrance. When I go grab a roll of toilet paper from under the bathroom sink, I scope a box of tampons.

Before I know it, Daisy's a regular at our pad, kicking it on the couch when I come home. Beady with his arm around her. All proud like she's some real find. She brings some pots and pans and tells Beady she's gonna teach him how to cook rice just like his mom's. One day she shows up with a plant in a hanger made out of twisted strips of wire. They hook it to the handle of one of the kitchen drawers. Every time I walk by, it rocks, and it makes me want to toss it out the fucking balcony.

"Where's your kid's dad?" I ask her one night.

"Chino," she says. That voice of hers rattly. "Armed robbery."

Beady's left to get more beer, and it's just her and me. He's been gone only a few minutes, and I'm already feeling weird. The way she looks at me. Those crooked pencil eyebrows making her whole face look lopsided.

I'm leaning up against the wall in the kitchen, and she's sitting on the counter. Right near the sink. Wrinkled miniskirt riding her thighs. She shifts, spreads her legs, and I get a look at her patch.

"Can I ask you something?" she goes.

I shrug my shoulders, staring her down.

"What do you got against me?" She smooths her hair back. "You're throwing me some mean looks."

I stay quiet.

"I like you. In high school I had a crush on this cute-ass white dude. Something about you reminds me of him."

I keep mad-dogging her.

She sighs, shrugs her shoulders, pushes her tube top up, trying to act decent all of a sudden. Like she just heard about shame. "Beady says you guys are tight."

"You got that right," I say. "I know him better than anybody."

She says, "I'm not here to mess with what you guys got going."

"Then why are you here?"

"He treats me real fine."

When Beady gets home, they go straight to his bedroom and close the door.

The next day, I'm doing an opening shift when the phone rings. It's Beady, and he asks if I can talk.

"Yeah," I say. "Just pricing shit."

"Can I come in today? To do a hit?"

He tells me he's hurting for cash. "Fuck. All my money's been going to wining and dining Daisy."

"Didn't I say?"

"Come on, man."

It's risky today, I tell him. Because I won't be the only one on the floor. Management's getting real suspicious, I say. Inventory's coming up off. So they're clocking people they recognize that come in a lot.

"They could recognize you," I say. "Blow your cover."

So he goes, "I'll send Daisy in. They don't know her. Then she can go later tonight to return."

I stay quiet.

"Come on, bro. I'm *begging* you."

"Fuck," I say. "Fine. Send her ass in at eleven. That's when Bill's going to the bank."

It's me and this rookie named Mark on the floor when eleven rolls around. Bill's left me in charge. When I see Daisy walking in, I tell Mark to go look for something in the back.

"A headset for a cell phone," I tell the rookie. "Special order. Customer called and said they'd be by in a few to pick it up." As soon as he goes in the back, I tell Daisy, "All right, grab some shit, and I'll throw it in a bag."

Only she's moving real slow. So I say, "Quick."

I'd stacked up the printers by the main aisle. There's only five. She goes over and picks one up. "Beady said to get one of these."

"You can't," I say. "They'll know one's missing."

"But this is what Beady told me to get," she says.

I can hear the rookie's footsteps in the back stockroom, and I know he's about to come out.

Stupid bitch is standing there in the middle of the store holding this huge box, no customers around, no employees. That stupid fucking look on her face.

"Shit," I say. "Fine. Just go. Get your ass out of here."

She walks out the front door just as Mark comes out of the stockroom.

"I couldn't find anything," he goes.

"It's cool," I go. "I'll look later."

After Bill gets back, the rookie clocks out and takes off.

Sure enough, Bill notices one of the printers gone. "So we sold one, huh?" he says.

"Guess so," I say. I tell him the rookie must have when I was out back looking for something.

"You left him on the floor alone?"

"Only for a minute. Customer called checking on an order. He was pissed."

Bill says I need to practice more floor control. "We're thinking of moving you up to key holder. But you have to prove yourself and can't be making dumb mistakes like that, Shawn."

"Sorry," I say.

Later that night, Beady and Daisy come to the apartment, a hundred bucks richer.

"We got you something," Beady says. He hands me a balloon of speed.

I snort my lines and sit on the couch to watch some television.

Daisy laughs, goes, "Oh my God. That was too easy."

Fucking great, I think. Now she's in on it. Now I'm gonna be risking it for this fool.

I go to my bedroom and slam the door shut.

*　　*　　*

The thing about living around so many Mexicans is that you start to pick up their ways. The streets and cities and mountains around here have Spanish names, so already, right there you learn some words. From Beady, I get all the cuss words and I can say the name of the state in Mexico his family's from without an accent. You wake up hungover and menudo suddenly sounds good. Around Christmastime, you start to crave tamales. At birthday parties, you get a piñata for the runt and stuff it with candy,

break off a broom handle so that they can have something to whack it with.

In high school, I dated this girl named Beatrice. I went with her once to this store on Rancho when her parents were having money problems. Her dad was laid off, and the mom couldn't get a job because she hardly spoke English. When she finally did find something, it was janitor work. Barely enough for them to make it.

So she went to this store. Shelves with statues of saints and fat gods I didn't recognize decked out in robes and feathers with rags wrapped around their heads. Wooden idols and figures of animals I couldn't make out. Incense sticks hanging from pegs on the walls so everywhere there was this strong smell of church, of holiness.

Beatrice bought a candle called a "Road Opener" with three different colors of wax in it. The woman that worked there poured some smelly oil into it, told Beatrice to take a folded dollar bill and stick it under the candle and to light it for five days straight. She sold her a rabbit's foot and said to rub it all the time, to concentrate and pray.

I don't know if it ever worked, though, because we stopped hooking up. Last time I saw Beatrice was a while ago. She was sitting at the bus stop. Dressed in a nurse's uniform and reading a magazine.

So I'm in the shopping center, checking out this new tattoo shop that just opened up because I'm thinking about getting some new ink done on my forearm. "I got too much skin," I tell the guy there. I show him the Celtic cross tattooed on my right bicep.

"What are you thinking about?" the guy goes.

"Don't know," I go. "Maybe something religious. I'm thinking about changing my ways." I laugh.

I spend some time looking through the books they got, showing all these different pictures of tats they've done on people. I check out the stencils on the walls. But all they got are pictures of Jesus all scarred up and bleeding. I don't wanna get one of those because it'll look like I'm just biting off of Beady.

"See anything you like?" the guy says.

"Not really."

"Go next door," he says. "The old lady sells these prayer cards with all these saints. Got all these sweet religious pictures."

I step in there and that smell hits me, and I remember Beatrice and that candle. Not the one she bought. But this other one. The words "Stay Away" floating across the top. I browse around, the old lady sitting behind the counter watching television. I think it's the same lady from way back when. But my memory's hazy from the speed I did earlier today.

"What do you need?" she says, lowering the television and getting up.

"I need a candle," I say, forgetting about the tat, scanning the rows of statues and idols. "There." I point to the one I saw years ago. "I need to get rid of someone."

"Okay," she says. "Is this person doing harm?"

"Yeah," I tell her. "She's destructive."

She tells me to use something sharp like a key or a knife to carve the name of the person I'm trying to get rid of into the top of the candle. "When she leaves, all those bad vibes will go along with her."

She says it would help if I take something from the person I'm looking to chase away and put it by the candle. A piece of cloth that I can tie around it, she says. Or a picture. Keep it there while it's lit for ten days.

No one's home when I get back. Beady's room's a mess. Piles of clothes and wrappers from fast food places are all over the floor. I have to dig through some of his stuff, feeling my way through piles of his boxers and dirty socks. I'm careful, though. Because, even though it's all messy, I don't want Beady to find out I'm going through his shit. So I set his boxers aside, the elastic bands all stretched out and wasting away. He needs new ones. Every time he comes out of the shower and he's walking around the apartment, they creep down. Sometimes he holds them up with his hand. Other times he just lets them fall off and strolls around ass naked. "Don't have nothing you don't," is what he says when I tell him to cover up.

I find a pair of panties tangled around one of his muscle shirts. So I take that and head back to my room. In the closet, I put the candle on a piece of cardboard from the box I use to keep my clothes, then carve her name into the wax just like the lady said. I use my hands to tear the panties up into pieces. I tie one of the strips around the candle. When I light it, my closet glows red and spooky.

I know Beady. Know him so good I can practically get into that head of his. I know his ways and he knows mine. We're family, Beady and me. That's the way we've always seen each other. That's what this scab don't get. That

Beady and me have been doing just fine by ourselves. That we don't need someone like her coming in and messing up what we got, what we've kept for ourselves.

Around me, there's shit that's unsettled, but that's the way it's always been. Everything with me's temporary. That's what I'm used to. All the things I own are thrown all over the place. Like someone opened up this box with my name on the side of it, turned it over, and shook everything out. And my stuff, I'm talking about my clothes, my shoes, my belongings, just came tumbling down from the sky and landed here in this place. And that was it. Some voice said to me, You're here, Shawn. This is you for now.

It's the same way with Beady. Which is why we operate the way we do, why we got it good here when it's just the two of us. When we're not tied to nothing or no one. And we're moving and going and getting it done. Taking what we need to get by day by day. Fucking with our setup only makes too much bad happen.

.   .   .

After work, I decided not to go home. I knew Daisy would be there. So instead, I went to this bar Beady and I go to sometimes called the Lickety Split. They had this chick there decked out in a one-piece bathing suit, "Official Corona Girl" written on a sash draped over her tits. She went around, getting all hugged up next to the men sitting on the stools, passing out bottle openers.

"Buenas noches," she said, handing me one.

I took it and gave it back. "Don't got no use for this," I said, mad-dogging her until she walked away. I stayed there, tossing back a few beers, getting a good buzz going. I thought about the time Beady and me were here, and we sat at the back booth and I carved my initials into the wood top.

I take my time getting home and walk in pretty late. Beady's snoring in his room. In the hallway, right by his door, I see her sandals. The impressions of her crooked toes in the padding make me gag.

My back's gotten used to lying on top of a bunch of blankets I use as a bed. So I'm there, wearing nothing, smoking a cigarette. I left my bedroom door open. From the hallway, I can see the moonlight coming from the living room, the shadows of the blinds making sharp lines going across the walls.

A few minutes later, I hear Beady's bedroom door squeak open. Daisy's standing in the hallway in one of his old football jerseys.

"Hey," she whispers, leaning up against the door frame. The shadows from the blinds are falling on her face, and I'm wishing they were razors or knives. "You awake in there?"

"I'm awake." I grab a shirt to cover myself. I offer her a cigarette.

"I don't smoke," she says.

Crazy bitch, I think. She shoots up speed, but she don't smoke? "Suit yourself," I say.

"Why are you sneaking in all quiet and late?" She walks over and sits on the floor near where I'm lying. When Beady's jersey hikes up a few inches, I can see she's got nothing else on underneath. She takes a good look at me lying there, my T-shirt covering my dick.

"Felt like it," I say. "What are you, my warden?"

She laughs. "No. Just that I was hoping to see you tonight, Shawn."

"Why?"

"You're fun to be around. To look at." She gives me another long sweep. She pulls the jersey off and straddles me. "Do I make you nervous?"

I stay quiet. She traces the outline of the Irish flag tattooed across my chest, then tickles my nipple. I don't even get a little hard. When I look away, she takes her hand and moves my face so that I'm looking right at her.

"I do, don't I?" she goes. "I make you nervous."

And I'm thinking how could Beady find this face attractive? How could he find this body sexy, enough to be giving it to her almost every night since she started showing herself around here?

"You make me sick, to be honest," I say.

I let the cigarette drop and burn the carpet when I take my hands and push her off of me. The shirt falls off, and I'm standing there naked. I grab her and shove her hard against the wall.

"Here's what I want," I say to her. "I want you to leave me alone."

She doesn't look scared or shocked or nothing. Her eyebrows are rubbed away, and without them she looks like an iguana. I'm expecting a forked tongue to come whipping out of that mouth of hers.

I take Beady's jersey and throw it at her. "Leave us alone, puta."

When I hear the door slam shut, I go over to my closet and light the can-

dle. With my head propped up on a pillow, I smoke and watch the flame, hoping she's feeling the hate.

I don't think she told Beady what happened in my bedroom last night. He's going around acting lovesick, saying Daisy makes him feel "real." Beady says the scab told him she understands me. That sometimes people just don't see eye to eye.

I tell Beady, "What? She think she's fuckin' Oprah now?"

                   *   *   *

I'm scheduled to work a mid-shift today. When I get to the store, Bill and the assistant manager, Karen, are both there, standing by the register. As I'm heading for the stockroom door, I see Mark leaning up against a computer desk we use to display shit.

"Don't clock in, Shawn," Bill says. "I want to go over some things with you."

He leads me out to the parking lot. A few minutes later, Karen and Mark follow us out.

"Tell me about that printer you said Mark sold," he says.

I lean up against the hood of a Toyota, watching the other employees running around the sales floor. The rookie's standing there, his arms crossed. He's trying to mad-dog me. Like he's a real bad-ass. I laugh and shake my head at him.

"What?" I say, getting up in his face.

He backs away.

Karen's got a clipboard with some notes on it, and she's holding the yellow copy of the journal tape management pulls out every night to check stock and balance the books.

"You said Mark sold it," Karen says, taking her glasses off and biting the left tip.

I say nothing.

"Mark says he heard someone come in that day, the day you said you went to the back to check on an order. He also doesn't remember hearing the register door pop open," Bill says.

Karen puts her glasses back on, says, "Printer wasn't sold that day. I checked." She holds that clipboard and the journal tape up. "But someone returned one later that night. Got cash back."

"You can tell us now what really happened," Bill says. "Because I think we already know."

So they make me sign this paper saying I'm guilty of gross misconduct, and they hand me my last paycheck. Bill says that, by law, they have to give me my pay.

"But if it were up to me," he says, "I'd keep it and call things even."

Karen starts saying how they know I'm behind all the shit that's been missing and how, because of what I did, the rest of the employees are gonna have to pay.

"Your actions only end up hurting innocent people," she tells me.

Rookie Mark says, "Yeah. Don't implicate me in your schemes."

"Suck my dick," I go to him.

Karen shakes her head. The rookie turns around and heads back in the store.

"I'm disappointed," Bill says. "Shawn, I liked you. You were hardworking, and you knew this job. We wanted to promote you."

"Yeah, well . . . sorry," I say. "Sorry about all this, Bill."

I hand him my vest. But I keep the nametag.

At the liquor store, I cash my last paycheck. I buy five lottery tickets and a twelve-pack of beer. The thing is I'm not even that mad at the stupid bitch for blowing our cover. I almost saw it coming, and that's the thing that gets me about all this. When she was standing there hugging that big box, I said to myself, This ain't good. I think I'm fucking pissed at myself for letting it go on without doing anything to stop or change it.

At home, I pound some beers, turn the radio up, try to imagine myself doing something else. I sit out on the balcony and settle in, take my shoes off, kick my feet up on the railing. It feels good right now, I think. This not having to work, not having to be anywhere. It's nice and quiet. I got a good buzz going. Later I'll go score some speed. Get to spinning nice and early. Don't matter if it's by myself. I can take Beady's car while he's in the bedroom fucking the scab. Maybe take a cruise out to the desert until I run out of gas.

I head back in and grab another beer. I turn the radio up, and I stand there in the living room. There's shit everywhere—pizza boxes and empty soda cups with the straws still poking out of the tops, Beady's dirty sock and shirts, a pair of my Dickies with the underwear still in them from when I

was passed out drunk and Beady stripped my ass and dragged me to my room, junk mail, one of Beady's rubbers. There's more of her shit. Blouses with the armpits stained white. A box of shoes. A statue of a unicorn on the kitchen counter. When I stumble to the bathroom to take a piss I see strands of hair stuck to the side of the toilet.

I walk between my room and his, hugging the wall to keep myself from falling over. He'll be coming home soon, I know. He'll find me here like this. All passed out and broken and messed up. He'll lift me up by the shoulders, my feet dragging on the carpet, and put me to bed so I can sleep heavy and deep and long for once in my life.

Feast of
Saint Francis of Assisi

Founder of the Franciscan Order

Patron of the poor, peace, animals, birds, ecology,

families, tailors, needle workers, and merchants.

Invoked against fire and dying alone.

Rodrigo Abel Zamora was born in Michoacán, the youngest of four children. His brothers, Leonardo and Moisés, were both in the United States. Leonardo was a waiter in a restaurant in Buffalo. Moisés worked construction and was always moving around—Tacoma, Chicago, Nashville. It was hard to keep track of where he was, and months went by without any word from him. His sister, Noemi, had moved with her husband to Veracruz, where they owned a small business that rebuilt motors for farm equipment.

Just before his fifteenth birthday, Rodrigo told his parents he was moving to Tijuana. He hoped to cross into the United States like his brothers.

"I'm going to California," he said. "There's nothing here." Things in San Miguel were hopeless. Every day someone left the pueblo. Houses had emptied out, and there was no work.

His mother gave him an address. Her comadre Margarita's daughter Araceli and her husband had left San Miguel the year before for Tijuana. "Araceli said she'd be there for us if we needed," his mother said. "Go there. Stay with them."

His father tucked a roll of bills in the boy's pocket. "Be careful," he said. "That city, it's dangerous." He patted his son on the back and watched him board the bus from the terminal lobby.

The bus to Tijuana traveled all day, along narrow roads that curved around mountainsides. Looking out the window, he saw deep ravines, the charred hulls of cars lying below like old bones. White crosses staked into the ground floated past, and he made a game of keeping count of how many he saw.

Tijuana was nothing like San Miguel. There were cars and buses everywhere. Wild dogs with bloated stomachs roamed the streets. Houses stood

stacked on top of one another on hillsides that crumbled when the rains came.

"Aquí," Rodrigo said to the taxista, giving him the address his mother had written down.

The house had a yard surrounded by a fence made of chicken wire, and geraniums grew inside plastic tubs on the steps leading up to the front door. "They left," the lady that answered said, barricading the door with her legs. Five pairs of hands poked out from behind her.

"Where?" he asked.

"I don't know. Everyone comes and goes around here. Are you a relative?"

"Yes," he said. "I need a place to stay. And work."

"El dompe," she said. "There's work in the dompe. You can't stay here. We're seven. The house, it's small. We're piled up."

That first day at the dompe, Rodrigo met Félix. He was older with callused hands that lifted old tires and wood planks with ease. When he saw Rodrigo, Félix winked at him and stuck his hand out.

"¿Qué onda?" he said. "I'm Félix."

"Rodrigo."

He held Rodrigo's hand, felt his arm. "You're strong," he said. "That's good. How old are you?"

"Fifteen," Rodrigo said.

"Are you all alone?"

Rodrigo nodded.

"Watch me," he said, pointing to his eyes with two fingers. "I'll take care of you. I'll help you."

He showed Rodrigo what to look for in the trash—rubber, plastic, anything shiny or made of glass, clothes and shoes.

Rodrigo found shelter in a ditch. He slept on scraps of cardboard and ate very little. He made sure not to spend the money his father gave him too quickly, and he hid it in his shoe. That week he was beaten and robbed, the pesos gone.

"I'll give you money," Félix said to Rodrigo when the boy told him what had happened. "But you have to give *me* something back." He grabbed Rodrigo's hand and placed it between his legs. From his pocket, Félix pulled

out a wad of crumpled bills. "Andale," he whispered. "Just touch me. That's it." He pointed to an abandoned building with dark windows. "I told you. I'll take care of you."

Rodrigo looked around. People with soot-covered faces hauled piles of trash and combed through the smoldering rubble. He thought of his mother and father back home, waiting for money. He knew coyotes were expensive; his brothers had written this in their letters. Sifting through all this it would take years to raise so much.

He heard voices in the rafters of the abandoned building that night and watched birds nesting on the metal beams supporting the roof. Félix took his shirt off and asked the boy to do the same. He only wanted Rodrigo to touch him. His chest. Between his legs. That was all.

"Ya," Felix said when they finished. He gave the boy some money, enough for him to buy something to eat. "Don't tell anyone," he said. "The men. They'll make fun of me. Beat me up. And you."

A week later, he saw a young woman with long tangled hair wearing leather huaraches by Felix's side. She was pregnant, her blouse tight against her stomach, her belly button a round nub.

"Meet me," Félix said, when the woman left his side to go to the bathroom behind a stack of crates. He pointed to the building.

Rodrigo went that night and found Félix kneeling on the floor, crying and shaking.

"Perdóname, señor," he said and kissed the crucifix around his neck. "I'm sick," he told Rodrigo. "The girl. She's my wife. And I love her. She's having my baby. I don't want to burn in hell."

He handed Rodrigo a bundle of pesos tied together with an oily piece of string. "Leave," he said. "You'll tempt me if you stay here. I can't look at you anymore. Watch yourself. The callejones. They're dangerous." He swept his arm over the lights of the city gleaming through the windows. "Leave. I don't want to see you."

"But I can't," the boy said. "I don't know anyone here. I'm alone. What will I do?"

"You're young. You'll find work. Go." He grabbed a fistful of dirt and threw it at the boy. He cried out and said, "It wasn't my fault. It was you, Diablo. You came here. Tempted me. I was here first. Go." He got up and

chased the boy out of the building, throwing rocks and bottles at him until
Rodrigo was far away.

He thought about going back to San Miguel. To the emptying streets and
the desolate homes. But Félix and the things they'd done were too fresh in
Rodrigo's mind.

I can't go back. I can't face them.

What Félix gave him was only enough to last a few days. He bought a
bottle of glass cleaner and found sheets of newspapers near a bus stop. He
stood at busy intersections, cleaning the windshields of passing cars. Many
of them just drove off without paying. Some drivers shouted curses and
threatened him. Cops chased him away. Sometimes he had to buy them off,
losing everything he'd earned in that day.

He was standing near the entrance to a store one morning gathering
scraps of paper and old newspapers when a boy reached over and pressed
several pesos into Rodrigo's hand. The boy smelled good. He was clean. He
wore nice pants with white shoes. Sunglasses covered his eyes. He studied
Rodrigo for a long time, then whispered, "Do you need work? Do you need
to make money?"

Rodrigo nodded.

"Vamos."

Rodrigo followed him.

His name was Chino, and he led him to a bar called Estrellitas. There
were boys there, all of them skinny, all of them in tight shirts and red shorts.
There were older men there, too, watching a boy on a platform dancing
naked. Rodrigo saw doors high above the dance floor behind a metal railing
that circled the perimeter of the room. Each door had a different number
painted on it, and white light bulbs burned beside them like eerie full
moons.

Rodrigo followed Chino into a booth below the stairs to the second
floor. The man sitting there was the owner, Ignacio. He instructed Rodrigo
to sit.

"You're looking for work?" he asked. "Looking to make money?"

Rodrigo nodded.

"Good," he said. "You're very handsome. You could make money here. If
you are good and my clients like you."

Chino led Rodrigo up to one of the rooms and told him to shower and change and comb his hair. Chino said their job was to entertain the customers. Some of them were powerful and rich.

"A lot of them come from los Estados Unidos," Chino said. "You have to keep this a secret. You can't tell anyone about these men. If you leave here and don't come back, Ignacio will find you and kill you. Wherever you go, he'll find you. I've seen him do it. Entiendes?"

"Sí," Rodrigo said.

"Have you ever done this before? Been with men?"

He thought of Félix. The abandoned warehouse. His wife's belly. A baby kicking around inside. "No," he said.

"Don't be nervous," Chino said. "The nice ones, they treat you real good. They just want to be with you. There are some, though. They will ask you to do things."

"What kinds of things?"

"Things, okay? You can't say no. If you do, Ignacio will kick you out. He'll go after you and kill you. You're lucky. He likes you. I can tell. I've worked here for four years. Since I was twelve. You can make good money. You're safe here. From all that caca out there. The police, they don't bother us. Ignacio pays them. Where are you from?"

Chino smoked a cigarette and blew out through the shutters of the room. When he saw the smoke, Rodrigo thought of the ribbons of mist hovering around the green hills that surrounded San Miguel.

"Michoacán," Rodrigo said.

"You haven't been in Tijuana long, right?"

"No," he said.

"If you go back out there, they'll eat you up. You don't matter out there." Chino lifted his shirt, revealing a scar like a pink worm burrowing beneath his skin. He wiggled his fingers and Rodrigo saw a stump, round and soft. "In here, you'll be safe. There's food. You'll make money. And Ignacio knows people. He can even help you cross the frontera. Get you papers."

Rodrigo thought of his mother patting tortillas, his father wandering through the dead fields of San Miguel. *I'll stay for now. I'll make some money. Save up.*

Rodrigo and the others were free to leave Estrellitas during the day as

long as they were back by nine at night. Chino took Rodrigo shopping. He bought two pairs of pants with his first few earnings. Then a pair of boots. Nice button-down shirts with the next. And bracelets and a chain. Chino showed him where to wire money. Rodrigo wrote letters and told his mother and father not to worry. The city was being good to him, he wrote. Very good. *And I hope to cross over soon with the help of a coyote. A very well-known one. Very safe. My boss knows many people. My job here, it's good.* Still, every night, he returned to the club, sad, missing his mother and father. Estrellitas was his home for now. He was safe. He was free to come and go as he pleased, as long as he came back on time.

Some of Rodrigo's clients were kind. They hugged him and petted his hands. Some taught him English words and told him about the United States. But there were others who wanted Rodrigo to do more than just talk and lie close. One made the boy urinate on his face. A man named Eric brought a thick braided belt and spanked Rodrigo with it. *But the money,* Rodrigo reminded himself every time. *It's good. I've made a lot. More than I would ever have made in the dompes or cleaning windows.*

Rodrigo had been at Estrellitas for a year when Dwight showed up. Dwight with hair on his chin the color of yellow cornsilk. Dwight who wore sunglasses inside the dark club. Dwight who bragged about his muscles. He showed Rodrigo the bulldog with squatty gray legs tattooed on his left biceps and the anchor across his back. It had an insignia with red letters that Dwight made Rodrigo memorize: USMC.

Their first night, nothing happened. They just sat on the bed and talked. Dwight told the boy his life was empty and that no one understood him.

"This macho bullshit, it's all an act. I'm married. But she's not satisfying me anymore. My true feelings, I'm repressing them," he said.

Repressing. Rodrigo repeated the word, memorized it. *Someday I'll use this word. Up there. In California.*

The next time they sat on the bed and kissed. Dwight put his head on Rodrigo's chest and cried.

"You understand me like no one else," Dwight said. "I'm taking you away. Keeping you for myself. Don't want none of these fuckers having their way with what's mine."

Rodrigo didn't understand. *Fuckers.* He repeated the word in his head. *You understand. No one else.*

A few days later, a man with a belly so big it spilled over his waistband, shading his boots, showed up at the club.

"Go with him," Ignacio said. "He'll take you to Dwight."

Rodrigo was told to pack up all his things and leave with this stranger. Maybe Dwight was at another club across the city or the state. Ignacio owned a circuit of places like this, scattered throughout the pueblos of the north, all along the frontera. Chino told him they all work together. The police. The Migra. Even some priests lure homeless boys in off the street and pass them off to Ignacio or some other jefe who trades pollos. That's how it happened for Rodrigo, how he crossed the border into California. A circuit of men—Border Patrol agents, cops, coyotes—slip things by. They work in secret, communicate by hand gestures, wear certain colors, drive certain cars. All of them get paid. Ignacio makes sure of it. Some of them don't want money at all. Instead they ask for a boy for a whole night. Every time he was ordered to be with a man who didn't have to pay or one who wasn't one of his regulars, Rodrigo wondered whose pasaje he was paying for, which boy he had helped sneak across.

Dwight was waiting for him on this side with a blanket and clothes. He took Rodrigo out for cheeseburgers and fries. They drove in the dark over long freeways, their numbers painted on blue and red crests—15, 215, 10. He saw the names of cities—San Diego, Los Angeles, Las Vegas, Riverside, San Bernardino. The car looped over a ramp supported by tall columns, and they pulled off the freeway. They passed a sign that read Buffalo. He thought of Leonardo. *Could he be there?* He wanted to ask Dwight to stop.

They came to the rows of houses, all of them small and pressed close together with flat roofs. They pulled into a driveway and got out. The duplex had a cramped kitchen. Some of the cabinets were missing doors, and the countertop was cracked and broken. In the living room, pushed up against the far wall, was a faded blue couch with lumpy cushions. The bedroom was at the end of the hall and had a high window. Dwight had to stand on a chair to reach the latch in order to open it. In the center on the floor there was a mattress with sheets Dwight had brought from his home. Cockroaches, with translucent wings on their backs like capes, roamed freely around the place.

"Temporary," he said to Rodrigo. "Until the divorce. Then it'll be just you and me. You understand, don't you?"

Understand. Rodrigo repeated the word to himself.

Dwight had stocked the refrigerator and cupboards with food and had bought a can of Raid to kill the roaches. On the floor of the bedroom there were pads of paper and pens. Next to these was a book of games and cross-word puzzles and another one, thick, with a black cover. It was titled *1,001 Big Questions.* "If you get bored," Dwight said. He tucked money in between the pages and told him. "For *emergencia. Comprende?*"

Rodrigo nodded.

They walked down to the end of the block. A phone booth with a rusted door stood under a streetlight that shone hazy yellow. Dwight had written a string of numbers on a sheet of paper.

"In case of something, page me," he said. "Dial this." He took Rodrigo's hand and guided his finger over each of the ten numbers. "After you hear the beep, punch these three more." He guided the boy's hand again, and Rodrigo's finger pushed the silver buttons with blackened numbers, his ear pressed against an oily receiver. "It's a secret code, okay?" Dwight said. "You're my secret."

Secret, the boy repeated. *Code.*

They walked back to the duplex. They sat on the couch and kissed and touched each other. Dwight unzipped his pants and pushed the boy's head down between his legs. When Dwight finished, he cleaned himself up and splashed water on his face.

"I won't be back until next weekend," he said. "Sit tight and lie low till I come. Don't go out. You could get lost. And Migra's been known to do sweeps around here." Then he roared off in his car.

That first night, Rodrigo couldn't sleep. He heard strange noises—the whistle of a distant train, voices shouting down the street, pipes hissing and groaning within the walls. He kept the hall light on to keep the cockroaches away and left the bedroom door open. He tried to fall asleep, breathing in the smell of soap on the pillowcases to soothe him. Rodrigo imagined Dwight's wife washing and hanging them out to dry in the sun.

The rest of the week he cried, thinking about his mother and father. *They don't even know I've left the country. I could be dead, and they wouldn't know.* He thought of his brothers. *Moisés moved around too much, but Leonardo, he stayed still because of his job.*

Maybe Dwight could take me to Buffalo. Rodrigo remembered the green street sign. Buffalo. *If I find him, what will I say, though? About how I got here? What will I say if he asks?*

He didn't understand the book or the crossword puzzles. Instead, to pass the time, he listened to the two girls who sat on the stoop next to his duplex. They had dark skin and beaded braids as violet as bougainvillea petals woven into their scalps. They talked loud, fast English. He tried to memorize the words they said and listened to the way their voices sounded when they laughed.

Dwight came back that Friday night.

"Got the whole weekend to ourselves, Rod. Told my wife I'd be in San Diego till Sunday. Shit, she don't care, man. All she does is sit around the house, playing cards, gambling my savings away at San Jacinto."

He brought a pizza, and they ate. Afterward, they went out for a ride around town. They drove along the río. The moon reflected in the water broken and warped, its light silvery, reminding him of the tinsel cords strung around the zócalo of San Miguel on Noche Santa. He saw the image of La Virgen de Guadalupe painted on the side of a wall, girls and boys standing in line near the entrance of a building with red, white, and green neon bands coiling around a marquee that read *El Yanquee: Donde Se Reunen Las Bandas Sinaloenses.* They drove by a restaurant, and Rodrigo smelled carne asasda, pollo a la parilla, carnitas. Dwight turned the music up and sang out loud, revving the engine at an intersection.

The weekend after, when he showed up again, Rodrigo waited until Dwight was inside before asking him to take him to Buffalo. But something was wrong. When the boy reached out to touch Dwight, he slapped his hand away. He sat on the floor and smoked small white rocks from a glass pipe that lit up blue and mysterious.

"Fucking two years sober out the fucking window," he said, sobbing. Rodrigo tried to understand him. Dwight took his shirt off and cried into the bulldog on his biceps. He stood up and paced, punching the walls and kicking the sofa.

His face and hands turned red. He yelled, waving his arms around and cursing. He pulled Rodrigo by the hair down the hall into the bedroom. He ripped the boy's pants off and pushed him down onto the mattress. He bent

him over, the boy's face pressed into the pillows. Rodrigo reached out, swatting the air with his left hand as Dwight raped him. When he finished, Dwight put his pants back on and collapsed on top of Rodrigo. Then he got up, ran out to his car, and took off. He didn't come back for two weeks.

            *   *   *

The boy stopped talking after that.

Two hours had passed. No customers had come to the door, peering in, looking for Perla. She hadn't flipped the sign over, hadn't set up the register. Instead, she had taken the blanket from the shelf behind the counter and covered Rodrigo up, the faint scent of roses from the "Serenidad" spray still lingering in the threads.

She had found him that morning huddled by the front door. His face was pressed against the iron bars and when Perla bent down to look at him, she saw the greenish bruises below his eye, the purple and red swirls around his neck. *Fingers.* Perla knew. She had seen them before. Consuelo Acosta's husband used to beat her, and she would come in looking for spells to chase his temper away, stretching the collar of her blouse or jacket over her neck to hide the marks, dabbing concealer to cover the black eyes.

Rodrigo's lip was split open. When he tried to smile, it cracked, and he winced. He spit on the ground and cursed in Spanish. Rodrigo trembled so much, Perla was afraid he was in shock. She had to carry him in, tucking her shoulder under his armpit, her arm around his waist, lifting him over the threshold, his feet hovering over the floor. He was so light it made her cry.

What am I supposed to do? He looks like he was trampled by a herd of horses. He was so small; his body swam in the folds of the blanket. He needed help. He needed to see a doctor. She remembered the business card with Teresa's cell phone number tucked away in her wallet. *I could call her.* Or maybe she should take the boy to the police first. They needed to report this man, this Dwight. *He's out there. Probably looking for him. He could be watching us right now. I should call them.* But the boy would say no. To Teresa. To the police. He was an illegal. Nobody but Perla and that man Dwight knew he was here. So she sat with him, cleaning his cuts, dampening a cloth with rubbing alcohol, pressing it against his wounds.

Keep him warm. That's all Perla could think about. *Keep him warm.* She pre-

pared him a té de manzanilla and lit some candles around the botánica to soothe and relax him.

"You don't have to talk anymore," she told Rodrigo, placing the cup in his hand. "I'll sit here with you. You've told me enough."

"No," he said. "I tell you. I trust you."

The boy trembled. *Don't lose him,* she told herself again and again. *Don't lose him.* His face was swollen and blue as an overripe plum. She held his hand and squeezed back her tears.

"Did Dwight give you the burns? On the back of your hand?" She dabbed the bloody scratches on his arms with a cloth, moist and heavy with alcohol. She touched his hands, her fingers running over the scars, trying to erase them.

The boy shook his head. "I do them myself. Because I wanted to die. Catch myself on fire."

Perla's own hands trembled at the thought of the boy lighting up like a match. Of skin melting his ears shut, his eyes. She remembered Agripina. She squeezed the cloth, and alcohol dripped to the floor.

"Dwight. He changed," Rodrigo said, putting his té down. "He scared me. Smoking the drugs. Sleeping for a long time. Almost for days. After the first time, when he raped me, Dwight made me not leave. He came by more. There all the time. I can't go outside."

"Why did you stay? Why didn't you run away?"

"I know nobody here. I don't know where I am. I was afraid of leaving that place. Dwight said if I do people will know I'm a mojado. The cops, they will take me back to Ignacio. The priests, they will take me back to Ignacio. Ignacio will kill me because I'm no good to him. All used up. He's killed other boys. All week long I sit in there alone. Dwight made me close the curtains. The cucaracahas running all around. Making me afraid to sleep. I look out the window when I hear the girls outside talking and playing music. I try to learn English from them. So I can run away."

"How was it that you came here? To see me those times? To leave the note?"

"I snuck out. First time when he was gone. Other times when he was sleeping off his drug. I wanted to pray. I don't want to go to the church because what if the priests find me? So I come here because I remember the

Virgen on the wall. I look through the window, and I see the santos. For a long time I was afraid to come in. I just walk by. The first time when Dwight was crazy, I was scared. I wanted help. I trust you. You're not a priest or a police or a doctor. You look like my Abuelita Josefa."

"You disappeared. Where were you? The last time I saw you was in March. You left me that note in May." Perla got up and walked over to the register. She took the note and showed it to him. "It's now late September. What happened? I wanted to go find you. But I didn't know where you lived."

He said after he came back from leaving the note, one of the neighbors, a woman living in the duplex where the two girls sat, told Dwight she saw him coming back with books and sheets of paper tucked under his arm.

"Dwight got so mad. Hit me. Said he was going to send me back to Estrellitas. I say no. Ignacio will kill me."

So Dwight brought a friend to keep an eye on the boy.

Rodrigo didn't know the man's name. He was much older that Dwight, with thick rimmed glasses, and a bald head that was pale red and spotted with brown freckles. He wore a tank top, and so many gray hairs covered his back that it was hard to see his skin. He smoked cigarettes, one after another. He had yellow teeth and fingernails thick as a rooster's beak. The old man watched the boy during the day. He brought a sleeping bag, some clothes, and a television. There was a stuffed bunny rabbit with floppy ears that the man kept on the floor next to the television. When Rodrigo accidentally kicked it over one day, the man slapped him hard and made him pick it up.

Rodrigo went for days without being able to leave his room. The man sat in front of the television, drinking beers and smoking, watching the place like a guard dog. The only time Rodrigo was allowed to come out was to eat. Only then could he see the sunlight and remember things like day and trees and wind and grass.

"Dwight bought a lock for the door, and the old man only let me come out to use the bathroom. He never did nothing to me. When Dwight came back at night, they smoked their drugs. Dwight had sex with me. Then hit me. Spit on me. Go to the bathroom on me. The old man could hear me crying. But he never did nothing."

Perla wanted him to stop now, to sit quietly and let her clean his scrapes and cuts. She wanted to bandage the scratches and rub rose oil and aloe vera on his chapped lips, but she let him go on.

"One night," he continued, "I hear them talking. I'm lying on the floor after Dwight was finished with me. And I'm hurting so much. I'm so weak. Nothing to eat. I can't get up. I'm wanting to die because why did this happen to me? Fucking dump a body. Dwight was saying that. Fucking dump a body."

The whole botánica was warm now from the candles. *How could you?* she thought, looking at the images of Saint Michael Archangel, San Judas, Juan Soldado. *How could you let this happen here?*

"They kept talking. And I'm lying there like that. Bloody and feeling like I'm dead."

He heard Dwight's car pull away and down the street. He would be gone until the next day, Rodrigo knew. He was alone with the old man again.

"They will kill me when he comes back," he said to Perla.

It was pitch black because Dwight had taken the bulbs from the fixtures. He could taste blood on his tongue. He crawled around, staying close to the ground, close to the band of light from the old man's television coming through the crack at the bottom of the locked door. The light glowed bright green, and Rodrigo remembered the robe of the Virgen on the botánica's wall. The papers with Perla's writings. The book of saints. How much she reminded him of Abuela Josefa and Mexico and his family.

"I crawled around in the room. It's dark. And I was naked and cold. I wanted to die because there's no one for me."

He stumbled while putting his pants on. He was dazed and hit the wall with his head. The old man heard. He unlocked the door and stepped in. Rodrigo could not see his face, only his shadow filling the doorway. A hand reached out to hit him, and he fell to the floor again. The old man threw himself on top of him.

All he could do was reach out, around him, his hand falling into the light of the television, the light tinting his fingers green. The man held Rodrigo's legs down with one hand, choked him with the other.

"My jacket," Rodrigo said, crying. "I feel it in the dark. A big lump. The bag of shells and rocks you put there. I take it. Squeeze like a fist. And swing

and swing. I hear crunching, feel his hands go loose. His glasses fall off and break. I swing and swing. Over and over until he won't move. I only have time to get my boots and my clothes. And I run out into the yard. No one sees me. It's late. I run and run. Past the street into a field. I stay where it's dark. No cars. I change, and I run. I stay down by the río. Hiding during the day. All day yesterday. At night I come here. For you. Because I miss my mamá and papá. You are like my Abuelita Josefa."

Rodrigo pulled the blankets off and rose slowly. His hands shook as he reached into the jacket's pocket for the pouch. It was stained with blood. She untied the string and poured out the shells and stones. They had shattered into small pieces, spilling out onto the floor of the botánica, dusting Perla's shoes.

.   .   .

He could be making all this up. But why? That wouldn't explain the bruises and scratches. Did he do them himself? Like the burns? Teresa. I should call Teresa. She knows. Drugs? Was he doing drugs? He could be in shock. Head trauma from too many beatings. Fluids collecting around his brain. Swelling his head up like a balloon.

It was midnight now. She watched him sleep, his feet hanging over the edge of the couch, a picture of Guillermo floating above the boy's bruised body. He wanted to stay at the botánica, to sleep there on the floor. He was afraid to leave. "Dwight. Out there," he told Perla, pointing to the empty parking lot. "He'll kill me."

"No," she told him. "Not as long as you're with me. I don't live that far. Just on the other side of the field. We have to go," she said. "We can't stay here."

So they waited until dark to leave.

At home, Perla drew all the curtains and locked the doors. She ran a hot bath for the boy. While he soaked she said, "I'll find something for you to wear."

Perla had kept all of Guillermo's clothes—his slacks and shirts, the ties and silk handkerchiefs with his initials embroidered in the corners. She rummaged through piles of his things in the hall closet to find a pair of sweatpants. From one of the hangers, she took an old flannel shirt.

He said he wasn't hungry, but she forced him to eat. She made warm tor-

tillas and scrambled eggs, heated more té, valeriana, to calm him. He sat in the kitchen while Perla cleared the dishes and wiped down the counter.

"I don't know what to do, señora," he said just before he fell asleep. "Do I go back there? To my parents? Or do I stay here? Look for my brothers?"

"Don't worry," she told him. "Mañana. Mañana. Right now, try and sleep."

His eyes fluttered before shutting completely. She didn't go to her room. Instead, Perla sat in the easy chair all night. Her eyes drifted from the boy sprawled out on the couch to the front door's bronze knob, the baseball bat resting on her lap.

If you have followed us, I'm not afraid. I'm ready for you. Andale. Here I am.

She woke to sunlight filtering through the cracks in the curtains. Rodrigo was already awake. She walked into the kitchen and saw him outside, leaning against the back porch column, looking out onto the wet blades of grass. He was still in Guillermo's clothes, the sleeves of the shirt covering his hands, the sweats rolled up and kicking around his ankles. The Santa Anas stirred the palm fronds, and they waved back and forth, sweeping the sky clean.

A ghost? But I touched his hand. Saw his blood. What do I do with him? she asked the wind.

It gave no answer. The palm fronds shuddered.

●　　　●　　　●

She led the boy down the dirt path through the lot. Dust devils swirled around them, catching scraps of paper and Styrofoam cups, sending them soaring up toward the sky.

Two men sat on the hood of a car near the tattoo shop. One talked on his cell phone. The other had a silver spike poking out from his chin, and black rubber rings stretched out his earlobes. Black thorns twisted around his biceps. Wolves breathing fire, crosses, and Chinese writing covered his forearms and legs. He watched as Perla unlocked the iron gate.

"Hold up, bro," the one talking on the phone said, and he covered its mouthpiece with a finger. "Excuse me," he said to Perla. "What time do they open?"

"Around noon," she said. Perla unlocked and opened the door. When

she turned back, she saw Rodrigo standing there, motionless, staring at the two men.

He shuddered when Perla reached out to lead him in. He said, "They're here for me. They're taking me back to Dwight."

"What do you mean?"

"He has tattoos like his." He pointed.

Perla looked at them.

"They're going to kill me," he shouted.

"Wait, Shawn," the man said into his phone again and cradled it between his shoulder and chin. "What'd you say, bro?" He walked up to Rodrigo, who backed away.

"He's sick," Perla said to the man. When she pressed her hand against his chest to keep him from coming closer to the boy, the cell phone fell and hit the concrete. "He doesn't know what he's saying."

"Let it go, Beady," his friend with the tattoos said. "He's fucking high."

But Rodrigo had moved too fast. When she turned around to lead him in, she saw him running away, back across the field. Past the house. Down the street. Perla watched the red and black checks of Guillermo's shirt fading into the hazy air, the dark patch of Rodrigo's hair growing smaller and smaller.

"Do you know what you did?" she shouted to the two men. "He's sick. He needs help. You chased him away."

They ignored her and sat there until the tattoo shop opened.

She stood in front of the botánica the whole morning and only went in when customers pulled up. She stayed open late, waiting until the tattoo shop was closed before going home. That night she slept out in the living room and left the porch light on, watching the shadows of moths dance across the stucco ceiling, wishing she could will them to fly off and find him.

Saturday morning, Perla left a box of cereal, a can of juice, two slices of bread, and a banana wrapped in a plastic bag next to the mailbox. On a piece of paper she left a note telling him to come to the shop. She looked for signs near the front door of the botánica that would tell her whether he'd come back and waited there for her like he'd done before. But there was nothing.

In the afternoon she walked over to the donut shop and asked Vithu and Alice if they'd seen anyone matching Rodrigo's description.

"I come at four in the morning to make the donuts," Vithu said, stepping outside to smoke. He swept his hand across the parking lot. "No cars. Nothing. I'm sorry."

"I've only seen some homeless guys," Alice said. "Sitting out on the tables. But they were older."

On Sunday, Perla woke early. She walked down the street to San Salvador's. She looked behind trash cans and under cars. She stood at the bus stop, lingering until the number 17 pulled up. When no one got off, she peered through the tinted windows and tried to recognize his face among the shadows of the passengers.

She made it to the church ten minutes early and took a seat in one of the pews at the back. By the time the bells chimed for the eighth time, San Salvador's was full. The congregation stood as the procession of altar boys carrying crucifixes and candles made their way to the front with Father Madrid following behind them, smiling and bowing his head. Reaching the altar, Father Madrid blessed himself and proceeded with the Mass. Perla's mind drifted.

Maybe I should have brought him here. Had him talk with Father Madrid. But he's afraid of churches, of priests.

A woman in a purple jacket and thick glasses rose and walked up to the lectern. She adjusted the microphone. Her voice was shaky when she spoke. "A reading from the Book of Habakkuk," she said. Everyone sat down.

She cleared her throat and began.

> *"How long, O LORD? I cry for help*
> *but you do not listen!*
> *I cry out to you, 'Violence!'*
> *but you do not intervene."*

She looked up and scanned the crowd. A baby cried. Someone behind Perla blew his nose.

> *"Why do you let me see ruin;*
> *why must I look at misery?*

Destruction and violence are before me;
there is strife, and clamorous discord.
This is why the law is benumbed,
and judgment is never rendered:
Because the wicked circumvent the just;
this is why judgment comes forth perverted."

The woman stepped away from the lectern and returned to her seat. The choir rose and sang from the balcony above.

Though she tried to concentrate on the Mass, she thought only of the boy. Everything he'd been through. How he'd trembled and bled. The things that had been done to him. All for what? He hadn't hurt anyone. *Why did you leave? I could have taken care of you.*

"Justice comes from within us. Look around." Father Madrid's voice rang loud, booming throughout the church. The embroidered sleeves of his surplice billowed out as he stretched his arms. "Do you see ruin? Do you see misery? Do you see something that needs to be changed? Then ask yourself: Am I doing enough? We must pray, yes. But we must also act. Take responsibility. For your community. For one another. For yourself. Let us go forth and do what is within our power to make things better. Instead of asking God simply to remove our obstacles, let us ask Him to give us the strength to remove them ourselves. Instead of throwing our hands up and saying 'It's too late, I can't do a thing,' let us implore Him to give us the ability to fix it, to change it. Instead of asking Him to solve our problems, let us ask Him to give us the wisdom and clarity to arrive at our own solutions."

Perla cupped her hands and rested them on her lap, the elastic cuffs of her sweater biting into her wrists. She bowed her head and closed her eyes.

When it came time for the Communion, Perla remained seated and watched the congregation rise row by row. People squeezed past her to reach the aisle, joining the single line inching toward the altar. The heads of many of the older women were covered in black and white lace mantillas. The men wore dark blue slacks and clean pressed shirts.

There were so few left Perla recognized. She remembered how there had been a time when she'd counseled parishioners outside near the drinking fountains before Mass, or had sat with them in the pews afterward, giving them recetas and novenas she carried in her purse.

Where did you go?

There had been the Lunas. Sofía and Julio and their six children had packed up and left for Arizona because there Julio could find more work and the family could buy a new house. There was Luz Peña and her blind mother, Carmen, who fell too many times, so that Luz finally had to put her in a home. There was Mr. Slusser, the war veteran who carried his medals around in his pocket, who retired to Washington to live with his son. There were the Pérezes, who moved to Las Vegas, and the Bustamantes, who flew back to the Philippines.

Perla placed her hands on the edge of the pew in front of her. She lowered her head again and listened to the slow shuffling of feet across the thick red carpet.

Why did you leave? she repeated, over and over, to herself. *Why? Why? I could have helped. I could have helped.*

When Mass ended, Perla got up and anointed her forehead with Holy Water. She felt it drying into her skin and imagined it mixing with her blood, giving her wisdom and strength and courage. One by one the congregants filed out. Father Madrid stood out on the front steps shaking hands as they exited.

"It's good to see you, señora," he said to Perla.

"You, too, Father."

"Tell me how things are with your business."

"Good. Same, you know?" She wanted to say something. About the boy. About what she knew. What he'd told her. Instead she said, "I'm still there."

"I'm glad." He took her hand and pressed it in between his own. They were warm, his fingers smooth. She thought of Darío. When he'd first touched her years ago, his palm pressed firmly on her forehead, puffing on a cigar to summon a spirit. "Your store, it's important," Father Madrid said. "It's good for the community. Like I said during my homily." He smiled.

"Thank you."

He raised his hand and blessed her. Perla walked down the steps into the street.

She wasn't going to wait anymore. *I'm going out and finding you myself. Buffalo Street. I'll start there. Stay put. I'm coming to you.*

She pressed the crosswalk button and waited for the light to turn green.

*   *   *

He has to be here. Somewhere.

The blocks of houses and apartment buildings slowly gave way to tire re-pair shops, a taquería, the Panadería Flor de Jalisco, the Excelsior Liquor Store as she walked up Buffalo. She zipped up her jacket and secured her wallet in the front pocket of her slacks.

When she reached the freeway overpass, Perla looked up and saw pi-geons nesting on the support beams, picking at their feathers. Someone coughed behind her, and she turned toward a cluster of eucalyptus trees growing in the narrow ditch running parallel to the sidewalk. The ground sloped down at an angle, and Perla braced herself to keep from falling as she made her way down there. She stepped into a clearing of dirt pounded flat, and the tree branches formed a green canopy above. A doll's head was nailed to one of the tree trunks. Its eyes had been poked out and its mouth scored. There was a cart stuffed with rags and crushed aluminum cans, a sleeping bag, and an overturned bucket with an unlit candle on top of it. Across from her stood a man in a jacket and red pin-striped pants. He was barefoot, his feet black as boot soles.

"Fuck," he shouted at Perla. "Come for your legs?" He raised his hand. "Fuck that. Fuck your legs. Spread your legs."

The rock he held had sharp edges flecked with bronze. She crouched down, shielding her head with both arms when she saw it fly out of his hand. It hit the ground behind her, shattering a baby food jar.

"Bitch," the man yelled. "Bitch. Bitch."

She turned and ran, the branches, heavy with the scent of eucalyptus, scratching her face and hands. *Balms. I could make an ointment with these branches. Doesn't matter if they're coated with train and car exhaust. It would work. I could still smooth out his scars with my hands.*

She made her way up the incline, only turning when she'd reached the sidewalk above to see if the man had followed her. But there were only the swaying branches, a cough, more cursing, and the rush of traffic as she hur-ried back home.

At dusk, Perla walked up and down her street calling Rodrigo's name. She stood out on the curb, holding a blanket, waiting for him. A few min-

utes later, Rosa passed by. She wore a sweatshirt and shorts with running shoes.

"Is everything okay?"

"Fine," Perla said, still shaken from her encounter with the homeless man beneath the trees.

"Are you sure, señora?" Rosa took a sip from the water bottle she held.

Perla gripped the blanket. "I was helping a customer. A boy. He ran away from me."

"Why?"

"I don't know. I was trying to help him," she said. Perla spread the blanket out on the lawn and sat down.

"I'll sit with you," Rosa said. "Keep you company."

An hour passed before Perla said to Rosa, "You should go. It's getting late. Danielle. Miguel. They probably need you."

"They're at his mom's," Rosa said. "I can get the keys to the van. We could drive around and look for him if you want." She got up.

Perla said, "No, it's too dark now. Maybe tomorrow." She placed her face in her hands and sighed. "I was trying to help him. Just help him. That's all."

"Well, if you need me, I'll be home, okay?" Rosa rose and walked down the sidewalk, the sound of her footsteps mixing with the shrill drone of the crickets in the ivy across the street.

∘   ∘   ∘

On Monday, she closed up the botánica at five-thirty. She took Rancho Avenue, heading south toward Agua Mansa Road. On the way, she passed a car raised on cinder blocks, passed houses with yards cluttered with toys and empty laundry detergent drums.

It was before six when she got to Galena Court. Perla followed the road, curving around like a horseshoe. She stopped in front of a house where a statue of Saint Francis stood in the center of the yard. There was an altar near the front door, and flowers were arranged in empty veladoras drained of their wax. At the foot of the altar, metal coffee cans with holes punched into their sides held stems of aloe vera plants. She stood on the sidewalk and prayed:

Lord, make me an instrument of your peace.
Where there is hatred, let me sow love;
where there is injury, pardon;
where there is doubt, faith;
where there is despair, hope;
where there is darkness, light;
and where there is sadness, joy.

O Divine Master, grant that I may not so much seek
to be consoled as to console;
to be understood as to understand;
to be loved as to love.
For it is in giving that we receive;
it is in pardoning that we are pardoned;
and it is in dying that we are born to eternal life. Amen.

From the house, a girl walked across the yard and placed an envelope into a mailbox numbered 144. She wore house slippers with cracked soles. She reached the door again and was about to turn the knob when Perla shouted, "Excuse me?"

The girl turned around. Her eyebrows were as thin as dental floss, and blue eyeshadow dusted her lids. She looked at Perla, the edge of her hip bone, sharp as a chisel, poking through the thin fabric of her jeans.

She said nothing.

"I'm looking for someone. A boy. His name's Rodrigo," Perla told her.

"You a cop or Social Services?" She sighed, rolled her eyes. "I ain't saying nothing. Not ratting no one out. Don't want no trouble. I don't know nothing." The girl placed her hand on the door's knob and began turning it. From inside came the sound of a radio playing music.

"A boy. Named Rodrigo," Perla insisted.

The girl walked down the stone steps, past Saint Francis, and toward Perla. "Why you looking for him? He your shorty?"

"Shorty?" Perla asked, confused.

"Kid. He your kid?"

"No. He's someone I care about."

"What's he look like?"

Perla tried to remember Rodrigo's features. "Thin. Very thin. Very gentle boy."

"That don't help." The girl laughed. "Now I know for sure you're not the jura. When the jura rolls up in their shiny black-and-whites they know quick who they're scoping out. Got stacks of flyers and everything sometimes even. The jura lives here, man. Since before my husband and me moved in we heard about Galena and the crazy shit that goes down here. But what are you gonna do? Gotta live, right? Even if it's in this place. With stabbings and break-ins and shit." The girl folded her arms. Bracelets dangled from her wrists.

Then Perla remembered. *The police. The old man. The pouch.* "Break-ins," she repeated. "Like what happened to that old man? Maybe a week ago? Did you know about that?"

"Yup." The girl shook her head. "Whole block did. Cops. Ambulance. Fire trucks even though nothing was burning. They wheeled him out on a stretcher."

"Where did it happen?"

The girl led Perla back behind her house. They walked between rows and rows of damp work shirts and skirts, baby socks and jeans hanging on clotheslines, to a clearing in the middle of the yard the duplexes shared. In the center stood a birch tree, its trunk carved with initials and crooked hearts. They walked on a concrete footpath between two of the units. Screen doors banged open and shut. Silhouettes floated by behind lace curtains or in between the slits of miniblinds. She heard water running and dishes clanking. The air was thick with the smell of chorizo and chiles.

"There," the girl said, pointing to the unit across the street. She turned around and walked back toward the birch tree, disappearing behind the damp laundry.

The screen door hung off its hinges. She could see the gurney's tracks in the grass. Perla jiggled the handle and tried to push the front door open, but it didn't give. She followed the path around the house. There was a trash can full of garbage—empty soda bottles, the cardboard flap of a box of Rice Krispies, bags of potato chips, cans of soup. Footprints were pressed into the muddy ground near a purple sage bush. Steps led up to the back door. It was ajar.

Someone's here.

Perla backed away slowly. She felt the wallet inside her pocket, heavy like a stone. She remembered the crazy man the day before, the rock flying past, barely missing her face. She followed the path back around and crossed the street again.

Just before Galena Court spilled back out onto Agua Mansa Road there was a phone booth. A directory hung from a gun metal gray chain and words were scratched into the strips of paint and on the windows: "SUK," "MANSA FLATS, Y QUE?," "AQUA IZ A FINE RUCA." She reached for her wallet, opened it, and found the business card where Teresa had written her cell phone number. Perla dropped coins in the slot and dialed the number. The buttons stuck when she pressed them. There were clicks, then static, before she heard short rings. Teresa's voice said, "Hello?"

"Teresa, it's me, Perla."

"Hey. What a coincidence. I was just thinking of you today. I need to come by and get more tea." A car drove past the phone booth, loud music thumping from its speakers. Teresa asked, "What is that? Where are you?"

She hesitated. "In a phone booth. Galena Court."

"Galena Court? What are you doing around there? At this time?"

"A customer," Perla told her. "A patient. I was trying to help. But I couldn't."

"What? Who?" Teresa asked.

"Rodrigo," she said. "I couldn't." Her voice trembled, and she began to cry.

Perla recounted everything—the club, the boy being smuggled across, Dwight, the bruises, the burn marks, the duplex where he was held. "I think someone's in there. I saw a garbage can. Footprints. That man Dwight could be in there. Or Rodrigo. He could be sick. In shock or traumatized. When he saw those men by the botánica, he got so scared. He ran. I tried to get him to stay." Her hands shook. "But he left. If he's around here, I can still help."

"Okay," Teresa said. "Okay. Okay. Calm down. Let's think. Juntas. You and me. On the phone. Are you sure this boy was being honest with you? That he wasn't trying to trick you or anything? You believe him? Everything he told you?"

"Yes, I do. That's why I'm here. I'm trying to help him. I just don't know how, what to do."

"Don't move. Stay there," Teresa insisted. "Give me fifteen minutes, okay? Fifteen." There was shuffling in the background, then something slamming shut. "Stay put. Don't try and go back there. Stay there, señora. In that phone booth. I'm coming to you. I'm on my way."

Perla hung up and stood there, gripping the receiver's handle, wishing there was a way she could call the boy and tell him she was there. That she wanted to help him. That he wasn't alone. That he shouldn't be afraid.

The streetlights flickered on, one by one, as Teresa pulled up and parked near the phone booth. "You did the right thing," she said, hugging Perla. "Calling me like that."

Perla said, "I need to know what to do. In case he's in there. But you didn't have to come down here. It's dark. Dangerous."

"You were upset. I could hear it in your voice. I don't want anything happening to you." Her cell phone rang, and she reached into her pocket. "I'm sorry," she said, looking at the light-up screen. "It's Craig." She pushed a button and said, "Hey, honey." She opened her jeep's hatch and pulled out a first-aid kit. "No," she said into the phone. "Helping a friend . . . I don't know . . . I might be a while . . . I'll call you when I'm on my way . . . I love you, too." She hung up and placed the phone back in her pocket.

Teresa walked around the passenger's side of the car and reached into the glove compartment. "Pepper spray," she said, holding a small black cylinder with a bright red nozzle. "Just in case." She felt around the floor beneath the seat and gave Perla a flashlight. "Vamos."

They left the car and walked back across the street.

Perla showed her the duplex, the darkened windows, the gurney's tracks in the grass. "Here," she said, pointing to the trash can behind the house and the footprints in the mud near the sage bush. "See? Someone might be in there."

Teresa walked up the steps first and nudged the door with her right shoulder. It creaked open and, as she stepped into the kitchen, she aimed the can of pepper spray at the dark air inside. "Come on," Teresa whispered, holding out her hand to Perla. She took it, switched on the flashlight, and followed.

Perla felt as if she had inhaled a handful of thorns; the air smelled of disinfectant, bug spray, and stale tobacco. There was a stove with chrome

burners and an empty space where a refrigerator must once have been. Perla focused the flashlight on the windowsill dotted with flies, their legs curled into tiny question marks. A round table was pushed up against the far wall, and scraps of cardboard padded its four feet. The sink dripped, a halo of rust encircling the drain.

"I don't think anyone's here," Teresa said. "Watch out. Don't bump into anything."

"Okay," Perla said. She pointed with the flashlight to the pepper spray. "Have you ever used it?"

"Once. I practiced on a face Craig drew on a box."

They walked through a graveyard of dead cockroaches in the living room doorway. Thin beams from the streetlights filtered through the gaps in the blinds covering the front windows, filling the room with a sad blue haze.

"Jesus," Teresa said, letting go of Perla's hand. "This is a pit." She took a few steps forward, touching the walls. "He said they had him locked in a room?"

Perla pointed the flashlight down the hallway. "There."

"Let's have a look."

It was much darker inside the room. The mattress was pushed up against the wall, the sheets unfolded, the pillows flattened.

Teresa squeezed Perla's hand. "Don't let go," she said. "I've got you, señora. I'm right here."

Perla aimed the flashlight at the floor. Her eyes traced a pattern of red dots small as rosary beads fanning out, stretching toward the closet with its missing doors.

"Look," Teresa said. "You see that? It's blood."

Perla imagined the struggle. The old man on top of the boy. Rodrigo's feet kicking. His hand reaching out to grab the pouch.

"He said he hit the man with the shells and stones I gave him," Perla said. "That was probably where they fought." She let go of Teresa's hand.

"What's that?" Teresa asked, pointing the flashlight at something poking out from beneath the mattress. "Look. It's a journal or something."

Perla recognized the cover immediately. It was the book of saints she had lent Rodrigo. She bent down and reached for it. Teresa stood behind her, holding the flashlight steady above her head.

Pressed between images of Saint Margaret of Antioch and Saint Martha were crumpled sheets of loose paper. She saw the curves and slants of her own handwriting, the dried golden rivers of her words. *Perla Maria Portillo. Seventy-two years of age. Born here in Agua Mansa, California. I run the botánica.* When Perla reached out to touch them, to feel the hardened gel, the raised tail of an *n* in the word *Botánica* or the loop of the *o* in Guillermo's name, those letters, those words, liquefied, pulsed, and came to life again.

"Let's go," Teresa said. She placed her hand gently on Perla's shoulder and led her out. "There's nothing here."

Perla gathered the frayed and tattered papers and closed the book. She watched her shadow, long and thin like a ghost, stretch over the wall, then fade into the darkness the room caught and held.

Charity

The summer before sixth grade Travis and his mother, Ruby Dean, moved into the house at the end of my block. The people who had rented it before never bothered to plant any grass out front because they always parked their cars on what should have been the lawn. It was just a small patch of mud and weeds surrounded by a chain link fence.

On the curb, they'd left a mattress that lay there until the day the moving van pulled up and Travis and his mother got out. Our place was three houses down on the opposite side of the street. I sat on the porch, sucking on ice cubes and watching them unload boxes.

That night I rode my bike to the end of the block. On the curb, cardboard boxes were piled on top of one another where the mattress had been. There were no lights on, and it looked as if no one was home. I parked my bike next to the boxes and sat on the curb. I pulled out a candy bar that was in my pocket and ate it. After I'd finished, I tossed the wrapper on the ground.

"You just gonna leave that wrapper there, love?" I heard a voice say. I turned to see a woman standing in the middle of the dirt yard in a purple silk kimono. She crossed her arms and walked over to me. I kept my head down, staring at her terry cloth house slippers, her toes peeking out from the front.

"Lose your tongue?" she asked.

"No," I said.

"You shy?"

I shrugged my shoulders. "Sometimes."

"Sometimes?" She laughed. "What's your name, honeybun?"

"Roberto."

"I knew a Roberto once. Italian guy. You Italian?"

"No," I said. "I'm American."

"There's nobody left that's *American*."

"My parents are Mexican," I said.

"You know Spanish?"

"Sometimes."

"You're a riot, kid. I'm Ruby. Ruby Dean."

She stuck her hand out, and I reached over the top of the fence to shake it. I heard my mother's voice down the street, calling my name.

"I have to go," I said to Ruby. "It was nice meeting you." I bent down to pick up the candy wrapper, and I shoved it in my pocket.

"Pick up after yourself," she shouted as I pedaled away. "I'm not always gonna be quick to catch you."

I said, "Okay."

When I got to our driveway my mother was shaking her head.

"What?" I asked. "I wasn't even doing anything."

"I saw you. We don't know those people," she said. "So don't bother them, entiendes?"

"Yeah, I get it." I parked my bike in the garage, between the wall and our van, and I went inside.

*   *   *

There wasn't much to do that summer. My best friend, Nick, was in Mexico visiting his grandmother, so I found myself watching television for hours. The more I watched, though, the more restless I became. There was an empty field that wasn't too far from my house. I would go there almost every afternoon to ride my bike, smashing beetles with my tires, pretending I was racing in a tournament.

The day I met Travis, I was coming back from the field. He was standing in the middle of his yard on top of an overturned milk crate. He held a green hose with a bright copper nozzle and was watering the mud. When I rode by, he nodded at me.

I stopped my bike. "It's just mud," I said, pointing. "Why are you watering mud?"

"What's it to you what I water? See that?" He pointed to a tuft of grass a few feet away from where I stood. "That's grass, in case you don't know what it looks like. If I water this mud the grass'll get bigger and keep growing."

"You need fertilizer." I pointed toward my house. My father and I had spent that Saturday cutting the grass. The tracks from the mower's wheels were still visible on the lawn. "It won't grow without it."

"I bet it will, and it'll make yours look like shit," he said, trying to spray me with the hose. "Get out of here, or I'll kick your ass."

That night after dinner, I sat with my father on the porch. He was concentrating hard on a crossword puzzle. My eyes traced the evenly spaced vertical rows our mower's wheels had left in the grass. The sprinkler heads popped out from the ground and began watering the yard and my mother's plants. I looked at the hedges lining our driveway, their neat boxy shapes, the roses, and the bougainvillea vines clinging to the columns of our porch. After my father finished his crossword puzzle, he went into the kitchen and sat with my mother, who was listening to the radio.

In the garage, I took the bag of fertilizer we had opened that weekend and secured the top flap with masking tape. Draping the bag over my bike's handlebars, I pedaled toward Travis's house. An El Camino with a bumper sticker that read "My Other Car's a UFO" was parked in their driveway. I knocked on the door long enough for my knuckles to feel raw before Ruby answered. She stood in the doorway, in the same kimono and house slippers. She wasn't wearing a bra, and her left breast was showing, the nipple big and pink as a tongue. She covered herself and smoothed back her hair.

"Darling. What can I do you for?"

"I'm looking for the boy that was watering the grass, I mean, the yard here today." I pointed behind me, still looking at her breast.

"Yard?" She laughed. "Are you high, kid? It's mud. You're looking for Travis, my son. What's he done to you?"

I put the bag of fertilizer on the ground. "I wanted to give this fertilizer to him. To help him grow the lawn. I mean the mud." I pointed to the clump of grass. "That."

"You're joking, right?"

"No," I said. "I'm not."

"Well that has got to be the sweetest thing I've ever heard. Let me see if he's here." She stepped away from the door. I tried to get a better look inside, but it was too dark to see anything. Ruby called out for Travis a few more times before finally giving up.

"Guess he's taken off," she said. "Could you come back tomorrow? I got a friend here right now." I heard someone sneeze.

"Can you give him this?" I touched the bag of fertilizer.

"Sure, love. I sure will." She winked at me before closing the door.

I rode down the street just in time to see my mother coming out of our house wheeling the garbage can out to the curb.

*   *   *

My father was at work, and my mother had gone grocery shopping. The smog was so bad that my eyes were stinging. I was standing over the kitchen sink dousing them with cold water when the doorbell rang.

Travis stood on my porch in a pair of cutoff jeans, a stained tank top, and a baseball cap with the brim pulled down low. He was bony and taller than me and wore plastic sunglasses. The first thing he said when he saw me behind the screen door was, "My mom made me come over to thank you for the bag of fertilizer."

"It works good," I said.

"It's used. Don't you have a new one?"

"My dad keeps them in the toolshed, and the toolshed's locked." I opened the screen door. "Sorry," I said. I pointed to our lawn. "He says it's the best."

"What's he, some kind of gardener or what?"

"No," I said. "He sells insurance."

"I'm thirsty," Travis said. "You got anything to drink in there?"

I went to the kitchen and filled two glasses with cherry punch from the pitcher in our refrigerator. Into each glass, I dropped ice cubes, and they popped and hissed as I walked back out to the porch. We sat on the steps, our legs stretched out under the sun.

"Aren't you gonna invite me in? My mom says it's rude when people don't even ask you in."

"I'm not allowed to have people over when I'm alone."

"Why not?"

"I'm just not."

He had a scab on his elbow that he picked at. When it bled, he asked if I had a bandage.

"No," I said. "I don't." I lied.

"Shit." He got up and walked over to the hose and turned it on. He let the water run over the cut, and pale red swirls trickled down his arm. "There," he said. "That works."

•   •   •

That summer, my mother was volunteering down at the library. They held a reading series for kids each Monday, Wednesday, and Friday from ten to two. I'd go with her, roaming the tall stacks and reading all my favorite books, sitting in the overstuffed chairs, enjoying the air-conditioning while she turned the pages of a book and made funny voices to groups of kids sitting around her in a semicircle. The librarians who worked there liked to tease me a lot, asking if I had a girlfriend yet.

"I don't want to go with you next time," I told my mother one day as we drove home.

"Why?"

"Those women bug me."

"Fine," she said as we pulled up to the driveway. "But we'll ask your father, too."

My father wrote down all the emergency numbers I'd need on an index card and showed me how to turn off the main gas line in case of an earthquake. My first day alone, I sat out back, swinging on our hammock, chewing on a plastic straw. It got boring, so at about twelve-thirty I walked over to Travis's house to see how the lawn was coming along.

The same El Camino was in the driveway, and I parked my bike next to it. This time I didn't knock on the front door. I was afraid of seeing Ruby's nipple again. Instead, I walked around back, past metal trash cans filled to the top with garbage. Travis was sitting under a tree, his back to me. He held twigs in both hands and was beating them violently against the trunk of the tree, his head jerking back like he was having a convulsion.

"Hey," I said, touching his shoulder. His hand swung around, and the twig he was holding whipped me on the arm.

I pulled it back quickly and winced from the pain.

"Shit," he said. "Why the fuck are you sneaking up on me like that?" He got up and looked at my arm. "You'll be all right," he said, punching me on the shoulder.

"What were you doing?" I asked.

"What'd it look like?"

I stayed quiet.

"I was playing the drums." He tossed the twigs on the ground and threw his hands up. "The drums! My mom's friend Roy plays in a band, and he says that if I get good he'll take me on tour with him." He pointed to the El Camino. "Says he's gotten laid more times in that car than in any place in the world. He calls it the 'Pussy Prowler,' and he's gonna teach me to drive it someday."

The house had a sunporch with an aluminum door that didn't shut all the way, and we walked through it into the kitchen. There were still boxes everywhere, and it was difficult to see anything because the curtains were drawn. I made out shapes here and there—a cactus in one corner of the dining room, a sewing machine on the kitchen counter. I walked with my hands reached out, trying not to bump into anything.

There was no furniture in the living room except for two lawn chairs near the front window and a wooden console table pushed up against the opposite wall. On the console, next to a lamp with a torn shade, there was a pair of bronze baby shoes.

"Those are mine," Travis said. He walked over to a pile of pictures in between the two chairs. "This is my dad." He held a picture of a man in a crew cut and uniform. "He's in the Army."

"Where is he?" I asked.

He looked like Travis. They both had hair the color of dry weeds.

"He's in Japan," Travis said. "He's been there for two years and doesn't call because it's expensive, and he says the international operators are all assholes. He wrote us a letter four weeks ago saying he's gonna be sending for us soon."

I handed the picture back to him.

A door opened down the hall, and Ruby and a man came out of the bedroom. He was holding a guitar and led her by the hand.

"Didn't I say you should play outside when Roy's here?" she said to Travis. She winked at me. "Roberto, love. How are you, sweetpea?"

"Good," I said, looking down at my shoes.

She introduced me to Roy, who said, "Roy Campos. Howdy, kid."

Travis and I walked back to the kitchen, and he asked if I was hungry.

"Sort of," I said.

He opened the refrigerator and pulled out two packets of string cheese from a bin. Using his teeth, he opened both of them and handed one to me.

He said, "I'll show you my room."

There were no curtains, and strips of aluminum foil covered the windows. In the center of the room was the mattress the previous owners had left by the curb, a thin sheet draped over it.

He said, "This is my favorite part." He ran across the room and tumbled down onto the mattress. "I'm gonna use some sticks I found out back and tie some rope around the mattress. When I'm done we can pretend like we're wrestlers."

"Okay," I said, looking at the sagging mattress, the coils sticking out of the side.

"Are you thirsty?" he asked.

"Yeah," I said. "A little."

We walked back out to the kitchen.

Roy sat at the dining table drinking a can of beer, and Ruby was by the sink smearing butter on flour tortillas.

"¿Qué pasa?" Roy said to Travis. "Have a seat."

Travis opened a cabinet door and brought out a small plastic cup. He gave it to Roy. From a paper bag next to him, Roy pulled out another can of beer. He opened it up, filled the cup, and slid it across the table to Travis.

After he finished the cup, Travis wiped his mouth and said, "It's too warm."

"I forgot I had it in the car," Roy said. He watched Ruby, who was biting into her tortilla. Roy turned to me and said, "You look like a sharp pistol, Roberto."

"Thank you," I said, though I didn't know what he meant. The guitar was against the wall, and he picked it up and started strumming. He wore dark brown construction boots with faded red laces and a flannel shirt with the sleeves torn off.

"Do you know how to play?" Roy asked when he saw me looking at him.

"No," I said. "But my dad likes music."

Ruby took bites of her tortilla and stood over the kitchen sink, staring out the window at the tree Travis had been practicing the drums on. "Don't teach the poor kid," she said. "You don't got the know-how."

Roy just ignored her. "You must got music flowing through your blood, kid." He took the plastic cup and poured some more beer into it. "Travis, get another one."

Ruby said, "Stop ordering him around, Roy."

He waved a hand up at her and said, "Relax, will you? We're just having some fun here."

Travis returned with another cup that Roy also filled with beer.

"A toast," he said. "To Roberto."

Roy and Travis raised their cups. I slowly lifted mine and took a deep breath before swallowing it as quickly as I could.

"That's it," Roy said, slapping me on the back a few times and clapping his hands. "You like it?"

"I guess."

Travis held out his cup and said, "Gimme more."

"Sorry. Bar's closed," Roy said. "Only one drink per customer."

Ruby put the tortillas back in the refrigerator. She turned to Roy and said, "Didn't you say you were gonna help me chop down that mangy tree out back? It's crawling with bugs."

He continued strumming his guitar, ignoring her altogether.

After a while, Ruby walked over to the table and pulled out the last two cans of beer from the paper bag next to Roy.

"I'll be in my room," she said.

"Be right there," Roy said.

"Don't feel much like sharing." She walked down the hall and slammed her bedroom door shut.

* * *

I felt the thud of Roy's big hand slapping my back the whole way home. The taste of beer still coated the inside of my mouth. I even felt a little giddy and had trouble steering my bike down the street. All of this gave me a thrill. I was eleven, and I suddenly felt rebellious and dangerous, capable of trouble.

My first impulse when I got back home was to brush my teeth and gargle with mouthwash until my gums hurt. Instead, I sat on the porch and waited for my mom.

She kissed me on the forehead. I tried to breathe heavily and sighed a few times, hoping she'd catch a whiff of the beer. Instead she asked what I'd done that afternoon.

"I saw that new kid that lives on the corner," I said, sighing again.

"From that ugly house?"

I nodded.

She was more concerned about the lawn. "They need to do something with that yard. Plant flowers. It's an eyesore."

When my father came home that evening he asked if I had seen the opened bag of fertilizer.

"I gave it to the new kid," I said.

"What for?"

"Because." I felt cocky, crossed my arms. "They're going to plant grass. Everyone's always saying that yard looks crappy."

"You should have asked first, okay?"

"Yeah," I told him. "Sorry."

After a while, he said, "Is there a father?"

"He's in the Army," I said. "He's in Japan."

"What's she like?" my mother asked. "I saw her the other morning as I drove by. I waved, but she didn't see me."

I thought about Ruby's flashy smile, her winks, her smooth, pink nipple. "She's nice," I said.

"Does she work?" my mother said.

"I don't know."

"Try to find out."

My father shook his head and rolled his eyes.

·   ·   ·

That Friday morning Travis came over and said I needed to take him to Best Donuts in the Prospect Shopping Center.

"It's too far to walk," he said. "I don't have a bike."

"What do you need to go for?" I asked.

"Breakfast. I can sit on the handlebars. Come on. I'll buy you a donut. My mom gave me a shitload of money." From his pocket, he pulled out a folded ten-dollar bill.

"That's not a lot," I said.

"More than what you got."

"I got more."

"Bullshit," Travis said. "Come on. Let's go."

My parents had made me promise that I would stay close to home when they were gone. Something bad could happen, my mother said. I could get kidnapped or hurt somehow. I looked around my house. Upstairs in my room, I'd picked up my clothes and made my bed. In the living room, the TV was off because there was nothing worth seeing.

Everything around me was quiet and clean. I could feel the heat coming from outside as I stood there watching Travis from behind the screen door. He was sweating, his cheeks as red as my bike's reflectors.

"I'm not supposed to ride past the end of the block," I said.

"Are your parents here?"

"No."

"Then who's gonna tell?"

I said nothing.

"Stop being a pussy."

"Shut up."

"It's ain't that far," he said. "If you don't wanna go, at least let me borrow your bike."

"Fine, I'll take you," I said, reluctantly.

It was slow going when we started out. Travis sat on the handlebars and was heavier than I expected. It was hard to steer, and we fell off a few times and wobbled down Rancho until we eventually made it.

There were only two stores left in the Prospect Shopping Center: Best Donuts, which was owned and run by a Cambodian family whose son was in my grade; and the Botánica Oshún. There were boards up in the windows of the ninety-nine-cent store, and a sign that read:

Moved to a New Location.
Come Visit Us at 4140 Barton Rd #3F, Grand Terrace.

Except for the telephone poles along the sidewalk, there was nowhere to lock up my bike. On a table in the botánica's window stood a statue about the size of a fire hydrant of a saint I didn't recognize. Dimes were taped across his mouth and over both his eyes, and he wore a faded velvet robe with dollar bills pinned along its front, secured by small safety pins. I leaned my bike there, under the glass window.

I told Travis, "I'll wait out here." I held on to my bike.

"Quit being a pussy. Nothing'll happen to it. We won't be long."

I stood there without moving.

"Fine," he said. "Wait then."

He came out with a bag and we sat on the curb near my bike and hardly spoke as we passed a glazed bar between us like a peace pipe until it was gone. The curb began to bother us, and we got up. Travis looked at the saint in the botánica's window.

"Why's it got dimes stuck to his mouth?"

I shrugged. "To keep it quiet?"

"Jesus Christ." He slapped his forehead with the palm of his hand. "It's a statue. What do they sell in there?"

"My mother brought me here once to buy a rosary and some white candles when I made my first Holy Communion."

"Come on." Travis tugged my shirt's sleeve. "Let's go in."

There were no other customers. After we closed the front door, Travis turned to me and said, "Are you scared?"

"Why should I be?" I punched him on the arm. "I've been in scarier places than this."

"Prove it," he said.

"Shut up," I said. I shook my head just as a woman walked out from behind a curtain.

She didn't say anything, just watched us as we strolled through the store and peered into the cases. When Travis picked up a small key chain with a picture of Jesus on it from a bin sitting on a bookcase, she said, "Those are a dollar."

He put it down and walked over to me standing in front of a postcard display.

"Ask her about the dimes on the statue," he whispered.

"You," I said.

"Chickenshit."

"What's with that statue in the window?" he asked the woman.

"What do you mean what's with it?" she responded, putting her glasses on.

"Why's it got dimes taped to its mouth?"

"It's Saint Anthony of Padua. He helps when you need to find something or when you need money. Those are ofrendas."

"What?" he asked.

"Offerings," she responded. "Money."

Travis looked over at me. "He thought the dimes were to keep him quiet."

"No," she said, watching us. "He helps."

"How?" I asked her.

"You have to pray. Light a candle. Concentrate." She pointed to her temple.

Then Travis tapped me on the shoulder. "My mom needs her breakfast," he said. "We better go."

When we got back to Travis's, we found Ruby sitting at the dining table in nothing but a bra and panties. I noticed a tattoo on her left shoulder that spelled out *Rebel*. She had pulled the curtains back and the whole kitchen was bright and warm.

Travis tossed the bag of donuts on the table near Ruby. "Are you okay?" he said in a low and serious voice that I hadn't ever heard him use before.

She laughed. "No. Fuck no. I've let myself get old. Ugly," she shouted, slapping the table's top.

I backed into the corner near the cactus and tried not to look at her.

"When I was younger, I was a different girl." She reached into her purse and pulled out a pack of cigarettes. She lit one and blew the smoke up toward the ceiling. "I had charisma. That's what your daddy said. That's why he fell for me. He said I had charisma, and that I could have had any man I wanted. Look at me." She swept her arm across the room, fanning smoke. "I got so much charisma, don't I? So much I got no man. I still ain't heard from your daddy. Part of me don't even care if I do anymore. Roy's gone."

She got up and walked to the counter and tossed the cigarette in the sink.

Ruby gripped the edge of the counter, and I could see her white knuckles, the purple netting of veins under her skin. "When I told him he should stick around more, maybe bring some clothes over and spend the night once or twice, he got pissed. Said I was trying to claw my way into his life. Said I was too old for him anyways and that he had this chick on the side named Maribel, so I told him to fuckin' die. I felt so good saying that. Fuckin' die, I said. And your dick's small, anyways."

She walked past us through the sunporch and out to the back. Travis and I followed her. In the middle of the yard, the tree towered in front of the three of us. Ruby pulled out a machete from a toolbox. She took three swings before she finally hit the tree.

Travis reached into the toolbox and pulled out a pair of hedge clippers that looked just like my father's and he joined her, both of them taking swings.

Ruby turned to me. Her eyes were swollen from crying. I thought about Roy, imagined him getting drunk and making out with some other woman in the back of his El Camino, then taking off to serenade someone else. Travis looked at me, his cheeks red. He gripped the hedge clippers tightly, and his other hand was balled up in a fist.

Ruby blew a few strands of hair away from her face, then licked her lips. "You just gonna stand there like that? Or are you gonna help?"

I found a pair of scissors and started swinging with them.

                    *   *   *

He didn't have to ask me twice. That night he tapped on my bedroom window and said he needed a ride. It was past midnight, and my parents were asleep in their room. Travis loosened the fasteners that secured the window's screen by bending them with the tips of his fingers, and I jumped out.

We took my bike from the garage and rode in silence the whole way, past dark streets and darker houses, hiding behind trash cans and in the shadows of trees when a car passed by or a dog barked. The empty fertilizer bag was slung over his shoulder.

By the time we reached the Prospect Center, I was drenched in sweat from all the pedaling. From the bag, Travis pulled out a heavy rock. He stood in front of the window with the statue and all I remember seeing is the

rock flying out of his hand, flying through the near black sky, the glass shattering and the pieces falling to the ground.

He cradled the statue in his arms and climbed up on the handlebars. I held the back of his shirt to keep him from falling forward and tried to steer with one hand.

"Pedal faster," he said.

I dropped him off in front of his house, and he walked away without saying anything to me. The statue's money flapped in the breeze, and when a bill fell to the ground, Travis bent down to pick it up. Even from my bike, I could see that the dollar bills pinned to the statue were fake.

I didn't see much of Travis the rest of the summer. Every time I'd go over to ask if he could come out, Ruby would answer and say that he was resting or that she had him doing chores out back and couldn't be disturbed.

Then that fall they moved away. The only thing they left behind was the statue. They'd placed it out on the curb, leaning it against the mailbox. The fake dollar bills were gone but the safety pins remained. I decided I was going to return it to the botánica. From my driveway, I watched as a man in a truck pulled up to their house. He took the statue and placed it upright on the truck's bed, using pieces of twine to keep it from falling out. When he pulled away, I got on my bike and followed him, pedaling as fast as I could. Waving my hand in the air, I tried to get the driver's attention. I whistled a few times but gave up when I heard loud music coming from the cab. I rounded the corner just in time to see the statue toppling over and banging against the side of the bed before tumbling out onto the street and breaking apart. The driver didn't notice. He just kept going. I stopped and got off my bike. One by one, I picked up the pieces, forming a neat pile of white stones on a patch of green grass.

Feast of
Saint Gregory the Wonder Worker

Bishop and Confessor

Patron of desperate situations and forgotten

and impossible causes.

Invoked against earthquakes and floods.

It was early morning. Perla dressed and combed her hair in front of the bathroom sink. On the third shelf of the medicine cabinet were her pills, Teresa's name on each bottle in small black letters along the bottom half of the labels. She hadn't talked with her since last month, after they'd come back from Galena Court.

"It's not your fault," Teresa had told her. "You reached out, tried to help." They had stood in the kitchen drinking lemon tea sweetened with piloncillo. She had tried to calm Perla down, to keep her from blaming herself for what happened to Rodrigo.

Teresa's lucky, Perla thought as she took her pills. *She has X-rays and blood tests. All that expensive equipment. Nurses who keep files and call patients. I have none of that.* She had things of earth and sky. Things born of root and bone and flesh. She had sprays and amulets, saints and gods with tempers and needs. She had teas and colored veladoras and remedios scrawled on tattered index cards. *He needed something else. And I didn't have a candle for it.*

      ·   ·   ·

Her first customer was a thin girl wearing a tight turtleneck sweater. Her pants hugged her hips, inching down low enough for her thong panties to show. In the strip of skin just above her waist was the tattooed image of a winged unicorn. The girl's hair was dyed bright red with stripes of purple and green, and she smelled of cloves. A pink bear squeezing a heart covered one side of her purse.

"Do you sell anything with fairies?" the girl asked.

"Glass figurines." Perla led her to a shelf near the window.

The girl pointed to a pixie with flowers in her hair sitting on a rock. "Could I see that one?"

Perla took it from the shelf and set it on the counter for the girl to examine.

"I love fairies," she said, looking at it. "How much is it?"

"This one is ten dollars."

"Tight," she said. "I'm gonna be next door for a while. After I'll come by to get it."

She left just as Alfonso's truck pulled up outside. Perla watched as he climbed out and crossed the parking lot. He looked taller than she remembered, and he had grown a mustache and lost some weight.

"¿Qué tal?" he said, stepping behind the counter to hug her. "It's so good to see you."

"You, too." Perla smiled at him and patted his hand. "I've missed having you around. It's lonely here without you." She led him to the chairs near the door.

"I can't stay long," he said. "I wanted to stop in and see how things were in the old place. It looks different to me in here. Smaller."

"It's still the same. But next door's changed."

"Tatuajes, eh? They do tatuajes?" He took his baseball cap off. "Are they nice?"

"They're okay. The owner, he says hi sometimes. They can be loud, though." She pointed to the television. "The needles they use. I hear them buzzing all day. Make these wavy white lines on the TV when it's on." Perla pointed to a statue resting on top of the set. "But I have Santa Clara there for help."

He rose and walked over to the window where the San Antonio statue used to be. Perla had left the space empty since the break-in, afraid the same thing would happen if she put something there.

"And San Antonio?" he asked

"I was robbed," she said. "They busted the window. Took him."

He shook his head, whistling through half-closed lips.

She watched his eyes sweep over the whole of the botánica, passing over the cracked and chipped paint on the ceiling, bubbling in some spots from too much moisture, the mismatched glass cases, the outdated cash register, the overstocked shelves.

He whistled again, then sat back down next to her.

"How are things over in your new place? What's it like?" Perla leaned in, took his hand, and held it.

"It's good," he said. "Really good. Business is better. The owners of the plaza are nice. They have security guards who sit up in a little tower in the middle of the parking lot. At night, they patrol. It's real safe. Real clean. We're happy there."

"I'm glad," she said. "I miss you, but I'm glad the business is better."

"If I would have stayed here, we would have gone under. It was a hard decision, but we had to go." Alfonso got up and said, "Speaking of which, I have to run."

"Stay a little longer," Perla pleaded.

"I can't. I'm on my way to Riverside." He looked at his watch. "I have an appointment." He put his baseball cap on. "I'll stop in again soon, okay? When I'm not in a hurry. In the meantime, if you need something, call us. You have our house number. Here, let me give you the store number." He reached for a scrap of paper and wrote it down. Perla tucked it in her pocket.

She put her arms around him and kissed his forehead. "Andale," she said. "Go. I'll see you soon then."

"Yes," he said. "I'll be back. When I have more time."

Alfonso walked out the door to his truck.

She needed some fresh air. The botánica was empty. Perla locked up and walked toward Best Donuts. She passed by the tattoo shop. Beaded curtains covered the windows. Magazines were stacked on top of a coffee table across from a leopard-print couch with red pillows. The girl who had been in earlier in the morning sat on a chair. Her pant leg was rolled up, and a man with fuzzy sideburns sat beside her on a stool with wheels. He wore latex gloves and was passing an electric needle over a patch of skin on her calf. When the man looked up from the girl's leg and saw Perla standing there, she quickly stepped away and continued walking toward the donut shop.

She wasn't hungry and didn't want to go inside. Instead she stood in the doorway and watched Alice take the empty pastry racks and stack them on top of one another. Perla went over to the newspaper vending machines a few feet away. Her eyes fell on an article printed on the front page of the *Agua Mansa Courier*:

Two San Bernardino County police officers discovered a badly burned body along the banks of the Santa Ana River near the Pepper

Avenue Bridge yesterday morning. The unidentified body was that of a young male, slightly built, and approximately 5′4″ in height. Anyone with information as to the victim's identity is asked to call the San Bernardino County Sheriff's Department.

*   *   *

The last time she'd opened the closet was when Rodrigo had spent the night. His clothes—stained jeans, a blue sweater, and his jacket—were in a plastic bag next to Guillermo's boots, tan and stained with oil and paint. She took the boots, went out into the living room, and sat on the couch.

Despite wearing two pairs of socks, they still fit too loose. She pulled the laces tight, feeling them squeeze the circulation around her ankles, and knotted them. The boots were heavy with steel-toed tips, and when she stood and tried to lift a foot up, her muscles strained. She went out to the garage and found the backpack stuffed into a storage bin. Perla grabbed a pair of sneakers and socks and went into the kitchen for a white candle and a white cloth.

Along the streetlights lining Rancho Boulevard, the city had strung red-, white-, and blue-striped banners tied to the posts with gold cords. On each was written: AGUA MANSA SUPPORTS ITS BRAVE TROOPS. GOD BLESS AMERICA. The banners flapped violently in the chilled morning wind, and their shadows bent and whipped across the concrete like long black lassos as Perla made her way toward the río.

The sun peeked just above the hills near the arroyo. The sky was purple, and the clouds shone bright yellow. Utility trucks and buses rumbled across the bridge, doing sixty down La Cadena toward Highgrove. She looked at the tall columns. Thick concrete blocks anchored them to the sandy river bottom. Paper bags and old tires were caught in the weeds along the banks.

Like where they found you.

She secured the backpack to her shoulder and followed a trail down the embankment. In the distance, other trails disappeared between weeds and bushes. Some led to the concrete blocks underneath the bridge. Others melted into the water. Still others looped back around into themselves. Reeds bent over the widest section of the river, sprouting up like small is-lands. She set the bag on the ground, then reached inside for an empty may-

onnaise jar. The color of Guillermo's boots changed from tan to dark brown when she stepped into the water. It rose just above her ankles, soaking the insides of the boots, her socks, her toes, as she went farther out, past the long green shoots hugging the shore. Where the water was the deepest, the clearest, Perla crouched down and jabbed at the sediment with her finger, and plumes of brown soil rose up. She scooped up some water in the jar and screwed the lid back on.

She turned back now, and walked up the embankment, water sloshing in the boots. She leaned against the rocks at the edge of the rise and, from the backpack, took out the dry sneakers and socks she had brought and changed into them. She wrapped the wet boots and socks in a plastic bag and placed them in the backpack, then zipped it up.

She heard the slow groan of tractors and looked across the river, saw them churning land and felt the ground quiver as the cranes scooped out mounds of dirt to level out the soil. The roofs of the two-story houses pointed up at the sky like arrows. They rose past the brick wall that separated the perimeter of the new development from the path of the arroyo. Perla imagined what it must have looked like hundreds of years ago: the river wide and deep, dark blue and teeming with fish, tribes of hunters living in round huts woven from straw and grass, animals grazing in the fields where houses would soon be.

The sun's white light bounced off the water. Beneath the bridge, the river was little more than a few scattered puddles. It didn't move. It settled around the tall grasses and old crates tossed from the side of the road, and she pictured it continuing to the ocean, gathering force as other tributaries merged with it, widening it, the water swift and strong, carving and smoothing out the sides of hills and mountains.

* * *

A school bus stopped near the Galena Court street sign. Children climbed up the steps, one by one, when the double doors swung opened. The driver wore a sweater draped over her shoulders, and music played from a radio near the steering wheel. The bus pulled away, the heads of the children bouncing up and down in their seats.

Sale circulars and flyers were taped to the screen door's handle. She

made her way around the back. Laundry hung on the clotheslines—sheets with faded images of bears and butterflies, a waitress uniform, towels, and bibs.

From the backpack, she took the white cloth and draped it on the steps leading to the back door. In the center, she placed the jar of river water next to the white candle that she lit. She followed the concrete walkway around the house, sprinkling Holy Water from the vials she'd filled after Mass and reciting the Twenty-third Psalm. Next to the purple sage bush by the back steps, she cleared a spot by brushing away some dried leaves and pulling up a bundle of weeds. She flattened the soil with her knuckles. With her finger she drew a small circle. In the center she placed the stone head of Elegguá.

The knob was missing from the door, and splinters poked her wrist when she reached out to touch the hole in the wood. She could see into the kitchen. Perla looked down at her altar. The río water had settled now. She stared at the top of Elegguá's head, took a deep breath, then pushed the door open and went in.

The kitchen table was gone; only the scraps of cardboard remained, kicked into a corner behind the back door. The dead cockroaches had been swept away. The floor in the living room was stained, and broken shards of glass crunched under her feet. In the center of the room was a bike with a missing wheel. There were plastic soda bottles, sleeping bags, and a green kerosene lantern on top of a plywood stand. By the door was a trash bag stuffed with garbage, brown liquid seeping out of one side onto the floor. Graffiti covered the walls. Someone had written: TURK, WHERE ARE YOU GOING? THIS IS HOME.

The air smelled of garbage and cigarettes. She continued down the hall and stepped into the bathroom. The tiles by the toilet were cracked and broken. There were yellow spots of urine in the bathtub, soiled baby diapers, and syringes in a trash can.

The mattress was still in the bedroom, but it was stripped of the sheets and pillowcases. She avoided stepping on the spot stained with blood, walking around it to the door. In a corner of the closet beside a paper bag stuffed with fast food wrappers she saw a pile of clothes: underwear; a shirt with a grinning orange cat; a pair of jeans with daisies sewn into the knees. The sleeves were buried beneath a black trench coat with metal clasp buttons. The flannel material was still soft, the colors still bright and

deep. She recognized the pattern—black and red checks. They were the sleeves of Guillermo's shirt, the one she had given Rodrigo to wear the day he vanished.

Perla's hands shook as she took the sleeves and placed them inside the backpack.

Outside, the concrete path was dry, the drops of Holy Water long since evaporated. The water inside the jar had settled, and the white candle burned low and warm in the glass votive. Eleggúa watched everything from the bushes with his cowrie shell eyes. She didn't know what to think anymore—whether to stay or go, whether to call the police office in San Bernardino or not. She knelt beside the altar and cried.

        •   •   •

Before opening on Saturday, Perla walked to Wyatt Elementary. She sat down on the bleachers in the park next to the school. The playground was empty. In the distance, the wind pushed the swings, and she imagined phantom children sitting on the seats, kicking their legs, pumping themselves higher and higher.

When you were alive, viejo, I came here every afternoon and watched the kids running around on the asphalt, chasing big red balls and crows that flew down from the sky. Sometimes I brought my lunch and sat from morning until their last recess. From these benches, I could never see their faces, so I would pick one out from the crowd and say to myself, "That one there. That's ours." I'd imagine myself standing over by the gate with all the other parents. Waiting there. For our baby.

Perla got up and walked over, pressing her hands against the fence separating the park from the school. She knew he was gone now. She could feel it. She ached, remembering his bruises, the way his face looked, swollen and blue from the beatings. She saw the teeth marks on his back and the cigarette burns on his hands.

That wasn't him. He's fine. He's still alive. He found his brother. She squeezed her eyes shut tight and gripped the metal fence and concentrated. *His brother will take care of him now. He'll be fine. He'll go to school. Learn things. Grow up and be successful. His parents will be proud.*

Perla breathed in deep and exhaled. She wished that life for him. She wished it again and again.

She moved away from the fence and sat back down. She looked out

across the asphalt playground stretching before her, flat and smooth, like a wide road without lanes.

There were no customers waiting when she got back to the botánica. She looked at the chipped corners of the display case, the nicks and scratches on the wooden bookcases, the silver strips of duct tape patching up a hole in the wall, and the clunky rotary phone sitting on a stack of phone books, some dating back to when the area code was still 714.

She reached for the book of saints she had taken that night at the duplex with Teresa. Rubber bands were stretched over the cover to keep the sheets of paper from falling out. She touched it and began removing the rubber bands but stopped herself.

A snow globe sat at the very edge of the main glass counter across from her. Perla had bought it from a deaf girl who handed her a card asking for a donation. Inside, there was a small blue lake shaped like a kidney bean with miniature ducks swimming on its surface. White and blue swirls of powder swished about—covering the tops of the fake plastic trees and people by the lake, the cars, the mountain peaks in the background—when she turned it upside down. They were lucky to be in there, she told herself. In that perfect world, where people breathed water instead of air, where nothing ever changed and you could only go so far, where the only interruption was the occasional shake right before a downpour of glitter.

Braceras

Our house is crowded with naked bodies. Some lean against the walls. The ones that don't have legs, the ones that are just torsos with heads, lie on top of the dining table near my mom's sewing machine. Bare arms are scattered around my dad's favorite recliner; I imagine women trapped beneath the floor trying to claw their way out.

My mom started sewing about a year ago to earn some extra cash and to busy herself. She said she was at that age when women need things to do, things to keep their hands and minds busy and going once their children are grown. She sews up tears in nurse's uniforms and cheerleading outfits, alters skirts, and lets out waistbands. Her clientele consists mainly of the neighbors on our block and, every now and again, the stray person off the street who happens to come across the flyers taped around town.

This morning, I find her working on Norma Sánchez's quinceañera dress. She takes a spool of thread, unwinds a piece, and breaks it off with her teeth. She's beautiful even in the dull morning light. Her hair's pinned up, and curls fall down and cradle the backs of her ears. She wears her nice charcoal pants and a lavender blouse with a pattern of orchids along the collar. She's all done up, waiting. My dad's blowing into town.

He's gone all the time. We go months without seeing or hearing from him. When he comes home, he sticks around for a few days, sits in his recliner, and watches soccer on TV. He takes my mom out to a restaurant, then they come home, play their oldies, and dance around the house in their

slippers, sipping vodka tonics and smoking cigarettes, the air in the kitchen looking like El Yanquee nightclub, heavy with love.

He takes off in the middle of the night without saying goodbye. He calls us from the road the next day. "I'm delivering to Sacramento. Then it's on to Seattle. I'll send some cash in the mail," he says. We'll get a money order from him, more than enough to last until he blows back in again.

He's always moving. That's the way it's been with that man, my mom says. Pata de perro, she calls him. Vago. Ever since we started going out, he's been like this, she says. I knew it when I married him.

I know some things about him, too, I want to say.

It gets me mad, him not being around like he should. There are times I want to tell my mom to just kick him to the curb. To move on and stop depending on him. He's never around. When he is, he acts real big and bad, trying to lay down the law. Calling shots. Lecturing me about the way I dress or about doing something with my life like my kid brother who's in the Marines.

"What are you gonna do? Paint for the rest of your life? Be some hippie starving artist?" he tells me when I'm out in the garage assembling my supplies.

"So now you're my guidance counselor? Why don't you try being around first instead of away doing who knows what?"

He shoots me a look and gets real close to me, his face flushed. "Watch that mouth, desgraciada. Don't forget who pays for all this. That makes me the man of the house."

"I know what you are," I say, putting my paintbrushes down. "I got your number," I say. "I don't go for your good guy act. They all do. But I don't. No, sir."

*   *   *

Everyone in Agua Mansa knows my dad, Enrique Medina. Enrique the big-rig driver. Enrique who parks the rig in the empty lot at the end of our block when he's home. He's the nicest man. A real sweet guy you want on your side. You need something, Enrique can get it for you. He's solid. A good citizen. Honest. He'll never shade you. Last Friday of every month is when Enrique rolls back into town, people say. Go to the Lickety Split. The booth in

the back by the jukebox. You'll find him there. Playing cards and knocking back some cold pistos. Telling stories about his life on the road. Go up to him, tell him you need something—a good mechanic, a coyote to smuggle a cousin or paisano over, a few bills until the check comes. He's hooked up. A straight-up Santa Claus. Enrique Medina's everywhere. He's real connected, they say. He should run for mayor. Real suave with his fancy watches and rings, his silk shirts and bolo ties, and those cowboy boots with shiny silver tips.

He's a real together guy, they say. Takes great care of that family of his. His wife only works because she wants to. She doesn't need to. His son's a Marine. But the daughter. She's a problem. Was in a few fights when she was in high school and got suspended. Just paints murals around town. Riding around on that chopper of hers. A studded leather jacket and combat boots like some thug. She's been a handful for Don Enrique. Poor man. He works so hard to give the family everything and she goes and acts up like that. How could she? He's such a sweet papá. It must break his heart sometimes.

Growing up, I used to believe all the talk about my dad. My brother and I always had everything we needed. Not like our friends whose parents struggled to pay their bills. We never had to worry. It was a fun childhood. Stacks of Christmas presents wrapped up all sweet and nice. Birthday parties with cakes and piñatas spinning from the patio beams. Whenever he came home from one of his long hauls, there was always a present for me beside him in the rig's cab. Me climbing those chrome steps. Hot engine air blasting up my legs. My dad smiling, behind the wheel. Blowing the horn and my brother and I would cheer and clap our hands. It was all real perfect.

This one time my mom got sick. She had to be in the hospital for a week. Some stomach infection. I was four, and Raúl had just turned two. We were still too young to be in school, and there was no one around to take care of us. One morning, he woke us up early. He changed Raúl's Pampers and left him in his pajamas. He made me get dressed and then stood behind me near the kitchen sink. He sprayed my hair with water the way my mom would and combed it, brushing so hard he tugged back the corners of my eyes. But by the time we were walking out the door, the ponytail had started to unravel, and my hair poofed out on one side.

We took a drive in his Nova and ended up in Rialto, in front of this faded

ocher house. The backyard was a dirt lot, and there was an old trailer parked under a lemon tree.

My dad had a key. He opened the door, and we walked in.

Stuffed animals and dolls were arranged on the love seat against the far wall. On the TV was a picture of a boy a year or two older than me. He was dressed in a white shirt and a navy tie. Stuck to one side of the frame was a red ribbon. Second Prize, it read, Jefferson Elementary, First Grade Spelling Bee.

My dad pushed some of the stuffed animals aside and told me to sit down. "Watch tu brother," he said as Raúl tried to crawl under the coffee table. "I'll be back."

He walked down the hall. A few minutes later, my dad came out with this woman who was dressed in a pair of tight jeans with a label that read *Kit Kats* sewn onto the back pocket. Her auburn hair was swept up in a bun, all neat with bobby pins and clips. She was younger than my mom. She bent down and took my hand.

"¿Eres Lluvia?" she said.

I nodded.

"¿Y qué pasó aquí?" She touched my ponytail and the side of my head.

My father laughed. "I tried it."

"Hmm. We'll fix it." She winked at me and smiled.

After my father left, she picked Raúl up, and we walked down the hall. We passed the room that must have belonged to the boy. There was a blanket with a race car on it draped over the bed and a radio and a stack of books on the floor. The woman led us to a room at the end of the hallway. She sat my brother on her bed. Near the door was a small vanity. There were tubes of lipstick in gold and silver cases. Bottles of perfume and jars of powders and creams sat on top of a glass tray. I saw tweezers and nail files and a bag of cotton balls.

When my brother fell asleep, she took some pillows and arranged them around his body. "So he won't roll over and fall off," she whispered.

She led me to the bathroom and undid my ponytail. She took a wooden stool and placed it in front of her.

"Anda," she said, gently nudging me.

I stepped on it, the edge of the sink coming just below my chin. She

combed my hair back, and I watched her face and mine framed by the mirror's thin silver border. The shower curtain behind her had a pattern of flamingos frozen in flight. She gathered and swept up loose strands of my hair the way my mother did every morning.

On the day my mom was to be released, my father brought along Raúl's stroller. He gave the woman some money and kissed my brother and me goodbye before leaving. After he woke from his nap, the woman placed Raúl in the stroller, and we walked to a McDonald's a few blocks away. She bought us Happy Meals and sat at a booth inside the restaurant while we jumped around the Playland with our shoes off. She watched us through the window the whole time—her elbow resting on the table, her chin in the palm of her hand. She smiled and blew kisses at us. Raúl was wearing shorts. When he fell on the ground and hurt his knee and cried, she ran out to him. She poured her cup of soda out on the ground. She took some of the ice cubes and wrapped them in a napkin. She placed them over his scrape and tried to calm him down.

She picked Raúl up, showing him a picture of Ronald McDonald and Grimace painted on one side of the slide. "Mira. Mira a los payasos," she said in a silly voice. She took Raúl's hand and made him wave at them. He laughed.

On our way home, we stopped off at the grocery store. My brother was out of apple juice, so we got him a carton and a box of animal crackers. When she asked what I wanted, I pointed to a display of construction paper, colored pencils, and rulers near the registers.

Back at her house, I sat on the floor and spread my papers out. I drew a picture for her of the Playland—the jungle gym, the ball pit, and a slide spiraling up to the sky where I'd sketched billowy clouds and a sun with a smiling face. I showed the three of us next to the slide holding hands.

I was sleeping when my father came back. I got up from the couch and walked into the kitchen. She was leaning up against the stove. My father had one arm around her waist. His other hand was shoved inside her blouse, moving around under the tight black fabric. He was kissing her neck. Her eyes were open, and she was looking at the refrigerator door. She'd taped the drawing I'd given her there, right next to a school lunch menu printed on fluorescent fuchsia paper.

Before we left, she hugged us tight and kissed our cheeks. She made sure

to wipe away her lipstick marks and smoothed back my hair, then buttoned my brother's jacket.

"Be good to your mamá," she said. "She'll still be weak."

On the car ride from the hospital, my mom whispered, her voice small and scratchy, that she was glad to be going home. She coughed and spit into a paper cup the nurse had given her. I reached over the seat and put my hand on her shoulder. She took it and with her other hand flipped the sun visor down and adjusted the mirror so that she could see me. She tilted her head to one side.

"I missed you," she said.

She spent the next few days in her robe and walked around the house in those booties they give you at the hospital, the ones with the rubber padding on the soles.

When she was feeling better, she combed my hair in the bathroom. I couldn't bring myself to look at her reflection. At least not right away.

*   *   *

A natural, my art teacher Miss López had called me when she saw the pencil sketch of a poodle I drew when I was a freshman. A natural artist.

"You gotta nurture this power," Miss López told me.

That's what she called it: power.

"You know the Clínica Mujer?" she asked me a few weeks before graduation. We were behind the art building soaking paintbrushes in laundry detergent buckets full of cold water.

"On Alta Vista?"

"Yeah."

"What of it?"

"Well, they asked me to paint this mural on the side of their building. Why don't you help me? I'll pay you."

"I've never painted a mural before."

"Relax. It's easy," she said. "You ever painted a room in your house before?"

"Once," I said.

"It's the same thing. Except you're doing it outdoors and doing it on a scaffold using more than one color of paint."

"Fine," I said. "I could use some extra cash."

The mural was of a group of women holding a banner reading "Al Futuro." To the Future. We used vibrant colors, greens and yellows and reds. We put a rainbow in the sky and hot air balloons and doves perched on the branches of citrus trees. We included all different types of women—Latina, black, white, Asian. We showed their faces strong, their eyes looking straight ahead. They're holding hands, all of them united.

Miss López was the one who suggested I start up the mural thing around here. After we finished up at the Clínica Mujer, she turned to me and said, "You're good at this. Why don't you keep at it? You could paint murals for restaurants and shops. It's great advertising for them."

"Alone?"

"Yeah. Alone. You can use my supplies to get started."

I inherited drums of exterior acrylic paints, tackle boxes full of paintbrushes with wide fat angles and thin tips, drop cloths, and industrial-sized cans of turpentine. Her scaffold was made out of two A-frame ladders and two thick sheets of plywood.

"It's kind of a pain in the ass," she said, showing me how to set it up, how to adjust the ends of the pieces of plywood on each rung of the ladders. "It's not very wide. But it's easy to transport because it's collapsible."

I got my neighbor Frankie D to help me move everything from Miss López's garage to mine.

"What you setting out to do, girl?" Frankie said, laughing. "Opening a paint supply shop?"

"I'm gonna dress this town up," I said.

"With used cans of paint?"

"No, stupid. With murals."

I start first by looking at the space. I try to get a feel of the rhythm around it, try to sense the flow of energy to figure out what colors I should use, what shades of green or red or brown. I touch the walls with my palms, become familiar with the bumps and grooves, with the cracks and chips.

None of that seems to matter, though. Because the trend around Agua Mansa, especially with the veterano cholo types, is low-riders and eagles and Aztec princes and princesses decked out in feathered headdresses and skimpy loincloths. Like right now, the piece I'm doing for Lucky's Quick

Mart is an eagle in flight with American and Mexican flags in the background, the word UNITY written across the bottom. I've done so many like this that it's automatic for me. But Miss López told me to try not to resist. Muralists, she says, are artists of the people. Their work is public art, art that needs to reflect the people, their hopes and desires.

I stop and look at my watch. It's later than I thought. I'm glad because I can't wait to get home today. My dad left early this morning, and I don't have to worry about dealing with his attitude.

When he drove off, my mom cried again, of course.

"He forget that?" I asked, pointing at a shirt of his she held.

She nodded. "And you know me. I always get like this when he leaves."

"Let it go. He'll be fine."

"I know. It's just, you hear these stories. About accidents on the road. I always think, 'What if next time he doesn't come back?' Sometimes at night I lie in bed thinking of him. Out there. All alone."

He's not alone, I wanted to tell her. He's probably got a lady in every city from here to Seattle. I probably got a grip of half brothers and sisters. I thought about the woman in Rialto years ago. The picture of that boy resting on top of the TV.

Instead I stayed quiet. I let her keep seeing what she wants to. Just like Raúl. Every time I try and get him to talk to me about Dad, he changes the subject or makes up an excuse about having to go.

Let them, I think to myself. Let them see what they want.

The eagle's giant wings are spread out across the side of the store, and they look so real, like they could carry me away across that painted sky, far bluer than the hazy one above me now. Drums of paint crowd the top of the scaffold, and I move them to one side and step back to survey my work. Gathered in the parking lot is a flock of seagulls. They look different from the ones I remember seeing at the beach the last time I was there. These are dingy, their feathers messy and ruffled. They're awkward and clumsy, picking over piles of trash, out of place in the middle of the asphalt.

From below the scaffold, a voice says, "Hey." An old woman stands there, holding two plastic shopping bags filled with groceries. Thick-rimmed sunglasses cover her eyes, and I can see my face in their lenses. "How much do you charge?"

"Depends," I say.

"I want a mural on my building. He says your prices are good. How much?"

"Depends on what you want. On the detail. On any of the supplies I may need."

"Okay," she says.

"What are you looking for?"

"A Virgen. The Virgen of Guadalupe."

"Where?"

"Botánica Oshún in the Prospect Center." She pauses. "Do you know how there's that one side that faces the empty field?" She points across the parking lot in the direction of the gulls.

"What of it?"

"People are dumping sofas and broken chairs, leaning them on the wall and taking off. It's getting full of graffiti and cuss words."

"I've got about two more days here. I can come by later this week to check it out."

"Good," she says. "I'll be expecting you."

      *   *   *

I stand in the bathroom washing smeared paint from my arms. In the medicine cabinet, there's a shelf with his shaving creams and gels, his razor blade with stubble still caught in the blade. I want to take all that and chuck it out the window.

After I'm done eating, the phone rings, and my mom grabs it. She says something before hanging up. She stands there with her head cocked at an angle, and it makes me remember the car ride from the hospital.

"Who was it? Telemarketer?" I ask, washing my plate in the sink.

"No," she says. "It's just this voice. A woman."

"Wrong number." I put my plate on the rack to dry. "Why are you spacing?"

"She was asking for your father."

I stay quiet.

"It's nothing," she says. "Just nobody."

She walks over to the sewing machine and goes at it. She doesn't let up all night. I hear the whirring from my room. Stopping. Starting. Stopping. Starting. And it sounds painful and angry. I turn my stereo on and flip

through some CDs stacked on the floor—Rammstein, Wumpscut, Skinny Puppy. I put one in and blast it, taking in the fast industrial beats. Like buzz-saws and jackhammers battling it out with drums and heavy guitar riffs. I stomp around my room until I'm sweating and out of breath, singing along to KMFDM's "Juke-Joint Jezebel."

*   *   *

Mom's still asleep when I hop on my Yamaha and head off to the botánica. When I get there, the old woman's standing behind the counter opening up a white jar.

The first thing she says to me is, "Keep it simple."

"Duh," I whisper.

"I want a sweet Virgen." She fills small plastic Ziploc bags full of green powder. "Something special," she tells me.

None of the pictures I had of the Virgin were very detailed, and it was hard getting a clear shot of her face. I was going through a shoe box of old photos and came across this one of my mom sitting on a chair in a house I didn't recognize. It must have been at a cousin's party, I guessed. I could see balloons in the background and a boy wearing a party hat. In the picture, my mom looks to one side, her mouth open. She's laughing. Her hands are clasped over her knee. She's real young. I can tell this was way before my father.

That's the face I use for the Virgin. The image itself is the standard one, like any you'll find on a thousand other walls. La Virgen's in the center of a circle of gold and yellow rays. She wears a deep crimson dress and, over that, an emerald cape with gold trim and a pattern of gold stars that covers her head and body. Her hands are cupped under her chin in prayer. Her face looks away to the side, her eyes downcast. An angel holds the crescent moon on which she stands.

"This is what I got," I say.

I unfold the sketch and hand it over. She walks over to the window where the light is better. I stroll around the store, looking into the glass cases where red and aqua stones are displayed next to necklaces of feather and yarn. I see jade pendants and ankhs and crucifixes. I flip through the novenas and prayer cards of Saint Christopher, Saint Martín de Porres, and

Saint Ignatius, arranged in a clear tray with individual slots. A small figurine of an angel wielding a sword stands guard on the other side of the register. Cut pieces of glass encircle the statue's base, and the sunlight bouncing off them casts rainbows across the ceiling.

"It's nice," the old woman says, handing it back over to me. "Very nice."

"When should I start?"

"You always dress like that when you work?" She reaches over the counter, tugs at the straps of my overalls, and glances at my boots.

"Yeah. Do you always dress *like that*?" I point.

"Yes. I'm comfortable. Are you comfortable?"

"I'm fine," I say. "I'm always fine."

"Then you should start now before all the good light is gone." She points at the door. "I'll pay you up front tomorrow. Cash." She turns away from me and continues filling her plastic bags. "Anything else you need, just let me know."

     ⬚   ⬚   ⬚

For a small fee, Frankie D helps me haul all my supplies to the sites where I do my murals.

"Why'd ya get that thing?" he says, pointing to my Yamaha. "If you knew you were gonna be dragging all this shit, you shoulda just bought a pickup. Hell, a rig like your old man's."

"I like to feel free," I say. "I like the wind in my face."

He helps me set up the ladders. When I tell him it's fine, that I can handle it, he says, "I don't mind. Got nowhere to go. Precious took the baby to the park."

When we're done, Frankie picks up his tools and pulls out of the parking lot toward home.

I don't see much of the old lady the first few days on the job. She seems to spend a good part of the day in the store while I'm working. She leaves the back door open for me in case I need to go to the bathroom. I cut through there, past the shelves stocked with rolls of paper towels and jugs of glass cleaner. A small Shiva statue sits on the second shelf. It's in between bottles of hand soap and a box of trash bags, and every time I walk by, I touch its forehead with my thumb.

Today she comes out of the store and hands me a glass of lemonade and

watches as I work on the rays around the Virgin's shoulders. It's morning and already I can tell that the day's going to be a warm one.

"You've got a pretty name," she says. "Who chose it?"

"My dad," I say, turning to look at her. "What's it to you?"

"I'm just wondering. Does he like your murals?"

"What's with the twenty questions?"

"Nothing. I'm just curious."

"Haven't seen you since I started. Where've you been hiding yourself?"

"Doing work," she says.

"It's just you that runs the place?"

"Just me."

The Yamaha's parked a few feet away. I take a sip of the lemonade and watch her go over to it. She touches the gas tank, runs her hands across the seat, stoops over and examines the chrome tailpipe and the back tire.

She asks, "You like motorbikes?"

"That's why I got one," I say, finishing up the lemonade and crunching a piece of ice.

"Why?" She doesn't look up at me when she asks this.

"Why what?"

"Why do you like them? Don't you get scared zooming around so fast? I've seen how these things fly. Why didn't you get a car instead?"

"Because I don't like getting stuck in traffic, okay? I like my bike. I like to be able to get on it and take off."

"Where to?"

I hand her the glass of lemonade. "Here. Thanks."

I turn around and continue painting.

A few days later, the old woman brings out a lawn chair. She sets it up directly behind me and pops open an umbrella. Last night she watched a segment on the news about sunburns and skin cancer.

"I have to be careful," she says, adjusting herself in her chair, draping a towel over her shoulders. From her pocket, she takes out the same pair of sunglasses she was wearing the day she commissioned me and puts them on. "Don't you get scared? Working out in the sun?"

"No."

She calls me hija and says she has an oil inside the shop. "It doesn't have sunscreen, hija. But it can give you some protection."

"I'm cool," I say. "Look." I hold both arms out. "See? No cancer here."

"Huh. Not yet. Then ten years from now you get this spot and next thing you know it's all over."

She keeps the towel wrapped around her shoulders and walks back into the shop. A few minutes later she comes out holding a small vial and a glass of lemonade.

"Come down." She goes over and sits back in her chair.

"I'm working here."

"Yes," she says. "You're working for me. I'm the boss. And if I say you come down here, you come down here." She unscrews the cap and pours some into her hand and rubs with both palms.

"What is it?" I ask

"It's an oil for strength. To attract good vibes. Give me your arms."

"How am I supposed to drink the lemonade?"

"After," she says.

I stand before her and hold out both arms. She begins by kneading the oil into my skin. I smell mint and cucumber, and it makes my skin feel cool. My muscles expand and relax. She pinches my knuckles, unravels the knots I feel there.

"Thanks," I say when she finishes.

"Es nada."

I turn around and face the mural. The Virgin's body's already sketched in, the traces of black lines forming the hands and the head. She looks out across the junk field.

From behind the old woman says, "You're Enrique Medina's little girl, aren't you?"

"Yeah."

"He's real popular around here."

"So I hear."

"He gets around, your father. All over the place."

I say, "It's what he does. What he's good at."

"Yeah," she says. "I know."

For a long time we're silent. Then I ask, "What do you think? You like how it's coming along?"

"It's nice," she says.

"Good," I say. "Because I'm not changing a thing."

She laughs at me. "I like you," she says. "You've got a strong spirit."

*   *   *

The house is empty when I get home. Everything's eerie with just me and the mannequins standing around, greeting me when I shut the door. I decide to take a shower and clean up before dinner. When I walk into my mom's room to grab a clean towel from the stack on her bed, I notice a bottle of pills on the dresser.

"What's going on?" I ask, holding the pills when she gets home.

She shakes her head and sits on the couch. "That," she says, tiredly. "That's nothing."

"Looks like a lot more than nothing." I stand in front of her when she doesn't answer. "Mamá?" I say softly when I see she's crying.

At first, she says, it felt like nothing. Abdominal pains. Like when you've eaten something that didn't agree with you.

"I took Tylenol," she says. "And it went away." She looks at me and hesitates before going on.

"But?"

"I thought it was a yeast infection. So I bought something at the farmacia. But nada. The doctor ran a test a week ago. She says it's an infection. She gave me antibiotics."

"That's it?" I look at the pills.

She stays quiet, kneading her purse's straps.

I sit next to her. "Tell me, Mom."

"She says it's gonorrhea."

"Jesus," I say. "Jesus Christ."

"She said I better call all the people I've slept with. I'm not some puta coming off the street, I told her. Maybe I got it from using a public toilet, I said. Or touching a doorknob."

"That fucker," I say.

"Who?"

"Him. Dad. That pig. That whore."

She shakes her head. "It wasn't him."

"What do you mean? Yeah it was. You don't get this by sitting on a toilet. It was Dad."

"Leave him out of this. I'll take care of it. He's a good man. Worked hard. You and your brother had everything. It's not his fault."

"It's not his fault? So whose is it? Yours? Are you running around screwing other men?"

"No," she shouts. "No." Her purse falls on the floor.

"Then?"

"Don't disrespect your father."

"He's disrespected you. This family. Open your eyes. He's fucking other women. Has been for years. Stop defending him. Stop painting this picture of him all sweet and perfect."

She gets up from the couch and walks over to the mannequins. "Why do you say all these things? Where are you getting this from?"

"Everyone around here knows, Mom," I say. "Everyone except you."

She takes the bottle and hurls it against the wall. It shatters, and the pills fall to the ground, rolling under the dining table and the couches, his recliner, and the TV. She throws herself on the floor, pounding on it with her hands, scratching it until some of her nails break. I crouch beside her, and I hold her in my arms. I hold and hold her.

         ·   ·   ·

The mural's done. The old woman comes out with a camera. She adjusts her glasses and takes some snapshots.

"Stand there," she orders me. "To the side."

I lean up against the wall, my thumbs hooked to the belt loops of my carpenter pants. She snaps a few like that before having me push the bike in front of the mural. I sit on it, and she snaps more, the camera clicking fast.

She gives me an extra hundred bucks and tells me, "Stop looking like a biker. Go to a school. Study art."

"I can't," I say. "I don't wanna leave my mom."

"You don't want to leave your mom. Your mom doesn't want to leave your father."

I look up at her, surprised. I flip my baseball cap backward and say, "What do you know?"

"I know your father's a cabrón."

"Everybody around here's a cabrón."

"It's more complicated, isn't it? There are feelings involved. History. There's too much history."

Before I leave, the old woman writes my address down and says she's going to mail me some copies of the pictures. She says she recited a prayer for me and my mom last night. To help us in our situation. She lit a candle to Saint Rita of Cascia, she says. The patrona of difficult marriages, of sickness and desperate causes.

"Tell your mamá," she says as I start my motorcycle up and rev the engine. "Tell her La Santa Rita will help her."

.   .   .

"I'm cutting off his balls," I say to my brother when he calls. I'm in the house alone. My mom's at the market. "I swear I'm cutting off his balls the next time he walks through the door."

"That's real mature, Lluvia," he says.

"There you go taking his side again."

"I'm not," he says. "See, this is why I hate talking with you about this. Because you always accuse me of defending him."

"You do. You should be pissed. Pissed he did this to her. That he's been lying all these years."

"I am pissed. I'm just saying to put yourself in her shoes. Imagine how frustrated and confused she's feeling right now. What would she do if she kicked him out?"

"She'd *do* just fine," I say. I look out and see my mom putting her purse and some grocery bags on the dining table.

"Who is it?" she asks.

"Raúl," I say.

"Here," she says, reaching out to take the receiver from my hand. "Hi," she says. "I know," she tells him. "I do. I will, I will. I love you."

She hangs up the phone and is quiet for a long time. She goes over to the dining table and starts putting the groceries away.

"Your father's coming in tonight. He called when you were out this morning," she tells me. "I don't know what to do."

I look at the naked mannequins, posed like beauty pageant contestants, their smiles painfully awkward, their eyes blank and empty. "I wanna take you somewhere," I say.

"Now?"

"Now," I say, leading her by the hand out to my motorcycle.

"Let's take the car," she says when I start it up. "You know that thing scares me."

"No," I tell her. "Get on." I give her my helmet.

"I have to put the groceries away. I have things to do before your father gets here."

"Just get on, Mom." I rev the engine, and she steps back. "Come on."

She looks back at the house, then at me. She puts the helmet on, climbs on the bike, and we take off down our street.

The botánica's closed when we pull up to the shopping center. I park my bike in front of the mural and shine the headlight on the wall, illuminating the image.

"Look, Mom," I say. "Look what I made."

She walks up to the wall slowly and touches the fresh paint—the harsh grays and blacks of metal and stone, the muted greens and browns of earth and soil, the gentle blues and purples of water and sky, and the gleaming golds and silvers of light and Heaven.

In the far background are the sharp and jagged peaks of the San Bernardino Mountains, with white veins trickling down their sides for snow. Stretching from the mountains are fields of citrus trees. The groves fade into new housing tracts, the trees themselves transforming into the skeletons of houses. The dirt rows where migrant farmworkers pick lemons and oranges melt into the concrete streets of Agua Mansa. The city spreads out before you, a grid of gray avenues and boulevards lined with shops and buildings—Tina's Taco Haven, the Agua Mansa Palms, San Salvador's church, our house. The streets are shaded with eucalyptus trees and pines and oaks, electrical wires tangled among their branches. There are cell phone towers disguised as palm trees, their steel trunks tagged with graffiti. A paletero pushes his ice cream cart down Redondo. Ranflas cruise up Descanso. On Meridian, a school bus releases a group of kids carrying Dora the Explorer and Spider-Man back-packs. The 10 runs from left to right with cars and motorcycles and trucks. The north–south streets run down, flowing like tributaries into the Santa Ana in the foreground, widening and expanding it. The río skirts the border of the city, passing through channels and the tall green stalks of wild horsetail and arundo canes. In the bottom right corner, just as the wall is about to end, the

water changes. It becomes a strip of turquoise fabric tumbling from the lap of Santa Ana herself, who sits on a bench stitching gold stars onto it by hand.

High above, past the branches and power lines, La Virgen floats on a bed of clouds sprinkled with roses in the center of the sky. The angel still holds her up, his fingers still curled around the crescent moon on which she stands. I kept the dark crimson robe and the emerald cloak dotted with stars. But now, instead of cupped, her hands are open, her arms stretched out. She looks straight ahead and over us all.

"It's you," I say. "Do you see?"

My mother is silent, then she says, "It's me." She says it defiantly. "It's me. Me."

"There was this picture I found of you," I say. "You're so happy in it. You're not wearing a wedding ring. It was before you got married, before Dad."

"I knew what he was when I married him," she tells me. "And that makes me mad the most. I knew and ignored it. I told myself I could change him."

"None of it's your fault," I say.

She turns around and looks out across the junk field. She says, "I keep thinking about those other women. Just like me. Out there somewhere. Waiting for him to get back to them."

"What do you wanna do?"

She puts the helmet on and buttons up her denim jacket. "I don't want us to be there when he comes home tonight. Let's go."

"Where to?" I ask, starting the bike up.

"Let's go," she repeats, getting on. "Let's take off."

My hands squeeze the grips. I rev the engine and we drive away.

I take the freeway on-ramp, and we head west on the 10 toward the ocean. I'm doing ninety, one hundred, then one hundred and fifteen, weaving in and out of traffic so fast that everything's just flashes of color. There's only us and the roar of the engine and the wind. My mother shouts and squeezes my waist tight, and she doesn't let go until we're far enough away.

Feast of
Nuestra Señora de Guadalupe

Holy Mother and Queen of the Americas

Patroness of Mexico, the Americas,

and the New World.

The sirens woke her at one in the morning. Perla got up and stood in the hallway, the water heater gurgling in the closet by the bathroom. In the backyard, lights throbbed, turning the leaves of the avocado tree pink then green then pink again. She tried to look over the fence but could see nothing. After a few minutes she gave up and went back to bed.

The morning was cold and clear and the sky bright blue. Dewdrops covering the tips of the creosote bushes sprinkled her legs as Perla walked through the lot toward the shopping center. On the street corner stood a middle-aged woman and a young girl. The girl held her arm around the woman's waist, and now and again she would stroke the woman's shoulder. Both of their heads were bent, staring at something on the concrete.

On her way to the donut shop to get her morning coffee, Perla passed the tattoo parlor. A fiberglass Santa Claus with a tan button nose and bright red cheeks stood guard near the entrance. Alfonso had never been in the habit of decorating the ninety-nine-cent store for Christmas, but he had moved, and these loud men were now next door. So much around her had changed this year. The botánica had been vandalized and robbed. Rodrigo was gone. *Only me. I'm still the same. Still around.*

Inside Best Donuts, Alice was placing maple bars in a pink box lined with waxed paper. "Did you hear what happened?" she asked, pointing toward the corner with a pair of metal tongs. "Some kid. Coming home last night. He was hit by a car and died on the spot. My grandpa was here baking. Said he heard tires screeching. Didn't think much about it. When he was outside smoking a while later, there were all these cops everywhere."

Perla looked through the lace patterns of snowflakes airbrushed on the windows at the women on the corner. An old man was with them now, arranging a bouquet of flowers around a wooden cross staked into the ground.

"Awful, isn't it?" Alice said. She handed Perla her coffee and left to help someone standing at the edge of the counter.

Perla opened at nine-fifteen. Her first customer was Nancy Pérez.

"How's everything with your father?" Perla asked.

"Worse." Nancy paused, then said, "He's in a coma. Darrell and I are driving to Vegas tonight. You know? I've been a real jerk all these years. I feel so bad. For everything."

Nancy's eyes filled with tears. She put a pair of sunglasses on and crossed her arms. "Anyway, I thought I'd stop by. Maybe buy something. A candle or whatever."

Perla sold her a scapular of Saint Jude for her father to wear, a prayer card of Santa Bárbara, and a white candle to light. She placed these in a paper bag and set it before Nancy.

Nancy opened the bag and peered inside. "My mom will appreciate this. I'll tell her you say hello."

"Please do," Perla said. "And tell her I'm sorry. I'm sorry what I told you to do last time you were in here didn't work."

Nancy looked down at the ground and shook her head. "It was too late by then. But you did all you could. Thank you."

She walked out the front door and drove away.

Later on, Perla helped a woman whose daughter was in the service. From her purse, the woman pulled out a wallet and pointed to a picture of a girl in a military uniform with medals pinned to her lapels. Behind her was a furled American flag, the folds thick.

"She's going away," the woman said. "Her name's Catalina Gómez. She's being sent to the war. I want to give her something. Protection."

Perla reached for the tackle box on the shelf behind the register. She sifted through the compartments filled with silver medallas until she found the one she was looking for.

"Here," she told the woman. "San Cristóbal." Perla threaded a leather shoestring through the eyelet of the medal. "Tell her to wear it all the time. It's the only way it can keep her safe."

When the woman handed Perla a five-dollar bill to pay, Perla took it and gave it back to her. "No," she said. "No."

The woman bowed her head and clasped the medal in both hands. "Once she's home safe," she said, smiling, sweeping her arm across

the store, "we'll have a party. And you, everyone, everyone will be invited."

A couple who were leaving the state came in next. They needed help selling their house, they told Perla.

"Where are you going?" she asked them.

"Para Washington," the man said. "Mucho trabajo." When he smiled, Perla saw a thin ribbon of gold outlining a front tooth.

"We have to sell the house fast," his wife said. "My mom, she told me we should buy a statue of San José and bury it in the front yard. Will that work?"

"Bury him upside down," Perla explained, taking the saint from the shelf. "Then the property will sell right away."

It was late afternoon and she was shelving some candles when Rosa arrived.

"I think I'm almost ready for another cut," Perla said to her, tucking loose strands of hair behind her ears.

"Okay. Sure," Rosa said. "You know, I have enough. To rent out a station."

"That's good. Will you be working in a salon now?"

"Eventually. But I'm gonna have to wait awhile." Rosa paused, then touched her stomach. "See, I'm pregnant again, and it looks like I'm gonna have twins. Twins!" she shouted and laughed out loud.

Perla took her hand. "Rosita, that's great."

Rosa said, "I was gonna wait to tell her, but I called my mom right after I found out. We talked for a long time, and she apologized, you know? For the way she acted. She said she was proud of me. Of my life. She said I'd sacrificed a lot, and I'd made good choices."

Perla said, "I'm glad you two are talking again. You'll need her help when they come." She pointed to Rosa's stomach.

"Not just hers. You told me way back then. You said to come back here when I needed this." She pointed to the shelves. "Well, I'm gonna need it. And I'll need your help, too. So get ready, okay?"

After she left, Perla took the book of saints from the shelf below the register. She pressed it against her chest and tried to remember what she had written on all those scraps of paper. Perla pictured him, forming her words over and over, chanting her life like a prayer.

She went over to the front window to watch the crowd on the corner. A man in a baseball cap sat on a lawn chair, sipping out of a sports bottle, talk-

ing on a cell phone. Girls in sweatshirts and boys in football jackets held each other or buried their hands in their faces and cried. There was a teddy bear squeezing a heart next to the cross on the ground, and balloons and poems and prayers written on pieces of paper were taped to the street sign.

She opened the door and walked across the parking lot.

Near the corner the woman and the girl stood beside the old man who held a handkerchief up to his nose. The girl looked up at her. She pointed to the book of saints Perla held and asked, "Are you from the church?"

"No," Perla said. "I just wanted to find out. What happened?" She looked over at the old man and the woman. "Qué pasó?"

"Lo mataron," the old man said. "Lo mataron anoche." He pointed to the cross where the name *Joey Ramírez* was written in thick black letters.

The woman was heavy with curly brown hair and chapped lips. She wore a sweater with the word *Forgiven* knitted across the chest. Dark purple spots covered the bottom part of the sweater. "My son," she responded. "Joey. My son. He was coming home from his girlfriend's house last night. Crossing." She pointed to the street. "A car ran him over and took off."

"Venía llegando," the old man said. He tried to adjust and straighten the cross when a gust of wind blew it over. He took his shoe off and used it to drive the cross further into the ground.

"They need stoplights here. Not stop signs. They just drive through those," the girl said, twisting her hair into a bun and tying it with an elastic band wrapped around her wrist. "But nobody's gonna do nothing. If there'd been a stoplight here my brother wouldn't have been killed. Nobody'll do nothing, though. Just watch."

Three boys standing by her whispered to one another and shook their heads. They looked away when the dead boy's mother began to cry and wring her hands.

"He was walking across the street when the car hit him," she shouted. "And it threw him off the road. He crawled. He crawled here. And he died right here. His blood," she said. She pointed to the stains on her sweater, then to a spot on the concrete where no one stood.

Seven-day veladoras surrounded it, one lined up next to the other, forming the outline of a body. Nuestra Señora de la Caridad del Cobre, La Mano Poderosa, San Martín de Porres, and Santa Marta outlined part of his left arm. There was San Judas Tadeo on the heel of his left foot, La Anima Sola

near his inner thigh, and El Santo Niño de Atocha by one knee. El Sagrado Corazón, El Cristo Rey, and San Martín Caballero crowned his head and shaped part of a shoulder.

Someone had leaned a picture of Joey against the stop sign. In it, he knelt, wearing gold football pants and a purple jersey. A helmet sat on the grass in front of him. In the background were empty bleachers.

"So much of his blood on the sidewalk. And they washed it away and it went down into the gutter. His blood is in the gutter." The woman pointed to her sweater again.

"I'm sorry," Perla said, gripping the book. "Did they catch who did it?"

The old man said, "No."

"Why would they do that? Hit someone and leave?" the girl said, untying her hair again, and it fell around her shoulders. "Pieces of shit. I hope someone they know gets run over."

"Lena," the old man said. "Cálmate."

"I'm pissed, Grandpa." Lena kicked the metal street sign over and over with the tip of her sandal. "I'm fucking pissed."

"My Joey," the woman cried out. "He never hurt nobody. He was coming home. Just coming home." She turned away from the crowd and took a few steps toward the shopping center's driveway.

Perla walked up behind her. She touched the woman's hand and said, "Why don't you come inside." She pointed to the store. "Let me make you some tea."

Perla led her into the botánica and seated her in the fold-up chair near Santa Bárbara. "There," she said. "Rest now."

"Yes. Okay."

"I'm Perla."

"I'm Angela," she responded. Her hands trembled.

Perla set the book on the counter and went to the kitchenette. From the cupboard beside the sink, she took a mug, filled it with water, and heated it in the microwave. She made Angela manzanilla tea and poured in a few drops of whiskey from the bottle tucked under the sink.

"Here," she said, handing her the mug. "This will relax you."

Angela took sips, looking around the botánica, at the shelves, the statues, the packets of incense and herbs hanging on the pegboard. "It's nice in here. It's peaceful," she said, her voice fast, her words catching in her throat.

She got up, paced around the store, and stood in front of the Santa Bár-

bara statue. She leaned over the arrangement of candles and the bouquet of flowers gathered at the base and touched the figure's face. "The last thing I said to my Joey. What was it? The last thing. I can't remember. I was in the kitchen sewing a hole in Lena's cheerleading outfit. He left. Out the door. He walked past me. He was wearing a lot of cologne. I remember the smell. Why can't I remember? We didn't fight. We got alone fine. I love Rocío. I liked her for my son. I wasn't mad that he was going to see her. I think I said something," she said. "But I can't remember. If only I hadn't been concentrating so much on that tear in Lena's outfit. I could remember what I said. What did I say?" She looked at Perla, then at Santa Bárbara.

"My husband died many years ago," Perla told her, in the words she had once written for Rodrigo. "At home. He died in our bed. The night before, he'd been up watching a movie on TV. He was always watching TV late into the night. I rolled over and told him to turn down the volume. I was so mad and sleepy that I yelled. It was the last thing I said to him. He turned it off, then rolled over and kissed me. It was dark, and he couldn't see me lying next to him so his kiss landed on my ear. All I remember is the feeling of his breath blowing into my ear."

Angela sat back down. The mug wobbled in her hand when she drew it to her mouth to drink. She said softly, "We've only been here a little over a year. My husband. The father of my babies. We're separated. He wants me back. I only wanted to get away from him. That's why we came here. My Joey, he was so happy about the move because he'd gotten into trouble at his old school. He was excited. New friends. A new start, he'd say. For all of us. He was turning seventeen this year." She touched her blood-caked sweater.

Everywhere inside the botánica things were piled on top of one another, stacked high, thrown together. There were the cases and shelves and all the merchandise in the stockroom. There were boxes lining the floor behind the register, spilling over with bags of incense sticks, bottles of bath salts, and the candles from the day's delivery. Rows of statues stood in frozen meditation, a long and ancient line of martyrs and prophets, healers and teachers. *So much*, Perla thought. *There's still so much left.*

Perla leaned in close and asked her, "Do you know who I am?"

Angela's hands still touched her son's dried blood. She shook her head slowly.

"I can walk on water. The dead," Perla told her. "Spirits and saints. They talk to me. I just have to listen."

Angela lowered her head and began to weep.

"Look at me," Perla said, placing the rosary around Angela's neck. "I'm here to tell you something. I'm here to tell you your baby, he's fine. Where he is."

On the counter were rosaries in small white boxes lined with padding. She had sold or given away so many over the years and wondered where they were—if they were hanging from the rearview mirrors of cars like Teresa's or stuffed in drawers or just maybe someone was holding one now, pressing the beads and concentrating on the Mysteries.

"Don't worry," Perla said. Taking a pad and pencil, she wrote something down from memory—a receta, a saint's name, a prayer for the dead. "Listen to me," Perla told her. "Listen now. I'll help. I'll tell you what to do."

Angela stopped crying and wiped her tears away as she held the rosary.

Outside, night was falling, and the faces of the people gathered on the corner were gray as stone and indistinguishable in the approaching darkness. Some paced restlessly, and others huddled together for warmth. Perla watched the silhouettes of the candles on the sidewalk, the specks of light in the glass cylinders burning distant and lonely.

Perla felt them there, all those who had come and gone, who had sought her help and guidance. She felt them standing with her, their fingers wrapping around her own, their hands working with hers. From the shelves she took two veladoras—one plain white, the other green with a picture of the Virgen de Guadalupe. She struck a match and the flame extended out like a torch, lighting both candles at the same time. She handed the white veladora to Angela, then took the other.

"Follow me," Perla told her.

They walked out of the shop and across the parking lot. There were a few people scattered about, wandering between the empty field and the cluster of candles on the corner. The front door of the tattoo shop opened and two men wearing latex gloves, their fingertips stained with green and black ink, approached and hovered near the group. They wore dark blue work shirts, their pants creased and stiff, and they smiled and hugged Angela and said something to her. Alice and her grandfather joined them. Her apron was dusted white with flour, and she wiped her hands before taking

Angela's. The jade pendant around her neck caught the light from the veladoras when she reached out to hug Lena. Alice's grandfather stood near Angela, smoking, his face wrinkled and small, as he watched the traffic on Rancho slow down. One by one, the cars turned off their engines and headlights. People got out and made their way to the corner. Some cut through the empty lot, stepping through the scrub, carrying flowers and lit candles.

Little by little the crowd grew until it filled the empty field, spilling into the parking lot and onto the street. There were members of San Salvador's church there, co-workers and friends of Angela, Joey's high school principal and some of his teachers. A reporter from the *Agua Mansa Courier* went around interviewing everyone, writing things down in a small notebook.

Perla thought about the scraps of paper she had given Rodrigo. What would she say about him if anyone ever asked? What would she come to remember about all that had happened here?

She watched Rosa walking through the crowd with Miguel Angel and Danielle, stopping now and again to let others pass in front of them, as they made their way to the altar. They placed some flowers there and the card that Danielle herself had made. Perla imagined the babies growing inside Rosa. She saw their lungs taking shape, tissues forming their brains, and a web of thin blue and red veins netting around a pair of small new hearts.

So many. So many of them.

Perla began moving through the crowd, reciting a prayer, touching their hands and faces when the people gathered around her. They had felt ache and disappointment and had borne witness to passing and loss. This was just a moment, Perla told them. Death was always stirring. It hid in the wind, in those palm trees, on the banks of the Santa Ana río. But if you stood there long enough, if you stood there and watched and listened, you could see what that river had once been, and you could see so much life in the still waters that remained.

Perla and Angela added their candles to the rest, and the light from the veladoras grew. A yellow glow rose up from the ground where they were clustered. It burst out in thick beams, shooting up to the sky, curving around the edges of buildings and houses and bending between tree branches and power lines, before it found its way back down. It descended upon them, and Perla watched as, one by one, they each shone brighter, wiser and forever changed, stronger now.

Acknowledgments

So many people helped me to get here. So many were with me from the very first word. So many joined in the middle or at the very end. I thank you all.

To my agent, Elyse Cheney, for her faith and brave support of this project and of me from the moment we met and for patiently listening to what I had to say. To my editor, Kate Medina, for guiding and pushing, for taking a chance on a kid from Tijuana, for seeing what I couldn't, and for never settling. To Stephanie Hanson for never failing to give the kinds of comments and input every writer dreams of. To everyone at Random House who got behind and pushed, who wrapped their many arms around this book and me. To Robin Rolewicz for the warm wishes and for doing so much behind the scene. Thank you, Abby Plesser, for your wisdom and grace and presence throughout, for keeping things moving swift and steady, and for the phone and e-mail pats on the back that kept me smiling.

I couldn't have asked for a better team.

To Geoffrey Wolff for never failing to tell me that I had the chops to pull this off, for the long talks in his office, and for reminding me what true commitment and artistry are. To Michelle Latiolais for being a brilliant master of language and mood and for showing me again and again until I got it right. To Arielle Read for so, so much. Your advice and encouragement always got me through. Mil gracias, "mi corazón." To the International Center for Writing and Translation and the Humanities Center for their generous financial support, which allowed me to do research for this book. To Judith Ashton, Laura Gómez, and Julie Tilton at San Bernardino Valley College for getting

things going way back then and for showing me how to persevere and how to matter in this world.

I'm better because of you.

To Amanda Rea for never letting me believe otherwise and for the keen eye and witty retorts. To Ariana Simard for being interested from the very beginning. To Kristen Williams for the Dump Cakes and Hello Dollies, for the fried shrimp and lasagna and the down-home East Texas love that kept me happy and full. To Michael Jaime-Becerra for being first, for opening the door and letting me follow, for his graciousness and his big heart, and for the uncanny coincidences that bind us. Only you and I get it, compa. To everyone in the MFA Program at UCI for the critiques and camaraderie. To Sandra Cisneros and my fellow Macondistas, the wild bunch straight out of San Antonio, Texas. To Leslie Larson and Carla Trujillo for their advice and for the long conversations that made me feel better. To Liliana Valenzuela for her brilliant job of translating this novel.

You've filled me up big-time.

To the Shallers of Glendora, Dusty and my best friend Mike, for all the fun we had getting here, and for the more we'll have getting there. To Jason Spivak for his guidance and friendship, for carefully keeping tabs on me from so far away, and for taking me along on those gigs during the Hollywood years. Jefe, un abrazo fuerte. To Elle Thornberry for the rowdy life that kept me insane and uncontrolled, tattooed and angry, for the bar fights and loud music, and for the wild times that made those nights gleam.

You've stayed with me and always will.

To Susan Straight for the books and stories, for the food of the soul that is inspiration and sweet hope, for the beats and rhythms to dance to words, for teaching me to look where no one else could, for teaching me to listen when no one else would, and for making me write it all down. To Kyle for making me reach, for seeing the potential when I was too exhausted, and for carrying so much of this with me as I fought to give a voice to these ghosts. I couldn't have done this without you. To my mother, Maria Luz, for giving so much and asking so little, and for always believing when everyone else had given up. To the memory of my father and my grandparents for crossing when it was rough, for working with their hands and dreaming with their souls so that I could do this, and for shining a light.

This I give to you. With everything. Everything.